THE YEAR'S BEST SCIENCE FICTION

TWELFTH ANNUAL COLLECTION

Gardner Dozois, Editor

ST. MARTIN'S PRESS ❧ NEW YORK

For Ellen Datlow

Library of Congress Catalog Card Number: 85-645716

ISBN 0-312-13222-0 (hardcover)
ISBN 0-312-13221-2 (paperback)

First Edition: July 1995

10 9 8 7 6 5 4 3 2

Acknowledgment is made for permission to print the following material:

"Forgiveness Day," by Ursula K. Le Guin. Copyright © 1994 by Ursula K. Le Guin. First published in *Asimov's Science Fiction*, November 1994. Reprinted by permission of the author and the author's agent, Virginia Kidd.

"The Remoras" by Robert Reed. Copyright © 1994 by Mercury Press, Inc. First published in *The Magazine of Fantasy & Science Fiction*, May 1994. Reprinted by permission of the author.

"Nekropolis" by Maureen F. McHugh. Copyright © 1994 by Bantam Doubleday Dell Magazines. First published in *Asimov's Science Fiction*, April 1994. Reprinted by permission of the author.

"Margin of Error" by Nancy Kress. Copyright © 1994 by Omni Publication International, Ltd. First published in *Omni,*October 1994. Reprinted by permission of the author.

"Cilia-of-Gold" by Stephen Baxter. Copyright © 1994 by Bantam Doubleday Dell Magazines. First published in *Asimov's Science Fiction*, August 1994. Reprinted by permission of the author.

"Going After Old Man Alabama" by William Sanders. Copyright © 1994 by William Sanders. First published in *Tales from the Great Turtle* edited by Piers Anthony and Richard Gilliam (Tor Books). Reprinted by permission of the author.

"Melodies of the Heart" by Michael F. Flynn. Copyright © 1994 by Bantam Doubleday Dell Magazines. First published in *Analog Science Fiction/Science Fact*, January 1994. Reprinted by permission of the author.

"The Hole in the Hole" by Terry Bisson. Copyright © 1994 by Bantam Doubleday Dell Magazines. First published in *Asimov's Science Fiction*, February 1994. Reprinted by permission of the author.

"Paris in June" by Pat Cadigan. Copyright © 1994 by Omni Publication International, Ltd. First published in *Omni*, June 1994. Reprinted by permission of the author.

"Flowering Mandrake" by George Turner. Copyright © 1994 by George Turner. First published in *Alien Shores*, ed. Peter McNamara and Margaret Winch (Aphelion). Reprinted by permission of the author and the author's agent, Cherry Weiner.

"None So Blind" by Joe Haldeman. Copyright © 1994 by Bantam Doubleday Dell Magazines. First published in *Asimov's Science Fiction*, November 1994. Reprinted by permission of the author.

"Cocoon" by Greg Egan. Copyright © 1994 by Bantam Doubleday Dell Magazines. First published in *Asimov's Science Fiction*, May 1994. Reprinted by permission of the author.

"Seven Views of Olduvai Gorge" by Mike Resnick. Copyright © 1994 by Mercury Press, Inc. First published in *The Magazine of Fantasy & Science Fiction*, October/November 1994. Reprinted by permission of the author.

"Dead Space for the Unexpected" by Geoff Ryman. Copyright © 1994 by *Interzone/Nexus*. First published in *Interzone 88*, October 1994. Reprinted by permission of the author.

"Cri de Coeur" by Michael Bishop. Copyright © 1994 by Bantam Doubleday Dell Magazines. First published in *Asimov's Science Fiction*, September 1994. Reprinted by permission of the author.

CONTENTS

ACKNOWLEDGMENTS

The editor would like to thank the following people for their help and support: first and foremost, Susan Casper, for doing much of the thankless scut work involved in producing this anthology; Michael Swanwick, Janet Kagan, Ellen Datlow, Virginia Kidd, Sheila Williams, Ian Randal Strock, Scott L. Towner, Tina Lee, David Pringle, Kristine Kathryn Rusch, Dean Wesley Smith, Pat Cadigan, David S. Garnett, Charles C. Ryan, Chuq von Rospach, Susan Allison, Ginjer Buchanan, Lou Aronica, Betsy Mitchell, Beth Meacham, Claire Eddy, David G. Hartwell, Mike Resnick, Bob Walters, Tess Kissinger, Steve Pasechnick, Richard Gilliam, Susan Ann Protter, Lawrence Person, Dwight Brown, Darrell Schweitzer, Don Keller, Robert Killheffer, Greg Cox, and special thanks to my own editor, Gordon Van Gelder.

Thanks are also due to Charles N. Brown, whose magazine *Locus* (Locus Publications, P.O. Box 13305, Oakland, CA 94661, $40.00 for a one-year subscription [twelve issues] via second class; credit card orders [510] 339-9198) was used as a reference source throughout the Summation, and to Andrew Porter, whose magazine *Science Fiction Chronicle* (Science Fiction Chronicle, P.O. Box 022730, Brooklyn, NY 11202-0056, $30.00 for a one-year subscription [twelve issues]; $36.00 first class) was also used as a reference source throughout.

SUMMATION
1994

For the most part, this was a gray, quiet year, solidly sunk in the traditional mid-decade doldrums. As usual, there were plenty of omens to be found, both positive and negative, and plenty of prognosticators eager to read the entrails for you—and again, also as usual, what conclusions you reached about whether things were looking good or looking bad for science fiction depended on which evidence you selectively chose to examine, and what weight you arbitrarily decided to give to it. Sometimes the future of SF publishing seems like Schrö-dinger's Cat—not only can't you know what's going to be in the box until you open it, but I sometimes suspect that our expectations help to *determine* what we're going to find in there when we finally do pop the lid. Whether we find a live cat or a dead cat in the box is going to be determined, in some small part at least, by our own actions, by how determined we are *not* to settle for lowest-common-denominator entertainment, by how ready we are to insist loudly and vocally on adult entertainment of intelligence and then to *back* that demand with cash money out of our wallets, and finally by how resourceful and creative people at every level of the publishing world can be in learning to overcome the daunting (but not, I hope, insurmountable) problems that lie in wait in the new century to come.

Whatever's going to happen in that new century, *this* year, in the closing decade of the current century, was a relatively quiet one. The game of Editorial Musical Chairs that has been underway for the last couple of years seems to have mostly played itself out—for the moment. (There were some exceptions, of course—Chris Miller was forced out of Avon by a corporate realignment that did away with her job, Janna Silverstein left Bantam for a job with Wizards of the Coast and Anne L. Groell left Avon to take the empty chair at Bantam.) Some established book lines died, such as the acclaimed Dell Abyss imprint, which was pretty much abandoned after the resignation of editor Jeanne Cavelos, and other lines, such as the last year's newly launched Del Rey Discovery program, are seemingly being allowed to languish away. On the other hand, some lines which were seen as being threatened last year got reprieves *this* year, such as the AvoNova line, which was left in place and relatively undisturbed after the long-rumored sale of Avon fell through (it had been feared that the rumored new owners would dismantle it) . . . and some lines that were even reported to have died last year rose again from the grave in 1994, as Harcourt Brace thought better of killing its SF line *after* the last possible minute, and rehired editor Michael Kandel, who had left only months before. New or revamped SF lines were also launched this year or enjoyed their first year of publication, including the very promising-looking new HarperPrism line, edited by John Silbersack, the new Tor, Orb, and Forge lines, edited by Patrick Nielsen Hayden, and the "relaunched" Warner line, now called Warner Aspect, edited by Betsy Mitchell. New lines were also launched or are in the process of being launched by new players in the publishing game: White Wolf, primarily a gaming company up until recently, sharply increased its presence in the SF and fantasy book area (Stephen Pagel, formerly science fiction buyer for B. Dalton's and the Barnes & Noble superstores, moved to White Wolf this year as Director of Sales; he will also be doing some editing for them—this will probably be good for White Wolf, but it might be bad for SF in general, as Pagel was primarily responsible for increasing the sale of SF at those chains by almost 25 percent in the last two years); and Wizards of the Coast, the Seattle-based gaming company responsible for the immensely popular trading card/fantasy game *Magic: The Gathering* hired Janna Silverstein away from Bantam to launch a new line of Fantasy and SF books; most of the books from these lines will probably be gaming-related, but some of them probably will be (and already have been, in the case of White Wolf) regular fantasy/SF/horror titles. One major magazine died this year, another seemed to be on its deathbed, and a third underwent a bizarre surprise transformation—while, at the same time, a half-dozen or more *new* magazines were struggling to establish themselves. The overall number of genre books published this year went down slightly for the third year in a row, but there were still more than 1,700 genre titles published, so the difference was hardly noticeable. There were enormous amounts of crap published during 1994, with media tie-in books, sharecropper books, gaming-oriented books, next-volume-in-infinitely-expansible-fantasy-trilogy books, wet-dream mercenary space-war fantasies, *Star Trek* books, *Star Trek: The Next Generation* books, *Star Trek: Deep Space Nine* books, *Star Trek: Voyager* books, *Tek War* books, and so on and so on, taking up ever-increasing amounts of room on bookstore shelves—and yet, in spite of all that, adult SF and fantasy novels of quality and intelligence continued to be published. Electronic publishing remained for the most part a dream for the 21st Century—and yet, at the same time, the first tentative steps that *might* make it a practical reality were being taken, here and there, one small incremental step at a time.

What you find in that box doesn't *have* to be a dead, rotting cat.

Only seven years left until the 21st Century! Until THE FUTURE! . . . that fabulous formless place where thousands of science fiction books and stories have been set. Will it be a glorious dream, or a hideous nightmare? It'll be interesting to open the box and see.

It was a grim year in the magazine market, with a massive hike in postage rates and the quickly escalating cost of paper affecting every magazine in existence to one extent or another. Many magazines throughout the entire marketplace were hit hard, and the science fiction market was no exception, with some major magazines dying or hovering just this side of death, and other magazines going through significant upheavals, the ultimate effects of which are impossible to predict as yet. And yet, at the same time that older magazines were faltering and dying, many *new* magazines were struggling to be born, ignoring, either bravely or naively, the overwhelming odds against them succeeding *either*.

Most of the big stories in this market this year involved death or drastic change. *Aboriginal SF,* which has been struggling for some time now and only managed to produce one "double" issue in 1994, was put up for sale, found no new buyer, and was finally declared officially dead in the early spring of 1995. *Amazing,* which had abandoned its large-size format in 1993, produced three digest-sized issues this year, and then "suspended publication" again; *Amazing* was also shopped around throughout the year and also found no one willing to buy it, at least as far as we know at the time of this writing. If *Amazing* does *not* find a new buyer, and quickly, then the odds are pretty good that it will die too, ending a remarkable sixty-eight-year run. Just as I was finishing the first draft of this Summation, there was a late-breaking news story of *major* proportions, major enough to get me to rework this section at the last possible moment: in a press release distributed in early March, *Omni* announced that it was immediately ceasing publication of its regular monthly edition, ending its seventeen-year history in that format. Instead, *Omni* "will convert its monthly editions to interactive online information services and begin publishing special quarterly 'super' editions this fall." The quarterly print version of *Omni,* supposedly featuring "expanded editorial content," including more stories per issue, will be "relaunched" in October, and will be sold only on newsstands; mail subscriptions to the magazine will be phased out beginning with the May issue. Ellen Datlow will stay on as the magazine's fiction editor.

Reverberations from this bombshell are still washing back and forth through the field even as I type, and so it's still hard to see through the smoke and discern what this news really means. The *Omni* press release puts the most positive spin possible on the decision to cease publication of the monthly print edition, saying that even though *Omni* is in a period "of growing advertising and stable circulation," they were making the decision to shift their primary emphasis to an electronic online format as a deliberate attempt to "get a jump on the new millennium," adding that "electronic publication, supplemented by high-quality print on a supportive basis, represents the future pathway for growth of this important brand name." Some industry insiders were skeptical, theorizing that the decision may actually be more sharply motivated by escalating production costs for the monthly print format than by a desire to explore exciting new markets, and that *Omni* may just be putting the best face possible on a decision they would have been forced to make anyway. It seems to me, though, that with a circulation of 787,000 (a circulation that had actually gone *up* almost 11% from the previous year), *Omni* should still be able to make a profit in *spite* of its no-doubt massive production costs . . . so perhaps we should give the *Omni* people the benefit of the doubt, and take their statement at face value.

Whatever the motivation behind the transformation, *Omni* will be the first really major general-interest magazine to try to establish an electronic online version of itself (*Wired* does have an online version, *HotWired,* but *Wired* is more specifically aimed at the intensive computer-user audience than are most magazines, including *Omni*), and it will be extremely interesting to see what kind of a success they can make for themselves in that format. If they make a really impressive go of it, we can expect to see other magazines take the plunge as well.

It was a gray year as well for the three major digest magazines, *Analog*, *Asimov's Science Fiction*, and *The Magazine of Fantasy & Science Fiction*, which all continued to lose circulation, although none of them suffered the kind of disastrous plunge that hit *Amazing* in 1992, when their circulation went down 61.6 percent from the previous year. So far, the circulation losses of the three digests have been relatively small—but this continued loss of blood is worrisome. The traditional digest-sized magazines really are the center of the field in some ways, or come as close to being a coherent center as the field *has* these days, anyway—a place where writers can hammer out a consensus as to what science fiction is like now and where it's going, and know that their work will be seen by the majority of serious core SF readers, as well as being seen by (and *influencing*) their peers. This is why the serious evolution of science fiction writing has always taken place at the short-story level; in a way—and this has been true as long as there has *been* a science fiction genre, certainly back to the days when Robert Heinlein and Isaac Asimov were the unknown new writers— it usually doesn't matter all that much what Big Novels by which Big Name Authors are sitting on the top of nationwide bestseller lists: most of the *really* evolutionary work is being done by young new writers at the short-story level, usually in the digest magazines. If we should lose most of the SF magazines, *particularly* the traditional digest magazines, it would be a disaster for the field, perhaps even one that would spell the eventual death of the genre *as* a genre, eliminating most of the continuity from one literary generation to another, and making it much more difficult for new writers to get into print and successfully develop their talents. Science fiction novels might continue to appear as usual for years after the magazines disappeared, as if nothing had happened, but, sooner or later, cut off at its roots, the genre would wither, or become so attenuated that it would shred and blow away on the wind in a thousand different directions. Some people tell you that the death of the genre *as* a genre would be a good thing, a liberating thing, but I don't agree with them—science fiction has built on *other* science fiction for decades, and, although that kind of force-breeding has produced weaknesses, it is also the source of science fiction's very special strengths, and some of the blossoms that have bloomed in that hothouse have been rare and wonderful indeed.

Asimov's Science Fiction, whose overall circulation had risen by 1.4 percent in 1993, lost 5.4 in circulation overall this year, with a decline of 3,000 in subscriptions, and a decline in copies sold on the newsstand of 1,000. *Analog* lost 3.8 percent in overall circulation, 2,000 in subscriptions, 1,000 on the newsstand. *The Magazine of Fantasy & Science Fiction* lost almost 10 percent of its overall circulation, 4,186 in subscriptions, 1,503 on the newsstand. *Asimov's Science Fiction* and *Analog* got a new president and publisher, Joachim P. Rosler, who replaced Christoph Haas-Heye. *The Magazine of Fantasy & Science Fiction* lost popular columnists John Kessel and Bruce Sterling; Robert Killheffer will replace Kessel as the primary book reviewer.

The British magazine *Interzone* completed its fourth full year as a monthly publication. Overall circulation dropped somewhat, and the literary quality seemed to have slipped a little, perhaps because they are now publishing a noticeably higher percentage of fantasy than they used to, most of it undistinguished. On the whole, though, the average quality of the stories remained high, and they are still one of the most reliable magazines in which to find first-rate material—myself, I think they should deemphasize the fantasy, and concentrate on science fiction again, particularly science fiction of the new ''British hard SF'' school, for which they are one of the natural homes. *Interzone* ''merged'' with the semiprozine *Nexus* this year, producing an issue devoted to material that had been originally produced for *Nexus,* and undergoing an internal ''redesign'' by former *Nexus* editor Paul Brazier—as far as I can tell, all the redesign did was make the magazine uglier and considerably harder to read, being one of those hip design jobs sported by magazines such as *Wired,* where the object seems to be to make the presentation of the text as confusing and hard to follow as possible. Since most of the *Interzone* audience is probably more interested in actually *reading* the text than in admiring its clever use as design elements, this may turn out to be a mistake.

Two of the newer SF magazines—*Science Fiction Age* and *Tomorrow,* both large-size magazines—successfully completed their second full years of publication. The overall circulation of *Science Fiction Age* remained more or less steady, losing about 4,400 newsstand sales but gaining about 4,800 in subscriptions— its overall circulation, though, is only about 62,000, and I continue to wonder if it can really be profitable, considering how expensive it must be to produce (a slick, full-color, large-format magazine like *Science Fiction Age* is *much* more expensive to produce than a digest-sized magazine like *Asimov's* or *F&SF,* which means that you have to *earn* a lot more to break even); of course, the upscale advertising that they're attracting might make up the difference. *Tomorrow's* circulation, already tiny by comparison with that of *Science Fiction Age* (*Science Fiction Age,* backed by a publishing company, obviously has much more money behind it than does *Tomorrow,* which is basically a one man show, and has only that man's own financial resources to back it), declined somewhat rather than growing this year, a bad sign. Last year I said that *Tomorrow* seemed to have published better fiction than *Science Fiction Age,* to a noticeable degree, in spite of the greater financial resources of the other magazine. This year, the differences in the quality of the fiction published in the two magazines seemed less marked, with *Science Fiction Age* seeming to improve somewhat and *Tomorrow* worsening by a similar degree. The overall quality of the stories in both magazines was somewhat lackluster—certainly not up to the average standard of, say, *F&SF,* or *Interzone*—but each magazine did publish their share of good work, including, in both cases, several of the year's first-rate stories. *Science Fiction Age* launched a companion magazine this year, *Realms of Fantasy,* edited by veteran editor Shawna McCarthy, another slick, large-size, full-color magazine, looking much like *Science Fiction Age,* in fact, except devoted to fantasy rather than science fiction. So far, *Realms of Fantasy* hasn't managed to produce anything really exceptional—most of the really innovative, Cutting-Edge fantasy is still being published in digest magazines like *F&SF* or *Asimov's,* or in anthologies like

Xanadu or *Tales from the Great Turtle*—but it's early days yet, and McCarthy is a shrewd and energetic editor, so I wouldn't be surprised to see a dramatic improvement in quality here in days to come. In any event, *Realms of Fantasy* is the first professional magazine devoted entirely to fantasy to come along for a good number of years, and as such is a welcome addition to the field.

Pulphouse: A Fiction Magazine managed to publish only one issue in 1994, but announced a much more realistic quarterly publication schedule (they had originally, several years back, announced that the magazine was going to be published on an unheard-of *weekly* schedule), and there are signs that this magazine may be coming out of the doldrums now that the financial upheavals at parent company Pulphouse Publishing seem to be subsiding. Original editor Dean Wesley Smith, who stepped down in 1993 and was replaced by Jonathan E. Bond, returned as editor this year, something I think is a good sign, since I disliked the direction in which Bond was taking the magazine, almost completely away from fantasy and science fiction toward the fields of "dark suspense" and non-supernatural "psychological horror." Smith seems to have reversed this trend, to some degree, at least, and perhaps things are looking up for *Pulphouse: A Fiction Magazine*. It'll be interesting to see what they can do in 1995. *Weird Tales* lost the license to its title in the middle of the year, and was forced to change its title to *Worlds of Fantasy and Horror*; it only published two issues this year, one under the old title and one under the new title, and in spite of having won a World Fantasy Award last year, continued to lose circulation, declining by about 3,000 copies. Let's hope they can do better in the coming year.

There were a slew of new magazines, with more in the pipeline, but we'll mention them below, in the semiprozine section; as it is, we've already mentioned several magazines here that by rights—using the yardstick of paid circulation—should have been discussed in the semiprozine section rather than in the professional section.

As usual, short SF also appeared in many magazines outside genre boundaries, from *Wired* to *The New Yorker*. *Playboy* in particular, under fiction editor Alice K. Turner, continues to run a relatively large amount of SF. There was also a slew of new SF media magazines, too many to mention individually.

As most of you probably know, I, Gardner Dozois, am also the editor of a prominent SF magazine, *Asimov's Science Fiction*. And that, as I've mentioned before, does pose a problem for me in compiling this summation, particularly the magazine-by-magazine review that follows. As the editor of *Asimov's*, I could be said to have a vested interest in the magazine's success, so that anything negative I said about another SF magazine (particularly another digest-sized magazine, my direct competition), could be perceived as an attempt to make my own magazine look good by tearing down the competition. Aware of this constraint, I've decided that nobody can complain if I only say *positive* things about the competition . . . and so, once again, I've limited myself to a listing of some of the worthwhile authors published by each.

Omni published good fiction this year by Pat Cadigan, Nancy Kress, Howard Waldrop, Bruce McAllister, Kate Wilhelm, Garry Kilworth, Kathe Koja, Allen Steel, and others. *Omni*'s fiction editor is Ellen Datlow.

The Magazine of Fantasy & Science Fiction featured good work by Mike Resnick, Robert Reed, Mary Rosenblum, Nina Kiriki Hoffman, L. Timmel Duchamp, David Gerrold, Ursula K. Le Guin, R. Garcia y Robertson, Ben Bova, Elizabeth Hand, Daniel Marcus, Carrie Richerson, Pati Nagle, and others. *F&SF*'s editor is Kristine Kathryn Rusch.

Asimov's Science Fiction featured good work by Ursula K. Le Guin, Maureen F. McHugh, Brian Stableford, Michael Bishop, Mary Rosenblum, Michael Swanwick, Mike Resnick, Brian W. Aldiss, Lisa Goldstein, R. Garcia y Robertson, Eliot Fintushel, Alexander Jablokov, Terry Bisson, John Brunner, and others. *Asimov's Science Fiction*'s editor is Gardner Dozois.

Analog featured good work by Michael F. Flynn, G. David Nordley, Geoffrey A. Landis, Charles L. Harness, Rick Shelley, Jack McDevitt, Bud Sparhawk, Ben Bova, Jerry Oltion, Stephen Goldin, and others. *Analog*'s longtime editor is Stanley Schmidt.

Amazing featured good work by Ursula K. Le Guin, Pamela Sargent, George Guthridge, Terry A. McGarry, and others. *Amazing*'s editor is Kim Mohan.

Interzone featured good work by Geoff Ryman, Greg Egan, Brian Stableford, Katharine Kerr, Stephen Baxter, Chris Beckett, Leigh Kennedy, Paul Di Filippo, Kim Newman, Garry Kilworth, and others. *Interzone*'s editor is David Pringle, now "assisted" by Paul Brazier.

Tomorrow published good work by Ursula K. Le Guin, Robert Reed, Eliot Fintushel, M. Shayne Bell, R. Garcia y Robertson, Michael H. Payne, Cynthia Ward, Felicity Savage, Norman Spinrad, and others. *Tomorrow*'s editor is Algis Budrys.

Science Fiction Age published good work by Martha Soukup, Barry N. Malzberg, Rick Wilber, Daniel Marcus, Robin Wilson, Bruce Boston, Geoffrey A. Landis, Gregory Benford, and others. *Science Fiction Age*'s editor is Scott Edelman.

Aboriginal Science Fiction featured interesting work in its final issue by K. D. Wentworth, J. Brooke, and others. The editor of the now-defunct *Aboriginal Science Fiction* was Charles C. Ryan.

Weird Tales, which changed its name in mid-year to *Worlds of Fantasy and Horror,* published good work by Tanith Lee, Ian R. MacLeod, Jeff VanderMeer, and others. *Worlds of Fantasy and Horror*'s editor is Darrell Schweitzer.

Pulphouse: A Fiction Magazine published interesting work by Steven Utley, Ray Vukcevich, Barry N. Malzberg, Carrie Richerson, and others. *Pulphouse: A Fiction Magazine*'s editor is Dean Wesley Smith.

(Subscription addresses follow for those magazines hardest to find on the newsstands: *The Magazine of Fantasy & Science Fiction*, Mercury Press, Inc., 143 Cream Hill Road, West Cornwall, CT, 06796, annual subscription—$26.00 in U.S.; *Asimov's Science Fiction*, Dell Magazines Fiction Group, P.O. Box 5130, Harlan, IA, 51593-5130—$39.97 for thirteen issues; *Interzone*, 217 Preston Drove, Brighton BN1 6FL, United Kingdom—$52.00 for an airmail one-year—twelve issues—subscription; *Analog*, Dell Magazines Fiction Group, P.O. Box 5133, Harlan, IA, 51593-5133—$39.97 for thirteen issues; *Tomorrow*, Box 6038 Evanston, IL 60204—$18.00 for a one-year (6 issues) subscription; *Pulphouse: A Fiction Magazine*, P.O. Box 1227, Eugene, OR 97440—$15 per year (4 issues) in the U.S.; *Worlds of Fantasy and Horror,* Terminus Publishing Company, 123 Crooked Lane, King of Prussia, PA 19406-2570—$16.00 for 4 issues in the U.S.

The fact that sophisticated desktop publishing technology is now cheap enough to be affordable by almost anyone, and that almost anyone can use it to produce a magazine that at least *looks* like a professional product, has opened the floodgates this year on a torrent of new magazines, most of them fiction semiprozines, many of them slick full-size productions, some of them even getting national newsstand distribution. Since the chances are that most of them run on a shoe-string budget and are probably severely undercapitalized, I expect most of them will die off like the proverbial flies. A few may have a chance of survival; we'll see.

Among the new fiction semiprozines, most of them SF-oriented, that are struggling to establish themselves, are *Crank!, Expanse, Offworld, Harsh Mistress Science Fiction Adventures* (which changed its name this year to *Absolute Magnitude*), the revamped version of *Galaxy, Mindsparks, Sirius Visions,* and so forth.

Of these, by far the best, in terms of literary quality, and the only one that I would have no reservations about recommending—although it is perhaps also the one the furthest out on the fringes of science fiction—was *Crank!,* edited by Bryan Cholfin, which this year featured one of 1994's best stories, Ursula K. Le Guin's "The Matter of Seggri," as well as thoroughly professional (although often decidedly *odd*) work by Jonathan Lethem, Chan Davis, Gene Wolfe, A. A. Attanasio, Lisa Tuttle, Terry Bisson, R. A. Lafferty, and others; they announced four issues this year, managed to produce two—this is a very promising magazine that deserves to survive, and I wish them well. *Absolute Magnitude, The Magazine of Science Fiction Adventures* (formerly *Harsh Mistress SF*), changed more than its name, going from a cheap-looking digest to a slick, full-size magazine with full-color covers that is one of the best-*looking* products on the newsstands; to date, the fiction inside has been less impressive than the covers, although they have published professional-level fiction by Don D'Ammassa, Hal Clement, Barry B. Longyear, and others—they produced two issues this year, one under each name. *Pirate Writings, Tales of Fantasy, Mystery & Science Fiction,* also changed from a digest-sized to a large-size format, and although it's not quite as slick-looking as *Absolute Magnitude,* the writing has been a tad livelier, perhaps because of its wider scope, with interesting work by Paul Di Filippo, Jane Yolen, Daniel Hatch, Jessica Amanda Salmonson, and others— they promised three issues, produced two, and announced a change to quarterly publication in future. *Expanse* is another nice-looking full-size magazine, but produced little of professional-level quality this year; they promised four issues, and actually produced two. Alas, I find it impossible to recommend the revamped version of *Galaxy,* which, in spite of featuring mostly professional authors, produced very little original fiction (there were a lot of reprints) that was worthwhile this year, with much of it downright awful; perhaps this is because, unlike any other magazine, almost all of it was in the form of short-short stories, a page or two apiece, which is a *very* difficult form in which to produce good work; the magazine also deserves mention as having more ads per issue than any other magazine I've ever seen, which I suppose reflects its origins (still very apparent) as a New Age catalog—*Galaxy* produced its announced six bimonthly issues this year. I was also not terribly impressed by *Sirius Visions, A Speculative Fiction Magazine Specializing in the Literature of Hope,* a "magazine" in a curious tabloid-sized newspaper format, which is published eight times a year on "Celtic holidays" such as Samhain, Beltane, and Lugnassugh, although it at least has published some professional-level fiction by Kristine Kathryn Rusch, Sue Storm, and others; I've seen the "Samhain" issue, don't know if there were any others. *Offworld* produced only one issue this year, and is already rumored to be dead. *Mindsparks* looks more like a fanzine than most of the slicker-looking magazines mentioned above, and has mostly been of note to date for some very professional-level (in fact, often quite technically sophisticated) nonfiction essays; there is less emphasis here on fiction, although they have published professional-level work by G. David Nordley, K. D. Wentworth, and others.

Another promising new fiction semiprozine was launched in early 1995; we'll talk more about it next year, but on the strength of the first issue, which I've already seen, I'm going to go out on a limb (*none* of the magazines here may be in existence by the end of 1995, including the one I'm about to mention—that's the nature of the semiprozine market) and recommend *Century,* a new bimonthly fiction magazine edited by Robert K. J. Killheffer. Judging from the stuff in their first issue, *Century* looks like it's going to be a thoroughly professional-level magazine, operating at a level of literary sophistication and eclecticism matched in the semiprozine field only by *Crank!*. So take a chance and subscribe now—maybe *your* money will make the difference between survival and death for this promising new magazine.

(It's interesting to note that most of these new magazines—*Absolute Magnitude, Pirate Writings, Sirius Visions, Galaxy,* even, to some extent, *Tomorrow*—are all self-consciously "retro" in sensibilities, dissatisfied with the current state of SF and harking back toward the "Good Old Days" when stories were less sophisticated and more "optimistic," untainted with sex and negativity, and all promising to deliver good old-fashioned action/adventure space-opera stuff [almost none of them, with the occasional exception of *Tomorrow, do* deliver it, in any reasonably competent form, but that's another story], the sort of thing that made your pulses pound when you were fourteen. In this climate, it's interesting to see new magazines like *Crank!* and *Century*—which actually is calling for *greater* literary complexity and higher levels of literary sophistication than is usually found in the genre today—swimming against the current, and I hope that this brave and audacious act proves to be a successful strategy for them.)

Things were chaotic among the longer-established semiprozines, with many of them dying or struggling. The most significant loss here was probably Steve Pasechnick's *Strange Plasma,* which published two issues this year, featuring good work by Michaela Roessner, Colin Greenland, Jim Marino, Kathleen Ann Goonan, R. A. Lafferty, and others, and then announced that it was ceasing publication. *New Pathways* and *Whispers* have also died, meaning that most of the most prominent of the older fiction semiprozines are gone. Of the remaining long-established SF fiction semiprozines, the best probably are the Canadian magazine *On Spec,* and two Australian magazines, *Aurealis* and *Eidolon.* Unfortunately, while two editions of *Eidolon* were supposedly produced in 1994, we never saw them, and we've heard nothing about *Aurealis* at all this year, which makes me wonder if they're still being produced. *On Spec* has been fairly reliable over the last few years, although this year it did produce only three issues out of a promised four; still, the magazing contains an interestingly eclectic mix of fiction, and the covers have improved over the last year or so to the point where they are probably the most handsome of any of the digest-sized semiprozines; worth your support. *Aberrations* is one of the most reliably published of the fiction semiprozines, bringing out twelve issues this year—unfortunately, the content is dreadful, usually a queasy combination of hardcore pornography and hardcore splatterpunk horror; not recommended. There was a one-shot "avant-garde" magazine called *Proud Flesh* out this year. As is usual with magazines that make a great fuss about how much more daring they are than the timid, stodgy old prozines, and how they'll bring us dangerous visions too controversial for the prozines to publish, in practice these dangerous vissions seem for the most part to be merely sniggering juvenile jokes about sex, including here a sequel to "The Frankenstein Penis" (from *Semiotext(e) SF*), called "The Dracula Vagina." That seems kind of disappointing, considering all the really controversial issues that society is going to have to deal with in the near future. *Grue, The Leading Edge,* and *Xizquil* produced only single issues this year, while *Space & Time, Deathrealm,* and *Next Phase* produced two. I didn't see *Tales of the Unanticipated, 2 A.M.,* or *Weirdbook,* or any of the British semiprozines such as *Back Brain Recluse, REM,* or *Strange Attractor,* and it's hard to tell which of these titles—if any—are still alive. *Marion Zimmer Bradley's Fantasy Magazine,* in its seventh year now, is another reliably published magazine, getting out their promised four issues this year as usual, but I continue to be unimpressed by the overall quality of the fiction, which frequently doesn't reach really professional levels. I haven't been following the horror semiprozines closely of late, but in that market *Cemetery Dance,* one of the most prominent of them, seems to have run into a bad patch because of the illness of the editor, and only managed three issues in 1994.

If you are looking for news and/or an overview of what's happening in the genre, then, as always, Charles N. Brown's *Locus* and Andy Porter's *SF Chronicle* remain your best bet among that sub-class of semiprozines known as "news-zines." *The New York Review of Science Fiction* (whose editorial staff includes David G. Hartwell, Donald G. Keller, Robert Killheffer, and Gordon Van Gelder) is more of a "criticalzine" than a "newszine," and by now has established itself as a fixture in this market; by far the most reliably published of the "criticalzines," it kept to its twelve-issue schedule once again this year. Some people profess to find *The New York Review of Science Fiction* dull, and some of it *is* dull; every issue, there's at least one piece that strikes me as extremely dull—but the magazine is also eclectic enough that I almost always find something in every issue that strikes me as interesting and absorbing, too. I'm also aware that the magazine publishes a varied enough mix of different types of material that something I find dull may strike someone *else* as fascinating, and vice versa. Steve Brown's *Science Fiction Eye* is almost always entertaining and interesting, *if* you can find it—but they only published one issue this year out of a scheduled three, which is pretty much par for the course for them. *Nova Express*—edited by Lawrence Person, Glen Cox, and Dwight Brown—is also entertaining, when you can find it, but there was no issue produced in 1994, although they keep promising one for 1995. If the new criticalzine called *Non-Stop Magazine*, which debuted in 1993, published an issue this year, I didn't see it, but I did receive a Winter 1995 issue just before this volume went to press. More reliable—they at least managed five out of their scheduled six issues—is another newish criticalzine, *Tangent*, which devotes itself to reviewing short fiction. The quality of the criticism still varies widely here, from profession-ally competent to embarrassingly amateuristic (although they seem to have gotten rid of their *most* inept reviewers), but this is a very important addition to the critical scene, since very little short fiction gets reviewed on a regular basis anywhere in the genre, except in Mark Kelly's column in *Locus*—and in *Tangent*. Anyone who's interested in short fiction should support this one.

(*Locus*, Locus Publications, Inc., P.O. Box 13305, Oakland, CA 94661—$50.00 for a one-year first-class subscription, 12 issues; *Science Fiction Chroni-cle*, Algol Press, P.O. Box 022730, Brooklyn, NY 11202-0056—$30.00 for 1 year, 12 issues, $36.00 first class; *The New York Review of Science Fiction*, Dragon Press, P.O. Box 78, Pleasantville, NY 10570—$30.00 per year; *Science Fiction Eye*, Box 18539, Asheville, NC 28814—$10.00 for one year; *Nova Express*, White Car Publications, P.O. Box 27231, Austin, TX 78755-2231—$10 for a one-year (four-issue) subscription; *Tangent*, 5779 Norfleet, Raytown, MO 64133—$20 for one year, four issues, make all monies payable to David A. Truesdale; *On Spec, the Canadian Magazine of Speculative Writing*, P.O. Box 4727, Edmonton, AB, Canada T6E 5G6—$18 for a one-year subscription; *Crank!*, Broken Mirrors Press, P.O. Box 380473, Cambridge, MA 02238—$12 for four issues; *Century*, P.O. Box 9270, Madison, WI 53715-0270—$27 for a one-year subscription; *Non-Stop Magazine*, Box 981, Peck Slip Station, New York, NY, 10272-0981—$18 for one year, four issues; *Aurealis, the Australian Magazine of Fantasy and Science Fiction*, Chimaera Publications, P.O. Box 538, Mt. Waverley, Victoria 3149, Australia—$24 for a four-issue (quarterly) subscription, "all money orders for overseas subscriptions should be in Austra-lian dollars"; *Eidolon, the Journal of Australian Science Fiction and Fantasy*, Eidolon Publications, P.O. Box 225, North Perth, Western Australia 6006—$34 (Australian) for $4 issues overseas, payable to Richard Scriven; *Back Brain Recluse*, P.O. Box 625, Sheffield S1 3GY, United Kingdom—$18 for four issues; *REM*, REM Publications, 19 Sandringham Road, Willesden, London NW2 5EP, United Kingdom—7.50 pounds sterling for four issues; *Xizquil*, P.O. Box 2885, Reserve, NM, 87830—$10 for three issues; *Strange Attractor: Horror, Fantasy, & Slipstream*, 111 Sundon Road, Houghton Regis, Beds. LU5 5NL, United Kingdom—7.75 pounds sterling for four issues; *Cemetery Dance*, P.O. Box 858, Edgewood, MD 21040—$15 for four issues (one year), $25 for eight issues (two years), "checks or money orders should be payable to Richard T. Chizmar only!"; *Pirate Writings, Tales of Fantasy, Mystery & Science Fiction*, 53 Whitman Ave., Islip, NY 11751, all checks payable to "Pirate Writings Publishing"—$15.00 for four issues; *Absolute Magnitude, The Magazine of Science Fiction Adventures*, P.O. Box 13, Greenfield, MA 01302, four issues for $14, all checks payable to "D.N.A. Publications"; *Argonaut Science Fiction*, P.O. Box 4201, Austin, TX 78765—$8 for two issues); *Grue Magazine*, Hells Kitchen Productions, Box 370, Times Square Sta., New York, NY 10108— $13.00 for three issues; *Expanse*, P.O. Box 43547, Baltimore, MD 21236-0547—$16 for four issues; *Sirius Visions*, Claddagh Press, 1075 NW Murray Road, Suite 161, Portland, OR 97229, eight issues for $16.50; *Galaxy Magazine*, The Institute for the Development of the Harmonious Human Being, Inc., P.O. Box 370, Nevada City, CA 95959—$18 for a one-year subscription (6 issues); *The Leading Edge*, 3163 JKHB, Provo, UT 84602—$8 for three issues; *Tales of the Unanticipated*, P.O. Box 8036, Lake Street Station, Minneapolis, MN 55408—$15.00 for four issues; *Mindsparks*, Molecudyne Research, P.O. Box 1379, Laurel, MD 20725-1379, four issues for $18; *Proud Flesh: Fiction for the Last Millennium*, Chris DeVito, 402 West Washington Street #2, Champaign, IL 61820-3456, $4.50 for the single issue.)

This was a fairly disappointing year for original anthologies, at least for science fiction anthologies—many of them contained one or two good stories, but the overall level of most of them was not particularly high. There were a couple of strong fantasy anthologies, an encouraging trend that has persisted for a few years now. There were few shared-world anthologies, but many theme anthologies, many of them predictably weak. And, although new anthology series were being born, some of the most prominent series died.

Turning to the established SF anthology series, *Universe 3* (Bantam Spectra), edited by Karen Haber and Robert Silverberg, was one of the year's stronger anthologies overall, and *still* struck me as mostly disappointing, with many of the stories dull and curiously bland. There *was* some good stuff here, though, mostly the more offbeat material. The best story here is probably Brian W. Aldiss's "The Madonna of Futurity," followed by Alex Jeffers's "Composition with Barbarian and Animal," which is deliberately and almost perversely slow-paced, but which does create a lush atmosphere and mood, with some sharp details, and Phillip C. Jennings's "Going West"—the Jennings story is also perverse, in its own way, frustratingly answering none of the puzzles that it raises in the course of the story, but with some vivid and *highly* unusual world-building and conceptualization. (Jennings's story is *also* perverse in *casually taking it for granted* that normal, red-blooded, American boys would, of course, all be eager to have sex with two-ton alien walruses . . . Nothing perverted *here*—they're all *girl* two-ton alien walruses, after all. Nothing *kinky* . . . This is slipped in (to coin a phrase) in such a casual, matter-of-fact manner that he *almost* gets away with it.) There was also interesting work here by Terry Boren, Paul Di Filippo, Wil McCarthy, Barry N. Malzberg, and E. Michael Blake. So there *is* good work here, even first-rate work . . . and yet, somehow you put

Universe 3 down with the feeling that it didn't really generate a lot of excitement, certainly not as much as has been generated by other Haber & Silverberg *Universe* volumes. An announcement was made at year's end that Bantam is dropping the *Universe* series; this is a real blow to the field, which not only loses yet another market, but a series that, when it was good, was *very* good, and, at its worst, was never less than competent and professional, and certainly always worth its cover price. The anthology market took another body blow this year with the news that Gollancz is also dropping the British anthology series *New Worlds,* which makes the current volume, *New Worlds 4* (Gollancz), edited by David Garnett, the last in the series. Unfortunately, *New Worlds* is going out on a low note rather than a high note. *New Worlds 4* is a highly uneven anthology, with some good stuff, but also with some Really Stupid stuff, including a *very* long version of the old story about how somebody's penis detaches itself from his body and scurries away, and a Barrington Bayley story that features the invention of what amounts to the Sodomy Drive, where you can only navigate hyperspace by the seat of your pants, as it were—except that nobody's wearing pants, if you see what I mean. (Nudge, nudge, wink, wink.) On the other hand, there *are* two first-rate stories here, Ian McDonald's story of starcrossed love between human and alien, "Legitimate Targets," and Lisa Tuttle's furiously despairing "And the Poor Get Children." Plus worthwhile work from Michael Moorcock and Garry Kilworth, an interesting-but-positively-dripping-with-ennui story by Graham Charnock, and a story by Robert Holdstock that could have been quite good if he had taken his material seriously and managed to avoid the broad winks into the wings. On the whole, a disappointing ending to a series that has been intermittently brilliant. *L. Ron Hubbard Presents Writers of the Future, Volume X* (Bridge), edited by Dave Wolverton, is, as always, mostly minor stories by novice writers, some of whom might be worth keeping an eye on in days to come. There was no volume in the *Synergy* anthology series out in 1994, for the fourth year in a row, and, in spite of the editor's assertions to the contrary, I think that it's reasonable to assume that this series is dead; he'll have to prove me wrong at this point by actually bringing a volume out.

Promised for next year is a new *Full Spectrum* volume, the series thankfully seeming to have survived the departure of all of its original editors for other publishing houses, and the launch of a new anthology series from Tor called *Starlight,* edited by Patrick Nielsen Hayden, which sounds quite promising. It's a sobering thought that, if not for *Full Spectrum* and the upcoming *Starlight,* there would now be no continuing science fiction annual original anthology series left in the field at all; at one time, there were a half-dozen or more of them. Next year will also see the launch of the first-ever professional online original anthology; *Neon Visions,* edited by Ellen Datlow, will appear on *Omni*'s electronic online magazine on America Online, and will present six original novellas, one per month, with each story online for one month and then archived for six months, so that they can be downloaded by anyone who has access to the online *Omni* through America Online. This is a fascinating experiment, and how successful it is will be a telling indicator of just how soon (if at all) electronic publishing will blossom into a major force in the publishing world.

Turning to the nonseries SF anthologies, it was a fairly weak year here overall as well, although again most of the anthologies contained at least one or two good stories. I guess in a way Mike Resnick's "Alternate" anthologies *are* a series, although not an officially recognized and acknowledged one. If you *do* consider them to be a series, then the series started strongly several years back with *Alternate Presidents,* and has been slowly running out of steam through the subsequent volumes—*Alternate Kennedys, Alternate Warriors*—with each one a little weaker than its predecessor. This trend is actually slightly reversed by this year's entry, *Alternate Outlaws* (Tor), edited by Mike Resnick, which I thought was somewhat stronger overall than last year's *Alternate Warriors*— but still nowhere as strong as *Alternate Presidents* had been. Why is this? For my money, it's because most of the stories in *Alternate Presidents* were solidly science-fictional extrapolations of legitimate Alternate History themes, things that actually *could* have happened. That's still true of the best stories in *Alternate Outlaws,* such as Walter Jon Williams's "Red Elvis" and Allen Steele's "Riders in the Sky" . . . but with every book the percentage of wildly improbable if not impossible (and sometimes downright silly) scenarios has gone up ("Suppose Mother Teresa formed an outlaw gang with Einstein and Albert Schweitzer!" "Suppose Carmen Miranda and Humphrey Bogart and Edward G. Robinson started robbing banks together!" "Suppose Queen Elizabeth the First became a pirate!"), much of it obviously wink-wink in-jokes between Resnick and his authors, and although this sort of thing *can* be entertaining, and sometimes *is* here, it also doesn't usually make for truly first-rate science fiction stories that you can remember more than a day or two down the road. In addition to the Williams and Steele stories mentioned above, *Alternate Outlaws* also contains entertaining work (yes, some of it fairly improbable, although most of it tends toward the more possible end of the Alternate History spectrum) by Maureen F. McHugh, Frank M. Robinson, Katharine Kerr, Martha Soukup, Judith Tarr, and others. There are apparently more "Alternate" anthologies in the pipeline, but I do begin to wonder if this series hasn't already lived out its natural life span. Almost all of the above remarks apply just as well, if not better, to *By Any Other Fame* (DAW), edited by Mike Resnick and Martin H. Greenberg, another anthology which, instead of exploring feasible Alternate History scenarios, mostly plays somewhat silly "What If" games with celebrities—"What if Groucho Marx had been chosen to play Rhett Butler?" . . . "What if Elvis became the President of the United States?" . . . "What if Humphrey Bogart was a private detective and Raymond Chandler was a movie star?" . . . and so on. As with *Alternate Outlaws,* there *is* some good stuff here, but it's mostly the stories that treat the theme the most seriously that deliver the most worthwhile material. The best story here is probably Jack C. Haldeman's "South of Eden, Somewhere Near Salinas," although the stories by Nancy Kress, Beth Meacham, Barry N. Malzberg, and Janet Kagan were also worthwhile; on the whole, this is probably somewhat weaker than *Alternate Outlaws,* though, while covering much the same sort of ground. *Alternate Worldcons* (Pulphouse Publishing, Box 1227, Eugene, OR 97440—$10 for *Alternate Worldcons*), edited by Mike Resnick, is more a fannish joke than an anthology that will appeal to the general readership—stories about what would have happened if other fan groups than the groups that *actually* won had won the bidding to put on a particular year's World Science Fiction Convention—and most of the stories in it will be unrewarding (if not incomprehensible) to those who are not hard-core convention-going fans, being mostly excuses to assemble lots of fannish in-jokes; the only piece here that might appeal to a wider readership is Kristine Kathryn Rusch's heartfelt poem, "ApocalypseCon."

Some of the same sort of ground that is covered in *Alternate Outlaws* and *By Any Other Fame* is also covered in *Alien Pregnant By Elvis* (DAW), edited by Esther M. Friesner and Martin H. Greenberg, an aggressively tongue-in-cheek anthology built around the premise that the things that you read in the headlines of supermarket tabloid newspapers are actually *true*—which, of course, means that many of the same celebrities who were featured in the two Resnick anthologies are put through a round of even sillier shenanigans here (for a dead man, poor old Elvis certainly has been kept busy the last couple of years—there was an anthology devoted to Elvis stories last year, another such anthology *this* year, and at least four of the year's original anthologies had Elvis stories in them, plus assorted magazine appearances). This is a totally frivolous anthology, of course, not meant to be taken seriously for a minute, and, if you keep that in mind, the stories in it are entertaining enough to make the book worth buying, although you'll have forgotten almost all of them an hour after reading them; this is one of those anthologies (there were several this year) that should be read one story at a time over a period of days, *not* read all in one sitting, which would be like sitting down and eating several gallons of caramel popcorn all at once—there was entertaining work here by Allen Steele, Lawrence Watt-Evans, Kristine Kathryn Rusch, Kate Daniel, George Alec Effinger, and Esther M. Friesner herself, among others. On the other hand, *Future Quartet: Earth in the Year 2042: A Four-Part Invention* (AvoNova), edited by Charles Sheffield, wants you to take it very seriously indeed, and, as a result, perhaps comes across as too frowningly solemn; certainly the four stories here (they are matched with four somewhat fictionalized "essays," by the same authors), all admirable attempts at forecasting future social problems with an eye to perhaps *preventing* them, while earnest and well-intentioned, are also mostly gray and rather dull; this also shouldn't be read all in one sitting, although here, rather than eating too much popcorn at one sitting, the analogy would be to eating huge quantities of something much heavier and more indigestible, a whole pot roast, perhaps— although all the stories contain interesting and substantial social speculations, the most entertaining *story* here, considered *as* a story, is, not surprisingly, by that veteran entertainer, Frederik Pohl.

One of the few shared-world anthologies this year was *Hotel Andromeda* (Ace), edited by Jack L. Chalker, an anthology of stories set in a "Galactic Grand Hotel." Most of the comments above about *Alien Pregnant By Elvis* apply just as well to *Hotel Andromeda*, and it's another of those books you're not going to want to read in one sitting, unless you *like* eating gallons of caramel popcorn at one go—which, perhaps, some people *do*. Another shared-world anthology, of a sort, anyway, was *Elric: Tales of the White Wolf* (White Wolf), edited by Edward E. Kramer, an anthology of stories about Michael Moorcock's famous sword & sorcery hero Elric of Melniboné, by Karl Edward Wagner, Neil Gaiman, Nancy A. Collins, Moorcock himself, and others. There was also a new *Wild Cards* "Mosaic Novel" this year, *Marked Cards,* edited by R. R. Martin (Baen).

There were also several examples this year of that curious subgenre, the "regional" anthology—SF stories ostensibly written by authors who all come from one particular region of the country, or written *about* one particular region of the country; in 1994, we also had an unusual number of "regional" anthologies featuring stories written by authors from *other* countries, as well. Perhaps the best of these "regional" anthologies, and certainly one of the best science fiction anthologies of the year in general, was the long-awaited *Future Boston* (Tor), edited by D. Alexander Smith. This anthology collects most of the "Future Boston" stories—set in a slowly sinking Boston that has become the world's intergalactic trading port—that first appeared in various SF magazines in the late 1980s and early 1990s, but also adds unpublished stories and newly written connecting sections in order to create what has become known in the trade as a "mosaic novel"—and, unlike most such, it manages to work pretty well as one, too; obviously a lot of thought and effort has gone into the creation of the background setting and scenario, and into the integrating of the material as well, much more so than is usually put into these sorts of projects. Most of the "Future Boston" stories that work best as stand-alone pieces were already published, of course, but some of the unpublished stories are quite good as well, the connecting pieces are interesting, and they really do add to the strength of the overall book— this really is one of those rare cases where the sum of the parts adds up to be greater than the whole. And even if it were *not,* you'd still have a collection of the original "Future Boston" stories, which included some of the best short work of the late 1980s. So this one is well worth your money, featuring good new material by Alexander Jablokov, Steven Popkes, Resa Nelson, Sarah Smith, David Alexander Smith, and others, as well as memorable reprints by Jablokov, Popkes, David Alexander Smith, Geoffrey A. Landis, and others.

As worthwhile and substantial in some ways, and also one of the best science fiction anthologies of the year, is *Alien Shores* (Aphelion), edited by Peter McNamara and Margaret Winch, a massive mixed original and reprint anthology of stories by Australian SF writers. The level of quality is perhaps more uneven here than in *Future Boston,* with some mediocre and even downright bad stories mixed in with the good ones, but it does contain one of the year's best stories, "Flowering Mandrake," by George Turner, plus good new stories by Sean McMullen, Stephen Dedman, Chris Simmons, Leanne Frahm, Lucy Sussex, and others, as well as good reprints by Greg Egan, Damien Broderick, Rosaleen Love, Terry Dowling, and others. Even if the overall level of quality were not as high as it is, though, this would still be a fascinating book for the look it gives us into what science fiction can be like in the hands of people from a very different culture and mindset. The same kind of insight can be gained from the two other books of Australian SF that were published (or at least came to my attention) this year—which I'll mention here for symmetry's sake, and also for your convenience in case you decide to check out Australian SF in a systematic way, although technically, being reprint anthologies, they should be covered in the reprint anthology section (where I'll mention them again)—*Mortal Fire: Best Australian SF* (Coronet Books), edited by Terry Dowling and Van Ikin, which contains good reprint material by Greg Egan, George Turner, A. Bertram Chandler, Cherry Wilder, David Lake, Damien Broderick, Sean McMullen, Terry Dowling, and others, and *Metaworlds: Best Australian Science Fiction* (Penguin Australia), edited by Paul Collins, which features good reprint stuff by many of the same authors in *Mortal Fire* and *Alien Shores*—Greg Egan, George Turner, Stephen Dedman, Terry Dowling, Sean McMullen, Damien Broderick, Rosaleen Love, David Lake, Leanne Frahm—although no specific stories are duplicated, an indication of the depth of field that exists in the Australian SF market these days.

There were also two anthologies of Canadian SF this year. *Prairie Fire: New Canadian Speculative Fiction,* edited by Candas Jane Dorsey and G. N. Louise Jonasson, a special book version of the Canadian magazine *Prairie Fire,* produced for ConAdien, this year's Worldcon, shows the Canadian tradition to be less oriented toward hard scientific concepts and updated space-opera than is the Australian tradition, at least in this volume, which leans more heavily toward softer "speculative fiction" than toward core SF; there is interesting work here (although not all of it necessarily science fiction by most accepted genre definitions) by Maria Billion, Keith Scott, Peter Watts, Derryl Murphy, Andrew Weiner, and others. *Northern Stars: The Anthology of Canadian Science Fiction* (Tor), a mixed original and reprint anthology edited by David G. Hartwell and Glenn Grant, gives us, not surprisingly, a look at a Canadian tradition that is much more solidly science fictional than the work in *Prairie Fire,* closer to— although, fascinatingly, by no means entirely synonymous with—the tradition of work in the United States and Britain. The original stories here are somewhat weak, but that's balanced by the presence of many strong reprint stories by writers such as Phyllis Gotlieb, Elisabeth Vonarburg, Spider Robinson, Charles de Lint, Andrew Weiner, Robert Charles Wilson, Eileen Kerrnaghan, Robert J. Sawyer, and others, including two really outstanding stories, William Gibson's "The Winter Market" and Candas Jane Dorsey's unjustly overlooked "(Learning About) Machine Sex."

Rounding out the year's "regional" SF anthologies was *Washed by a Wave of Wind: Science Fiction from the Corridor* (Signature Books), edited by M. Shayne Bell, ostensibly an anthology of stories by writers who live in Utah and southeastern Idaho—"the Corridor"—although they have to stretch the definition to "or has lived" there to get in people like Orson Scott Card, who don't anymore. (I've heard this book referred to, sarcastically, as *Great Science Fiction by Mormons,* but although most of the writers here *do* seem to be Mormons, that may be an accident of geography, and, in any case, is *not* the official organizing principle given.) The original fiction here, unfortunately, tends to be rather weak, although there is interesting work by Dave Wolverton, D. William Shunn, and others, and the anthology also features strong reprint work by M. Shayne Bell, Michaelene Pendleton, and, especially, Orson Scott

Card, whose huge novella "Pageant Wagon" is the kingpiece of the book. There was also a horror anthology of stories set in the South (mostly in New Orleans and its surrounding areas), *South from Midnight* (Southern Fried Press), edited by Richard Gilliam, Martin H. Greenberg, and Thomas R. Hanlon.

Turning to the fantasy anthologies, there was another edition in the *Xanadu* series this year, *Xanadu 2* (Tor), edited by Jane Yolen. This one was perhaps slightly less substantial than last year's volume, but still delivered a pleasing mix of different *styles* of fantasy, over a nicely eclectic range of tone and mood, and featured strong work by Megan Lindholm, Delia Sherman, Ursula K. Le Guin, Jessica Amanda Salmonson, Patricia A. McKillip, and others; let's hope that this series will continue for many years, because I think that it is contributing something valuable to the contemporary scene.

Encouragingly, the year also featured several strong and very eclectic fantasy (mostly) anthologies. For instance, it's hard to know where to categorize the British anthology *Blue Motel: Narrow Houses Volume 3* (Little, Brown), edited by Peter Crowther. Ostensibly it's a horror anthology, but it contains a lot of stuff that doesn't fit into the horror category at all, including a very strong SF story by Ursula K. Le Guin, another of her recent crop of Hainish stories, "Betrayals," which I'd have to rank as perhaps the third best Le Guin story this year, right behind "Forgiveness Day" and "The Matter of Seggri"—and which looks very out-of-place indeed in a horror anthology, making you wonder how in the world it got there. That's not the end of the unclassifiable stuff, though. *Blue Motel* also features another good SF story, by Kathleen Ann Goonan, a strange fantasy by Brian W. Aldiss which mingles Greek myth with the dreams of a condemned modern-day prisoner, a mystery-horror Hitchcock homage with distinct surreal elements by Ian McDonald, and a totally surreal and totally unclassifiable fantasy by Michael Moorcock. The rest of the anthology is mostly made up of standard English ghost story stuff, more what you would have expected, although still perhaps slightly more cozy and less gruesome than the usual hardcore horror anthology, which is one reason, along with its eclecticism, why I arbitrarily decided to review it here under fantasy. It's definitely a worthwhile anthology, one of the year's better ones, in fact—a shame that Le Guin didn't publish "Betrayals" somewhere where most of the people who'd like to read it would have a chance of finding it, though. Another quite eclectic anthology, in spite of what would seem like a fairly restrictive theme, was *Tales from the Great Turtle: Fantasy in the Native American Tradition* (Tor), edited by Piers Anthony and Richard Gilliam. I hadn't expected much, going in, since Native American themes had already been overused to the point of cliché in fantasy in the last few years, but I was pleasantly surprised by the range of different types of materials and different styles and attacks here—ranging from stories similar to traditional Native American folktales to harder-edged stories set in the modern world to stories set in the borderland between science fiction and wild surrealism—and *Tales from the Great Turtle* may well be the best fantasy anthology of the year, and one of the year's best in any category. My favorite from the book is William Sanders's "Going After Old Man Alabama," a nicely quirky backwoods fantasy with a wry flavor to it somewhat reminiscent of the work of Terry Bisson or the early R. A. Lafferty. My second favorite is Kristine Kathryn Rusch's powerful "Monuments to the Dead." The book also features a chunk of Jack Dann's famous unpublished novel, *Counting Coup*—unfortunately, it is just that, a chunk, and doesn't really stand on its feet as an individual work of fiction, but it's worth reading anyway, and gives you a feel for what the rest of the (alas, unpublished!) novel is like. There is also strong, quirky work here by Owl Goingback, Jane Yolen, Ed Gorman, Steve Rasnic Tem, Caroline Rhodes, Esther M. Friesner, Rick Wilber, Pamela Sargent, Gerald Hausman, Nicholas A. DiChario, and others. All in all, only a few mediocre-to-bad pieces here, making it a good value for your money; it's a nice-looking hardcover, too, with an unusually creative cover design. The other candidate for best fantasy anthology of the year was *Black Thorn, White Rose* (AvoNova Morrow), edited by Ellen Datlow and Terri Windling, another anthology of "updated" fairy tales told with modern sensibilities, a sequel to last year's *Snow White, Blood Red*. This isn't quite as strong overall as *Snow White, Blood Red* had been, but it is still one of the year's best fantasy anthologies, with an entertaining and satisfyingly varied selection of stories, many of them straddling that ambiguous borderland where fairy-tale fantasy shades into horror; in fact, a legitimate argument could be made for considering it a horror anthology, but I do think that, on balance, it *feels* more like a fantasy anthology than a horror anthology, which is why I'm mentioning it here. The best story in *Black Thorn, White Rose* is Howard Waldrop's strange mixture of backwoods humor, fairy tale, and Damon Runyonesque riffs, "The Sawing Boys," but there is also strong work here by Nancy Kress, Patricia C. Wrede, Michael Kandel, Jane Yolen, Roger Zelazny, Peter Straub, and Susan Wade, among others. Not quite in the same league as *Tales from the Great Turtle* or *Black Thorn, White Rose*, but still an enjoyable and eclectic anthology whose contents include fantasy, Alternate History, horror, and science fiction, was *Weird Tales from Shakespeare* (DAW), edited by Katharine Kerr and Martin H. Greenberg. This is another of those anthologies that, given the rather silly concept—stories about Shakespeare, or stories that play in one way or another with Shakespeare's material—is actually better than you'd expect it to be, although the bulk of the stories are not meant to be taken seriously. The best story in *Weird Tales from Shakespeare* is Gregory Feeley's "Aweary of the Sun," but there is also worthwhile material by Brian Aldiss, Josepha Sherman, Laura Resnick, Esther M. Friesner, Mike Resnick, Gregory Benford, Kate Elliot, and others. Another eating-a-gallon-of-caramel-popcorn-at-one-sitting anthology is *Deals with the Devil* (DAW), edited by Mike Resnick, Martin H. Greenberg, and Loren D. Estleman, which delivers just what it *says* it's going to deliver, most of the stories lightweight to *extremely* lightweight, a few of them more substantial than you'd think, the majority of them reasonably entertaining; the best work here is by Gregory Feeley, Frank M. Robinson, Pat Cadigan, Judith Tarr, George Alec Effinger, Laura Resnick, David Gerrold, Anthony Lewis, and Mike Resnick himself. There was also yet another Christmas anthology this year, joining the crowded shelf of such titles that have been brought out in the last few years, a mixed reprint and original anthology called *Christmas Magic* (Tor), edited by David G. Hartwell. Most of the originals here are rather weak, but the bulk of the book is reprint material, and there are strong reprint stories here from Donald E. Westlake, Alexander Jablokov, Janet Kagan, Robert Frazier and James Patrick Kelly, Howard Waldrop, William Browning Spencer, Harlan Ellison, Nina Kiriki Hoffman, and others.

I haven't been following the horror field as closely as I once did, but it seemed to me that the most prominent horror anthology of the year may have been *Little Deaths* (Millennium), edited by Ellen Datlow. I've frankly grown tired of the standard "Erotic Horror" anthology, especially the gross-out splatterpunk fuck-'em-in-the-intestines-while-they-die sort, which have proliferated so greatly in the last couple of years as to almost form a subgenre of their own (interestingly, in spite of the violence toward women and hostility *for* women that seems to be an integral part of these sorts of books, many of the authors who most frequently write for them *are* women, an odd social phenomenon), but *Little Deaths* is done with a good deal more literary sophistication and variety of tone than is the standard product. My favorite story here was Nicola Griffith's novella "Yaguara," followed by Lucius Shepard's "The Last Time"; the book also features strong work by M. John Harrison, Pat Cadigan, Jack Womack, Sarah Clemens, and others. Unfortunately, the Griffith, the Shepard, and the Harrison stories, some of the best stories in the anthology, have all been cut out of the upcoming American edition (I read the British edition), meaning that the book you get is going to be *considerably* weaker than the book you *could* have gotten, which is a shame. Also getting a lot of attention in the horror market this year was *Love in Vein: Twenty Original Tales of Vampiric Erotica* (HarperPrism), edited by Poppy Z. Brite, which leans toward the grotesque, splatterpunk end of the field, but which is occasionally leavened by welcome touches of intelligence and style. There was less such leavening in *The King Is Dead: Tales of Elvis Postmortem* (Delta), edited by Paul M. Sammon, a mixed reprint and original anthology that is pretty solidly hardcore splatterpunk in sensibility, although there *is* some stuff here that doesn't rely on the grotesque, by writers such as Harlan Ellison, Chet Williamson, Michael Reaves, and others. Ironically, the two best stories here, "Bubba Ho-Tep," by Joe R. Lansdale and "Donna Rae," by Neal Barrett Jr., demonstrate the strengths *and* the weaknesses of splatterpunk, both full of headlong energy and strong, shaggy, irreverent humor, and both spoiling some of their impact (for old farts like me, anyway) by indulging in material that is too obviously there for no real reason *other* than to shock the reader, deliberate gross-out-for-the-sake-of-grossing-people-out stuff, like a little boy picking his nose and showing it to a roomful of his mother's friends having a tea party. On the whole, then, I'd have to say that this book is less successful than *last* year's Elvis anthology *Elvis Rising: Stories on the King,* and certainly more concentrated on horror than that anthology was, which also featured science fiction, fantasy, and mainstream stories. (It's interesting to notice the similarities—and the differences—between *The King Is Dead* and *Alien Pregnant by Elvis*: both anthologies rely heavily on stories inspired by tabloid newspaper headlines, but the mood and tone of those stories are very different from one book to the other.) Mention should also be made of *The Best of Whispers* (Borderlands Press), edited by Stuart David Schiff, a mixed reprint and original anthology of stories from the well-known (and now, alas, defunct), horror/fantasy semiprozine that includes original work by Whitley Strieber, Ray Bradbury, Lucius Shepard, Melanie Tem, and others, and strong reprints by Fritz Leiber, Karl Edward Wagner, Connie Willis, Ramsey Campbell, and David J. Schow. Other original horror anthologies this year included: *Borderlands 4* (Borderlands Press), edited by Elizabeth and Thomas Monteleone; *Return to the Twilight Zone* (DAW), edited by Carol Serling; *Dark Destiny: The World of Darkness* (White Wolf), edited by Edward E. Kramer; and the above-mentioned *South from Midnight*. (It should be mentioned that some of the anthologies that I have pigeonholed above as fantasy anthologies—for instance, *Blue Motel* and *Black Thorn, White Rose*, and even, to a somewhat lesser extent, *Deals with the Devil*—could validly have been listed as horror anthologies instead; and, if they *were* so listed, then *Blue Motel* and *Black Thorn, White Rose* would certainly have to be ranked along with *Little Deaths* as the top horror anthologies of the year (although which *order* I'd rank them in, I have no idea). Listing them as fantasy anthologies instead was a subjective decision on my part, and a case could be made for either categorization.)

An associational anthology that might be of interest to some genre readers is *The Mysterious West* (HarperCollins), edited by Tony Hillerman—the gimmick here is that this is a book of mystery stories with Western settings, written by well-known mystery writers, but some of those writers, such as Bill Pronzini, Ed Gorman, and Carole Nelson Douglas, will be familiar to the SF readership as well, and a few of the stories even have mild fantastic elements (one being narrated by a cat, for instance).

In terms of literary quality, 1994 seemed to be a pretty good year for novels, perhaps even better than 1993, although somewhat fewer strong first novels were published than last year.

As far as the numbers are concerned, the newsmagazine *Locus* estimates 1,109 original books and 627 reprints, for an overall total of 1,736 SF/fantasy/horror books published in 1994, declining by 5 percent from 1993's total, the third year in a row of decline—although, for all the grim recessionary talk that has preoccupied the field during the last couple of years, if you compare this to 1993's total of 1,820 titles, it's clear that this decline has by no means been an *enormous* one; what usually happens is that the death of one already established publishing line is balanced by the launching of a *new* line somewhere else, leaving the overall totals roughly the same. (It should be emphasized that this total does *not* include the gaming and media-related books; if it did, the overall total would be far higher.) Original SF/fantasy/horror *novels* make up 616 of the titles in that overall total. According to *Locus,* there were 204 SF novels published in 1994 (as opposed to 263 in 1993), 234 fantasy novels published in 1994 (as opposed to 267 published in 1993), and 178 horror novels published in 1994 (as opposed to 175 in 1993—it's interesting to note that although adult horror titles declined, the explosion in the Young Adult horror market more than made up the difference; 38 percent of all horror books are now Young Adult titles, up from 30 percent last year). Hardcover books accounted for 39 percent of the total this year, trade paperbacks for 20 percent, and mass-market paperbacks for 41 percent—five years ago, trade paperbacks accounted for only 7 percent of the total, while mass-market paperbacks made up 50 percent, so obviously the trade paperback format has grown at the expense of the mass-market paperback format. Many if not most adult SF and fantasy novels seem to come out in hardcover these days, with a mass-market or trade paperback reprint following; there are noticeably fewer original mass-market paperbacks than there were only a few years ago; some publishers have almost phased-out the paperback original, with Tor, for instance, now doing 76 percent of its original titles as hardcovers—that's high, but Bantam/Doubleday/Dell is doing 38 percent of its originals as hardcovers, and Random/Ballantine/Del Rey/Fawcett is doing 40 percent of its originals as hardcovers, so obviously Tor is not alone in following this trend. Maybe the original mass-market paperback is on the way out, or at least destined to be squeezed down to a far smaller share of the market.

Even restricting myself to the SF novels alone, it's obviously just about impossible for any one individual—let alone somebody with all of the huge amounts of reading that I have to do at shorter lengths for *Asimov's* and for this anthology—to read and evaluate *all* of the more than 200 new science fiction novels that came out in 1994, or even a really significant fraction of them.

Therefore, as usual, I'm going to limit myself to listing those novels that have received a lot of attention and acclaim in 1994, including: *The Iron Dragon's Daughter*, Michael Swanwick (Morrow/AvoNova); *Green Mars*, Kim Stanley Robinson (Bantam Spectra); *Heavy Weather*, Bruce Sterling (Bantam Spectra); *Wildlife*, James Patrick Kelly (Tor); *Slow Funeral*, Rebecca Ore (Tor); *Brittle Innings*, Michael Bishop (Bantam); *Solis*, A. A. Attanasio (HarperCollins); *Beggars and Choosers*, Nancy Kress (Tor); *Permutation City*, Greg Egan (Millennium); *Furious Gulf*, Gregory Benford (Bantam Spectra); *Half the Day Is Night*, Maureen F. McHugh (Tor); *Red Dust*, Paul M. McAuley (Morrow/AvoNova); *Temporary Agency*, Rachel Pollack (St. Martin's Press); *Ring*, Stephen Baxter (HarperCollins UK); *Mother of Storms*, John Barnes (Tor); *Larque on the Wing*, Nancy Springer (Morrow/AvoNova); *Love & Sleep*, John Crowley (Bantam); *The Stars are Also Fire*, Poul Anderson (Tor); *Somewhere East of Life*, Brian W. Aldiss (Carroll & Graf); *North Wind*, Gwyneth Jones (Gollancz); *Feersum Endjinn*, Iain M. Banks (Orbit); *Hot Sky at Midnight*, Robert Silverberg (Bantam Spectra); *Genetic Soldier*, George Turner (Morrow/AvoNova); *Mysterium*, Robert Charles Wilson (Bantam Spectra); *Pasquale's Angel*, Paul J. McAuley (Gollancz); *Caldé of the Long Sun*, Gene Wolfe (Tor); *Summer of Love*, Lisa Mason (Bantam Spectra); *The Engines of God*, Jack McDevitt (Ace); *The Voices of Heaven*, Frederik Pohl (Tor); *Towing Jehovah*, James Morrow (Harcourt Brace); *Summer King, Winter Fool*, Lisa Goldstein (Tor); *Happy Policeman*, Patricia Anthony (Harcourt Brace); *Worldwar: In the Balance*, Harry Turtledove (Del Rey); *Terminal Café*, Ian McDonald (Bantam Spectra); *Foreigner*, C. J. Cherryh (Warner Aspect); *Random Acts of Senseless Violence*, Jack Wamack (Grove Atlantic); *End of an Era*, Robert J. Sawyer (Ace); *Climbing Olympus*, Kevin J. Anderson (Warner Aspect); *Shadow's End*, Sheri S. Tepper (Bantam Spectra);

The Jericho Iteration, Allen Steele (Ace); *Mirror Dance,* Lois McMaster Bujold (Baen); *Merlin's Wood,* Robert Holdstock (HarperCollins UK); *The Carnival of Destruction,* Brian Stableford (Carroll & Graf); *Fires of Eden,* Dan Simmons (Putnam); *Insomnia,* Stephen King (Viking); and *The Dolphins of Pern,* Anne McCaffery (Del Rey).

It didn't seem to be quite as strong a year for first novels as last year, although some excellent first novels did appear. The first novels that stirred up the most excitement and acclaim this year were *Queen City Jazz,* Kathleen Ann Goonan (Tor), *Gun, with Occasional Music,* Jonathan Lethem (Harcourt Brace), and *Vurt,* Jeff Noon (Crown), the Arthur C. Clarke Award winner this year, which pulled reviews ranging from admiringly positive to almost rabidly negative. Other first novels included: *This Side of Judgment,* J. R. Dunn (Harcourt Brace); *The Imperium Game,* K. D. Wentworth (Del Rey); *Voices in the Light,* Sean McMullen (Aphelion); *Changing Fate,* Elisabeth Waters (DAW): *The Woman Between the Worlds,* F. Gwynplaine MacIntyre (Dell); *Aggressor Six,* Wil McCarthy; *Witch and Wombat,* Carolyn Cushman (Warner Questar); *Love Bite,* Sherry Gottlieb (Warner); *The Child Queen,* Nancy McKenzie (Del Rey); *Aurian,* Maggie Furey (Bantam Spectra); and *Brother to Dragons, Companion to Owls,* Jane Lindskold (AuoNova). The Del Rey Discovery line, which had stirred up a lot of excitement last year with acclaimed and award-winning first novels by writers such as Nicola Griffith and Mary Rosenblum (Griffith won the Tiptree Award, Rosenblum the Compton Crook Award), seemed to generate less of interest this year, and I get the feeling that it's being phased out, or at least is being allowed to peter out—which, if true, is a shame, since it was a very promising line.

It looked to me, although this is a subjective opinion, gathered from reading the reviews and listening to reader reaction, as if 1994 was a pretty good year for novels, although there was no clear favorite, no single book that dominated the category in the way that other books have done in years past. It's anyone's guess what will end up winning the major awards, although *Green Mars* and *The Iron Dragon's Daughter* seem to be favorites in some quarters. And, of course, SFWA's bizarre "rolling eligibility" rule allows books from 1993 such as Greg Bear's *Moving Mars* to be pitted against the 1994 novels for the Nebula Award, which complicates things even more, and makes it even more difficult to predict who is going to win what. (*Green Mars,* of course, already won last year's Hugo Award, and is now up for *this* year's Nebula Award, just to confuse things further. I wonder if anyone else has noticed that Kim Stanley Robinson won the Nebula and the Hugo Awards last year with *two separate books*? I can't think of any other case where the same author won the Nebula Award with one book and the Hugo Award with *another* book, in the same year!)

As can be seen from a glance at the list above, Tor had another very strong year (perhaps even stronger than last year), as did Bantam Spectra. The HarperCollins line is also beginning to show up on the list, as is stuff from the revamped Warner Aspect line and from the AvoNova line, which was spared from a shakeup that might have resulted in its demise when the sale of Morrow/Avon fell through. And, in another positive bit of news, the Harcourt Brace line, which was reported to be dead last year after the dismissal of editor Michael Kandel, has hired Kandel back again as a "consultant" and seems not to be dead after all—and is also placing some strong books on the list.

And for those who voice the often-heard complaint that there's no science in science fiction anymore, it should be noted that in the list above the books by Egan, Sterling, Kelly, Robinson, Attanasio, Benford, Baxter, Turner, Silverberg, Kress, McHugh, Banks, Anderson, McAuley, Pohl, Steele, and a number of others, are clearly and unequivocally science fiction by any reasonable definition—and that a few, especially the Egan, the Benford, the Robinson, and the Baxter, are "hard" science fiction as hard and pure as it is ever likely to get. In spite of all the moaning about how SF is being diluted (and, by implication, ruined) by fantasy, there is still plenty of pure-quill core science fiction to be found if you look for it. (Although it should *also* be said that in some cases, as in Swanwick's *The Iron Dragon's Daughter*, the admixture of fantasy with science fiction, far from "ruining" SF, is instead producing some exciting and viable new hybrids, and opening up new horizons.)

Associational items that might be of interest to SF readers this year included: Norman Spinrad's near-future thriller about terrorism and the uses of electronic media, *Pictures of 11* (Bantam), which makes an interesting companion to his classic SF media novel, *Bug Jack Barron*; two historical novels by Judith Tarr *Throne of Isis* and *The Eagle's Daughter*, both from Tor; and Richard Matheson's horror-western, *Shadow on the Sun* (Berkley). I'm not sure *where* to mention the illustrated book version of Harlan Ellison's screenplay version of Isaac Asimov's collection *I, Robot*, called *I, Robot: The Illustrated Screenplay* (Warner Aspect)—but since it's a screenplay that reads like a novel, and is as long as most novels, perhaps this is as appropriate a place as any. To be fair, I'll also mention it in the art books section.

Another interesting milestone to note is that *HotWired*, the online electronic-magazine version of *Wired*, announced plans to serialize Alexander Besher's novel *RIM: A Novel of Virtual Reality*, with added hypertext links and multimedia enhancements, the first time this has been done (in quite this way, anyway), as far as I know. People keep telling me that Electronic Publishing in any significant form is decades away, if it ever comes at all—but I dunno. Seemed to me you could see the seeds of it everywhere this year, if you looked around.

1994 didn't seem to be as strong a year overall for short-story collections as 1993 had been—the publication last year of the massive Cordwainer Smith retrospective collection *The Rediscovery of Man* was enough all by itself to tip the balance in favor of 1993—but there still *were* some excellent collections published this year. The best collections of the year were: *A Fisherman of the Inland Sea*, Ursula K. Le Guin (HarperPrism); *The Breath of Suspension*, Alexander Jablokov (Arkham House); *Unconquered Countries*, Geoff Ryman (St. Martin's Press); *The Coming of Vertumnus*, Ian Watson (Gollancz); and *Travellers in Magic*, Lisa Goldstein (Tor). Also first-rate were: *Crashlander*, Larry Niven (Del Rey); *Otherness*, David Brin (Bantam Spectra); *Women and Ghosts*, Alison Lurie (Doubleday); *A Knot in the Grain and Other Stories*,

Robin McKinley (Morrow Greenwillow); *The Girl Who Heard Dragons,* Anne McCaffery (Tor); *The Early Fears,* Robert Bloch (Fedogan & Bremer); and *The Passage of Light: The Recursive Science Fiction of Barry N. Malzberg,* Barry N. Malzberg (NESFA Press). Special mention should be made of a hard-to-categorize item, *Mind Fields: The Art of Jacek Yerka/The Fiction of Harlan Ellison* (Morpheus International), a collection of stories by Ellison, each matched with the painting by Yerka that inspired it.

Sharply reversing the trend for the last several years, most of the best collections this year were published by mainline trade houses such as Bantam Spectra and HarperPrism and Tor, while relatively few were published by the small presses, which until now had dominated this category throughout the last part of the '80s and the early '90s; Arkham House and NESFA Press, however, remain important sources of major new collections, especially Arkham House, which in the last couple of years has published collections by many of the hottest new writers in SF. It'll be very interesting to see if this trend continues; since I'd like to see the total of collections published annually go *up* sharply (you'd be surprised by a list of some of the authors, even popular ones, who have never *had* a collection, especially a collection from a mainline trade publisher), I'd be pleased to see both the trade publishers *and* the small presses increase the number of collections they bring out every year—there's certainly room for expansion.

Since very few small-press titles will be findable in the average bookstore, or even in the average chain store, mail order is your best bet, and so I'm going to list the addresses of the small-press publishers mentioned above: Arkham House, P.O. Box 546, Sauk City, WI 53583—$20.95 for *The Breath of Suspension*; NESFA Press, P.O. Box 809, Framingham, MA 07101-0203—$14.00 for *The Passage of the Light: The Recursive Science Fiction of Barry N. Malzberg*; Morpheus International, 200 N. Robertson Blvd. #326, Beverly Hills, CA 90211—$24.95 for *Mind Fields: The Art of Jacek Yerka/The Fiction of Harlan Ellison*.

The reprint anthology market had another solid year in 1994, with a larger-than-usual number of big "historical overview"–type anthologies, all of them excellent values. As usual in this category, some of the best bets for your money were the various "Best of the Year" anthologies, and the annual Nebula Award anthology, *Nebula Awards 28* (Harcourt Brace Jovanovich), edited by James Morrow. Science fiction is at the moment still being covered by only one "Best of the Year" anthology series, the one you are holding in your hand, but a *new* "Best" series covering science fiction, to be edited by David G. Hartwell and Kathryn Cramer, has been announced for next year—this additional coverage from what will no doubt be a very different aesthetic perspective than mine is certainly a good thing for the genre at large, and it will be very interesting to see Hartwell and Cramer's idea of which of 1995's stories are worthy of inclusion in a "Best" anthology; certainly the field is wide and various enough for there to be room for volumes representing different tastes than my own. This year there were still three Best of the Year anthologies covering horror: Karl Edward Wagner's long-running *Year's Best Horror Stories* (DAW), this year up to volume XXII, an entry in a newer British series, *The Best New Horror 5* (Carroll & Graf), edited by Stephen Jones and Ramsey Campbell, and the Ellen Datlow half of a mammoth volume covering both horror *and* fantasy, *The Year's Best Fantasy and Horror* (St. Martin's Press), edited by Ellen Datlow and Terri Windling, this year up to its Seventh Annual Collection. Unfortunately, Karl Edward Wagner's *The Year's Best Horror Stories* has died with him; the series will not be continued next year, which brings to a sad close the longest-running "Best" anthology series in the SF/fantasy/horror end of the industry, and which puts DAW Books entirely out of the business of publishing "Best of the Year" series—at one time, they were publishing *three* such "Best" series, one covering science fiction, one covering fantasy, and one covering horror, but now all those series are dead. I continue to think that the expansion of the market for fantasy, and especially the recent expansion of the short fiction fantasy market with specialized magazines such as *Realms of Fantasy* and anthology series such as *Xanadu,* indicates that fantasy ought to merit more coverage than just the Windling half of the Datlow/Windling anthology, that someone ought to start an annual "Best" volume devoted to fantasy alone (or, perhaps, that the Datlow/Windling volume ought to be split into two separate books), but so far this is a suggestion that has fallen upon deaf ears.

Turning to the retrospective "historical overview" anthologies, there was a retrospective Nebula volume this year, *Nebula Award-Winning Novellas* (Barnes & Noble), edited by Martin H. Greenberg (although I continue to question the wisdom of singling some award winners out as "better" than others, which is the implication of this volume and the recent *SuperHugos* anthology), and a new Hugo-winners volume, *The New Hugo Winners, Volume III* (Baen), edited by Connie Willis. There was also a retrospective anthology of stories from *F&SF, The Best from Fantasy & Science Fiction: A 45th Anniversary Anthology* (St. Martin's Press), edited by Edward L. Ferman & Kristine Kathryn Rusch, an anthology that belongs in the library of every serious student of science fiction. Also first-rate was another "historical overview" anthology, this one covering fantasy, *The Oxford Book of Fantasy Stories* (Oxford), edited by Tom Shippey. A retrospective anthology with a somewhat more specialized slant was *New Eves: SF About the Extraordinary Women of Today and Tomorrow* (Longmeadow Press), edited by Janrae Frank, Jean Stine, and Forrest J. Ackerman—some of the stories in this anthology of stories by women about women have dated rather badly, but the book does also contain more recent work by strong contemporary writers such as Ursula K. Le Guin, Joanna Russ, Mary Rosenblum, Karen Joy Fowler, Octavia Butler, Nancy Kress, Maureen F. McHugh, and others, and, in any case, even the "dated" material is of historical interest . . . and importance, in a genre rapidly forgetting its own history. Noted without comment is *another* big retrospective "historical overview" anthology, *Modern Classic Short Novels of Science Fiction* (St. Martin's Press), edited by Gardner Dozois.

Without doubt, by far the most controversial "historical overview" anthology of the year is *The Ascent of Wonder: The Evolution of Hard SF* (Tor), edited by David G. Hartwell and Kathryn Cramer, which managed to generate at least as much heat and light, especially in the form of "flamewars" on the various computer networks, as last year's fiercely controversial *The Norton Book of Science Fiction*. Ironically, most of the howls of protest seemed to be coming from core fans of "Hard SF," who were outraged by the inclusion of writers such as J. G. Ballard, Kate Wilhelm, and Philip K. Dick as "Hard SF" writers. This is definitely an anthology with an ideological axe to grind, and I have no intention of attempting to analyze—let alone argue with—the intricate structures of theory advanced by Hartwell and Cramer to justify their definitions of what qualifies as "Hard SF," although no, the anthology's inclusions don't always make sense to *me*, either—but I'm not sure, in the long run, that any of that really *matters*. As I said last year in defense of *The Norton Book of Science Fiction*, another book whose contents you could certainly quibble with and second-guess (as critics probably *will* be doing, for years to come), what is overshadowed by the controversy over who's been included and who's been left out is that, like *The Norton Book* before it, *The Ascent of Wonder* is an enormous book jam-packed with excellent stories by excellent writers. Considered just as a pure reading value—ignoring all the polemics and the conflicting aesthetic arguments—*The Ascent of Wonder* is certainly one of the very best buys for your money available in the field this year, and certainly deserves a place on your library shelf just as a reference anthology alone, whether or not you agree with Hartwell and Kramer's overview of the evolution of "Hard SF" or their opinion as to who ought to be in a "Hard SF" anthology.

You could also argue with the selections in *Future Primitive: The New Ecoptoias* (Tor), edited by Kim Stanley Robinson, a few of which seemed far enough off the ostensible theme that they ought to be in some other anthology altogether—but again, it's a good reading value for your money, and includes quirky and not frequently reprinted stories by Howard Waldrop, Gene Wolfe, Pat Murphy, R. A. Lafferty, Ursula K. Le Guin, Robert Silverberg, and others. *Omni Visions Two* (Omni Books), edited by Ellen Datlow, is another interesting and worthwhile reprint anthology, featuring good stories by Kate Wilhelm, Howard Waldrop, Frederik Pohl, Robert Silverberg, Jack Dann, Michael Swanwick, and others. Two good reprint anthologies of stories from little-seen Australian writers (already mentioned above) are *Mortal Fire, Best Australian SF* (Coronet Books), edited by Terry Dowling and Van Ikin, and *Metaworlds* (Penguin Australia), edited by Paul Collins—although you'll probably have to haunt well-stocked SF specialty bookstores, or mail order, to find them. There was also a good reprint (mostly) anthology of Canadian SF, also mentioned above, *Northern Stars* (Tor), edited by David G. Hartwell and Glenn Grant. There was also a reprint anthology of science fictional vampire stories, *Tomorrow Sucks* (Baen), edited by Greg Cox and T. K. F. Weisskopf, and Jack Zipes edited a reprint fantasy anthology, *The Outspoken Princess and The Gentle Knight: Timely Fairy Tales for Tumultuous Times* (Bantam). Two anthologies of mostly reprint stories were *Animal Brigade 3000* (Ace) and *Commando Brigade 3000* (Ace), both edited by Martin Harry Greenberg and Charles Waugh.

Noted without comment are: *Horses!* (Ace), edited by Jack Dann and Gardner Dozois; and *Isaac Asimov's Cyberdreams* (Ace), edited by Gardner Dozois and Sheila Williams.

This seemed to be a moderately weak year in the SF-oriented nonfiction and reference book field, although perhaps any year would look weak by comparison with a year like 1993, which saw the publication of the landmark volume *The Encyclopedia of Science Fiction*. There was, however, a fair amount of general nonfiction that might be of interest to SF readers. Most of the SF reference works this year were rather specialized, and many of the critical books difficult for the average non-scholarly reader to wade through, but the most prominent items in this category this year included: *Science Fiction and Fantasy Book Review Annual 1991* (Greenwood), edited by Robert A. Collins and Robert Latham; *The Fabulous Realm: A Literary-Historical Approach to British Fantasy, 1780–1990* (Scarecrow Press), by Karen Patricia Smith; *The Work of Jack Vance: An Annotated Bibliography and Guide* (Underwood-Miller), by Jerry Hewett and Daryl F. Mallett; *Science Fiction in the 20th Century* (Oxford Opus), by Edward James; *Odd Genre: A Study in Imagination and Evolution* (Greenwood), by John J. Pierce; *Science Fiction Before 1900: Imagination Discovers Technology* (Macmillan/Twayne), by Paul Alkon; *The Dystopian Impulse in Modern Literature: Fiction as Social Criticism* (Greenwood), by M. Keith Booker; two literary biographies/studies, *Roald Dahl: A Biography* (Farrar Straus Giroux), by Jeremy Treglown and *Olaf Stapledon: Speaking for the Future* (Syracuse University Press), by Robert Crossley; and another study of fairy tales, *Fairy Tale As Myth/Myth as Fairy Tale*, Jack Zipes (University Press of Kentucky). Of more general interest and perhaps more accessible for the average reader were: Isaac Asimov's posthumously published autobiography, *I. Asimov: A Memoir* (Doubleday), by Isaac Asimov (although I remain convinced that Isaac intended the title to be *I, Asimov*, a humorous reference to his famous collection *I, Robot*, and not the dry *I. Asimov* title it was published under); a book of transcriptions of interviews given by Samuel R. Delany at various points in time, *Silent Interviews: On Language, Race, Sex, Science Fiction, and Some Comics* (Wesleyan University Press), by Samuel R. Delany; and a sort of dictionary/guide to Gene Wolfe's *Book of the New Sun* novels, *Lexicon Urthus: A Dictionary for the Urth Cycle* (Sirius Fiction), by Michael Andre-Driussi—still somewhat specialized, but less dry by virtue of its subject matter than some of the more academic studies above.

There were several good values in the art book field this year, including *The Art of James Christensen: A Journey of the Imagination* (Greenwich Workshop), James Christensen; *Ship of Dreams*, Dean Morrissey (Abrams/Mill Pond Press); *The Fantastic Art of Jacek Yerka*, Jacek Yerka (Morpheus International); *Spectrum: The Best in Contemporary Fantastic Art* (Underwood Books), edited by Cathy Burnett and Arnie Fenner, a sort of "Best of the Year" compilation of last year's fantastic art, an interesting concept; *Virgil Finlay's Far Beyond* (Charles F. Miller), Virgil Finlay; *Mermaids and Magic Shows* (Paper Tiger), David Delamare; *Horripilations: The Art of J. K. Potter* (Paper Tiger), J. K. Potter; and, just in case you had any doubts, a cartoon book proving that Gahan Wilson is *Still Weird* (Forge). Mention should be made here of a couple of unusual items: the black-humored *Lady Cottington's Pressed Fairy Book* (Turner) by Terry

Jones and Brian Froud, which is just what it *says* that it is, complete with Pressed Fairies that fall out of the book when you open it, which can get you some odd looks in bookstores; and *I, Robot: The Illustrated Screenplay* (Warner Aspect), by Harlan Ellison—as I mentioned the text under novels, I suppose it's only fair to mention the *artwork* here, and, in fact, the illustrations, by newcomer Mark Zug, are stunning, vivid and painterly, and suggest that Zug could perhaps rival the accomplishments of a Michael Whelan if he continues to work in the field of fantastic art.

There were scads of books this year about *Star Trek* in one or the other of its incarnations, including biographies of Gene Roddenberry and various cast members, but I'm not going to bother to list them here. If you want to find them all, all you have to do is go into your local bookstore, where, no doubt, they will be piled up in stacks halfway to the ceiling.

Turning to the general genre-related nonfiction field, there was a fair amount of stuff this year that will probably be of interest to most genre readers. Perhaps the scariest such item is the hair-raising *The Hot Zone* (Random House), which tells the frightening story of how the ultra-deadly virus Ebola Zaire—which is not only highly contagious, but kills nine out of ten of its victims, very rapidly—*almost* got loose in the general population of Washington, D.C., in 1989, a disaster that could have killed tens of millions of people nationwide (the recently released film, *Outbreak*, is obviously inspired by this incident); you won't sleep well nights after reading *this* one, especially when you realize that a *successful* outbreak of Ebola could happen at any time—and that, if it *did*, there would be very little authorities could do to stop the spread of the virtus. Ebola is only *one* of the biological catastrophes laying in wait for us that are described in *The Coming Plague* (Farrar Straus Giroux), by Laurie Garrett, which also deals with everything from the recent outbreaks of so-called "flesh-eating bacteria" to the spread of Hanta virus and drug-resistant tuberculosis, and on to the terrifying possibility that soon bacteria will develop resistance to *all* known antibiotics, something that is already close to happening, as antibiotics become useless one after the other, with appalling speed. Reading these books emphasizes again how precarious is our existence upon this earth; you don't need an atomic war or the impact of a dinosaur-killer asteroid to wipe out the human race (or, at the very least, destroy much of our present civilization)—all you need is a killer virus striking into a population that has no immunity for it, something that becomes more and more possible in these days of jet travel between continents, when someone exposed in Africa or South America to a rare virus that's never made it out of the jungle before can be coughing in an airport waiting room in New York City a few hours later (a theory unsettling like this—minus the jet planes and the airplane waiting rooms, of course—is now being advanced by some scientists to explain what *really* killed the dinosaurs, with the famous asteroid strike reduced to being just the coup de grâce). After these harrowing scenarios, the benign future of space exploration and colonization mapped out in *Pale Blue Dot: A Vision of the Human Future in Space* (Random House), by Carl Sagan, seems almost wistfully Utopian; assuming that human civilization *can* manage to turn aside or survive the various biological/ecological/social catastrophes that are lying in wait for it in the next few decades, though, Sagan offers a reasonable blueprint for what we ought to do in space and why we ought to do it, and this book is certainly a must for anyone interested in the exploration of space, or who believes in the hopeful future humanity could achieve there—which probably still includes a majority of genre readers, even in these fearful End-of-the-Millennium days. Another fascinating book that will probably be of interest to most genre readers is *The Human Animal: A Personal View of the Human Species* (Crown), by Desmond Morris, an examination of the biological basis for human behavior, and the instinctual/biological reasons why human cultures and social institutions have evolved in the way that they have. Not everyone will agree with everything Morris has to say here—he tends to generalize too widely from too little data in some places, and has a distinctly "human" tendency to ignore or downplay things that don't agree with his theory—but the book is absolutely packed with fascinating information (did you know, for instance, that there are *two* kinds of sperm, with two distinctly different functions, released in the human male ejaculation? Well, you *would* if you'd read this book!), and much of Morris's theorizing is not only ingenious but convincing—reading the book, for instance, has swayed me toward giving a lot more credibility to the theory that humanity evolved from shoreline-dwelling semiaquatic apes, a highly controversial theory that I had considered unlikely before, but for which Morris musters a formidable body of logical evidence. Another controversial book that gleefully attempts to overturn many of today's "accepted" scientific theories is *Out of Control: The Rise of Neo-Biological Civilization* (Addison-Wesley), by Kevin Kelly, which challenges such cherished genre notions as the idea that the human mind and personality can be succesfully "uploaded" into a computer, and even dares to champion a modified form of that most-sneered-at theory of the 20th Century, Lamarckian evolution, which may not be quite as totally discredited as most people think. It may be that in these two books we are getting a preview of the coming paradigm-shifts that will establish the new scientific consensus of the 21st Century—until the *next* paradigm-shift comes along to destroy *it*, of course! (For instance, our understanding of cosmology has just been destroyed by recent astronomical observations nobody can as yet understand or reconcile with current theory, leaving just about *everything* in question, including such scientific dogma as the Big Bang Theory of creation, which had been sacrosanct throughout the last half of the century. These are certainly "interesting times" for science, with many of the accepted paradigms under attack, and that makes for interesting *reading* for us.) Another book that is jam-packed with fascinating data, *Ancient Inventions* (Ballantine Books), by Peter James and Nick Thorpe, may be a bit further removed from the central concerns of the field, but will probably interest many genre readers anyway, dealing as it does with the *technologies* of the ancient world, many of them turning out to be surprisingly "modern"—for instance, they were using steam engines in ancient Greece, electric batteries in ancient Iraq, flush-toilets in ancient Crete, and condoms in ancient Rome long before their present-day equivalents were invented! Also richly informative and immensely entertaining is *The Cartoon History of the Universe II* (Doubleday), by Larry Gonick, a compilation of volumes 8 through 13 of Gonick's famous comic book series. The quality of the artwork in this series sharply declined after volume 6 in the original sequence, unfortunately, but the *text* still remains funny, erudite, insightful, and amazingly well-researched—in fact, if you read this volume and its predecessor, you will know far more about history and the roots of culture than (alas) the average college graduate.

1994 is being touted as a record year for genre films, at the box office, at least, although most of them didn't impress me much artistically. And, if you limit your definition of ''genre'' films to ''science fiction'' films, you find that genre films really didn't even do all *that* well at the box office, either. Most of the ''genre'' films that made a lot of money in 1994 were *fantasy* films—the block-buster animated film *The Lion King* (which has *already* earned enough to win it a place on the highest-grossing-films-of-all-time list), *The Santa Clause, the Flintstones, The Mask, Interview With the Vampire* . . . even *Forrest Gump* and Schwarzenegger's *True Lies,* which, while not genre films in the accepted sense, were certainly fantasies of *some* sort. If you look just at *science fiction* films, as opposed to fantasy films, the year begins to look less successful, even by money-earning standards. *Star Trek Generations,* the long-awaited film combining the casts of the original *Star Trek* and *Star Trek: The Next Generation,* was the biggest grosser among the science fiction films, and even it, although it did okay, didn't elicit the kind of monumental box office–blockbuster business that it had been hoped it would attract. In fact, reaction to *Star Trek Generations* in general has been surprisingly lackluster, with most of the hardcore *Star Trek* fans I've talked to either disliking it outright or, at best, not responding to it with much enthusiasm—even those who liked it the most seem to be only lukewarm about it. (Considering the lackluster response to *Star Trek Generations,* there has been some talk about whether or not there *will* be another *Star Trek* theatrical film; if there *isn't,* then Paramount, which deliberately scuttled the highly successful *Star Trek: The Next Generation* in order to move the cast into theatrical films, may have, ironically enough, killed this cash cow and wasted a highly popular ensemble cast for nothing.) Next down the list as a money earner was *Stargate,* which seems to have aroused even less enthusiasm, being widely regarded as a handsomely mounted film with great special effects, poor writing, and a badly muddled plotline. Reaction was even poorer to *Robert A. Heinlein's The Puppet Masters,* a film version of the classic SF novel that emphasized the gooshey horror-movie, *Alien*-like aspects of the storyline, and that was generally felt to be a disappointment, in spite of a good performance by Donald Sutherland. *Timecop* was a somewhat slicker and more intelligent version of the usual Jean-Claude Van Damme film, which still allowed plenty of room for Jean-Claude to beat people up. *Mary Shelley's Frankenstein* (which can be considered to be SF if you wink at the science), a well-intentioned attempt to return to an at least somewhat more ''authentic'' version of the classic story, flopped badly at the box office. *Junior,* a man-gets-pregnant comedy starring Arnold Schwarzenegger, was another box office bomb. And that was about it for science fiction films this year.

Not really much of a year for genre films then, if you exclude fantasy films—and even most of the fantasy films, with the possible exception of *The Lion King*, were not terribly successful *artistically* (did anyone really *need* a live-action version of *The Flintstones*?), however much money they pulled in. (And, of course, there were also fantasy films that did mediocre-to-poor box office business this year, including *The Shadow*, a misguided remake of *Miracle on 34th Street*, and Indiana Jonesish live-action version of *The Jungle Book*, the combined live-action and animated feature *The Pagemaster*, and the animated film *The Swan Princess*.)

All of the big-budget blockbuster films that were promised last year are still looming somewhere over the horizon: the new *Star Wars* movie, the new *Indiana Jones* movie, the new Stanley Kubrick SF movie, the new *Batman* movie, Kevin Costner's *Waterworld* (already the most expensive movie ever made, and still climbing, and being referred to derisively in the industry as *Fishtar* or *Kevin's Gate*), the *Jurassic Park* sequel, and so forth. Maybe we'll actually see some of them next year.

Turning to television, the big story of the year was the launching of the new *Star Trek* series, *Star Trek: Voyager*, which in turn was used to launch the new Paramount network. I have mixed feelings about *Star Trek: Voyager*. I didn't much warm to Kate Mulgrew (an actress I've never much liked anyway) as Captain Janeway (although, to be fair, many other people *do* seem to have liked her). However, I did like many of the other cast members, who seem to have quite a bit of potential as performers, particularly the actor who plays Kim, the actor who plays the little warthog-like alien, and the actor who plays the Vulcan Security Officer. And the shows are already more entertaining and action-oriented than the dull-as-dishwater *Star Trek: Deep Space Nine*. On the other hand, the writing and plotting on "Voyager" have so far ranged from mediocre to down-right bad, with the premiere episode in particular having holes in the plot-logic you could fly a starship through. And *Star Trek: Voyager* also suffers from a high level of scientifically illiterate gobbledegook and technical double-talk, an even *higher* level than is standard for most *Star Trek* shows—the episode wherein a character's lungs are stolen and then successfully replaced with a pair of "hologram lungs," for instance, is already infamous among *Trek* fans, as is the show wherein the ship is receiving messages beamed "out of the event horizon of a black hole" [!].

So, I don't know. The production values are up to the usual high standard, the crew is likeable, and a few of the actors seem to have the potential to be effective and entertaining performers. If they can only improve the *writing*, the show may have a shot at being worth watching. Standards of quality in the writing seem to have slumped in the last few years throughout the entire *Star Trek* empire, with poor writing also being responsible for blunting a lot of the potential of the *Star Trek Generations* theatrical film, and producer Rick Berman really should know better, since he was the one mostly responsible for *improving* the quality of the writing on *Star Trek: The Next Generation* in the first place—improving it to the point where, at its height several seasons back, it was very probably the best science fiction show on television, and maybe the best ever put on television. But the level of writing quality was dropping fast in the seasons just before the cancellation of *Star Trek: The Next Generation,* and never *have* risen to a terribly high level in the first place on *Star Trek: Deep Space Nine,* or, so far, on *Star Trek: Voyager.* You can do without expensive special effects if you have to in a science fiction show, but you can't do without good *writing,* and I think that this is a lesson that needs to be relearned by those in charge of the *Star Trek* empire.

To be fair, we should give *Star Trek: Voyager* a reasonable chance to improve. After all, *Star Trek: The Next Generation* was so bad as to be nearly unwatchable in its first few seasons, and then improved dramatically later on, and it's not impossible that the same thing could happen with *Star Trek: Voyager.* Already, in its unimproved-upon form, I like it better than *Star Trek: Deep Space Nine.* (The question has also been raised if *Star Trek: Deep Space Nine* and *Star Trek: Voyager* can hold the loyalty of the core *Star Trek* audience over the long haul, now that the immensely popular *Star Trek: The Next Generation,* the direct descendant of the original *Star Trek* show, is off the air. It's really too early to tell, but neither of the new *Trek* shows seem to be as popular with the *Trek* fans I've talked to as *Star Trek: The Next Generation* was, for what that's worth.)

There were plenty of other genre shows on television this year, perhaps more than ever before, most of them unimpressive. One of the new shows, *Earth 2,* had an interesting premise, but quickly bogged down in a morass of overly complex soap-opera-like plotting, with the endlessly trekking characters never really seeming to *get* anywhere or accomplish anything. *SeaQuest DSV,* frankly, stinks, as does a new show called *Space Precinct,* and as did the already-cancelled *RoboCop. TekWar* has its supporters, but hasn't impressed me much. *M.A.N.T.I.S., Highlander,* and *Forever Knight* are just live-action comic books, although *M.A.N.T.I.S.* has a few clever touches. *Mystery Science Theater 3000* seems to have grown a bit stale, and *Northern Exposure* is clearly on its last legs. *Babylon 5* survived a shaky patch last year, and seems to be doing better this year; it also, against the odds, seems to be slowly winning against its direct rival, a show very similar in concept and format, *Star Trek: Deep Space Nine*— or, at least, most people *I've* talked to seem to prefer *Babylon 5* to *Deep Space Nine*; I suspect that the ratings are still higher for *Star Trek: Deep Space Nine,* though, since it has the momentum of the *Star Trek* empire behind it. *The Adventures of Briscoe County, Jr.* died, in spite of an enthusiastic cult following, and *Lois and Clark* survived, although, at year's end, it was rumored to be on the chopping block. Speaking of cult followings, *The X-Files* probably has the most enthusiastic cult following of any genre show this side of *Star Trek,* and many people will go so far as to call it the best genre show on television; I myself will admit that it is usually smart, sassy, and stylish, and sometimes even scary, although the "science" is often absurd, and sometimes their tongues get pushed a little *too* deeply into their cheeks. After going through a bad patch late last year where it looked as though it would be cancelled, *The X-Files* has come back strong this year, even being featured on the cover of *TV Guide,* and looks as if it might grow into a genuine hit.

TV movies with genre elements this year included an Alternate History piece called *Fatherland*, about the Nazis having won World War II, an eight-hour miniseries version of Stephen King's *The Stand*, a two-hour reprise of the old series *Alien Nation*, and *Witch Hunt*, an extremely disappointing sequel to *Cast a Deadly Spell*, a TV movie from a few years back that had considerably more wit and style than the follow-up did.

The 52nd World Science Fiction Convention, ConAdian, was held in Winnipeg, Manitoba, Canada, from September 1 to September 5, 1994, and drew an estimated attendance of 3,500, making it the smallest North American worldcon in years. The 1994 Hugo Awards, presented at ConAdian, were: Best Novel, *Green Mars*, by Kim Stanley Robinson; Best Novella, "Down in the Bottomlands," by Harry Turtledove; Best Novelette, "Georgia on My Mind," by Charles Sheffield; Best Short Story, "Death on the Nile," by Connie Willis; Best Nonfiction, *The Encyclopedia of Science Fiction*, edited by John Clute and Peter Nicholls; Best Professional Editor, Kristine Kathryn Rusch; Best Professional Artist, Bob Eggleton; Best Original Artwork, Space Fantasy Commemorative Stamp Booklet, by Stephen Hickman; Best Dramatic Presentation, *Jurassic Park*; Best Semiprozine, *Science Fiction Chronicle*; Best Fanzine, *Mimosa*, edited by Dick and Nicki Lynch; Best Fan Writer, David Langford; Best Fan Artist, Brad W. Foster; plus the John W. Campbell Award for Best New Writer to Amy Thomson.

The 1993 Nebula Awards, presented at a banquet at the River Valley Inn in Eugene, Oregon, on April 23, 1994, were: Best Novel, *Red Mars*, by Kim Stanley Robinson; Best Novella, "The Night We Buried Road Dog," by Jack Cady; Best Novelette, "Georgia on My Mind," by Charles Sheffield; Best Short Story, "Graves," by Joe Haldeman.

The World Fantasy Awards, presented at the Twentieth Annual World Fantasy Convention in New Orleans, Louisiana, on October 30, 1994, were: Best Novel, *Glimpses*, by Lewis Shiner; Best Novella, "Under the Crust," by Terry Lamsley; Best Short Fiction, *The Lodger*, Fred Chappell; Best Collection, *Alone with the Horrors*, by Ramsey Campbell; Best Anthology, *Full Spectrum 4*, edited by Lou Aronica, Amy Stout, and Betsy Mitchell; Best Artist (tie), Alan Clarke and J. K. Potter; Special Award (Professional), to Underwood-Miller; Special Award (Nonprofessional), Marc Michaud, for Necronomicon Press; plus a Life Achievement Award to Jack Williamson.

The 1994 Bram Stoker Awards, presented by the Horror Writers of America during a meeting June 3 to June 5 in Las Vegas, Nevada, were: Best Novel, *The Throat*, by Peter Straub; Best First Novel, *The Thread That Binds the Bones*, by Nina Kiriki Hoffman; Best Collection, *Alone with the Horrors*, by Ramsey Campbell; Best Novella, "The Night We Buried Road Dog," by Jack Cady; Best Novelette, "Death in Bangkok," Dan Simmons; Best Short Story, "I Hear the Mermaids Singing," by Nancy Holder; Best Nonfiction, *Once Around the Bloch*, by Robert Bloch; plus a Life Achievement Award to Joyce Carol Oates.

There was no winner of the 1993 John W. Campbell Memorial Award, the first time in the history of this award that a winner has not been declared.

The 1993 Theodore Sturgeon Award for Best Short Story was won by "Fox Magic," by Kij Johnson.

The 1993 Philip K. Dick Memorial Award (tie) went to *Growing Up Weightless,* by John M. Ford and *Elvissey,* by Jack Womack.

The 1993 Arthur C. Clarke award was won by *Vurt,* by Jeff Noon.

The 1993 James Tiptree, Jr. Award was won by *Ammonite,* by Nicola Griffith.

The 1994 James Tiptree, Jr. Award (tie) was won by *Larque on the Wing,* by Nancy Springer and "The Matter of Seggri," by Ursula K. Le Guin.

The 1993 Compton Crook Award was won by *The Drylands,* by Mary Rosenblum.

* * *

Dead in 1994 were: Famous horror, fantasy, and suspense writer **Robert Bloch**, 77, author of the classic novel *Psycho* and the classic story "Yours Truly, Jack the Ripper," as well as dozens of other novels and collections, and many screenplays, winner of the Hugo, the Edgar Award, the Bram Stoker Award, and the World Fantasy Convention's Lifetime Achievement Award, one of the best loved figures in the fantasy, horror, and science fiction genres; well-known horror writer and editor **Karl Edward Wagner**, 48, World Fantasy Award-winner, author of the "Kane" series, and, for the last fifteen years, the editor of the prestigious and highly influential anthology series *The Year's Best Horror Stories,* a friend; **Raymond Z. Gallun**, 83, one of the few remaining stars from the "Superscience" era of the 1930s, a prolific writer for the SF pulps of that day, and author of *People Minus X* and *The Eden Cycle*; **Raymond F. Jones**, veteran author, best known for his work in *Astounding* in the 1940s and 1950s, author of the novel *This Island Earth,* which inspired the well-known film; **Robert Shea**, 61, writer and editor, best known as coauthor of the *Illuminatus* trilogy; **Rick Raphael**, 74, SF writer, author of *Code Three*; **Pierre Boulle**, 81, French author, best known for his novels *Planet of the Apes* and *The Bridge on the River Kwai*; **James Clavell**, 69, author of *Shōgun* and *King Rat*; **Gerd Prokop**, 61, German SF writer; **Lydia Langstaff**, fan and beginning SF writer; **Donald Swann**, 70, composer and pianist who composed music for the J. R. R. Tolkien song-cycle *The Road Goes Ever On* and who wrote an opera version of C. S. Lewis's *Perelandra*; **Sean Spacher**, 51, prominent fan artist and sculptor; **Walter Lantz**, 93, cartoonist, creator of Woody Woodpecker; **Don Thompson**, 58, well-known comics fan, coeditor of *The Comic Buyer's Guide,* as well as coeditor of *All in Color for a Dime* and *The Comic-Book Book*; **Ella Parker**, 75, well-known British fan legendary for her kindness and hospitality, one of the many beneficiaries of which was an unknown fan at his first convention, who later became the editor of this anthology series; **Bill Benthake**, 76, longtime SF fan; **Morris Scott Dollens**, 74, fan and fan artist; **Harry C. Bigglestone**, 47, fan and convention organizer; **Burt Lancaster**, 80, famous film actor, best known to genre audiences for his roles in *The Island of Dr. Moreau* and *Seven Days in May*; **John Candy**, 43, comic and film actor, best known to genre audiences for his roles in *Splash* and the soap-opera fantasy *Delirious*; **Peter Cushing**, 81, film actor, best known to genre audiences for his role in *Star Wars,* as well as for dozens of horror movies such as *The Mummy* and *The Curse of Frankenstein*; **Jessica Tandy**, 85, best known to genre audiences for her roles in *The Birds* and *Cocoon*; **Raul Julia**, 54, film actor, best known for his roles in *The Addams Family* and *Addams Family Values*; **Cesar Romero**, 86, best known to genre audiences for his role as The Joker in television's original *Batman* series; **William Conrad**, 73, television and radio actor, perhaps best known to genre audiences as the voice of the narrator on *The Bullwinkle Show*; **Terence Young**, 79, director, among other films, of two of the best James Bond movies, *Dr. No* and *From Russia With Love*; **Noah Berry Jr.**, film and television actor, perhaps best known for his role on TV's "The Rockford Files," as well as his role in the early SF film *Rocketship X-M*; **Annette Pelz McComas**, 83, widow of SF editor J. Francis McComas, as well as editor of *The Eureka Years: Boucher and McComas's Magazine of Fantasy and Science Fiction 1949–1954*; **Pat Killough**, 49, husband of SF writer Lee Killough; **Felicity Brunner**, 82, mother of SF writer John Brunner; **Bette Fast**, wife of writer Howard Fast and mother of writer Jonathan Fast; **Thelma D. Hamm**, 89, widow of SF figure E. Everett Evans; and **Verna Smith Trestrail**, 73, daughter of SF writer E. E. Smith.

THE YEAR'S BEST SCIENCE FICTION

TWELFTH
ANNUAL
COLLECTION

FORGIVENESS DAY

Ursula K. Le Guin

Ursula K. Le Guin is one of the best-known and most universally respected SF writers in the world today. Her famous novel *The Left Hand of Darkness* may have been the most influential SF novel of its decade, and shows every sign of becoming one of the enduring classic of the genre—even ignoring the rest of Le Guin's work, the impact of this one novel alone on future SF and future SF writers would be incalculably strong. (Her 1968 fantasy novel, *A Wizard of Earthsea*, would be almost as influential on future generations of High Fantasy writers.) *The Left Hand of Darkness* won both the Hugo and Nebula Awards in 1970 as did Le Guin's monumental novel *The Dispossessed* a few years later. Her novel *Tehanu* won her another Nebula in 1990, and she has also won three other Hugo Awards and a Nebula Award for her short fiction, as well as the National Book Award for Children's literature for her novel *The Farthest Shore*, part of her acclaimed Earthsea trilogy. Her other novels include *Planet of Exile, The Lathe of Heaven, City of Illusions, Rocannon's World, The Beginning Place, A Wizard of Earthsea, The Tombs of Atuan*, and the controversial multimedia novel (it sold with a tape cassette of music, and included drawings and recipes) *Always Coming Home*. She has published four story collections: *The Wind's Twelve Quarters, Orsinian Tales, The Compass Rose*, and *Buffalo Gals and Other Animal Presences*. Her most recent books are the novel *Searoad*, and a new collection, *A Fisherman of the Inland Sea*. Her stories have appeared in our Second, Fifth, and Eighth Annual Collections.

Here she returns to the star-spanning, Hainish-settled interstellar community known as the Ekumen, the same fictional universe as her famous novels *The Left Hand of Darkness* and *The Dispossessed*, for a thoughtful and passionate story of clashing cultural values, politics, violence, religion, and terror—and of the star-crossed relationship of a man and a woman who are literally worlds apart . . .

Solly had been a space brat, a Mobile's child, living on this ship and that, this world and that; she'd traveled five hundred lightyears by the time she was ten. At twenty-five she had been through a revolution on Alterra, learned *aiji* on Terra and farthinking from an old hilfer on Rokanan, breezed through the Schools on Hain, and survived an assignment as Observer in murderous, dying Kheakh, skipping another half-millennium at near lightspeed in the process. She was young, but she'd been around.

She got bored with the Embassy people in Voe Deo telling her to watch out

I

for this, remember that; she was a Mobile herself now, after all. Werel had its quirks—what world didn't? She'd done her homework, she knew when to curtsey and when not to belch, and vice versa. It was a relief to get on her own at last, in this gorgeous little city, on this gorgeous little continent, the first and only Envoy of the Ekumen to the Divine Kingdom of Gatay.

She was high for days on the altitude, the tiny, brilliant sun pouring vertical light into the noisy streets, the peaks soaring up incredibly behind every building, the dark-blue sky where great near stars burned all day, the dazzling nights under six or seven lolloping bits of moon, the tall black people with their black eyes, narrow heads, long, narrow hands and feet, gorgeous people, her people! She loved them all. Even if she saw a little too much of them.

The last time she had had completely to herself was a few hours in the passenger cabin of the airskimmer sent by Gatay to bring her across the ocean from Voe Deo. On the airstrip she was met by a delegation of priests and officials from the King and the Council, magnificent in scarlet and brown and turquoise, and swept off to the Palace, where there was a lot of curtseying and no belching, of course, for hours—an introduction to his little shrunken old majesty, introductions to High Muckamucks and Lord Hooziwhats, speeches, a banquet—all completely predictable, no problems at all, not even the impenetrable giant fried flower on her plate at the banquet. But with her, from that first moment on the airstrip and at every moment thereafter, discreetly behind or beside or very near her, were two men: her Guide and her Guard.

The Guide, whose name was San Ubattat, was provided by her hosts in Gatay; of course he was reporting on her to the government, but he was a most obliging spy, endlessly smoothing the way for her, showing her with a bare hint what was expected or what would be a gaffe, and an excellent linguist, ready with a translation when she needed one. San was all right. But the Guard was something else.

He had been attached to her by the Ekumen's hosts on this world, the dominant power on Werel, the big nation of Voe Deo. She had promptly protested to the Embassy back in Voe Deo that she didn't need or want a bodyguard. Nobody in Gatay was out to get her and even if they were she preferred to look after herself. The Embassy sighed. Sorry, they said. You're stuck with him. Voe Deo has a military presence in Gatay, which after all is a client state, economically dependent. It's in Voe Deo's interest to protect the legitimate government of Gatay against the native terrorist factions, and you get protected as one of their interests. We can't argue with that.

She knew better than to argue with the Embassy, but she could not resign herself to the Major. His military title, rega, she translated by the archaic word "Major," from a skit she'd seen on Terra. That Major had been a stuffed uniform, covered with medals and insignia. It puffed and strutted and commanded, and finally blew up into bits of stuffing. If only this Major would blow up! Not that he strutted, exactly, or even commanded, directly. He was stonily polite, woodenly silent, stiff and cold as rigor mortis. She soon gave up any effort to talk to him; whatever she said, he replied Yessum or Nomum with the prompt stupidity of a man who does not and will not actually listen, an officer officially incapable of humanity. And he was with her in every public situation, day and night, on the street, shopping, meeting with businessmen and officials, sightseeing, at court, in the balloon ascent above the mountains—with her everywhere, everywhere but bed.

Even in bed she wasn't quite as alone as she would often have liked; for the Guide and the Guard went home at night, but in the anteroom of her bedroom slept the Maid—a gift from His Majesty, her own private asset.

She remembered her incredulity when she first learned that word, years ago, in a text about slavery. "On Werel, members of the dominant caste are called *owners*; members of the serving class are called *assets*. Only owners are referred to as men and women; assets are called bondsmen, bondswomen."

So here she was, the owner of an asset. You don't turn down a king's gift. Her asset's name was Rewe. Rewe was probably a spy too, but it was hard to believe. She was a dignified, handsome woman some years older than Solly and about the same intensity of skin-color, though Solly was pinkish-brown and Rewe was bluish-brown. The palms of her hands were a delicate azure. Rewe's manners were exquisite and she had tact, astuteness, an infallible sense of when she was wanted and when not. Solly of course treated her as an equal, stating right out at the beginning that she believed no human being had a right to dominate, much less own, another, that she would give Rewe no orders, and that she hoped they might become friends. Rewe accepted this, unfortunately, as a new set of orders. She smiled and said yes. She was infinitely yielding. Whatever Solly said or did sank into that acceptance and was lost, leaving Rewe unchanged: an attentive, obliging, gentle physical presence, just out of reach. She smiled, and said yes, and was untouchable.

And Solly began to think, after the first fizz of the first days in Gatay, that she needed Rewe, really needed her as a woman to talk with. There was no way to meet Owner women, who lived hidden away, "at home," they called it. All bondswomen but Rewe were somebody else's property, not hers to talk to. All she ever met was men. And eunuchs.

That had been another thing hard to believe, that a man would voluntarily trade his virility for a little social standing; but she met such men all the time in King Hotat's court. Born assets, they were freed from slavery by becoming eunuchs, and as such often rose to positions of considerable power and trust among their owners. The eunuch Tayandan, majordomo of the palace, ruled the king, who didn't rule, but figureheaded for the Council. The Council was made up of various kinds of lord but only one kind of priest, Tualites. Only assets worshipped Kamye, and the original religion of Gatay had been suppressed when the monarchy became Tualite a century or so ago. If there was one thing she really disliked about Werel, aside from slavery and genderdominance, it was the religions. The songs about Lady Tual were beautiful, and the statues of her and the great temples in Voe Deo were wonderful, and the *Arkamye* seemed to be a good story though longwinded; but the deadly self-righteousness, the intolerance, the stupidity of the priests, the hideous doctrines that justified every cruelty in the name of the faith! As a matter of fact, Solly said to herself, was there anything she *did* like about Werel?

And answered herself instantly: I love it, I love it. I love this weird little bright sun and all the broken bits of moons and the mountains going up like ice walls and the people—the people with their black eyes without whites like animals' eyes, eyes like dark glass, like dark water, mysterious—I want to love them, I want to know them, I want to reach them!

But she had to admit that the pissants at the Embassy had been right about one thing: being a woman was tough on Werel. She fit nowhere. She went about alone, she had a public position, and so was a contradiction in terms: proper women stayed at home, invisible. Only bondswomen went out in the streets, or met strangers, or worked at any public job. She behaved like an asset, not like an owner. Yet she was something very grand, an envoy of the Ekumen, and Gatay very much wanted to join the Ekumen and not to offend its envoys. So the officials and courtiers and businessmen she talked to on the business of the Ekumen did the best they could: they treated her as if she were a man.

The pretense was never complete and often broke right down. The poor old king groped her industriously, under the vague impression that she was one of his bedwarmers. When she contradicted Lord Gatuyo in a discussion, he stared with the blank disbelief of a man who has been talked back to by his shoe. He had been thinking of her as a woman. But in general the disgenderment worked, allowing her to work with them; and she began to fit herself into the game, enlisting Rewe's help in making clothes that resembled what male owners wore in Gatay, avoiding anything that to them would be specifically feminine. Rewe was a quick, intelligent seamstress. The bright, heavy, close-fitted trousers were practical and becoming, the embroidered jackets were splendidly warm. She liked wearing them. But she felt unsexed by these men who could not accept her for what she was. She needed to talk to a woman.

She tried to meet some of the hidden owner women through the owner men, and met a wall of politeness without a door, without a peephole. What a wonderful idea; we will certainly arrange a visit when the weather is better! I should be overwhelmed with the honor if the Envoy were to entertain Lady Mayoyo and my daughters, but my foolish, provincial girls are so unforgivably timid—I'm sure you understand. Oh, surely, surely, a tour of the inner gardens—but not at present, when the vines are not in flower! We must wait until the vines are in flower!

There was nobody to talk to, nobody, until she met Batikam the Makil.

It was an event: a touring troupe from Voe Deo. There wasn't much going on in Gatay's little mountain capital by way of entertainment, except for temple dancers—all men, of course—and the soppy fluff that passed as drama on the Werelian network. Solly had doggedly entered some of these wet pastels, hoping for a glimpse into the life "at home"; but she couldn't stomach the swooning maidens who died of love while the stiffnecked jackass heroes, who all looked like the Major, died nobly in battle, and Tual the Merciful leaned out of the clouds smiling upon their deaths with her eyes slightly crossed and the whites showing, a sign of divinity. She had noticed that Werelian men never entered the network for drama. Now she knew why. But the receptions at the palace and the parties in her honor given by various lords and businessmen were pretty dull stuff: all men, always, because they wouldn't have the slavegirls in while the Envoy was there; and she couldn't flirt even with the nicest men, couldn't remind them that they were men, since that would remind them that she was a woman not behaving like a lady. The fizz had definitely gone flat by the time the makil troupe came.

She asked San, a reliable etiquette advisor, if it would be all right for her to attend the performance. He hemmed and hawed and finally, with more than usually oily delicacy, gave her to understand that it would be all right so long as she went dressed as a man. "Women, you know, don't go in public. But sometimes, they want so much to see the entertainers, you know? Lady Amatay used to go with Lord Amatay, dressed in his clothes, every year; everybody knew, nobody said anything—you know. For you, such a great person, it would be all right. Nobody will say anything. Quite, quite all right. Of course, I come with you, the rega comes with you. Like friends, ha? You know, three good men friends going to the entertainment, ha? Ha?"

Ha, ha, she said obediently. What fun!—But it was worth it, she thought, to see the makils.

They were never on the network. Young girls at home were not to be exposed to their performances, some of which, San gravely informed her, were unseemly. They played only in theaters. Clowns, dancers, prostitutes, actors, musicians, the makils formed a kind of subclass, the only assets not personally owned. A talented slave boy bought by the Entertainment Corporation from his owner was thenceforth the property of the Corporation, which trained and looked after him the rest of his life.

They walked to the theater, six or seven streets away. She had forgotten that the makils were all transvestites, indeed she did not remember it when she first saw them, a troop of tall slender dancers sweeping out onto the stage with the precision and power and grace of great birds wheeling, flocking, soaring. She watched unthinking, enthralled by their beauty, until suddenly the music changed and the clowns came in, black as night, black as owners, wearing fantastic trailing skirts, with fantastic jutting jewelled breasts, singing in tiny, swoony voices, "Oh do not rape me please kind Sir, no no, not now!" They're men, they're men! Solly realized then, already laughing helplessly. By the time Batikam finished his star turn, a marvelous dramatic monologue, she was a fan. "I want to meet him," she said to San at a pause between acts. "The actor—Batikam."

San got the bland expression that signified he was thinking how it could be arranged and how to make a little money out of it. But the Major was on guard, as ever. Stiff as a stick, he barely turned his head to glance at San. And San's expression began to alter.

If her proposal was out of line, San would have signaled or said so. The Stuffed Major was simply controlling her, trying to keep her as tied down as one of "his" women. It was time to challenge him. She turned to him and stared straight at him. "Rega Teyeo," she said, "I quite comprehend that you're under orders to keep me in order. But if you give orders to San or to me, they must be spoken aloud, and they must be justified. I will not be managed by your winks or your whims."

There was a considerable pause, a truly delicious and rewarding pause. It was difficult to see if the Major's expression changed; the dim theater light showed no detail in his blueblack face. But there was something frozen about his stillness that told her she'd stopped him. At last he said, "I'm charged to protect you, Envoy."

"Am I endangered by the makils? Is there impropriety in an Envoy of the Ekumen congratulating a great artist of Werel?"

Again the frozen silence. "No," he said.

"Then I request you to accompany me when I go backstage after the performance to speak to Batikam."

One stiff nod. One stiff, stuffy, defeated nod. Score one! Solly thought, and sat back cheerfully to watch the lightpainters, the erotic dances, and the curiously touching little drama with which the evening ended. It was in archaic poetry, hard to understand, but the actors were so beautiful, their voices so tender that she found tears in her eyes and hardly knew why.

"A pity the makils always draw on the *Arkamye*," said San, with smug, pious disapproval. He was not a very highclass owner, in fact he owned no assets; but he was an owner, and a bigoted Tualite, and liked to remind himself of it. "Scenes from the *Incarnations of Tual* would be more befitting such an audience."

"I'm sure you agree, Rega," she said, enjoying her own irony.

"Not at all," he said, with such toneless politeness that at first she did not realize what he had said; and then forgot the minor puzzle in the bustle of finding their way and gaining admittance to the backstage and to the performers' dressingroom.

When they realized who she was, the managers tried to clear all the other performers out, leaving her alone with Batikam (and San and the Major, of course); but she said no, no, no, these wonderful artists must not be disturbed, just let me talk a moment with Batikam. She stood there in the bustle of doffed costumes, half-naked people, smeared makeup, laughter, dissolving tension after the show, any backstage on any world, talking with the clever, intense man in elaborate archaic woman's costume. They hit it off at once. "Can you come to my house?" she asked. "With pleasure," Batikam said, and his eyes did not flick to San's or the Major's face: the first bondsman she had yet met who did not glance to her Guard or her Guide for permission to say or do anything, anything at all. She glanced at them only to see if they were shocked. San looked collusive, the Major looked rigid. "I'll come in a little while," Batikam said, "I must change."

They exchanged smiles, and she left. The fizz was back in the air. The huge stars hung clustered like grapes of fire. A moon tumbled over the icy peaks, another jigged like a lopsided lantern above the curlicue pinnacles of the palace. She strode along the dark street, enjoying the freedom of the male robe she wore and its warmth, making San trot to keep up; the Major, longlegged, kept pace with her. A high, trilling voice called, "Envoy!" and she turned with a smile, then swung round, seeing the Major grappling momentarily with someone in the shadow of a portico. He broke free, caught up to her without a word, seized her arm in an iron grip and dragged her into a run. "Let go!" she said, struggling;

she did not want to use an aiji break on him, but nothing less was going to get her free.

He pulled her nearly off balance with a sudden dodge into an alley; she ran with him, letting him keep hold on her arm. They came unexpectedly out into her street and to her gate, through it, into the house, which he unlocked with a word—how did he do that?—"What is all this?" she demanded, breaking away easily, holding her arm where his grip had bruised it.

She saw, outraged, the last flicker of an exhilarated smile on his face. Breathing hard, he asked, "Are you hurt?"

"Hurt? Where you yanked me, yes—what do you think you were doing?"

"Keeping the fellow away."

"What fellow?"

He said nothing.

"The one who called out? Maybe he wanted to talk to me!"

After a moment the Major said, "Possibly. He was in the shadow. I thought he might be armed. I must go out and look for San Ubattat. Please keep the door locked until I come back." He was out the door as he gave the order; it never occurred to him that she would not obey, and she did obey, raging. Did he think she couldn't look after herself? that she needed him interfering in her life, kicking slaves around, "protecting" her? Maybe it was time he saw what an aiji fall looked like. He was strong and quick, but had no real training. This kind of amateur interference was intolerable, really intolerable; she must protest to the Embassy again.

As soon as she let him back in with a nervous, shamefaced San in tow, she said, "You opened my door with a password. I was not informed that you had right of entrance day and night."

He was back to his military blankness. "Nomum," he said.

"You are not to do so again. You are not to seize hold of me ever again. I must tell you that if you do I will injure you. If something alarms you, tell me what it is and I will respond as I see fit. Now will you please go."

"With pleasure, mum," he said, wheeled, and marched out.

"Oh, Lady—Oh, Envoy," San said, "that was a dangerous person, extremely dangerous people, I am so sorry, disgraceful," and he babbled on. She finally got him to say who he thought it was, a religious dissident, one of the Old Believers who held to the original religion of Gatay and wanted to cast out or kill all foreigners and unbelievers. "A bondsman?" she asked with interest, and he was shocked—"Oh, no, no, a real person, a man—but most misguided, a fanatic, a heathen fanatic! Knifemen, they call themselves. But a man, Lady—Envoy, certainly a man!"

The thought that she might think that an asset might touch her upset him as much as the attempted assault. If such it had been.

As she considered it, she began to wonder if, since she had put the Major in his place at the theater, he had found an excuse to put her in her place by "protecting" her. Well, if he tried it again he'd find himself upside down against the opposite wall.

"Rewe!" she called, and the bondswoman appeared instantly as always. "One of the actors is coming. Would you like to make us a little tea, something like that?'' Rewe smiled, said, ''Yes,'' and vanished. There was a knock at the door. The Major opened it—he must be standing guard outside—and Batikam came in.

It had not occurred to her that the makil would still be in women's clothing, but it was how he dressed offstage too, not so magnificently, but with elegance, in the delicate, flowing materials and dark, subtle hues that the swoony ladies in the dramas wore. It gave considerable piquancy, she felt, to her own male costume. Batikam was not as handsome as the Major, who was a stunning-looking man till he opened his mouth; but the makil was magnetic, you had to look at him. He was a dark greyish brown, not the blueblack that the owners were so vain of (though there were plenty of black assets, too, Solly had noticed: of course, when every bondswoman was her owner's sexual servant). Intense, vivid intelligence and sympathy shone in his face through the makil's stardust-black makeup, as he looked around with a slow, lovely laugh at her, at San, and at the Major standing at the door. He laughed like a woman, a warm ripple, not the ha, ha of a man. He held out his hands to Solly, and she came forward and took them. ''Thank you for coming, Batikam!'' she said, and he said, ''Thank you for asking me, Alien Envoy!''

''San,'' she said, ''I think this is your cue?''

Only indecision about what he ought to do could have slowed San down till she had to speak. He still hesitated a moment, then smiled with unction and said, ''Yes, so sorry, a very good night to you, Envoy! Noon hour at the Office of Mines tomorrow, I believe?'' Backing away, he backed right into the Major, who stood like a post in the doorway. She looked at the Major, ready to order him out without ceremony, how dare he shove back in!—and saw the expression on his face. For once his blank mask had cracked, and what was revealed was contempt. Incredulous, sickened contempt. As if he was obliged to watch someone eat a turd.

''Get out,'' she said. She turned her back on both of them. ''Come on, Batikam; the only privacy I have is in here,'' she said, and led the makil to her bedroom.

He was born where his fathers before him were born, in the old, cold house in the foothills above Noeha. His mother did not cry out as she bore him, since she was a soldier's wife, and a soldier's mother, now. He was named for his greatuncle, killed in the first Tribal Mutiny on Yeowe. He grew up in the stark discipline of a poor household of pure veot lineage. His father, when he was on leave, taught him the arts a soldier must know; when his father was on duty the old Asset-Sergeant Habbakam took over the lessons, which began at five in the morning, summer or winter, with worship, shortsword practice, and a cross-country run. His mother and grandmother taught him the other arts a man must know, beginning with good manners before he was two, and after his second birthday going on to history, poetry, and sitting still without talking.

The child's day was filled with lessons and fenced with disciplines; but a child's day is long. There was room and time for freedom, the freedom of the farmyard and the open hills. There was the companionship of pets, foxdogs, running dogs, spotted cats, hunting cats, and the farm cattle and the greathorses; not much companionship otherwise. The family's assets, other than Habbakam and the two housewomen, were serfs, sharecropping the stony foothill land that they and their owners had lived on forever. Their children were light-skinned, shy, already stooped to their lifelong work, ignorant of anything beyond their fields and hills. Sometimes they swam with Teyeo, summers, in the pools of the river. Sometimes he rounded up a couple of them to play soldiers with him. They stood awkward, uncouth, smirking when he shouted "Charge!" and rushed at the invisible enemy. "Follow me!" he cried shrilly, and they lumbered after him, firing their tree-branch guns at random, pow, pow. Mostly he went alone, riding his good mare Tasi or afoot with a hunting cat pacing by his.

A few times a year visitors came to the estate, relatives or fellow-officers of Teyeo's father, bringing their children and their housepeople. Teyeo silently and politely showed the child guests about, introduced them to the animals, took them on rides. Silently and politely, he and his cousin Gemat came to hate each other; at age fourteen they fought for an hour in a glade behind the house, punctiliously following the rules of wrestling, relentlessly hurting each other, getting bloodier and wearier and more desperate, until by unspoken consent they called it off and returned in silence to the house, where everyone was gathering for dinner. Everyone looked at them and said nothing. They washed up hurriedly, hurried to table. Gemat's nose leaked blood all through the meal; Teyeo's jaw was so sore he could not open it to eat. No one commented.

Silently and politely, when they were both fifteen, Teyeo and Rega Toebawe's daughter fell in love. On the last day of her visit they escaped by unspoken collusion and rode out side by side, rode for hours, too shy to talk. He had given her Tasi to ride. They dismounted to water and rest the horses in a wild valley of the hills. They sat near each other, not very near, by the side of the little quiet-running stream. "I love you," Teyeo said. "I love you," Emdu said, bending her shining black face down. They did not touch or look at each other. They rode back over the hills, joyous, silent.

When he was sixteen Teyeo was sent to the Officers' Academy in the capital of his province. There he continued to learn and practice the arts of war and the arts of peace. His province was the most rural in Voe Deo; its ways were conservative, and his training was in some ways anachronistic. He was of course taught the technologies of modern warfare, becoming a first-rate pod pilot and an expert in telereconnaissance; but he was not taught the modern ways of thinking that accompanied the technologies in other schools. He learned the poetry and history of Voe Deo, not the history and politics of the Ekumen. The Alien presence on Werel remained remote, theoretical to him. His reality was the old reality of the veot class, whose men held themselves apart from all men not soldiers and in brotherhood with all soldiers, whether owners, assets, or enemies. As for women, Teyeo considered his rights over them absolute, binding him absolutely to responsible chivalry to women of his own class and protective, merciful treatment of bondswomen. He believed all foreigners to be basically hostile, untrustworthy heathens. He honored the Lady Tual, but worshipped the

Lord Kamye. He expected no justice, looked for no reward, and valued above all competence, courage, and self-respect. In some respects he was utterly unsuited to the world he was to enter, in others well prepared for it, since he was to spend seven years on Yeowe fighting a war in which there was no justice, no reward, and never even an illusion of ultimate victory.

Rank among veot officers was hereditary. Teyeo entered active service as a rega, the highest of the three veot ranks. No degree of ineptitude or distinction could lower or raise his status or his pay. Material ambition was no use to a veot. But honor and responsibility were to be earned, and he earned them quickly. He loved service, loved the life, knew he was good at it, intelligently obedient, effective in command; he had come out of the Academy with the highest recommendations, and being posted to the capital, drew notice as a promising officer as well as a likeable young man. At twenty-four he was absolutely fit, his body would do anything he asked of it. His austere upbringing had given him little taste for indulgence but an intense appreciation of pleasure, so the luxuries and entertainments of the capital were a discovery of delight to him. He was reserved and rather shy, but companionable and cheerful. A handsome young man, in with a set of other young men very like him, for a year he knew what it is to live a completely privileged life with complete enjoyment of it. The brilliant intensity of that enjoyment stood against the dark background of the war in Yeowe, the slave revolution on the colony planet, which had gone on all his lifetime, and was now intensifying. Without that background, he could not have been so happy. A whole life of games and diversions had no interest for him; and when his orders came, posted as a pilot and division commander to Yeowe, his happiness was pretty nearly complete.

He went home for his thirty-day leave. Having received his parents' approbation, he rode over the hills to Rega Toebawe's estate and asked for his daughter's hand in marriage. The rega and his wife told their daughter that they approved his offer and asked her, for they were not strict parents, if she would like to marry Teyeo. "Yes," she said. As a grown, unmarried woman, she lived in seclusion in the women's side of the house, but she and Teyeo were allowed to meet and even to walk together, the chaperone remaining at some distance. Teyeo told her it was a three-year posting; would she marry in haste now, or wait three years and have a proper wedding? "Now," she said, bending down her narrow, shining face. Teyeo gave a laugh of delight, and she laughed at him. They were married nine days later—it couldn't be sooner, there had to be some fuss and ceremony, even if it was a soldier's wedding—and for seventeen days Teyeo and Emdu made love, walked together, made love, rode together, made love, came to know each other, came to love each other, quarreled, made up, made love, slept in each other's arms. Then he left for the war on another world, and she moved to the women's side of her husband's house.

His three-year posting was extended year by year, as his value as an officer was recognized and as the war on Yeowe changed from scattered containing actions to an increasingly desperate retreat. In his seventh year of service an order for compassionate leave was sent out to Yeowe Headquarters for Rega Teyeo, whose wife was dying of complications of berlot fever. At that point, there was no headquarters on Yeowe; the Army was retreating from three directions toward the old colonial capital; Teyeo's division was fighting a rear-guard defense in the seamarshes; communications had collapsed.

Command on Werel continued to find it inconceivable that a mass of ignorant slaves with the crudest kind of weapons could be defeating the Army of Voe Deo, a disciplined, trained body of soldiers with an infallible communications network, skimmers, pods, every armament and device permitted by the Ekumenical Convention Agreement. A strong faction in Voe Deo blamed the setbacks on this submissive adherence to alien rules. The hell with Ekumenical Conventions. Bomb the damned brownies back to the mud they were made of. Use the biobomb, what was it for, anyway? Get our men off the foul planet and wipe it clean. Start fresh. If we don't win the war on Yeowe, the next revolution's going to be right here on Werel, in our own cities, in our own homes! The jittery government held on against this pressure. Werel was on probation, and Voe Deo wanted to lead the planet to Ekumenical status. Defeats were minimized, losses were not made up, skimmers, pods, weapons, men were not replaced. By the end of Teyeo's seventh year, the Army on Yeowe had been essentially written off by its government. Early in the eighth year, when the Ekumen was at last permitted to send its Envoys to Yeowe, Voe Deo and the other countries that had supplied auxiliary troops finally began to bring their soldiers home.

It was not until he got back to Werel that Teyeo learned his wife was dead.

He went home to Noeha. He and his father greeted each other with a silent embrace, but his mother wept as she embraced him. He knelt to her in apology for having brought her more grief than she could bear.

He lay that night in the cold room in the silent house, listening to his heart beat like a slow drum. He was not unhappy, the relief of being at peace and the sweetness of being home were too great for that; but it was a desolate calm, and somewhere in it was anger. Not used to anger, he was not sure what he felt. It was as if a faint, sullen red flare colored every image in his mind, as he lay trying to think through the seven years on Werel, first as a pilot, then the ground war, then the long retreat, the killing and the being killed. Why had they been left there to be hunted down and slaughtered? Why had the government not sent them reinforcements? The questions had not been worth asking then, they were not worth asking now. They had only one answer: We do what they ask us to do, and we don't complain. I fought every step of the way, he thought, without pride. The new knowledge sliced keen as a knife through all other knowledge— And while I was fighting, she was dying. All a waste, there on Yeowe. All a waste, here on Werel. He sat up in the dark, the cold, silent, sweet dark of night in the hills. "Lord Kamye," he said aloud, "help me. My mind betrays me."

During the long leave home he sat often with his mother. She wanted to talk about Emdu, and at first he had to force himself to listen. It would be easy to forget the girl he had known for seventeen days seven years ago, if only his mother would let him forget. Gradually he learned to take what she wanted to give him, the knowledge of who his wife had been. His mother wanted to share all she could with him of the joy she had had in Emdu, her beloved child and friend. Even his father, retired now, a quenched, silent man, was able to say,

"She was the light of the house." They were thanking him for her. They were telling him that it had not all been a waste.

But what lay ahead of them? Old age, the empty house. They did not complain, of course, and seemed content in their severe, placid round of daily work; but for them the continuity of the past with the future was broken.

"I should remarry," Teyeo said to his mother. "Is there anyone you've noticed . . . ?"

It was raining, a grey light through the wet windows, a soft thrumming on the eaves. His mother's face was indistinct as she bent to her mending.

"No," she said. "Not really." She looked up at him, and after a pause asked, "What . . . where do you think you'll be posted?"

"I don't know."

"There's no war now," she said, in her soft, even voice.

"No," Teyeo said. "There's no war."

"Will there be . . . ever? do you think?"

He stood up, walked down the room and back, sat down again on the cushioned platform near her; they both sat straightbacked, still except for the slight motion of her hands as she sewed; his hands lay lightly one in the other, as he had been taught when he was two.

"I don't know," he said. "It's strange. It's as if there hadn't been a war. As if we'd never been in Yeowe—the Colony, the Uprising, all of it. They don't talk about it. It didn't happen. We don't fight wars. This is a new age; they say that often on the net. The age of peace, brotherhood across the stars. So, are we brothers with Yeowe, now? Are we brothers with Gatay and Bambur and the Forty States? Are we brothers with our assets? I can't make sense of it; I don't know what they mean. I don't know where I fit in." His voice too was quiet and even.

"Not here, I think," she said. "Not yet."

After a while he said, "I thought . . . children . . ."

"Of course. When the time comes." She smiled at him. "You never could sit still for half an hour . . . Wait. Wait and see."

She was right, of course; and yet what he saw on the net and in town tried his patience and his pride. It seemed that to be a soldier now was a disgrace. Government reports, the news and the analyses, constantly referred to the army and particularly the veot class as fossils, costly and useless, Voe Deo's principal obstacle to full admission to the Ekumen. His own uselessness was made clear to him when his request for a posting was met by an indefinite extension of his leave on half pay. At thirty-two, they appeared to be telling him, he was superannuated.

Again he suggested to his mother that he should accept the situation, settle down, and look for a wife. "Talk to your father," she said. He did so; his father said, "Of course your help is welcome, but I can run the farm well enough for a while yet. Your mother thinks you should go to the capital, to Command. They can't ignore you if you're there. After all. After seven years' combat— your record—"

Teyeo knew what that was worth, now. But he was certainly not needed here, and probably irritated his father with his ideas of changing this or that way things were done. They were right, he should go to the capital and find out for himself what part he could play in the new world of peace.

His first halfyear there was grim. He knew almost no one at Command or in the barracks; his generation was dead, or invalided out, or home on half pay. The younger officers, who had not been in Yeowe, seemed to him a cold, buttoned-up lot, always talking money and politics; little businessmen, he privately thought them. He knew they were afraid of him—of his record, of his reputation; whether he wanted to or not he reminded them that there had been a war that Werel had fought and lost; a civil war; their own race fighting against itself, class against class. They wanted to dismiss it as a meaningless quarrel on another world, nothing to do with them.

Teyeo walked the streets of the capital, watched the thousands of bondsmen and bondswomen hurrying about their owners' business, and wondered what they were waiting for.

"The Ekumen does not interfere with the social, cultural, or economic arrangements and affairs of any people," the Embassy and the government spokesmen repeated. "Full membership for any nation or people that wishes it is contingent only on absence, or renunciation, of certain specific methods and devices of warfare," and there followed the list of terrible weapons, most of them mere names to Teyeo, but a few of them inventions of his own country: the biobomb, as they called it, and the neuronics.

He personally agreed with the Ekumen's judgment on such devices, and respected their patience in waiting for Voe Deo and the rest of the Werel to prove not only compliance with the ban, but acceptance of the principle. But he very deeply resented their condescension. They sat in judgment on everything Werelian, viewing from above. The less they said about the division of classes, the clearer their disapproval was. "Slavery is of very rare occurrence in Ekumenical worlds," said their books, "and disappears completely with full participation in the Ekumenical policy." Was that what the Alien Embassy was really waiting for?

"By our Lady!" said one of the young officers—many of them were Tualites, as well as businessmen—"the Aliens are going to admit the muddies before they admit us!" He was sputtering with indignant rage, like a redfaced old rega faced with an insolent bondsoldier. "Yeowe—a damned planet of savages, tribesmen, regressed into barbarism—preferred over us!"

"They fought well," Teyeo observed, knowing he should not say it as he said it, but not liking to hear the men and women he had fought against called muddies. Assets, rebels, enemies, yes.

The young man stared at him and after a moment said, "I suppose you love 'em, eh? The muddies?"

"I killed as many as I could," Teyeo replied politely, and then changed the conversation; the young man, though nominally Teyeo's superior at Command, was an oga, the lowest rank of veot, and to snub him further would be illbred.

They were stuffy, he was touchy; the old days of cheerful good fellowship were a faint, incredible memory. The bureau chiefs at Command listened to his request to be put back on active service and sent him endlessly on to another department. He could not live in barracks, but had to find an apartment, like a civilian. His half pay did not permit him indulgence in the expensive pleasures of the city. While waiting for appointments to see this or that official, he spent his days in the library net of the Officers Academy. He knew his education had been incomplete and was out of date. If his country was going to join the Ekumen, in order to be useful he must know more about the Alien ways of thinking and the new technologies. Not sure what he needed to know, he floundered about in the network, bewildered by the endless information available, increasingly aware that he was no intellectual and no scholar and would never understand Alien minds, but doggedly driving himself on out of his depth.

A man from the Embassy was offering an introductory course in Ekumenical history in the public net. Teyeo joined it, and sat through eight or ten lecture and discussion periods, straight-backed and still, only his hands moving slightly as he took full and methodical notes. The lecturer, a Hainishman who translated his extremely long Hainish name as Old Music, watched Teyeo, tried to draw him out in discussion, and at last asked him to stay in after session. "I should like to meet you, Rega," he said, when the others had dropped out.

They met at a cafe. They met again. Teyeo did not like the Alien's manners, which he found effusive; he did not trust his quick, clever mind; he felt Old Music was using him, studying him as a specimen of The Veot, The Soldier, probably The Barbarian. The Alien, secure in his superiority, was indifferent to Teyeo's coldness, ignored his distrust, insisted on helping him with information and guidance, and shamelessly repeated questions Teyeo had avoided answering. One of these was, "Why are you sitting around here on half pay?"

"It's not by my own choice, Mr. Old Music," Teyeo finally answered, the third time it was asked; he was very angry at the man's impudence, and so spoke with particular mildness. He kept his eyes away from Old Music's eyes, bluish, with the whites showing like a scared horse. He could not get used to Aliens' eyes.

"They won't put you back on active service?"

Teyeo assented politely. Could the man, however alien, really be oblivious to the fact that his questions were grossly humiliating?

"Would you be willing to serve in the Embassy Guard?"

That question left Teyeo speechless for a moment; then he committed the extreme rudeness of answering a question with a question. "Why do you ask?"

"I'd like very much to have a man of your capacity in that corps," said Old Music, adding with his appalling candor, "Most of them are spies or blockheads. It would be wonderful to have a man I knew was neither. It's not just sentry-duty, you know. I imagine you'd be asked by your government to give information; that's to be expected. And we would use you, once you had experience and if you were willing, as a liaison officer. Here or in other countries. We would not, however, ask you to give information to us. Am I clear, Teyeo? I want no misunderstanding between us as to what I am and am not asking of you."

"You would be able . . . ?" Teyeo asked cautiously.

Old Music laughed and said, "Yes. I have a string to pull in your Command. A favor owed. Will you think it over?"

Teyeo was silent a minute. He had been nearly a year now in the capital and his requests for posting had met only bureaucratic evasion and, recently, hints that they were considered insubordinate. "I'll accept now, if I may," he said, with a cold deference.

The Hainishman looked at him, his smile changing to a thoughtful, steady gaze. "Thank you," he said. "You should hear from Command in a few days."

So Teyeo put his uniform back on, moved back to the City Barracks, and served for another seven years on alien ground. The Ekumenical Embassy was, by diplomatic agreement, a part not of Werel but of the Ekumen—a piece of the planet that no longer belonged to it. The Guardsmen furnished by Voe Deo were protective and decorative, a highly visible presence on the Embassy grounds in their white and gold dress uniform. They were also visibly armed, since protest against the Alien presence still broke out erratically in violence.

Rega Teyeo, at first assigned to command a troop of these guards, soon was transferred to a different duty, that of accompanying members of the Embassy staff about the city and on journeys. He served as a bodyguard, in undress uniform. The Embassy much preferred not to use their own people and weapons, but to request and trust Voe Deo to protect them. Often he was also called upon to be a guide and interpreter, and sometimes a companion. He did not like it when visitors from somewhere in space wanted to be chummy and confiding, asked him about himself, invited him to come drinking with them. With perfectly concealed distaste, with perfect civility, he refused such offers. He did his job and kept his distance. He knew that that was precisely what the Embassy valued him for. Their confidence in him gave him a cold satisfaction.

His own government had never approached him to give information, though he certainly learned things that would have interested them. Voe Dean intelligence did not recruit their agents among veots. He knew who the agents in the Embassy Guard were; some of them tried to get information from him, but he had no intention of spying for spies.

Old Music, whom he now surmised to be the head of the Embassy's intelligence system, called him in on his return from a winter leave at home. The Hainishman had learned not to make emotional demands on Teyeo, but could not hide a note of affection in his voice greeting him. "Hullo, Rega! I hope your family's well? Good. I've got a particularly tricky job for you. Kingdom of Gatay. You were there with Kemehan two years ago, weren't you? Well, now they want us to send an Envoy. They say they want to join. Of course the old king's a puppet of your government; but there's a lot else going on there. A strong religious separatist movement. A Patriotic Cause, kick out all the foreigners, Voe Deans and Aliens alike. But the king and council requested an Envoy, and all we've got to send them is a new arrival. She may give you some problems till she learns the ropes. I judge her a bit headstrong. Excellent material, but young, very young. And she's only been here a few weeks. I requested you, because she needs your experience. Be patient with her, Rega. I think you'll find her likeable."

He did not. In seven years he had got accustomed to the Aliens' eyes and their various smells and colors and manners; protected by his flawless courtesy and his stoical code, he endured or ignored their strange or shocking or troubling behavior, their ignorance and their different knowledge. Serving and protecting the foreigners entrusted to him, he kept himself aloof from them, neither touched nor touching. His charges learned to count on him and not to presume on him. Women were often quicker to see and respond to his Keep Out signs than men; he had an easy, almost friendly relationship with an old Terran Observer whom he had accompanied on several long investigatory tours. "You are as peaceful to be with as a cat, Rega," she told him once, and he valued the compliment. But the Envoy to Gatay was another matter.

She was physically splendid, with clear redbrown skin like that of a baby, glossy swinging hair, a free walk—too free: she flaunted her ripe, slender body at men who had no access to it, thrusting it at him, at everyone, insistent, shameless. She expressed her opinion on everything with coarse self-confidence. She could not hear a hint and refused to take an order. She was an aggressive, spoiled child with the sexuality of an adult, given the responsibility of a diplomat in a dangerously unstable country. Teyeo knew as soon as he met her that this was an impossible assignment. He could not trust her or himself. Her sexual immodesty aroused him as it disgusted him; she was a whore whom he must treat as a princess. Forced to endure and unable to ignore her, he hated her.

He was more familiar with anger than he had used to be, but not used to hating. It troubled him extremely. He had never in his life asked for a reposting, but on the morning after she had taken the makil into her room, he sent a stiff little appeal to the Embassy. Old Music responded to him with a sealed voice-message through the diplomatic link: "Love of god and country is like fire, a wonderful friend, a terrible enemy; only children play with fire. I don't like the situation. There's nobody here I can replace either of you with. Will you hang on a while longer?"

He did not know how to refuse. A veot did not refuse duty. He was ashamed at having even thought of doing so, and hated her again for causing him that shame.

The first sentence of the message was enigmatic, not in Old Music's usual style but flowery, indirect, like a coded warning. Teyeo of course knew none of the intelligence codes either of his country or of the Ekumen. Old Music would have to use hints and indirection with him. "Love of god and country" could well mean the Old Believers and the Patriots, the two subversive groups in Gatay, both of them fanatically opposed to foreign influence; the Envoy could be the child playing with fire. Was she being approached by one group or the other? He had seen no evidence of it, unless the man in the shadows that night had been not a knifeman but a messenger. She was under his eyes all day, her house watched all night by soldiers under his command. Surely the makil, Batikam, was not acting for either of those groups. He might well be a member of Hame, the asset liberation underground of Voe Deo, but as such would not endanger the Envoy, since the Hame saw the Ekumen as their ticket to Yeowe and to freedom.

Teyeo puzzled over the words, replaying them over and over, knowing his own stupidity faced with this kind of subtlety, the ins and outs of the political labyrinth. At last he erased the message and yawned, for it was late; bathed, lay down, turned off the light, said under his breath, "Lord Kamye, let me hold with courage to the one noble thing!" and slept like a stone.

The makil came to her house every night after the theater. Teyeo tried to tell himself there was nothing wrong in it. He himself had spent nights with the makils, back in the palmy days before the war. Expert, artistic sex was part of their business. He knew by hearsay that rich city women often hired them to come supply a husband's deficiencies. But even such women did so secretly, discreetly, not in this vulgar, shameless way, utterly careless of decency, flouting the moral code, as if she had some kind of right to do whatever she wanted wherever and whenever she wanted it. Of course Batikam colluded eagerly with her, playing on her infatuation, mocking the Gatayans, mocking Teyeo—and mocking her, though she didn't know it. What a chance for an asset to make fools of all the owners at once!

Watching Batikam, Teyeo felt sure he was a member of Hame. His mockery was very subtle; he was not trying to disgrace the Envoy. Indeed his discretion was far greater than hers. He was trying to keep her from disgracing herself. The makil returned Teyeo's cold courtesy in kind, but once or twice their eyes met and some brief, involuntary understanding passed between them, fraternal, ironic.

There was to be a public festival, an observation of the Tualite Feast of Forgiveness, to which the Envoy was pressingly invited by the King and Council. She was put on show at many such events. Teyeo thought nothing about it except how to provide security in an excited holiday crowd, until San told him that the festival day was the highest holy day of the old religion of Gatay, and that the Old Believers fiercely resented the imposition of the foreign rites over their own. The little man seemed genuinely worried. Teyeo worried too when, next day, San was suddenly replaced by an elderly man who spoke little but Gatayan and was quite unable to explain what had become of San Ubattat. "Other duties, other duties call," he said in very bad VoeDean, smiling and bobbing, "very great relishes time, aha? Relishes duties call."

During the days that preceded the festival tension rose in the city; graffiti appeared, symbols of the old religion smeared across the walls; a Tualite temple was desecrated, after which the Royal Guard was much in evidence in the streets. Teyeo went to the palace and requested, on his own authority, that the Envoy not be asked to appear in public during a ceremony that was "likely to be troubled by inappropriate demonstrations." He was called in and treated by a Court official with a mixture of dismissive insolence and conniving nods and winks, which left him really uneasy. He left four men on duty at the Envoy's house that night. Returning to his quarters, a little barracks down the street which had been handed over to the Embassy Guard, he found the window of his room open and a scrap of writing, in his own language, on his table: *Fest F is set up for assasnation.*

He was at the Envoy's house promptly the next morning and asked her asset to tell her he must speak to her. She came out of her bedroom pulling a white wrap around her naked body. Batikam followed her, half-dressed, sleepy, and amused. Teyeo gave him the eye-signal *go*, which he received with a serene, patronizing smile, murmuring to the woman, "I'll go have some breakfast. Rewe? have you got something to feed me?" He followed the bondswoman out of the room. Teyeo faced the Envoy and held out the scrap of paper.

"I received this last night, ma'am," he said. "I must ask you not to attend the festival tomorrow."

She considered the paper, read the writing, and yawned. "Who's it from?"

"I don't know, ma'am."

"What's it mean? *Assassination*? They can't spell, can they?"

After a moment, he said, "There are a number of other indications—enough that I must ask you—"

"Not to attend the festival of Forgiveness, yes. I heard you." She went to a windowseat and sat down, her robe falling wide to reveal her legs; her bare, brown feet were short and supple, the soles pink, the toes small and orderly. Teyeo looked fixedly at the air beside her head. She twiddled the bit of paper. "If you think it's dangerous, Rega, bring a guardsman or two with you," she said, with the faintest tone of scorn. "I really have to be there. The King requested it, you know. And I'm to light the big fire, or something. One of the few things women are allowed to do in public here. . . . I can't back out of it." She held out the paper, and after a moment he came close enough to take it. She looked up at him smiling; when she defeated him she always smiled at him. "Who do you think would want to blow me away, anyhow? The Patriots?"

"Or the Old Believers, ma'am. Tomorrow is one of their holidays."

"And your Tualites have taken it away from them? Well, they can't exactly blame the Ekumen, can they?"

"I think it possible that the government might permit violence in order to excuse retaliation, ma'am."

She started to answer carelessly, realized what he had said, and frowned. "You think the Council's setting me up? What evidence have you?"

After a pause he said, "Very little, ma'am. San Ubattat—"

"San's been ill. The old fellow they sent isn't much use, but he's scarcely dangerous! Is that all?" He said nothing, and she went on, "Until you have real evidence, Rega, don't interfere with my obligations. Your militaristic paranoia isn't acceptable when it spreads to the people I'm dealing with here. Control it, please! I'll expect an extra guardsman or two tomorrow; and that's enough."

"Yes, ma'am," he said, and went out. His head sang with anger. It occurred to him now that her new guide had told him San Ubattat had been kept away by religious duties, not by illness. He did not turn back. What was the use? "Stay on for an hour or so, will you, Seyem?" he said to the guard at her gate, and strode off down the street, trying to walk away from her, from her soft brown thighs and the pink soles of her feet and her stupid, insolent, whorish voice giving him orders. He tried to let the bright icy sunlight air, the stepped streets snapping with banners for the festival, the glitter of the great mountains and the clamor of the markets fill him, dazzle and distract him; but he walked seeing his own shadow fall in front of him like a knife across the stones, knowing the futility of his life.

"The veot looked worried," Batikam said in his velvet voice, and she laughed, spearing a preserved fruit from the dish and popping it, dripping, into his mouth.

"I'm ready for breakfast now, Rewe," she called, and sat down across from Batikam. "I'm starving! He was having one of his phallocratic fits. He hasn't saved me from anything lately. It's his only function, after all. So he has to invent occasions. I wish, I wish he was out of my hair. It's so nice not to have poor little old San crawling around like some kind of pubic infestation. If only I could get rid of the Major now!"

"He's a man of honor," the makil said; his tone did not seem ironical.

"How can an owner of slaves be an honorable man?"

Batikam watched her from his long, dark eyes. She could not read Werelian eyes, beautiful as they were, filling their lids with darkness.

"Male hierarchy members always yatter about their precious honor," she said. "And 'their' women's honor, of course."

"Honor is a great privilege," Batikam said. "I envy it. I envy him."

"Oh, the hell with all that phony dignity, it's just pissing to mark your territory. All you need envy him, Batikam, is his freedom."

He smiled. "You're the only person I've ever known who was neither owned nor owner. That is freedom. *That* is freedom. I wonder if you know it?"

"Of course I do," she said. He smiled, and went on eating his breakfast, but there had been something in his voice she had not heard before. Moved and a little troubled, she said after a while, "You're going away soon."

"Mind-reader. Yes. In ten days, the troupe goes on to tour the Forty States."

"Oh, Batikam, I'll miss you! You're the only man, the only person here I can talk to—let alone the sex—"

"Did we ever?"

"Not often," she said, laughing, but her voice shook a little. He held out his hand; she came to him and sat on his lap, the robe dropping open. "Little pretty Envoy breasts," he said, lipping and stroking, "little soft Envoy belly. . . . " Rewe came in with a tray and softly set it down. "Eat your breakfast, little Envoy," Batikam said, and she disengaged herself and returned to her chair, grinning.

"Because you're free you can be honest," he said, fastidiously peeling a pinifruit. "Don't be too hard on those of us who aren't and can't." He cut a slice and fed it to her across the table. "It has been a taste of freedom to know you," he said. "A hint, a shadow . . . "

"In a few years at most, Batikam, you *will* be free. This whole idiotic structure of masters and slaves will collapse completely when Werel comes into the Ekumen."

"If it does."

"Of course it will."

He shrugged. "My home is Yeowe," he said.

She stared, confused. "You come from Yeowe?"

"I've never been there," he said, "I'll probably never go there. What use have they got for makils? But it is my home. Those are my people. That is my freedom. When will you see. . . . " His fist was clenched; he opened it with a soft gesture of letting something go. He smiled and returned to his breakfast. "I've got to get back to the theater," he said, "we're rehearsing an act for the Day of Forgiveness."

She wasted all day at court. She had made persistent attempts to obtain permission to visit the mines and the huge government-run farms on the far side of the mountains, from which Gatay's wealth flowed; she had been as persistently foiled—by the protocol and bureaucracy of the government, she had thought at first, their unwillingness to let a diplomat do anything but run round to meaning-less events; but some businessmen had let something slip about conditions in the mines and on the farms that made her think they might be hiding a more brutal kind of slavery than any visible in the capital. Today she got nowhere, waiting for appointments that had not been made. The old fellow who was standing in for San misunderstood most of what she said in VoeDean, and when she tried to speak Gatayan he misunderstood it all, through stupidity or intent. The Major was blessedly absent most of the morning, replaced by one of his soldiers, but turned up at court, stiff and silent and set-jawed, and attended her until she gave up and went home for an early bath.

Batikam came late that night. In the middle of one of the elaborate fantasy games and role-reversals she had learned from him and found so exciting, his caresses grew slower and slower, soft, dragging across her like feathers, so that she shivered with unappeased desire and, pressing her body against his, realized that he had gone to sleep. "Wake up," she said, laughing and yet chilled, and shook him a little. The dark eyes opened, bewildered, full of fear.

"I'm sorry," she said at once, "go back to sleep, you're tired. No, no, it's all right, it's late." But he went on with what she now, whatever his skill and tenderness, had to see was his job.

In the morning at breakfast she said, "Can you see me as an equal, do you, Batikam?"

He looked tired, older than he usually did. He did not smile. After a while he said, "What do you want me to say?"

"That you do."

"I do," he said quietly.

"You don't trust me," she said, bitter.

After a while he said, "This is Forgiveness Day. The Lady Tual came to the men of Asdok, who had set their hunting cats upon her followers. She came among them riding on a great hunting cat with a fiery tongue, and they fell down in terror, but she blessed them, forgiving them." His voice and hands enacted the story as he told it. "Forgive me," he said.

"You don't need any forgiveness!"

"Oh, we all do. It's why we Kamyites borrow the Lady Tual now and then. When we need her. So, today you'll be the Lady Tual, at the rites?"

"All I have to do is light a fire, they said," she said anxiously, and he laughed. When he left she told him she would come to the theater to see him, tonight, after the festival.

The horse-race course, the only flat area of any size anywhere near the city, was thronged, vendors calling, banners waving; the Royal motorcars drove straight into the crowd, which parted like water and closed behind. Some rickety-looking bleachers had been erected for lords and owners, with a curtained section for ladies. She saw a motorcar drive up to the bleachers; a figure swathed in red cloth was bundled out of it and hurried between the curtains, vanishing. Were there peepholes for them to watch the ceremony through? There were women in the crowds, but bondswomen only, assets. She realized that she, too, would be kept hidden until her moment of the ceremony arrived: a red tent awaited her, alongside the bleachers, not far from the roped enclosure where priests were chanting. She was rushed out of the car and into the tent by obsequious and determined courtiers.

Bondswomen in the tent offered her tea, sweets, mirrors, makeup, and hair-oil, and helped her put on the complex swathing of fine red and yellow cloth, her costume for her brief enactment of Lady Tual. Nobody had told her very clearly what she was to do, and to her questions the women said, "The priests will show you, Lady, you just go with them. You just light the fire. They have it all ready." She had the impression that they knew no more than she did; they were pretty girls, court assets, excited at being part of the show, indifferent to the religion. She knew the symbolism of the fire she was to light; into it faults and transgressions could be cast and burnt up, forgotten. It was a nice idea.

The priests were whooping it up out there; she peeked out—there were indeed peepholes in the tent fabric—and saw the crowd had thickened. Nobody except in the bleachers and right against the enclosure ropes could possibly see anything, but everybody was waving red and yellow banners, munching fried food, and making a day of it, while the priests kept up their deep chanting. In the far right of the little, blurred field of vision through the peephole was a familiar arm: the Major's, of course. They had not let him get into the motorcar with her. He must have been furious. He had got here, though, and stationed himself on guard. "Lady, Lady," the court girls were saying, "here come the priests now," and they buzzed around her making sure her headdress was on straight and the damnable, hobbling skirts fell in the right folds. They were still plucking and patting as she stepped out of the tent, dazzled by the daylight, smiling and trying to hold herself very straight and dignified as a Goddess ought to do; she really didn't want to fuck up their ceremony.

Two men in priestly regalia were waiting for her right outside the tent door. They stepped forward immediately, taking her by the elbows and saying, "This way, this way, Lady." Evidently she really wouldn't have to figure out what to do. No doubt they considered women incapable of it, but in the circumstances it was a relief. The priests hurried her along faster than she could comfortably walk in the tight-drawn skirt. They were behind the bleachers now; wasn't the enclosure in the other direction? A car was coming straight at them, scattering the few people who were in its way. Somebody was shouting; the priests suddenly began yanking her, trying to run; one of them yelled and let go her arm, felled by a flying darkness that had hit him with a jolt—she was in the middle of a melee, unable to break the iron hold on her arm, legs imprisoned in the skirt, and there was a noise, an enormous noise, that hit her head and bent it down, she couldn't see or hear, blinded, struggling, shoved face first into some dark place with her face pressed into a stifling, scratchy darkness and her arms held locked behind her.

A car, moving. A long time. Men, talking low. They talked in Gatayan. It was very hard to breathe. She did not struggle; it was no use. They had taped her arms and legs, bagged her head. After a long time she was hauled out like a corpse and carried quickly, indoors, down stairs, set down on a bed or couch, not roughly though with the same desperate haste. She lay still. The men talked, still almost in whispers. It made no sense to her. Her head was still hearing that enormous noise, had it been real? had she been struck? She felt deaf, as if inside a wall of cotton. The cloth of the bag kept getting stuck on her mouth, sucked against her nostrils as she tried to breathe.

It was plucked off; a man stooping over her turned her so he could untape her arms, then her legs, murmuring as he did so, "Don't to be scared, Lady, we don't to hurt you," in VoeDean. He backed away from her quickly. There were four or five of them; it was hard to see, there was very little light. "To wait here," another said, "everything all right. Just to keep happy." She was trying to sit up, and it made her dizzy. When her head stopped spinning, they were all gone. As if by magic. Just to keep happy.

A small very high room. Dark brick walls, earthy air. The light was from a little biolume plaque stuck on the ceiling, a weak, shadowless glow. Probably quite sufficient for Werelian eyes. Just to keep happy. I have been kidnaped. How about that. She inventoried: the thick mattress she was on; a blanket; a door; a small pitcher and a cup; a drainhole, was it, over in the corner? She swung her legs off the mattress and her feet struck something lying on the floor at the foot of it—she coiled up, peered at the dark mass, the body lying there. A man. The dark uniform, the skin so black she could not see the features, but she knew him. Even here, even here, the Major was with her.

She stood up unsteadily and went to investigate the drainhole, which was simply that, a cement-lined hole in the floor, smelling slightly chemical, slightly foul. Her head hurt, and she sat down on the bed again to massage her arms and ankles, easing the tension and pain and getting herself back into herself by touching and confirming herself, rhythmically, methodically. I have been kidnaped. How about that. Just to keep happy. What about him?

Suddenly knowing that he was dead, she shuddered and held still.

After a while she leaned over slowly, trying to see his face, listening. Again she had the sense of being deaf. She heard no breath. She reached out, sick and shaking, and put the back of her hand against his face. It was cool, cold. But warmth breathed across her fingers, once, again. She crouched on the mattress and studied him. He lay absolutely still, but when she put her hand on his chest she felt the slow heartbeat.

"Teyeo," she said in a whisper. Her voice would not go above a whisper.

She put her hand on his chest again. She wanted to feel that slow, steady beat, the faint warmth; it was reassuring. Just to keep happy.

What else had they said. Just to wait. Yes. That seemed to be the program. Maybe she could sleep. Maybe she could sleep and when she woke up the ransom would have come. Or whatever it was they wanted.

She woke up with the thought that she still had her watch, and after sleepily studying the tiny silver readout for a while decided she had slept three hours; it was still the day of the Festival, too soon for ransom probably, and she wouldn't be able to go to the theater to see the makils tonight. Her eyes had grown accustomed to the low light and when she looked she could see, now, that there was dried blood all over one side of the man's head. Exploring, she found a hot lump like a fist above his temple, and her fingers came away smeared. He had got himself crowned. That must have been him, launching himself at the priest, the fake priest, all she could remember was a flying shadow and a hard thump and an oof! like an aiji attack, and then there had been the huge noise that confused everything. She clicked her tongue, tapped the wall, to check her hearing. It seemed to be all right; the wall of cotton had disappeared. Maybe she had been crowned herself? She felt her head, but found no lumps. The man must have a concussion, if he was still out after three hours. How bad? When would the men come back?

She got up and nearly fell over, entangled in the damned Goddess skirts. If only she was in her own clothes, not this fancy dress, three pieces of flimsy stuff you had to have servants to put on you! She got out of the skirt piece, and used the scarf piece to make a kind of tied skirt that came to her knees. It wasn't warm in this basement or whatever it was; it was dank and rather cold. She walked up and down, four steps turn, four steps turn, four steps turn, and did some warmups. They had dumped the man onto the floor. How cold was it? Was shock part of concussion? People in shock needed to be kept warm. She dithered a long time, puzzled at her own indecision, at not knowing what to do. Should she try to heave him up onto the mattress? Was it better not to move him? Where the hell were the men? Was he going to die?

She stooped over him and said sharply, "Rega! Teyeo!" and after a moment he caught his breath.

"Wake up!" She remembered now, she thought she remembered, that it was important not to let concussed people lapse into a coma. Except he already had.

He caught his breath again, and his face changed, came out of the rigid immobility, softened; his eyes opened and closed, blinked, unfocused. "Oh Kamye," he said very softly.

She couldn't believe how glad she was to see him. Just to keep happy. He evidently had a blinding headache, and admitted that he was seeing double. She helped him haul himself up onto the mattress and covered him with the blanket. He asked no questions, and lay mute, lapsing back to sleep soon. Once he was settled she went back to her exercises, and did an hour of them. She looked at her watch. It was two hours later, the same day, the Festival day. It wasn't evening yet. When were the men going to come?

They came early in the morning, after the endless night that was the same as the afternoon and the morning. The metal door was unlocked and thrown clanging open, and one of them came in with a tray while two of them stood with raised, aimed guns in the doorway. There was nowhere to put the tray but the floor, so he shoved it at Solly, said, "Sorry, Lady!" and backed out; the door clanged shut, the bolts banged home. She stood holding the tray. "Wait!" she said.

The man had waked up and was looking groggily around. After finding him in this place with her she had somehow lost his nickname, did not think of him as the Major, yet shied away from his name. "Here's breakfast, I guess," she said, and sat down on the edge of the mattress. A cloth was thrown over the wicker tray; under it was a pile of Gatayan grainrolls stuffed with meat and greens, several pieces of fruit, and a capped water-carafe of thin, fancily beaded metal alloy. "Breakfast, lunch, and dinner, maybe," she said. "Shit. Oh well. It looks good. Can you eat? Can you sit up?"

He worked himself up to sit with his back against the wall, and then shut his eyes.

"You're still seeing double?"

He made a small noise of assent.

"Are you thirsty?"

Small noise of assent.

"Here." She passed him the cup. By holding it in both hands he got it to his mouth, and drank the water slowly, a swallow at a time. She meanwhile devoured three grainrolls one after the other, then forced herself to stop, and ate a pinifruit. "Could you eat some fruit?" she asked him, feeling guilty. He did not answer. She thought of Batikam feeding her the slice of pini at breakfast, when, yesterday, a hundred years ago.

The food in her stomach made her feel sick. She took the cup from the man's relaxed hand—he was asleep again—and poured herself water, and drank it slowly, a swallow at a time.

When she felt better she went to the door and explored its hinges, lock, and surface. She felt and peered around the brick walls, the poured concrete floor, seeking she knew not what, something to escape with, something. . . . She should do exercises. She forced herself to do some, but the queasiness returned, and a lethargy with it. She went back to the mattress and sat down. After a while she found she was crying. After a while she found she had been asleep. She needed to piss. She squatted over the hole and listened to her urine fall into it. There was nothing to clean herself with. She came back to the bed and sat down on it, stretching out her legs, holding her ankles in her hands. It was utterly silent.

She turned to look at the man; he was watching her. It made her start. He looked away at once. He still lay half propped up against the wall, uncomfortably, but relaxed.

"Are you thirsty?" she asked.

"Thank you," he said. Here where nothing was familiar and time was broken off from the past, his soft, light voice was welcome in its familiarity. She poured him a cup full and gave it to him. He managed it much more steadily, sitting up to drink. "Thank you," he whispered again, giving her back the cup.

"How's your head?"

He put his hand to the swelling, winced, and sat back.

"One of them had a stick," she said, seeing it in a flash in the jumble of her memories—"a priest's staff. You jumped the other one."

"They took my gun," he said. "Festival." He kept his eyes closed.

"I got tangled in those damn clothes. I couldn't help you at all. Listen. Was there a noise, an explosion?"

"Yes. Diversion, maybe."

"Who do you think these boys are?"

"Revolutionaries. Or . . ."

"You said you thought the Gatayan government was in on it."

"I don't know," he murmured.

"You were right, I was wrong, I'm sorry," she said with a sense of virtue at remembering to make amends.

He moved his hand very slightly in an it-doesn't-matter gesture.

"Are you still seeing double?"

He did not answer; he was phasing out again.

She was standing, trying to remember Selish breathing exercises, when the door crashed and clanged, and the same three men were there, two with guns, all young, black-skinned, short-haired, very nervous. The lead one stooped to set a tray down on the floor, and without the least premeditation Solly stepped on his hand and brought her weight down on it. "You wait!" she said. She was staring straight into the faces and gun-muzzles of the other two. "Just wait a moment, listen! He has a head injury, we need a doctor, we need more water, I can't even clean his wound, there's no toilet paper, who the hell are you people anyway?"

The one she had stomped was shouting, "Get off! Lady to get off my hand!" but the others heard her. She lifted her foot and got out of his way as he came up fast, backing into his buddies with the guns. "All right, lady, we are sorry to have trouble," he said, tears in his eyes, cradling his hand. "We are Patriots. You send messish to this Pretender, like our messish. Nobody is to hurt. All right?" He kept backing up, and one of the gunmen swung the door to. Crash, rattle.

She drew a deep breath and turned. Teyeo was watching her. "That was dangerous," he said, smiling very slightly.

"I know it was," she said, breathing hard. "It was stupid. I can't get hold of myself. I feel like pieces of me. But they shove stuff in and run, damn it! We have to have some water!" She was in tears, the way she always was for a moment after violence or a quarrel. "Let's see, what have they brought this time." She lifted the tray up onto the mattress; like the other, in a ridiculous semblance of service in a hotel or a house with slaves, it was covered with a cloth. "All the comforts," she murmured. Under the cloth was a heap of sweet pastries, a little plastic handmirror, a comb, a tiny pot of something that smelled like decayed flowers, and a box of what she identified after a while as Gatayan tampons.

"It's things for the lady," she said. "God damn them, the stupid Goddamn pricks! A mirror!" She flung the thing across the room. "Of course I can't last a day without looking in the mirror! God *damn* them!" She flung everything else but the pastries after the mirror, knowing as she did so that she would pick up the tampons and keep them under the mattress and, oh, God forbid, use them if she had to, if they had to stay here, how long would it be? ten days or more—"Oh, God," she said again. She got up and picked everything up, put the mirror and the little pot, the empty water jug and the fruit-skins from the last meal, onto one of the trays and set it beside the door. "Garbage," she said in VoeDean. Her outburst, she realized, had been in another language; Alterran, probably. "Have you any idea," she said, sitting down on the mattress again, "how hard you people make it to be a woman? You could turn a woman against being one!"

"I think they meant well," Teyeo said. She realized that there was not the faintest shade of mockery, even of amusement in his voice. If he was enjoying her shame, he was ashamed to show her that he was. "I think they're amateurs," he said.

After a while she said, "That could be bad."

"It might." He had sat up and was gingerly feeling the knot on his head. His coarse, heavy hair was blood-caked all around it. "Kidnaping," he said. "Ransom demands. Not assassins. They didn't have guns. Couldn't have got in with guns. I had to give up mine."

"You mean these aren't the ones you were warned about?"

"I don't know." His explorations caused him a shiver of pain, and he desisted. "Are we very short of water?"

She brought him another cup full. "Too short for washing. A stupid Goddamn mirror when what we need is water!"

He thanked her and drank and sat back, nursing the last swallows in the cup. "They didn't plan to take me," he said.

She thought about it and nodded. "Afraid you'd identify them?"

"If they had a place for me they wouldn't put me in with a lady." He spoke without irony. "They had this ready for you. It must be somewhere in the city."

She nodded. "The car ride was half an hour or less. My head was in a bag, though."

"They've sent a message to the Palace. They got no reply, or an unsatisfactory one. They want a message from you."

"To convince the government they really have me? Why do they need convincing?"

They were both silent.

"I'm sorry," he said, "I can't think." He lay back. Feeling tired, low, edgy after her adrenaline rush, she lay down alongside him. She had rolled up the Goddess' skirt to make a pillow; he had none. The blanket lay across their legs.

"Pillow," she said. "More blankets. Soap. What else?"

"Key," he murmured.

They lay side by side in the silence and the faint unvarying light.

Next morning about eight, according to Solly's watch, the Patriots came into the room, four of them; two stood on guard at the door with their guns ready; the other two stood uncomfortably in what floor space was left, looking down at their captives, both of whom sat crosslegged on the mattress. The new spokesman spoke better VoeDean than the others. He said they were very sorry to cause the lady discomfort and would do what they could to make it comfortable for her, and she must be patient and write a message by hand to the Pretender King, explaining that she would be set free unharmed as soon as the King commanded the Council to rescind their treaty with Voe Deo.

"He won't," she said. "They won't let him."

"Please do not discuss," the man said with frantic harshness. "This is writing materials. This is the message." He set the papers and a stylo down on the mattress, nervously, as if afraid to get close to her.

She was aware of how Teyeo effaced himself, sitting without a motion, his head lowered, his eyes lowered; the men ignored him.

"If I write this for you I want water, a lot of water, and soap and blankets and toilet paper and pillows and a doctor, and I want somebody to come when I knock on that door, and I want some decent clothes. Warm clothes. Men's clothes."

"No doctor!" the man said. "Write it! Please! Now!" He was jumpy, twitchy, she dared push him no further. She read their statement, copied it out in her large, childish scrawl—she seldom handwrote anything—and handed both to the spokesman. He glanced over it and without a word hurried the other men out. Clash went the door.

"Should I have refused?"

"I don't think so," Teyeo said. He stood up and stretched, but sat down again looking dizzy. "You bargain well," he said.

"We'll see what we get. Oh, God. What is going *on?*"

"Maybe," he said slowly, "Gatay is unwilling to yield to these demands. But when Voe Deo—and your Ekumen—get word of it, they'll put pressure on Gatay."

"I wish they'd get moving. I suppose Gatay is horribly embarrassed, saving face by trying to conceal the whole thing—is that likely? How long can they keep it up? What about your people? Won't they be hunting for you?"

"No doubt," he said, in his polite way.

It was curious how his stiff manner, his manners, which had always shunted her aside, cut her out, here had quite another effect; his restraint and formality reassured her that she was still part of the world outside this room, from which they came and to which they would return, a world where people lived long lives.

What did long life matter? she asked herself, and didn't know. It was nothing she had ever thought about before. But these young Patriots lived in a world of short lives. Demands, violence, immediacy, and death, for what? for a bigotry, a hatred, a rush of power.

"Whenever they leave," she said in a low voice, "I get really frightened."

Teyeo cleared his throat and said, "So do I."

Exercises.

"Take hold—no, take *hold*, I'm not made of glass!—Now—"

"Ha!" he said, with his flashing grin of excitement, as she showed him the break, and he in turn repeated it, breaking from her.

"All right, now you'd be waiting—here"—thump—"see?"

"Ai!"

"I'm sorry—I'm sorry, Teyeo—I didn't think about your head—Are you all right? I'm really sorry—"

"Oh, Kamye," he said, sitting up and holding his black, narrow head between his hands. He drew several deep breaths. She knelt penitent and anxious.

"That's," he said, and breathed some more, "that's not, not fair play."

"No of course it's not, it's aiji—all's fair in love and war, they say that on Terra—Really, I'm sorry, I'm terribly sorry, that was so stupid of me!"

He laughed, a kind of broken and desperate laugh, shook his head, shook it again. "Show me," he said. "I don't know what you did."

Exercises.

"What do you do with your mind?"

"Nothing."

"You just let it wander?"

"No. Am I and my mind different beings?"

"So . . . you don't focus on something? You just wander with it?"

"No."

"So you *don't* let it wander."

"Who?" he said, rather testily.

A pause.

"Do you think about—"

"No," he said. "Be still."

A very long pause, maybe a quarter hour.

"Teyeo, I can't. I itch. My mind itches. How long have you been doing this?"

A pause, a reluctant answer: "Since I was two."

He broke his utterly relaxed motionless pose, bent his head to stretch his neck and shoulder muscles. She watched him.

"I keep thinking about long life, about living long," she said. "I don't mean just being alive a long time, hell, I've been alive about eleven hundred years, what does that mean, nothing. I mean . . . Something about thinking of life as long makes a difference. Like having kids does. Even thinking about having kids. It's like it changes some balance. It's funny I keep thinking about that now, when my chances for a long life have kind of taken a steep fall. . . ."

He said nothing. He was able to say nothing in a way that allowed her to go on talking. He was one of the least talkative men she had ever known. Most men were so wordy. She was fairly wordy herself. He was quiet. She wished she knew how to be quiet.

"It's just practice, isn't it?" she asked. "Just sitting there."

He nodded.

"Years and years and years of practice. . . . Oh, God. Maybe . . ."

"No, no," he said, taking her thought immediately.

"But why don't they *do* something? What are they *waiting* for? It's been nine *days!*"

From the beginning, by unplanned, unspoken agreement, the room had been divided in two: the line ran down the middle of the mattress and across to the facing wall. The door was on her side, the left; the shithole was on his side, the right. Any invasion of the other's space was requested by some almost invisible cue and permitted the same way. When one of them used the shit-hole the other unobtrusively faced away. When they had enough water to take cat-baths, which was seldom, the same arrangement held. The line down the middle of the mattress was absolute. Their voices crossed it, and the sounds and smells of their bodies. Sometimes she felt his warmth; Werelian body temperature was somewhat higher than hers, and in the dank, still air she felt that faint radiance as he slept. But they never crossed the line, not by a finger, not in the deepest sleep.

Solly thought about this, finding it, in some moments, quite funny. At other moments it seemed stupid and perverse. Couldn't they both use some human comfort? The only time she had touched him was the first day, when she had helped him get onto the mattress, and then when they had enough water she had cleaned his scalp-wound and little by little washed the clotted, stinking blood out of his hair, using the comb, which had after all been a good thing to have, and pieces of the Goddess' skirt, an invaluable source of washcloths and bandages. Then once his head healed, they practiced aiji daily; but aiji had an impersonal, ritual purity to its clasps and grips that was a long way from creature comfort. The rest of the time his bodily presence was clearly, invariably uninvasive and untouchable.

He was only maintaining, under incredibly difficult circumstances, the rigid restraint he had always shown. Not just he, but Rewe too; all of them, all of them but Batikam; and yet was Batikam's instant yielding to her whim and desire the true contact she had thought it? She thought of the fear in his eyes, that last night. Not restraint, but constraint.

It was the mentality of a slave society: slaves and masters caught in the same trap of radical distrust and self-protection.

"Teyeo," she said, "I don't understand slavery. Let me say what I mean," though he had shown no sign of interruption or protest, merely civil attention. "I mean, I do understand how a social institution comes about and how an individual is simply part of it—I'm not saying why don't you agree with me in seeing it as wicked and unprofitable, I'm not asking you to defend it or renounce it. I'm trying to understand what it feels like to believe that two-thirds of the human beings in your world are actually, rightfully your property. Five-sixths, in fact, including women of your caste."

After a while he said, "My family owns about twenty-five assets."

"Don't quibble."

He accepted the reproof.

"It seems to me that you cut off human contact. You don't touch slaves and slaves don't touch you, in the way human beings ought to touch—in mutuality. You have to keep yourselves separate, always working to maintain that boundary.

Because it isn't a natural boundary—it's totally artificial, manmade. I can't tell owners and assets apart physically. Can you?''

''Mostly.''

''By cultural, behavioral clues—right?''

After thinking a while, he nodded.

''You are the same species, race, people, exactly the same in every way, with a slight selection toward color. If you brought up an asset child as an owner it would *be* an owner in every respect, and vice versa. So you spend your lives keeping up this tremendous division that doesn't exist. What I don't understand is how you can fail to see how appallingly wasteful it is. I don't mean economically!''

''In the war,'' he said, and then there was a very long pause; though Solly had a lot more to say, she waited, curious. ''I was on Yeowe,'' he said, ''you know, in the civil war.''

That's where you got all those scars and dents, she thought; for however scrupulously she averted her eyes, it was impossible not to be fairly familiar with his spare, onyx body by now, and she knew that in aiji he had to favor his left arm, which had a considerable chunk out of it ju't above the bicep.

''The slaves of the Colonies revolted, you know, some of them at first, then all of them. Nearly all. So we Army men there were all owners. We couldn't send asset soldiers, they might defect. We were all veots and volunteers. Owners fighting assets. I was fighting my equals. I learned that pretty soon. Later on I learned I was fighting my superiors. They defeated us.''

''But that—'' Solly said, and stopped; she did not know what to say.

''They defeated us from beginning to end,'' he said. ''Partly because my government didn't understand that they could. That they fought better and harder and more intelligently and more bravely than we did.''

''Because they were fighting for their freedom!''

''Maybe so,'' he said in his polite way.

''So . . .''

''I wanted to tell you that I respect the people I fought.''

''I know so little about war, about fighting,'' she said, with a mixture of contrition and irritation. ''Nothing, really. I was on Kheakh, but that wasn't war, it was racial suicide, mass slaughter of a biosphere. I guess there's a difference. . . . That was when the Ekumen finally decided on the Arms Convention, you know. Because of Kheakh and Orint destroying themselves. The Terrans had been pushing for the Convention for ages. Having nearly committed suicide themselves a while back. I'm half Terran. My ancestors rushed around their planet slaughtering each other. For millennia. They were masters and slaves, too, some of them, a lot of them. . . . But I don't know if the Arms Convention was a good idea. If it's right. Who are we to tell anybody what to do and not to do? The idea of the Ekumen was to offer a way. To open it. Not to bar it to anybody.''

He listened intently, but said nothing until after some while. ''We learn to . . . close ranks. Always. You're right, I think, it wastes . . . energy, the spirit. You are open.''

His words cost him so much, she thought, not like hers that just came dancing out of the air and went back into it; he spoke from his marrow. It made what he said a solemn compliment, which she accepted gratefully, for as the days went on she realized occasionally how much confidence she had lost and kept losing: self-confidence, confidence that they would be ransomed, rescued, that they would get out of this room, that they would get out of it alive.

"Was the war very brutal?"

"Yes," he said. "I can't . . . I've never been able to—to see it—Only something comes like a flash—" He held his hands up as if to shield his eyes. Then he glanced at her, wary. His apparently cast-iron self-respect was, she knew now, vulnerable in many places.

"Things from Kheakh that I didn't even know I saw, they come that way," she said. "At night." And after a while, "How long were you there?"

"Seven years."

She winced. "Were you lucky?"

It was a queer question, not coming out the way she meant, but he took it at value. "Yes," he said. "Always. The men I went there with were killed. Most of them in the first few years. We lost three hundred thousand men on Yeowe. They never talk about it. Two-thirds of the veot men in Voe Deo were killed. If it was lucky to live, I was lucky." He looked down at his clasped hands, locked into himself.

After a while she said softly, "I hope you still are."

He said nothing.

"How long has it been?" he asked, and she said, clearing her throat, after an automatic glance at her watch, "Sixty hours."

Their captors had not come yesterday at what had become a regular time, about eight in the morning. Nor had they come this morning.

With nothing left to eat and now no water left, they had grown increasingly silent and inert; it was hours since either had said anything. He had put off asking the time as long as he could prevent himself.

"This is horrible," she said, "this is so horrible. I keep thinking . . ."

"They won't abandon you," he said. "They feel a responsibility."

"Because I'm a woman?"

"Partly."

"Shit."

He remembered that in the other life her coarseness had offended him.

"They've been taken, shot. Nobody bothered to find out where they were keeping us," she said.

Having thought the same thing several hundred times, he had nothing to say.

"It's just such a horrible *place* to die," she said. "It's sordid. I stink. I've stunk for twenty days. Now I have diarrhea because I'm scared. But I can't shit anything. I'm thirsty and I can't drink."

"Solly," he said sharply. It was the first time he had spoken her name. "Be still. Hold fast."

She stared at him.

"Hold fast to what?"

He did not answer at once and she said, "You won't let me touch you!"

"Not to me—"

"Then to what? There isn't anything!" He thought she was going to cry, but she stood up, took the empty tray, and beat it against the door till it smashed into fragments of wicker and dust. "Come! God damn you! Come, you bastards!" she shouted. "Let us out of here!"

After that she sat down again on the mattress. "Well," she said.

"Listen," he said.

They had heard it before: no city sounds came down to this cellar, wherever it was, but this was something bigger, explosions, they both thought.

The door rattled.

They were both afoot when it opened: not with the usual clash and clang, but slowly. A man waited outside; two men came in. One, armed, they had never seen; the other, the tough-faced young man they called the spokesman, looked as if he had been running or fighting, dusty, worn out, a little dazed. He closed the door. He had some papers in his hand. The four of them stared at one other in silence for a minute.

"Water," Solly said. "You bastards!"

"Lady," the spokesman said, "I'm sorry." He was not listening to her. His eyes were not on her. He was looking at Teyeo, for the first time. "There is a lot of fighting," he said.

"Who's fighting?" Teyeo asked, hearing himself drop into the even tone of authority, and the young man respond to it as automatically: "Voe Deo. They sent troops. After the funeral, they said they would send troops unless we surrendered. They came yesterday. They go through the city killing. They know all the Old Believer centers. Some of ours." He had a bewildered, accusing note in his voice.

"What funeral?" Solly said.

When he did not answer, Teyeo repeated it: "What funeral?"

"The lady's funeral, yours. Here—I brought netprints—A state funeral. They said you died in the explosion."

"What God-damned explosion?" Solly said in her hoarse, parched voice, and this time he answered her: "At the Festival. The Old Believers. The fire, Tual's fire, there were explosives in it. Only it went off too soon. We knew their plan. We rescued you from that, lady," he said, suddenly turning to her with that same accusatory tone.

"Rescued me, you asshole!" she shouted, and Teyeo's dry lips split in a startled laugh, which he repressed at once.

"Give me those," he said, and the young man handed him the papers.

"Get us water!" Solly said.

"Stay here, please. We need to talk," Teyeo said, instinctively holding on to his ascendancy. He sat down on the mattress with the net prints. Within a few minutes he and Solly had scanned the reports of the shocking disruption of the Festival of Forgiveness, the lamentable death of the Envoy of the Ekumen in a terrorist act executed by the cult of Old Believers, the brief mention of the death of a Voe Dean Embassy guard in the explosion, which had killed over seventy priests and onlookers, the long descriptions of the state funeral, reports of unrest, terrorism, reprisals, then reports of the Palace gratefully accepting offers of assistance from Voe Deo in cleaning out the cancer of terrorism. . . .

"So," he said finally. "You never heard from the Palace. Why did you keep us alive?"

Solly looked as if she thought the question lacked tact, but the spokesman answered with equal bluntness, "We thought your country would ransom you."

"They will," Teyeo said. "Only you have to keep your government from knowing we're alive. If you—"

"Wait," Solly said, touching his hand. "Hold on. I want to think about this stuff. You'd better not leave the Ekumen out of the discussion. But getting in touch with them is the tricky bit."

"If there are Voe Dean troops here, all I need is to get a message to anyone in my command, or the Embassy Guards."

Her hand was still on his, with a warning pressure. She shook the other one at the spokesman, finger outstretched: "You kidnaped an Envoy of the Ekumen, you asshole! Now you have to do the thinking you didn't do ahead of time. And I do too, because I don't want to get blown away by your God-damned little government for turning up alive and embarrassing them. Where are you hiding, anyhow? Is there any chance of us getting out of this room, at least?"

The man, with that edgy, frantic look, shook his head. "We are all down here now," he said. "Most of the time. You stay here safe."

"Yes, you'd better keep your passports safe!" Solly said. "Bring us some water, damn it! Let us talk a while. Come back in an hour."

The young man leaned toward her suddenly, his face contorted. "What the hell kind of lady you are," he said. "You foreign filthy stinking cunt."

Teyeo was on his feet, but her grip on his hand had tightened: after a moment of silence, the spokesman and the other man turned to the door, rattled the lock, and were let out.

"Oaf," she said, looking dazed.

"Don't," he said, "don't—" He did not know how to say it. "They don't understand," he said. "It's better if I talk."

"Of course. Women don't give orders. Women don't talk. Shitheads! I thought you said they felt so responsible for me!"

"They do," he said. "But they're young men. Fanatics. Very frightened." And you talk to them as if they were assets, he thought, but did not say.

"Well so am I frightened!" she said, with a little spurt of tears. She wiped her eyes and sat down again among the papers. "God," she said. "We've been dead for twenty days. Buried for fifteen. Who do you think they buried?"

Her grip was powerful; his wrist and hand hurt. He massaged the place gently, watching her.

"Thank you," he said. "I would have hit him."

"Oh, I know. Goddamn chivalry. And the one with the gun would have blown your head off. Listen, Teyeo. Are you sure all you have to do is get word to somebody in the Army or the Guard?"

"Yes, of course."

"You're sure your country isn't playing the same game as Gatay?"

He stared at her. As he understood her, slowly the anger he had stifled and denied, all these interminable days of imprisonment with her, rose in him, a fiery flood of resentment, hatred, and contempt.

He was unable to speak, afraid he would speak to her as the young Patriot had done.

He went around to his side of the room and sat on his side of the mattress, somewhat turned from her. He sat cross-legged, one hand lying lightly in the other.

She said some other things. He did not listen or reply.

After a while she said, "We're supposed to be talking, Teyeo. We've only got an hour. I think those kids might do what we tell them, if we tell them something plausible—something that'll work."

He would not answer. He bit his lip and held still.

"Teyeo, what did I say? I said something wrong. I don't know what it was. I'm sorry."

"They would—" He struggled to control his lips and voice. "They would not betray us."

"Who? The Patriots?"

He did not answer.

"Voe Deo, you mean? Wouldn't betray us?"

In the pause that followed her gentle, incredulous question, he knew that she was right; that it was all collusion among the powers of the world; that his loyalty to his country and service was wasted, as futile as the rest of his life. She went on talking, palliating, saying he might very well be right. He put his head into his hands, longing for tears, dry as stone.

She crossed the line. He felt her hand on his shoulder.

"Teyeo, I am very sorry," she said. "I didn't mean to insult you! I honor you. You've been all my hope and help."

"It doesn't matter," he said. "If I—If we had some water."

She leapt up and battered on the door with her fists and a sandal.

"Bastards, bastards," she shouted.

Teyeo got up and walked, three steps and turn, three steps and turn, and halted on his side of the room. "If you're right," he said, speaking slowly and formally, "we and our captors are in danger not only from Gatay but from my own people, who may . . . who have been furthering these anti-Government factions, in order to make an excuse to bring troops here . . . to *pacify* Gatay. That's why they know where to find the factionalists. We are . . . we're lucky our group was . . . was genuine."

She watched him with a tenderness that he found irrelevant.

"What we don't know," he said, "is what side the Ekumen will take. That is . . . There really is only one side."

"No, there's ours, too. The underdogs. If the Embassy sees Voe Deo pulling a takeover of Gatay, they won't interfere, but they won't approve. Especially if it involves as much repression as it seems to."

"The violence is only against the anti-Ekumen factions."

"They still won't approve. And if they find out I'm alive they're going to be quite pissed at the people who claimed I went up in a bonfire. Our problem is how to get word to them. I was the only person representing the Ekumen in Gatay. Who'd be a safe channel?"

"Any of my men. But . . ."

"They'll have been sent back; why keep Embassy Guards here when the Envoy's dead and buried? I suppose we could try. Ask the boys to try, that is." Presently she said wistfully, "I don't suppose they'd just let us go—in disguise? It would be the safest for them."

"There is an ocean," Teyeo said.

She beat her head. "Oh, why don't they bring some *water* . . ." Her voice was like paper sliding on paper. He was ashamed of his anger, his grief, himself. He wanted to tell her that she had been a help and hope to him too, that he honored her, that she was brave beyond belief; but none of the words would come. He felt empty, worn out. He felt old. If only they would bring water!

Water was given them at last; some food, not much and not fresh. Clearly their captors were in hiding and under duress. The spokesman—he gave them his war-name, Kergat, Gatayan for Liberty—told them that whole neighborhoods had been cleared out, set afire, that Voe Dean troops were in control of most of the city including the palace, and that almost none of this was being reported in the net. "When this is over Voe Deo will own my country," he said with disbelieving fury.

"Not for long," Teyeo said.

"Who can defeat them?" the young man said.

"Yeowe. The idea of Yeowe."

Both Kergat and Solly stared at him.

"Revolution," he said. "How long before Werel becomes New Yeowe?"

"The assets?" Kergat said, as if Teyeo had suggested a revolt of cattle or of flies. "They'll never organize."

"Look out when they do," Teyeo said mildly.

"You don't have any assets in your group?" Solly asked Kergat, amazed. He did not bother to answer. He had classed her as an asset, Teyeo saw. He understood why; he had done so himself, in the other life, when such distinctions made sense.

"Your bondswoman, Rewe," he asked Solly—"was she a friend?"

"Yes," Solly said, then, "No. I wanted her to be."

"The makil?"

After a pause she said, "I think so."

"Is he still here?"

She shook her head. "The troupe was going on with their tour, a few days after the Festival."

"Travel has been restricted since the Festival," Kergat said. "Only government and troops."

"He's Voe Dean. If he's still here, they'll probably send him and his troupe home. Try and contact him, Kergat."

"A makil?" the young man said, with that same distaste and incredulity. "One of your Voe Dean homosexual clowns?"

Teyeo shot a glance at Solly: Patience, patience.

"Bisexual actors," Solly said, disregarding him; but fortunately Kergat was determined to disregard her.

"A clever man," Teyeo said, "with connections. He could help us. You and us. It could be worth it. If he's still here. We must make haste."

"Why would he help us? He is Voe Dean."

"An asset, not a citizen," Teyeo said. "And a member of Hame, the asset underground, which works against the government of Voe Deo. The Ekumen admits the legitimacy of Hame. He'll report to the Embassy that a Patriot group has rescued the Envoy and is holding her safe, in hiding, in extreme danger. The Ekumen, I think, will act promptly and decisively. Correct, Envoy?"

Suddenly reinstated, Solly gave a short, dignified nod. "But discreetly," she said. "They'll avoid violence, if they can use political coercion."

The young man was trying to get it all into his mind and work it through. Sympathetic to his weariness, distrust, and confusion, Teyeo sat quietly waiting. He noticed that Solly was sitting equally quietly, one hand lying in the other. She was thin and dirty and her unwashed, greasy hair was in a lank braid. She was brave, like a brave mare, all nerve; she would break her heart before she quit.

Kergat asked questions; Teyeo answered them, reasoning and reassuring. Occasionally Solly spoke, and Kergat was now listening to her again, uneasily, not wanting to, not after what he had called her. At last he left, not saying what he intended to do; but he had Batikam's name and an identifying message from Teyeo to the Embassy: "Half-pay veots learn to sing old songs quickly."

"What on earth!" Solly said when Kergat had gone.

"Did you know a man named Old Music, in the Embassy?"

"Ah! Is he a friend of yours?"

"He has been kind."

"He's been here on Werel from the start. A First Observer. Rather a powerful man.—Yes, and 'quickly,' all right . . . My mind really isn't working at all. I wish I could lie down beside a little stream, in a meadow, you know, and drink. All day. Every time I wanted to, just stretch my neck out and slup, slup, slup. . . . Running water . . . In the sunshine . . . Oh God, oh God, sunshine. Teyeo, this is very difficult. This is harder than ever. Thinking that there maybe is really a way out of here. Only not knowing. Trying not to hope and not to not hope. Oh, I am so tired of sitting here!"

"What time is it?"

"Half-past twenty. Night. Dark out. Oh God, darkness! Just to be in the darkness. . . . Is there any way we could cover up that damned biolume? Partly? To pretend we had night, so we could pretend we had day?"

"If you stood on my shoulders, you could reach it. But how could we fasten a cloth?"

They pondered, staring at the plaque.

"I don't know. Did you notice there's a little patch of it that looks like it's dying? Maybe we don't have to worry about making darkness. If we stay here long enough. Oh, God!"

"Well," he said after a while, curiously self-conscious, "I'm tired." He stood up, stretched, glanced for permission to enter her territory, got a drink of water, returned to his territory, took off his jacket and shoes, by which time her back was turned, took off his trousers, lay down, pulled up the blanket, and said in his mind, "Lord Kamye, let me hold fast to the one noble thing." But he did not sleep.

He heard her slight movements; she pissed, poured a little water, took off her sandals, lay down.

A long time passed.

"Teyeo."

"Yes."

"Do you think . . . that it would be a mistake . . . under the circumstances . . . to make love?"

A pause.

"Not under the circumstances," he said, almost inaudibly. "But—in the other life—"

A pause.

"Short life versus long life," she murmured.

"Yes."

A pause.

"No," he said, and turned to her. "No, that's wrong." They reached out to each other. They clasped each other, cleaved together, in blind haste, greed, need, crying out together the name of God in their different languages and then like animals in the wordless voice. They huddled together, spent, sticky, sweaty, exhausted, reviving, rejoined, reborn in the body's tenderness, in the endless exploration, the ancient discovery, the long flight to the new world.

He woke slowly, in ease and luxury. They were entangled, his face was against her arm and breast; she was stroking his hair, sometimes his neck and shoulder. He lay for a long time aware only of that lazy rhythm and the cool of her skin against his face, under his hand, against his leg.

"Now I know," she said, her half-whisper deep in her chest, near his ear, "that I don't know you. Now I need to know you." She bent forward to touch his face with her lips and cheek.

"What do you want to know?"

"Everything. Tell me who Teyeo is. . . ."

"I don't know," he said. "A man who holds you dear."

"Oh, God," she said, hiding her face for a moment in the rough, smelly blanket.

"Who is God?" he asked sleepily. They spoke VoeDean, but she usually swore in Terran or Alterran; in this case it had been Alterran, *seyt*, so he asked, "Who is Seyt?"

"Oh—Tual—Kamye—what have you. I just say it. It's just bad language. Do you believe in one of them? I'm sorry! I feel like such an oaf with you, Teyeo. Blundering into your soul, invading you—We *are* invaders, no matter how pacificist and priggish we are—"

"Must I love the whole Ekumen?" he asked, beginning to stroke her breasts, feeling her tremor of desire and his own.

"Yes," she said, "yes, yes."

*   *   *

It was curious, Teyeo thought, how little sex changed anything. Everything was the same, a little easier, less embarrassment and inhibition; and there was a certain and lovely source of pleasure for them, when they had enough water and food to have enough vitality to make love. But the only thing that was truly different was something he had no word for. Sex, comfort, tenderness, love, trust, no word was the right word, the whole word. It was utterly intimate, hidden in the mutuality of their bodies, and it changed nothing in their circumstances, nothing in the world, even the tiny wretched world of their imprisonment. They were still trapped. They were getting very tired and were hungry most of the time. They were increasingly afraid of their increasingly desperate captors.

"I will be a lady," Solly said. "A good girl. Tell me how, Teyeo."

"I don't want you to give in," he said, so fiercely, with tears in his eyes, that she went to him and held him in her arms.

"Hold fast," he said.

"I will," she said. But when Kergat or the others came in she was sedate and modest, letting the men talk, keeping her eyes down. He could not bear to see her so, and knew she was right to do so.

The doorlock rattled, the door clashed, bringing him up out of a wretched, thirsty sleep. It was night or very early morning. He and Solly had been sleeping close entangled for the warmth and comfort of it; and seeing Kergat's face now he was deeply afraid. This was what he had feared, to show, to prove her sexual vulnerability. She was still only half-awake, clinging to him.

Another man had come in. Kergat said nothing. It took Teyeo some time to recognize the second man as Batikam.

When he did, his mind remained quite blank. He managed to say the makil's name. Nothing else.

"Batikam?" Solly croaked. "Oh, my God!"

"This is an interesting moment," Batikam said in his warm actor's voice. He was not transvestite, Teyeo saw, but wore Gatayan men's clothing. "I meant to rescue you, not to embarrass you, Envoy, Rega. Shall we get on with it?"

Teyeo had scrambled up and was pulling on his filthy trousers. Solly had slept in the ragged pants their captors had given her. They both had kept on their shirts for warmth.

"Did you contact the Embassy, Batikam?" she was asking, her voice shaking, as she pulled on her sandals.

"Oh, yes. I've been there and come back, indeed. Sorry it took so long. I don't think I quite realized your situation here."

"Kergat has done his best for us," Teyeo said at once, stiffly.

"I can see that. At considerable risk. I think the risk from now on is low. That is . . ." He looked straight at Teyeo. "Rega, how do you feel about putting yourself in the hands of Hame?" he said. "Any problems with that?"

"Don't, Batikam," Solly said. "Trust him!"

Teyeo tied his shoe, straightened up, and said, "We are all in the hands of the Lord Kamye."

Batikam laughed, the beautiful full laugh they remembered.

"In the Lord's hands, then," he said, and led them out of the room.

In the *Arkamye* it is said, "To live simply is most complicated."

Solly requested to stay on Werel, and after a recuperative leave at the seashore was sent as Observer to South Voe Deo. Teyeo went straight home, being informed that his father was very ill. After his father's death, he asked for indefinite leave from the Embassy Guard, and stayed on the farm with his mother until her death two years later. He and Solly, a continent apart, met only occasionally during those years.

When his mother died, Teyeo freed his family's assets by act of irrevocable manumission, deeded over their farms to them, sold his now almost valueless property at auction, and went to the capital. He knew Solly was temporarily staying at the Embassy. Old Music told him where to find her. He found her in a small office of the palatial building. She looked older, very elegant. She looked at him with a stricken and yet wary face. She did not come forward to greet him or touch him. She said, "Teyeo, I've been asked to be First Mobile on Yeowe."

He stood still.

"Just now—I just came from talking on the ansible with Hain—" She put her face in her hands. "Oh, my God!" she said.

He said, "My congratulations, truly, Solly."

She suddenly ran at him, threw her arms around him, and cried, "Oh, Teyeo, and your mother died, I never thought, I'm so sorry, I never, I never do—I thought we could—What are you going to do? Are you going to stay there?"

"I sold it," he said. He was enduring rather than returning her embrace. "I thought I might return to the service."

"You sold your *farm?* But I never saw it!"

"I never saw where you were born," he said.

There was a pause. She stood away from him, and they looked at each other.

"You would come?" she said.

"I would," he said.

Several years after Yeowe entered the Ekumen, Mobile Solly Agat Terwa was sent as an Ekumenical liaison to Terra; later she went from there to Hain, where she served with great distinction as a Stabile. In all her travels and posts she was accompanied by a Werelian army officer some years older than herself, a very handsome man, as reserved as she was outgoing. People who knew them knew their passionate pride and trust in each other. Solly was perhaps the happier person, rewarded and fulfilled in her work; but Teyeo had no regrets. He had lost his world, but he had held fast to the one noble thing.

THE REMORAS

Robert Reed

Here's a story that takes us where *no* one has ever gone before, boldly or otherwise— on a circuit around the Galaxy itself, in a spaceship many times bigger than the Earth, with a passenger list full of jaded immortals, both human and alien. Even on such a ship and on such a journey, though, there are paths you can follow that will take you where you never expected to be able to go, and where none of your peers will want to *follow* . . .

A relatively new writer, Robert Reed is a frequent contributor to *The Magazine of Fantasy & Science Fiction* and *Asimov's Science Fiction*, and has also sold stories to *Universe, New Destinies, Tomorrow, Synergy,* and elsewhere. His books include the novels *The Lee Shore, The Hormone Jungle, Black Milk, The Remarkables,* and *Down the Bright Way.* His most recent book is the novel *Beyond the Veil of Stars.* Upcoming is a new novel, *An Exaltation of Larks.* His stories have appeared in our Ninth, Tenth, and Eleventh Annual Collections. He lives in Lincoln, Nebraska.

Quee Lee's apartment covered several hectares within one of the human districts, some thousand kilometers beneath the ship's hull. It wasn't a luxury unit by any measure. Truly wealthy people owned as much as a cubic kilometer for themselves and their entourages. But it had been her home since she had come on board, for more centuries than she could count, its hallways and large rooms as comfortable to her as her own body.

The garden room was a favorite. She was enjoying its charms one afternoon, lying nude beneath a false sky and sun, eyes closed and nothing to hear but the splash of fountains and the prattle of little birds. Suddenly her apartment interrupted the peace, announcing a visitor. "He has come for Perri, miss. He claims it's most urgent."

"Perri isn't here," she replied, soft gray eyes opening. "Unless he's hiding from both of us, I suppose."

"No, miss. He is not." A brief pause, then the voice said, "I have explained this to the man, but he refuses to leave. His name is Orleans. He claims that Perri owes him a considerable sum of money."

What had her husband done now? Quee Lee could guess, halfway smiling as she sat upright. *Oh, Perri . . . won't you learn . . .* ? She would have to dismiss this Orleans fellow herself, spooking him with a good hard stare. She rose and dressed in an emerald sarong, then walked the length of her apartment, never hurrying, commanding the front door to open at the last moment but leaving the security screen intact. And she was ready for someone odd. Even someone sordid, knowing Perri. Yet she didn't expect to see a shiny lifesuit more than two meters tall and nearly half as wide, and she had never imagined such a face gazing down at her with mismatched eyes. It took her a long moment to realize this was a Remora. An authentic Remora was standing in the public walkway, his vivid round face watching her. The flesh was orange with diffuse black blotches that might or might not be cancers, and a lipless, toothless mouth seemed to flow into a grin. What would bring a Remora here? They never, never came down here . . . !

"I'm Orleans." The voice was sudden and deep, slightly muted by the security screen. It came from a speaker hidden somewhere on the thick neck, telling her, "I need help, miss. I'm sorry to disturb you . . . but you see, I'm desperate. I don't know where else to turn."

Quee Lee knew about Remoras. She had seen them and even spoken to a few, although those conversations were eons ago and she couldn't remember their substance. Such strange creatures. Stranger than most aliens, even if they possessed human souls. . . .

"Miss?"

Quee Lee thought of herself as being a good person. Yet she couldn't help but feel repelled, the floor rolling beneath her and her breath stopping short. Orleans was a human being, one of her own species. True, his genetics had been transformed by hard radiations. And yes, he normally lived apart from ordinary people like her. But inside him was a human mind, tough and potentially immortal. Quee Lee blinked and remembered that she had compassion as well as charity for everyone, even aliens . . . and she managed to sputter, "Come in." She said, "If you wish, please do," and with that invitation, her apartment deactivated the invisible screen.

"Thank you, miss." The Remora walked slowly, almost clumsily, his lifesuit making a harsh grinding noise in the knees and hips. That wasn't normal, she realized. Orleans should be graceful, his suit powerful, serving him as an elaborate exoskeleton.

"Would you like anything?" she asked foolishly. Out of habit.

"No, thank you," he replied, his voice nothing but pleasant.

Of course. Remoras ate and drank only self-made concoctions. They were permanently sealed inside their lifesuits, functioning as perfectly self-contained organisms. Food was synthesized, water recycled, and they possessed a religious sense of purity and independence.

"I don't wish to bother you, miss. I'll be brief."

His politeness was a minor surprise. Remoras typically were distant, even arrogant. But Orleans continued to smile, watching her. One eye was a muscular pit filled with thick black hairs, and she assumed those hairs were light sensitive. Like an insect's compound eye, each one might build part of an image. By contrast, its mate was ordinary, white and fishy with a foggy black center. Mutations could do astonishing things. An accelerated, partly controlled evolution was occurring inside that suit, even while Orleans stood before her, boots stomping on the stone floor, a single spark arcing toward her.

Orleans said, "I know this is embarrassing for you—"

"No, no," she offered.

"—and it makes me uncomfortable too. I wouldn't have come down here if it wasn't necessary."

"Perri's gone," she repeated, "and I don't know when he'll be back. I'm sorry."

"Actually," said Orleans, "I was hoping he would be gone."

"Did you?"

"Though I'd have come either way."

Quee Lee's apartment, loyal and watchful, wouldn't allow anything nasty to happen to her. She took a step forward, closing some of the distance. "This is about money being owed? Is that right?"

"Yes, miss."

"For what, if I might ask?"

Orleans didn't explain in clear terms. "Think of it as an old gambling debt." More was involved, he implied. "A very old debt, I'm afraid, and Perri's refused me a thousand times."

She could imagine it. Her husband had his share of failings, incompetence and a self-serving attitude among them. She loved Perri in a controlled way, but his flaws were obvious. "I'm sorry," she replied, "but I'm not responsible for his debts." She made herself sound hard, knowing it was best. "I hope you didn't come all this way because you heard he was married." Married to a woman of some means, she thought to herself. In secret.

"No, no, no!" The grotesque face seemed injured. Both eyes became larger, and a thin tongue, white as ice, licked at the lipless edge of the mouth. "Honestly, we don't follow the news about passengers. I just assumed Perri was living with someone. I know him, you see . . . my hope was to come and make my case to whomever I found, winning a comrade. An ally. Someone who might become my advocate." A hopeful pause, then he said, "When Perri does come here, will you explain to him what's right and what is not? Can you, please?" Another pause, then he added, "Even a lowly Remora knows the difference between right and wrong, miss."

That wasn't fair, calling himself lowly. And he seemed to be painting her as some flavor of bigot, which she wasn't. She didn't look at him as lowly, and morality wasn't her private possession. Both of them were human, after all. Their souls were linked by a charming and handsome, manipulative user . . . by her darling husband . . . and Quee Lee felt a sudden anger directed at Perri, almost shuddering in front of this stranger.

"Miss?"

"How much?" she asked. "How much does he owe you, and how soon will you need it?"

Orleans answered the second question first, lifting an arm with a sickly whine coming from his shoulder. "Can you hear it?" he asked. As if she were deaf. "My seals need to be replaced, or at least refurbished. Yesterday, if possible."

The arm bent, and the elbow whined. "I already spent my savings rebuilding my reactor."

Quee Lee knew enough about lifesuits to appreciate his circumstances. Remoras worked on the ship's hull, standing in the open for hours and days at a time. A broken seal was a disaster. Any tiny opening would kill most of his body, and his suffering mind would fall into a protective coma. Left exposed and vulnerable, Orleans would be at the mercy of radiation storms and comet showers. Yes, she understood. A balky suit was an unacceptable hazard on top of lesser hazards, and what could she say?

She felt a deep empathy for the man.

Orleans seemed to take a breath, then he said, "Perri owes me fifty-two thousand credits, miss."

"I see." She swallowed and said, "My name is Quee Lee."

"Quee Lee," he repeated. "Yes, miss."

"As soon as Perri comes home, I'll discuss this with him. I promise you."

"I would be grateful if you did."

"I will."

The ugly mouth opened, and she saw blotches of green and gray-blue against a milky throat. Those were cancers or perhaps strange new organs. She couldn't believe she was in the company of a Remora—the strangest sort of human— yet despite every myth, despite tales of courage and even recklessness, Orleans appeared almost fragile. He even looked scared, she realized. That wet orange face shook as if in despair, then came the awful grinding noise as he turned away, telling her, "Thank you, Quee Lee. For your time and patience, and for everything."

Fifty-two thousand credits!

She could have screamed. She would scream when she was alone, she promised herself. Perri had done this man a great disservice, and he'd hear about it when he graced her with his company again. A patient person, yes, and she could tolerate most of his flaws. But not now. Fifty thousand credits was no fortune, and it would allow Orleans to refurbish his lifesuit, making him whole and healthy again. Perhaps she could get in touch with Perri first, speeding up the process . . .?

Orleans was through her front door, turning to say good-bye. False sunshine made his suit shine, and his faceplate darkened to where she couldn't see his features anymore. He might have any face, and what did a face mean? Waving back at him, sick to her stomach, she calculated what fifty-two thousand credits meant in concrete terms, to her. . . .

. . . wondering if she should . . . ?

But no, she decided. She just lacked the required compassion. She was a particle short, if that, ordering the security screen to engage again, helping to mute that horrid grinding of joints as the Remora shuffled off for home.

The ship had many names, many designations, but to its long-term passengers and crew it was referred to as *the ship*. No other starship could be confused for it. Not in volume, nor in history.

The ship was old by every measure. A vanished humanoid race had built it, probably before life arose on Earth, then abandoned it for no obvious reason. Experts claimed it had begun as a sunless world, one of the countless jupiters that sprinkled the cosmos. The builders had used the world's own hydrogen to fuel enormous engines, accelerating it over millions of years while stripping away its gaseous exterior. Today's ship was the leftover core, much modified by its builders and humans. Its metal and rock interior was laced with passage-ways and sealed environments, fuel tanks and various ports. There was room enough for hundreds of billions of passengers, though there were only a fraction that number now. And its hull was a special armor made from hyperfibers, kilometers thick and tough enough to withstand most high-velocity impacts.

The ship had come from outside the galaxy, passing into human space long ago. It was claimed as salvage, explored by various means, then refurbished to the best of its new owners' abilities. A corporation was formed; a promotion was born. The ancient engines were coaxed to life, changing the ship's course. Then tickets were sold, both to humans and alien species. Novelty and adventure were the lures. One circuit around the Milky Way; a half-million-year voyage touring the star-rich spiral arms. It was a long span, even for immortal humans. But people like Quee Lee had enough money and patience. That's why she purchased her apartment with a portion of her savings. This voyage wouldn't remain novel for long, she knew. Three or four circuits at most, and then what? People would want something else new and glancingly dangerous. Wasn't that the way it always was?

Quee Lee had no natural lifespan. Her ancestors had improved themselves in a thousand ways, erasing the aging process. Fragile DNAs were replaced with better genetic machinery. Tailoring allowed a wide-range of useful proteins and enzymes and powerful repair mechanisms. Immune systems were nearly perfect; diseases were extinct. Normal life couldn't damage a person in any measurable way. And even a tragic accident wouldn't need to be fatal, Quee Lee's body and mind able to withstand frightening amounts of abuse.

But Remoras, despite those same gifts, did not live ordinary lives. They worked on the open hull, each of them encased in a lifesuit. The suits afforded extra protection and a standard environment, each one possessing a small fusion plant and redundant recycling systems. Hull life was dangerous in the best times. The ship's shields and laser watchdogs couldn't stop every bit of interstellar grit. And every large impact meant someone had to make repairs. The ship's builders had used sophisticated robots, but they proved too tired after several billions of years on the job. It was better to promote—or demote—members of the human crew. The original scheme was to share the job, brief stints fairly dispersed. Even the captains were to don the lifesuits, stepping into the open when it was safest, patching craters with fresh-made hyperfibers. . . .

Fairness didn't last. A kind of subculture arose, and the first Remoras took the hull as their province. Those early Remoras learned how to survive the huge radiation loads. They trained themselves and their offspring to control their damaged bodies. Tough genetics mutated, and they embraced their mutations. If an eye was struck blind, perhaps by some queer cancer, then a good Remora would evolve a new eye. Perhaps a hair was light-sensitive, and its owner, purely by force of will, would culture that hair and interface it with the surviving optic nerve, producing an eye more durable than the one it replaced. Or so Quee Lee had heard, in passing, from people who acted as if they knew about such things.

Remoras, she had been told, were happy to look grotesque. In their culture, strange faces and novel organs were the measures of success. And since disaster could happen anytime, without warning, it was unusual for any Remora to live long. At least in her sense of long. Orleans could be a fourth or fifth generation Remora, for all she knew. A child barely fifty centuries old. *For all she knew.* Which was almost nothing, she realized, returning to her garden room and undressing, lying down with her eyes closed and the light baking her. Remoras were important, even essential people, yet she felt wholly ignorant. And ignorance was wrong, she knew. Not as wrong as owing one of them money, but still. . . .

This life of hers seemed so ordinary, set next to Orleans' life. Comfortable and ordinary, and she almost felt ashamed.

Perri failed to come home that next day, and the next. Then it was ten days, Quee Lee having sent messages to his usual haunts and no reply. She had been careful not to explain why she wanted him. And this was nothing too unusual, Perri probably wandering somewhere new and Quee Lee skilled at waiting, her days accented with visits from friends and parties thrown for any small reason. It was her normal life, never anything but pleasant; yet she found herself thinking about Orleans, imagining him walking on the open hull with his seals breaking, his strange body starting to boil away . . . that poor man . . . !

Taking the money to Orleans was an easy decision. Quee Lee had more than enough. It didn't seem like a large sum until she had it converted into black-and-white chips. But wasn't it better to have Perri owing her instead of owing a Remora? She was in a better place to recoup the debt; and besides, she doubted that her husband could raise that money now. Knowing him, he probably had a number of debts, to humans and aliens both; and for the nth time, she wondered how she'd ever let Perri charm her. What was she thinking, agreeing to this crazy union?

Quee Lee was old even by immortal measures. She was so old she could barely remember her youth, her tough neurons unable to embrace her entire life. Maybe that's why Perri had seemed like a blessing. He was ridiculously young and wore his youth well, gladly sharing his enthusiasms and energies. He was a good, untaxing lover; he could listen when it was important; and he had never tried milking Quee Lee of her money. Besides, he was a challenge. No doubt about it. Maybe her friends didn't approve of him—a few close ones were openly critical—but to a woman of her vintage, in the middle of a five thousand century voyage, Perri was something fresh and new and remarkable. And Quee Lee's old friends, quite suddenly, seemed a little fossilized by comparison.

"I love to travel," Perri had explained, his gently handsome face capable of endless smiles. "I was born on the ship, did you know? Just weeks after my parents came on board. They were riding only as far as a colony world, but I stayed behind. My choice.'' He had laughed, eyes gazing into the false sky of her ceiling. ''Do you know what I want to do? I want to see the entire ship, walk every hallway and cavern. I want to explore every body of water, meet every sort of alien—''

''Really?''

''—and even visit their quarters. Their homes.'' Another laugh and that infectious smile. ''I just came back from a low-gravity district, six thousand kilometers below. There's a kind of spidery creature down there. You should see them, love! I can't do them justice by telling you they're graceful, and seeing holos isn't much better.''

She had been impressed. Who else did she know who could tolerate aliens, what with their strange odors and their impenetrable minds? Perri was remarkable, no doubt about it. Even her most critical friends admitted that much, and despite their grumbles, they'd want to hear the latest Perri adventure as told by his wife.

''I'll stay on board forever, if I can manage it.''

She had laughed, asking, ''Can you afford it?''

''Badly,'' he had admitted. ''But I'm paid up through this circuit, at least. Minus day-by-day expenses, but that's all right. Believe me, when you've got millions of wealthy souls in one place, there's always a means of making a living.''

''Legal means?''

''Glancingly so.'' He had a rogue's humor, all right. Yet later, in a more sober mood, he had admitted, ''I do have enemies, my love. I'm warning you. Like anyone, I've made my share of mistakes—my youthful indiscretions—but at least I'm honest about them.''

Indiscretions, perhaps. Yet he had done nothing to earn her animosity.

''We should marry,'' Perri had proposed. ''Why not? We like each other's company, yet we seem to weather our time apart too. What do you think? Frankly, I don't think you need a partner who shadows you day and night. Do you, Quee Lee?''

She didn't. True enough.

''A small tidy marriage, complete with rules,'' he had assured her. ''I get a home base, and you have your privacy, plus my considerable entertainment value.'' A big long laugh, then he had added, ''I promise. You'll be the first to hear my latest tales. And I'll never be any kind of leech, darling. With you, I will be the perfect gentleman.''

Quee Lee carried the credit chips in a secret pouch, traveling to the tubecar station and riding one of the vertical tubes toward the hull. She had looked up the name *Orleans* in the crew listings. The only Orleans lived at Port Beta, no mention of him being a Remora or not. The ports were vast facilities where taxi craft docked with the ship, bringing new passengers from nearby alien worlds. It was easier to accelerate and decelerate those kilometer-long needles. The ship's own engines did nothing but make the occasional course correction, avoiding dust clouds while keeping them on their circular course.

It had been forever since Quee Lee had visited a port. And today there wasn't even a taxi to be seen, all of them off hunting for more paying customers. The nonRemora crew—the captains, mates and so on—had little work at the moment, apparently hiding from her. She stood at the bottom of the port—a lofty cylinder capped with a kilometer-thick hatch of top-grade hyperfibers. The only other tourists were aliens, some kind of fishy species encased in bubbles of liquid water or ammonia. The bubbles rolled past her. It was like standing in a school of small tuna, their sharp chatter audible and Quee Lee unable to decipher any of it. Were they mocking her? She had no clue, and it made her all the more frustrated. They could be making terrible fun of her. She felt lost and more than a little homesick all at once.

By contrast, the first Remora seemed normal. Walking without any grinding sounds, it covered ground at an amazing pace. Quee Lee had to run to catch it. To catch her. Something about the lifesuit was feminine, and a female voice responded to Quee Lee's shouts.

"What what what?" asked the Remora. "I'm busy!"

Gasping, Quee Lee asked, "Do you know Orleans?"

"Orleans?"

"I need to find him. It's quite important." Then she wondered if something terrible had happened, her arriving too late—

"I do know someone named Orleans, yes." The face had comma-shaped eyes, huge and black and bulging, and the mouth blended into a slit-like nose. Her skin was silvery, odd bunched fibers running beneath the surface. Black hair showed along the top of the faceplate, except at second glance it wasn't hair. It looked more like ropes soaked in oil, the strands wagging with a slow stately pace.

The mouth smiled. The normal-sounding voice said, "Actually, Orleans is one of my closest friends!"

True? Or was she making a joke?

"I really have to find him," Quee Lee confessed. "Can you help me?"

"Can I help you?" The strange mouth smiled, gray pseudoteeth looking big as thumbnails, the gums as silver as her skin. "I'll take you to him. Does that constitute help?" And Quee Lee found herself following, walking onto a lifting disk without railing, the Remora standing in the center and waving to the old woman. "Come closer. Orleans is up there." A skyward gesture. "A good long way, and I don't think you'd want to try it alone. Would you?"

"Relax," Orleans advised.

She thought she was relaxed, except then she found herself nodding, breathing deeply and feeling a tension as it evaporated. The ascent had taken ages, it seemed. Save for the rush of air moving past her ears, it had been soundless. The disk had no sides at all—a clear violation of safety regulations—and Quee Lee had grasped one of the Remora's shiny arms, needing a handhold, surprised to feel rough spots in the hyperfiber. Minuscule impacts had left craters too tiny to see. Remoras, she had realized, were very much like the ship itself—enclosed biospheres taking abuse as they streaked through space.

"Better?" asked Orleans.

"Yes. Better." A thirty kilometer ride through the port, holding tight to a Remora. And now this. She and Orleans were inside some tiny room not five hundred meters from the vacuum. Did Orleans live here? She nearly asked, looking at the bare walls and stubby furniture, deciding it was too spare, too ascetic to be anyone's home. Even his. Instead she asked him, "How are *you*?"

"Tired. Fresh off my shift, and devastated."

The face had changed. The orange pigments were softer now, and both eyes were the same sickening hair-filled pits. How clear was his vision? How did he transplant cells from one eye to the other? There had to be mechanisms, reliable tricks . . . and she found herself feeling ignorant and glad of it. . . .

"What do you want, Quee Lee?"

She swallowed. "Perri came home, and I brought what he owes you."

Orleans looked surprised, then the cool voice said, "Good. Wonderful!"

She produced the chips, his shiny palm accepting them. The elbow gave a harsh growl, and she said, "I hope this helps."

"My mood already is improved," he promised.

What else? She wasn't sure what to say now.

Then Orleans told her, "I should thank you somehow. Can I give you something for your trouble? How about a tour?" One eye actually winked at her, hairs contracting into their pit and nothing left visible but a tiny red pore. "A tour," he repeated. "A walk outside? We'll find you a lifesuit. We keep them here in case a captain comes for an inspection." A big deep laugh, then he added, "Once every thousand years, they do! Whether we need it or not!"

What was he saying? She had heard him, and she hadn't.

A smile and another wink, and he said, "I'm serious. Would you like to go for a little stroll?"

"I've never . . . I don't know . . . !"

"Safe as safe can be." Whatever that meant. "Listen, this is the safest place for a jaunt. We're behind the leading face, which means impacts are nearly impossible. But we're not close to the engines and their radiations either." Another laugh, and he added, "Oh, you'll get a dose of radiation, but nothing important. You're tough, Quee Lee. Does your fancy apartment have an autodoc?"

"Of course."

"Well, then."

She wasn't scared, at least in any direct way. What Quee Lee felt was excitement and fear born of excitement, nothing in her experience to compare with what was happening. She was a creature of habits, rigorous and ancient habits, and she had no way to know how she'd respond *out there*. No habit had prepared her for this moment.

"Here," said her gracious host. "Come in here."

No excuse occurred to her. They were in a deep closet full of lifesuits—this was some kind of locker room, apparently—and she let Orleans select one and dismantle it with his growling joints. "It opens and closes, unlike mine," he explained. "It doesn't have all the redundant systems either. Otherwise, it's the same."

On went the legs, the torso and arms and helmet; she banged the helmet against the low ceiling, then struck the wall with her first step.

"Follow me," Orleans advised, "and keep it slow."

Wise words. They entered some sort of tunnel that zigzagged toward space, ancient stairs fashioned for a nearly human gait. Each bend had an invisible field that held back the ship's thinning atmosphere. They began speaking by radio, voices close, and she noticed how she could feel through the suit, its pseudoneurons interfacing with her own. Here gravity was stronger than earth-standard, yet despite her added bulk she moved with ease, limbs humming, her helmet striking the ceiling as she climbed. Thump, and thump. She couldn't help herself.

Orleans laughed pleasantly, the sound close and intimate. "You're doing fine, Quee Lee. Relax."

Hearing her name gave her a dilute courage.

"Remember," he said, "your servomotors are potent. Lifesuits make motions large. Don't overcontrol, and don't act cocky."

She wanted to succeed. More than anything in recent memory, she wanted everything as close to perfect as possible.

"Concentrate," he said.

Then he told her, "That's better, yes."

They came to a final turn, then a hatch, Orleans pausing and turning, his syrupy mouth making a preposterous smile. "Here we are. We'll go outside for just a little while, okay?" A pause, then he added, "When you go home, tell your husband what you've done. Amaze him!"

"I will," she whispered.

And he opened the hatch with an arm—the abrasive sounds audible across the radio, but distant—and a bright colored glow washed over them. "Beautiful," the Remora observed. "Isn't it beautiful, Quee Lee?"

Perri didn't return home for several more weeks, and when he arrived—"I was rafting Cloud Canyon, love and didn't get your messages!"—Quee Lee realized that she wasn't going to tell him about her adventure. Nor about the money. She'd wait for a better time, a weak moment, when Perri's guard was down. "What's so important, love? You sounded urgent." She told him it was nothing, that she'd missed him and been worried. How was the rafting? Who went with him? Perri told her, "Tweewits. Big hulking baboons, in essence." He smiled until she smiled too. He looked thin and tired; but that night, with minimal prompting, he found the energy to make love to her twice. And the second time was special enough that she was left wondering how she could so willingly live without sex for long periods. It could be the most amazing pleasure.

Perri slept, dreaming of artificial rivers roaring through artificial canyons; and Quee Lee sat up in bed, in the dark, whispering for her apartment to show her the view above Port Beta. She had it projected into her ceiling, twenty meters overhead, the shimmering aurora changing colors as force fields wrestled with every kind of spaceborn hazard.

"What do you think, Quee Lee?"

Orleans had asked the question, and she answered it again, in a soft awed voice. "Lovely." She shut her eyes, remembering how the hull itself had stretched off into the distance, flat and gray, bland yet somehow serene. "It is lovely."

"And even better up front, on the prow," her companion had maintained. "The fields there are thicker, stronger. And the big lasers keep hitting the comets tens of millions of kilometers from us, softening them up for us." He had given a little laugh, telling her, "You can almost feel the ship moving when you look up from the prow. Honest."

She had shivered inside her lifesuit, more out of pleasure than fear. Few passengers ever came out on the hull. They were breaking rules, no doubt. Even inside the taxi ships, you were protected by a hull. But not up there. Up there she'd felt exposed, practically naked. And maybe Orleans had measured her mood, watching her face with the flickering pulses, finally asking her, "Do you know the story of the first Remora?"

Did she? She wasn't certain.

He told it, his voice smooth and quiet. "Her name was Wune," he began. "On Earth, it's rumored, she was a criminal, a registered habitual criminal. Signing on as a crew mate helped her escape a stint of psychological realignment—"

"What crimes?"

"Do they matter?" A shake of the round head. "Bad ones, and that's too much said. The point is that Wune came here without rank, glad for the opportunity, and like any good mate, she took her turns out on the hull."

Quee Lee had nodded, staring off at the far horizon.

"She was pretty, like you. Between shifts, she did typical typicals. She explored the ship and had affairs of the heart and grieved the affairs that went badly. Like you, Quee Lee, she was smart. And after just a few centuries on board, Wune could see the trends. She saw how the captains were avoiding their shifts on the hull. And how certain people, guilty of small offenses, were pushed into double-shifts in their stead. All so that our captains didn't have to accept the tiniest, fairest risks."

Status. Rank. Privilege. She could understand these things, probably too well.

"Wune rebelled," Orleans had said, pride in the voice. "But instead of overthrowing the system, she conquered by embracing it. By transforming what she embraced." A soft laugh. "This lifesuit of mine? She built its prototype with its semi-forever seals and the hyperefficient recyke systems. She made a suit that she'd never have to leave, then she began to live on the hull, in the open, sometimes alone for years at a time."

"Alone?"

"A prophet's contemplative life." A fond glance at the smooth gray terrain. "She stopped having her body purged of cancers and other damage. She let her face—her beautiful face—become speckled with dead tissues. Then she taught herself to manage her mutations, with discipline and strength. Eventually she picked a few friends without status, teaching them her tricks and explaining the peace and purpose she had found while living up here, contemplating the universe without obstructions."

Without obstructions indeed!

"A few hundred became the First Generation. Attrition convinced our great captains to allow children, and the Second Generation numbered in the thousands. By the Third, we were officially responsible for the ship's exterior and the deadliest parts of its engines. We had achieved a quiet conquest of a world-sized realm, and today we number in the low millions!"

She remembered sighing, asking, "What happened to Wune?"

"An heroic death," he had replied. "A comet swarm was approaching. A repair team was caught on the prow, their shuttle dead and useless—"

"Why were they there if a swarm was coming?"

"Patching a crater, of course. Remember. The prow can withstand almost any likely blow, but if comets were to strike on top of one another, unlikely as that sounds—"

"A disaster," she muttered.

"For the passengers below, yes." A strange slow smile. "Wune died trying to bring them a fresh shuttle. She was vaporized under a chunk of ice and rock, in an instant."

"I'm sorry." Whispered.

"Wune was my great-great-grandmother," the man had added. "And no, she didn't name us Remoras. That originally was an insult, some captain responsible. Remoras are ugly fish that cling to sharks. Not a pleasing image, but Wune embraced the word. To us it means spiritual fulfillment, independence and a powerful sense of self. Do you know what I am, Quee Lee? I'm a god inside this suit of mine. I rule in ways you can't appreciate. You can't imagine how it is, having utter control over my body, my self . . . !"

She had stared at him, unable to speak.

A shiny hand had lifted, thick fingers against his faceplate. "My eyes? You're fascinated by my eyes, aren't you?"

A tiny nod. "Yes."

"Do you know how I sculpted them?"

"No."

"Tell me, Quee Lee. How do you close your hand?"

She had made a fist, as if to show him how.

"But which neurons fire? Which muscles contract?" A mild, patient laugh, then he had added, "How can you manage something that you can't describe in full?"

She had said, "It's habit, I guess. . . ."

"Exactly!" A larger laugh. "I have habits too. For instance, I can willfully spread mutations using metastasized cells. I personally have thousands of years of practice, plus all those useful mechanisms that I inherited from Wune and the others. It's as natural as your making the fist."

"But my hand doesn't change its real shape," she had countered.

"Transformation is my habit, and it's why my life is so much richer than yours." He had given her a wink just then, saying, "I can't count the times I've re-evolved my eyes."

Quee Lee looked up at her bedroom ceiling now, at a curtain of blue glows dissolving into pink. In her mind, she replayed the moment.

"You think Remoras are vile, ugly monsters," Orleans had said. "Now don't deny it. I won't let you deny it."

She hadn't made a sound.

"When you saw me standing at your door? When you saw that a Remora had come to *your* home? All of that ordinary blood of yours drained out of your face. You looked so terribly pale and weak, Quee Lee. Horrified!"

She couldn't deny it. Not then or now.

"Which of us has the richest life, Quee Lee? And be objective. Is it you or is it me?"

She pulled her bedsheets over herself, shaking a little bit.

"You or me?"

"Me," she whispered, but in that word was doubt. Just the flavor of it. Then Perri stirred, rolling toward her with his face trying to waken. Quee Lee had a last glance at the projected sky, then had it quelched. Then Perri was grinning, blinking and reaching for her, asking:

"Can't you sleep, love?"

"No," she admitted. Then she said, "Come here, darling."

"Well, well," he laughed. "Aren't you in a mood?"

Absolutely. A feverish mood, her mind leaping from subject to subject, without order, every thought intense and sudden, Perri on top of her and her old-fashioned eyes gazing up at the darkened ceiling, still seeing the powerful surges of changing colors that obscured the bright dusting of stars.

They took a second honeymoon, Quee Lee's treat. They traveled halfway around the ship, visiting a famous resort beside a small tropical sea; and for several months, they enjoyed the scenery and beaches, bone-white sands dropping into azure waters where fancy corals and fancier fishes lived. Every night brought a different sky, the ship supplying stored images of nebulas and strange suns; and they made love in the oddest places, in odd ways, strangers sometimes coming upon them and pausing to watch.

Yet she felt detached somehow, hovering overhead like an observer. Did Remoras have sex? she wondered. And if so, how? And how did they make their children? One day, Perri strapped on a gill and swam alone to the reef, leaving Quee Lee free to do research. Remoran sex, if it could be called that, was managed with electrical stimulation through the suits themselves. Reproduction was something else, children conceived in vitro, samples of their parents' genetics married and grown inside a hyperfiber envelope. The envelope was expanded as needed. Birth came with the first independent fusion plant. What an incredible way to live, she realized; but then again, there were many human societies that seemed bizarre. Some refused immortality. Some had married computers or lived in a narcotic haze. There were many, many spiritual splinter groups . . . only she couldn't learn much about the Remoran faith. Was their faith secret? And if so, why had she been allowed a glimpse of their private world?

Perri remained pleasant and attentive.

"I know this is work for you," she told him, "and you've been a delight, darling. Old women appreciate these attentions."

"Oh, you're not old!" A wink and smile, and he pulled her close. "And it's not work at all. Believe me!"

They returned home soon afterward, and Quee Lee was disappointed with her apartment. It was just as she remembered it, and the sameness was depressing. Even the garden room failed to brighten her mood . . . and she found herself wondering if she'd ever lived anywhere but here, the stone walls cold and closing in on her.

Perri asked, "What's the matter, love?"

She said nothing.

"Can I help, darling?"

"I forgot to tell you something," she began. "A friend of yours visited . . . oh, it was almost a year ago."

The roguish charm surfaced, reliable and nonplussed. "Which friend?"

"Orleans."

And Perri didn't respond at first, hearing the name and not allowing his expression to change. He stood motionless, not quite looking at her; and Quee Lee noticed a weakness in the mouth and something glassy about the smiling eyes. She felt uneasy, almost asking him what was wrong. Then Perri said, "What did Orleans want?" His voice was too soft, almost a whisper. A sideways glance, and he muttered, "Orleans came here?" He couldn't quite believe what she was saying. . . .

"You owed him some money," she replied.

Perri didn't speak, didn't seem to hear anything.

"Perri?"

He swallowed and said, "Owed?"

"I paid him."

"But . . . but what happened . . . ?"

She told him and she didn't. She mentioned the old seals and some other salient details, then in the middle of her explanation, all at once, something obvious and awful occurred to her. What if there hadn't been a debt? She gasped, asking, "You did owe him the money, didn't you?"

"How much did you say it was?"

She told him again.

He nodded. He swallowed and straightened his back, then managed to say, "I'll pay you back . . . as soon as possible . . ."

"Is there any hurry?" She took his hand, telling him, "I haven't made noise until now, have I? Don't worry." A pause. "I just wonder how you could owe him so much?"

Perri shook his head. "I'll give you five thousand now, maybe six . . . and I'll raise the rest. Soon as I can, I promise."

She said, "Fine."

"I'm sorry," he muttered.

"How do you know a Remora?"

He seemed momentarily confused by the question. Then he managed to say, "You know me. A taste for the exotic, and all that."

"You lost the money gambling? Is that what happened?"

"I'd nearly forgotten, it was so long ago." He summoned a smile and some of the old charm. "You should know, darling . . . those Remoras aren't anything like you and me. Be very careful with them, please."

She didn't mention her jaunt on the hull. Everything was old news anyway, and why had she brought it up in the first place? Perri kept promising to pay her back. He announced he was leaving tomorrow, needing to find some nameless people who owed him. The best he could manage was fifteen hundred credits. "A weak down payment, I know." Quee Lee thought of reassuring him—he seemed painfully nervous—but instead she simply told him, "Have a good trip, and come home soon."

He was a darling man when vulnerable. "Soon," he promised, walking out the front door. And an hour later, Quee Lee left too, telling herself that she was going to the hull again to confront her husband's old friend. What was this mysterious debt? Why did it bother him so much? But somewhere during the long tube-car ride, before she reached Port Beta, she realized that a confrontation would just further embarrass Perri, and what cause would that serve?

"What now?" she whispered to herself.

Another walk on the hull, of course. If Orleans would allow it. If he had the time, she hoped, and the inclination.

His face had turned blue, and the eyes were larger. The pits were filled with black hairs that shone in the light, something about them distinctly amused. "I guess we could go for a stroll," said the cool voice. They were standing in the same locker room, or one just like it; Quee Lee was unsure about directions. "We could," said Orleans, "but if you want to bend the rules, why bend little ones? Why not pick the hefty ones?"

She watched the mouth smile down at her, two little tusks showing in its corners. "What do you mean?" she asked.

"Of course it'll take time," he warned. "A few months, maybe a few years . . ."

She had centuries, if she wanted.

"I know you," said Orleans. "You've gotten curious about me, about *us*." Orleans moved an arm, not so much as a hum coming from the refurbished joints. "We'll make you an honorary Remora, if you're willing. We'll borrow a lifesuit, set you inside it, then transform you partway in a hurry-up fashion."

"You can? How?"

"Oh, aimed doses of radiation. Plus we'll give you some useful mutations. I'll wrap up some genes inside smart cancers, and they'll migrate to the right spots and grow. . . ."

She was frightened and intrigued, her heart kicking harder.

"It won't happen overnight, of course. And it depends on how much you want done." A pause. "And you should know that it's not strictly legal. The captains have this attitude about putting passengers a little bit at risk."

"How much risk is there?"

Orleans said, "The transformation is easy enough, in principle. I'll call up our records, make sure of the fine points." A pause and a narrowing of the eyes. "We'll keep you asleep throughout. Intravenous feedings. That's best.

You'll lie down with one body, then waken with a new one. A better one, I'd like to think. How much risk? Almost none, believe me.''

She felt numb. Small and weak and numb.

"You won't be a true Remora. Your basic genetics won't be touched, I promise. But someone looking at you will think you're genuine."

For an instant, with utter clarity, Quee Lee saw herself alone on the great gray hull, walking the path of the first Remora.

"Are you interested?"

"Maybe. I am."

"You'll need a lot of interest before we can start," he warned. "We have expenses to consider, and I'll be putting my crew at risk. If the captains find out, it's a suspension without pay." He paused, then said, "Are you listening to me?"

"It's going to cost money," she whispered.

Orleans gave a figure.

And Quee Lee was braced for a larger sum, two hundred thousand credits still large but not unbearable. She wouldn't be able to take as many trips to fancy resorts, true. Yet how could a lazy, prosaic resort compare with what she was being offered?

"You've done this before?" she asked.

He waited a moment, then said, "Not for a long time, no."

She didn't ask what seemed quite obvious, thinking of Perri and secretly smiling to herself.

"Take time," Orleans counseled. "Feel sure."

But she had already decided.

"Quee Lee?"

She looked at him, asking, "Can I have your eyes? Can you wrap them up in a smart cancer for me?"

"Certainly!" A great fluid smile emerged, framed with tusks. "Pick and choose as you wish. Anything you wish."

"The eyes," she muttered.

"They're yours," he declared, giving a little wink.

Arrangements had to be made, and what surprised her most—what she enjoyed more than the anticipation—was the subterfuge, taking money from her savings and leaving no destination, telling her apartment that she would be gone for an indeterminate time. At least a year, and perhaps much longer. Orleans hadn't put a cap on her stay with them, and what if she liked the Remoran life? Why not keep her possibilities open?

"If Perri returns?" asked the apartment.

He was to have free reign of the place, naturally. She thought she'd made herself clear—

"No, miss," the voice interrupted. "What do I tell him, if anything?"

"Tell him . . . tell him that I've gone exploring."

"Exploring?"

"Tell him it's my turn for a change," she declared; and she left without as much as a backward glance.

* * *

Orleans found help from the same female Remora, the one who had taken Quee Lee to him twice now. Her comma-shaped eyes hadn't changed, but the mouth was smaller and the gray teeth had turned black as obsidian.

Quee Lee lay between them as they worked, their faces smiling but the voices tight and shrill. Not for the first time, she realized she wasn't hearing their real voices. The suits themselves were translating their wet mutterings, which is why throats and mouths could change so much without having any audible effect.

"Are you comfortable?" asked the woman. But before Quee Lee could reply, she asked, "Any last questions?"

Quee Lee was encased in the lifesuit, a sudden panic taking hold of her. "When I go home . . . when I'm done . . . how fast can I . . . ?"

"Can you?"

"Return to my normal self."

"Cure the damage, you mean." The woman laughed gently, her expression changing from one unreadable state to another. "I don't think there's a firm answer, dear. Do you have an autodoc in your apartment? Good. Let it excise the bad and help you grow your own organs over again. As if you'd suffered a bad accident. . . ." A brief pause. "It should take what, Orleans? Six months to be cured?"

The man said nothing, busy with certain controls inside her suit's helmet. Quee Lee could just see his face above and behind her.

"Six months and you can walk in public again."

"I don't mean it that way," Quee Lee countered, swallowed now. A pressure was building against her chest, panic becoming terror. She wanted nothing now but to be home again.

"Listen," said Orleans, then he said nothing.

Finally Quee Lee whispered, "What?"

He knelt beside her, saying, "You'll be fine. I promise."

His old confidence was missing. Perhaps he hadn't believed she would go through with this adventure. Perhaps the offer had been some kind of bluff, something no sane person would find appealing, and now he'd invent some excuse to stop everything—

—but he said, "Seals tight and ready."

"Tight and ready," echoed the woman.

Smiles appeared on both faces, though neither inspired confidence. Then Orleans was explaining: "There's only a slight, slight chance that you won't return to normal. If you should get hit by too much radiation, precipitating too many novel mutations . . . well, the strangeness can get buried too deeply. A thousand autodocs couldn't root it all out of you."

"Vestigial organs," the woman added. "Odd blemishes and the like."

"It won't happen," said Orleans.

"It won't," Quee Lee agreed.

A feeding nipple appeared before her mouth.

"Suck and sleep," Orleans told her.

She swallowed some sort of chemical broth, and the woman was saying, "No, it would take ten or fifteen centuries to make lasting marks. Unless—"

Orleans said something, snapping at her.

She laughed with a bitter sound, saying, "Oh, she's asleep . . . !"

And Quee Lee was asleep. She found herself in a dreamless, timeless void, her body being pricked with needles—little white pains marking every smart cancer—and it was as if nothing else existed in the universe but Quee Lee, floating in that perfect blackness while she was remade.

"How long?"

"Not so long. Seven months, almost."

Seven months. Quee Lee tried to blink and couldn't, couldn't shut the lids of her eyes. Then she tried touching her face, lifting a heavy hand and setting the palm on her faceplate, finally remembering her suit. "Is it done?" she muttered, her voice sloppy and slow. "Am I done now?"

"You're never done," Orleans laughed. "Haven't you been paying attention?"

She saw a figure, blurred but familiar.

"How do you feel, Quee Lee?"

Strange. Through and through, she felt very strange.

"That's normal enough," the voice offered. "Another couple months, and you'll be perfect. Have patience."

She was a patient person, she remembered. And now her eyes seemed to shut of their own volition, her mind sleeping again. But this time she dreamed, her and Perri and Orleans all at the beach together. She saw them sunning on the bone-white sand, and she even felt the heat of the false sun, felt it baking hot down to her rebuilt bones.

She woke, muttering, "Orleans? Orleans?"

"Here I am."

Her vision was improved now. She found herself breathing normally, her wrong-shaped mouth struggling with each word and her suit managing an accurate translation.

"How do I look?" she asked.

Orleans smiled and said, "Lovely."

His face was blue-black, perhaps. When she sat up, looking at the plain gray locker room, she realized how the colors had shifted. Her new eyes perceived the world differently, sensitive to the same spectrum but in novel ways. She slowly climbed to her feet, then asked, "How long?"

"Nine months, fourteen days."

No, she wasn't finished. But the transformation had reached a stable point, she sensed, and it was wonderful to be mobile again. She managed a few tentative steps. She made clumsy fists with her too-thick hands. Lifting the fists, she gazed at them, wondering how they would look beneath the hyperfiber.

"Want to see yourself?" Orleans asked.

Now? Was she ready?

Her friend smiled, tusks glinting in the room's weak light. He offered a large mirror, and she bent to put her face close enough . . . finding a remade face staring up at her, a sloppy mouth full of mirror-colored teeth and a pair of hairy pits for eyes. She managed a deep breath and shivered. Her skin was lovely, golden or at least appearing golden to her. It was covered with hard white lumps, and her nose was a slender beak. She wished she could touch herself, hands stroking her faceplate. Only Remoras could never touch their own flesh. . . .

"If you feel strong enough," he offered, "you can go with me. My crew and I are going on a patching mission, out to the prow."

"When?"

"Now, actually." He lowered the mirror. "The others are waiting in the shuttle. Stay here for a couple more days, or come now."

"Now," she whispered.

"Good." He nodded, telling her, "They want to meet you. They're curious what sort of person becomes a Remora."

A person who doesn't want to be locked up in a bland gray room, she thought to herself, smiling now with her mirrored teeth.

They had all kinds of faces, all unique, myriad eyes and twisting mouths and flesh of every color. She counted fifteen Remoras, plus Orleans, and Quee Lee worked to learn names and get to know her new friends. The shuttle ride was like a party, a strange informal party, and she had never known happier people, listening to Remora jokes and how they teased one another, and how they sometimes teased her. In friendly ways, of course. They asked about her apartment—how big; how fancy; how much—and about her long life. Was it as boring as it sounded? Quee Lee laughed at herself while she nodded, saying, "No, nothing changes very much. The centuries have their way of running together, sure."

One Remora—a large masculine voice and a contorted blue face—asked the others, "Why do people pay fortunes to ride the ship, then do everything possible to hide deep inside it? Why don't they ever step outside and have a little look at where we're going?"

The cabin erupted in laughter, the observation an obvious favorite.

"Immortals are cowards," said the woman beside Quee Lee.

"Fools," said a second woman, the one with comma-shaped eyes. "Most of them, at least."

Quee Lee felt uneasy, but just temporarily. She turned and looked through a filthy window, the smooth changeless landscape below and the glowing sky as she remembered it. The view soothed her. Eventually she shut her eyes and slept, waking when Orleans shouted something about being close to their destination. "Decelerating now!" he called from the cockpit.

They were slowing. Dropping. Looking at her friends, she saw a variety of smiles meant for her. The Remoras beside her took her hands, everyone starting to pray. "No comets today," they begged. "And plenty tomorrow, because we want overtime."

The shuttle slowed to nothing, then settled.

Orleans strode back to Quee Lee, his mood suddenly serious. "Stay close," he warned, "but don't get in our way, either."

The hyperfiber was thickest here, on the prow, better than ten kilometers deep, and its surface had been browned by the ceaseless radiations. A soft dry dust clung to the lifesuits, and everything was lit up by the aurora and flashes of laser light. Quee Lee followed the others, listening to their chatter. She ate a little meal of Remoran soup—her first conscious meal—feeling the soup moving down her throat, trying to map her new architecture. Her stomach seemed the same, but did she have two hearts? It seemed that the beats were wrong. Two hearts nestled side by side. She found Orleans and approached him. "I wish I could pull off my suit, just once. Just for a minute." She told him, "I keep wondering how all of me looks."

Orleans glanced at her, then away. He said, "No."

"No?"

"Remoras don't remove their suits. Ever."

There was anger in the voice and a deep chilling silence from the others. Quee Lee looked about, then swallowed. "I'm not a Remora," she finally said. "I don't understand. . . ."

Silence persisted, quick looks exchanged.

"I'm going to climb out of this . . . eventually . . . !"

"But don't say it now," Orleans warned. A softer, more tempered voice informed her, "We have taboos. Maybe we seem too rough to have them—"

"No," she muttered.

"—yet we do. These lifesuits are as much a part of our bodies as our guts and eyes, and being a Remora, a true Remora, is a sacred pledge that you take for your entire life."

The comma-eyed woman approached, saying, "It's an insult to remove your suit. A sacrilege."

"Contemptible," said someone else. "Or worse."

Then Orleans, perhaps guessing Quee Lee's thoughts, made a show of touching her, and she felt the hand through her suit. "Not that you're anything but our guest, of course. Of course." He paused, then said, "We have our beliefs, that's all."

"Ideals," said the woman.

"And contempt for those we don't like. Do you understand?"

She couldn't, but she made understanding sounds just the same. Obviously she had found a sore spot.

Then came a new silence, and she found herself marching through the dust, wishing someone would make angry sounds again. Silence was the worst kind of anger. From now on, she vowed, she would be careful about everything she said. Every word.

The crater was vast and rough and only partway patched. Previous crew had brought giant tanks and the machinery used to make the patch. It was something of an artform, pouring the fresh liquid hyperfiber and carefully curing it. Each shift added another hundred meters to the smooth crater floor. Orleans stood with Quee Lee at the top, explaining the job. This would be a double shift, and she was free to watch. "But not too closely," he warned her again, the tone vaguely parental. "Stay out of our way."

She promised. For that first half-day, she was happy to sit on the crater's lip, on a ridge of tortured and useless hyperfiber, imagining the comet that must have made this mess. Not large, she knew. A large one would have blasted a crater too big to see at a glance, and forty crews would be laboring here. But it hadn't been a small one, either. It must have slipped past the lasers, part of a swarm. She watched the red beams cutting across the sky, their heat producing new colors in the aurora. Her new eyes saw amazing details. Shock waves as violet phosphorescence; swirls of orange and crimson and snowy white. A beautiful deadly sky, wasn't it? Suddenly the lasers fired faster, a spiderweb of beams overhead, and she realized that a swarm was ahead of the ship, pinpointed by the navigators somewhere below them . . . tens of millions of kilometers ahead, mud and ice and rock closing fast . . . !

The lasers fired even faster, and she bowed her head.

There was an impact, at least one. She saw the flash and felt a faint rumble dampened by the hull, a portion of those energies absorbed and converted into useful power. Impacts were fuel, of a sort. And the residual gases would be concentrated and pumped inside, helping to replace the inevitable loss of volatiles as the ship continued on its great trek.

The ship was an organism feeding on the galaxy.

It was a familiar image, almost cliché, yet suddenly it seemed quite fresh. Even profound. Quee Lee laughed to herself, looking out over the browning plain while turning her attentions inward. She was aware of her breathing and the bump-bumping of wrong hearts, and she sensed changes with every little motion. Her body had an odd indecipherable quality. She could feel every fiber in her muscles, every twitch and every stillness. She had never been so alive, so self-aware, and she found herself laughing with a giddy amazement.

If she was a true Remora, she thought, then she would be a world unto herself. A world like the ship, only smaller, its organic parts enclosed in armor and forever in flux. Like the passengers below, the cells of her body were changing. She thought she could nearly feel herself evolving . . . and how did Orleans control it? It would be astonishing if she could re-evolve sight, for instance . . . gaining eyes unique to herself, never having existed before and never to exist again . . . !

What if she stayed with these people?

The possibility suddenly occurred to her, taking her by surprise.

What if she took whatever pledge was necessary, embracing all of their taboos and proving that she belonged with them? Did such things happen? Did adventurous passengers try converting—?

The sky turned red, lasers firing and every red line aimed at a point directly overhead. The silent barrage was focused on some substantial chunk of ice and grit, vaporizing its surface and cracking its heart. Then the beams separated, assaulting the bigger pieces and then the smaller ones. It was an enormous drama, her exhilaration married to terror . . . her watching the aurora brightening as force fields killed the momentum of the surviving grit and atomic dust. The sky was a vivid orange, and sudden tiny impacts kicked up the dusts around her. Something struck her leg, a flash of light followed by a dim pain . . . and she wondered if she was dead, then how badly she was wounded. Then she blinked and saw the little crater etched above her knee. A blemish, if that. And suddenly the meteor shower was finished.

Quee Lee rose to her feet, shaking with nervous energy.

She began picking her way down the crater slope. Orleans' commands were forgotten; she needed to speak to him. She had insights and compliments to share, nearly tripping with her excitement, finally reaching the worksite and gasping, her air stale from her exertions. She could taste herself in her breaths, the flavor unfamiliar, thick and a little sweet.

"Orleans!" she cried out.

"You're not supposed to be here," groused one woman.

The comma-eyed woman said, "Stay right there. Orleans is coming, and don't move!"

A lake of fresh hyperfiber was cooling and curing as she stood beside it. A thin skin had formed, the surface utterly flat and silvery. Mirror-like. Quee Lee could see the sky reflected in it, leaning forward and knowing she shouldn't. She risked falling in order to see herself once again. The nearby Remoras watched her, saying nothing. They smiled as she grabbed a lump of old hyperfiber, positioning herself, and the lasers flashed again, making everything bright as day.

She didn't see her face.

Or rather, she did. But it wasn't the face she expected, the face from Orleans' convenient mirror. Here was the old Quee Lee, mouth ajar, those pretty and ordinary eyes opened wide in amazement.

She gasped, knowing everything. A near-fortune paid, and nothing in return. Nothing here had been real. This was an enormous and cruel sick joke; and now the Remoras were laughing, hands on their untouchable bellies and their awful faces contorted, ready to rip apart from the sheer brutal joy of the moment . . . !

"Your mirror wasn't a mirror, was it? It synthesized that image, didn't it?" She kept asking questions, not waiting for a response. "And you drugged me, didn't you? That's why everything still looks and feels wrong."

Orleans said, "Exactly. Yes."

Quee Lee remained inside her lifesuit, just the two of them flying back to Port Beta. He would see her on her way home. The rest of the crew was working, and Orleans would return and finish his shift. After her discovery, everyone agreed there was no point in keeping her on the prow.

"You owe me money," she managed.

Orleans' face remained blue-black. His tusks framed a calm icy smile. "Money? Whose money?"

"I paid you for a service, and you never met the terms."

"I don't know about any money," he laughed.

"I'll report you," she snapped, trying to use all of her venom. "I'll go to the captains—"

"—and embarrass yourself further." He was confident, even cocky. "Our transaction would be labeled illegal, not to mention disgusting. The captains will be thoroughly disgusted, believe me." Another laugh. "Besides, what can anyone prove? You gave someone your money, but nobody will trace it to any of us. Believe me.''

She had never felt more ashamed, crossing her arms and trying to wish herself home again.

"The drug will wear off soon,'' he promised. ''You'll feel like yourself again. Don't worry.''

Softly, in a breathless little voice, she asked, ''How long have I been gone?''
Silence.

"It hasn't been months, has it?''

"More like three days.'' A nod inside the helmet. ''The same drug distorts your sense of time, if you get enough of it.''

She felt ill to her stomach.

"You'll be back home in no time, Quee Lee.''

She was shaking and holding herself.

The Remora glanced at her for a long moment, something resembling remorse in his expression. Or was she misreading the signs?

"You aren't spiritual people,'' she snapped. It was the best insult she could manage, and she spoke with certainty. ''You're crude, disgusting monsters. You couldn't live below if you had the chance, and this is where you belong.''

Orleans said nothing, merely watching her.

Finally he looked ahead, gazing at the endless gray landscape. ''We try to follow our founder's path. We try to be spiritual.'' A shrug. ''Some of us do better than others, of course. We're only human.''

She whispered, ''Why?''

Again he looked at her, asking, ''Why what?''

"Why have you done this to me?''

Orleans seemed to breathe and hold the breath, finally exhaling. ''Oh, Quee Lee,'' he said, ''you haven't been paying attention, have you?''

What did he mean?

He grasped her helmet, pulling her face up next to his face. She saw nothing but the eyes, each black hair moving and nameless fluids circulating through them, and she heard the voice saying, ''This has never, never been about you, Quee Lee. Not you. Not for one instant.''

And she understood—perhaps she had always known—struck mute and her skin going cold, and finally, after everything, she found herself starting to weep.

Perri was already home, by chance.

"I was worried about you,'' he confessed, sitting in the garden room with honest relief on his face. ''The apartment said you were going to be gone for a year or more. I was scared for you.''

"Well,'' she said, ''I'm back.''

Her husband tried not to appear suspicious, and he worked hard not to ask certain questions. She could see him holding the questions inside himself. She watched him decide to try the old charm, smiling now and saying, ''So you went exploring?''

"Not really.''

"Where?"

"Cloud Canyon," she lied. She had practiced the lie all the way from Port Beta, yet it sounded false now. She was halfway startled when her husband said:

"Did you go into it?"

"Partway, then I decided not to risk it. I rented a boat, but I couldn't make myself step on board."

Perri grinned happily, unable to hide his relief. A deep breath was exhaled, then he said, "By the way, I've raised almost eight thousand credits already. I've already put them in your account."

"Fine."

"I'll find the rest too."

"It can wait," she offered.

Relief blended into confusion. "Are you all right, darling?"

"I'm tired," she allowed.

"You look tired."

"Let's go to bed, shall we?"

Perri was compliant, making love to her and falling into a deep sleep, as exhausted as Quee Lee. But she insisted on staying awake, sliding into her private bathroom and giving her autodoc a drop of Perri's seed. "I want to know if there's anything odd," she told it.

"Yes, miss."

"And scan him, will you? Without waking him."

The machine set to work. Almost instantly, Quee Lee was being shown lists of abnormal genes and vestigial organs. She didn't bother to read them. She closed her eyes, remembering what little Orleans had told her after he had admitted that she wasn't anything more than an incidental bystander. "Perri was born Remora, and he left us. A long time ago, by our count, and that's a huge taboo."

"Leaving the fold?" she had said.

"Every so often, one of us visits his home while he's gone. We slip a little dust into our joints, making them grind, and we do a pity-play to whomever we find."

Her husband had lied to her from the first, about everything.

"Sometimes we'll trick her into giving even more money," he had boasted. "Just like we've done with you."

And she had asked, "Why?"

"Why do you think?" he had responded.

Vengeance, of a sort. Of course.

"Eventually," Orleans had declared, "everyone's going to know about Perri. He'll run out of hiding places, and money, and he'll have to come back to us. We just don't want it to happen too soon, you know? It's too much fun as it is."

Now she opened her eyes, gazing at the lists of abnormalities. It had to be work for him to appear human, to cope with those weird Remora genetics. He wasn't merely someone who had lived on the hull for a few years, no. He was a full-blooded Remora who had done the unthinkable, removing his suit and living below, safe from the mortal dangers of the universe. Quee Lee was the latest of his ignorant lovers, and she knew precisely why he had selected her. More than money, she had offered him a useful naiveté and a sheltered ignorance . . . and wasn't she well within her rights to confront him, confront him and demand that he leave at once . . . ?

"Erase the lists," she said.

"Yes, miss."

She told her apartment, "Project the view from the prow, if you will. Put it on my bedroom ceiling, please."

"Of course, miss," it replied.

She stepped out of the bathroom, lasers and exploding comets overhead. She fully expected to do what Orleans anticipated, putting her mistakes behind her. She sat on the edge of her bed, on Perri's side, waiting for him to wake on his own. He would feel her gaze and open his eyes, seeing her framed by a Remoran sky. . . .

. . . and she hesitated, taking a breath and holding it, glancing upwards, remembering that moment on the crater's lip when she had felt a union with her body. A perfection; an intoxicating sense of self. It ʳ as induced by drugs and ignorance, yet still it had seemed true. It was a perception worth any cost, she realized; and she imagined Perri's future, hounded by the Remoras, losing every human friend, left with no choice but the hull and his left-behind life. . . .

She looked at him, the peaceful face stirring.

Compassion. Pity. Not love, but there was something not far from love making her feel for the fallen Remora.

"What if . . . ?" she whispered, beginning to smile.

And Perri smiled in turn, eyes closed and him enjoying some lazy dream that in an instant he would surely forget.

NEKROPOLIS

MAUREEN F. McHUGH

Here's a hard-eyed and compelling look at the price of freedom, from one of SF's most acclaimed new writers . . .

Born in Ohio, Maureen F. McHugh spent some years living in Shijiazhuang in the People's Republic of China, an experience that has been one of the major shaping forces on her fiction to date. Upon returning to the United States, she made her first sale in 1989, and has since made a powerful impression on the SF world with a relatively small body of work, becoming a frequent contributor to *Asimov's Science Fiction*, as well as selling to *The Magazine of Fantasy & Science Fiction*, *Alternate Warriors*, *Aladdin*, and other markets. In 1992, she published one of the year's most widely acclaimed and talked-about first novels, *China Mountain Zhang*, which received the prestigious Tiptree Memorial Award. She has had stories in our Tenth and (in collaboration with David B. Kisor) Eleventh Annual Collections. Her most recent book is a new novel, *Half the Day Is Night*. She lives with her family in Twinsburg, Ohio.

How I came to be jessed. Well, like most people who are jessed, I was sold. I was twenty-one, and I was sold three times in one day, one right after another. First to a dealer who looked at my teeth and in my ears and had me scanned for augmentation; then to a second dealer where I sat in the back office drinking tea and talking with a gap-toothed boy who was supposed to be sold to a restaurant owner as a clerk; and finally that afternoon to the restaurant owner. The restaurant owner couldn't really have wanted the boy anyway, since the position was for his wife's side of the house.

I have been with my present owner since I was twenty-one. That was pretty long ago, I am twenty-six now. I was a good student, I got good marks, so I was purchased to oversee cleaning and supplies. This is much better than if I were a pretty girl and had to rely on looks. Then I would be used up in a few years. I'm rather plain, with a square jaw and unexceptional hair.

I liked my owner, liked my work. But now I would like to go to him and ask him to sell me.

"Diyet," he would say, taking my hand in his fatherly way, "Aren't you happy here?"

"Mardin-salah," I would answer, my eyes demurely on my toes. "You are like a father and I have been only too happy with you." Which is true even beyond being jessed. I don't think I would mind being part of Mardin's household even if I were unbound. Mostly Mardin pays no attention to me, which is how I prefer things. I like my work and my room. I like being jessed. It makes things simpler.

All would be fine if it were not for the new one.

I have no problems with AI. I don't mind the cleaning machine, poor thing, and as head of the women's household, I work with the household intelligence all the time. I may have had a simple, rather conservative upbringing, but I have come to be pretty comfortable with AI. The Holy Injunction doesn't mean that all AI is abomination. But AI should not be biologically constructed. AI should not be made in the image of humanity.

It thinks of itself. It has a name. It has gender.

It thinks it is male. And it's head of the men's side of the house, so it thinks we should work together.

It looks human male, has curly black hair and soft honey-colored skin. It flirts, looking at me sideways out of black, vulnerable gazelle eyes. Smiling at me with a smile which is not in the slightest bit vulnerable. "Come on, Diyet," it says, "we work together. We should be friends. We're both young, we can help each other in our work."

I do not bother to answer.

It smiles wickedly (although I know it is not wicked, it is just something grown and programmed. Soulless. I am not so conservative that I condemn cloning, but it is not a clone. It is a biological construct.). "Diyet," it says, "I think you are too pure. A Holy Sister."

"Don't sound foolish," I say.

"You need someone to tease you," it says, "you are so solemn. Tell me, is it because you are jessed?"

I do not know how much it knows, does it understand the process of jessing? "The Mashahana says that just as a jessed hawk is tamed, not tied, so shall the servant be bound by affection and duty, not chains."

"Does the Mashahana say it should not make you sad, Diyet?"

Can something not human blaspheme?

In the morning, Mardin calls me into his office. He offers me tea, translucent green and fragrant with flowers, which I sip, regarding my sandals and my pink toenails. He pages through my morning report, nodding, making pleased noises, occasionally slurping his tea. Afternoons and evenings, Mardin is at his restaurant. I have never been in it, but I understand that it is an exceptional place.

"What will you do this afternoon?" he asks.

It is my afternoon free. "My childhood friend, Kari, and I will go shopping, Mardin-salah."

"Ah," he says, smiling. "Spend a little extra silver," he says, "buy yourself earrings or something. I'll see the credit is available."

I murmur my thanks. He makes a show of paging through the report, and the sheets of paper whisper against each other.

"And what do you think of the harni, Akhmim? Is he working out?"

"I do not spend so much time with it, Mardin-salah. Its work is with the men's household."

"You are an old-fashioned girl, Diyet, that is good." Mardin-salah holds the report a little farther away, striking a very dignified pose in his reading. "Harni have social training, but no practice. The merchant recommended to me that I send it out to talk and meet with people as much as possible."

I wriggle my toes. He has stopped referring to it as if it were a person, which is good, but now he is going to try to send it with me. "I must meet my friend Kari at her home in the Nekropolis, Mardin-salah. Perhaps it is not a good place to take a harni." The Nekropolis is a conservative place.

Mardin-salah waves his hand airily. "Everything is in order, Diyet," he says, referring to the reports in front of him. "My wife has asked that you use a little more scent with the linens."

His wife thinks I am too cheap. Mardin-salah likes to think that he runs a frugal household. He does not, money hemorrhages from this house, silver pours from the walls and runs down the street into the pockets of everyone in this city. She wanted to buy *it*, I am certain. She is like that, she enjoys toys. Surrounds herself with things, projects still more things, until it is difficult to know what is in her quarters and what comes out of the walls. She probably saw it and had to have it, the way she had to have the little long-haired dog with the overbite, her little lion dog—nasty little thing that Fadina has to feed and bathe. Fadina is her body servant.

I hope Mardin will forget about the harni, but he doesn't. There is no respite. I must take it with me.

It is waiting for me after lunch. I am wearing lavender and pale yellow, with long yellow ribbons tied around my wrists.

"Jessed, Diyet," it says. "You wouldn't have me along if you weren't."

Of course I am jessed. I always wear ribbons when I go out. "The Mashahana says ribbons are a symbol of devotion to the Most Holy, as well as an earthly master."

It runs its long fingers through its curly hair, shakes its head, and its golden earring dances. Artifice, the pretense of humanity. Although I guess even a harni's hair gets in its eyes. "Why would you choose to be jessed?" it asks.

"You wouldn't understand," I say, "come along."

It never takes offense, never worries about offending. "Can you tell the difference between the compulsion and your own feelings?" it asks.

"Jessing only heightens my natural tendencies," I say.

"Then why are you so sad?" it asks.

"I am not sad!" I snap.

"I am sorry," it says immediately. Blessedly, it is silent while we go down to the tube. I point which direction we are going and it nods and follows. I get a seat on the tube and it stands in front of me. It glances down at me. Smiles. I fancy it looks as if it feels pity for me. (Artifice. Does the cleaning machine feel sorry for anyone? Even itself? Does the household intelligence? The body chemistry of a harni may be based on humanity, but it is carefully calculated.)

It wears a white shirt. I study my toenails.

The tube lets us off at the edge of the Nekropolis, at the Moussin of the White Falcon. Mourners in white stand outside the Moussin, and I can faintly smell the incense on the hot air. The sun is blinding after the cool dark tube, and the Moussin and the mourners' robes are painful to look at. They are talking and laughing. Often, mourners haven't seen each other for years, family is spread all across the country.

The harni looks around, as curious as a child or a jackdaw. The Nekropolis is all white stone, the doorways open onto blackness.

I grew up in the Nekropolis. We didn't have running water, it was delivered every day in a big lorritank and people would go out and buy it by the *karn*, and we lived in three adjoining mausoleums instead of a flat, but other than that, it was a pretty normal childhood. I have a sister and two brothers. My mother sells paper funeral decorations, so the Nekropolis is a very good place for her to live, no long tube rides every day. The part we lived in was old. Next to my bed were the dates for the person buried behind the wall, 3673 to 3744. All of the family was dead hundreds of years ago, no one ever came to this death house to lay out paper flowers and birds. In fact, when I was four, we bought the rights to this place from an old woman whose family had lived here a long time before us.

Our house always smelled of cinnamon and the perfume my mother used on her paper flowers and birds. In the middle death-house, there were funeral arrangements everywhere, and when we ate we would clear a space on the floor and sit surrounded. When I was a little girl, I learned the different uses of papers; how my mother used translucent tissue for carnations, stiff satiny brittle paper for roses, and strong paper with a grain like linen for arrogant falcons. As children, we all smelled of perfume, and when I stayed the night with my friend Kari, she would wrap her arms around my waist and whisper in my neck, "You smell so good."

I am not waiting for the harni. It has to follow, it has no credit for the tube ride. If it isn't paying attention and gets lost, it will have to walk home.

When I glance back a block and a half later, it is following me, its long curly hair wild about its shoulders, its face turned artlessly toward the sun. Does it enjoy the feeling of sunlight on skin? Probably, that is a basic biological pleasure. It must enjoy things like eating.

Kari comes out, running on light feet. "Diyet!" she calls. She still lives across from my mother but now she has a husband and a pretty two-year-old-daughter, a chubby toddler with black hair and clear skin the color of amber. Tariam, the little girl, stands clinging to the doorway, her thumb in her mouth. Kari grabs my wrists and her bracelets jingle. "Come out of the heat!" She glances past me and says, "Who is this?"

The harni stands there, one hand on his hip, smiling.

Kari drops my wrists and pulls a little at her rose colored veil. She smiles, thinking of course that I have brought a handsome young man with me.

"It is a harni," I say and laugh, shrill and nervous. "Mardin-salah asked me to bring him with me."

"A harni?" she asks, her voice doubtful.

I wave my hand. "You know the mistress, always wanting toys. He is in charge of the men's household." "He," I say. I meant "it." "It is in charge." But I don't correct myself, not wanting to call attention to my error.

"I am called Akhmim," it says smoothly. "You are a friend of Diyet's?"

Its familiarity infuriates me. Here I am, standing on the street in front of my mother's house, and it is pretending to be a man, with no respect for my reputation. If it is a man, what am I doing escorting a strange man? And if people know it is a harni, that is as bad. In the Nekropolis, people do not even like AI like the cleaning machine.

"Kari," I say, "Let's go."

She looks at the harni a moment more, then goes back to her little girl, picks her up, and carries her inside. Normally I would go inside, sit and talk with her mother, Ena. I would hold Tariam on my lap and wish I had a little girl with perfect tiny fingernails and such a clean, sweet milk smell. It would be cool and dark inside, the environment controlled, and we would eat honeysweets and drink tea. I would go across the street, see my mother and youngest brother, who is the only one at home now.

The harni stands in the street, looking at the ground. It seems uncomfortable. It does not look at me; at least it has the decency to make it appear we are not together.

Kari comes out, bracelets ringing. While we shop, she does not refer to the harni, but, as it follows us, she glances back at it often. I glance back and it flashes a white smile. It seems perfectly content to trail along, looking at the market stalls with their red canopies.

"Maybe we should let him walk with us," Kari says. "It seems rude to ignore him."

I laugh, full of nervousness. "It's not human."

"Does it have feelings?" Kari asks.

I shrug. "After a fashion. It is AI."

"It doesn't look like a machine," she says.

"It's not a machine," I say, irritated with her.

"How can it be AI if it is not a machine?" she presses.

"Because it's *manufactured*. A technician's creation. An artificial combination of genes, grown somewhere."

"Human genes?"

"Probably," I say. "Maybe some animal genes. Maybe some that they made up themselves, how would I know?" It is ruining my afternoon. "I wish it would offer to go home."

"Maybe he can't," Kari says. "If Mardin-salah told him to come, he would have to, wouldn't he?"

I don't really know anything about harni.

"It doesn't seem fair," Kari says. "Harni," she calls, "come here."

He tilts his head, all alert. "Yes, mistress?"

"Are harni prescripted for taste?" she inquires.

"What do you mean, the taste of food?" he asks. "I can taste, just as you do, although," he smiles, "I personally am not overly fond of cherries."

"No, no," Kari says. "Colors, clothing. Are you capable of helping make choices? About earrings for example?"

He comes to look at the choices, and selects a pair of gold and rose enamel teardrops and holds them up for her. "I think my taste is no better than that of the average person," he says, "but I like these."

She frowns, looks at him through her lashes. She has got me thinking of it as "him." And she is flirting with him! Kari! A married woman!

"What do you think, Diyet?" she asks. She takes the earrings, holds one beside her face. "They are pretty."

"I think they're gaudy."

She is hurt. In truth, they suit her.

She frowns at me. "I'll take them," she says. The stallman names a price.

"No, no, no," says the harni, "you should not buy them, this man is a thief." He reaches to touch her, as if he would pull her away, and I hold my breath in shock—if the thing should touch her!

But the stallman interrupts with a lower price. The harni bargains. He is a good bargainer, but he should be, he has no compassion, no concern for the stallkeeper. Charity is a human virtue. The Mashahana says, "A human in need becomes every man's child."

Interminable, this bargaining, but finally, the earrings are Kari's. "We should stop and have some tea," she says.

"I have a headache," I say, "I think I should go home."

"If Diyet is ill, we should go," the harni says.

Kari looks at me, looks away, guilty. She *should* feel guilt.

I come down the hall to access the Household AI and the harni is there. Apparently busy, but waiting for me. "I'll be finished in a minute and out of your way," it says. Beautiful fingers, wrist bones, beautiful face, and dark curling hair showing just where its shirt closes; it is constructed elegantly. Lean and long-legged, like a hound. When the technician constructed it, did he know how it would look when it was grown? Are they designed aesthetically?

It takes the report and steps aside, but does not go on with its work. I ignore it, doing my work as if it were not there, standing so it is behind me.

"Why don't you like me?" it finally asks.

I consider my answers. I could say it is a thing, not something to like or dislike, but that isn't true. I like my bed, my things. "Because of your arrogance," I say to the system.

A startled hiss of indrawn breath. "My . . . arrogance?" it asks.

"Your presumption." It is hard to keep my voice steady, every time I am around the harni I find myself hating the way I speak.

"I . . . I am sorry, Diyet," it whispers. "I have so little experience, I didn't realize I had insulted you."

I am tempted to turn around and look at it, but I do not. It does not really feel pain, I remind myself. It is a thing, it has no more feelings than a fish. Less.

"Please, tell me what I have done?"

"Your behavior. This conversation, here," I say. "You are always trying to make people think that you are human."

Silence. Is it considering? Or would it be better to say processing?

"You blame me for being what I am," the harni says. It sighs. "I cannot help being what I am."

I wait for it to say more, but it doesn't. I turn around, but it is gone.

After that, every time it sees me, if it can it makes some excuse to avoid me. I do not know if I am grateful or not. I am very uncomfortable.

My tasks are not complicated; I see to the cleaning machine, and set it loose in the women's household when it will not inconvenience the mistress. I am jessed to Mardin, although I serve the mistress. I am glad I am not jessed to her; Fadina is, and she has to put up with a great deal. I am careful never to blame the mistress in front of her. Let her blame the stupid little dog for crapping on the rug. She knows that the mistress is unreasonable, but of course, emotionally, she is bound to affection and duty.

On Friday mornings, the mistress is usually in her rooms, preparing for her Sunday *bismek*. On Friday afternoons, she goes out to play the Tiles with her friends and gossip about husbands and the wives who aren't there. I clean on Friday afternoons. I call the cleaning machine and it follows me down the hallway like a dog, snuffling along the baseboards for dust.

I open the door and smell attar of roses. The room is different, white marble floor veined with gold and amethyst, covered with purple rugs. Braziers and huge open windows looking out on a pillared walkway, beyond that vistas down to a lavender sea. It's the mistress' *bismek* setting. A young man is reading a letter on the walkway, a girl stands behind him, her face is tear-stained.

Interactive fantasies. The characters are generated from lists of traits, they're projections controlled by whoever is game-mistress of the *bismek* and fleshed out by the household AI. Everyone else comes over and becomes characters in the setting. There are poisonings and love affairs. The mistress' setting is in ancient times and seems to be quite popular. Some of her friends have two or three identities in the game.

She usually turns it off when she goes out. The little cleaning machine stops. It can read the difference between reality and the projection, but she has ordered it never to enter the projection because she says the sight of the thing snuffling through walls damages her sense of the alternate reality. I reach behind the screen and turn the projection off so that I can clean. The scene disappears, even the usual projections, and there is the mistress' rooms and their bare walls. "Go ahead," I tell the machine and start for the mistress' rooms to pick up things for the laundry.

To my horror, the mistress steps out of her bedroom. Her hair is loose and long and disheveled, and she is dressed in a day robe, obviously not intending to go out. She sees me in the hall and stops in astonishment. Then her face darkens, her beautiful, heavy eyebrows folding toward her nose, and I instinctively start to back up. "Oh, Mistress," I say, "I am sorry, I didn't know you were in, I'm sorry, let me get the cleaning machine and leave, I'll just be out of here in a moment, I thought you had gone out to play the Tiles, I should have checked with Fadina, it is my fault, mistress—''

"Did you turn them off?" she demands. "You stupid girl, *did you turn Zarin and Nisea off?*''

I nod mutely.

"Oh Holy One," she says. "Ugly, incompetent girl! Are you completely lacking in sense? Did you think they would be there and I wouldn't be here? It's difficult enough to prepare without interference!''

"I'll turn it back on," I say.

"Don't touch anything!" she shrieks. "FADINA!" The mistress has a very popular *bismek* and Fadina is always explaining to me how difficult it is for the mistress to think up new and interesting scenarios for her friends' participation.

I keep backing up, hissing at the cleaning machine, while the mistress follows me down the hall shrieking "FADINA!" and because I am watching the mistress I back into Fadina coming in the door.

"Didn't you tell Diyet that I'd be in this afternoon?" the mistress says.

"Of course," Fadina says.

I am aghast. "You did not!" I say.

"I did, too," Fadina says. "You were at the access. I distinctly told you and you said you would clean later.''

I start to defend myself and the mistress slaps me in the face. "Enough of you, girl," she says. And then the mistress makes me stand there and berates me, reaching out now and then to grab my hair and yank it painfully, because of course she believes Fadina when the girl is clearly lying to avoid punishment. I cannot believe that Fadina has done this to me; she is in terror of offending the mistress, but she has always been a good girl, and I am innocent. My cheek stings, and my head aches from having my hair yanked, but, worse, I am so angry and so, so humiliated.

Finally we are allowed to leave. I know I should give Fadina a piece of my mind, but I just want to escape. Out in the hall, Fadina grabs me so hard that her nails bite into the soft part under my arm. "I told you she was in an absolute frenzy about Saturday," she whispers. "I can't believe you did that! And now she'll be in a terrible mood all evening and I'm the one who will suffer for it!''

"Fadina," I protest.

"Don't you 'Fadina' me, Diyet! If I don't get a slap out of this, it will be the intervention of the Holy One!''

I have already gotten a slap, and it wasn't even my fault. I pull my arm away from Fadina and try to walk down the hall without losing my dignity. My face is hot and I am about to cry. Everything blurs in tears, so I duck into the linens and sit down on the hamper. I want to leave this place, I don't want to work for that old woman. I realize that my only friend in the world is Kari and now we are so far apart, and I feel so hurt and lonely that I just sob.

The door to the linens opens and I turn my back thinking, "Go away, whoever you are.''

"Oh, excuse me," the harni says.

At least *it* will go away. But the thought that the only thing around is the harni makes me feel even lonelier. I cannot stop myself from sobbing.

"Diyet," it says hesitantly, "are you all right?"

I can't answer. I want it to go away, and I don't.

After a moment, it says from right behind me, "Diyet, are you ill?"

I shake my head.

I can feel it standing there, perplexed, but I don't know what to do and I can't stop crying and I feel so foolish. I want my mother. Not that she would do anything other than remind me that the world is not fair. My mother believes in facing reality. Be strong, she always says. And that makes me cry harder.

After a minute, I hear the harni leave, and awash in self pity, I even cry over that. My feelings of foolishness are beginning to outweigh my feelings of unhappiness, but perversely enough I realize that I am enjoying my cry. That it has been inside me, building stronger and stronger, and I didn't even know it.

Then someone comes in again, and I straighten my back again, and pretend to be checking towels. The only person it could be is Fadina.

It is the harni, with a box of tissues. He crouches beside me, his face full of concern. "Here," he says.

Embarrassed, I take one. If you didn't know, you would think he was a regular human. He even smells of clean man-scent. Like my brothers.

I blow my nose, wondering if harni ever cry. "Thank you," I say.

"I was afraid you were ill," he says.

I shake my head. "No, I am just angry."

"You cry when you are angry?" he asks.

"The mistress is upset at me and it's Fadina's fault, but I had to take the blame." That makes me start to cry again, but the harni is patient and he just crouches next to me in among the linens, holding the box of tissues. By the time I collect myself, there is a little crumpled pile of tissues and some have tumbled to the floor. I take two tissues and start folding them into a flower, like my mother makes.

"Why are you so nice to me when I am so mean to you?" I ask.

He shrugs. "Because you do not want to be mean to me," he says. "It makes you suffer. I am sorry that I make you so uncomfortable."

"But you can't help being what you are," I say. My eyes are probably red. Harni never cry, I am certain. They are too perfect. I keep my eyes on the flower.

"Neither can you," he says. "When Mardin-salah made you take me with you on your day off, you were not even free to be angry with him. I knew that was why you were angry with me." He has eyes like Fhassin, my brother (who had long eyelashes like a girl, just like the harni).

Thinking about Mardin-salah makes my head ache a little and I think of something else. I remember and cover my mouth in horror. "Oh no."

"What is it?" he asks.

"I think . . . I think Fadina did tell me that the mistress would be in, but I was, was thinking of something else, and I didn't pay attention." I was standing at the access, wondering if the harni was around, since that was where I was most likely to run into him.

"It is natural enough," he says, unnatural thing that he is. "If Fadina weren't jessed, she would probably be more understanding."

He is prescribed to be kind, I remind myself. I should not ascribe human motives to an AI. But I haven't been fair to him, and he is the only one in the whole household sitting here among the linens with a box of tissues. I fluff out the folds of the flower and put it among the linens. A white tissue flower, a funeral flower.

"Thank you . . . Akhmim." It is hard to say his name.

He smiles. "Do not be sad, Diyet."

I am careful and avoid the eye of the mistress as much as I can. Fadina is civil to me, but not friendly. She says hello to me, politely, and goes on with whatever she is doing.

It is Akhmim, the harni, who stops me one evening and says, "The mistress wants us for *bismek* tomorrow." It's not the first time I've been asked to stand in, but usually it's Fadina who lets me know and tells me what I'm supposed to do. Lately, however, I have tried to be kind to Akhmim. He is easy to talk to, and like me he is alone in the household.

"What are we supposed to be?" I ask.

The harni flicks his long fingers dismissively, "Servants, of course. What's it like?"

"Bismek?" I shrug. "Play-acting."

"Like children's games?" he asks, looking doubtful.

"Well, yes and no. It's been going on a couple of years now and there are hundreds of characters," I say. "The ladies all have roles, and you have to remember to call them by their character names and not their real names, and you have to pretend it's all real. All sorts of things happen; people get in trouble and they all figure out elaborate plots to get out of trouble and people get strange illnesses and everybody professes their undying affection. The mistress threw her best friend in prison for awhile, Fadina said that was very popular."

He looks at me for a moment, blinking his long eyelashes. "You are making fun of me, Diyet," he says, doubtful.

"No," I say laughing, "it is true." It is, too. "Akhmim, no one is ever really hurt or uncomfortable."

I think he cannot decide whether to believe me or not.

Saturday afternoon, I am dressed in a pagan-looking robe that leaves one shoulder bare. And makes me look ridiculous, I might add. I am probably a server. Projections are prettier than real people, but they aren't very good at handing out real food.

I am in the mistress' quarters early. The scent of some heavy, almost bitter incense is overwhelming. The cook is laying out real food, using our own service, but the table is too tall to sit at on the floor, and there are candles and brass bowls of dates to make it look antique. Without the projection, the elaborate table looks odd in the room, which is otherwise empty of furniture. Akhmim is helping, bringing in lounging chairs so that the guests can recline at the table. He is dressed in a white robe that comes to his knees and brown sandals that have elaborate crisscross ties, and, like me, his shoulder is bare. But the harni looks graceful. Maybe people really did wear clothes like this. I am embarrassed to be seen by a man with my shoulder and neck bare. Remember, I think, Akhmim is what he is, he is not really a man or he wouldn't be here. The mistress wouldn't have a man at *bismek*, not in her quarters. Everyone would be too uncomfortable, and Mardin-salah would never allow it.

Akhmim looks up, smiles at me, comes over. "Diyet," he says, "Fadina says that the mistress is in a terrible mood."

"She is always in a terrible mood when she is nervous," I say.

"I'm nervous."

"Akhmim!" I say, laughing, "don't worry."

"I don't understand any of this playing pretend," he wails softly, "I never had a childhood!"

I take his hand and squeeze it. If he were a man, I would not touch him. "You'll do fine. We don't have to do much anyway, just serve dinner. Surely you can manage that, probably better than I can."

He bites his lower lip, and I am suddenly so reminded of my brother Fhassin I could cry. But I just squeeze his hand again. I'm nervous, too, but not about serving dinner. I have avoided the mistress since the incident with the cleaning machine.

Fadina comes in and turns on the projection, and suddenly the white marble room glows around us, full of servants and musicians tuning up. I feel better, able to hide in the crowd. Akhmim glances around. "It *is* exciting," he says thoughtfully.

There are five guests, Fadina greets them at the door and takes them back to the wardrobe to change. Five middle-aged women, come to pretend. I tell Akhmim their character names as they come in so that he knows what to call them.

The musicians start playing; projections, male and female, recline on projected couches. I know some of their names. Of course, they have projected servers and projected food. I wish I knew what the scenario was, usually Fadina tells me ahead of time, but she doesn't talk much to me these days. Pretty soon the mistress comes in with the real guests, and they all find the real couches, where they can talk to each other. First is bread and cheese, already on the table, and Akhmim has to pour wine, but I just stand there, next to a projected servant. Even this close she seems real, exotic with her pale hair. I ask her what her name is and she whispers, "Miri." Fadina is standing next to the mistress' couch, she glares at me. I'm not supposed to make the household AI do extra work.

The first part of the meal is boring. The mistress' friends get up once in awhile to whisper to each other or a projection, and projections do the same thing. There's some sort of intrigue going on, people look very tense and excited. Akhmim and I glance at each other and he smiles. While I am serving, I whisper to him, "Not so bad, is it?"

The two lovers I turned off are at this dinner, I guess they are important characters right now. The mistress' friends are always there, but the projections change so fast. The girl is apparently supposed to be the daughter of one of the mistress' friends. It will be something to do with the girl, I imagine.

Almost two hours into the dinner, the girl is arguing with her lover and stands up to leave—her eyes roll back in her head and she falls to the marble floor, thrashing. There is hysterical activity, projected characters rushing to the girl, the woman whose character is supposed to be the mother of the girl behaving with theatrical dignity in the circle of real women. The male lover is hysterical, kneeling and sobbing. It makes me uncomfortable, both the seizures and the reactions. I look for Akhmim, he is standing against the wall, holding a pitcher of wine, observing. He looks thoughtful. The girl's lover reaches onto the table and picks up her wine glass while everybody else watches him. The action is so highlighted that only an idiot would fail to realize that it's supposed to be important. The "mother" shrieks suddenly, "Stop him! It's poison!" And there is more hysterical activity, but they are too late. The lover drinks down the wine. The "mother" is "held back" by her friends, expeditious since the other characters are projections and she would look foolish trying to touch them.

I am embarrassed by the melodrama, by the way these women play with violence. I look back at Akhmim, but he's still observing. What does he think, I wonder.

There is a call for a physician, projections rush to and fro. There is a long, drawn-out death scene for the girl, followed by an equally long death for the lover. The women are openly sobbing, even Fadina. I clasp my hands together, squeeze them, look at the floor. Finally, everything is played out. They sit around the "dining room" and discuss the scenario and how masterful it was. The mistress looks drained but pleased. One by one the women pad back and change, then let themselves out until only the mistress and the "mother" are left.

"It was wonderful," she keeps telling the mistress.

"As good as when Hekmet was ill?" the mistress asks.

"Oh, yes. It was wonderful!" Finally they go back to change, Fadina following to help, and Akhmim and I can start clearing the dishes off the table.

"So what did you think," I ask, "was it what you expected?"

Akhmim makes a noncommittal gesture.

I stack plates and dump them on a tray. Akhmim boosts the tray, balancing it at his shoulder like a waiter. He is really much stronger than he looks. "You don't like it," he says finally.

I shake my head.

"Why not, because it's not real?"

"All this violence," I say. "Nobody would want to live this way. Nobody would want these things to happen to them." I am collecting wine glasses, colored transparent blue and rose like soap bubbles.

He stands looking at me, observing me the way he did the women, I think. What do we look like to harni? He is beautiful, the tray balanced effortlessly, the muscles of his bare arm and shoulder visible. He looks pagan enough in his white robe, with his perfect, timeless face. Even his long curly hair seems right.

I try to explain. "They entertain themselves with suffering."

"They're only projections," he says.

"But they seem real, the whole point is to forget they're projections, isn't it?" The glasses ring against each other as I collect them.

Softly he says, "They are bored women, what do they have in their lives?"

I want him to understand how I am different. "You can't tell me it doesn't affect the way they see people, look at the way the mistress treats Fadina!" Akhmim tries to interrupt me, but I want to finish what I am saying. "She wants excitement, even if it means watching death. Watching a seizure, that's not entertaining, not unless there's something wrong. It's decadent, what they do, it's . . . it's sinful! Death isn't entertainment."

"Diyet!" he says.

Then the mistress grabs my hair and yanks me around and all the glasses in my arms fall to the floor and shatter.

Sweet childhood. Adulthood is salty. Not that it's not rewarding, mind you, just different. The rewards of childhood are joy and pleasure, but the rewards of adulthood are strength. I am punished, but it is light punishment, not something that demands so much strength. The mistress beats me. She doesn't really hurt me much, it's noisy and frightening, and I cut my knee where I kneel in broken glass, but no serious damage. I am locked in my room and only allowed punishment food: bread, tea, and a little cheese, but I can have all the paper I want, and I fill my rooms with flowers. White paper roses, white iris with petals curling down to reveal their centers, snowy calla lilies like trumpets and poppies and tulips of luscious paper with nap like velvet. My walls are white and the world is white, filled with white flowers.

"How about daisies," Akhmim asks. He comes to bring me my food and my paper.

"Too innocent," I say. "Daisies are only for children."

Fadina recommended to the mistress that Akhmim be my jailer. She thinks that I hate to have him near me, but I couldn't have asked for better company than the harni. He's never impatient, never comes to me asking for attention to his own problems. He wants to learn how to make flowers. I try to teach him but he can never learn to do anything but awkwardly copy my model. "You make them out of your own head," he says. His clever fingers stumble and crease the paper or turn it.

"My mother makes birds, too," I say.

"Can you make birds?" he asks.

I don't want to make birds, just flowers.

I think about the Nekropolis. Akhmim is doing his duties and mine, too, so he is busy during the day and mostly, I am alone. When I am not making flowers I sit and look out my window, watching the street, or I sleep. It is probably because I am not getting so much to eat, but I can sleep for hours. A week passes, then two. Sometimes I feel as if I have to get out of this room, but then I ask myself where I would want to go and I realize that it doesn't make any difference. This room, the outside, they are all the same place, except that this room is safe.

The place I want to go is the Nekropolis, the one in my mind, but it's gone. I was the eldest, then my sister, Larit, then my brother, Fhassin, and then the baby boy, Michim. In families of four, underneath the fighting, there is always pairing, two and two. Fhassin and I were a pair. My brother. I think a lot about Fhassin and about the Nekropolis, locked in my room.

I sleep, eat my little breakfast that Akhmim brings me, sleep again. Then I sit at the window or make flowers, sleep again. The only time that is bad is late afternoon, early evening, when I have slept so much that I can't sleep any more and my stomach is growling and growling. I feel fretful and teary. When Akhmim comes in the evening with dinner he bruises my senses until I get accustomed to his being there; his voice has so many shades, his skin is so much more supple, so much more oiled and textured than paper, that he overwhelms me.

Sometimes he sits with his arms around my shoulders and I lean against him. I pretend intimacy doesn't matter because he is only a harni, but I know that I am lying to myself. How could I ever have thought him safe because he was made rather than born? I understood from the first that he wasn't to be trusted, but actually it was I that couldn't be trusted.

He is curious about my childhood, he says he never was a child. To keep him close to me I tell him everything I can remember about growing up, all the children's games, teach him the songs we skipped rope to, the rhymes we used to pick who was it, everybody with their fists in the center, tapping a fist on every stress as we chanted:

> ONCE my SIS-ter HAD a HOUSE,
> THEN she LEFT it TO a MOUSE,
> SING a SONG
> TELL a LIE
> KISS my SIS-ter
> SAY good-BYE

"What does it mean," he asks, laughing.

"It doesn't mean anything," I explain, "it's a way of picking who is it. Who is the fox, or who holds the broom while everybody hides." I tell him about fox and hounds, about how my brother Fhassin was a daredevil and one time to get away he climbed to the roof of Kari's grandmother's house and ran along the roofs and how our mother punished him. And of how we got in a fight and I pushed him and he fell and broke his collarbone.

"What does Kari do?" he asks.

"Kari is married," I say. "Her husband works, he directs a lorritank, like the one that delivers water."

"Did you ever have a boyfriend?" he asks.

"I did, his name was Zard."

"Why didn't you marry?" he asks. He is so innocent.

"It didn't work," I say.

"Is that why you became jessed?"

"No," I say.

He is patient, he waits.

"No," I say again. "It was because of Shusilina."

And then I have to explain.

Shusilina moved into the death house across the street, where Kari's grand had lived until he died. Kari's grand had been a soldier when he was young, and to be brave for the Holy he had a Serinitin implant, so that when he was old he didn't remember who he was anymore. And when he died, Shusilina and her husband moved in. Shusilina had white hair and had had her ears pointed and she wanted a baby. I was only twenty, and trying to decide whether I should marry Zard. He had not asked me, but I thought he might, and I wasn't sure what I should answer. Shusilina was younger than me, nineteen, but she wanted a baby, and that seemed terribly adult. And she had come from outside the Nekropolis, and had pointed ears, and everybody thought she was just a little too good for herself.

We talked about Zard, and she told me that after marriage everything was not milk and honey. She was very vague on just what she meant by that, but I should know that it was not like it seemed now, when I was in love with Zard. I should give myself over to him, but I should hold some part of myself private, for myself, and not let marriage swallow me.

Now I realize that she was a young bride trying to learn the difference between romance and life, and the conversations are obvious and adolescent, but then it seemed so adult to talk about marriage this way. It was like something sacred, and I was being initiated into mysteries. I dyed my hair white.

My sister hated her. Michim made eyes at her all the time but he was only thirteen. Fhassin was seventeen and he laughed at Michim. Fhassin laughed at all sorts of things. He looked at the world from under his long eyelashes, so in contrast with his sharp-chinned face and monkey grin. That was the year Fhassin, who had always been shorter than everybody, almost shorter than Michim, suddenly grew so tall. He was visited by giggling girls, but he never took any of them seriously.

It was all outside, not inside the family. In the evenings we sat on the floor in the middle of our three death houses and made paper flowers. We lived in a house filled with perfume. I was twenty, Larit was nineteen, but nobody had left my mother's house, and we never thought that was strange. But it was, the way we were held there.

So when did Fhassin stop seeing her as silly and begin to see Shusilina as a person? I didn't suspect it. The giggling girls still came by the house, and Fhassin still grinned and didn't really pay much attention. They were careful, meeting in the afternoon when her husband was building new death-houses at the other end of the Nekropolis and the rest of us were sleeping.

I think Fhassin did it because he was always a daredevil, like walking on the roofs of the death-houses, or the time he took money out of our mother's money pot so he could sneak out and ride the Tube. He was lost in the city for hours, finally sneaking back onto the Tube and risking getting caught as a free-farer.

No, that isn't true. The truth must be that he fell in love with her. I had never really been in love with Zard, maybe I have never been in love with anyone. How could I understand? I couldn't stand the thought of leaving the family to marry Zard, how could *he* turn his back on the family for Shusilina? But some alchemy must have transformed him, made him see her as something other than a vain and silly girl—yes, it's a cliché to call her a vain and silly girl, but that's what she was. She was married, and it wasn't very exciting anymore, not nearly as interesting as when her husband was courting her. Fhassin made her feel important, look at the risk he was taking, for her. For her!

But what was going on in Fhassin? Fhassin despised romantic love, sentimentality.

Her husband suspected, laid in wait and caught them, the neighborhood poured out into the street to see my brother, shirtless, protecting Shusilina whose hair was all unbound around her shoulders. Fhassin had a razor, and was holding off her screaming husband. The heat poured all over his brown, adolescent shoulders and chest. We stood in the street, sweating. And Fhassin was laughing, deadly serious, but laughing. He was so alive. Was it the intensity? Was that the lure for Fhassin? This was my brother, who I had known all my life, and he was a stranger.

I realized that the Nekropolis was a foreign place, and I didn't know anyone behind the skinmask of their face.

They took my brother and Shusilina, divorced her from her husband for the adultery trial, and flogged them both, then dumped them in prison for seven years. I did not wait for Zard to ask me to marry him—not that he would have, now. I let my hair go black. I became a dutiful daughter. When I was twenty-one, I was jessed, impressed to feel duty and affection for whoever would pay the fee of my impression.

Akhmim doesn't understand. He has to go. I cry when he's gone.

Finally, after twenty-eight days, I emerge from my room, white and trembling like Iqurth from the tomb, to face the world and my duties. I don't know what the mistress has told Mardin, but I am subjected to a vague lecture I'm sure Mardin thinks of as fatherly. Fadina avoids meeting my eyes when she sees me. The girl who works with the cook watches the floor. I move like a ghost through the woman's quarters. Only the mistress sees me, fastens her eyes on me when I happen to pass her, and her look is cruel. If I hear her, I take to stepping out of the hall if I can.

Friday afternoon, she is playing the Tiles, and I take the cleaning machine to her room. I have checked with Fadina, to confirm that she is not in, but I cannot convince myself that she has left. Perhaps Fadina has forgotten, perhaps the mistress has not told her. I creep in and stand listening. The usual projection is on—not *bismek* but the everyday clutter of silks and fragile tables with silver lace frames, antique lamps, paisley scarves and cobalt pottery. The cleaning machine will not go in. I stop and listen, no sound but the breeze through the window hangings. I creep through the quarters, shaking. The bed is unmade, a tumble of blue and silver brocade. That's unusual, Fadina always makes it. I think about making it, but I decide I had better not, do what I always do or the mistress will be on me. Best do only what is safe. I pick up the clothes off the floor and creep back and turn off the projection. The machine starts.

If she comes back early what will I do? I stand by the projection switch, unwilling to leave even to put the clothing in the laundry. If she comes back, when I hear her, I will snap on the projection machine. The cleaning machine will stop and I will take it and leave. It is the best I can do.

The cleaning machine snuffles around, getting dust from the window sills and table tops, cleaning the floor. It is so slow. I keep thinking I hear her and snapping on the projection. The machine stops and I listen, but I don't hear anything so I snap the projection off and the cleaning machine starts again. Finally the rooms are done, and the cleaning machine and I make our escape. I have used extra scent on the sheets in the linen closet, the way she likes them, and I have put extra oil in the rings on the lights and extra scent in the air freshener. It is all a waste, all that money, but that's what she likes.

I have a terrible headache. I go to my room and wait and try to sleep until the headache is gone. I am asleep when Fadina bangs on my door and I feel groggy and disheveled.

"The mistress wants you," she snaps, glaring at me.

I can't go.

I can't *not* go. I follow her without doing up my hair or putting on my sandals.

The mistress is sitting in her bedroom, still dressed up in saffron and veils. I imagine she has just gotten back. "Diyet," she says, "did you clean my rooms?"

What did I disturb? I didn't do anything to this room except pick up the laundry and run the cleaning machine; is something missing? "Yes, mistress," I say. Oh, my heart.

"Look at this room," she hisses.

I look, not knowing what I am looking for.

"Look at the bed!"

The bed looks just the same as it did when I came in, blankets and sheets tumbled, shining blue and silver, the scent of her perfume in the cool air.

"Come here," the mistress commands, "kneel down." I kneel down so that I am not taller than she is. She looks at me for a moment, so angry that she doesn't seem able to speak. Then, I see it coming but I can't do anything, up comes her hands and she slaps me. I topple sideways, mostly from surprise. "Are you too stupid to even know to make a bed?"

"Fadina always makes your bed," I say. I should have made it, I should have. Holy One, I am such an idiot.

"So the one time Fadina doesn't do your work you are too lazy to do it yourself?"

"Mistress," I say, "I was afraid to—"

"You *should* be afraid!" she shouts. She slaps me, both sides of my face, and shouts at me, her face close to mine. On and on. I don't listen, it's just sound. Fadina walks me to the door. I am holding my head up, trying to maintain some dignity. "Diyet," Fadina whispers.

"What?" I say, thinking maybe she has realized that it's the mistress, that it's not my fault.

But she just shakes her head, "Try not to upset her, that's all. Just don't upset her." Her face is pleading, she wants me to understand.

Understand what? That she is jessed? As Akhmim says, we are only what we are.

But I understand what it is going to be like now. The mistress hates me, and there's nothing I can do. The only way to escape is to ask Mardin to sell me off, but then I would have to leave Akhmim. And since he's a harni he can't even ride the Tube without someone else providing credit. If I leave, I'll never see him again.

The room is full of whispers. The window is open and the breeze rustles among the paper flowers. There are flowers everywhere, on the dresser, the chairs. Akhmim and I sit in the dark room, lit only by the light from the street. He is sitting with one leg underneath him. Like some animal, a panther, indolent.

"You'll still be young when I'm old," I say.

"No," he says. That is all, just the one word.

"Do you get old?"

"If we live out our natural span. About sixty, sixty-five years."

"Do you get wrinkles? White hair?"

"Some. Our joints get bad, swell, like arthritis. Things go wrong." He is so quiet tonight. Usually he is cheerful.

"You are so patient," I say.

He makes a gesture with his hands, "It does not matter."

"Is it hard for you to be patient?"

"Sometimes," he says. "I feel frustration, anger, fear. But we are bred to be patient."

"What's wrong?" I ask. I sound like a little girl, my voice all breathy.

"I am thinking. You should leave here."

The mistress is always finding something. Nothing I do is right. She pulls my hair, confines me to my room. "I can't," I say, "I'm jessed."

He is so still in the twilight.

"Akhmim," I say, suddenly cruel, "do you want me to go?"

"Harni are not supposed to have 'wants,' " he says, his voice flat. I have never heard him say the word "harni." It sounds obscene. It makes me get up, his voice. It fills me with nervousness, with aimless energy. If he is despairing, what is there for me? I leave the window, brush my fingers across the desk, hearing the flowers rustle. I touch all the furniture, and take an armload of flowers, crisp and cool, and I drop them in his lap. "What?" he says. I take more flowers and throw them over his shoulders. His face is turned up at me, lit by the light from the street, full of wonder. I gather flowers off the chair, drop them on him. There are flowers all over the bed, funeral flowers. He reaches up, flowers spilling off his sleeves, and takes my arms to make me stop, saying, "Diyet, what?" I lean forward and close my eyes.

I wait, hearing the breeze rustle the lilies, the poppies, the roses on the bed. I wait forever. Until he finally kisses me.

He won't do any more than kiss me. Lying among all the crushed flowers he will stroke my face, my hair, he will kiss me, but that is all. "You have to leave," he says, desperately. "You have to tell Mardin, tell him to sell you."

I won't leave. I have nothing to go to.

"Do you love me because you have to? Is it because you are a harni and I am a human and you have to serve me?" I ask.

He shakes his head.

"Do you love me because of us?" I press. There are no words for the questions I am asking him.

"Diyet," he says.

"Do you love the mistress?"

"No," he says.

"You should love the mistress, shouldn't you, but you love me."

"Go home, go to the Nekropolis. Run away," he urges, kissing my throat, tiny little kisses, as if he has been thinking of my throat for a long time.

"Run away? From Mardin? What would I do for the rest of my life? Make paper flowers?"

"What would be wrong with that?"

"Would you come with me?" I ask.

He sighs and raises up on his elbow. "You should not fall in love with me."

This is funny. "This is a fine time to tell me."

"No," he says, "it is true." He counts on his fine fingers, "One, I am a harni, not a human being, and I belong to someone else. Two, I have caused all of your problems, if I had not been here, you would not have had all your troubles. Three, the reason it is wrong for a human to love a harni is because harni-human relationships are bad paradigms for human behavior, they lead to difficulty in dealing with human-to-human relationships—"

"I don't *have* any human-to-human relationships," I interrupt.

"You will, you are just young."

I laugh at him. "Akhmim, you're younger than *I* am! Prescripted wisdom."

"But wisdom nonetheless," he says, solemnly.

"Then why did you kiss me?" I ask.

He sighs. It is such a human thing, that sigh, full of frustration. "Because you are so sad."

"I'm not sad right now," I say. "I'm happy because you are here." I am also nervous. Afraid. Because this is all so strange, and even though I keep telling myself that he's so human, I am afraid that underneath he is really alien, more unknowable than my brother. But I want him to stay with me. And I am happy. Afraid but happy.

My lover. "I want you to be my lover," I say.

"No." He sits up. He is beautiful, even disheveled. I can imagine what I look like. Maybe he does not even like me, maybe he has to act this way because I want it. He runs his fingers through his hair, his earring gleams in the light from the street.

"Do harni fall in love?" I ask.

"I have to go," he says. "We've crushed your flowers." He picks up a lily whose long petals have become twisted and crumpled and tries to straighten it out.

"I can make more. Do you have to do this because I want you to?"

"No," he says very quietly. Then more clearly, like a recitation, "Harni don't have feelings, not in the sense that humans do. We are loyal, flexible, and affectionate."

"That makes you sound like a smart dog," I say, irritated.

"Yes," he says, "that is what I am, a smart dog, a very smart dog. Good night, Diyet."

When he opens the door, the breeze draws and the flowers rustle, and some tumble off the bed, trying to follow him.

* * *

"Daughter," Mardin says, "I am not sure that this is the best situation for you."
He looks at me kindly. I wish Mardin did not think that he had to be my father.

"Mardin-salah?" I say, "I don't understand, has my work been unsatisfactory?" Of course my work has been unsatisfactory, the mistress hates me. But I am afraid they have somehow realized what is between Akhmim and me—although I don't know how they could. Akhmim is avoiding me again.

"No, no," he waves his hand airily, "your accounts are in order, you have been a good and frugal girl. It is not your fault."

"I . . . I am aware that I have been clumsy, that perhaps I have not always understood what the mistress wished, but Mardin-salah, I am improving!" I am getting better at ignoring her, I mean. I don't want him to feel inadequate. Sitting here, I realize the trouble I've caused him. He hates having to deal with the household in any but the most perfunctory way. I am jessed to this man, his feelings matter to me. Rejection of my services is painful. This has been a good job, I have been able to save some of my side money so that when I am old I won't be like my mother, forced to struggle and hope that the children will be able to support her when she can't work anymore.

Mardin is uncomfortable. The part of me that is not jessed can see that this is not the kind of duty that Mardin likes. This is not how he sees himself; he prefers to be the benevolent patriarch. "Daughter," he says, "you have been exemplary, but wives. . . ." he sighs. "Sometimes, child, they get whims, and it is better for me, and for you, if we find you some good position with another household."

At least he hasn't said anything about Akhmim. I bow my head because I am afraid I will cry. I study my toes. I try not to think of Akhmim. Alone again. Oh Holy One, I am so tired of being alone. I will be alone my whole life, jessed women do not marry. I cannot help it, I start to cry. Mardin takes it as a sign of my loyalty and pats me gently on the shoulder. "There, there, child, it will be all right."

I don't want Mardin to comfort me. The part of me that watches, that isn't jessed, doesn't even really *like* Mardin—but at the same time, I want to make him happy, so I gamely sniff and try to smile. "I, I know you know what is best," I manage. But my distress makes him uncomfortable. So he says when arrangements are made he will tell me.

I look for Akhmim, to tell him, but he stays in the men's side of the house, away from the middle where we eat, and far away from the women's side.

I begin to understand. He didn't love me, it was just that he was a harni, and it was *me* . . . I led him to myself. Maybe I am no better than Shusilina, with her white hair and pointed ears. So I work, what else is there to do? And I avoid the mistress. Evidently Mardin has told her he is getting rid of me, because the attacks cease. Fadina even smiles at me, if distantly. I would like to make friends with Fadina again, but she doesn't give me a chance. So I will never see him again. He isn't even that far from me, and I will never see him again.

There is nothing to be done about it. Akhmim avoids me. I look across the courtyard or across the dining room at the men's side, but I almost never see him. Once in awhile he's there, with his long curly hair and his black gazelle eyes, but he doesn't look at me.

I pack my things. My new mistress comes. She is a tall, gray-haired woman with slightly pop-eyes. She has a breathy voice and a way of hunching her shoulders as if she wished she were actually a very small woman. I am supposed to give her my life? It is monstrous.

We are in Mardin's office. I am upset. I want desperately to leave, I am so afraid of coming into a room and finding the mistress. I am trying not to think of Akhmim. But what is most upsetting is the thought of leaving Mardin. Will the next girl understand that he wants to pretend that he is frugal, but that he really is not? I am nearly overwhelmed by shame because I have caused this. I am only leaving because of my own foolishness, and I have failed Mardin, who only wanted peace.

I will not cry. These are impressed emotions. Soon I will feel them for this strange woman. Oh Holy, what rotten luck to have gotten this woman for a mistress. She wears bronze and white—bronze was all the fashion when I first came and the mistress wore it often—but this is years after and these are second-rate clothes, a young girl's clothes and not suited to my mistress at all. She is nervous, wanting me to like her, and all I want to do is throw myself at Mardin's feet and embarrass him into saying that I can stay.

Mardin says, "Diyet, she has paid the fee." He shows me the credit transaction and I see that the fee is lower than it was when I came to Mardin's household. "I order you to accept this woman as your new mistress."

That's it. That's the trigger. I feel a little disoriented. I never really noticed how the skin under Mardin's jaw was soft and lax. He is actually rather nondescript. I wonder what it must be like for the mistress to have married him. She is tall and vivid, if a bit heavy, and was a beauty in her day. She must find him disappointing. No wonder she is bitter.

My new mistress smiles tentatively. Well, she may not be fashionable, the way my old mistress was, but she looks kind. I hope so, I would like to live in a kind household. I smile back at her.

That is it. I am impressed.

My new household is much smaller than the old one. The mistress' last housekeeper was clearly inefficient. I am busy for days, just trying to put things in order. I must be frugal, there is much less money in this house. It is surprising how much I have gotten accustomed to money at Mardin's house; this is much more like I grew up.

I do inventories of the linens and clean all the rooms from top to bottom. At first I am nervous, but my new mistress is not like the old one at all. She watches me work as if astounded, and she is never offended if she walks in her room and I have the cleaning machine going. I learn not to work too much around her, she is oddly sensitive about it. She won't say anything, but she will start to make funny little embarrassed/helpful gestures, or suggest that I get myself some tea. Her husband is an old man. He smiles at me and tells me very bad jokes, puns, and I have to laugh to be polite. I would like to avoid him because he bores me nearly to tears. They have a daughter who is a terror. She is in trouble all the time. She spends money, takes her mother's credit chip without asking—they have been forced to put a governor on daily purchases and they are in the process of locking the girl out of the parents' credit.

The daughter is nice enough to me, but her politeness is false. She argues with her mother about spending money on getting a jessed servant instead of sending her to school. But the daughter's marks at academy are dreadful and the mistress says she will not waste money on more.

Akhmim. I think of him all the time.

Emboldened by my mistress' approval, I rearrange the furniture. I take some things she has—they are not very nice—and put them up. I re-program the household AI. It is very limited, insufficient for anything as complicated as *bismek*, but it can handle projections, of course. I remember the things my old mistress used to like and I put around cobalt blue vases and silver framed pictures. Marble floors would overwhelm these rooms, but the tile I pick is nice.

My days are free on Tuesday and half-a-day Sunday. Tuesday my mistress apologizes to me. They are a little tight on credit and she cannot advance my leisure allowance until Sunday, do I mind?

Well, a little, but I say I don't. I spend the afternoon making flowers.

When I make flowers I think of Akhmim and myself on the bed surrounded by crushed carnations and iris. It isn't good to think about Akhmim, he doesn't miss me, I'm sure. He is a harni, always an owned thing, subject to the whims of his owners. If they had constructed him with lasting loyalties, his life would be horrible. Surely when the technician constructed his genes, he made certain that Akhmim would forget quickly. He told me that harni do not love. But he also told me that they did. And he told he didn't love the old mistress, but maybe he only said that because he had to, because I did not love the old mistress and his duty is to make humans happy.

I put the flowers in a vase. My mistress is delighted, she thinks they are lovely.

Long lilies, spiked stamens and long petals like lolling tongues. Sometimes feelings are in me that have no words, and I look at the paper flowers and want to rip them to pieces.

On Sunday, my mistress has my leisure allowance. Mardin used to add a little something extra, but I realize that in my new circumstances I can't expect that. I go to the Moussin of the White Falcon, on the edge of the Nekropolis, to listen to the service.

Then I take the tube to the street of Mardin's house. I don't even intend to walk down the street, but of course I do. And I stand outside the house, looking for a sign of Akhmim. I'm afraid to stand long, I don't want anyone to see me. What would I tell them, that I'm homesick? I'm jessed.

I like to take something to do on the tube, so the ride is not so boring. I have brought a bag full of paper to make flowers. I think I'll earn a little money on the side by making wreaths. I am not allowed to give it to my mistress, that's against the law. It's to protect the jessed that this is true.

In the Nekropolis, we lived in death houses, surrounded by death. Perhaps it isn't odd that I'm a bit morbid, and perhaps that is why I pull a flower out of my bag and leave it on a window sill on the men's side of the house. After all, something did die, although I can't put in words exactly what it was. I don't really know which window is Akhmim's, but it doesn't matter, it's just a gesture. It only makes me feel foolish.

Monday I wake early and drink hot, strong mate. I take buckets of water and scrub down the stone courtyard. I make a list of all the repairs that need to be done. I take the mistress' printouts and bundle them. She saves them, she subscribes to several services and she feels that they might be useful. My old mistress would have quite a lot to say about someone who would save printouts. The mistress goes out to shop, and I clean everything in her storage. She has clothes she should throw out, things fifteen years old and hopelessly out of date. (I remember when I wore my hair white. And later when we used to wrap our hair in veils, the points trailing to the backs of our knees. We looked so foolish, so affected. What are young girls wearing now? How did I get to be so old, I'm not even thirty.)

I put aside all the things I should mend, but I don't want to sit yet. I run the cleaning machine, an old clumsy thing even stupider than the one at Mardin's. I push myself all day, a whirlwind. There is not enough in this house to do, even if I clean the cleaning machine, so I clean some rooms twice.

Still, when it is time to sleep, I can't. I sit in my room making a funeral wreath of carnations and tiny, half-open roses. The white roses gleam like satin.

I wake up on my free day, tired and stiff. In the mirror, I look ghastly, my hair tangled and my eyes puffy. Just as well the harni never saw me like this, I think. But I won't think of Akhmim any more. That part of my life is over, and I have laid a flower at its death house. Today I will take my funeral wreaths around and see if I can find a shop that will buy them. They are good work, surely someone will be interested. It would just be pocket money, take a little of the strain off my mistress, she would not feel then as if she wasn't providing extras for me if I can provide them for myself.

I take the tube all the way to the Nekropolis, carefully protecting my wreaths from the other commuters. All day I walk through the Nekropolis, talking to stall keepers, stopping sometimes for tea, and when I have sold the wreaths, sitting for awhile to watch the people, letting my tired mind empty.

I am at peace, now I can go back to my mistress.

The Mashahana tells us that the darkness in ourselves is a sinister thing. It waits until we relax, it waits until we reach the most vulnerable moments, and then it snares us. I want to be dutiful, I want to do what I should. But when I go back to the tube, I think of where I am going; to that small house and my empty room. What will I do tonight? Make more paper flowers, more wreaths? I am sick of them. Sick of the Nekropolis.

I can take the tube to my mistress' house, or I can go by the street where Mardin's house is. I'm tired, I'm ready to go to my little room and relax. Oh, Holy One, I dread the empty evening. Maybe I should go by the street just to fill up time. I have all this empty time in front of me. Tonight and tomorrow and the week after and the next month and down through the years as I never marry and become a dried-up woman. Evenings spent folding paper. Days clean-ing someone else's house. Free afternoons spent shopping a bit, stopping in tea shops because my feet hurt. That is what lives *are*, aren't they? Attempts to fill our time with activity designed to prevent us from realizing that there *is* no meaning? I sit at a tiny table the size of a serving platter and watch the boys hum by on their scooters, girls sitting behind them, clutching their waists with one hand, holding their veils with the other, while the ends stream and snap behind them, glittering with the shimmer of gold (this year's fashion).

So I get off the tube and walk to the street where Mardin lives. And I walk up the street past the house. I stop and look at it. The walls are pale yellow stone. I am wearing rose and sky blue, but I have gone out without ribbons on my wrists.

"Diyet," Akhmim says, leaning on the window sill, "you're still sad."

He looks so familiar and it is so easy, as if we do this every evening. "I live a sad life," I say, my voice even. But my heart is pounding. To see him! To talk to him!

"I found your token," he says.

"My token," I repeat, not understanding.

"The flower. I thought today would be your free day so I tried to watch all day. I thought you had come and I missed you." Then he disappears for a moment, and then he is sitting on the window sill, legs and feet outside, and he jumps lightly to the ground.

I take him to a tea shop. People look at us, wondering what a young woman is doing unescorted with a young man. Let them look. "Order what you want," I say, "I have some money."

"Are you happier?" he asks. "You don't look happier, you look tired."

And he looks perfect, as he always does. Have I fallen in love with him precisely because he *isn't* human? I don't care, I feel love, no matter what the reason. Does a reason for a feeling matter? The feeling I have for my mistress may be there only because I am impressed, but the *feeling* is real enough.

"My mistress is kind," I say, looking at the table. His perfect hand, beautiful nails and long fingers, lies there.

"Are you happy?" he asks again.

"Are you?" I ask.

He shrugs. "A harni does not have the right to be happy or unhappy."

"Neither do I," I say.

"That's *your* fault. Why did you do it?" he asks. "Why did you choose to be jessed? You were free." His voice is bitter.

"It's hard to find work in the Nekropolis, and I didn't think I would ever get married."

He shakes his head. "Someone would marry you. And if they didn't, is it so awful not to get married?"

"Is it so awful to be jessed?" I ask.

"Yes."

That is all he says. I suppose to him it looks as if I threw everything away, but how can he understand how our choices are taken from us? He doesn't even understand freedom and what an illusion it really is.

"Run away," he says.

Leave the mistress? I am horrified. "She needs me, she cannot run that house by herself and I have cost her a great deal of money. She has made sacrifices to buy me."

"You could live in the Nekropolis and make funeral wreaths," he urges. "You could talk to whomever you wished and no one would order you around."

"I don't want to live in the Nekropolis," I say.

"Why not?"

"There is nothing there for me!"

"You have friends there."

"I wouldn't if I ran away."

"Make new ones," he says.

"Would you go?" I ask.

He shakes his head. "I'm not a person, I can't live."

"What if you could make a living, would you run away?"

"Yes," he says, "yes." He squares his shoulders defiantly and looks at me. "If I could be human, I would be." He is shaming me.

Our tea comes. My face is aflame with color, I don't know what to say. I don't know what to think. He feels morally superior. He thinks he knows the true worth of something I threw away. He doesn't understand, not at all.

"Oh Diyet," he says softly, "I am sorry. I shouldn't say these things to you."

"I didn't think you could have these feelings," I whisper.

He shrugs again. "I can have any feelings," he says. "Harni aren't jessed."

"You told me to think of you as a dog," I remind him. "Loyal."

"I am loyal," he says. "You didn't ask who I was loyal to."

"You're supposed to be loyal to the mistress."

He drums the table with his fingers, *taptaptaptap*, *taptaptaptap*. "Harni aren't like geese," he says, not looking at me. His earring is golden, he is rich and fine-looking. I had not realized at my new place how starved I had become for fine things. "We don't impress on the first person we see." Then he shakes his head. "I shouldn't talk about all this nonsense. You must go, I must go back before they miss me."

"We have to talk more," I say.

"We have to go," he insists. Then he smiles at me and all the unhappiness disappears from his face. He doesn't seem human anymore, he seems pleasant; *harni*. I get a chill. He is so alien. I understand him less than I understand people like my old mistress. We get up and he looks away as I pay.

Outside Mardin's house I tell him, "I'll come back next Tuesday."

It's good I did so much before, because I sleepwalk through the days. I leave the cleaning machine in the doorway where the mistress almost trips over it. I forget to set the clothes in order. I don't know what to think.

I hear the mistress say to the neighbor, "She is a godsend, but so moody. One day she's doing everything, the next day she can't be counted on to remember to set the table."

What right does she have to talk about me that way? Her house was a pigsty when I came.

What am I thinking? What is wrong with me that I blame my mistress? Where is my head? I feel ill, my eyes water and head fills. I can't breathe, I feel heavy. I must be dutiful. I used to have this feeling once in a while when I was first jessed, it's part of the adjustment. It must be the change. I have to adjust all over again.

I find the mistress, tell her I'm not feeling well, and go lie down.

The next afternoon, just before dinner, it happens again. The day after that is fine, but then it happens at mid-morning of the third day. It is Sunday and I have the afternoon off. I force myself to work through the morning. My voice is hoarse, my head aches. I want to get everything ready since I won't be there to see to dinner in the afternoon. White cheese and olives and tomatoes on a platter. My stomach rebels and I have to run to the bathroom.

What is wrong with me?

I go to the moussin in the afternoon, lugging my bag, which is heavy with paper, and sit in the cool dusty darkness, nursing my poor head. I feel as if I should pray. I should ask for help, for guidance. The moussin is so old that the stone is irregularly worn, and through my slippers I can feel the little ridges and valleys in the marble. Up around the main worship hall here are galleries hidden by arabesques of scrollwork. Kari and I used to sit up there when we were children. Above that, sunlight flashes through clerestory windows. Where the light hits the marble floor it shines hard, hurting my eyes and my head. I rest my forehead on my arm, turned sideways on the bench so I can lean on the back. With my eyes closed I smell incense and my own scent of perfume and perspiration.

There are people there for service, but no one bothers me. Isn't that amazing?

Or maybe it is only because anyone can see that I am impure.

I get tired of my own melodrama. I keep thinking that people are looking at me, that someone is going to say something to me. I don't know where to go.

I don't even pretend to think of going back to my room. I get on the tube and go to Mardin's house. I climb the stairs from the tube—these are newer, but, like the floor of the moussin, they are unevenly worn, sagging in the centers from the weight of this crowded city. What would it be like to cross the sea and go north? To the peninsula, Ida, or north from there, into the continent? I used to want to travel, to go to a place where people had yellow hair, to see whole forests of trees. Cross the oceans, learn other languages. I told Kari that I would even like to taste dog, or swine, but she thought I was showing off. But it's true, once I would have liked to try things.

I am excited, full of energy and purpose. I can do anything. I can understand Fhassin, standing in the street with his razor, laughing. It is worth it, anything is worth it for this feeling of being alive. I have been jessed, I have been asleep for so long.

There are people on Mardin's street. It's Sunday and people are visiting. I stand in front of the house across the street. What am I going to say if someone opens the door? I am waiting to meet a friend. What if they don't leave, what if Akhmim sees them and doesn't come out. The sun bakes my hair, my head. Akhmim, where are you? Look out the window. He is probably waiting on the mistress. Maybe there is a *bismek* party and those women are poisoning Akhmim. They could do anything, they *own* him. I want to crouch in the street and cover my head in my hands, rock and cry like a widow woman from the Nekropolis. Like my mother must have done when my father died. I grew up without a father, maybe that's why I'm so wild. Maybe that's why Fhassin is in prison and I'm headed there. I pull my veil up so my face is shadowed. So no one can see my tears.

Oh my head. Am I drunk? Am I insane? Has the Holy One, seeing my thoughts, driven me mad?

I look at my brown hands. I cover my face.

"Diyet?" He takes my shoulders.

I look up at him, his beautiful familiar face, and I am stricken with terror. What is he? What am I trusting my life, my future to?

"What's wrong," he asks, "are you ill?"

"I'm going insane," I say. "I can't stand it, Akhmim, I can't go back to my room—"

"Hush," he says, looking up the street and down. "You have to. I'm only a harni. I can't do anything, I can't help you."

"We have to go. We have to go away somewhere, you and I."

He shakes his head. "Diyet, please. You must hush."

"You said you wanted to be free," I say. My head hurts so bad. The tears keep coming even though I am not really crying.

"I can't be free," he says. "That was just talk."

"I have to go now," I say. "I'm jessed, Akhmim, it is hard, if I don't go now I'll never go."

"Your mistress—"

"DON'T TALK ABOUT HER!" I shout. If he talks about her I may not be able to leave.

He looks around again. We are a spectacle, a man and a woman on the street.

"Come with me, we'll go somewhere, talk," I say, all honey. He cannot deny me, I see it in him. He has to get off the street. He would go anywhere. Any place is safer than this.

He lets me take him into the tube, down the stairs to the platform. I clutch my indigo veil around my face. We wait in silence, he has his hands in his pockets. He looks like a boy from the Nekropolis, standing there in just his shirt, no outer robe. He looks away, shifts his weight from one foot to the other, ill at ease. So human. Events are making him more human. Taking away all the uncertainties.

"What kind of genes are in you?" I ask.

"What?" he asks.

"What kinds of genes?"

"Are you asking for my chart?" he says.

I shake my head. "Human?"

He shrugs. "Mostly. Some artificial sequences."

"No animal genes," I say. I sound irrational because I can't get clear what I mean. The headache makes my thoughts skip, my tongue thick.

He smiles a little. "No dogs, no monkeys."

I smile back, he is teasing me. I am learning to understand when he teases. "I have some difficult news for you, Akhmim. I think you are a mere human being."

His smile vanishes. He shakes his head. "Diyet," he says. He is about to talk like a father.

I stop him with a gesture. My head still hurts.

The train whispers in, sounding like wind. Oh the lights. I sit down, shading my eyes, and he stands in front of me. I can feel him looking down at me. I look up and smile, or maybe grimace. He smiles back, looking worried. At the Moussin of the White Falcon, we get off. Funny that we are going into a cemetery to live. But only for awhile, I think. Somehow I will find a way we can leave. We'll go north, across the sea, up to the continent, where we'll be strangers. I take him through the streets and stop in front of a row of death houses, like the Lachims', but an inn. I give Akhmim money and tell him to rent us a place for the night. "Tell them your wife is sick," I whisper.

"I don't have any credit. If they take my identification, they'll know," he says.

"This is the Nekropolis," I say. "They don't use credit. Go on. Here you are a man."

He frowns at me but takes the money. I watch him out of the corner of my eye, bargaining, pointing at me. Just pay, I think, even though we have so little money. I just want to lie down, to sleep. And finally he comes out and takes me by the hand and leads me to our place. A tiny place of rough whitewashed walls, a bed, a chair, a pitcher of water and two glasses. "I have something for your head," he says. "The man gave it to me." He smiles ruefully. "He thinks you are pregnant."

My hand shakes when I hold it out. He puts the white pills in my hand and pours a glass of water for me. "I'll leave you here," he says. "I'll go back. I won't tell anyone that I know where you are."

"Then you were lying to me," I say. I don't want to argue, Akhmim, just stay until tomorrow. Then it will be too late. "You said if you could be free, you would. You *are* free."

"What can I do? I can't live," he says in anguish. "I can't get work!"

"You can sell funeral wreaths. I'll make them."

He looks torn. It is one thing to think how you will act, another to be in the situation and do it. And I know, seeing his face, that he really is human, because his problem is a very human problem. Safety or freedom.

"We will talk about it tomorrow," I say. "My head is aching."

"Because you are jessed," he says. "It is so dangerous. What if we don't make enough money? What if they catch us?"

"That is life," I say. I will go to prison. He will be sent back to the mistress. Punished. Maybe made to be conscript labor.

"Is it worth the pain?" he asks in a small voice.

I don't know, but I can't say that. "Not when you have the pain," I say, "but afterward it is."

"Your poor head." He strokes my forehead. His hand is cool and soothing.

"It's all right," I say. "It hurts to be born."

MARGIN OF ERROR

Nancy Kress

Born in Buffalo, New York, Nancy Kress now lives in Brockport, New York. She began selling her elegant and incisive stories in the mid-seventies, and has since become a frequent contributor to *Asimov's Science Fiction*, *The Magazine of Fantasy & Science Fiction*, *Omni*, and elsewhere. Her books include the novels *The Prince of Morning Bells*, *The Golden Grove*, *The White Pipes*, *An Alien Light*, and *Brain Rose*, and the collection *Trinity and Other Stories*. She is also a regular contributor to *Writer's Digest* and has written one book on fiction writing, *Beginnings*, *Middles and Ends*. Her most recent books are the novel version of her Hugo and Nebula-winning story, *Beggars in Spain*, a sequel, *Beggars and Choosers*, and a new collection, *The Aliens of Earth*. She has also won a Nebula Award for her story "Out of All Them Bright Stars." She has had stories in our Second, Third, Sixth, Seventh, Eighth, Ninth, Tenth, and Eleventh Annual Collections.

In the chilling little story that follows, she reaffirms the truth of that old saying about revenge. It *is* a dish best served cold.

Paula came back in a blaze of glory, her institute uniform with its pseudomilitary medals crisp and bright, her spine straight as an engineered diamond-fiber rod. I heard her heels clicking on the sidewalk and I looked up from the bottom porch step, a child on my lap. Paula's face was genemod now, the blemishes gone, the skin fine-pored, the cheekbones chiseled under green eyes. But I would have known that face anywhere. No matter what she did to it.

"Karen?" Her voice held disbelief.

"Paula," I said.

"*Karen?*" This time I didn't answer. The child, my oldest, twisted in my arms to eye the visitor.

It was the kind of neighborhood where women sat all morning on porches or stoops, watching children play on the sidewalk. Steps sagged; paint peeled; small front lawns were scraped bare by feet and tricycles and plastic wading pools. Women lived a few doors down from their mothers, both of them growing heavier every year. There were few men. The ones there were didn't seem to stay long.

I said, "How did you find me?"

"It wasn't hard," Paula said, and I knew she didn't understand my smile.

Of course it wasn't hard. I had never intended it should be. This was undoubtedly the first time in nearly five years that Paula had looked.

She lowered her perfect body onto the porch steps. My little girl, Lollie, gazed at her from my lap. Then Lollie opened her cupped hands and smiled. "See my frog, lady?"

"Very nice," Paula said. She was trying hard to hide her contempt, but I could see it. For the sad imprisoned frog, for Lollie's dirty face, for the worn yard, for the way I looked.

"Karen," Paula said, "I'm here because there's a problem. With the project. More specifically with the initial formulas, we think. With a portion of the nanoassembler code from five years ago, when you were . . . still with us."

"A problem," I repeated. Inside the house, a baby wailed. "Just a minute."

I set Lollie down and went inside. Lori cried in her crib. Her diaper reeked. I put a pacifier in her mouth and cradled her in my left arm. With the right arm I scooped Timmy from his crib. When he didn't wake, I jostled him a little. I carried both babies back to the porch, deposited Timmy in the portacrib, and sat down next to Paula.

"Lollie, go get me a diaper, honey. And wipes. You can carry your frog inside to get them."

Lollie went; she's a sweet-natured kid. Paula stared incredulously at the twins. I unwrapped Lori's diaper and Paula grimaced and slid farther away.

"Karen . . . are you listening to me? This is *important*!"

"I'm listening."

"The nanocomputer instructions are off, somehow. The major results check out, obviously . . ." *Obviously*. The media had spent five years exclaiming over the major results. ". . . but there are some odd foldings in the proteins of the twelfth-generation nanoassemblers." Twelfth generation. The nanocomputer attached to each assembler replicates itself every six months. That was one of the project's checks and balances on the margin of error. It had been five and a half years. Twelfth generation was about right.

"Also," Paula continued, and I heard the strain in her voice, "there are some unforeseen macrolevel developments. We're not sure yet that they're tied to the nanocomputer protein folds. What we're trying to do now is cover all the variables."

"You must be working on fairly remote variables if you're reduced to asking me."

"Well, yes, we are. Karen, do you have to do that *now*?"

"Yes." I scraped the shit off Lori with one edge of the soiled diaper. Lollie danced out of the house with a clean one. She sat beside me, whispering to her frog. Paula said, "What I need . . . what the project needs . . ."

I said, "Do you remember the summer we collected frogs? We were maybe eight and ten. You'd become fascinated reading about that experiment where they threw a frog in boiling water but it jumped out, and then they put a frog in cool water and gradually increased the temperature to boiling until the stupid frog just sat there and died. Remember?"

"Karen . . ."

"I collected sixteen frogs for you, and when I found out what you were going to do with them, I cried and tried to let them go. But you boiled eight of them anyway. The other eight were controls. I'll give you that—proper scientific method. To reduce the margin of error, you said."

"Karen . . . we were just kids . . ."

I put the clean diaper on Lori. "Not all kids behave like that. Lollie doesn't. But you wouldn't know that, would you? Nobody in your set has children. You should have had a baby, Paula." She barely hid her shudder. But, then, most of the people we knew felt the same way. She said, "What the project needs is for you to come back and work on the same small area you did originally. Looking for something—anything—you might have missed in the proteincoded instructions to successive generations of nanoassemblers."

"No," I said.

"It's not really a matter of choice. The macrolevel problems—I'll be frank, Karen. It looks like a new form of cancer. Unregulated replication of some very weird cells."

"So take the cellular nanomachinery out." I crumpled the stinking diaper and set it out of the baby's reach. Closer to Paula.

"You know we can't do that! The project's irreversible!"

"Many things are irreversible," I said. Lori started to fuss. I picked her up, opened my blouse, and gave her the breast. She sucked greedily. Paula glanced away. She has had nanomachinery in her perfect body, making it perfect, for five years now. Her breasts will never look swollen, blue-veined, sagging.

"Karen, listen . . ."

"No . . . you listen." I said quietly. "Eight years ago you convinced Zweigler I was only a minor member of the research team, included only because I was your sister. I've always wondered, by the way, how you did that—were you sleeping with him, too? Seven years ago you got me shunted off into the minor area of the project's effect on female gametes—which nobody cared about because it was already clear there was no way around sterility as a side effect. Nobody thought it was too high a price for a perfect, self-repairing body, did they? Except me." Paula didn't answer. Lollie carried her frog to the wading pool and set it carefully in the water. I said, "I didn't mind working on female gametes, even if it was a backwater, even if you got star billing. I was used to it, after all. As kids, you were always the cowboy; I got to be the horse. You were the astronaut, I was the alien you conquered. Remember? One Christmas you used up all the chemicals in your first chemistry set and then stole mine."

"I don't think trivial childhood incidents matter in . . ."

"Of course you don't. And I never minded. But I did mind when five years ago you made copies of all my notes and presented them as yours, while I was so sick during my pregnancy with Lollie. You claimed *my* work. Stole it. Just like the chemistry set. And then you eased me off the project."

"What you did was so minor . . ."

"If it was so minor, why are you here asking for my help now? And why would you imagine for half a second I'd give it to you?" She stared at me, calculating. I stared back coolly. Paula wasn't used to me cool. I'd always been

the excitable one. Excitable, flighty, unstable—that's what she told Zweigler.
A security risk.

Timmy fussed in his portacrib. I stood up, still nursing Lori, and scooped
him up with my free arm. Back on the steps, I juggled Timmy to lie across Lori
on my lap, pulled back my blouse, and gave him the other breast. This time
Paula didn't permit herself a grimace.

She said, "Karen, what I did was wrong. I know that now. But for the sake
of the project, not for me, you have to . . ."

"You *are* the project. You have been from the first moment you grabbed the
headlines away from Zweigler and the others who gave their life to that work.
'Lovely Young Scientist Injects Self With Perfect-Cell Drug!' 'No Sacrifice Too
Great To Circumvent FDA Shortsightedness, Heroic Researcher Declares.' "

Paula said flatly, "You're jealous. You're obscure and I'm famous. You're
a mess and I'm beautiful. You're . . ."

"A milk cow? While you're a brilliant researcher? Then solve your own
research problems."

"This was your area . . ."

"Oh, Paula, they were *all* my areas. I did more ᴏf the basic research than
you did, and you know it. But you knew how to position yourself with Zweigler,
to present key findings at key moments, to cultivate the right connections. And,
of course, I was still under the delusion we were partners. I just didn't realize
it was a barracuda partnering a goldfish."

From the wading pool Lollie watched us with big eyes. "Mommy . . ."

"It's okay, honey. Mommy's not mad at you. Look, better catch your frog—
he's hopping away."

She shrieked happily and dove for the frog. Paula said softly, "I had no idea
you were so angry after all this time. You've changed, Karen."

"But I'm not angry. Not any more. And you never knew what I was like
before. You never bothered to know."

"I knew you never wanted a scientific life. Not the way I did. You always
wanted kids. Wanted . . . *this*." She waved her arm around the shabby yard.
David left eighteen months ago. He sends money. It's never enough.

"I wanted a scientific establishment that would let me have both. And I wanted
credit for my work. I wanted what was mine. How did you do it, Paula—end
up with what was yours and what was mine, too?"

"Because you were distracted by baby shit and frogs!" Paula yelled, and I
saw how scared she really was. Paula didn't make admissions like that. A tactical
error. I watched her stab desperately for a way to retain the advantage. A way
to seize the offensive. I seized it first. "You should have left David alone. You
already had Zweigler; you should have left me David. Our marriage was never
the same after that."

She said, "I'm dying, Karen."

I turned my head from the nursing babies to look at her.

"It's true. My cellular machinery is running wild. The nanoassemblers are
creating weird structures, destructive enzymes. For five years they replicated
perfectly and now. . . . For five years it all performed *exactly* as it was programmed to . . ."

I said, "It still does."

Paula sat very still. Lori had fallen asleep. I juggled her into the portacrib and nestled Timmy more comfortably on my lap. Lollie chased her frog around the wading pool. I squinted to see if Lollie's lips were blue.

Paula choked out, "You programmed the assembler machinery in the ovaries to . . ."

"Nobody much cares about women's ovaries. Only fourteen percent of college-educated women want to muck up their lives with kids. Recent survey result. Less than one percent margin of error."

". . . you actually sabotaged . . . hundreds of women have been injected by now, maybe *thousands* . . ."

"Oh, there's a reverser enzyme," I said. "Completely effective if you take it before the twelfth-generation replication. You're the only person that's been injected that long. I just discovered the reverser a few months ago, tinkering with my old notes for something to do in what your friends probably call my idle domestic prison. That's provable, incidentally. All my notes are computer-dated."

Paula whispered, "Scientists don't *do* this . . ."

"Too bad you wouldn't let me be one."

"Karen . . ."

"Don't you want to know what the reverser is, Paula? It's engineered from human chorionic gonadotropin. The pregnancy hormone. Too bad you never wanted a baby."

She went on staring at me. Lollie shrieked and splashed with her frog. Her lips *were* turning blue. I stood up, laid Timmy next to Lori in the portacrib, and buttoned my blouse.

"You made an experimental error twenty-five years ago," I said to Paula. "Too small a sample population. Sometimes a frog jumps out."

I went to lift my daughter from the wading pool.

CILIA-OF-GOLD

Stephen Baxter

One of the young SF writers who are revitalizing the ''hard-science'' story here at the beginning of the nineties, British writer Stephen Baxter is fast making a reputation for himself as an author whose work often pushes the Cutting Edge of science. He writes genuinely ''hard'' SF which also treats the reader to the kind of immense vistas, cosmic scope, and fast-paced action associated with the Superscience space opera writers of yesteryear. Baxter made his first sale to *Interzone* in 1987, and since then has become one of that magazine's most frequent contributors, as well as making sales to *Asimov's Science Fiction, Zenith, New Worlds,* and elsewhere. His first novel, *Raft,* was released in 1991 to wide and enthusiastic response, and has been followed with two more novels, *Timelike Infinity, Anti-Ice,* and *Ring.* A new novel, *Flux,* has just been published, and *another* new novel, *The Time Ships,* has just been published in England.

Here he takes us to a mining colony on Mercury, in company with a trouble-shooting mission that runs into troubles *considerably* more bizarre than anyone could ever have *anticipated* having to deal with . . .

The people—though exhausted by the tunnel's cold—had rested long enough, Cilia-of-Gold decided.

Now it was time to fight.

She climbed up through the water, her flukes pulsing, and prepared to lead the group further along the Ice-tunnel to the new Chimney cavern.

But, even as the people rose from their browsing and crowded through the cold, stale water behind her, Cilia-of-Gold's resolve wavered. The Seeker was a heavy presence inside her. She could *feel* its tendrils wrapped around her stomach, and—she knew—its probes must already have penetrated her brain, her mind, her *self.*

With a beat of her flukes, she thrust her body along the tunnel. She couldn't afford to show weakness. Not now.

''Cilia-of-Gold.''

A broad body, warm through the turbulent water, came pushing out of the crowd to bump against hers: it was Strong-Flukes, one of Cilia-of-Gold's Three-mates. Strong-Flukes's presence was immediately comforting. ''Cilia-of-Gold. I know something's wrong.''

Cilia-of-Gold thought of denying it; but she turned away, her depression deepening. "I couldn't expect to keep secrets from you. Do you think the others are aware?"

The hairlike cilia lining Strong-Flukes's belly barely vibrated as she spoke. "Only Ice-Born suspects something is wrong. And if she didn't, we'd have to tell her." Ice-Born was the third of Cilia-of-Gold's mates.

"I can't afford to be weak, Strong-Flukes. Not now."

As they swam together, Strong-Flukes flipped onto her back. Tunnel water filtered between Strong-Flukes's carapace and her body; her cilia flickered as they plucked particles of food from the stream and popped them into the multiple mouths along her belly. "Cilia-of-Gold," she said. "I *know* what's wrong. You're carrying a Seeker, aren't you?"

" . . . Yes. How could you tell?"

"I love you," Strong-Flukes said. "*That's* how I could tell."

The pain of Strong-Flukes's perception was as sharp, and unexpected, as the moment when Cilia-of-Gold had first detected the signs of the infestation in herself . . . and had realized, with horror, that her life must inevitably end in madness, in a purposeless scrabble into the Ice over the world. "It's still in its early stages, I think. It's like a huge heat, inside me. And I can feel it reaching into my mind. Oh, Strong-Flukes . . ."

"Fight it."

"I can't. I—"

"You can. You *must*."

The end of the tunnel was an encroaching disk of darkness; already Cilia-of-Gold felt the inviting warmth of the Chimney-heated water in the cavern beyond.

This should have been the climax, the supreme moment of Cilia-of-Gold's life.

The group's old Chimney, with its fount of warm, rich water, was failing; and so they had to flee, and fight for a place in a new cavern.

That, or die.

It was Cilia-of-Gold who had found the new Chimney, as she had explored the endless network of tunnels between the Chimney caverns. Thus, it was she who must lead this war—Seeker or no Seeker.

She gathered up the fragments of her melting courage.

"You're the best of us, Cilia-of-Gold," Strong-Flukes said, slowing. "Don't ever forget that."

Cilia-of-Gold pressed her carapace against Strong-Flukes's in silent gratitude.

Cilia-of-Gold turned and clacked her mandibles, signaling the rest of the people to halt. They did so, the adults sweeping the smaller children inside their strong carapaces.

Strong-Flukes lay flat against the floor and pushed a single eyestalk toward the mouth of the tunnel. Her caution was wise; there were species who could home in on even a single sound-pulse from an unwary eye.

After some moments of silent inspection, Strong-Flukes wriggled back along the Ice surface to Cilia-of-Gold.

She hesitated. "We've got problems, I think," she said at last.

The Seeker seemed to pulse inside Cilia-of-Gold, tightening around her gut. "What problems?"

"This Chimney's inhabited already. By *Heads*."

Kevan Scholes stopped the rover a hundred yards short of the wall-mountain's crest.

Irina Larionova, wrapped in a borrowed environment suit, could tell from the tilt of the cabin that the surface here was inclined upward at around forty degrees—shallower than a flight of stairs. This "mountain," heavily eroded, was really little more than a dust-clad hill, she thought.

"The wall of Chao Meng-Fu Crater," Scholes said briskly, his radio-distorted voice tinny. "Come on. We'll walk to the summit from here."

"Walk?" She studied him, irritated. "Scholes, I've had one hour's sleep in the last thirty-six; I've traveled across ninety million miles to get here, via tugs and wormhole transit links—and you're telling me I have to *walk* up this damn hill?"

Scholes grinned through his faceplate. He was AS-preserved at around physical-twenty-five, Larionova guessed, and he had a boyishness that grated on her. *Damn it*, she reminded herself, *this "boy" is probably older than me.*

"Trust me," he said. "You'll love the view. And we have to change transports anyway."

"Why?"

"You'll see."

He twisted gracefully to his feet. He reached out a gloved hand to help Larionova pull herself, awkwardly, out of her seat. When she stood on the cabin's tilted deck, her heavy boots hurt her ankles.

Scholes threw open the rover's lock. Residual air puffed out of the cabin, crystallizing. The glow from the cabin interior was dazzling; beyond the lock, Larionova saw only darkness.

Scholes climbed out of the lock and down to the planet's invisible surface. Larionova followed him awkwardly; it seemed a long way to the lock's single step.

Her boots settled to the surface, crunching softly. The lock was situated between the rover's rear wheels: the wheels were constructs of metal strips and webbing, wide and light, each wheel taller than she was.

Scholes pushed the lock closed, and Larionova was plunged into sudden darkness.

Scholes loomed before her. He was a shape cut out of blackness. "Are you okay? Your pulse is rapid."

She could hear the rattle of her own breath, loud and immediate. "Just a little disoriented."

"We've got all of a third of a gee down here, you know. You'll get used to it. Let your eyes dark-adapt. We don't have to hurry this."

She looked up.

In her peripheral vision, the stars were already coming out. She looked for a bright double star, blue and white. There it was: Earth, with Luna.

And now, with a slow grandeur, the landscape revealed itself to her adjusting eyes. The plain from which the rover had climbed spread out from the foot of the crater wall-mountain. It was a complex patchwork of crowding craters, ridges and scarps—some of which must have been miles high—all revealed as a glimmering tracery in the starlight. The face of the planet seemed *wrinkled*, she thought, as if shrunk with age.

"These wall-mountains are over a mile high," Scholes said. "Up here, the surface is firm enough to walk on; the regolith dust layer is only a couple of inches thick. But down on the plain the dust can be ten or fifteen yards deep. Hence the big wheels on the rover. I guess that's what five billion years of a thousand-degree temperature range does for a landscape. . . ."

Just twenty-four hours ago, she reflected, Larionova had been stuck in a boardroom in New York, buried in one of Superet's endless funding battles. And now this . . . wormhole travel was bewildering. "Lethe's waters," she said. "It's so—desolate."

Scholes gave an ironic bow. "Welcome to Mercury," he said.

Cilia-of-Gold and Strong-Flukes peered down into the Chimney cavern.

Cilia-of-Gold had chosen the cavern well. The Chimney here was a fine young vent, a glowing crater much wider than their old, dying home. The water above the Chimney was turbulent, and richly cloudy; the cavern itself was wide and smooth-walled. Cilia-plants grew in mats around the Chimney's base. Cutters browsed in turn on the cilia-plants, great chains of them, their tough little arms slicing steadily through the plants. Sliding through the plant mats Cilia-of-Gold could make out the supple form of a Crawler, its mindless, tube-like body wider than Cilia-of-Gold's and more than three times as long. . . .

And, stalking around their little forest, here came the Heads themselves, the rulers of the cavern. Cilia-of-Gold counted four, five, six of the Heads, and no doubt there were many more in the dark recesses of the cavern.

One Head—close to the tunnel mouth—swiveled its huge, swollen helmet-skull toward her.

She ducked back into the tunnel, aware that all her cilia were quivering.

Strong-Flukes drifted to the tunnel floor, landing in a little cloud of food particles. *"Heads,"* she said, her voice soft with despair. "We can't fight Heads."

The Heads' huge helmet-skulls were sensitive to heat—fantastically so, enabling the Heads to track and kill with almost perfect accuracy. Heads *were* deadly opponents, Cilia-of-Gold reflected. But the people had nowhere else to go.

"We've come a long way to reach this place, Strong-Flukes. If we had to undergo another journey—" *through more cold, stagnant tunnels* "—many of us couldn't survive. And those who did would be too weakened to fight.

"No. We have to stay here—to *fight* here."

Strong-Flukes groaned, wrapping her carapace close around her. "Then we'll all be killed."

Cilia-of-Gold tried to ignore the heavy presence of the Seeker within her—

and its prompting, growing more insistent now, that she *get away* from all this, from the crowding presence of people—and she forced herself to *think*.

Larionova followed Kevan Scholes up the slope of the wall-mountain. Silicate surface dust compressed under her boots, like fine sand. The climbing was easy—it was no more than a steep walk, really—but she stumbled frequently, clumsy in this reduced gee.

They reached the crest of the mountain. It wasn't a sharp summit: more a wide, smooth platform, fractured to dust by Mercury's wild temperature range.

"Chao Meng-Fu Crater," Scholes said. "A hundred miles wide, stretching right across Mercury's South Pole."

The crater was so large that even from this height its full breadth was hidden by the tight curve of the planet. The wall-mountain was one of a series that swept across the landscape from left to right, like a row of eroded teeth, separated by broad, rubble-strewn valleys. On the far side of the summit, the flanks of the wall-mountain swept down to the plain of the crater, a full mile below.

Mercury's angry sun was hidden beyond the curve of the world, but its corona extended delicate, structured tendrils above the far horizon.

The plain itself was immersed in darkness. But by the milky, diffuse light of the corona, Larionova could see a peak at the center of the plain, shouldering its way above the horizon. There was a spark of light at the base of the central peak, incongruously bright in the crater's shadows: that must be the Thoth team's camp.

"This reminds me of the Moon," she said.

Scholes considered this. "Forgive me, Dr. Larionova. Have you been down to Mercury before?"

"No," she said, his easy, informed arrogance grating on her. "I'm here to oversee the construction of Thoth, not to sightsee."

"Well, there's obviously a superficial similarity. After the formation of the main System objects five billion years ago, all the inner planets suffered bombardment by residual planetesimals. That's when Mercury took its biggest strike: the one which created the Caloris feature. But after that, Mercury was massive enough to retain a molten core—unlike the Moon. Later planetesimal strikes punched holes in the crust, so there were lava outflows that drowned some of the older cratering.

"Thus, on Mercury, you have a mixture of terrains. There's the most ancient landscape, heavily cratered, and the *planitia:* smooth lava plains, punctured by small, young craters.

"Later, as the core cooled, the surface actually shrunk inward. The planet lost a mile or so of radius."

Like a dried-out tomato. "So the surface *is* wrinkled."

"Yes. There are *rupes* and *dorsa:* ridges and lobate scarps, cliffs a couple of miles tall and extending for hundreds of miles. Great climbing country. And in some places there are gas vents, chimneys of residual thermal activity." He turned to her, corona light misty in his faceplate. "So Mercury isn't really so much like the Moon at all. . . . Look. You can see Thoth."

She looked up, following his pointing arm. There, just above the far horizon, was a small blue star.

She had her faceplate magnify the image. The star exploded into a compact sculpture of electric blue threads, surrounded by firefly lights: the Thoth construction site.

Thoth was a habitat to be placed in orbit close to Sol. Irina Larionova was the consulting engineer contracted by Superet to oversee the construction of the habitat.

Thoth's purpose was to find out what was wrong with the Sun.

Recently, anomalies had been recorded in the Sun's behavior; aspects of its interior seemed to be diverging, and widely, from the standard theoretical models. Superet was a loose coalition of interest groups on Earth and Mars, intent on studying problems likely to impact the longterm survival of the human species.

Problems in the interior of mankind's only star clearly came into the category of things of interest to Superet.

Irina Larionova wasn't much interested in any of Superet's semi-mystical philosophizing. It was the work that was important, for her: and the engineering problems posed by Thoth were fascinating.

At Thoth, a Solar-interior probe would be constructed. The probe would be one Interface of a wormhole terminal, loaded with sensors. The Interface would be dropped into the Sun. The other Interface would remain in orbit, at the center of the habitat.

The electric-blue bars she could see now were struts of exotic matter, which would eventually frame the wormhole termini. The sparks of light moving around the struts were GUTships and short-haul tugs. She stared at the image, wishing she could get back to some real work.

Irina Larionova had had no intention of visiting Mercury herself. Mercury was a detail, for Thoth. Why would *anyone* come to Mercury, unless they had to? Mercury was a piece of junk, a desolate ball of iron and rock too close to the Sun to be interesting, or remotely habitable. The two Thoth exploratory teams had come here only to exploit: to see if it was possible to dig raw materials out of Mercury's shallow—and close-at-hand—gravity well, for use in the construction of the habitat. The teams had landed at the South Pole, where traces of water-ice had been detected, and at the Caloris Basin, the huge equatorial crater where—it was hoped—that ancient impact might have brought iron-rich compounds to the surface.

The tugs from Thoth actually comprised the largest expedition ever to land on Mercury.

But, within days of landing, both investigative teams had reported anomalies.

Larionova tapped at her suit's sleeve-controls. After a couple of minutes an image of Dolores Wu appeared in one corner of Larionova's faceplate. *Hi, Irina,* she said, her voice buzzing like an insect in Larionova's helmet's enclosed space.

Dolores Wu was the leader of the Thoth exploratory team in Caloris. Wu was Mars-born, with small features and hair greyed despite AntiSenescence treatments. She looked weary.

"How's Caloris?" Larionova asked.

Well, we don't have much to report yet. We decided to start with a detailed gravimetric survey . . .

"And?"

We found the impact object. We think. It's as massive as we thought, but much—much—too small, Irina. It's barely a mile across, way too dense to be a planetesimal fragment.

"A black hole?"

No. Not dense enough for that.

"Then what?"

Wu looked exasperated. *We don't know yet, Irina. We don't have any answers. I'll keep you informed.*

Wu closed off the link.

Standing on the corona-lit wall of Chao Meng-Fu Crater, Larionova asked Kevan Scholes about Caloris.

"Caloris is *big*," he said. "Luna has no impact feature on the scale of Caloris. And Luna has nothing like the Weird Country in the other hemisphere . . ."

"The what?"

A huge planetesimal—or *something*—had struck the equator of Mercury, five billion years ago, Scholes said. The Caloris Basin—an immense, ridged crater system—formed around the primary impact site. Whatever caused the impact was still buried in the planet, somewhere under the crust, dense and massive; the object was a gravitational anomaly which had helped lock Mercury's rotation into synchronization with its orbit.

"Away from Caloris itself, shock waves spread around the planet's young crust," Scholes said. "The waves focused at Caloris' antipode—the point on the equator diametrically opposite Caloris itself. And the land there was shattered, into a jumble of bizarre hill and valley formations. *The Weird Country.* . . . Hey. Dr. Larionova."

She could *hear* that damnable grin of Schole's. "What now?" she snapped.

He walked across the summit toward her. "Look up," he said.

"Damn it, Scholes—"

There was a pattering against her faceplate.

She tilted up her head. Needle-shaped particles swirled over the wall-mountain from the planet's dark side and bounced off her faceplate, sparkling in corona light.

"What in Lethe is that?"

"Snow," he said.

Snow . . . On Mercury?

In the cool darkness of the tunnel, the people clambered over each other; they bumped against the Ice walls, and their muttering filled the water with crisscrossing voice-ripples. Cilia-of-Gold swam through and around the crowd, coaxing the people to follow her will.

She felt immensely weary. Her concentration and resolve threatened continually to shatter under the Seeker's assault. And the end of the tunnel, with the deadly Heads beyond, was a looming, threatening mouth, utterly intimidating.

At last the group was ready. She surveyed them. All of the people—except the very oldest and the very youngest—were arranged in an array which filled the tunnel from wall to wall; she could hear flukes and carapaces scraping softly against Ice.

The people looked weak, foolish, eager, she thought with dismay; now that she was actually implementing it her scheme seemed simple-minded. Was she about to lead them all to their deaths?

But it was too late for the luxury of doubt, she told herself. Now, there was no other option to follow.

She lifted herself to the axis of the tunnel, and clacked her mandibles sharply. "Now," she said, "it is time. The most important moment of your lives. And you must *swim*! Swim as hard as you can; swim for your lives!"

And the people responded.

There was a surge of movement, of almost exhilarating *intent*. The people beat their flukes as one, and a jostling mass of flesh and carapaces scraped down the tunnel.

Cilia-of-Gold hurried ahead of them, leading the way toward the tunnel mouth. As she swam she could feel the current the people were creating, the plug of cold tunnel water they pushed ahead of themselves.

Within moments the tunnel mouth was upon her.

She burst from the tunnel, shooting out into the open water of the cavern, her carapace clenched firm around her. She was plunged immediately into a clammy heat, so great was the temperature difference between tunnel and cavern.

Above her the Ice of the cavern roof arched over the warm Chimney mouth. And from all around the cavern, the helmet-skulls of Heads snapped around toward her.

Now the people erupted out of the tunnel, a shield of flesh and chitin behind her. The rush of tunnel water they pushed ahead of themselves washed over Cilia-of-Gold, chilling her anew.

She tried to imagine this from the Heads' point of view. This explosion of cold water into the cavern would bring about a much greater temperature difference than the Heads' heat-sensor skulls were accustomed to; the Heads would be *dazzled*, at least for a time: long enough—she hoped—to give her people a fighting chance against the more powerful Heads.

She swiveled in the water. She screamed at her people, so loud she could feel her cilia strain at the turbulent water. "*Now*! Hit them now!"

The people, with a roar, descended toward the Heads.

Kevan Scholes led Larionova down the wall-mountain slope into Chao Meng-Fu Crater.

After a hundred yards they came to another rover. This car was similar to the one they'd abandoned on the other side of the summit, but it had an additional fitting, obviously improvised: two wide, flat rails of metal, suspended between the wheels on hydraulic legs.

Scholes helped Larionova into the rover and pressurized it. Larionova removed her helmet with relief. The rover smelled, oppressively, of metal and plastic.

While Scholes settled behind his controls, Larionova checked the rover's data desk. An update from Dolores Wu was waiting for her. Wu wanted Larionova to come to Caloris, to see for herself what had been found there. Larionova sent a sharp message back, ordering Wu to summarize her findings and transmit them to the data desks at the Chao site.

Wu acknowledged immediately, but replied: *I'm going to find this hard to summarize, Irina.*

Larionova tapped out: *Why?*

We *think we've found an artifact.*

Larionova stared at the blunt words on the screen.

She massaged the bridge of her nose; she felt an ache spreading out from her temples and around her eye sockets. She wished she had time to sleep.

Scholes started the vehicle up. The rover bounced down the slope, descending into shadow. "It's genuine water-ice snow," Scholes said as he drove. "You know that a day on Mercury lasts a hundred and seventy-six Earth days. It's a combination of the eighty-eight-day year and the tidally locked rotation, which—"

"I know."

"During the day, the Sun drives water vapor out of the rocks and into the atmosphere."

"What atmosphere?"

"You really don't know much about Mercury, do you? It's mostly helium and hydrogen—only a billionth of Earth's sea-level pressure."

"How come those gases don't escape from the gravity well?"

"They do," Scholes said. "But the atmosphere is replenished by the solar wind. Particles from the Sun are trapped by Mercury's magnetosphere. Mercury has quite a respectable magnetic field: the planet has a solid iron core, which . . ."

She let Scholes' words run on through her head, unregistered. *Air from the solar wind, and snow at the South Pole . . .*

Maybe Mercury was a more interesting place than she'd imagined.

"Anyway," Scholes was saying, "the water vapor disperses across the planet's sunlit hemisphere. But at the South Pole we have this crater: Chao Meng-Fu, straddling the Pole itself. Mercury has no axial tilt—there are no seasons here—and so Chao's floor is in permanent shadow."

"And snow falls."

"And snow falls."

Scholes stopped the rover and tapped telltales on his control panel. There was a whir of hydraulics, and she heard a soft crunch, transmitted into the cabin through the rover's structure.

Then the rover lifted upward through a foot.

The rover lurched forward again. The motion was much smoother than before, and there was an easy, hissing sound.

"You've just lowered those rails," Larionova said. "I knew it. This damn rover is a sled, isn't it?"

"It was easy enough to improvise," Scholes said, sounding smug. "Just a couple of metal rails on hydraulics, and Vernier rockets from a cannibalized tug to give us some push. . . ."

"It's astonishing that there's enough ice here to sustain this."

"Well, that snow may have seemed sparse, but it's been falling steadily—for five billion years . . . Dr. Larionova, there's a whole frozen ocean here, in Chao Meng-Fu Crater: enough ice to be detectable even from Earth."

Larionova twisted to look out through a viewport at the back of the cabin. The rover's rear lights picked out twin sled tracks, leading back to the summit of the wall-mountain; ice, exposed in the tracks, gleamed brightly in starlight.

Lethe, she thought. *Now I'm skiing. Skiing, on Mercury. What a day.*

The wall-mountain shallowed out, merging seamlessly with the crater plain. Scholes retracted the sled rails; on the flat, the regolith dust gave the ice sufficient traction for the rover's wide wheels. The rover made fast progress through the fifty miles to the heart of the plain.

Larionova drank coffee and watched the landscape through the viewports. The corona light was silvery and quite bright here, like moonlight. The central peak loomed up over the horizon, like some approaching ship on a sea of dust. The ice-surface of Chao's floor—though pocked with craters and covered with the ubiquitous regolith dust—was visibly smoother and more level than the plain outside the crater.

The rover drew to a halt on the outskirts of the Thoth team's sprawling camp, close to the foothills of the central peak. The dust here was churned up by rover tracks and tug exhaust splashes, and semi-transparent bubble-shelters were hemispheres of yellow, homely light, illuminating the darkened ice surface. There were drilling rigs, and several large pits dug into the ice.

Scholes helped Larionova out onto the surface. "I'll take you to a shelter," he said. "Or a tug. Maybe you want to freshen up before—"

"Where's Dixon?"

Scholes pointed to one of the rigs. "When I left, over there."

"Then that's where we're going. Come on."

Frank Dixon was the team leader. He met Larionova on the surface, and invited her into a small opaqued bubble-shelter nestling at the foot of the rig.

Scholes wandered off into the camp, in search of food.

The shelter contained a couple of chairs, a data desk, and a basic toilet. Dixon was a morose, burly American; when he took off his helmet there was a band of dirt at the base of his wide neck, and Larionova noticed a sharp, acrid stink from his suit. Dixon had evidently been out on the surface for long hours.

He pulled a hip flask from an environment suit pocket. "You want to drink?" he asked. "Scotch?"

"Sure."

Dixon poured a measure for Larionova into the flask's cap, and took a draught himself from the flask's small mouth.

Larionova drank; the liquor burned her mouth and throat, but it immediately took an edge off her tiredness. "It's good. But it needs ice."

He smiled. "Ice we got. Actually, we have tried it; Mercury ice is good, as clean as you like. We're not going to die of thirst out here, Irina."

"Tell me what you've found, Frank."

Dixon sat on the edge of the desk, his fat haunches bulging inside the leggings of his environment suit. "Trouble, Irina. We've found trouble."

"I know that much."

"I think we're going to have to get off the planet. The System authorities—and the scientists and conservation groups—are going to climb all over us, if we try to mine here. I wanted to tell you about it, before—"

Larionova struggled to contain her irritation and tiredness. "That's *not* a problem for Thoth," she said. "Therefore it's not a problem for me. We can tell Superet to bring in a water-ice asteroid from the Belt, for our supplies. You know that. Come on, Frank. Tell me why you're wasting my time down here."

Dixon took another long pull on his flask, and eyed her.

"There's *life* here, Irina," he said. "Life, inside this frozen ocean. Drink up; I'll show you."

The sample was in a case on the surface, beside a data desk.

The thing in the case looked like a strip of multicolored meat: perhaps three feet long, crushed and obviously dead; shards of some transparent shell material were embedded in flesh that sparkled with ice crystals.

"We found this inside a two-thousand-yard-deep core," Dixon said.

Larionova tried to imagine how this would have looked, intact and mobile. "This means nothing to me, Frank. I'm no biologist."

He grunted, self-deprecating. "Nor me. Nor any of us. Who expected to find life, on Mercury?" Dixon tapped at the data desk with gloved fingers. "We used our desks' medico-diagnostic facilities to come up with this reconstruction," he said. "We call it a *mercuric*, Irina."

A Virtual projected into space a foot above the desk's surface; the image rotated, sleek and menacing.

The body was a thin cone, tapering to a tail from a wide, flat head. Three parabolic cups—*eyes?*—were embedded in the smooth "face," symmetrically placed around a lipless mouth. . . . No, not eyes, Larionova corrected herself. Maybe some kind of sonar sensor? That would explain the parabolic profile.

Mandibles, like pincers, protruded from the mouth. From the tail, three fins were splayed out around what looked like an anus. A transparent carapace surrounded the main body, like a cylindrical cloak; inside the carapace, rows of small, hairlike cilia lined the body, supple and vibratile.

There were regular markings, faintly visible, in the surface of the carapace.

"Is this accurate?"

"Who knows? It's the best *we* can do. When we have your clearance, we can transmit our data to Earth, and let the experts get at it."

"Lethe, Frank," Larionova said. "This looks like a fish. It looks like it could *swim*. The streamlining, the tail—"

Dixon scratched the short hairs at the back of his neck and said nothing.

"But we're on Mercury, damn it, not in Hawaii," Larionova said.

Dixon pointed down, past the dusty floor. "Irina. It's not all frozen. There are *cavities* down there, inside the Chao ice-cap. According to our sonar probes—"

"Cavities?"

"Water. At the base of the crater, under a couple of miles of ice. Kept liquid by thermal vents, in crust-collapse scarps and ridges. Plenty of room for swimming. . . . We speculate that our friend here swims on his back—" he tapped the desk surface, and the image swiveled "—and the water passes down, between his body and this carapace, and he uses all those tiny hairs to filter out particles of food. The trunk seems to be lined with little mouths. See?" He flicked the image to another representation; the skin became transparent, and Larionova could see blocky reconstructions of internal organs. Dixon said, "There's no true stomach, but there is what looks like a continuous digestive tube passing down the axis of the body, to the anus at the tail."

Larionova noticed a thread-like structure wrapped around some of the organs, as well as around the axial digestive tract.

"Look," Dixon said, pointing to one area. "Look at the surface structure of these lengths of tubing, here near the digestive tract."

Larionova looked. The tubes, clustering around the digestive axis, had complex, rippled surfaces. "So?"

"You don't get it, do you? It's *convoluted*—like the surface of a brain. Irina, we think that stuff must be some equivalent of nervous tissue."

Larionova frowned. *Damn it, I wish I knew more biology.* "What about this thread material, wrapped around the organs?"

Dixon sighed. "We don't know, Irina. It doesn't seem to fit with the rest of the structure, does it?" He pointed. "Follow the threads back. There's a broader main body, just here. We think maybe this is some kind of parasite, which has infested the main organism. Like a tapeworm. It's as if the threads are extended, vestigial limbs. . . . "

Leaning closer, Larionova saw that tendrils from the worm-thing had even infiltrated the brain-tubes. She shuddered; if this was a parasite, it was a particularly vile infestation. Maybe the parasite even modified the mercuric's behavior, she wondered.

Dixon restored the solid-aspect Virtual.

Uneasily, Larionova pointed to the markings on the carapace. They were small triangles, clustered into elaborate patterns. "And what's this stuff?"

Dixon hesitated. "I was afraid you might ask that."

"Well?"

". . . We think the markings are artificial, Irina. A deliberate tattoo, carved into the carapace, probably with the mandibles. Writing, maybe: those look like symbolic markings, with information content."

"Lethe," she said.

"I know. This fish was smart," Dixon said.

The people, victorious, clustered around the warmth of their new Chimney. Recovering from their journey and from their battle-wounds, they cruised easily over the gardens of cilia-plants, and browsed on floating fragments of food.

It had been a great triumph. The Heads were dead, or driven off into the labyrinth of tunnels through the Ice. Strong-Flukes had even found the Heads' principal nest here, under the silty floor of the cavern. With sharp stabs of her mandibles, Strong-Flukes had destroyed a dozen or more Head young.

Cilia-of-Gold took herself off, away from the Chimney. She prowled the edge of the Ice cavern, feeding fitfully.

She was a hero. But she couldn't bear the attention of others: their praise, the warmth of their bodies. All she seemed to desire now was the uncomplicated, silent coolness of Ice.

She brooded on the infestation that was spreading through her.

Seekers were a mystery. Nobody knew *why* Seekers compelled their hosts to isolate themselves, to bury themselves in the Ice. What was the point? When the hosts were destroyed, so were the Seekers.

Perhaps it wasn't the Ice itself the Seekers desired, she wondered. Perhaps they sought, in their blind way, something *beyond* the Ice. . . .

But there *was* nothing above the Ice. The caverns were hollows in an infinite, eternal Universe of Ice. Cilia-of-Gold, with a shudder, imagined herself burrowing, chewing her way into the endless Ice, upward without limit. . . . Was that, finally, how her life would end?

She hated the Seeker within her. She hated her body, for betraying her in this way; and she hated herself.

"Cilia-of-Gold."

She turned, startled, and closed her carapace around herself reflexively.

It was Strong-Flukes and Ice-Born, together.

Seeing their warm, familiar bodies, here in this desolate corner of the cavern, Cilia-of-Gold's loneliness welled up inside her, like a Chimney of emotion.

But she swam away from her Three-mates, backward, her carapace scraping on the cavern's Ice wall.

Ice-Born came toward her, hesitantly. "We're concerned about you."

"Then don't be," she snapped. "Go back to the Chimney, and leave me here."

"No," Strong-Flukes said quietly.

Cilia-of-Gold felt desperate, angry, confined. "You know what's wrong with me, Strong-Flukes. I have a *Seeker.* It's going to kill me. And there's nothing any of us can do about it."

Their bodies pressed close around her now; she longed to open up her carapace to them and bury herself in their warmth.

"We know we're going to lose you, Cilia-of-Gold," Ice-Born said. It sounded as if she could barely speak. Ice-Born had always been the softest, the most loving, of the Three, Cilia-of-Gold thought, the warm heart of their relationship. "And—"

"Yes?"

Strong-Flukes opened her carapace wide. "We want to be Three again," she said.

Already, Cilia-of-Gold saw with a surge of love and excitement, Strong-Flukes's ovipositor was distended: swollen with one of the three isogametes which would fuse to form a new child, their fourth. . . .

A child Cilia-of-Gold could never see growing to consciousness.

"No!" Her cilia pulsed with the single, agonized word.

Suddenly the warmth of her Three-mates was confining, claustrophobic. She had to get away from this prison of flesh; her mind was filled with visions of the coolness and purity of *Ice*: of clean, high *Ice*.

"Cilia-of-Gold. Wait. Please—"

She flung herself away, along the wall. She came to a tunnel mouth, and she plunged into it, relishing the tunnel's cold, stagnant water.

"Cilia-of-Gold! *Cilia-of-Gold!*"

She hurled her body through the web of tunnels, carelessly colliding with walls of Ice so hard that she could feel her carapace splinter. On and on she swam, until the voices of her Three-mates were lost forever.

We've dug out a large part of the artifact, Irina, Dolores Wu reported. *It's a mash of what looks like hull material.*

"Did you get a sample?"

No. We don't have anything that could cut through material so dense. . . . Irina, we're looking at something beyond our understanding.

Larionova sighed. "Just tell me, Dolores," she told Wu's data desk image.

Irina, we think we're dealing with the Pauli Principle.

Pauli's Exclusion Principle stated that no two baryonic particles could exist in the same quantum state. Only a certain number of electrons, for example, could share a given energy level in an atom. Adding more electrons caused complex shells of charge to build up around the atom's nucleus. It was the electron shells—this consequence of Pauli—that gave the atom its chemical properties.

But the Pauli principle *didn't* apply to photons; it was possible for many photons to share the same quantum state. That was the essence of the laser: billions of photons, coherent, sharing the same quantum properties.

Irina, Wu said slowly, *what would happen if you could turn off the Exclusion Principle, for a piece of baryonic matter?*

"You can't," Larionova said immediately.

Of course not. Try to imagine anyway.

Larionova frowned. What if one could lase mass? "The atomic electron shells would implode, of course."

Yes.

"All electrons would fall into their ground state. Chemistry would be impossible."

Yes. But you may not care . . .

"Molecules would collapse. Atoms would fall into each other, releasing immense quantities of binding energy."

You'd end up with a superdense substance, wouldn't you? Completely non-reactive, chemically. And almost unbreachable, given the huge energies required to detach non-Pauli atoms.

Ideal hull material, Irina. . . .

"But it's all impossible," Larionova said weakly. "You *can't* violate Pauli."

Of course you can't, Dolores Wu replied.

* * *

Inside an opaqued bubble-shelter, Larionova, Dixon and Scholes sat on fold-out chairs, cradling coffees.

"If your mercuric was so smart," Larionova said to Dixon, "how come he got himself stuck in the ice?"

Dixon shrugged. "In fact it goes deeper than that. It looked to us as if the mercuric burrowed his way up into the ice, deliberately. What kind of evolutionary advantage could there be in behavior like that? The mercuric was certain to be killed."

"Yes," Larionova said. She massaged her temples, thinking about the mercuric's infection. "But maybe that thread-parasite had something to do with it. I mean, some parasites change the way their hosts behave."

Scholes tapped at a data desk; text and images, reflected from the desk, flickered over his face. "That's true. There are parasites which transfer themselves from one host to another—by forcing a primary host to get itself eaten by the second."

Dixon's wide face crumpled. "Lethe. That's disgusting."

"The lancet fluke," Scholes read slowly, "is a parasite of some species of ant. The fluke can make its host climb to the top of a grass stem and then lock onto the stem with its mandibles—and wait until it's swallowed by a grazing sheep. Then the fluke can go on to infest the sheep in turn."

"Okay," Dixon said. "But why would a parasite force its mercuric host to burrow up into the ice of a frozen ocean? When the host dies, the parasite dies too. It doesn't make sense."

"There's a lot about this that doesn't make sense," Larionova said. "Like, the whole question of the existence of life in the cavities in the first place. There's no *light* down there. How do the mercurics survive, under two miles of ice?"

Scholes folded one leg on top of the other and scratched his ankle. "I've been going through the data desks." He grimaced, self-deprecating. "A crash course in exotic biology. You want my theory?"

"Go ahead."

"The thermal vents—which cause the cavities in the first place. The vents are the key. I think the bottom of the Chao ice-cap is like the mid-Atlantic ridge, back on Earth.

"The deep sea, a mile down, is a desert; by the time any particle of food has drifted down from the richer waters above it's passed through so many guts that its energy content is exhausted.

"But along the Ridge, where tectonic plates are colliding, you have hydrothermal vents—just as at the bottom of Chao. And the heat from the Atlantic vents supports life: in little colonies, strung out along the mid-Atlantic Ridge. The vents form superheated fountains, smoking with deep-crust minerals that life can exploit: sulphides of copper, zinc, lead, and iron, for instance. And there are very steep temperature differences, and so there are high energy gradients—another prerequisite for life."

"Hmm." Larionova closed her eyes and tried to picture it. *Pockets of warm water, deep in the ice of Mercury; luxuriant mats of life surrounding mineral-*

rich hydrothermal vents, browsed by Dixon's mercuric animals. . . . Was it possible?

Dixon asked, "How long do the vents persist?"

"On Earth, in the Ridge, a couple of decades. Here we don't know."

"What happens when a vent dies?" Larionova asked. "That's the end of your pocket world, isn't it? The ice chamber would simply freeze up."

"Maybe," Scholes said. "But the vents would occur in rows, along the scarps. Maybe there are corridors of liquid water, within the ice, along which mercurics could migrate."

Larionova thought about that for a while.

"I don't believe it," she said.

"Why not?"

"I don't see how it's possible for life to have *evolved* here in the first place." In the primeval oceans of Earth, there had been complex chemicals, and electrical storms, and . . .

"Oh, I don't think that's a problem," Scholes said.

She looked at him sharply. Maddeningly, he was grinning again. "Well?" she snapped.

"Look," Scholes said with grating patience, "we've two anomalies on Mercury: the life forms here at the South Pole, and Dolores Wu's artifact under Caloris. The simplest assumption is that the two anomalies are connected. Let's put the pieces together," he said. "Let's construct a hypothesis. . . . "

Her mandibles ached as she crushed the gritty Ice, carving out her tunnel upward. The rough walls of the tunnel scraped against her carapace, and she pushed Ice rubble down between her body and her carapace, sacrificing fragile cilia designed to extract soft food particles from warm streams.

The higher she climbed, the harder the Ice became. The Ice was now so cold she was beyond cold; she couldn't even feel the Ice fragments that scraped along her belly and flukes. And, she suspected, the tunnel behind her was no longer open but had refrozen, sealing her here, in this shifting cage, forever.

The world she had left—of caverns, and Chimneys, and children, and her Three-mates—were remote bubbles of warmth, a distant dream. The only reality was the hard Ice in her mandibles, and the Seeker heavy and questing inside her.

She could feel her strength seeping out with the last of her warmth into the Ice's infinite extent. And yet *still* the Seeker wasn't satisfied; still she had to climb, on and up, into the endless darkness of the Ice.

. . . But now—impossibly—there was something *above* her, breaking through the Ice. . . .

She cowered inside her Ice-prison.

Kevan Scholes said, "Five billion years ago—when the solar system was very young, and the crusts of Earth and other inner planets were still subject to bombardment from stray planetesimals—a ship came here. An interstellar craft, maybe with FTL technology."

"Why? Where from?" Larionova asked.

"I don't know. How could I know that? But the ship must have been massive—with the bulk of a planetesimal, or more. Certainly highly advanced, with a hull composed of Dolores's superdense Pauli construction material."

"Hmm. Go on."

"Then the ship hit trouble."

"What kind of trouble?"

"I don't *know*. Come on, Dr. Larionova. Maybe it got hit by a planetesimal itself. Anyway, the ship crashed here, on Mercury—"

"Right." Dixon nodded, gazing at Scholes hungrily; the American reminded Larionova of a child enthralled by a story. "It was a disastrous impact. It caused the Caloris feature. . . . "

"Oh, be serious," Larionova said.

Dixon looked at her. "Caloris *was* a pretty unique impact, Irina. Extraordinarily violent, even by the standards of the system's early bombardment phase. . . . Caloris Basin is *eight hundred miles* across; on Earth, its walls would stretch from New York to Chicago."

"So how did anything survive?"

Scholes shrugged. "Maybe the starfarers had some kind of inertial shielding. How can we know? Anyway the ship was wrecked; and the density of the smashed-up hull material caused it to sink into the bulk of the planet, through the Caloris puncture.

"The crew were stranded. So they sought a place to survive. Here, on Mercury."

"I get it," Dixon said. "The only viable environment, long term, was the Chao Meng-Fu ice cap."

Scholes spread his hands. "Maybe the starfarers had to engineer descendants, quite unlike the original crew, to survive in such conditions. And perhaps they had to do a little planetary engineering too; they may have had to initiate some of the hydrothermal vents which created the enclosed liquid-water world down there. And so—"

"Yes?"

"And so the creature we've dug out of the ice is a degenerate descendant of those ancient star travelers, still swimming around the Chao sea."

Scholes fell silent, his eyes on Larionova.

Larionova stared into her coffee. "A 'degenerate descendant.' After *five billion years?* Look, Scholes, on Earth it's only three and a half billion years since the first prokaryotic cells. And on Earth, whole phyla—groups of species—have emerged or declined over periods less than a *tenth* of the time since the Caloris Basin event. Over time intervals like that, the morphology of species flows like hot plastic. So how is it possible for these mercurics to have persisted?"

Scholes looked uncertain. "Maybe they've suffered massive evolutionary changes," he said. "Changes we're just not seeing. For example, maybe the worm parasite is the malevolent descendant of some harmless creature the starfarers brought with them."

Dixon scratched his neck, where the suit-collar ring of dirt was prominent. "Anyway, we've still got the puzzle of the mercuric's burrowing into the ice."

"Hmm." Scholes sipped his cooling coffee. "I've got a theory about that, too."

"I thought you might," Larionova said sourly.

Scholes said, "I wonder if the impulse to climb up to the surface is some kind of residual yearning for the stars."

"What?"

Scholes looked embarrassed, but he pressed on: "A racial memory buried deep, prompting the mercurics to seek their lost home world. . . . Why not?"

Larionova snorted. "You're a romantic, Kevan Scholes."

A telltale flashed on the surface of the data desk. Dixon leaned over, tapped the telltale and took the call.

He looked up at Larionova, his moon-like face animated. "Irina. They've found another mercuric," he said.

"Is it intact?"

"More than that." Dixon stood and reached for his helmet. "This one isn't dead yet . . . "

The mercuric lay on Chao's dust-coated ice. Humans stood around it, suited, their faceplates anonymously blank.

The mercuric, dying, was a cone of bruised-purple meat a yard long. Shards of shattered transparent carapace had been crushed into its crystallizing flesh. Some of the cilia, within the carapace, stretched and twitched. The cilia looked differently colored from Dixon's reconstruction, as far as Larionova could remember: these were yellowish threads, almost golden.

Dixon spoke quickly to his team, then joined Larionova and Scholes. "We couldn't have saved it. It was in distress as soon as our core broke through into its tunnel. I guess it couldn't take the pressure and temperature differentials. Its internal organs seem to be massively disrupted. . . . "

"Just think." Kevan Scholes stood beside Dixon, his hands clasped behind his back. "There must be millions of these animals in the ice under our feet, embedded in their pointless little chambers. Surely none of them could dig more than a hundred yards or so up from the liquid layer."

Larionova switched their voices out of her consciousness. She knelt down, on the ice; under her knees she could feel the crisscross heating elements in her suit's fabric.

She peered into the dulling sonar-eyes of the mercuric. The creature's mandibles—prominent and sharp—opened and closed, in vacuum silence.

She felt an impulse to reach out her gloved hand to the battered flank of the creature: to *touch* this animal, this person, whose species had, perhaps, traveled across light years—and five billion years—to reach her. . . .

But still, she had the nagging feeling that something was wrong with Scholes' neat hypothesis. The mercuric's physical design seemed crude. Could this really have been a starfaring species? The builders of the ship in Caloris must have had some form of major tool-wielding capability. And Dixon's earlier study had shown that the creature had no trace of any limbs, even vestigially. . . .

Vestigial limbs, she remembered. *Lethe.*

Abruptly her perception of this animal—and its host parasite—began to shift; she could feel a paradigm dissolving inside her, melting like a Mercury snowflake in the Sun.

"Dr. Larionova? Are you all right?"

Larionova looked up at Scholes. "Kevan, I called you a romantic. But I think you were almost correct, after all. *But not quite.* Remember we've suggested that the *parasite*—the infestation—changes the mercuric's behavior, causing it to make its climb."

"What are you saying?"

Suddenly, Larionova saw it all. "I don't believe this mercuric is descended from the starfarers—the builders of the ship in Caloris. I think the rise of the mercurics' intelligence was a *later* development; the mercurics grew to consciousness *here*, on Mercury. I *do* think the mercurics are descended from something that came to Mercury on that ship, though. A pet, or a food animal— Lethe, even some equivalent of a stomach bacteria. Five billion years is time enough for anything. And, given the competition for space near the short-lived vents, there's plenty of encouragement for the development of intelligence, down inside this frozen sea."

"And the starfarers themselves?" Scholes asked. "What became of them? Did they die?"

"No," she said. "No, I don't think so. But they, too, suffered huge evolutionary changes. I think they did devolve, Scholes; in fact, I think they lost their awareness.

"But one thing persisted within them, across all this desert of time. And that was the starfarers' vestigial will to *return*—to the surface, one day, and at last to the stars. . . . "

It was a will which had survived even the loss of consciousness itself, somewhere in the long, stranded aeons: a relic of awareness long since transmuted to a deeper biochemical urge—*a will to return home*, still embedded within a once-intelligent species reduced by time to a mere parasitic infection.

But it was a home which, surely, could no longer exist.

The mercuric's golden cilia twitched once more, in a great wave of motion which shuddered down its ice-flecked body.

Then it was still.

Larionova stood up; her knees and calves were stiff and cold, despite the suit's heater. "Come on," she said to Scholes and Dixon. "You'd better get your team off the ice as soon as possible; I'll bet the universities have their first exploratory teams down here half a day after we pass Earth the news."

Dixon nodded. "And Thoth?"

"Thoth? I'll call Superet. I guess I've an asteroid to order. . . . "

And then, she thought, *at last I can sleep. Sleep and get back to work.*

With Scholes and Dixon, she trudged across the dust-strewn ice to the bubble shelters.

She could feel the Ice under her belly . . . but above her *there was no Ice*, no water even, an infinite *nothing* into which the desperate pulses of her blinded eyes disappeared without echo.

Astonishingly—impossibly—she *was*, after all, above the Ice. How could this be? Was she in some immense upper cavern, its Ice roof too remote to see? Was this the nature of the Universe, a hierarchy of caverns within caverns?

She knew she would never understand. But it didn't seem to matter. And, as her awareness faded, she felt the Seeker inside her subside to peace.

A final warmth spread out within her. Consciousness splintered like melting ice, flowing away through the closing tunnels of her memory.

GOING AFTER OLD MAN ALABAMA

William Sanders

Are you your brother's keeper? Or your neighbor's? Here's a clever, inventive, and offbeat tale that suggests that you *are*, or *should* be, even if you have to go to a great deal of trouble and travel a very long way, to some extremely odd places, in order *to* keep him—or keep him from making mischief, anyway . . .

William Sanders lives in Tahlequah, Oklahoma, where he is an active member of the traditional Nighthawk Keetoowah Society. A former powwow dancer and Cherokee gospel singer, he is the author of fifteen published books, many of them as Will Sundown, including Westerns and adventure books. As Sanders, he has published a few science fiction novels, including *Journey to Fusang* (a nominee for the Campbell Award) and *The Wild Blue and Gray*. His other books include the popular Taggart Roper mystery novels, *The Next Victim, A Death on 66,* and *Blood Autumn*.

Charlie Badwater was the most powerful medicine man in all the eastern Oklahoma hill country. Or the biggest witch, depending on which person you listened to; among Cherokees the distinction tends to be a little hazy.

Either way, when Thomas Cornstalk finally decided that something had to be done about Old Man Alabama, he didn't need to think twice before getting in his old Dodge pickup truck and driving over to Charlie Badwater's place. Thomas Cornstalk was no slouch of a medicine man himself, but in a situation like this you went to the man with the power.

Charlie Badwater lived by himself in a one-room log cabin at the end of a really bad dirt road, up near the head of Butcherknife Hollow. There was nobody in sight when Thomas Cornstalk drove up, but as he got down from the pickup cab a big gray owl fluttered down from the surrounding woods and disappeared into the deep shadows behind the cabin. A moment later the cabin door opened and Charlie Badwater stepped out into the sunlight. " *'Siyo, Tami, dohiju?''* he called.

Thomas Cornstalk half-raised a hand in casual greeting. He and Charlie Badwater went back a long way. " *'Siyo, Jali. Gado haduhne*? Catching any mice?'' he added dryly.

Charlie Badwater chuckled deep in his chest without moving his lips. ''Hey,'' he said, ''remember old Moses Otter?'' And they both chuckled together, remembering.

*   *   *

Moses Otter had been a mean old man with a permanent case of professional jealousy, especially toward anybody who might have enough power to make him look bad. Since Moses Otter had never in his life been more than a second-rate witch, this included a lot of people.

One of his nastier tricks had been to turn himself into an owl—he could do that all right, but then who can't?—and fly over the woods until he spotted a clearing where a possible rival was growing medicine tobacco. Now of course serious tobacco has to be grown absolutely unseen by anyone except the person who will be using it, so this had meant a great deal of frustration and ruined medicine all over the area. Quite a few people had tried to witch Moses Otter and put a stop to this crap, but his protective medicine had always worked.

Charlie Badwater, then a youthful and inexperienced unknown, had gone to Moses Otter's place and told him in front of several witnesses that if he enjoyed being a bird he could have a hell of a good time from now on. And had turned him on the spot into the mangiest, scabbiest turkey buzzard ever seen in Oklahoma; and Moses Otter, after a certain amount of flopping around trying to change himself back, had flown away, never to be seen again except perhaps as an unidentifiable member of a gang of roadkill-pickers down on the Interstate.

That, Thomas Cornstalk recalled, had been the point at which everybody had realized that Charlie Badwater was somebody special. Maybe they hadn't fully grasped just how great he would one day become, but the word had definitely gone out that Charlie Badwater was somebody you didn't want to screw around with.

Now, still chuckling, Charlie Badwater tilted his head in the direction of his cabin. "*Kawi jaduli*'? Got a pot just made."

They went inside the cabin and Thomas Cornstalk sat down at the little pine-board table while Charlie Badwater poured a couple of cups of hell-black coffee from a blue and white speckled metal pot. "Ought to be ready to walk by now," Charlie Badwater said. "Been on the stove a long time."

"Good coffee," Thomas Cornstalk affirmed, tasting. "Damn near eat it with a fork."

They sat at the table, drinking coffee and smoking hand-rolled cigarettes, not talking for the moment: a couple of fifty-some-odd-year-old full-bloods, similarly dressed in work shirts and Wal-Mart jeans and cheap nylon running shoes made in Singapore. Charlie Badwater had the classic lean, deep-chested, no-ass build of the mountain Cherokee, while Thomas Cornstalk was one of those heavyset, round-faced types who may or may not have some Choctaw blood from way back in old times. Their faces, however, were similarly weathered, their hands callused and scarred from years of manual labor. Charlie Badwater was missing the end joint of his left index finger. There were only three people who knew how he had lost it and two of them were dead and nobody had the nerve to ask the third one. Let alone Charlie.

They talked a little, finally, about this and that; routine inquiries about the health of relatives, remarks about the weather, the usual pleasantries that a couple of properly raised Cherokee men will exchange before getting down to the real point of a conversation. But Thomas Cornstalk, usually the politest of men, was worried enough to hold the small talk to the bare minimum required by decency.

"Gusdi nusdi," he said finally. "Something's the matter. I'm not sure what," he added, in response to the inquiry in Charlie Badwater's eyes. "It's Old Man Alabama."

"That old weirdo?" Charlie Badwater wrinkled his nose very slightly, as if smelling something bad. "What's he up to these days? Still nutty as a *kenuche* ball, I guess?"

"Who knows? That's what I came to talk with you about," Thomas Cornstalk said. "He's up to something, all right, and I think it's trouble."

Old Man Alabama was a seriously strange old witch—in his case there was no question at all about the definition—who lived on top of a mountain over in Adair County, not far from the Arkansas line. He wasn't Cherokee; he claimed to be the last surviving descendant of the Alabama tribe, and he often gibbered and babbled in a language he claimed was the lost Alabama tongue. It could have been; Thomas Cornstalk couldn't recognize a word of it, and he spoke sixteen Indian languages as well as English and Spanish—that was his special medicine, the ability to speak in different tongues; he could also talk with animals. On the other hand it might just as easily have been a lot of meaningless blather, which was what Thomas Cornstalk and a good many other people suspected.

There was also the inconvenient fact that there were still some Alabamas living on a reservation down in Texas, big as you please; but it had been a long time since anybody had pointed this out in Old Man Alabama's hearing. Not after what had happened to the last bigmouth to bring the subject up.

Whatever he was—Thomas Cornstalk had long suspected he was some kind of Creek or Seminole or maybe Yuchi, run off by his own people—Old Man Alabama was as crazy as the Devil and twice as nasty. That much was certain.

He was skinny and tall and he had long arms that he waved wildly about while talking, or for no apparent reason at all. Everything about him was long: long matted hair falling past his shoulders, long beaky nose, long bony fingers ending in creepy-looking long nails. He walked with a strange angling gait, one shoulder higher than the other, and he spat constantly, *tuff tuff tuff,* so you could follow him down a dirt road on a dry day by the little brown spots in the dust.

It was widely believed that he had a long tongue like a moth's, that he kept curled up in his mouth and only stretched out at night during unspeakable acts. That was another story people weren't eager to investigate first hand.

He also stank. Not the way a regular man smelled bad, even a very dirty regular man—though Old Man Alabama was sure as hell dirty enough—but a horrible, eye-watering stench that reminded you of things like rotten cucumbers and dead skunks on the highway in hot weather. That alone would have been reason enough for people to give him a wide berth, even if they hadn't been afraid of him.

And oh, yes, people *were* afraid of him. Mothers hid their pregnant daughters indoors when they saw him walking by the house, afraid that even a single direct look from those hooded reptilian eyes might cause monstrous deformities to the unborn.

Most people, in fact, avoided talking about him at all; it was well known that witches knew when they were being talked about, and the last thing people wanted was to draw the displeased attention of a witch as powerful and unpredictable as Old Man Alabama. It was a measure of the power of both Charlie Badwater and Thomas Cornstalk that they were willing to talk freely about him. Even so, Thomas Cornstalk would have been just as comfortable if Charlie Badwater hadn't spoken quite so disrespectfully about the old man.

"All I know," Thomas Cornstalk said, "he's been cooking up some kind of almighty powerful medicine up on that mountain of his. I go over that way pretty often, you know, got some relatives that call me up every time one of their kids gets a runny nose . . . anyway, sometimes you can hear these sounds, up where your ear can't quite get ahold of them, like those dog whistles, huh? And people see strange lights up on the mountain at night, and sometimes in the daytime the air looks sort of shimmery above the mountaintop, the way it does over a hot stove. Lots of smoke too, that's another thing. I got a smell or two when the wind was right and I don't know what the old man's burning up there but it's nothing I'd want in *my* medicine bag."

He paused, sipping his coffee, his eyes wandering about the interior of the cabin. Lots of medicine men live surrounded by all sorts of junk, their houses littered and smelly, walls and ceiling hung with bundles of dried herbs and feathers and skins and bones and other parts of birds and animals. Charlie Badwater's cabin, however, was as neat as a white doctor's office, everything stowed carefully away out of sight.

"I went up to see him, finally," Thomas Cornstalk said. "Or tried to, but he was either gone or hiding. I couldn't get close to the cabin. He's got the place circled—you know? You get to about ten or fifteen steps from the cabin and it starts to be harder and harder to walk, like you're stepping in molasses, till finally you can't go any farther. By then the cabin looks all rubbery, too, like it's melting. I had my pipe with me, and some good tobacco, and I tried every *igawesdi* I know for getting past a protective spell. Whatever Old Man Alabama has around that cabin, it's no ordinary medicine."

"Huh." Charlie Badwater was beginning to look interested. "See anything? I mean anything to suggest what's going on."

"Not a thing." Thomas Cornstalk pulled his shoulder blades together for a second. "Place made my skin crawl so bad, I got out pretty quick. Went home and smoked myself nearly black. Burned enough cedar for a Christmas-tree lot before I felt clean again."

"Huh," Charlie Badwater said again. He sat for a minute or so in silence, staring out through the open cabin door, though there was nothing out there but a stretch of dusty yard and the woods beyond.

"All right," he said at last, and got to his feet. "We better go pay Old Man Alabama a visit."

Thomas Cornstalk stood up too. "You want to go right now?" he said, a little surprised.

"Sure. You got something else you have to do?"

"No," Thomas Cornstalk admitted, after a moment's hesitation. He wasn't really ready for this, he thought, but maybe it was better to get on with it. The longer they waited, the better the chance that Old Man Alabama would find out they were coming, and do something unusually bad to try and stop them.

Charlie Badwater started toward the door. Thomas Cornstalk said, "You're not taking any stuff along? You know, medicine?"

Charlie Badwater patted his jeans pockets. "Got my pipe and some tobacco on me. I don't expect I'll need anything else."

Going out the door, following Charlie Badwater across the yard, Thomas Cornstalk shook his head in admiring wonder. That Charlie, he thought. Probably arm-wrestle the Devil left-handed, if he got a chance. Probably win, too.

They rode back down the dirt road in Thomas Cornstalk's old pickup truck. Charlie Badwater didn't own any kind of car or truck. He didn't have a telephone or electricity in his cabin, either. It was some mysteri' us but necessary part of his personal medicine.

The dirt track came out of the woods, after a mile or so of dust and rocks and sun-hardened ruts, and joined up with a winding gravel road that dipped down across the summer-dry bed of Butcherknife Creek and then climbed up the side of Turkeyfoot Ridge. On the far side of the ridge, the gravel turned into potholed county blacktop. Several miles farther along, they came out onto the Stilwell road. "Damn, Charlie," Thomas Cornstalk said, hanging a left, "you think you could manage to live further back in the woods?"

"Not without coming out on the other side," Charlie Badwater said.

The road up beside of Old Man Alabama's mountain was even worse than the one to Charlie Badwater's place. "I was here just this morning," Thomas Cornstalk said, fighting the wheel, "and I swear this mule track is in worse shape than it was then. And look at that," he exclaimed, and stepped on the brake pedal. "I know *that* wasn't there before—"

A big uprooted white oak tree was lying across the road. The road was littered with snapped-off limbs and still-green leaves. The two men in the pickup truck looked at each other. There hadn't been so much as a stiff breeze all day.

"Get out and walk, then," Charlie Badwater said after a minute. "We can use the exercise, I guess."

They got out and walked on up the road, climbing over the fallen tree. A little way beyond, the biggest rattlesnake Thomas Cornstalk had ever seen was lying in the road, looking at them. It coiled up and rattled its tail and showed its fangs but Charlie Badwater merely said, "*Ayuh jaduji,*" and the huge snake uncoiled and slid quietly off into the woods while Charlie and Thomas walked past.

"I always wondered," Thomas Cornstalk said as they trudged up the steep mountainside. "You suppose a rattlesnake really believes you're his uncle, when you say that?"

"Who knows? It doesn't matter how things work, Thomas. It just matters that they *do* work." Charlie Badwater grinned. "Talked to this professor from Northeastern State once, showed up at a stomp dance down at Redbird. He said Cherokees are pragmatists."

"What's that mean?"

"Beats me. I told him most of the ones I know are Baptists, with a few Methodists and of course there's a lot of people getting into those holy-roller outfits—" Charlie Badwater stopped suddenly in the middle of the road. "Huh," he grunted softly, as if to himself. Thomas Cornstalk couldn't remember ever seeing him look so surprised.

They had rounded the last bend in the road and had come in sight of Old Man Alabama's cabin. Except the cabin itself was barely in sight of all, in any normal sense. The whole clearing where the cabin stood was walled off by a kind of curtain of yellowish light, through which the outlines of the cabin showed only vaguely and irregularly. The sky looked somehow darker directly above the clearing, and all the surrounding trees seemed to have taken on strange and disturbing shapes. There was a high-pitched whining sound in the air, like the singing of a million huge mosquitoes.

"You were right, Thomas," Charlie Badwater said after a moment. "The old turd's gotten hold of something heavy. Who'd have thought it?"

"It wasn't like this when I was here this morning," Thomas Cornstalk said, looking around him and feeling very uneasy. "Not so *extreme*, like."

"Better have a look, then." Charlie Badwater took out a buckskin pouch and a short-stemmed pipe. Facing toward the sun, he poured a little tobacco from the pouch into his palm and began to sing, a strange-sounding song that Thomas Cornstalk had never heard before. Four times he sang the song through, pausing at the end of each repetition to blow softly on the tobacco. Then he stuffed the tobacco into the bowl of the pipe. It was an ordinary cheap briar pipe, the kind they sell off cardboard wall displays in country gas stations. In Cherokee medicine there is no particular reverence or importance placed on the pipe itself; the tobacco carries all the power, and then only if properly doctored with the right *igawesdi* words. Charlie Badwater could, if he had preferred, have simply rolled the tobacco into a cigarette and used that.

He lit the pipe with a plastic butane lighter and walked toward the cabin, puffing. Thomas Cornstalk followed, rather reluctantly. He didn't like this, but he would have followed Charlie Badwater to hell. Which, of course, might very well be where they were about to go.

Charlie Badwater pointed the stem of the pipe at the shimmering wall of light that blocked their way. Four times he blew smoke at the barrier, long dense streams of bluish white smoke that curled and eddied back strangely as they hit the bright curtain. On the fourth puff there was a sharp cracking sound and suddenly the curtain was gone and the humming stopped and there was only a weed-grown clearing and a tumbledown gray board shack badly in need of a new roof. Somewhere nearby a bird began singing, as if relieved.

"*Asuh,*" Thomas Cornstalk murmured in admiration.

"Make me think, I'll teach you that one some time," Charlie Badwater said. "It's not hard, once you learn the song . . . well, let's have a look around."

They walked slowly toward the cabin. There wasn't much to see. The yard was littered with an amazing assortment of junk—broken crockery and rusting pots and pans, chicken feathers and unidentifiable bones, bottles and cans, a wrecked chair with stuffing coming out of the cushions—but none of it suggested anything except that you wouldn't want Old Man Alabama living next door. A big pile of turtle shells lay on the sagging front porch. There was a rattlesnake skin nailed above the door.

"No smoke," Charlie Badwater said, studying the chimney. "Reckon he's gone? Well, one way to find out."

He stepped up onto the porch and turned to look back at Thomas Cornstalk, who hadn't moved. "Coming?"

"You go," Thomas Cornstalk said. "I'll wait out here for you. If it's all the same to you." He wouldn't have gone inside that cabin for a million dollars and a lifetime ticket to the Super Bowl. "Need to work on my tan," he added.

Charlie Badwater chuckled and disappeared through the cabin door. There was no sound of voices or anything else from within, so Thomas Cornstalk figured he must have been right about Old Man Alabama being gone. That didn't make much sense; why would the old maniac have put up such a fancy protective spell if he wasn't going to be inside? Come to think of it, *how* could he have laid on that barrier from the outside? As far as Thomas Cornstalk knew, a spell like that had to be worked from inside the protective circle. But nothing about this made any sense. . . .

Charlie Badwater's laugh came through the open cabin door. "You're not going to believe this," he called. "I don't believe it myself."

"What did you find?" Thomas Cornstalk said as Charlie came back out.

"About what you'd expect, mostly. A whole bunch of weird stuff piled every which way and hanging from the ceiling, all of it dirty as a pigpen and stinking so bad you can hardly breathe in there. Nothing unusual—considering who and what lives here—except these."

He held up a stack of books. Thomas Cornstalk stared. "Books?" he said in amazement. "What's Old Man Alabama doing with books? I know for a fact he can't read."

"Who knows? Maybe got them to wipe his ass with. Ran out of pine cones or whatever he uses." Charlie Badwater sat down on the edge of the porch and began flipping through the books. "Looks like he stole them from the school over at Rocky Mountain. Old bastard's a sneak thief on top of everything else."

"What kind of books are they? The kind with pictures of women? Maybe he's been out in the woods by himself too long."

"No, look, this is a history book. And this one has a bunch of pictures of old-time sailing ships, like in the pirate movies. Now why in the world—"

Charlie Badwater sat staring at the books for a couple of minutes, and then he tossed them aside and stood up. "I'm going to look around some more," he said.

Thomas Cornstalk followed him as he walked around the cabin. The area in back of the cabin looked much the same as the front yard, but then both men saw the blackened spot where a small fire had been burning. Large rocks had been placed in a circle around the fire place, and some of the rocks were marked with strange symbols or patterns. A tiny wisp of smoke, no greater than that from a cigarette, curled up from the ashes.

Charlie Badwater walked over and held his hand above the ashes, not quite touching the remains of the fire. Then he crouched way down and began studying the ground closely, slowly examining the entire area within the circle of stones and working his way back toward where Thomas Cornstalk stood silently watching. This was one of Charlie Badwater's most famous specialties: reading sign. People said he could track a catfish across a lake.

"He came out here," he said at last, "barefoot as usual, and he walked straight to that spot by the fire and walked around it—at least four times, it's pretty confused there—and then, well . . ."

"What? Where'd he go?"

"Far as I can tell, he just flew away. Or disappeared or something. He didn't walk back out of that circle of rocks, anyway. And whatever he did, it wasn't long ago that he did it. Those ashes are still warm."

A small dry voice said, "Looking for the old man?"

Thomas Cornstalk turned around. A great big blue jay was sitting on the collapsing eaves of Old Man Alabama's shack.

"Because," the jay said, speaking in that sarcastic way jays have, "I don't think you're going to find him. Not anytime soon, anyway. He left sort of drastic."

"Did you see what happened?" Thomas Cornstalk asked the jay.

Charlie Badwater had turned around too by now. He was looking from Thomas Cornstalk to the jay and back again. There was an odd look on his face; he seemed almost wistful. For all his power, all the fantastic things he could do, he had never been granted the ability to talk with animals—which is not something you can learn; you have the gift or you don't—and there are few things that can make a person feel quite as shut out as watching somebody like Thomas Cornstalk having a conversation with bird or beast.

"Hey," the jay said, "I got trapped in here when the old son of a bitch put that whatever-the-hell around the cabin. Tried to fly out, hit something like a wall in the air, damn near broke my beak. Thought I was going to starve to death in here, till you guys showed up. Tell your buddy thanks for turning the damn thing off."

"Ask him where Old Man Alabama went," Charlie Badwater said.

"I saw the whole thing," the jay said, not waiting for the translation. Thomas Cornstalk noticed that; he had suspected for some time that blue jays could understand Cherokee, even if they pretended not to. "Old guy walked out there mumbling to himself, stomped around the fire a little, made a lot of that racket that you humans call singing—hey, no offense, but even a boat-tailed grackle can sing better than that—and then all of a sudden he threw a bunch of stuff on the fire. There was a big puff of smoke and when it cleared away he was just as gone as you please."

"I knew it," Charlie Badwater said, when this had been interpreted for him. He squatted down by the fire and began picking up handfuls of ashes and blackened twigs and dirt, running the material through his fingers and sniffing it like a dog and occasionally putting a pinch in his mouth to taste it. "Ah," he said finally. "All right, I know what he used. Don't understand *why*—there are some combinations in there that shouldn't work at all, by any of the rules I know—but like I said, what works is what works."

He stood up and looked at the jay. "Ask him if he can remember the song."

"Sure," the jay said. "No problem. Not sure I can sing it, of course—"

"I'll be right back," Charlie Badwater said, heading for the cabin. A minute later Thomas Cornstalk heard him rummaging around inside. The jay said, "Was it something I said?"

In a little while Charlie Badwater came back, his arms full of buckskin bags and brown paper sacks. "Lucky for us he had plenty of everything," he said, and squatted down on the ground and took off his old black hat and turned it upside down on his knees and began taking things out of the bags: mostly dried leaves and weeds and roots, but other items too, not all of them easily identifiable. At one point Thomas Cornstalk was nearly certain he recognized a couple of human finger bones.

"All right," Charlie Badwater said, setting the hat carefully next to the dead fire and straightening up. "Now how does that song go?"

That part wasn't easy. The jay had a great deal of trouble forming some of the sounds; a crow would have been better at this, or maybe a mockingbird. The words weren't in any language Thomas Cornstalk had ever heard, and Charlie Badwater said he'd never heard a song remotely like this one.

At last, after many false starts and failed tries, Charlie Badwater got all the way through the song and the jay said, "That's it. He's got it perfect. No accounting for tastes, I guess."

Charlie Badwater was already piling up sticks from the pile of wood beside the ring of stones. He got out his lighter and in a few minutes the fire was crackling and flickering away. *"Ehena,"* he said over his shoulder. "Ready when you are."

"You want me in on this?"

"Of course. Let's go, Thomas. *Nula.*"

Thomas Cornstalk wasn't at all happy about this, but he walked across the circle to stand beside Charlie Badwater, who had picked up his hat and was holding it in front of him in both hands.

"This I've got to see," the jay commented from its perch on the roof. It had moved up to the ridgepole, probably for a better view. "You guys are crazier than the old man."

Charlie Badwater circled the fire four times, counterclockwise, like a stomp dancer, with Thomas Cornstalk pacing nervously behind him. After the fourth orbit he stopped, facing the sun, and began singing the song the jay had taught him. It sounded different now, somehow. The hair was standing up on Thomas Cornstalk's neck and arms.

Suddenly Charlie Badwater emptied the hat's contents onto the fire. There was a series of sharp fizzing and sputtering noises, and a big cloud of dense gray smoke surged up and surrounded both men. It was so thick that Thomas

Cornstalk couldn't see an inch in front of his face; it was like having his head under very muddy water, or being covered with a heavy gray blanket.

Other things were happening, too. The ground underfoot was beginning to shift and become soft; it felt like quicksand, yet he wasn't sinking into it. His skin prickled all over, not painfully but pretty unpleasantly, and he felt a little sick to his stomach.

The grayness got darker and darker, while the ground fell away completely, until Thomas Cornstalk felt himself to be floating through a great black nothingness. For some reason he was no longer frightened; he simply assumed that he had died and this was what it was like when you went to the spirit world. *"Ni, Jali,"* he called out.

"Ayuh ahni, Tami." The voice sounded close by, but strange, as if Charlie Badwater had fallen down a well.

"Gado nidagal' stani? What's going to happen?"

"Nigal' stisguh," came the cheerful reply. "Whatever . . ."

Thomas Cornstalk had no idea how long the darkness and the floating sensation lasted. His sense of time, the whole idea of time itself, had vanished in that first billow of smoke. But then suddenly the darkness turned to dazzling light and there was something solid under his feet again. Caught by surprise, he swayed and staggered and fell heavily forward, barely getting his arms up in time to protect his face.

He lay half-stunned for a moment, getting the breath back into his lungs and the sight back to his eyes. There was hard smooth planking against his hands; it felt like his own cabin floor, in fact, and at first he thought he must somehow be back home. Maybe the whole thing was a dream and he'd just fallen out of bed . . . but he rolled over and saw bright blue sky above him, crisscrossed by a lot of ropes and long poles. He sat up and saw that he was on the deck of a ship.

It was a ship such as he had only seen in books and movies: the old-fashioned kind, made of wood, with masts and sails instead of an engine. Off beyond the railing, blue water stretched unbroken to the horizon.

Beside him, Charlie Badwater's voice said, "Well, I have to admit this wasn't what I expected."

Thomas Cornstalk turned his head in time to see Charlie Badwater getting to his feet. That seemed like a good idea, so he did it too. The deck was tilted to one side and the whole ship was rolling and pitching, gently but distinctly, with the motion of the sea. Thomas Cornstalk's stomach began to feel a trifle queasy. He hadn't been aboard a ship since his long-ago hitch in the marines, but he remembered about seasickness. He closed his eyes for a second and forced his stomach to settle down. This was no time to lose control of any part of himself.

He said, "Where the hell are we, Charlie?"

From behind them came a harsh cackle. "Where? Wrong question."

The words were in English. The voice was dry and high-pitched, with an old man's quaver. Both men said, "Oh, shit," and turned around almost in unison.

Old Man Alabama was standing on the raised deck at the stern of the ship, looking down at them. His arms were folded and his long hair streamed and fluttered in the wind. His mouth was pulled back at the corners in the closest thing to a smile Thomas Cornstalk had ever seen on his face.

"Not *where*," he went on, and cackled again. "You ought to ask, *when* are we? Of course there's some *where* in it too—"

The horrible smile disappeared all at once. "Say," Old Man Alabama said in a different voice, "how did you two get here, anyway?"

"Same way you did," Charlie Badwater said, also in English. "It wasn't very hard."

"You're a liar." Old Man Alabama spat hard on the deck. "It took me years to learn the secret. How could you two stupid Cherokees—"

"A little bird told us," Thomas Cornstalk interrupted. He knew it was too easy but he couldn't resist.

"I used the same routine you did," Charlie Badwater said, "only I put in a following-and-finding *igawesdi*. You ought to have known you couldn't lose me, old man. What are you up to, anyway?"

Old Man Alabama unfolded his long arms and waved them aimlessly about. It made him look remarkably like a spider monkey Thomas Cornstalk had seen in the Tulsa zoo.

"Crazy Old Man Alabama," he screeched. "I know what you all said about me behind my back—"

"Hey," Charlie Badwater said, "I said it to your face too. Plenty of times."

"Loony old witch," Old Man Alabama went on, ignoring him. "Up there on his mountain, doing nickel-and-dime hexes and love charms, comes into town every now and then and scares the little kids, couldn't witch his way out of a wet paper sack. Yeah, well, look what the crazy old man went and did."

He stopped and shook himself all over. "I did it, too," he said. His voice had suddenly gone softer; it was hard to understand the words. "Nobody else ever even tried it, but I did it. Me."

He stared down at them for a minute, evidently waiting for them to ask him what exactly he'd done. When they didn't, he threw his hands way up over his head again and put his head back and screamed, "*Time*! I found out how to fly through time! Look around you, damn it—they don't have ships like this in the year we come from. Don't you know what you're looking at, here?" ·

Thomas Cornstalk was already glancing up and down the empty decks, up into the rigging and . . . empty decks? "What the hell," he said. "What happened to the people? The sailors and all?"

"Right," Charlie Badwater said. "You didn't sail this thing out here by yourself. Hell, you can't even paddle a canoe. I've seen you try."

Old Man Alabama let off another of his demented laughs. "There," he said, gesturing out over the rail. "There they are, boys. Fine crew they make now, huh?"

Thomas Cornstalk looked where the old man was pointing, but he couldn't see anything but the open sea and sky and a bunch of seagulls squawking and flapping around above the ship's wake. Then he got it. "Aw, hell," he said. "You didn't."

"Should have been here a little while ago," Old Man Alabama chortled, "when they were still learning how to fly. Two of them crashed into the water and a shark got them. Hee hee."

"But why?" Charlie Badwater said. "I mean, the part about traveling into the past, okay, I hate to admit it but I'm impressed. But then fooling around with this kind of childishness, turning a lot of poor damn sailors into sea birds? I know you hate white people, but—"

"Hah! Not just any bunch of sailors," Old Man Alabama said triumphantly. "Not just any white people, either. This is where it all *started*, you dumb blanket-asses! And I'm the one who went back and fixed it!"

He began to sing, a dreadful weird keening that rose and fell over a four-tone scale, without recognizable words. Charlie Badwater and Thomas Cornstalk looked at each other and then back at the old man. Thomas Cornstalk said, "You mean this ship—"

"Yes! It's old *Columbus*'s ship! Now the white bastards won't come at all!" Old Man Alabama's face was almost glowing. "And it was me, me, *me* that stopped them. Poor cracked Old Man Alabama, turns out to be the greatest Indian in history, that's all—"

"Uh, excuse me," Thomas Cornstalk said, "but if this is Columbus's ship, where are the other two?"

"Other two what?" Old Man Alabama asked irritably.

"Other two ships, you old fool," Charlie Badwater said. "Columbus had three ships."

"That's right," Thomas Cornstalk agreed. "I remember from school."

Old Man Alabama was looking severely pissed off. "Are you sure? Damn it, I went to a lot of trouble to make sure I got the right one. Gave this white kid from Tahlequah a set of bear claws *and* a charm to make his girlfriend put out— little bastard drove a hard bargain—for finding me the picture in that book. Told me what year it was and everything. I'm telling you, this is it." Old Man Alabama stomped his bare feet on the deck. "Columbus's ship. The *Mayflower*."

"You ignorant sack of possum poop," Charlie Badwater said. "You don't know squat, do you? Columbus's ship was named the *Santa Maria*. The *Mayflower* was a totally different bunch of *yonegs*. Came ashore up in Maine or somewhere like that."

"These schoolkids nowadays, they're liable to tell you anything," Thomas Cornstalk remarked. "Half of them can't read any better than you do. My sister's girl is going with this white boy, I swear he don't know any more than the average fencepost."

Old Man Alabama was fairly having a fit now. "No," he howled, flailing the air with his long skinny arms. "No, no, it's a lie—"

Charlie Badwater sighed and shook his head. "I bet this isn't even the *Mayflower*," he said to Thomas Cornstalk. "Let's have a look around."

They walked up and down the deserted main deck, looking. There didn't seem to be anything to tell them the name of the ship.

"I think they put the name on the stern," Thomas Cornstalk said. "You know, the hind end of the ship. They did when I was in the corps, anyway."

They climbed a ladder and crossed the quarterdeck, paying no attention to Old Man Alabama, who was now lying on the deck beating the planks with his fists. "Hang on to my belt or something, will you?" Thomas Cornstalk requested. "I don't swim all that good."

With Charlie Badwater holding him by the belt, he hung over the railing and looked at the name painted in big letters across the ship's stern. It was hard to make out at that angle, and upside down besides, but finally he figured it out.

"*Mary Celeste*," he called back over his shoulder. "That's the name. The *Mary Celeste*."

Charlie Badwater looked at Old Man Alabama. "*Mayflower*. Columbus. My Native American ass," he said disgustedly. "I should have let those white guys hang him, back last year."

Thomas Cornstalk straightened up and leaned back against the rail. "Well," he said, "what do we do now?"

Charlie Badwater shrugged. "Go back where we came from. *When* we came from."

"Can you do it?"

"Anything this old lunatic can do, I can figure out how to undo."

Thomas Cornstalk nodded, feeling much relieved. "Do we take him along?"

"We better. No telling what the consequences might be if we left him." Charlie Badwater stared at the writhing body on the deck at his feet. "You know the worst part? It was a hell of a great idea he had. Too bad it had to occur to an idiot."

"*Nasgiduh nusdi*," Thomas Cornstalk said. "That's how it is."

He looked along the empty decks once again. "You think anybody's ever going to find this boat? Come along in another ship, see this one floating out here in the middle of the ocean, nobody on board . . . man," he said, "that's going to make some people wonder."

"People need to wonder now and then," Charlie Badwater said. "It's good for their circulation."

He grinned at Thomas Cornstalk. "Come on," he said. "Let's peel this old fool off the deck and go home."

MELODIES OF THE HEART

Michael F. Flynn

Born in Easton, Pennsylvania, Michael F. Flynn has a BA in math from La Salle College and an MS for work in topology from Marquette University, and works as an industrial quality engineer and statistician. Since his first sale there in 1984, Flynn has become a mainstay of *Analog*, and one of their most frequent contributors. He has also made sales to *The Magazine of Fantasy & Science Fiction* and elsewhere, and is thought of as one of the best of the crop of new "hard science" writers. His first novel was the well-received *In the Country of the Blind*. It was followed by *Fallen Angels*, a novel written in collaboration with Larry Niven and Jerry Pournelle. His most recent book is the novel *The Nanotech Chronicles,* and a new novel, *Firestar,* is on the way, as is a collection of his short stories. His story "The Forest of Time" was in our Fifth Annual Collection. He lives in Edison, New Jersey.

In the poignant and fascinating novella that follows, Flynn invents a new and unique kind of time-travel—one that functions without you actually having to *go* anywhere . . .

I have never been to visit in the gardens of my youth. They are dim and faded memories, brittle with time: A small river town stretched across stony bluffs and hills. Cliffside stairs switchbacking to a downtown of marvels and magical stores. A little frame house nestled in a spot of green, with marigolds tracing its bounds. Men wore hats. Cars gleamed with chrome and sported tailfins enough to take flight. Grown-ups were very tall and mysterious. Sometimes, if you were good, they gave you a nickel, which you could rush to the corner grocery and buy red hot dollars and jawbreakers and licorice whips.

I don't remember the music, though. I know I should, but I don't. I even know what the tunes must have been; I've heard them often enough on Classic Rock and Golden Oldy shows. But that is now, my memories are silent.

I don't go back; I have never gone back. The town would all be different— grimier and dirtier and twenty years more run down. The house I grew up in was sold, and then sold again. Strangers live there now. The cliffside stairs have fallen into disrepair, and half the stores are boarded up and silent. The corner groceries are gone, and a nickel won't buy you squat. Grown-ups are not so tall.

They are still a mystery, though. Some things never change.

> *The music is dreamy.*
> *It's peaches and creamy.*
> *Oh! don't let my feet touch the ground. . . .*

I remember her as I always remember her: sitting against the wall in the garden sunshine, eyes closed, humming to herself.

The first time I saw Mae Holloway was my first day at Sunny Dale. On a tour of the grounds, before being shown to my office, the director pointed out a shrunken and bent old woman shrouded in a shapeless, palehued gown. "Our Oldest Resident." I smiled and acted as if I cared. What was she to me? Nothing, then.

The resident doctor program was new then. A conservative looking for a penny to pinch and a liberal looking for a middle-class professional to kick had gotten drunk together one night and come up with the notion that, if you misunderstood the tax code, your professional services could be extorted by the state. My sentence was to provide on-site medical care at the Home three days a week. Dr. Khan, who kept an office five miles away, remained the "primary care provider."

The Home had set aside a little room that I could use for a clinic. I had a metal desk, an old battered filing cabinet, a chair with a bad caster that caused the wheel to seize up—as if there were a Rule that the furniture there be as old and as worn as the inhabitants. For supplies, I had the usual medicines for aches and pains. Some digitalis. Ointments of one sort or another. Splints and bandages. Not much else. The residents were not ill, only old and tired. First aid and mortuaries covered most of their medical needs.

The second time I saw Mae Holloway was later that same day. The knock on the door was so light and tentative that at first I was unsure I had heard it. I paused, glanced at the door, then bent again over my medical journal. A moment later, the knock came again. Loud! As if someone had attacked the door with a hammer. I turned the journal down, open to the page I had been reading, and called out an invitation.

The door opened and I waited patiently while she shuffled across the room. Hobble, hobble, hobble. You would think old folks would move faster. It wasn't as though they had a lot of time to waste.

When she had settled into the hard plastic seat opposite my desk, she leaned forward, cupping both her hands over the knob of an old blackthorn walking stick. Her face was as wrinkled as that East Tennessee hill country she had once called home. "You know," she said—loudly, as the slightly deaf often do, "you oughtn't leave your door shut like that. Folks see it, they think you have someone in here, so they jes' mosey on."

That notion had been in the back of my mind, too. I had thought to use this time to keep up with my professional reading. "What may I do for you, Mrs. Holloway?" I said.

She looked away momentarily. "I think—" Her jaw worked. She took a breath. "I think I am going insane."

I stared at her for a moment. Just my luck. A nut case right off the bat. Then I nodded. "I see. And why do you say that?"

"I hear music. In my head."

"Music?"

"Yes. You know. Like this." And she hummed a few bars of a nondescript tune.

"I see—"

"That was 'One O'Clock Jump!' " she said, nearly shouting now. "I used to listen to Benny Goodman's band on 'Let's Dance!' Of course, I was younger then!"

"I'm sure you were."

"WHAT DID YOU SAY?"

"I SAID, 'I'M SURE YOU WERE'!" I shouted at her across the desk.

"Oh. Yes," she said in a slightly softer voice. "I'm sorry, but it's sometimes hard for me to hear over the music. It grows loud, then soft." The old woman puckered her face and her eyes drifted, becoming distanced. "Right now, it's 'King Porter.' A few minutes ago it was—"

"Yes, I'm sure," I said. Old folks are slow and rambling and forgetful; a trial to talk with. I rose, hooking my stethoscope into my ears, and circled the desk. Might as well get it over with. Mrs. Holloway, recognizing the routine, unfastened the top buttons of her gown.

Old folks have a certain smell to them, like babies; only not so pleasant. It is a sour, dusty smell, like an attic in the summer heat. Their skin is dry, spotted parchment, repulsive to the touch. When I placed the diaphragm against her chest, she smiled nervously. "I don't think you'll hear my music that way," she said.

"Of course not," I told her. "Did you think I would?"

She rapped the floor with her walking stick. Once, very sharp. "I'm no child, Doctor Wilkes! I have not been a child for a long, long time; so, don't treat me like one." She waved her hand up and down her body. "How many children do you know who look like me?"

"Just one," I snapped back. And instantly regretted the remark. There was no point in being rude; and it was none of her business anyway. "Tell me about your music," I said, unhooking my stethoscope and stepping away.

She worked her lips and glared at me for a while before she made up her mind to cooperate. Finally, she looked down at the floor. "It was one, two nights ago," she whispered. Her hands gripped her walking stick so tightly that the knuckles stood out large and white. She twisted it as if screwing it into the floor. "I dreamed I was dancing in the Roseland Ballroom, like I used to do years and years ago. Oh, I was once so light on my feet! I was dancing with Ben Wickham—he's dead now, of course; but he was one smooth apple and sure knew how to pitch woo. The band was a swing band—I was a swinger, did you know?—and they were playing Goodman tunes. 'Sing, Sing, Sing.' 'Stardust.' But it was so loud, I woke up. I thought I was still dreaming for a while, because I could still hear the music. Then I got riled. I thought, who could be playing their radio so loud in the middle of the night? So I took myself down the hall, room by room, and listened at each door. But the music stayed the same, no matter where I went. That's when I knowed . . . ." She paused, swallowed hard, looked into the corner. "That's when I knowed, knew, it was all in my head."

I opened the sphygmomanometer on my desk. Mae Holloway was over a hundred years old, according to the Home's director; well past her time to shuffle off. If her mind was playing tricks on her in her last years, well, that's what old minds did. Yet, I had read of similar cases of "head" music. "There are several possibilities, Mrs. Holloway," I said, speaking loudly and distinctly while I fastened the pressure cuff to her arm, "But the best bet is that the music really *is* all in your head."

I smiled at the *bon mot*, but all the wire went out of her and she sagged shapelessly in her chair. Her right hand went to her forehead and squeezed. Her eyes twisted tight shut. "Oh, no," she muttered. "Oh, dear God, no. It's finally happened."

Mossbacks have no sense of humor. "Please, Mrs. Holloway! I didn't mean 'in your head' like that. I meant the fillings in your teeth. A pun. Fillings sometimes act like crystal radios and pick up broadcast signals, vibrating the small bones of the middle ear. You are most likely picking up a local radio station. Perhaps a dentist could—"

She looked up at me and her eyes burned. "That was a wicked joke to pull, boy. It was cruel."

"I didn't mean it that way—"

"And I know all about fillings and radios and such," she snapped. "Will Hickey had that problem here five years ago. But that can't be why I hear music." And she extruded a ghastly set of false teeth.

"Well, then—"

"And what sort of radio station could it be? Swing tunes all the time, and only those that I know? Over and over, all night long, with no interruptions. No commercials. No announcements of song titles or performers." She raised her free hand to block her ear, a futile gesture, because the music was on the other side.

On the other side of the ear . . . ? I recalled certain case studies from medical school. Odd cases. "There are other possibilities," I said. "Neurological problems . . ." I pumped the bulb and she winced as the cuff tightened. She lowered her hand slowly and looked at me.

"Neuro . . . ?" Her voice trembled.

"Fossil memories," I said.

She shook her head. "I ain't—I'm not rememberin'. I'm hearin'. I know the difference."

I let the air out of the cuff and unfastened it. "I will explain as simply as I can. Hearing occurs in the brain, not the ear. Sound waves vibrate certain bones in your middle ear. These vibrations are converted into neural impulses and conveyed to the auditory cortex by the eighth cranial nerve. It is the auditory cortex that creates 'sound.' If the nerve were connected to the brain's olfactory region instead, you would 'smell' music."

She grunted. "Quite a bit of it smells, these days."

Hah, hah. "The point is that the sensory cortices can be stimulated without external input. Severe migraines, for example, often cause people to 'see' visions or 'hear' voices. And sometimes the stimulus reactivates so-called 'fossil' memories, which your mind interprets as contemporary. That may be what you are experiencing."

She looked a little to the side, not saying anything. I listened to her wheezy breath. Then she gave me a glance, quick, almost shy. "Then, you don't think I'm . . . you know . . . crazy?" Have you ever heard hope and fear fused into a single question? I don't know. At her age, I think I might prefer a pleasant fantasy world over the dingy real one.

"It's unlikely," I told her. "Such people usually hear voices, not music. If you were going insane, you wouldn't hear Benny Goodman tunes; you would hear Benny Goodman—probably giving you important instructions."

A smile twitched her lips and she seemed calmer, though still uneasy. "It's always been a bother to me," she said quietly, looking past me, "the notion that I might be—well, you know. All my life, it seems, as far back as I can remember."

Which was not that far, the director had told me that morning. "All your life. Why is that?"

She looked away and did not speak for a moment. When she did, she said, "I haven't had no, any, headaches, doc. And I don't have any now. If that's what did it, how come I can still hear the music?"

If she did not want to talk about her fears, that was fine with me. I was no psychiatrist, anyway. "I can't be sure without further tests, but a trigger event—possibly even a mild stroke—could have initiated the process." I had been carefully observing her motor functions, but I could detect none of the slackness or slurring of the voice typical of severe hemiplegia. "Dr. Wing is the resident neurologist at the hospital," I said. "I'll consult with him."

She looked suddenly alarmed, and shook her head. "No hospitals," she said firmly. "Folks go to hospitals, they die."

At her age, that was largely true. I sighed. "Perhaps at Khan's clinic, then. There really are some tests we should run."

That seemed to calm her somewhat, for she closed her eyes and her lips moved slightly.

"Have you experienced any loss of appetite, or episodes of drowsiness?" I asked. "Have you become irritable, forgetful, less alert?" Useless questions. What geezer did not have those symptoms? I would have to inquire among the staff to find out if there had been a recent change in her behavior.

And she wasn't listening any more. At least, not to me. "Thank you, Doctor Wilkes. I was so afraid. . . . That music. . . . But only a stroke, only a stroke. It's such a relief. Thank you. Such a relief."

A relief? Compared to madness, I suppose it was. She struggled to her feet, still babbling. When she left my office, hobbling once more over her walking stick, she was humming to herself again. I didn't know the tune.

> *Even though we're drifting down life's stream apart*
> *Your face I still can see in dream's domain;*
> *I know that it would ease my breaking heart*
> *To hold you in my arms just once again.*

It was dark when I arrived home. As I turned into the driveway I hit the dashboard remote, and the garage door rose up like a welcoming lover. I slid into the left-hand slot without slowing, easing the Lincoln to a halt just as the tennis ball, hanging by a string from the ceiling, touched the windshield. Brenda never understood that. Brenda always came to a complete stop in the driveway before raising the garage door.

I could see without looking that I had beaten her home again. And they said doctors kept long hours. . . . When I stepped from the car, I turned my back on the empty slot.

I stood for some moments at the door to the kitchen, jiggling the car keys in my hand. Then, instead of entering the house, I turned and left the garage through the backyard door. I had seen the second story light on as I came down the street. Deirdre's room. Tonight, for some reason, I couldn't face going inside just yet.

The back yard was a gloom of emerald and jade. The house blocked the glare of the street lamps, conceding just enough light to tease shape from shadow. I walked slowly through the damp grass toward the back of the lot. Glowing clouds undulated in the water of the swimming pool, as if the ground had opened up and swallowed the night sky. Only a few stars poked through the overcast. Polaris? Sirius? I had no way of knowing. I doubted that half a dozen people in the township knew the stars by name; or perhaps even that they had names. We have become strangers to our skies.

At the back of the lot, the property met a patch of woodland—a bit of unofficial greenbelt, undeveloped because it was inaccessible from the road. Squirrels lived there, and blue jays and cardinals. And possum and skunk, too. I listened to the rustle of the night dwellers passing through the carpet of dead leaves. Through the trees I could make out the lights of the house opposite. Distant music and muffled voices. Henry and Barbara Carter were throwing a party.

That damned old woman. Damn all of them. Shambling, crackling, brittle, dried-out old husks, clinging fingernail-tight to what was left of life. . . .

I jammed my hands in my pockets and stood there. For how long, I do not know. It might have been five minutes or half an hour. Finally the light on the second floor went out. Then I turned back to the house and reentered through the garage. The right-hand stall was still empty.

Consuela sat at the kitchen table near the French doors, cradling a ceramic mug shaped like an Olmec head. Half the live-in nurses in the country are Latin; and half of those are named Consuela. The odor of cocoa filled the room, and the steam from the cup wreathed her broad, flat face, lending it a sheen. More *Indio* than *Ladino*, her complexion contrasted starkly with her nurse's whites. Her jet-black hair was pulled severely back, and was held in place with a plain, wooden pin.

"Good evening, Nurse," I said. "Is Dee-dee down for the night?"

"Yes, Doctor. She is."

I glanced up at the ceiling. "I usually tuck her in."

She gave me an odd look. "Yes, you do."

"Well. I was running a little late today. Did she miss me?"

Consuela looked through the French doors at the back yard. "She did."

"I'll make it up to her tomorrow."

She nodded. "I'm sure she would like that."

I shed my coat and carried it to the hall closet. A dim night light glowed at the top of the stairwell. "Has Mrs. Wilkes called?"

"An hour ago." Consuela's voice drifted down the hallway from the kitchen. "She has a big case to prepare for tomorrow. She will be late."

I hung the coat on the closet rack and stood quietly still for a moment before closing the door. Another big case. I studied the stairs to the upper floor. Brenda had begun getting the big cases when Deirdre was eighteen months and alopecia had set in. Brenda never tucked Dee-dee into bed after that.

Consuela was washing her cup at the sink when I returned to the kitchen. She was short and dark and stocky. Not quite chubby, but with a roundness that scorned New York and Paris fashion. I rummaged in the freezer for a frozen dinner. Brenda had picked Consuela from among a dozen applicants. Brenda was tall and thin and blonde.

I put the dinner in the microwave and started the radiation. "I met an interesting woman today," I said.

Consuela dried her cup and hung it on the rack. "All women are interesting," she said.

"This one hears music in her head." I saw how that piqued her interest.

"We all do," she said, half-turned to go.

I carried my microwaved meal and sat at the table. "Not like this. Not like hearing a radio at top volume."

She hesitated a moment longer; then she shrugged and sat across the table from me. "Tell me of this woman."

I moved the macaroni and cheese around on my plate. "I spoke with Dr. Wing over the car phone. He believes it may be a case of 'incontinent nostalgia,' or Jackson's Syndrome."

I explained how trauma to the temporal lobe sometimes caused spontaneous upwellings of memory, often accompanied by "dreamy states" and feelings of profound and poignant joy. Oliver Sacks had written about it in one of his best-sellers. "Shostakovitch had a splinter in his left temporal lobe," I said. "When he cocked his head, he heard melodies. And there have been other cases. Stephen Foster, perhaps." I took a bite of my meal. "Odd, isn't it, how often the memories are musical."

Consuela nodded. "Sometimes the music is enough."

"Other memories may follow, though."

"Sometimes the music is enough," she repeated enigmatically.

"It should make the old lady happy, at least."

Consuela gave me a curious look. "Why should it make her happy?" she asked.

"She has forgotten her early years completely. This condition may help her remember." An old lady reliving her childhood. Suddenly there was bitterness in my mouth. I dropped my fork into the serving tray.

Consuela shook her head. "Why should it make her happy?" she asked again.

That little bird knew lots of things.
It did, upon my word. . . .

The Universe balances. For every Consuela Montejo there is a Noor Khan.

Dr. Noor Khan was a crane, all bones and joints. She was tall, almost as tall as I, but thin to the point of gauntness. She cocked her head habitually from side to side. That, the bulging eyes, and the hooked nose accentuated her bird-like appearance. A good run, a flapping of the arms, and she might take squawking flight—and perhaps appear more graceful.

"Mae Holloway. Oh, my, yes. She is a feisty one, is she not?" Khan rooted in her filing cabinet, her head bobbing as she talked. "Does she have a problem?"

"Incontinent nostalgia, it's sometimes called," I said. "She is experiencing spontaneous, musical recollections, possibly triggered by a mild stroke to the temporal lobes." I told her about the music and Wing's theories.

She bobbed her head. "Curious. Like *déjà vu* only different." Then, more sternly. "If she has had a stroke, even a mild one, I must see her at once."

"I've told her that, but she's stubborn. I thought since you knew her better. . . ."

Noor Khan sighed. "Yes. Well, the older we grow, the more set in our ways we become. Mae must be set in concrete."

It was a joke and I gave it a thin smile. *The older we grow. . . .*

The file she finally pulled was a thick one. I took the folder from her and carried it to her desk. I had nothing particular in mind, just a review of Holloway's medical history. I began paging through the records. In addition to Dr. Khan's notes, there were copies of records from other doctors. I looked up at Khan. "Don't you have patients waiting?"

She raised an eyebrow. "My office hours start at ten, so I have no patients at the moment. You need not worry that I am neglecting them."

If it was a reproof, it was a mild one, and couched in face-saving Oriental terms. I hate it when people watch me read. I always feel as if they were reading over my shoulder. I wanted to tell Khan that I would call her if I needed her; but it was, after all, her office and I was sitting at her desk, so I don't know what I expected her to do. "Sorry," I said. "I didn't mean to ruffle your feathers."

Holloway was in unusually good health for a woman of her age. Her bones had grown brittle and her eyes nearsighted—but no glaucoma; and very little osteoporosis. She had gotten a hearing aid at an age when most people were already either stone deaf or stone dead. Clinical evidence showed that she had once given birth, and that an anciently broken leg had not healed entirely straight. What right had she to enjoy such good health?

Khan had been on the phone. "Mae has agreed to come in," she told me as she hung up. "I will send the van to pick her up Tuesday. I wish I could do a CAT scan here. I would hate to force her in hospital."

"It's a waste, anyway," I muttered.

"What?"

I clamped my jaw shut. All that high technology, and for what? To add a few miserable months to lives already years too long? How many dollars per day of life was that? How much of it was productively returned? That governor, years ago. What was his name? Lamm? He said that the old had a duty to die and make room for the young. "Nothing," I said.

"What is wrong?" asked Khan.

"There's nothing wrong with me."

"That wasn't what I asked."

I turned my attention to the folder and squinted at the spidery, illegible handwriting on the oldest record: 1962, if the date was really what it looked like. Why did so many doctors have poor handwriting? Holloway's estimated age looked more like an eighty five than sixty-five. I waved the sheet of stationery at her. "Look at the handwriting on this," I complained. "It's like reading Sanskrit."

Khan took the letter. "I can read Sanskrit, a little," she said with a smile. "It's Doctor Bench's memoir, isn't it? Yes, I thought so. I found it when I assumed Dr. Rosenblum's practice a few years ago. Dr. Bench promised he would send Mrs. Holloway's older records, but he never did, so Howard had to start a medical history almost from scratch, with only this capsule summary."

I took the sheet back from her. "Why didn't Bench follow through?"

She shrugged. "Who knows? He put it off. Then one of those California brush fires destroyed his office. Medically, Mae is a blank before 1962."

Just like her mind. I thought. Just like her mind.

> *For the joy of eye and ear*
> *For the heart and mind's delight*
> *For the mystic harmony*
> *Linking sense to sound and sight. . . .*

The third time I saw Mae Holloway, she was waiting by the clinic door when I arrived to open it. Eyes closed, propped against the wall by her walking stick, she hummed an obscure melody. "Good morning, Mrs. Holloway," I said. "Feeling better today?"

She opened her eyes and squeezed her face into a ghastly pucker. "Consarn music kept me awake again last night."

I gave her a pleasant smile. "Too bad you don't hear Easy Listening." I stepped through the door ahead of her. I heard her cane tap-tap-tapping behind me and wondered if a practiced ear could identify an oldster by her distinctive cane tap. I could imagine Tonto, ear pressed to the ground. "Many geezer come this way, *kemo sabe.*"

Snapping open my briefcase, I extracted my journals and stacked them on the desk. Mae lowered herself into the visitor's chair. "Jimmy Kovacs will be coming in to see you later today. He threw his back out again."

I opened the issue of *Brain* that Dr. Wing had lent me. "Never throw anything out that you might need again later," I said, running my eye down the table of contents.

"You do study on those books, Doctor."

"I like to keep up on things."

I flipped the journal open to the article I had been seeking and began to read. After a few minutes, she spoke again. "If you spent half the time studying on people as you do studying on books, you'd be better at doctorin'."

I looked up scowling. Who was she to judge? A bent-up, shriveled old woman who had seen more years than she had a right to. "The body is an intricate machine,'' I told her. "The more thoroughly I understand its mechanisms, the better able I am to repair it.''

"A machine,'' she repeated.

"Like an automobile.''

"And you're jest an auto mechanic.'' She shook her head.

I smiled, but without humor. "Yes, I am. Maybe that's less glamorous than being a godlike healer, but I think it's closer to the truth.'' An auto mechanic. And some cars were old jalopies destined for the junk heap; so why put more work into them? I did not tell her that. And others were not built right to begin with. I did not tell her that, either. It was a cold vision, but in its way, comforting. Helplessness is greater solace than failure.

Mae grunted. "Mostly milk sours 'cause it's old.''

I scowled again. More hillbilly philosophy? Or simply an addled mind unable to hold to a topic? "Does it,'' I said.

She studied me for a long while without speaking. Finally, she shook her head. "Most car accidents are caused by the driver.''

"I'll pass that along to the National Transportation Safety Board.''

"What I mean is, you might pay as much attention to the driver as to the automobile.''

I sighed and laid the journal aside. "I take it that you want to tell me what is playing on your personal Top 40 today.''

She snorted, but I could see that she really did. I leaned back in my chair and linked my hands behind my head. "So, tell me, Mrs. Holloway, what is 'shaking'?''

She made fish faces with her lips. Mentally, I had dubbed her Granny Guppy when she did that. It was as if she had to flex her lips first to ready them for the arduous task of flapping.

" 'Does Your Mother Know You're Out, Cecelia?' ''

"What?'' It took a moment. Then I realized that it must have been a song title. Some popular ditty now thankfully forgotten by everyone save this one old lady. "Was that a favorite song of yours?'' I asked.

She shook her head. "Oh, mercy, no; but there was a year when you couldn't hardly avoid it.''

"I see.''

"And, let's see. . . .'' She stopped and cocked her head. The Listening Look, I called it. "Now it's 'The Red, Red Robin'—''

"Comes bob-bob-bobbing along?''

"Yes, that's the one. And already today I've heard 'Don't Bring Lulu' and 'Side by Side' and 'Kitten on the Keys' and 'Bye-bye Blackbird.' '' She made a pout with her lips. "I do wish the songs would play out entirely.''

"You told me they weren't your favorite songs.''

"Some are, some aren't. They're just songs I once heard. Sometimes they remind me of things. Sometimes it seems as if they *almost* remind me of things. Things long forgotten, but waiting for me, just around a corner somewhere.'' She shook herself suddenly. "Tin Pan Alley wasn't my favorite, though,'' she went on. "I was a sheba. I went for the wild stuff. The Charleston; the Black Bottom. All those side kicks. . . . I was a little old for that, but. . . . Those were wild days, I tell you. Hip flasks and stockings rolled down and toss away the corset.'' She gave me a wink.

This . . . *prune* had gone for the wild stuff? Though, grant her, she had had her youth once. It didn't seem fair that she should have it twice. "Sheba?" I asked.

"A sheba," she said. "A flapper. The men were sheiks. Because of that . . . what was his name?" She tapped her cane staccato on the floor. "Valentino, that was it. Valentino. Oh, those eyes of his! All the younger girls dreamed about having him; and I wouldn't have minded one bit, myself. He had It.''

"It?"

"It. Valentino drove the girls wild, he did. And a few boys, too. Clara Bow had It, too.''

"Sex appeal?"

"Pshaw. Sex appeal is for snugglepups. A gal didn't have It unless both sexes felt something. Women, too. Women were coming out back then. We could smoke, pet, put a bun on if we wanted to—least, 'til the dries put on the kabosh. We had the vote. Why we even had a governor, back in Wyoming, where I once lived. Nellie Taylor Ross. I met her once, did I tell you? Why I remember—''

Her sudden silence piqued me. "You remember what?"

"Doc?" Her voice quavered and her eyes looked right past me, wide as tunnels.

"What is it?"

"Doc? I can see 'em. Plain as day.''

"See whom, Mrs. Holloway?" Was the old biddy having a seizure right there in my office?

She looked to her left, then her right. "We're sitting in the gallery," she announced. "All of us wearing pants, too, 'stead o' dresses. And down there . . . down there . . .'' She aimed a shaking finger at a point somewhere below my desk. "That's Alice with the gavel. Law's sake! They're ghosts, Doc. They're ghosts all around me!''

"Mrs. Holloway," I said. "Mrs. Holloway, close your eyes.''

She turned to me. "What?"

"Close your eyes.''

She did. "I can still see 'em," she said, with a wonder that was close to terror. "I can still see 'em. Like my eyes were still open.'' She raised a shaking hand to her mouth. Her ragged breath slowly calmed and, more quietly, she repeated, "I can still see 'em.'' A heartbeat went by, then she sighed. "They're fading, now," she said. "Fading.'' Finally, she opened her eyes. She looked troubled. "Doc, what happened to me? Was it a hallucy-nation?"

I leaned back in my chair and folded my hands under my chin. "Not quite. Simply a non-musical memory.''

"But . . . it was so *real*, like I done traveled back in time.''

"You were here the whole time," I assured her with a grin.

She struck the floor with her cane. "I know that. I could see you just as plain as I could see Alice and the others.''

I sighed. Her sense of humor had dried out along with the rest of her. "Patients with your condition sometimes fall into 'dreamy states,' " I explained. "They see or hear their present and their remembered surroundings simultaneously, like a film that has been double-exposed. Hughlings Jackson described the symptom in 1880. He called it a 'doubling of consciousness.' " I smiled and tapped the journal Wing had given me. "Comes from studying on books," I said.

But she wasn't paying me attention. "I remember it all so clearly now. I'd forgotten. Alice Robertson of Oklahoma was the first woman to preside over the House of Representatives. June 20, 1921, it was. Temporary Speaker. Oh, those were a fine fifteen minutes, I tell you." She sighed and shook her head. "I wonder," she said. "I wonder if I might remember my Ma and Pa and my little brother. Zach . . . ? Was that his name? It's always been a trouble to me that I've forgotten. It don't seem right to forget your own kin."

An inverse square law, I suppose. Memories dim and blur with age, their strength depending on distance and mass. Too many of Mae's memories were too distant. They had passed beyond the horizon of her mind, and had faded like an old photograph left too long in the Sun. And yet sometimes, near the end, like ashes collapsing in a dying fire, the past can become brighter than the present.

"No," I said. "It don't seem right."

"And Mister. . . . Haven't thought on that man in donkey's years," she said. "Green Holloway was my man. I always called him Mister. He called me his Lorena."

"Lorena?"

Mae shrugged. "I don't remember why. There was a song. . . . He took the name from that. It was real popular, so I suppose I'll recollect it bye and bye. He was an older man, was Mister. I remember him striding up through Black's hell; gray and grizzled, but strong as splo. All brass and buckles in his state militia uniform. Company H, 5th Tennessee. Just that one scene has stayed with me all my life, like an ole brown photograph. Dear Lord, but that man had arms like cooper's bands. I can close my eyes and feel them around me sometimes, even today." She shivered and looked down.

"Splo?" I prompted.

"Splo," she repeated in a distracted voice. Then, more strongly, as if shoving some memory aside, "Angel teat. We called it apple john back then. Mister kept a still out behind the joe. Whenever he run off a batch, he'd invite the spear-side over and we'd all get screwed."

I bet. Whatever she had said. "Apple john was moonshine?" *High tail it, Luke. The revenooers are a-coming.* What kind of Barney Google life had she led up in those Tennessee hills? "So when you say you got screwed, you mean you got drunk, not, uh. . . ."

Mae sucked in her lips and gnawed on them. "It was good whilst we were together," she said at last. "Right good." Her lips thinned. "But Mister, he lit a shuck on me, just like all the others." She gave me a look, half angry, half wary; and I could almost see the shutter come down behind her eyes. "Ain't no use getting close to nobody," she said. "They're always gone when you need them. Why, I ain't, haven't seen Little Zach nigh unto. . . ." She looked momentarily confused. "Not for years and years. I loved that boy like he was more'n a brother; but he yondered off and never come back.'' She creaked to her feet. ''So, I'll just twenty-three skidoo, Jack. You got things to do; so do I.''

I watched her go, thinking she was right about one thing. Old milk does go sour.

> *There will I find a settled rest*
> *While others go and come.*
> *No more a stranger or a guest*
> *But like a child at home.*

Brenda's silver Beemer was parked in the garage when I got home. I pulled up beside it and contemplated its shiny perfection as I turned my engine off. Brenda was home. How long had it been, now? Three weeks? Four? It was hard to remember. Leave early; back late. That was our life. A quick peck in the morning and no-time-for-breakfast-dear. Tiptoes late at night, and the sheets rustle and the mattress sags; and it was hardly enough even to ruffle your sleep. Always on the run; always working late. One of us would have to slow down, or we might never meet at all.

My first thought was that I might give Consuela the night off. It had been so long since Brenda and I had been alone together. My second thought was that she had gotten in trouble at the office and had lost her job.

Doctors make good money. Lawyers make good money. Doctors married to lawyers make *very* good money. It was not enough.

''Brenda?'' I called as I entered the kitchen from the garage. ''I'm home!'' There was no one in the kitchen; though something tangy with orange and sage was baking in the oven. ''Brenda?'' I called again as I reached the hall closet.

A squeal from upstairs. ''Daddy's home!''

I hung up my overcoat. ''Hello, Dee-dee. Is Mommy with you?'' Unlikely, but possible. Stranger things have happened.

''No.'' Followed by a long silence; ''Connie is telling me a story, about a mule and an ox.''

Another silence, then footsteps on the stairs. Consuela looked at me over the banister as she descended.

''The mule and the ox?'' I said.

''Nothing,'' she replied curtly. ''An old Mayan folk tale.''

''Where's Brenda?'' I asked her. ''I know she's home; her car is in the garage.'' Maybe she was in the back yard, by the pool or in the woods.

No, she didn't like the woods; she was afraid of deer ticks.

''Mrs. Wilkes came home early,'' Consuela said, ''and packed a bag—''

Mentally, I froze. Not *this*. Not *now*. Without Brenda's income. . . . ''Packed a bag? Why?''

''She said she must go to Washington for a few days, to assist in an argument before the Supreme Court.''

''Oh.'' Sudden relief coupled with sudden irritation. She could have phoned. At the Home. In my car. I showed Consuela my teeth. ''The Supreme Court, you say. Well. That's quite a feather in her cap.''

''Were she an Indio, a feather in the cap might mean something.''

"Consuela. A joke? Did Brenda say when she would be back?"

Consuela hesitated, then shook her head. "She came home, packed her bag, gave me instructions. When the car arrived, she left."

And never said good-bye to Deedee. Maybe a wave from the doorway, a crueler good-bye than none at all. "What sort of instructions?" That wasn't the question I wanted to ask. I wanted to ask whose car picked her up. Whom she was assisting in Washington? Walther Crowe, the steeleyed senior partner with the smooth, European mannerisms? FitzPatrick, the young comer who figured so often on the society pages? But Consuela would not know; or, if she did, she would not say. There were some places where an outsider did not deliberately set herself.

"The sort of instructions," she replied, "that are unnecessary to give a professional. But they were only to let me know that I was her employee."

"You're angry." I received no answer. Then I asked, "Have you and Deedee eaten yet?"

"No." A short answer, not quite a retort.

"I didn't pull rank on you. Brenda did."

She shrugged and looked up at me with her head cocked to the side. "You are a doctor; I am a nurse. We have a professional relationship. Mrs. Wilkes is only an employer."

She was in a bad mood. I had never seen her angry before. I wondered what patronizing tone Brenda had used with her. I always made the effort to treat Consuela as an equal; but Brenda seldom did. Sometimes I thought Brenda was half-afraid of our Deirdre's nurse; though for what reason, I could not say. I glanced at the overcoat in the closet. "Would you and Dee-dee like to go out to eat?"

She gave me a thoughtful look; then shook her head. "She will not leave the house."

I glanced at the stairs. "No, she'll not budge, will she?" It was an old argument, never won. "She can play outside. She can go to school with the other children. There is no medical reason to stay in her—"

"There is something wrong with her heart."

"No, it's too soon for—"

"There is something wrong with her heart," she repeated.

"Oh." I looked away. "But. . . . We'll eat in the dining room today. The three of us. Whatever that is you have in the oven. I'll set the table with the good dinnerware."

"A special occasion?"

I shook my head. "No. Only maybe we each have a reason to be unhappy just now." I wondered if Brenda had left a message in the bedroom. Some hint as to when she'd return. I headed toward the dining room.

"The ox was weary of plowing," Consuela said.

"Eh?" I turned and looked back at her. "What was that?"

"The ox was weary of plowing. All day, up the field and down, while the farmer cracked the whip behind him. Each night in the barn, when the ox complained, the mule would laugh. 'If you detest the plowing so much, why do it?' 'It is my job, señor mule,' the ox would reply. 'Then do it and don't complain. Otherwise, refuse. Go on strike.' The ox thought about this and, several days later, when the farmer came to him with the harness, the ox would not budge. 'What is wrong, señor ox?' the farmer asked him. 'I am on strike,' the ox replied. 'All day I plow with no rest. I deserve a rest.' The farmer nodded. 'There is justice in what you say. You have worked hard. Yet the fields must be plowed before the rains come.' And so he hitched the mule to the plow and cracked the whip over him, and worked him for many weeks until the plowing was done.''

Consuela stopped, and with a slight gesture of the head turned for the kitchen.

Although entitled to two evenings a week off, Consuela seldom took them, preferring the solitude of her own room. She lived there quietly, usually with the hall door closed; always with the connecting door to Dee-dee's room open. Once a month she sent a check to Guatemala. She read books. Sometimes she played softly on a sort of flute: weird, serpentine melodies that she had brought with her from the jungle. More than once, the strange notes had caused Brenda to stop whatever she was doing, whether mending or reading law or even making love, and listen with her head cocked until the music stopped. Then she would shiver slightly, and resume whatever she had been doing as though nothing had happened.

Consuela had furnished her room with Meso-American bric-a-brac. Colorful, twisty things. Statuettes, wall hangings, a window treatment. Squat little figurines with secretive, knowing smiles. A garland of fabric flowers. An obsidian carving that suggested a panther in mid-leap. Brenda found it all vaguely disturbing, as if she expected chittering monkeys swinging from the bookshelves and curtains; as if Consuela had brought a part of the jungle with her into Brenda's clear, ordered, rational world. It wasn't proper, at all. It was somehow out of control.

"Did you like having dinner downstairs today?" I asked Dee-dee as I studied Consuela's room through the connecting door. The flute lay silent on Consuela's dresser top. It was the kind you blew straight into, with two rows of holes, one for each hand.

"It was OK, I guess." A weak voice, steady but faint.

I turned around. "Only OK?" There was an odd contrast here, a paradox. Although it was evening and Deirdre's room was shrouded in darkness, Consuela's room had seemed bright with rioting colors.

"Did I leave any toys downstairs?" A worried voice in the darkness. Anxious.

"No, I checked." I resolved to check again, just in case we had overlooked something that had rolled under the sofa. Brenda detested disorder. She did not like finding things out of place.

"Mommy won't mind, will she? That I ate downstairs."

I turned. "Not if we don't tell her. Mommy will be at the Supreme Court for a few days."

Dee-dee made a sound in her throat. No sorrow, no joy. Just acknowledgment. Mommy might never come home at all for all the difference it made in Dee-dee's life. "Ready to be tucked in?"

Dee-dee grinned a delicious smile and snuggled deeper into the sheets. It was a heartbreaking smile. I gave her back the best one I could muster, and took a long, slow step toward the bed. She shrieked and ducked under the covers. I waited until she peeked out and took another step. It was a game we played, every move as encrusted with ritual as a Roman Mass.

Hutchinson-Gilford Syndrome. Deedee's smile was snaggle-toothed. Her hair, sparse; her skin, thin and yellow.

Manifestations: Alopecia, onset at birth to eighteen months, with degeneration of hair follicles. Thin skin. Hypoplasia of the nails. . . . I had read the entry in *Smith's* over and over, looking for the one item I had missed, the loophole I had overlooked. It was committed to memory now; like a mantra. *Periarticular fibrosis; stiff or partially flexed prominent joints. Skeletal hypoplasia, dysphasia and degeneration.*

Dee-dee had weighed 2.7 kilos at birth. Her fontanel had ossified late, but the slowness of her growth had not become apparent until seven months. She lagged the normal growth charts by one-third. When she lost hair, it did not grow back. Her skin had brownish-yellow "liver" spots.

Natural history: Deficit of growth becomes severe after one year. The tendency to fatigue easily may limit participation in childhood activities. Intelligence and brain development are unimpaired.

Deirdre Wilkes was an alert, active mind trapped in a body aging far too quickly. A shrunken little gnome of a ten-year old. *Etiology: Unknown.* I hugged her and kissed her on the cheek. Then I tucked the sheets tightly under the mattress.

Prognosis: The life span is shortened by relentless arterial atheromatosis. Death usually occurs at puberty.

There were no papers delivered on Hutchinson-Gilford that I had not crawled through word after word, searching for the slightest whisper of a breakthrough. Some sign along the horizon of research. But there were no hints. There were no loopholes.

Prognosis: death.

There were no exceptions.

Deirdre could smile because she was only a child and could not comprehend what was happening to her body. She knew she would have to "go away" someday, but she didn't know what that really meant.

Smiling was the hardest part of the game.

> *Come along, Josephine, In my flying machine.*
> *We'll go up in the air. . . .*

How can I explain the feelings of dread and depression that enveloped me every time I entered Sunny Dale? I was surrounded by ancients. Bent, gray, hobbling creatures forever muttering over events long forgotten or families never seen. And always repeating their statements, always repeating their statements, as if it were I who were hard of hearing and not they. The Home was a waiting room for Death. Waiting and waiting, until they had done with waiting. Here is where the yellowed skin and the liver spots belonged. Here! Not on the frame of a ten-year-old.

*   *   *

The fourth time I saw Mae Holloway, she crept up behind me as I opened the door to the clinic. "Morning, doc," I heard her say.

"Good morning, Mrs. H.," I replied without turning around. I opened the door and stepped through. Inevitably, she followed, humming. I wondered if this was going to become a daily ritual. She planted herself in the visitor's chair. Somehow, it had become her own. "The show just ended," she announced. "Oh, it was a peach." She waved a hand at my desk. "Go on, set down. Make yourself pleasant."

It was my own fault, really. I had shown an interest in her tiresome recollections, and now she felt she had to share everything with me, as if I were one of her batty, old cronies. No good deed goes unpunished. Perhaps I was the only one who put up with her.

But I did have a notion that could wring a little use out of my sentence. I could write a book about Mae Holloway and her musical memories. People were fascinated with how the mind worked; or rather with how it failed to work. Sacks had described similar cases of incontinent nostalgia in one of his books; and if he could make the best-seller lists with a collection of neurological case studies, why not I? With fame, came money; and the things money could buy.

But my book would have to be something new, something different; not just a retelling of the same neurological tales. The teleology, perhaps. Sacks had failed to discover any meaning to the music his patients had heard, any reason *why* this tune or that was rememb-heard. If I kept a record, I might discover enough of a pattern to form the basis of a book. I rummaged in my desk drawer and took out a set of file cards that I had bought to make notes on my patients. Might as well get started. I poised my pen over a card. "What show was that?" I asked.

"*Girl of the Golden West*. David Belasco's new stage play." She shook her head. "I first seen it, oh, years and years ago, in Pittsburgh; before they made it a high falutin' opera. That final scene, where Dick Johnson is hiding in the attic, and his blood drips through the ceiling onto the sheriff. That was taken from real life, you know."

"Was it." I wrote *Girl of the Golden West* and *doubling episode* and made a note to look it up. Then I poised my pen over a fresh card. "I'd like to ask you a few questions about your music, Mrs. Holloway. That is, if you don't mind."

She gave me a surprised glance and looked secretly pleased. She fussed with her gown and settled herself into her seat. "You may fire when ready, Gridley."

"You *are* still hearing the music, aren't you, Mrs. Holloway?"

"Well, the songs aren't so loud as they were. They don't keep me awake anymore; but if I concentrate, I can hear 'em."

I made a note. "You've learned to filter them out, that's all."

"If You Talk in Your Sleep, Don't Mention My Name."

"What?"

" 'If You Talk in Your Sleep, Don't Mention My Name.' That was one of 'em. The tunes I been hearing. Go on, write that down. Songs were getting real speedy in those days. There was 'Mary Took the Calves to the Dairy Show' and 'This is No Place for a Minister's Son.' Heh-heh. The blues was all in a lather over 'em. That, and actor-folks actually kissing each other in the moving picture shows. They tried to get that banned. And the animal dances, too.''

''Animal dances?''

''Oh, there were a passel of 'em,'' she said. ''There was the kangaroo dip, the crab step, the fox trot, the fish walk, the bunny hug, the lame duck. . . . I don't remember them all.''

''The fox trot,'' I offered. ''I think people still dance that.''

Mae snorted. ''All the fire's out of it. You should have read what the preachers and the newspapers had to say about it back then. They sure were peeved; but the kids thought it was flossy. It was a way to get their parents' goat. 'Bug them,' I guess you say now.''

''Kids? Isn't the fox trot a ballroom dance for, well, you know—mature people?''

She made her sour-lemon face. ''Sure. Now. But today's old folks were yesterday's kids. And they still like the music they liked when they were young. Heh-heh. When you're ninety or a hundred, sonny, you'll be a-listening to that acid rock and telling your grandkids what hell-raisers you used to be. And they won't believe you, either. We tote the same bags with us all our lives, doc. The same interests; the same likes and dislikes. Those older'n us and those younger'n us, why, they have their own bags.'' A sudden scowl, halfway between fright and puzzlement, passed across her face like the shadow of a cloud. Then she hunched her shoulders. ''Me, I've got too many bags.''

She'd get no argument from me on that. ''Have you heard any other songs?'' I asked.

She folded her hands over the knob of her walking stick and rested her chin on them. ''Let's see. . . . Yesterday, I heard, heard 'Waiting for the Robert E. Lee' and 'A Perfect Day.' Those were real popular, once. And lots of Cohan songs. 'Oh, it was Mary, Mary, long before the fashion changed. . . . ' And 'Rosie O'Grady.' Then there was 'Memphis Blues.' Young folks thought it was 'hep.' Even better than ragtime.''

She shook her head. ''I never cottoned too well to those kids, though,'' she said. ''They remind me of the kids nowadays. A little too. . . . What do you say now? 'Close to the edge.' Ran wild when they were young 'uns, they did. Hung around barbershops. Hawked papers as newsies. Worked the growler for their old man.''

I looked up from my notes. ''Worked the growler?''

''Took the beer bucket to the saloon to get it filled. Imagine sending a child— even girls!—into a saloon! No wonder Carrie and the others wanted to close 'em up. Maybe folks my age were a little too stuck on ourselves, like the younger folks said; but at least we had principles. With us, it wasn't all just to have a good time. We fought for things worth fighting for. Suffrage. Prohibition. Birth control. Oh, those were times, I tell you. Maggie, making those speeches about birth control and standing up there on the stage that one time with the tape over her mouth, because they wouldn't let her talk. I helped her open that clinic of hers over in Brooklyn, though I never did care for her attitude about Jews and coloreds. Controlling 'undesirables' wasn't the real reason for birth control, anyway.''

"Mrs. Holloway!"

She looked at me and laughed. "Now, don't tell me *your* generation is shocked at such talk!"

"It's not that. It's—"

"That old folks wrangled over it, too? Well, folks aren't born old. We were young, too; and as full of piss and vinegar as anyone else. I read *Moral Physiology* when it first come out; though Mister did try mightily to discourage me. And, later, there was *The Unwelcomed Child*. Doc, if men had babies, birth control would never have been a crime."

Folks aren't born old. . . . I squared off my deck of index cards. "I suppose not." My generation had been as strong as any for civil rights and feminism. Certainly stronger than the hard-edged cynics coming up behind us. It sounded as if Mae had had a similar generational experience. Though, that would put her in the generation *before* the hell-raising Lost Generation. What was it called? The Missionary Generation? Maybe she was older than she looked; though that hardly seemed possible. "Let's get back to the songs—" I suggested.

"Yes, the songs," she said. "The songs. Why, I recollect a man had a right good voice. Now what was his name . . . ? A wonderful dancer, too."

"Ben Wickman?" I suggested.

"No. No, Ben was later. This was out Pittsburgh way. Joe Paxton. That was it." She tilted her head back. "He was a barnstormer, Joe was. He knew 'em all. Calbraith Rodgers, Glenn Curtiss, Pancho Barnes, even Wilbur Wright. Took me up once, through the Alleghenies. Oh, my, that was something, let me tell you. The wind in your face and the ground drifting by beneath you, and the golden Sun peeking between the shoulders of the hills. . . . And you felt you were dancing with the clouds." She sighed, and the light in her eyes slowly faded. "But he was like all the rest." Her face closed up; became hard. "I come on him one day packing his valise, and when I asked him why he was cutting out, all he could say was, 'How old is Ann?' "

"What?"

She blinked and focused moistened eyes on me. Slowly, before they could even fall, her tears vanished into the sand of her soul. "Oh, that's what everyone said back then. 'How old is Ann?' It meant 'Who knows?' Came from one of those brain teasers that ran in the *New York Press*. You know. 'If Mary is twice as old as Ann was when Mary . . . ' And it goes through all sorts of contortions and ends up 'How old is Ann?' Most folks hadn't the foggiest notion and didn't care, so they started saying 'How old is Ann?' when they didn't know the answer to something." She pushed down on her walking stick and started to rise.

"Wait. I still have a few questions."

"Well, I don't have any more answers. Joe, well, he turned out worthless in the end; but we had some high times together." Then she sighed and looked off into the distance. "And he did take me flying, once, when flying was more than just a ride."

> *As I was walking down the street,*
> *down the street, down the street,*

A handsome gal I chanced to meet.
Oh, she was fair to view.
Lovely Fan', won't you come out tonight,
*   come out tonight, come out tonight?*
Lovely Fan', won't you come out tonight,
*   and dance by the light of the moon?*

It was late in the evening—midnight, perhaps—and, dressed in housecoat and slippers, I was frowning over a legal pad and a few dozen index cards, a cup of cold coffee beside me on the kitchen table. I was surrounded by small, sourceless sounds. If you have been in a sleeping building at night, you know what I mean. Creaks and rustlings and the sighs of . . . what? Spirits? Air circulation vents? The soft groan of settling timbers. The breath of the wind against the windows. The staccato scritching of tiny night creatures dancing across the roof shingles. The distant rumble of a red-eye flight making its descent into the metropolitan area. Among such confused, muttering sounds, who can distinguish the pad of bare feet on the floor?

A gasp, and I turned.

I had never seen Consuela when she was not wearing nurse's whites. Perhaps once or twice, bundled in a coat as she sought one of her rare nights out; but never in a red and yellow flowing flowered robe. Never with her black hair unfastened and sweeping around her like a ravenfeather cape. She stood in the kitchen doorway, clenching the robe's collar in her fist.

"Consuela," I said.

"I—saw the light on. I thought you had already gone to sleep. So I—" Consuela flustered was a new sight, too. She turned to go. "I did not mean to disturb you."

"No, no. Stay a while." I laid my pen down and stretched. "I couldn't get to sleep, so I came down here to work a while." When she hesitated, I stood and pulled a chair out for her. She gave me a sidelong look, then bobbed her head once and took a seat. I wondered if she thought I might "try something." Late at night; wife away; both of us in pajamas, thoughts of bed in our minds. Hell, *I* wondered if I might try something. Brenda had grown more distant each year since Deirdre's birth.

But Consuela was not my type. She was too short, too wide, too dark. I studied her covertly while I handled her chair. Well, perhaps not "too." And she did have a liquid grace to her, like a panther striding through the jungle. Brenda's grace was of a different sort. Brenda was fireworks arcing and bursting across the night sky. You might get burnt, but never bitten.

"Would you like something to drink?" I asked when she had gotten settled. "Apple juice, orange juice." Too late for coffee; and a liqueur would have been inappropriate.

"Orange juice would be fine, thank you," she said.

I went to the refrigerator and removed the carafe. Like everyone else, we buy our OJ in wax-coated paperboard containers; but Brenda transferred the milk, the juices, and half a dozen other articles into carafes and canisters and other more appropriate receptacles. Most people shelved their groceries. We repackaged ours.

"Do you remember the old woman I told you about last week?"

"The one who hears music? Yes."

I brought the glasses to the table. "She's starting to remember other things, now." I told her about Mae's recollections, her consciousness doubling. "I've started to keep track of what she sees and hears," I said, indicating the papers on the table. "And I've sent to the military archives to see if they could locate Green Holloway's service records. Later this week, I plan to go into the City to check the census records at the National Archives."

Consuela picked up the legal pad and glanced at it. "Why are you doing this thing?"

"For verification. I'm thinking I might write a book."

She looked at me. "About Mrs. Holloway?"

"Yes. And I think I may have found an angle, too." I pointed to the pad she held. "That is a list of the songs and events Holloway has rememb-heard."

After a moment's hesitation, Consuela read through the list. She shook her head. "You are looking for meaning in this?" Her voice held a twist of skepticism in it. For a moment, I saw how my activities might look from her perspective. Searching for meaning in the remembered songs of a half-senile old woman. What should that be called, senemancy? Melodimancy? What sort of auguries did High Priest Wilkes find, eviscerating this morning's ditties?

"Not meaning," I said. "Pattern. Explanation. Some way to make sense of what she is going through."

Consuela gave me that blank look she liked to affect. "It may not make sense."

"But it almost does." I riffed the stack of index cards. Each card held information about a song Mae had heard. The composer, songwriter, performer; the date, the topic, the genre. Whether Mae had liked it or not. "The first time she came to me," I said, "she was 'rememb-hearing' swing tunes from the 1930s. A few days later, it was music of the 'Roaring Twenties.' Then the jazz gave way to George M. Cohan and the 'animal dance' music of the Mauve Decade. Do you see? The songs keep coming from earlier in her life."

"Memphis Blues," 1912. "A Perfect Day," 1910. "Mary Took the Calves to the Dairy Show," 1909. "Rosie O Grady," 1906. Songs my grandparents heard as children. "East side, west side, All around the town. . . ." I remembered how Granny used to sit my brother and me on her lap, one on each knee, and rock us back and forth while she sang that. I paused and cocked my head, listening into the silence of the night.

But I could hear nothing. I could remember *that* she sang it; but I could not remember the singing.

"It is a voyage," I said, loudly, to fill the silence. "A voyage of discovery up the stream of time."

Consuela shook her head. "Rivers have rapids," she said, "and falls."

> *Hello, my baby, hello, my honey,*
> *hello, my ragtime gal . . .*
> *Send me a kiss by wire,*
> *Baby, my heart's on fire.*

Mae's morning visit fell into a routine. She settled herself into her chair with an air of proprietorship and croaked out snatches of tunes while I wrote down what I could, recording the rest on a cheap pocket tape recorder I had purchased. She hummed "The Maple Leaf Rag" and "Grace and Beauty" and the "St. Louis Tickle." I suffered through her renditions of "My Gal Sal" and "The Rosary." ("A big hit," she assured me, "for over twenty-five years.") She rememb-heard the bawdy "Hot Time in the Old Town Tonight" (sounding grotesque on her ancient lips), the raggy "You've Been a Good Old Wagon, But You've Done Broke Down," and the poignant "Good-bye, Dolly Gray."

She frowned for a moment. "Or was that 'Nellie Gray'?" Then she shrugged. "Those were happy songs, mostly," she said. "Oh, they were such good songs back then. Not like today, all angry and shouting. Even the sad songs were sweet. Like 'Tell Them that You Saw Me' or 'She's Only a Bird in a Gilded Cage.' And Mister taught me 'Lorena,' once. I wish I could recollect that 'un. And 'Barbry Ellen.' I learned me that 'un when I was knee-high to a grasshopper. Pa told me it was the President's favorite song. The old President, from when his Pappy fought in the War. I haven't heard those yet. Or—'' She cocked her head to the side. "Well, dad-blast it!"

"What's wrong, Mrs. Holloway?"

"I'm starting to hear coon songs."

"Coon songs!"

She shook her head. "Coon songs. They was—were—all the rage. 'Coon, Coon, Coon' and 'All Coons Look Alike to Me' and 'If the Man in the Moon were a Coon.' Some of them songs were writ by coloreds themselves, because they had to write what was popular if they wanted to make any money."

"Mrs. Holloway . . . !"

"Never said I liked 'em," she snapped back. "I met plenty of coloreds in my time, and there's some good and some bad, just like any other folks. Will Biddle, he farmed two hollers over from my Pa when I was a sprout, and he worked as hard as any man-jack in the hills, and carried water for no man. My Pa said—my Pa. . . ." She paused, frowned and shook her head. "Pa?"

"What is it?"

"Oh."

"Mrs. Holloway?"

She spoke in a whisper, not looking at me, not looking at anything I could see. "I remember when my Pa died. Him a-laying on the bed, all wore out by life. Gray and wrinkled and toothless. And, dear Lord, how that ached me. I remember thinking how he'd been such a strong man. Such a strong man." She sighed. "It's an old apartment, and the wallpaper is peeling off'n the walls. There's a big dark water stain on one wall and the steam radiator is hissing like a cat."

"You don't remember where you were . . . are?" I asked, jotting a few quick notes.

She shook her head. "No. I'm humming 'In the Good Old Summertime.' Or maybe the tune is just running through my head. Pa, he. . . ." A tear formed in the corner of her eye. "He wants me to sing him the song."

"The song? What song is that?"

"An old, old song he used to love. 'Sing it to me one last time,' he says. And I can't sing at all because my throat's clenched up so tight. But he asks me again, and. . . . Those eyes of his! How I loved that old man." Mae's own eyes had glazed over as she lived the scene again in her mind. She reached out as if clasping another pair of hands in her own and croaked haltingly:

> *"I gaze on the moon as I tread the drear wild,*
> *And feel that my mother now thinks of her child . . .*
> *Be it ever so humble . . ."*

She could not finish. For a time, she sobbed softly. Then she brushed her eye with her sleeve and looked past me. "I never knew, doc. I never knew at all what a blessing it was to forget."

> *Come and sit by my side if you love me.*
> *Do not hasten to bid me adieu,*
> *But remember the bright Mohawk Valley*
> *And the girl that has loved you so true.*

Later that day, as I was leaving the Home, I noticed Mae sitting in the common room and paused a moment to eavesdrop. There were a handful of other residents moldering in chairs and rockers; but Mae sat singing quietly to herself and I thought what the hell, and pulled out my pocket tape recorder and stepped up quietly beside her.

It was a patriotic hymn. "America, the Beautiful." I'm sure you've heard it. Even I know the words to that one. Enough to know that Mae had them all wrong. *Oh beautiful for halcyon skies? Above the enameled plain?* And the choruses. . . . The way Mae sang it, "God shed his grace for thee" sounded more like a plea than a statement.

> *America! America! God shed his grace for thee*
> *Till selfish gain no longer stain The banner of the free!*

The faulty recollection disturbed me. If Mae's memories were unreliable, then what of my book? What if my whole rationale turned out wrong?

Her croakings died away and she opened her eyes and spotted me. "Heading home, doc?"

"It's been a long day," I said. There was no sign on her face of her earlier melancholy, except that maybe her cheeks sagged a little lower than before, her eyes gazed a little more sadly. She seemed older, somehow; if such a thing were possible.

She patted the chair next to her. "Hot foot it on over," she said. "You're just in time for the slapstick."

She was obviously having another doubling episode, and, in some odd way, I was being asked to participate. I looked at my watch, but decided that since our morning session had been cut short, I might as well make the time up now. My next visit was not until Friday. If I waited until then, these memories could be lost.

"Slapstick?" I asked, taking the seat she had offered.

"You never been to the Shows?" She tsk-ed and shook her head. "Well, Jee-whiskers. They been the place to go ever since Tony Pastor got rid of the cootchee-cootchee and cleaned up his acts. A young man can take his steady there now and make goo-goo eyes." She nudged me with her elbow. "A fellow can be gay with his fairy up in the balcony."

I pulled away from her. "I beg your pardon?"

"Don't you want to be gay?" she asked.

"I should hope not! I have a wife, a dau—"

Mae laughed suddenly and capped a gnarled hand over her mouth. So help me, she blushed. "Oh, my goodness, me! I didn't mean were you a *cake-eater.* I got all mixed up. I was sitting down front at the burly-Q and I was sitting here in the TV room with you. When we said 'be gay,' we meant let your hair down and relax. And a 'fairy' was your girl friend, what they used to call a chicken when I was younger. All the boys wanted to be gay blades, with their starched collars and straw hats and spats. And their moustaches! You never saw such moustaches! Waxed and curled and barbered." She chuckled to herself. "I was a regular daisy, myself." She closed her eyes and leaned back.

"A regular daisy?"

"A daisy," she repeated. "Like in the song. Gals was going out to work in them days. So they made a song about it. Now, let me see. . . ." She pouted and stared closed-eyed at the sky. "How did that go?" She began to sing in a cracked, quavery voice.

> *"My daughter's as fine a young girl as you'll meet*
> *In your travels day in and day out;*
> *But she's getting high-toned and she's putting on airs*
> *Since she has been working about. . . .*
> *When she comes home at night from her office,*
> *She walks in with a swag like a fighter;*
> *And she says to her ma, 'Look at elegant me!'*
> *Since my daughter plays on the typewriter.*
>
> *She says she's a 'regular daisy,'*
> *Uses slang 'til my poor heart is sore;*
> *She now warbles snatches from operas*
> *Where she used to sing 'Peggy O Moore.'*
> *Now the red on her nails looks ignited;*
> *She's bleached her hair 'til it's lighter.*
> *Now perhaps I should always be mad at the man*
> *That taught her to play the typewriter.*
>
> *She cries in her sleep, 'Your letter's to hand.'*
> *She calls her old father, 'esquire';*
> *And the neighbors they shout*
> *When my daughter turns out,*
> *'There goes Bridget Typewriter Maguire.' "*

When Mae was done, she laughed again and wiped tears from her eyes. "Law's sake," she said. "Girls a-working in the offices. I remember what a stir-up that was. Folks said secretarial was man's work, and women couldn't be good typewriters, no how. There was another song, 'Everybody Works But Father,' about how if women was to go to work, all the men would be out of jobs. Heh-heh. I swan! It weren't long afore one gal in four had herself a 'position,' like they used to say; and folks my age complained how the youngsters were 'going to pot.' '' She shook her head and chuckled.

"I always did find those kids more to my taste," she went on. "There was something about 'em; some spark that I liked. They knew how to have fun without that ragged edge that the next batch had. And they had, I don't know, call it a dream. They were out to change the world. They sure weren't wishy-washy like the other folks my age. 'Middle-aged,' that's what the kids back then called us. We were 'Professor Tweetzers' and 'Miss Nancys' and 'goo-goos.' And to tell you the truth, Doc, I thought they pegged it right. People my age grew up trying to imitate their parents; until they saw how much more fun the kids were having. Then they tried to be just like their kids. Heh-heh."

I grunted something noncommittal. Middle-aged crazy, just like my Uncle Larry. "I suppose there were a lot of 'mid-life crises' back then, too." I ventured. Uncle Larry had gone heavy into love beads and incense, radical politics. He grew a moustache and wore bell-bottoms. The whole hippie scene. Walked out on his wife for a young "chick" and thought it was all "groovy." I remember how pathetic those thirtysomething wannabes seemed to us in college.

Dad, now, he never had an "identity crisis." He always knew exactly who he was. He had gone off to Europe and saved the world, and then came back home and rebuilt it. Uncle Larry was too young to save the world in the Forties, and too old to save it in the Sixties. He was part of that bewildered, silent generation sandwiched between the heroes and the prophets.

"Neurasthenia," Mae said. "We called it neurasthenia back then. Seems everyone I knew was getting divorced or having an attack of 'the nerves.' Even the President was down in the mullygrubs when he was younger. Nervous breakdown. That's what you call it nowadays, isn't it? Now, T.R. There was a man with sand in him. Him and that 'strenuous life' he always preached about. Why, he'd fight a circle saw. Saw him that time in Milwaukee. Shot in the chest, and he still gave a stem-winder of a speech before he let them take him off. Did you know he got me in trouble one time?"

"Who, Teddy Roosevelt? How?"

"T.R., he was a-hunting and come on a bear cub; but he wouldn't shoot the poor thing because it wasn't the manly thing to do. So, some sharper started making stuffed animal dolls and called 'em Teddy's Bear. I given one to my neighbor child as a present." Mae slapped her knee. "Well, her ma had herself a conniption fit, 'cause the experts all said how animal dolls would give young 'uns the nightmares. And the other President who had the neurasthenia." Mae scowled and waved a hand in front of her face. "Oh, I know who it was," she said in an irritated voice. "That college professor. What was his name?"

"Wilson," I suggested, "Woodrow Wilson."

"That's the one. I think he was always jealous of T.R. He wouldn't let him take the Rough Riders into the Great War."

I started to make some comment, but Mae's mouth dropped open. "The war . . . ?'' she whispered. "The war! Oh, Mister. . . ." Her face crumpled. "Oh, Mister! You're too old!" She covered her face and began to weep.

She felt in her sleeves for a handkerchief; then wiped her eyes and looked at me. "I forgot," she said. "I forgot. It was the war. Mister went away to the war. That's why he never come back. He never run out on me, at all. He would have come back after it was over, if he'd still been alive. He would have.''

"I'm sure he would have," I said awkwardly.

"I told him he was too old for that sort of thing; but he just laughed and said it was a good cause and they needed men like him to spunk up the young 'uns. So he marched away one day and someone he never met before shot him dead, and I don't even know when and where it happened.''

"I'm sorry," I said, at a loss for anything else to say. A good cause? The War to End All Wars, nearly forgotten now; its players, comic-opera Ruritanians on herky-jerky black and white newsreels. The last war begun in innocence.

Her hands had twisted the handkerchief into a knot. She fussed with it, straightened it out on her lap, smoothed it with her hand. In a quiet voice, she said, "Tell me, doc. Tell me. Why do they have wars?''

I shook my head. Was there ever a good reason? To make the world safe for democracy? To stop the death camps? To free the slaves? Maybe. Those were better reasons than cheap oil. But up close, no matter what the reason, it was husbands and sons and brothers who never came home.

> Oh, them golden slippers, Oh, them golden slippers
> Golden slippers I'm gonna wear, Because they look so neat;
> Oh, them golden slippers, Oh, them golden slippers,
> Golden slippers I'm gonna wear To walk them golden streets.

Ever since our late evening encounter, Consuela had begun wearing blouses, skirts, and robes around the house instead of her nurse's whites. The colors were bright, even garish; the patterns, blocky and intricate. The costumes made the woman more open, less mysterious. It was as if, having once seen her *deshabille*, a barrier had come down. She had begun teaching Dee-dee to play the cane flute. Sometimes I heard them in the evening, the notes drifting down from above stairs, lingering in the air. Was it a signal, I wondered? I sensed that the relationship between Consuela and myself had changed; but in what direction, I did not know.

Dee-dee should have been in school. She should have been in fifth grade; and she should have come home on the school bus, full of laughter and bursting to tell us what she had learned that day. Brenda and I should have helped her with her homework, nursed her bruises, and hugged her when she cried. That was the natural order of things.

But Dee-dee lived in her room, played in the dark. She studied at home, tutored by Consuela or myself or by private instructors we sometimes hired. School and other children were far away. She was a prisoner, half of her mother's strained disapproval, half of her own withdrawal. Save for Consuela and myself and a few, brief contacts with Brenda, she had no other person in her short, bounded life. Who could dream what scenarios her dolls performed in the silence of her room?

I found the two of them at the kitchen table Consuela with her inevitable cocoa, Dee-dee with a glass of milk and a stack of graham crackers. There were cracker crumbs scattered across the Formica and a ring of white across Dee-dee's lip.

I beamed at her. "The princess has come down from her tower once more!"
She tucked her head in a little. "It's all right, isn't it?"

I kissed her on the forehead. How sparse her hair had grown! "Of course, it is!"

I settled myself across the table from Consuela. She was wearing an ivory blouse with a square-cut neck bordered by red stitching in the shape of flowers. "Thank you, nurse," I said. "She should be downstairs more often."

"Yes, I know."

Was there a hint of disapproval there? A slight drawing together of the lips? I wanted to make excuses for Brenda. It was not that Brenda made Dee-dee stay in her room, but that she never made her leave. It was Deirdre who stayed always by herself. "So, what did you do today, Dee-dee?"

"Oh, nothing. I read my schoolbooks. Watched TV. I helped Connie bake a cake."

"Did you? Sounds like a pretty busy day to me."

She and Consuela shared a grin with each other. "We played ball, a little, until I got tired. And then we played word games. I see something . . . blue! What is it?"

"The sky?"

"I can't see the sky from here. It's long and thin."

"Hmm. Long, thin and blue. Spaghetti with blueberry sauce?"

Dee-dee laughed. "No, silly. It has a knot in it."

"Hmm. I can't imagine what it could be." I straightened my tie and Dee-dee laughed again. I looked down at the tie and gave a mock start. "Wait! Long, thin, blue and a knot. . . . It's my belt!"

"No! It's your tie!"

"My tie? Why. . . ." I gave her a look of total amazement. "Why, you're absolutely, positively right. Now, why didn't I see that? It was right under my nose. Imagine missing something right under your nose!"

We played a few more rounds of "I see something" and then Dee-dee wandered back to the family room and settled on the floor in front of the TV. I watched her for a while as she stared at the pictures flickering there. I thought of how little time was left before cartoons would play unwatched.

Consuela placed a cup of coffee in front of me. I sipped from it absently while I sorted through the day's mail stacked on the table. "Brenda will be coming home on Monday," I said. Consuela already knew that and I knew that she knew, so I don't know why I said it.

But why Monday? Why not Friday? Why spend another weekend in Washington with Walther Crowe? I could think of any number of reasons, I could.

"Deirdre will be happy to have her mother back," Consuela said in flat tones.

I was looking at the envelopes, so I did not see her face. I knew what she meant, though. No more flute lessons; no more games downstairs. I reached across the table and placed my hand atop one of hers. It was warm, probably from holding the cocoa mug.

"Deirdre's mother never left," I said.

Consuela looked away. "I am only her nurse."

"You take care of her. That's more—" I caught myself. I had started to say that that was more than Brenda did; but there were some things that husbands did not say about their wives to other women. I noticed, however, that Consuela had not pulled her hand away from mine.

I released her hand. "Say, here's a letter from the National Archives." I said with forced heartiness, dancing away from the sudden abyss that had yawned open before me. Too many lives had been ruined by reading invitations where none were written.

Consuela stood and turned away, taking her cup to the sink. I slit the envelope open with my index finger and pulled out the yellow flimsy. *Veteran: Holloway, Green. Branch of Service: Infantry (Co. H, 5th Tennessee). Years of Service: 1918 or 1919.* It was the order form I had sent to the Military Service Records department after Mae's earlier recollection of her husband. As I unfolded it, Consuela came and stood beside me, reading over my shoulder. Somehow, it was not uncomfortable.

☑ *We were unable to complete your request as written.*

☑ *We found additional pension and military service files of the same name (or similar variations).*

☑ *The enclosed records are those which best match the information provided. Please resubmit, if these are not the desired files.*

I grunted and paged through the sheets. Company muster rolls. A Memorandum of Prisoner of War Records: *Paroled and exchanged at Cumberland Gap, Sept. 5 '62.*

The last page was a white photocopy of a form printed in an old-fashioned typeface. **Casualty Sheet**. The blanks were penned in by an elegant Spencerian hand. Name, *Green Holloway*. Rank, *Private*. Company *"H"*, Regiment 5"2. Division, 3"2. Corps, 23"2. Arm, *Inf*. State, *Tenn.*

Nature of casualty, *Bullet wound of chest (fatal).*

Place of casualty, *Resaca, Ga.*

Date of casualty, *May 14, 1864, the regiment being in action that date.*

Jno. T. Henry, Clerk

I tossed the sheets to the kitchen table. "These can't be right," I said.

Consuela picked them up. "What is wrong?"

"Right name, wrong war. These are for a Green Holloway who died in the Civil War."

Consuela raised an eyebrow. "And who served in the same company as your patient's husband?"

"State militia regiments were raised locally, and the same families served in them, generation after generation. Green here was probably 'Mister's' grandfather. Back then children were often given their grandparents' names.'' I took the photocopies from Consuela and stuffed them back in the envelope. ''Well, there was a waste of ten dollars.'' I dropped the envelope on the table.

Dee-dee called from the family room. ''What's this big book you brought home?''

''The Encyclopedia of Song,'' I said over my shoulder. ''It's to help me with a patient I have.''

''The old lady who hears music?''

I turned in my chair. ''Yes. Did Connie tell you about her?''

Dee-dee nodded her head. ''I wish I could hear music like that. You wouldn't need headphones or a Walkman, would you?''

I remembered that Mae had had two very unhappy recollections in one day. ''No,'' I said, ''but you don't get to pick the station, either.''

Later that evening, after Dee-dee had been tucked away, I spread my index cards and sheets of paper over the kitchen table, and arranged the tape recorder on my left where I could replay it as needed. The song encyclopedia lay in front of me, open to its index. A pot of coffee stood ready on my right.

Consuela no longer retreated to her own room after dinner. When I looked up from my work I could see her, relaxed on the sofa in the family room, quietly reading a book. Her shoes off, her legs tucked up underneath her, the way some women sit curled up. I watched her silently for a while. So serene, like a jaguar indolent upon a tree limb. She appeared unaware of my regard, and I bent again over my work before she looked up.

I soon verified that Mae's latest recollections were from the Gay Nineties. The earliest one, ''Ta-Ra-Ra Boom-der-ay,'' had been written in 1890, and the others dated from the same era. ''Good-bye, Dollie Gray,'' had been a favorite of the soldiers going off to fight in the Philippine ''insurrection,'' while ''Hot Time in the Old Town'' had been the Rough Riders' ''theme song.'' Mae's version of ''America the Beautiful,'' I discovered, was the original 1895 lyrics. Apparently, Katherine Lee Bates had written the song as much for protest as for patriotism.

When I had finished the cataloging I closed the songbook, leaned back in my chair, and stretched my arms over my head. Consuela looked up at the motion; I smiled at her and she smiled back. I checked my watch. ''Almost bed time,'' I said. Consuela said nothing, but nodded slightly.

Middle-aged?

The thought struck me like a discordant note and I turned back to my work. I ran the tape back and forth until I found what I was looking for. Yes. Mae had said that the ''young folks'' at the turn of the century had called her age-mates ''middle-aged.'' So Mae must have already been mature by then. How was that possible? At most, she might have been a teenager, one of the ''young folks,'' herself.

Unless she had looked old for her age.

God! I stabbed the shut-off button with my forefinger.

After a moment, I ran the tape through again, listening for Mae's descriptions of her peers and her younger contemporaries. "Wishy-washy." Folks her age had been wishy-washy. Yet, in an earlier session, she had described her age-mates as moralistic. I flipped through my written notes until I found it.

Yes, just as I remembered. But, psychologically, that made no sense. Irresolute twenty-somethings do not mature into forty-something moralists. The irresolute become the two-sides-to-every-question types; the mediators, the compromisers, the peace-makers. The ones both sides despise—and miss desperately when they are gone. The moralists are nocompromise world-savers. They preach "prohibition," not "temperance."

The wild youth Mae remembered from the Ragtime Era and the Mauve Decade—the hard-edged "newsies"—those were the young Hemingways, Bogies and Mae Wests; the "Blood-and-Guts" Pattons and the "Give-'em-Hell" Harrys. The Lost Generation, they had been called. The idealistic, young teeners and twenty-somethings of the Gay Nineties that Mae found so simpatico were the young FDR, W.E.B. DuBois and Jane Addams. The generation of "missionaries" out to save the world. They had all been "the kids" to her. But that would put Mae into the even older, Progressive Generation, a contemporary of T.R. and Edison and Booker T. Washington.

I drummed my pencil against the table top. That would make her 120 years old, or thereabouts. That wasn't possible, was it? I pushed myself from the table and went to the bookcase in the family room.

The Guinness Book of Records sat next to the dictionary, the thesaurus, the atlas and the almanac, all neatly racked together. Sometimes, Brenda's obsessive organizing paid off. I noticed that Dee-dee had left one of her own books, *The Boxcar Children*, on the shelf and made a mental note to return it to her room later.

According to *Guinness*, the oldest human being whose birth could be authenticated was Shigechiyo Izumi of Japan, who had died in 1986 at the ripe age of 120 years and 237 days. So, a few wheezing, stumbling geezers did manage to hang around that long. But not many. Actuarial tables suggested one life in two billion. So, with nearly six billion of us snorting and breathing and poking each other with our elbows, two or three such ancients were possible. Maybe, just maybe, Mae could match Izumi's record. The last surviving Progressive.

The oldest human being.

The oldest human being remembers.

The oldest human being remembers pop music of the last hundred years.

A Hundred-and-Twentysomething. Great book title. It had "best-seller" written all over it.

> *'Neath the chestnut tree, where the wild flow'rs grow,*
> *And the stream ripples forth through the vale,*
> *Where the birds shall warble their songs in spring,*
> *There lay poor Lilly Dale.*

On my next visit, Mae was not waiting by the office door for me to unlock it. So, after I had set my desk in order, I hung the "Back in a Minute" sign on the doorknob and went to look for her. Not that I was concerned. It was just that I had grown used to her garrulous presence.

I found Jimmy Kovacs in the common room watching one of those inane morning "news" shows. "Good morning, Jimmy. How's your back?"

He grinned at me. "Oh, I can't complain." He waited a beat. "They won't let me."

I smiled briefly. "Glad to hear it. Have you seen—"

"First hurt my back, oh, it must have been sixty-six, sixty-seven. Lifting forms."

"I know. You told me already. I'm looking for—"

"Not forms like paperwork. Though nowadays you could strain your back lifting them, too." He crackled at his feeble joke. It hadn't been funny the first two times, either. "No, I'm talking about those 600-pound forms we used to use on the old flatbed perfectors. Hot type. Blocks of lead quoined into big iron frames. Those days, printing magazines was a *job*, I tell you. You could smell the ink; you could feel the presses pounding through the floor and the heat from the molten lead in the linotypes." He shook his head. "I saw the old place once a few years back. A couple of prissy kids going ticky-ticky on those computer keyboards." He made typing motions with his two index fingers.

I interrupted before he could give me another disquisition on the decadence of the printing industry. I could just imagine the noise, the lead vapors, the heavy weight-lifting. Some people have odd notions about the Good Old Days. "Have you seen Mae this morning, Jimmy?"

"Who? Mae? Sure, I saw the old gal. She was headed for the gardens." He pointed vaguely.

Old gal? I chuckled at the pot calling the kettle black. But then I realized with a sudden shock that there were more years between Mae and Jimmy than there were between Jimmy and me. There was old, and then there was *old*. Perhaps we should distinguish more carefully among them—say "fogies," "mossbacks" and "geezers."

Mae was sitting in the garden sunshine, against the red brick back wall, upon a stone settee. I watched her for a few moments from behind the large plate glass window. The Sun was from her right, illuminating the red and yellow blossoms around her and sparkling the morning dew like diamonds strewn across the grass. The dewdrops were matched by those on her cheeks. She wore a green print dress with flowers, so that the dress, the grass and the flower beds; the tears and the dew, all blended together, like old ladies' garden camouflage.

She did not see me coming. Her eyes were closed tight, looking upon another, different world. I stood beside her, unsure whether to rouse her. Were those tears of joy or tears of sorrow? Would it be right to interrupt either? I compromised by placing my hand on her shoulder. Her dry, birdlike claw reached up and pressed itself against mine.

"Is that you, Doctor Wilkes?" I don't know how she knew that. Perhaps her eyes had not been entirely closed. She opened them and looked at me, and I could see that her regurgitated memories had been sorrowful ones. That is the problem with Jackson's syndrome. You remember. You can't help remembering. "Oh, Doctor Wilkes. My mama. My sweet, sweet mama. She's dead."

The announcement did not astonish me. Had either of Mae Holloway's parents been alive I would have been astonished. I started to tell her that, but my words came out surprisingly gently. "It happened a long time ago," I told her. "It's a hurt long over."

She shook her head. "No. It happened this morning. I saw Pa leaning over my bed. Oh, such a strong, young man he was! But he'd been crying. His eyes were red and his beard and hair weren't combed. He told me that my mama was dead at last and she weren't a-hurtin' no more."

Mae Holloway pulled me down to sit beside her on the hard, cold bench, and she curled against me for all the world like a little girl. I hesitated and almost pulled away; but I am not without pity, even for an old woman who half-thought she was a child.

"He told me it was my fault."

"What?" Her voice had been muffled against my jacket.

"He told me it was my fault."

"Who? Your father told you that? That was . . . cruel."

She spoke in a high-pitched, childish voice. "He tol' me that mama never gotten well since I was borned. There was something about my birthin' that hurt her inside. I was six and I never seen my mama when she weren't a-bed . . ."

She couldn't finish. Awkwardly, I put an arm around her shoulder. A husband who lost his wife to childbirth would blame the child, whether consciously or not. Especially a husband in the full flush of youth. Worse still, if it was a lingering death. If for years the juices of life had drained away, leaving a gasping, joyless husk behind.

If for years the juices of life had drained away, leaving a gasping, joyless husk behind.

"I have to get back to my office," I said, standing abruptly. "There may be a patient waiting. Is there anything I can get you? A sedative?"

She shook her head slowly back and forth several times. When she spoke, she sounded more like an adult Mae. "No. No, thank you. I ain't—haven't had these memories for so long that I got to feel them now, even when it pains me. There'll be worse coming back to me, bye and bye. And better, too. The Good Man'll help me bear it."

It wasn't until I was back behind my desk and had made some notes about her recollection for my projected book that I was struck with an annoying inconsistency. If Mae's mother had died from complications of childbirth, where did her "little brother Zach" come from?

Step-brother, probably. A young man like her father would have sought a new bride before too long. Eventually, we put tragedy behind us and get on with life. But if I was going to analyze the progress of Mae's condition, I would need to confirm her recollections. After all, memories are tricky things. The memories of the old, trickier than most.

> *Peaches in the summertime,*
> *Apples in the fall;*
> *If I can't have the girl I love,*
> *I won't have none at all.*

There was music in the air when I returned home, and I followed the thread of it through the garage and into the back yard, where I found Consuela sitting on a blanket of red, orange and brown, swathed in a flowing, pale green muumuu, and Deirdre beside her playing on the cane flute. Dee-dee's thin, knobby fingers moved haltingly and the notes were flat, but I actually recognized the tune. Something about a spider and a waterspout.

"Hello, Dee-dee. Hello, Consuela."

Deirdre turned. "Daddy!" she said. She pulled herself erect on Consuela's gown and hobbled across the grass to me. I crouched down and hugged her. "Dee-dee, you're outside playing."

"Connie said it was all right."

"Of course, it's all right. I wish you would come out more often."

A cloud passed across the sunshine. "Connie said no one can see me in the yard." A hesitation. "And Mommy's not home."

No one to tell her how awful she looked. No cruel, taunting children. No thoughtlessly sympathetic adults offering useless condolences. Nothing but Connie, and me, and the afternoon sun. I looked over Dee-dee's shoulder: "Thank you, nur—Thank you, Connie."

She blinked at my use of her familiar name, but made no comment. "The sunshine is good for her."

"She *is* my sunshine. Aren't you, Dee-dee?" *You are my sunshine, my only sunshine.* A fragment of a tune. Only, how did the rest of it go?

"Oh, Daddy. . . ."

"So, has Connie been teaching you to play the flute?"

"Yes. And she showed me lots of things. Did you know there are zillions of different bugs in our grass?"

"Are there?" *You make me happy when skies are grey.*

"Yeah. There's ants and centipedes and . . . and mites? And honey bees. Honey bees like these little white flowers." And she showed me a ball of clover she had tucked behind her ear.

"You better watch that," I said, "or the bees will come after you, too."

"Oh, Daddy. . . ."

"Because you're so sweet." *You'll never know, dear, how much I love you.*

"Daaddyy. I saw some spiders, too."

"Going up in the waterspout?"

She giggled. "There are different kinds of spiders, too. They're like eensy-weensy tigers, Connie says. They eat flies and other bugs. Yuck! I wouldn't want to be a spider, would you?"

"No."

"But you are!" Secret triumph in her voice. She had just tricked me, somehow. "There was this spider that was nothing but a little brown ball with legs *this* long!" She held her arms far enough apart to cause horror movie buffs to blanch. "They named it after you," she added with another giggle. "They call it a Daddy-long-legs. You're a daddy and you have long legs, so you must be a spider, too."

"Then . . . I've got you in my web!" I grabbed her and she squealed. "And now I'm going to gobble you up!" I started kissing her on the cheeks. She giggled and made a pretense of escape. I held her all the tighter. *Please don't take my sunshine away.*

We sat for a while on the blanket, just the three of us. Consuela told us stories from Guatemala. How a rabbit had gotten deeply into debt and then tricked his creditors into eating one another. How a disobedient child was turned into a monkey. Dee-dee giggled at that and said she would *like* to be a monkey. I told them about Mae Holloway.

"She didn't give me any new songs today," I said, "but she finally remembered something from her childhood." I explained how her mother had died and her father had blamed her for it.

"Poor girl!" Consuela said, looking past me. "It's not right for a little girl to grow up without a mother."

"Deirdre Wilkes! What on *earth* are you doing out*side* in the *dirt*?"

Dee-dee stiffened in my arms. I turned and saw Brenda in the open garage door, straight as a rod. A navy blue business suit with white ruffled blouse. Matching overcoat, hanging open. A suitbag slung from one shoulder, a briefcase clenched in the other hand. "Brenda," I said, standing up with Dee-dee in my arms. "We didn't expect you until Monday."

She looked at each of us. "Evidently not."

"Dee-dee was just getting a little sunshine."

Brenda stepped close and whispered. "The neighbors might see."

I wanted to say, So what? But I held my peace. You learn there are times when it is best to say nothing at all. You learn.

"Nurse." She spoke to Consuela. "Aren't you dressed a bit casually?"

"Yes, señora. It is after five." When she had to, Consuela could remember what was in her contract.

"A professional does not watch the clock. And a professional dresses appropriately for her practice. How do you think it would look if I went to the office in blouse and skirt instead of a suit? Take Deirdre inside. Don't you know there are all sorts of bugs and dirt out here? What if she were stung by a bee? Or bitten by a deer tick?"

"Brenda," I said, "I don't think—"

She turned to me. "Yes, exactly. You didn't think. How could you have allowed this, Paul? Look, in her hand. That's Nurse's whistle, or whatever it is. Has Deirdre been playing it? Putting it in her mouth? How unsanitary! And there are weeds in her hair. For God's sake, Paul, you're a doctor. You should have said something."

Sometimes I thought Brenda had been raised in a sterile bubble. The least little thing out of place, the least little thing done wrong, was enough to set her off. Dust was a hanging offense. She hadn't always been that way. At school, she'd been reasonably tidy, but not obsessed. It had only been in the last few years that cleanliness and order had begun to consume her life. Each year, I could see the watch spring wound tighter and tighter.

Consuela bundled up flute, blanket, and Dee-dee, and took them inside, leaving me alone with Brenda. I tried to give here a hug, and she endured it briefly. "Welcome home."

"Christ, Paul. I go away for two weeks and everything is falling apart."

"No, Nurse was right to bring her outside. Deirdre should have as much normal activity as possible. There is nothing wrong with her mind. It's just her body aging too fast." That wasn't strictly true. Hutchinson-Gilford was sometimes called *progeria*, but it differed in some of its particulars from normal senile aging.

Brenda swatted at a swarm of midges. "There are too many bugs out here," she said. "Let's go inside. Carry my suitbag for me."

I took it from her and followed her inside the house. She dropped her briefcase on the sofa in the living room and continued to the hall closet, where she shed her overcoat. "You're home early," I said again.

"That's right. Surprised?" She draped her overcoat across a hanger.

"Well. . . ." *Yes, I was.* "Did Crowe drop you off?"

She shoved the other coats aside with a hard swipe. "Yes." Then she turned and started up the stairs. I closed the closet door for her.

"How was Washington?" I asked. "Did you impress the Supremes?"

She didn't answer and I followed her up the stairs. I found her in our bedroom, shedding her travel clothes. I hung the suit bag on the closet door. "Did you hear me? I asked how—"

"I heard you." She dropped her skirt to the floor and sent it in the direction of the hamper with a flick of her foot. "Walther offered me a partnership."

"Did he?" I retrieved her skirt and put it in the hamper. "That's great news!" It was. Partners made a bundle. They took a cut of the fees the associates charged. "It opens up all sorts of opportunities."

Brenda gave me a funny look. "Yes," she said. "It does." If I hadn't known better, I would have said she looked distressed. It was hard to imagine Brenda being unsure.

"What's wrong?" I said.

"Nothing. It's just that there are conditions attached."

"What conditions? A probationary period? You've been an associate there for seven years. They should know your work by now."

"It isn't that."

"Then, what—"

Deirdre interrupted us. She stood in the doorway of our bedroom, one foot crossed pigeontoed over the other, a gnarled finger tucked in one shrunken check. "Mommy?"

Brenda looked at a point on the door jamb a quarter inch above Deedee's head. "What is it, honey?"

"I should tell you 'welcome home' and 'I missed you.' "

I could almost hear *Connie said . . .* in front of that statement and I wondered if Brenda could hear it, too.

"I missed you, too, honey," Brenda told the door knob.

"I've got to take my bath, now."

"Good. Be sure to get all that dirt washed off."

"OK, Mommy." A brief catch, and then, "I love you, Mommy."

Brenda nodded. "Yes."

Dee-dee waited a moment longer, then turned and bolted for the bathroom. I could hear Connie already running the water. I waited until the bathroom door closed before I turned to Brenda. "You could have told her that you loved her, too."

"I do," she said, pulling on a pair of slacks. "She knows I do."

"Not unless you tell her once in a while."

She flashed me an irritated look, but made no reply. She took a blouse from her closet and held it in front of her while she stood before the mirror. "Let's go out to eat tonight."

"Go out? Well, you know that Dee-dee doesn't like to leave the house, but—"

"Take Deirdre with us? Whatever are you thinking of, Paul? She would be horribly embarrassed. Think of the stares she'd get! No, Consuela can feed her that Mexican goulash she's cooking."

"Guatemalan."

"What?"

"It's Guatemalan, whatever it is."

"Do you have to argue with everything I say?"

"I thought, with you being just back and all, that the three of us—" *The four of us.* "—could eat dinner together, for a change."

"I won't expose Deirdre to the rudeness of strangers."

"No, not when she can get it at home." I don't know why I said that. It just came out.

Brenda stiffened. "What does that crack mean?"

I turned away. "Nothing."

"No, tell me!"

I turned back and faced her. "All right. You treat Dee-dee like a non-person. She's sick, Brenda, and it's not contagious and it's not her fault."

"Then whose fault is it?"

"That's lawyer talk. It's no one's fault. It just happens. We've been over that and over that. There is no treatment for progeria."

"And, oh, how it gnaws at you! *You can't cure her!*"

"No one can!"

"But especially you."

No one could cure Dee-dee. I knew that. It was helplessness, not failure. I had accepted that long ago. "And you're angry and bitter," I replied, "because there's nobody you can sue!"

She flung her blouse aside and it landed in a wad in the corner. "Maybe," she said through clenched teeth, "Maybe I'll take that partnership offer, after all."

It was not until much later that evening, as I lay awake in bed, Brenda a thousand miles away on the other side, that I remembered Consuela's remark. *It's not right for a little girl to grow up without a mother.* I wondered. Had she been making a comment, or making an offer?

> *I don't want to play in your yard*
> *I don't like you any more.*

You'll be sorry when you see me
Sliding down our cellar door.

The next time I saw Mae Holloway, we quarreled.

Perhaps it was her own constant sourness coming to the fore, or perhaps it was her fear of insanity returning. But it may have been a bad humor that I carried with me from Brenda's homecoming. We had smoothed things out, Brenda and I, but it was a fragile repair, the cracks plastered over with I-was-tired and I-didn't-mean-it, and we both feared to press too hard, lest it buckle on us. At dinner, she had told me about the case she had helped argue, and I told her about Mae Holloway and we both pretended to care. But it was all monologue. Listening holds fewer risks than response; and an attentive smile, less peril than engagement.

Mae wouldn't look at me when I greeted her. She stared resolutely at the floor, at the medicine cabinet, out the window. Sometimes, she stared into another world. I noticed how she gnawed on her lips.

"We have a couple of days to catch up on, Mrs. Holloway," I said. "I hope you've been making notes, like I asked."

She shook her head slowly, but in a distracted way. She was not responding to my statement, but to some inner reality. "I just keep remembering, doc. There's music all the time, and that double vision—"

"Consciousness doubling."

"It's like I'm in two places at once. Sometimes, I forget which is which and I try to step around things only I cain't, because they're only ghosts, only ghosts. And sometimes, I recollect things that couldn't have. . . ."

The "dreamy states" of Jackson patients often grow deeper and more frequent. In one woman, they had occupied nearly her entire day; and, in the end, they had crowded out her normal consciousness entirely. "I could prescribe something, if you like," I said. "These spells of yours are similar to epileptic seizures. So, there are drugs that—"

She shook her head again. "No. I won't take drugs." She looked directly at me at last. "Don't you understand? I've got to know. It's always been bits and pieces. Just flashes. A jimble-jamble that never made sense. Now. . . ." She paused and took a deep breath. "Now, at least, I'll know."

"Know what, Mrs. Holloway?"

"About . . . everything." She looked away again. Talking with her today was like pulling teeth.

"What about the songs, Mae? We didn't get anything useful on Wednesday and I wasn't here Tuesday or yesterday, so that's three days we have to catch up on."

Mae turned and studied me with lips as thin as broth. "You don't care about any of this, do you? It's all professional; not like you and I are friends. You don't care if'n I live or die; and I don't care if'n you do."

"Mrs. Holloway, I—"

"Good." She gave a sharp nod of her head. "That's jake with me. Because I don't like having friends," she said. "I decided a long time ago if'n I don't have 'em, I won't miss 'em when they cut out. So let's just keep this doc and old lady.'' Her stare was half admonition, half challenge, as if she dared me to leap the barriers she had set down around her.

I shrugged. Keep things professional. That was fine with me, too. A crabby old lady like her, it was no wonder they all ran out on her.

She handed over a crumpled, yellow sheet of lined paper, which I flattened out on my desk. She had written in a soft pencil, so I smeared some of the writing and smudged my palm. I set a stack of fresh index cards by and began to copy the song titles for later research. ''Where Did You Get That Hat?'' ''Comrades.'' ''The Fountain in the Park.'' ''Love's Old Sweet Song.'' While I worked, I could hear Mae humming to herself. I knew without looking that she had her eyes closed, that she was living more and more in another world, gradually leaving this one behind. ''White Wings.'' ''Walking for That Cake.'' ''My Grandfather's Clock.'' ''In the Gloaming.'' ''Silver Threads Among the Gold.'' ''The Mulligan Guard.'' Mae was her own Hit Parade. Though if the music did play continually, as she said, this list could only be a sample of what she had heard over the last three days. ''The Man on the Flying Trapeze.'' ''Sweet Genevieve.'' ''Champagne Charlie.'' ''You Naughty, Naughty Men.'' ''When You and I were Young, Maggie.'' ''Beautiful Dreamer.'' Three days' worth of unclaimed memories.

I noticed that she had recorded no doubling episodes, this time. Because she had not had any? It seemed doubtful, considering. But one entry had been crossed out; rubbed over with the pencil until there was nothing but a black smear and a small hole in the paper where the pencil point had worn through. I held it up to the light, but could make out nothing.

I heard Mae draw in her breath and looked up in time to see a mien on her face, almost of ecstasy. ''What is it?''

''I'm standing out in a meadow. There's a sparkling stream meandering through it, and great, grey, rocky mountains rearing all around. Yellow flowers shivering in the breeze and I think how awful purty and peaceful it is.'' She sighed. ''Oh, doc, sometimes, just for a second, we can be so happy.''

Jackson had often described his patients' ''dreamy states'' as being accompanied by intense feelings of euphoria; sudden bursts of childlike joy. No doubt some endorphin released in the brain.

''There's a fellow coming up toward me from the ranch,'' she continued, trepidation edging into her voice. ''My age, maybe a little older. Might be Mister's younger brother, because he favors him some. He's a-weeping something awful. I reach out to him and he puts his head on my shoulder and says. . . .'' Mae stopped and winced in pain. She sucked in her breath and held it. Then she let it out slowly. ''And he says how Sweet Annie is dead and the baby, too; and there was nothing the sawbones could do. Nothing at all. And I think, *Thank you, Goodman Lord. Thank you, that she won't suffer the way that Ma did.* And then a mockingbird takes wing from the aspen tree right in front of me and I think how awful peaceful the meadow is now that the screaming has stopped.''

She wiped at her nose with her sleeve. ''Listen to it. Can you hear it, doc? There ain't a sound but for the breeze and that old mockingbird.'' The look on her face changed somehow, changed subtly. "Listen to the mockingbird," she croaked. "Listen to the mockingbird. Oh, the mockingbird still singing o'er her grave. . . .''

Then she looked about in sudden surprise. "Land's sake! Now, how did I get here? Why, everybody's so happy; singing the mockingbird song and dancing all over the lawn and a-hugging each other." A smile slowly came over her face. She had apparently tripped from one doubling episode directly into another, due to some association with the song, and the imprinted emotions were playing back with it, overwriting the melancholy of the first episode. Or else she had seized on the remembered joy herself, and had wrapped herself in it against the cold.

"I'm a-wearing my Sanitary Commission uniform," she went on, preening her shabby, faded gown. She shot her cuffs, straightened something at her throat that wasn't there. "I was a nurse, you know; and when the news come that the war was finally over we all heighed over to the White House and had ourselves a party on the lawn, the whole kit 'n boodle of us. Then the President hisself come out and joined us." She turned in her seat and pointed toward the medicine cabinet. "Here he comes now!"

And in that instant, her joy became absolute terror. "Him?" Her smile stretched to a ghastly rictus and she cowered into her chair, covering her eyes with her hand. But you can't close your eyes to memory. You can't. "No! I kin still see him!" she said.

What was so terrifying about seeing President Wilson close up? "What's wrong, Mrs. Holloway?"

"They shot him."

"What, on the White House lawn? No president has been shot there." And certainly not Wilson.

She took her hands away from her eyes, glanced warily left, then right. Slowly, she relaxed, though her hands continued to tremble. Then, she looked at me. "No, the shooting happened later," she snapped, anger blossoming from her fear. Then she closed up and her eyes took on a haunted look. "I'm taking up too much of your time, doc," she said, creaking to her feet.

"No, you're not. Really," I told her.

"Then you're taking up too much of mine." I thought her blackthorn stick would punch holes in the floor tiles as she left.

After a moment's hesitation, I followed. She had recalled her father's death. She had remembered that her birth had killed her mother and that her father had blamed her for it. She had remembered her husband going off to war, never to return. Sad memories, sorrowful memories; but there was something about this new recollection that terrified her.

She thought she was going crazy.

It was easy to track her through the garden. Deep holes punched into the sod marked her trail among the flower beds. When I caught up with her, she was leaning over a plot of gold and crimson marigolds. "You know, I remember exactly where I was when President Kennedy was shot," I said by way of easing her into conversation.

Mae Holloway scowled and bent over the flower bed. "Don't make no difference no-how," she said. "He's dead either way, ain't he?" She turned her back on me.

"No particular reason." I had figured it out. She had seen McKinley, not Wilson; and her husband had fought in the Spanish-American War, not World War I.

She turned her dried-out face to me. "Think I'm getting senile, doc? Why aren't you back in your office reading on your books? You might have a patient to ignore."

"They'll find me if they need me."

"I tol' you the songs I been remembering. Why did you follow me out here, anyway?"

I had better things to do than have a bitter old woman berate me. "If you feel in a friendlier mood later," I said, "you know where to find me."

Back in my office, I began checking the latest tunes against the song encyclopedia. The mindless transcription kept me busy, so that I did not dwell on Mae's intransigence. Let her stew in her own sour juices.

But I soon noticed a disturbing trend in the data. "Champagne Charlie" was written in 1868. "You Naughty, Naughty Men" ("When married how you treat us and of each fond hope defeat us, and there's some will even beat us. . . .") had created a scandal at Niblo's Gardens in 1866. And "Beautiful Dreamer" dated from *1864*. Mae could not have heard those songs when they were new. Born in the early seventies at best, tucked away back in the hills of Tennessee—"So far back in the hollers," she had said one time, "that they had to pipe in the daylight."—She must have heard them later.

And if a little bit later, why not a whole lot later?

And there went the whole rationale for my book.

The problem with assigning dates to Mae's neurological hootenanny was that she could have heard the songs at any time. A melody written in the twenties, like "The Red, Red Robin," is heard and sung by millions of children today. Scott Joplin created his piano rags at the turn of the century; yet most people knew them from *The Sting*, a movie made in the seventies and set in the thirties, an era when ragtime had been long out of fashion.

(The telescoping effect of distance. From this far down the river of years, who can distinguish the Mauve Decade from the Thirties? Henry James and Upton Sinclair and Ernest Hemingway came of age in very different worlds; but they seem alike to us because they are just dead people in funny clothing, singing quaint, antique songs. "Old-fashioned" is enough to blur them together.)

Face it. Many of those old songs were still being sung and recorded when I was young. Lawrence Welk. Mitch Miller. Preservation Hall. Leon Redbone had warbled "Champagne Charlie" on the "Tonight Show" in front of God and everybody. Wasn't it far more likely that Mae had heard it then, than that she had heard it in 1868?

A Hundred-and-Twentysomething. I had deduced a remarkable age for Mae from the dates of the songs she remembered. If that was a will-o'-the wisp, what was the point? There was no teleology to interest the professionals; no hook to grab the public. How many people would care about an old woman's recollections? Not enough to make a best-seller.

And what right had that old bat, what right had anyone, to live so long when *children* were dying? What use were a few extra years remembering the past when there were others who would never have a future?

Damn! I saw that I had torn the index card. I rummaged in the drawer for tape, found none, and wondered if it made any sense to bother recopying the information. The whole effort was a waste of time. I picked up the deck of index cards and threw them. I missed the wastebasket and they fluttered like dead leaves across the room.

Oh, how old is she, Billy Boy, Billy Boy?
Oh, how old is she, charming Billy?
She's twice six and she's twice seven,
Forty-eight and eleven.
She's a young thing that cannot leave her mother.

I could have gone home, instead, and gotten an early start on the weekend.

I had planned to visit the National Archives today, but to continue the book project now seemed pointless. The whole rationale had collapsed; and Mae had withdrawn into that fearful isolation in which I had found her. Brenda had taken the day off to recuperate from her trip. She was probably waiting for me. There was no reason not to go home.

But, I closed the clinic at noon and took the Transit to Newark's Penn Station, where I transferred to the PATH train into the World Trade Center. From there a cab dropped me at Varick and Houston in lower Manhattan.

If we did not meet, we could not quarrel.

The young woman behind the information desk was a pixie: short, with serious bangs and serious, round glasses. Her name tag read SARA. "Green?" she said when I had explained my mission. "What an odd name. It might be a nickname. You know, like 'Red.' One of my grandfathers was called 'Blackie' because his family name was White." She took out a sheet of scratch paper and made some notes on it. "I'd suggest you start with the 1910 Census and look for Green Holloway in the Soundex."

"Soundex?" I said. "What is that?"

"It's like an Index, but it's based on sounds, not spelling. Which is good, since the enumerators didn't always spell the names right. Holloway might have been recorded as, oh, H-a-l-i-w-a-y, for example, or even H-a-l-l-a-w-a-y; but the Soundex code would be the same."

"I see. Clever."

She took out a brochure and jotted another note on the scratch pad. "Holloway would be . . . H. Then L is a 4, and the W and Y don't count. That's H400. There will be a lot of other names listed under H400, like Holly and Hall, but that should narrow your search." She filled out a request voucher for me. "Even with the Soundex," she said as she wrote, "there are no guarantees. There are all sorts of omissions, duplicates, wrong names, wrong ages. Dad missed his great-grandmother in the 1900 Census, because she was living with her son-in-law and the enumerator had listed her with the son-in-law's family name. One of my great-great-grandfathers 'aged' fourteen years between the 1870 and 1880 censuses; and his wife-to-be was listed twice in 1860. People weren't always home; so, the enumerator would try to get the information from a neighbor, who didn't always know. So you should always cross-check your information.''

She directed me to an empty carrel, and shortly after, an older man delivered the 1910 Soundex for Blount County, Tennessee. I threaded the microfilm spool into the viewer and spun forward, looking for H400. Each frame was an index card with the head of household on top and everyone else listed below with their ages and relationships.

I slowed when I started to see first names starting with G: Gary . . . George . . . Gerhard . . . Glenn . . . Granville . . . Gretchen . . . Gus . . . No Green. I backed up and checked each of the G's, one by one, thinking Green might be out of sequence.

Still, no luck. And I couldn't think of any other way "Green" might be spelled. Unless it was a nickname, in which case, forget it. I scrolled ahead to the M's. If the census taker had interviewed Mae, Green might be listed as "Mister."

But. . . . No "Mister." Then I checked the M's again, this time searching for "Mae" or "May," because if Mister had died in the Spanish-American War rather than World War I, Mae herself would have been listed as head of household in 1910.

Still nothing. It was a fool's errand, anyway. For all I knew, Mae was really Anna-Mae or Lulu-Mae or some other such Appalachianism, which would make finding her close to impossible.

I tried the 1900 Soundex next. But I came up dry on that, too. No Green, no Mister, no Mae. Eventually, I gave up.

I leaned back in the chair and stretched my arms over my head. Now what? *We lived so far back in the hollers they had to pipe in the daylight.* It could be that the census takers had flat out missed her. Or she had already left the hills by 1900. In which case, I did not know where to search. She had gone to Cincinnati, I remembered. And to California. At one time or another, she had mentioned San Francisco, and Chicago, and Wyoming, and even New York City. The old bag had a lot of travel stickers on her.

I took a walk to stretch my legs. If I left now, and the trains were on time, and the traffic was light, I could still be home in time to tuck Dee-dee in. But a check of the sidewalk outside the building showed the crowds running thick. The Financial District was getting an early start on the weekend. Not a good time to be leaving the City. Not a good time at all. Traffic heading for the tunnels sat at a standstill. Tightly-packed herds of humans trampled the sidewalks. I would have likened them to sheep, but for the in-your-face single-mindedness with which they marched toward their parking lots and subway entrances.

The trains would be SRO, packed in with tired, sweaty office workers chattering about Fashion Statements or Sunday's Big Game; or (the occasional Type A personality) hunched over their laptops, working feverishly on their next deal or their next angina, whichever came first.

Was there ever a time when the New York crowds thinned out? Perhaps there was a continual stream of drones flowing through the streets of Manhattan twenty-four hours a day. Or maybe they were simply walking around and around this one block just to fool me. A Potemkin Crowd.

I returned to the information desk. "I guess as long as I'm stuck here I'll check 1890." That would be before the Spanish-American War, so Green might be alive and listed.

"I'm sorry," Sara told me. "The 1890 Census was destroyed in a fire in 1921, and only a few fragments survived.

I sighed. "Dead end, I guess. I'm sorry I took up so much of your time."

"That's what I'm here for. You could try 1880, though, and look for parents. There's a partial Soundex for households with children aged ten and under. If the woman was born in the 1870s like you think. . . ."

I shook my head. "No. I know she was born a Murray, but I don't know her father's name." Checking each and every M600 for a young child named Mae was not an appealing task. I might only be killing time; but I had no intention of bludgeoning it to death. I'd have a better chance hunting Holloways, because Green's name was so out of the ordinary. But I'd have to go frame-by-frame there, too, since I didn't know his parents' names, either. That sort of painstaking research was the reason why God invented professionals.

Sara pointed to a row of shelves near the carrels. "There is one other option. There are printed indices of Heads of Households for 1870 and earlier."

I shook my head. "The grandparents? I don't know their names, either."

"Did she have a brother?"

"Zach," I said. "Just the two of them, as far as I know. At least, she's never mentioned any other siblings."

"Children sometimes were given their grandparents' names. Maybe her father's parents were Zach and Mae Murray. It's a shot in the dark, but what do you have to lose? If you don't look, you'll never find anything."

"OK, thanks." I wandered over to the row of index volumes and studied them. I was blowing off the time now and I knew it. Still, I could always strike it lucky.

The indices for Tennessee ran from 1820 through 1860. Thick, bound volumes on heavy paper. No Soundex here. I'd have to remember to check alternate spellings. I pulled out the volume for 1860 and flipped through the pages until I found Murray. Murrays were "thick as ticks on a hound dog's hide," but none of them were named Zach. However, when I checked H, I did find a "Green Holloway" in District 2, Greenback, Tennessee. Mister's grandfather? How many Green Holloways could there be? I copied the information and put in a request for the spool; then, just for luck, I checked 1850, as well.

The 1850 Census listed a "Greenberry Hollaway," also in District 2, Greenback P.O. I chuckled. Greenberry? Imagine sending a kid to school with a name like Greenberry!

Green appeared in the 1840 and 1830 indexes, too. And 1830 listed a "Josh Murry" in the same census district as Green. Mae's great-grandfather? Worth a look, anyway.

The trail ended there. The Blount County returns for 1820 were lost, and all the earlier censuses had been destroyed when the British burned Washington in 1814.

I put the volumes back on the shelf. There was a thick atlas on a reading stand next to the indices and, out of curiosity, I turned it open to Tennessee. It took me a while to find Greenback. When I finally did, I saw that it lay in Loudon County, not Blount.

"That doesn't make any sense," I muttered.

"What doesn't?" A shriveled, dried up old man with wire frame glasses was standing by my elbow waiting to use the atlas.

"The indices all say Blount County, but the town is in Loudon." I didn't bother to explain. It wasn't any of his business. There could be any number of reasons for the discrepancy. The Greenback post office could have serviced parts of Blount County.

The man adjusted his glasses and peered at the map. I stepped aside. "It's all yours," I said.

"Now, hold on, sonny." He opened his satchel, something halfway between a purse and a briefcase, and pulled out a dog-eared, soft-bound red book. He licked his forefinger and rubbed pages aside. He hummed and nodded as he read. "Here's your answer," he said, jabbing a finger at a table. "Loudon County was erected in 1870 from parts of Blount and neighboring counties. Greenback was in the part that became Loudon County. See?" He closed the book one-handed with a snap. "It's simple."

I guess if hanging around musty old records is your whole life, it's easy to sound like an expert. He looked like something the Archives would have in storage anyway. "Thanks," I said.

The whole afternoon had been a waste of time. I had been searching in the wrong county. Blast the forgetfulness of age! Mae had said she had been born in Blount County, so I had looked in Blount County. And all the while, the records were tucked safely away under Loudon.

I checked the clock on the wall. Four-thirty? Too late to start over. Time to pack it in and catch the train.

When I returned to my carrel, however, I found the spool for 1860 Blount County had already been delivered. I considered sending it back, but decided to give it a fast read before leaving. I mounted the spool and spun the fast forward, slowing when I reached District 2. About a third of the way through, I stopped.

Names	Age	Sex	Color	Occupation, etc.	Value of real estate	Value of personal property	Birthplace
Holloway, Green	56	M	W	Farmer	$800	$100	Tenn
" Mabel	37	F	"				"
" Zachary	22	M	"				"

Hah! There it was. Success—of sorts—at last!. This Green Holloway must have been the same one whose Civil War records I had gotten. Green and

Mabel Holloway begat Zach Holloway, who must have begat Green "Mister" Holloway. Jesus. If those ages were correct, Mabel was only fifteen when she did her begatting. Who said babies having babies was a modern thing? But, kids grew up faster back then. They took on a lot of adult responsibilities at fifteen or sixteen. Today, they behave like juveniles into their late twenties.

Now that I knew what I was looking for and where it was, it didn't take me very long to check the 1850 Census, as well.

Names	Age	Sex	Color	Occupation, etc.	Value of real estate	Birthplace
Holloway, Greenberry	45	M	W	Farmer	$250	Tenn
" Mae	32	F	"			"
" Zachy	12	M	"			"

Those names . . . the eerie coincidence gave me a queer feeling. And Mabel should have been twenty-seven, not thirty-two. (Or else she should have been forty-two in 1860.) But then I remembered Sara's cautions. How easy it was for enumerators to get names and ages wrong; and how the same names were used generation after generation.

Just one more spool, I promised myself. Then I head home.

Names of heads of families	Free white persons, including heads of families																					
	Males											Females										
	To 5	5-10	10-15	15-20	20-30	30-40	40-50	50-60	60-70	70-80	80-90	90-100	To 5	5-10	10-15	15-20	20-30	30-40	40-50	50-60	60-70	70-80	80-90	90-100
Greeny Holloway	1					1												1						

Uncle Sugar had been less nosy in 1840. The Census listed only heads of households. Everyone else was tallied by age bracket.

The "white female" was surely Mabel, and she was in her twenties. So her age in 1860 had been wrong. She must have been forty-two, not thirty-seven. Twenty-two, thirty-two, forty-two. That made sense. I folded the sheet with the information and stuffed it in my briefcase. Sara had been right about cross-checking the documentation. The census takers had not always gotten the straight skinny. Mabel had probably looked younger than her years in 1860 and a neighbor, asked for the data, had guessed low.

"She looks younger than her years." The phrase wriggled through my mind and I thought fleetingly of Dee-dee looking older than her years. For every yin there is a yang, and if the Universe did balance . . . if for some reason Mabel herself never spoke to the enumerator and a neighbor in the next holler guessed her age instead, the guess would be low. So, twenty-seven, thirty-two, thirty-seven made a weird kind of sense, too. And it actually agreed better with the written documents!

And what if she kept it up! I laughed to myself. Now there was a crazy thought! Aging five years to the decade, by 1870 she would have seemed . . . mmm, forty-two. And today? Add another sixty-odd years, and Mabel would appear to be. . . . A hundred and five or thereabouts. About as old as Mae seemed to be.

I paused with one arm in my jacket.

About as old as Mae seemed to be? I stared at the spool boxes stacked in the carrel, ready for pick-up.

Greenberry and Mabel. Green and Mae? No, it was absurd. A wild coincidence of names. *The census records are not that reliable. And it's only that Dee-dee is aging too fast that you even thought about someone aging too slow.* I took a few steps toward the door.

And the 1830 Census? I hadn't bothered checking it. What if it listed a Green Holloway aged twenty to twenty-nine and a "white female" *still* aged twenty to twenty-nine?

I turned and looked back at the reading room and my heart began to pound in my ears, and all of a sudden I knew why Dr. Bench had figured Mae for eighty-five three decades ago, and why Mae had feared for her sanity all her life.

> *So early in the month of May,*
> *As the green buds were a-swelling.*
> *A young man on his death-bed lay,*
> *For the love of Barbry Ellen.*

It was pitch-black out when I finally arrived home. There was a light on in the kitchen, none above stairs. I parked in the driveway and got out and walked around the end of the garage through the gate into the back yard. The crickets were chirruping like a swing with a squeaky hinge. Lightning bugs drifted lazily through the air. I walked all the way to the back of the yard, to the edge of the woods and leaned against a bent gum tree. The ground around me was littered with last year's prickly balls. I listened to the night sounds.

I had checked 1830 and found . . . I didn't know what I found. Nothing. Everything. A few tantalizing hints. Greenberry, Mabel and Zachary. Mister, Mae and . . . Zach? Not a younger brother, but a son? And another entry: *Wm. Biddle, Jr., a free man of color.* Mae had spoken of "Will Biddle who farmed two hollers over from us when I was a child. . . ." But in 1830? In *1830?*

There was a logical part of my mind that rejected those hints. Each had an alternative explanation. Coincidence of names. Clerical errors. Senile memory.

Sometimes we remember things only because we have been told them so often. I remember that I stepped in a birthday cake when I was two years old. It had been placed on the floor in the back of the family car and I had climbed over the seat and. . . . But do I *remember* it? Or do I remember my parents telling me the story—and showing me the snapshot—so many times over the years that it has become real to me. Mae could be remembering family tales she had heard, tales scrambled and made *hers* by a slowly short-circuiting brain.

But there was another part of me that embraced those hints; that wanted to believe that Mae had known Margaret Sanger, had voted for Teddy Roosevelt, had danced on the White House lawn in a Sanitary Commission uniform, because if they were true. . . .

I stepped away from the tree and a rabbit shot suddenly left to right in front of me. I watched it bound away . . . And spied figures moving about in the Carters's backyard. Henry and Barbara. I watched them for a while, wondering idly what they were up to. Then I recalled Henry's nickname for his wife—and a song that Mae had known.

I took the same route the rabbit had taken. Last year's dead leaves crackled and dry twigs snapped beneath my feet. I saw one of the Carters—Henry, I thought—come suddenly erect and look my way. I hoped he wouldn't call the police. Then I thought, Christ, they're newlyweds. What sort of backyard shenanigans was I about to walk in on?

I stopped and waved a hand. "That you, Henry? Barbara? It's Paul Wilkes."

A second shadow stood erect by the first. "What's wrong?" It was Barbara's voice.

"I—I saw you moving around back there and thought it might be prowlers. Is everything all right?"

"Sure," said Henry. "Come on out. You'll get tick-bitten if you stay in there."

"Why don't you have your yard light on?" I asked as I stepped from the woods. Stupid question. I could think of a couple of reasons. Brenda and I had once gone skinny dipping in our pool at three in the morning. *Stifled laughter and urgent play, and the water glistening like pearls on her skin.* That had been years ago, of course; but sometimes it was good to remember that there had once been times like that.

"It would spoil the viewing," Henry said.

Now that I was close enough, I saw that they had a telescope set up on a tripod. It was a big one. "Oh. Are you an astronomer?"

Henry shook his head. "I'm a genetic engineer, or I will be when I finish my dissertation. Barbry's going to be a biochemist. Astronomy is our hobby."

"I see." I felt uncomfortable, an intruder; but I had come there with a purpose. I made as if to turn away and then turned back. "Say, as long as I'm here, there is a question you might be able to answer for me."

"Sure." They were an obliging couple. The Moon was half-full, the air was spring evening cool, they did not really want me there interrupting whatever it was that the sky-gazing would have led to.

"I've heard Henry call you Barbry," I said to Barbara. "And . . . do you know a song called 'Barbry Ellen'?"

She laughed. "You mean 'Barbara Allen.' Sure. That's where Henry came up with the nickname. He's into folk singing. 'Barbry Ellen' is an older version."

"Well, someone told me it was the 'old president's favorite song,' and I wondered if you knew—"

"Which old president? That's easy. George Washington. You see, he had this secret crush on his best friend's wife, and—"

"George Washington? Are you sure?"

"Well, there might have been other presidents who liked it. But Washington's partiality is on the record, and the song has been out of vogue a long, long time.''

"Was that all you wanted to know?" asked Henry. There was something in his voice that sounded a lot like "good bye." He wasn't happy, I could tell. I had spoiled the mood for him.

"Yes, certainly," I said. "I thought you might have been prowlers." I backed away into the woods, then turned and walked quickly home.

I learned me that 'un when I was knee-high to a grasshopper. Pa told me it was the President's favorite song. The old President, from when his Pappy fought in the War.

The old President, from when his Pappy fought in the War.

> *Lost my partner, what'll I do?*
> *Lost my partner, what'll I do?*
> *Lost my partner, what'll I do?*
> *Skip to my love, my darling.*

Brenda drank tea. She always allowed the bag to steep for a precise five minutes (read the package) and always squeezed it dry with her tea spoon. She always disposed of the bag in the trash before drinking from the cup. When she drank, she held the saucer in her left hand and the cup in her right and hugged her elbows close to her body. She stood near the French doors in the family room, gazing out toward the back yard and the woods beyond. I had no idea if she had heard me.

"I said, I think I'll go over to Sunny Dale today and look in on Mrs. Holloway."

Brenda held herself so still she was nearly rigid. Not because she was reacting to what I had said. She always stood that way. She spent her life at attention.

"You didn't have any plans, did you?"

A small, precise shake of the head. "No. No plans. We never have any plans." A sip of tea that might have been measured in minims. "Maybe I'll go into the office, too. There are always cases to work on."

I hesitated a moment longer before leaving. When I reached the front door, I heard her call.

"Paul?"

"Yes?" Down the length of the hall I could see her framed by the glass doors at the far end. She had turned around and was facing me. "What?"

"Why do you have to go in today? It's a Saturday."

"It's . . . nothing I can talk about yet. A wild notion. It might be nothing more than a senile woman's ravings, but it might be the most important discovery of the century. Brenda, if I'm right, it could change our lives."

Even from where I stood I could see the faint smile that trembled on her lips. "Yes, it could, at that." She turned around and faced the glass again. "You do what you have to do, Paul. So will I."

It was odd, but I suddenly remembered how much we had once done together. Silly things, simple things. Football games, Scrabble, Broadway shows. Moments public and private. The party had asked Brenda to run for the state legislature one time, and I had urged her to accept, but the baby had been due and. . . . Somehow, now we stood at opposite ends of the house. I thought for a moment of asking her to come with me to the Home, but thought better of it. Brenda would find those old, grey creatures more distressing than I did. "Look," I said, "this should only take a couple of hours. I'll call you and we'll do something together this afternoon. Take in a movie, maybe."

She nodded in her distracted way. I saw that she had spilled tea into her saucer.

Once at the Home, I sought out Mae in her garden retreat, hoping that she was in a better mood than yesterday. I had a thousand questions to ask her. A dozen puzzles and one hope. But when she saw me coming, her face retreated into a set of tight lines: eyes, narrowed; mouth and lips, thin and disapproving.

"Go away," said Mae Holloway.

"I only wanted to ask a few—"

"I said, go away! Why are you always pestering me?"

"Don't mind her," said a voice by my elbow. "She's been that way since yesterday." I turned and saw Jimmy Kovacs, the retired printer. "Headache. Maybe you should give her something."

"You don't need a doctor to take aspirin."

He shook his head. "Aspirin didn't work. She needs something stronger. Might be a migraine. I had an allergy once. To hot dog meat. Every time I had a frank, my head felt like fireworks going off inside. So, my doc, he tells me—"

"I'll see what I can do," I said. Old folks chatter about little else than their ailments. They compare them the way young boys compare . . . well, you know what I mean. "Mine is bigger than yours." They have contests, oldsters do, to see who has the biggest illness. The winner gets to die.

I sat on the stone bench beside Mae. "Jimmy tells me you have a headache," I said.

"Jimmy should mind his own affairs."

"Where does it hurt?"

"In my haid, jackass. That's what makes it a headache."

"No, I mean is it all over or in one spot? Is it a dull ache or sharp points. Is it continual, or does it come in bursts? Do you see or hear anything along with the headache?"

She gave me a look. "How do you make a headache into such a contraption?"

I shrugged. "There are many things that can cause a headache. When did it start?" If I could relieve her pain, she might be willing to answer the questions I had about her family history.

She squinted at the ground, her face tight as a drum. I heard her suck in her breath. Bees danced among the flowers to our right; the fragrances hung in the air. "Yesterday afternoon," she said. "Yesterday afternoon, after you left. It was like the Sun come up inside my head. I was lying down for a nap when everything turned blind-white for a few seconds and I heard a chorus a-singing hymns. I thought I'd surely died and gone to heaven." She took a deep breath and massaged her left temple with her fingers. "Somedays I'ud as lief I were dead. All these here aches and pains. And I cain't do the things I used to. I used to dance. I used to love to dance, but I can't do that no more. And everybody who ever mattered to me is a longtime gone."

Her parents. Little Zach. Green Holloway. Gone a very long time, if I was right. Joe Paxton. Ben Wickham. There must have been plenty of others, besides. Folks in Cincinnati, in California, in Wyoming. She left a trail of alienation behind her every place she had ever been. It was a cold trail, in more ways than one.

"When the white light faded out, I saw it weren't an angel choir, after all. It were Christy's Minstrels that time when they come to Knoxville, and Mister and me and . . ." she frowned and shook her head. "Mister and me, we tarryhooted over to hear 'em. Doc, it was the clearest spell I ever had. I was a-settin' in the audience right down in front. I clean forgot I was a-bedded down here in Sunny Dale."

Sometimes migraines triggered visions. Some of the saints had suffered migraines and seen the Kingdom of God. "Yes?" I prompted.

"Well, Mister was a-settin' on my left holding my hand; and someone's man-child, maybe fifteen year, was press't up agin me on my right—oh, we was packed in almighty tight, I tell you—but, whilst I could see and hear as clear as I can see and hear you, I couldn't feel any of them touching me. When I thunk on it, I could feel that I was lying a-bed with the sheets over me."

I nodded. "You weren't getting any tactile memories, then. I think your—"

She didn't hear me. "The troupe was setting on benches, with each row higher than the one in front—Tiers, that be what they call 'em. They all stood to sing the medley, 'cept 'Mr. Interlocutor,' who sat in a chair front and center. Heh. That was the outdoin'est chair I ever did see. Like a king's throne, it was. They sang 'Jim Along Josie' and 'Ring, Ring the Banjo.' I h'ain't heard them tunes since who flung the chuck. The interlocutor was sided by the soloists on his right and the glee singers—what they later called barbershop singers—on the left." She gestured, moving both hands out from the center. "Then the banjo player and the dancer. Then there was four end-men, two t' either side. Those days, only the end-men were in the Ethiopian business."

"The Ethiopian business?"

"You know. Done up in black-face."

Images of Cantor singing "Mammy." Exaggerated lips; big, white, buggy eyes. An obscene caricature. "Black face!"

My disapproval must have shown in my voice, for Mae grew defensive. "Well, that was the only way us reg'lar folks ever got to hear nigra music back then," she said, rubbing her temple. "The swells could hear 'em any time; but the onlyest nigras I ever saw 'fore I left the hills was Willie Biddle and his kin, and they didn't do a whole lot of singing and dancing."

"Nigras?" That was worse than black-face. I tried to remind myself that Mae had grown up in a very different world.

Mae seemed to refocus. Her eyes lost the dreamy look. "What did I say? Nigra? Tarnation, that isn't right, any more, is it? They say 'coloreds' now."

"African-American. Or black."

She shook her head, then winced and rubbed her temple again. "They weren't mocking the col—the black folks. The minstrels weren't. Not then. It was fine music. Toe-tapping. And the banjo. Why, white folks took that up from the coloreds. But we'uns couldn't go to dark-town shows, and they couldn't come to us—not in them days. So, sometimes white folks dressed up to play black music. Daddy Rice, he was supposed to be the best, though I never did see him strut ''Jim Crow''; but James Bland, that wrote a lot of the tunes, was a black man his own self. I heard he went off to France later 'cause of the way the white folks was always greenin' him.''

"I see. Has your headache subsided since then?" *Minstrel shows*, I thought.

"It's all so mixed up. These memories I keep getting. It's like a kalidey-scope I had as a young-un. All those pretty beads and mirrors. . . .''

"Your headache, Mrs. Holloway. I asked if it was still the same." Try to keep old folks on the track. Go ahead, try it.

She grimaced. "Why, it comes and goes, like ocean waves. I seen the ocean once. Out in Californey. Now, that was a trek, let me tell you. Folks was poor on account of the depression, so I took shank's mare a long part of the way, just like Sweet Betsy.'' She sighed. "That was always a favorite of mine. Every time I heard it, it was like I could see it all in my mind. The singing around the campfire; the cold nights on the prairie. The Injuns a-whooping and a-charging.'' She began to sing.

"The Injuns come down in a great yelling horde.
And Betsy got skeered they would scalp her adored.
So behind the front wagon wheel Betsy did crawl.
And she fought off the Injuns with powder and ball.''

Mae tried to smile, but it was a weak and pained one. "I went back to Californey years later. I taken the *Denver Zephyr*, oh, my, in the 1920s I think it was. Packed into one of them old coach cars, cheek by jowl, the air so thick with cigar smoke. And when you opened the window, why you got coal ash in your face from the locomotive.''

"Look, why don't you come to the clinic with me and I'll see if I have anything for that headache of yours.''

She nodded and rose from her bench, leaning on her stick. She took one step and looked puzzled. Then she staggered a little. "Dizzy,'' she muttered. Then she toppled forward over her stick and fell to the ground. I leapt to my feet and grabbed her by the shoulders, breaking her fall.

"Hey!'' I said. "Careful! You'll break something.''

Her eyes rolled back up into her head and her limbs began to jerk uncontrolla-bly. I looked over my shoulder and saw Jimmy Kovacs hurrying up the garden path. "Quick,'' I said. "Call an ambulance! Call Dr. Khan! Tell her to meet us at the hospital.''

Jimmy hesitated. He looked at Mae, then at me. "What's wrong?'' he said.

"Hurry! I think she's having another stroke.''

Jimmy rushed off and I turned back to Mae. Check-out time, I thought. But why now? Why now?

I have always loved hospitals. They are factories of health, mass producers of treatments. The broken and defective bodies come in, skilled craftsmen go to work—specialists from many departments, gathered together in one location—and healthy and restored bodies emerge. Usually. No process is 100 percent efficient. Some breakdowns cannot be repaired. But it is more efficient to have the patients come to the doctor than to have the doctor waste time traveling from house to house. Only when health is mass produced can it be afforded by the masses.

Yet, I can see how some people would dislike them. The line is a thin one between the efficient and the impersonal.

Khan and I found Mae installed in the critical care unit. The ward was shaped like a cul-de-sac, with the rooms arranged in a circle around the nurses' station. White sheets, antiseptic smell. Tubes inserted wherever they might prove useful. Professionally compassionate nurses. Bill Wing was waiting for us there. With clipboard in hand and stethoscope dangling from his neck, he looked like an archetype for The Doctor. We shook hands and I introduced him to Khan. Wing led us out into the corridor, away from the patient. Mae was in a coma, but it was bad form to discuss her case in front of her, as if she were not there.

"It was not a stroke," he told us, "but a tumor. An astrocytoma encroaching on the left temporal lobe. It is malignant and deeply invasive." Wing spoke with an odd Chinese British accent. He was from Guangdong by way of Hong Kong.

I heard Khan suck in her breath. "Can it be removed?" she asked.

Wing shook his head. "On a young and healthy patient, maybe; though I would hesitate to perform the operation even then. On a woman this old and weak. . . ." He shook his head again. "I have performed a decompression to relieve some of the pressure, but the tumor itself is not removable."

Khan sighed. "So sad. But she has had a long life."

"How much longer does she have?" I asked.

Wing pursed his lips and looked inscrutable. "That is hard to say. Aside from the tumor, she is in good health—for a woman her age, of course. It could be tomorrow; it could be six months. She has a time bomb in her head, and no one knows how long the fuse is. We only know that the fuse—"

"Has been lit," finished Khan. Wing looked unhappy, but nodded.

"As the tumor progresses," he continued, "her seizures will become more frequent. I suspect there will be pain as the swelling increases." He paused and lowered his head slightly, an Oriental gesture.

"There must be something you can do," I said. Khan looked at me.

"Sometimes," she said, "there is nothing that can be done."

I shook my head. "I can't accept that." Holloway could not die. Not yet. Not now. I thought of all those secrets now sealed in her head. They might be fantasies, wild conclusions that I had read into partial data; but I had to know. I had to know.

"There is an end to everything." Noor Khan gazed toward the double doors that led to the medical CCU. "Though it is always hard to see the lights go out."

I drew my coat on. "I'm going to go to the University library for a while."

Khan gave me a peculiar look. "The library?" She shrugged. "I will stay by her side. You know how she feels about hospitals. She will be frightened when she recovers consciousness. Best if someone she knows is with her."

I nodded. "She may not regain consciousness for some time," I reminded her. "What about your patients?"

"Dr. Mendelson will handle my appointments tomorrow. I called him before I came over."

All right, let her play the martyr! I tugged my cap onto my head. Khan didn't expect thanks, did she? I could just picture the old crone's ravings. The hysteria. She would blame Khan, not thank her, for bringing her here.

As I reached the door, I heard Khan gasp. "She's singing!"

I turned. "What?"

Khan was hovering over the bed. She flapped an arm. "Come. Listen to this."

As if I had not listened to enough of her ditties. I walked to the bedside and leaned over. The words came soft and slurred, with pauses in between as she sucked in breath: "There was an old woman . . . at the foot of the hill. . . . If she ain't moved away . . . she's living there still. . . . Hey diddle . . . day-diddle . . . de-dum. . . ." Her voice died away into silence. Khan looked at me.

"What was that all about?"

I shook my head. "Another random memory," I said. "The tumor is busy, even if she is not."

It was not until mid-afternoon, buried deep in the stacks at the University library, that I remembered my promise to call Brenda. But when I phoned from the lobby, Consuela told me that she had gone out and that I was not to wait up for her.

> But the summer faded, and a chilly blast
> O'er that happy cottage swept at last;
> When the autumn song birds woke the dewy morn,
> Our little "Prairie Flow'r" was gone.

In the year before Deirdre was born, Brenda and I took a vacation trip to Boston and Brenda laid out an hour-by-hour itinerary, listing each and every site we planned to visit. Along the way, she kept detailed logs of gas, mileage, arrival and departure times at each attraction, expenses, even tips to bellboys. It did not stop her from enjoying Boston. She did not insist that we march in lockstep to the schedule. "It's a guide, not a straitjacket," she had said. Yet, she spent an hour before bed each night updating and revising the next day's itinerary. Like an itch demanding a scratch, like a sweet tooth longing for chocolate, satisfying the urge to organize gave her some deep, almost sensual pleasure.

Now, of course, everything was planned and scheduled, even small trips. Sometimes the plan meant more than the journey.

Brenda frowned as I pulled into the secluded lot and parked in front of an old, yellow, wood-frame building. A thick row of fir trees screened the office building from the busy street and reduced the sound of rushing traffic to a whisper.

"Paul, why are we stopping? What is this place?"

"A lab," I told her. "That phone call just before we left the house. Some work I gave them is ready."

"Can't you pick it up tomorrow when you're on duty?" she said. "We'll be late."

"We won't be late. The Sawyers never start on time, and there'll be three other couples to keep them busy."

"I hope that boy of theirs isn't there. He gives me the creeps, the way he stares at people."

"Maybe they changed his medication," I said. "Do you want to come in, or will you wait out here?"

"Is there a waiting area?"

"I don't know. I've never been here before."

Brenda gave a small sound, halfway between a cough and a sigh. Then she made a great show of unbuckling her seat belt.

"You don't have to come in if you don't want to," I said.

"Can you just get this over with?"

Inside the front door was a small lobby floored with dark brown tiles. The directory on the wall listed three tenants in white plastic, push-pin letters: a management consulting firm, a marriage counselor, and the genetics lab.

When Brenda learned that S/P Microbiology, was situated on the third floor, she rolled her eyes and decided to wait in the lobby. "Don't be long," she said, her voice halfway between an order, a warning and a plaintive plea to keep the schedule.

The receptionist at S/P was a young redhead wearing a headset and throat mike. He showed me to a chair in a small waiting room, gave me a not-too-old magazine to read, and spoke a few words into his mouthpiece. When the telephone rang, he touched his earpiece once and answered the phone while on his way back to his station. Clever, I thought, to have a receptionist not tied to a desk.

I was alone only for a moment before Charles Randolph Singer himself came out. He was a short, slightly rumpled-looking man a great deal younger than his reputation had led me to expect. His white lab coat hung open, revealing a pocket jammed full of pens and other instruments. "Charlie Singer," he said. "You're Doctor Wilkes?"

"Yes."

He shook my hand. "You sure did hand us one larruping good problem." Then he cocked his head sideways and looked at me. "Where'd you get the samples?"

"I'd . . . rather not say yet."

"Hunh. Doctor-patient crap, right? Well, you're paying my rent with this job, so I won't push it. Come on in back. I'll let Jessie explain things."

I followed Singer into a larger room lined with lab benches and machines. A desiccator and a centrifuge, a mass spec, a lot of other equipment I didn't recognize. A large aquarium filled with brackish water, fish and trash occupied one corner. The plastic beverage can rings and soda bottles were dissolving into a floating, liquid scum, which the fish calmly ignored.

"Jessie!" Singer said. "Wilkes is here."

A round-faced woman peered around the side of the mass spectrometer. "Oh," she said. "You." She was wearing a headset similar to the receptionist's.

"Jessica Burton-Peeler," said Singer introducing us, "is the second-best geneticist on the face of the planet."

Peeler smiled sweetly. "That was last year, Charlie." She spoke with a slight British accent.

Singer laughed and pulled a stick of gum from the pocket of his lab coat. He unwrapped it and rolled it into a ball between his fingers. "Tell Doctor Wilkes here what we found." He popped the wad of gum into his mouth.

"Would you like some tea or coffee, Doctor? I can have Eamonn bring you a cup."

"No, thanks. My wife is waiting downstairs. We were on our way to a dinner party, but I couldn't wait until tomorrow to find out."

Singer gave me a speculative look. "Find out what?"

"What you found out."

After a moment, Singer grunted and shrugged. "All right. We cultured all three cell samples," he said. "The 'B' sample was normal in all respects. The cells went through fifty-three divisions."

"Which is about average," Peeler added. "As for the other two . . . one of them divided only a dozen times—"

"The 'A' sample," I interjected.

"Yes," she said after a momentary pause. "The 'A' sample. But the 'C' sample . . . that one divided one hundred and twenty-three times."

I swallowed. "And that is . . . abnormal?"

"Abnormal?" Singer laughed. "Doc, that measurement is so far above the Gaussian curve that you can't even see abnormal from there."

"The 'A' sample wasn't normal, either," said Peeler quietly.

I looked at her, and she looked at me calmly and without expression. "Well," I said and coughed. "Well."

"So, what's next?" Singer demanded. "You didn't send us those tissue samples just to find out they were different. You already knew that—or you suspected it—when you sent them in. We've confirmed it. Now what?"

"I'd like you to compare them and find out how their DNA differs."

Singer nodded after a thoughtful pause. "Sure. If the reason is genetic. We can look for factors common to several 'normal' samples but different for your 'A' and 'C' samples. Run polymerase chain reactions. Tedious, but elementary."

"And then. . . ." I clenched and unclenched my fists. "I've heard you work on molecular modifiers."

"Nanomachines," said Singer. "I have a hunch it'll be a big field someday, and I'm planning to get in on the ground floor." He jerked a thumb over his shoulder at the aquarium. "Right now I'm working on a bacterium that eats plastic waste."

"Dear Lord," said Burton-Peeler in sudden wonder. "You want us to modify the DNA, don't you?"

Singer looked from me to his wife. "Modify the DNA?"

"Yes," I started to say.

Burton-Peeler pursed her lips. "Modify the 'A' sample, of course. Whatever factor we find in the 'C' sample that sustains the cell division . . . you want us to splice that into the short-lived sample."

I nodded, unable to speak. "I thought it might be possible to bring it up to normal."

Singer rubbed his jaw. "I don't know. Splicing bacterial DNA is one thing. Human DNA is another. A universe more of complexity. Of course, there is that business with the multiple sclerosis aerosol. They used a modified rhinovirus to carry the mucous-producing genes into the lungs. If the factor is gene specific, we could do something similar. Infect the cells with a retrovirus and—"

"Then you can do it?"

"Now hold on. I said no such thing. I said *maybe* it was possible, *if* the chips fall right. But there'll be some basic research needed. It will cost. A lot."

"I'll . . . find the money. Somehow."

Singer shook his head slowly. "I don't think you can find that much. You're talking about maybe three to five years research here."

"Three to—" I felt the pit of my stomach drop away. "I don't have three to five years." Dee-dee would be dead by then. And Mae, too, taking the secret in her genes with her.

"We'll do it at cost," said Burton-Peeler. Singer turned and looked at his wife. "What?"

"We'll do it at cost, Charlie, I'll tell you why later." She looked back to me. "Understand, we still cannot promise fast results. When you set off into the unknown, you cannot predict your arrival time."

Go for broke. Damn the torpedoes. "Just try is all I ask."

Burton-Peeler saw me out. On the landing to the stairwell she stopped. "You're the father of the young girl with progeria," she said. "I saw it in the paper a few years ago. The 'A' sample was hers, wasn't it?"

I nodded. "Yes, and the second sample was my own. For comparison." I turned to go.

Peeler stopped me with an arm on my sleeve. She looked into my eyes. "Whose was the third sample?" she asked.

I smiled briefly and sadly. "My faith, that the Universe balances."

In the lobby, Brenda was just handing a tea cup and saucer back to Singer's red-haired receptionist when she saw me coming. With a few brisk motions she collected her things and was already breezing out the door as I caught up with her.

"I'll drive," she said. "We're way behind schedule now, thanks to you."

I said nothing and she continued in what was supposed to be an idly curious tone. "Who was that woman with you? The one on the landing."

"Woman? Oh, that was Jessica Burton-Peeler. Singer's wife."

Brenda arched an eyebrow and made a little moue with her lips. "She's a little on the plump side," she said. "Do you find plump women attractive?"

I didn't have the time to deal with Brenda's insecurities. "Start the car," I told her. "We'll be late for dinner."

They say we are aged and gray, Maggie
As spray by the white breakers flung;

But to me you're as fair as you were, Maggie,
When you and I were young.

Mae Holloway lay between white sheets, coupled to tubes and wires. She lay with her eyes closed, and her arms limp by her sides atop the sheets. Her mouth hung half-open. She seemed grey and shrunken; drawn, like a wire through a die. Her meager white hair was nearly translucent.

She looked like a woman half her age.

Noor Khan was sitting near the wall reading a magazine. She looked up as I entered the room. "They told you?"

"That Mae has recovered consciousness? Yes. I'm surprised to see you still here."

Khan looked at the bed. "I have made arrangements. She has no family to keep watch."

"No," I agreed. "They are long gone." Longer than Khan could suppose. "Is she sleeping?"

She hesitated a moment, then spoke in a whisper. "Not really. I think that as long as she keeps her eyes closed she can pretend she is not in hospital. Those memories of hers . . . the consciousness-doubling, you called it. I think they play continually, now. The pressure from the tumor on the temporal lobe."

I nodded. Suppress all external stimuli and Mae could—in a biological kind of virtual reality—live again in the past. If we spoke too loudly, it would bring her back to a time and place she did not want. "Why don't you take a break?" I said. "I'll sit with her for a while."

Khan cocked her head to the side and looked at me. "You will?"

"Yes. Is that so surprising?"

She started to say something and then changed her mind. "I will be in the cafeteria." And then she fluttered out.

When she was gone, I pulled the chair up to the bedside and sat in it. "Mae? It's Doctor Wilkes." I touched her gently on the arm, and she seemed to flinch from the contact. "Mae?"

"I hear yuh," she said. Her voice was low and weak and lacked her usual snap. I had to lean close to hear her. "It'ud pleasure me if you'd company for a mite. It's been mighty lonely up hyar."

"Has it? But Doctor Khan—"

"I kilt the b'ar," she whispered, "but it stove up Pa something awful. He cain't hardly git around no more, so I got to be doin' for him." She paused as if listening. "I'm not so little as that, mister; I jest got me a puny bone-box. I ain't no yokum. I been over the creek. And I got me a Tennessee toothpick, too, in case you have thoughts about a little girl with a crippled-up Pa. What's yore handle, mister?"

"Mrs. Holloway," I said gently. "Don't you know me?"

Mae giggled. "Right pleased to meet you, Mister Holloway. Greenberry's a funny name, so I'll just call you Mister. If you'll set a spell, I'll whup up a bait to eat. H'ain't much, only squirrel, but I aim to go hunting tomorry and find a deer that'll meat us for a spell."

I pulled back and sat up straight in my chair. She was reliving her first meeting with Green Holloway. Was she too far gone into the quicksand of nostalgia to respond to me? "Mae," I said more loudly, shaking her shoulder. "It's Doctor Wilkes. Can you hear me?"

Mae gasped and her eyes flew open. "Whut . . . ? Where . . . ?" The eyes lighted on me and went narrow. "You."

"Me," I agreed. "How are you feeling, Mrs. Holloway?"

"I'm a-gonna die. How do you want me to feel?"

Relieved? Wasn't there a poem about weary rivers winding safe to the sea? But, no matter how long and weary the journey, can anyone face the sea at the end of it? "Mrs. Holloway, do you remember the time you were on the White House lawn and the president came out?"

Her face immediately became wary and she looked away from me. "What of it?"

"That president. It was Lincoln, wasn't it?"

She shook her head, a leaf shivering in the breeze.

I took a deep breath. "The Sanitary Commission was the Union Army's civilian medical corps. If you were wearing that uniforr , you were remembering the 1860s. That business on the lawn. It happened. I looked it up. The dancing. 'Listen to the Mockinbird.' Lincoln coming outside to join the celebration. The whole thing. You know it, but you won't admit it because it sounds impossible."

"Sounds impossible?" She turned her head and looked at me at last. "How could I remember Lincoln? I'm not *that* old!"

"Yes, you are, Mae. You are that old. It's just that those early memories have gone all blurry. It's become hard for you to tell the decades apart. Your oldest memories had faded entirely, until your stroke revived them."

"You're talking crazy."

"I think it must be a defense mechanism," I went on as if she had not spoken. "The blurring and forgetting. It keeps the mental desktop cleared of clutter by shoving the old stuff aside."

"Doc. . . ."

"But, every now and then, one of those old, faded memories would pop up, wouldn't it? Some impossible recollection. And you would think—"

"That I was going crazy." In a whisper, half to herself, she said, "I was always afraid of that, as long back as I can remember."

No wonder. Sporadic recollections of events generations past. Could a sane mind remember meeting Lincoln? "Mae. I found your name in the 1850 census."

She shook her head again. Disbelief. But behind it . . . hope? Relief that those impossible memories might be real? "Doc, how can it be possible?"

I spread my hands. "I don't know. Something in your genes. I have some people working on it, but . . . I think you have been aging slow. I don't know how that is possible. Maybe it has never happened before. Maybe you're the only one. Or maybe there were others and no one ever noticed. Maybe they were killed in accidents; or they really did go mad; or they thought they were recalling past lives. It doesn't matter. Mae, I've spent the last week in libraries and archives. You were born around 1800."

"No!"

"Yes. Your father was a member of Captain James Scott's settlement company. The Murrays, the Hammontrees, the Holloways, the Blacks and others. The overmountain men, they were called. They bought land near Six Mile Creek from the Overhill Cherokees."

I paused. Mae said nothing but she continued to look at me, slowly shaking her head. "Believe me," I said. "Your father's name was Josh, wasn't it?"

"Josiah. Folks called him Josh. I . . . I had forgotten my folks for such a long time; and now that I can remember, it pains me awful."

"Yes. I overheard. A bear mauled him."

"Doc, he was such a fine figure of a man. Right portly—I mean, handsome. He cut a swath wherever he walked. To see him laid up like that. . . . Well, it sorrowed me something fierce. And him always saying I shouldn't wool over him."

"He died sometime between 1830 and 1840, after you married Green Holloway."

She looked into the distance. "Mister, he was a long hunter. He come on our homestead one day and saw how things stood and stayed to help out. Said it wasn't fittin' for a young gal to live alone like that with no man to side her. 'Specially a button like I was. There was outlaws and renegades all up and down the Trace who wouldn't think twice about bothering a young girl. When Pa finally said 't was fittin,' we jumped the broom 'til the preacher-man come through." She stopped. "Doc?"

"Yes?"

"Doc, you must have it right. Because . . . because, how long has it been since folks lived in log cabins, and long hunters dressed up in buckskins?"

"A long time," I said. "A very long time."

"Seems like just a little while ago to me, but I know it can't be. The Natchez Trace? I just never gave it much thought."

Have you ever seen a neglected field overgrown with weeds? That was Mae's memory. Acres of thistle and briar. All perspective lost, all sense of elapsed time. "Your memories were telescoped," I said. "Remember when you sang 'Sweet Betsy from Pike' for me, and you said how real it all seemed to you? Well, after the Civil War, sometime during the Great Depression of the 1870s, you went out west, probably on one of the last wagon trains, after they finished the railroad. After that, I lost track."

She stayed quiet for a long time and I began to think she had dozed off. Then she spoke again.

"Sometimes I remember the Tennessee hills," she said in a faraway voice, "all blue and purple and cozy with family." She sighed. "I loved them mountains," she said. "We had us a hardscrabble, side-hill farm. The hills was tilted so steep we could plow both sides of an acre. And the cows had their legs longer on the one side than the other so's they could stand straight-up." She chuckled at the hillbilly humor. "Oh, it was a hard life. You kids today don't know. But in the springtime, when the piney roses and star-flowers and golden bells was in bloom, and the laurel hells was all purpled up; why, doc, you couldn't ask

God for a purtier sight.'' She sighed. ''And other times . . . other times, I remember a ranch in high-up, snow-capped mountains with longhorned cattle and vistas where God goes when He wants to feel small. There was a speakeasy in Chicago, where the jazz was hot; and a bawdy house in Frisco, where I was.'' She let her breath out slowly and closed her eyes again. ''I remember wearing bustles and bloomers, and linen and lace, and homespun and broadcloth. I've been so many people, I don't know who I am.''

She opened her eyes and looked at me. ''But I was always alone, except in them early years. With Mister. And with Daddy and my brother Zach.'' A tear dripped down the side of her face. I pulled a tissue from the box and blotted it up for her. ''There weren't nobody left for me. Nobody.''

I hesitated for a moment. Then I said, ''Mae, you never had a brother.''

''Now what are you talking about? I remember him clear as day.''

''I've checked the records. Your mother died and your father never remarried.''

Mae started to speak, then frowned. ''Pa did tell me oncet that he'd never hitch ag'in, because he loved the dust of Ma's feet and the sweat of her body more than he loved any other woman. But Zach—''

''Was your own child.''

She sucked in her breath between clenched teeth. ''No, he weren't! He was near my own age.''

''You remember Zach from 1861 when he followed your husband into the army. He was twenty-two then, and you . . . Well, you seemed to be thirty-seven to those around you. So, in your memory he seems like a brother. By the time you rejoined him on his ranch in Wyoming, he was even a bit older than your apparent age. Remember how you thought he resembled Mister? Well, that was because he was Mister's son. I think . . . I think that was when you started forgetting how the years passed for you. Mae, no one ever ran out on you. You just outlived them. They grew old and they died and you didn't. And after a while you just wouldn't dare get close to anyone.''

Tears squeezed from behind her eyes. ''Stop it! Every time you say something, you make me remember.''

''In all this time, Mae, you've never mentioned your child. You did have one; the clinical evidence is there. If Zach wasn't your boy, who was? Who was the boy sitting next to you at the minstrel show in Knoxville?''

She looked suddenly confused, and there was more to her confusion than the distance of time. ''I don't know.'' Her eyes glazed and she looked to her right. I knew she was re-seeing the event. ''Zach?'' she said. ''Is that you, boy? Zach? Oh, it is. It is.'' She refocused on me. ''He cain't hear me,'' she said plaintively. ''He hugged me, but I couldn't feel his arms.''

''I know. It's only a memory.''

''I want to feel his arms around me. They grow up so fast, you know. The young-uns. One day, they're a baby, cute as a button; the next, all growed up and gone for a soldier. All growed up. I could see it happening. All of 'em, getting older and older. I thought there was something wrong with me. That I'd been a bad girl, because I kilt my Ma; and the Good Man was punishing me by holding me back from the pearly gates. If'n I never grew old, I'd never die. And if I never died, I'd never see any of my kin-folk again. Doc, you can't know what it's like, knowing your child will grow old and wither like October corn and die right before your eyes."

For a moment, I could not breathe. "Oh, I know," I whispered. "I know."

"Zach. . . . I lived to see him turn to dust in the ground. He died in my own arms, a feeble, old man, and he asked me to sing 'Home, Sweet Home,' like I used to when he was a young 'un. Oh, little Zach!" And she began to cry in earnest. She couldn't move her arms to wipe the tears away, so I pulled another tissue from the box on the tray and dabbed at her cheeks.

She reached out a scrawny hand and clutched my arm. "Thank you, doc. Thank you. You helped me find my child again. You helped me find my boy."

And then I did an odd thing. I stood and bent low over the bed, and I kissed Mae Holloway on her withered cheek.

> *I'm going there to see my mother.*
> *She said she'd meet me when I come.*
> *I'm only going over Jordan,*
> *I'm only going over home.*

My days at the Home passed by in an anonymous sameness, dispensing medicines, treating aches and pains. Only a handful of people came to see me; and those with only trivial complaints. Otherwise, I sat unmolested in my office, the visitor's chair empty. I found it difficult even to concentrate on my journals. Finally, almost in desperation, I began making rounds, dropping in on Rosie and Jimmy and the others, chatting with them, enduring their pointless, rambling stories; sometimes suggesting dietary or exercise regimens that might improve their well-being. Anything to feel useful. I changed a prescription on Old Man Morton, now the Home's Oldest Resident, and was gratified to see him grow more alert. Sometimes you have to try different medications to find a treatment that works best for a particular individual.

Yet somehow those days seemed empty. The astonishing thing to me was how little missed Mae Holloway was by the other residents. Oh, some of them asked after her politely. Jimmy did. But otherwise it was as if the woman had evaporated, leaving not even a void behind. Partly, I suspected, it was because they were unwilling to face up to this reminder of their own mortality. But partly, too, it must have been a sense of relief that her aloof and abrasive presence was gone. If she never had any friends, Mae had told me, she wouldn't miss them when they were gone. But neither did they miss her.

I usually stopped at the hospital on my way home, sometimes to obtain a further tissue sample for Singer's experiments, sometimes just to sit with her. Often, she was sedated to relieve the pain of the tumor. More usually, she was dreaming; adrift on the river of years, connected to our world and time by only the slenderest of threads.

When she was conscious, she would spin her reminiscences for me and sing. "Rosalie, the Prairie Flower." "Cape Ann." "Woodsman, Spare that Tree." "Ching a Ring Chaw." "The Hunters of Kentucky." "Wait for the Wagon."

We agreed, Mae and I, that a wagon was just as suitable as a Chevrolet for courting pretty girls, and Phyllis and her wagon was the ancestor of Daisy and her bicycle, Lucille and her Oldsmobile, and Josephine and her flying machine. And someday, I suppose, Susie and her space shuttle.

It was odd to see Mae so at peace with her memories. She no longer feared them; no longer suppressed them. She no longer fled from them. Rather, she embraced them and passed them on to me. When she sang, "Roisin the Beau," she remarked casually how James Polk had used its melody for a campaign song. She recollected without flinching that she had voted for Zachary Taylor. "Old Rough and Ready," she said. "There was a man for you. 'Minds me some'at of that T.R. Too bad they pizened him, but he was out to break the slave power." It gave her no pause to recall how at New Orleans, "*There stood John Bull in martial pomp/And there stood Old Kentucky.*" It must have been an awful relief to acknowledge those memories, to relax in their embrace.

There were fond memories of her "bean," Green the Long Hunter. Of days spent farming or hunting or spinning woolen or cooking 'shine. Of nights spent 'setting' by the fire, smoking their pipes, reading to each other from the Bible. Quiet hours from a time before an insatiable demand for novelty—for something always to be *happening*—had consumed us. Green had even taken her down to Knoxville to see the touring company of *The Gladiator*, a stage play about Spartacus. Tales of slave revolts did not play well elsewhere in the South, but the mountaineers had no love for the wealthy flatland aristocrats.

She recalled meeting Walt Whitman, a fellow nurse in the Sanitary Commission. "A rugged fellow and all full of himself," she recalled, "but as kind and gentle with the men as any of the women-folk."

She still confused her son sometimes with a brother, with her father, with Green. He was younger, he was older, he was of her own age. But there were childhood memories, too, of the sort most parents have. How he had "spunked up with his gal," "spooned with his chicken," or "lollygagged with his peach," depending on the slang of the decade. How they had "crossed the wide prairie" together after the War and set up a ranch in Wyoming Territory. How he met and wed Sweet Annie, a real "piece of calico."

Not all the memories were pleasant—Sweet Annie had died screaming—but Mae relished them just the same. It was her life she was reclaiming, and a life consists of different parts good and bad. The parts make up a whole. I continued to record her tales and tunes, as much because I did not know what else to do as because of any book plans. I noticed that, while her doubling episodes often hopscotched through her life—triggered by associations and chance remarks— the music that played in her mind continued its slow and inexorable backward progression, spanning the 1840s and creeping gradually into the mid-thirties.

Slowly, a weird conviction settled on me. When the dates of her rememb-heard tunes finally reached 1800, she would die.

Time was running short. Most brain tumor patients did not survive a year from the time of first diagnosis; and Mae was so fragile to begin with that I doubted a whole year would be hers. Reports from Singer alternated between encouragement and frustration. Apparent progress would evaporate with a routine, follow-up test. Happenstance observation would open up a whole new line of inquiry. Singer submitted requests for additional cell samples almost daily. Blood, skin, liver. It seemed almost as if Mae might be used up entirely before Singer could pry loose the secret of her genes and splice that secret into my Deirdre.

I began to feel as if I were in a race with time. A weird sort of race in which time was speeding off in both directions. A young girl dying too old. An old woman dying too young.

One day, Wing was waiting for me when I entered the hospital. Seeing the flat look of concern on his face, my heart faltered. *Not yet*, I thought; *not yet*! My heart screeched, but I kept my own face composed. He took me aside into a small consultation room. Plaster walls with macro designs painted in happy, soothing colors. Comfortable chairs; green plants. An appallingly cheerful venue in which to receive bad news.

But it was not bad news. It was good news, of an odd and unexpected sort.

"Herpes?" I said when he had told me. "Herpes is a cure for brain tumors?" I couldn't help it. I giggled.

Wing frowned. "Not precisely. Culver-Blaese is a new treatment and outside my field of specialty, but let me explain it as Maurice explained it to me." Maurice LeFevre was the resident in genetic engineering, one of the first such residencies in the United States. "Several years ago," said Wing, "Culver and Blaese successfully extracted the gene for the growth enzyme, thymidine kinase, from the herpes virus, and installed it into brain tumor cells using a harmless retrovirus."

"I would think," I said dryly, "that an enzyme that facilitates reproduction is the last thing a brain tumor needs spliced into its code."

Wing blinked rapidly several times. "Oh, I'm sorry. You see it's the ganciclovir. I didn't make that clear?"

"Ganciclovir is—?"

"The chemical used to fight herpes. It reacts with thymidine kinase, and the reaction products interfere with cell reproduction. So if tumor cells start producing thymidine, injecting ganciclovir a few days later will gum up the tumor's reproduction and kill it. There have been promising results on mice and an initial trial with twenty human patients."

"What is 'promising'?"

"Complete remission in 75 percent of the cases, and appreciable shrinkage in all of them."

I sucked in my breath. I could hardly credit what Wing was telling me. Here was a treatment, a *deus ex machina*. Give Singer another year of live tissue experiments and he would surely find the breakthrough we sought. "What's the catch?" I asked. There had to be a catch. There was always a catch.

There were two.

"First," said Wing, "the treatment is experimental, so the insurance will not cover it. Second . . . well, Mrs. Holloway has refused."

"Eh? Refused? Why is that?"

Wing shook his head. "I don't know. She wouldn't tell me. I thought if I caught you before you went to see her—"

"That I could talk her into it?"

"Yes. The two of you are very close. I can see that."

Close? Mae and I? If Wing could see that, those thick eyeglasses of his were more powerful than the Hubble telescope. Mae had not been close to anyone since her son died. *Since her child died in her arms, an old, old man.* Inwardly, I shuddered. No wonder she had never gotten close to anyone since. No wonder she had lost an entire era of her life.

"I'll give it a try," I said.

When I entered her room, Mae was lying quietly in her bed, humming softly. Awake, I knew, but not quite present. Her face was curled into a smile, the creases all twisted around in unwonted directions. There was an air about her, something halfway between sleep and joy, a *calm* that had inverted all those years of sourness, stood everything on its head, and changed all her minus signs to plus.

Setting on her cabin porch, I imagined, gazing down the hillside at the laurel hells, and at a distant, pristine stream meandering through the holler below. At peace. At last.

I pulled the visitor's chair by the bedside and laid a hand lightly on her arm. She didn't stir. "Mae, it's me. I've come to set a spell with you."

"Howdy there, doc," she whispered. "Oh, it's such a lovely sunset. All heshed. I been telling Li'l Zach about the time his grandpap and Ol' Hickory went off t' fi't the Creeks. I was already fourteen when Pa went off, so I minded the cabin while he was away."

I leaned closer to her. "Mae, has Dr. Wing spoken to you about the new treatment?"

She took in a long, slow breath, and let it out as slowly. "Yes."

"He told me you refused."

"I surely did that."

"Why?"

"Why?" She opened her eyes and looked at me; looked sadly around the room. "I been hanging on too long. It's time to go home."

"But—"

"And what would it git me, anyways? Another year? Six months? Doc, even if I am nigh on to two hunnert year, like you say, and my bone-box only thinks it's a hunnert, *that's still older'n most folks git.* Even if that Doctor LeFevre can do what he says and rid me of this hyar tumor, there'll be a stroke afore long or my ticker'll give out, or something. Doc, *there ain't no point to it.* When I was young, when I was watching everyone I knew grow old and die, I wanted to go with them. I wanted to be with them. Why should I want to tarry now? If the Lord'll have me, I'm ready." She closed her eyes again and turned a little to the side.

"But, Mae—"

"And who'll miss me, beside?" she muttered.

"I will."

She rolled out flat again and looked at me. "You?"

"Yes. A little, I guess."

She snorted. "You mean you'll miss whatever you want that you're wooling me over. Always jabbing me with needles, like I was a pincushion. There's something gnawing away at you, Doc. I kin see it in your eyes when you think no one is looking. Kind of sad and angry and awful far away. I don't know what it is, but I know I got something to do with it."

I drew back under her speech. Her words were like slaps.

"And suppose'n they do it and they do git that thang outen my brain. Doc, what'll happen to my music? What'll happen to my memories?"

"I—"

"You done told me they come from that tumor a-pressing against the brain. What happens if it's not pressing any longer?"

"The memories might stay, now that they've been started, even with the original stimulus removed. It might have been a 'little stroke' that started it, just like we thought originally."

"But you can't guarantee it, can you?" She fixed me with a stare until I looked away.

"No. No guarantees."

"Then I don't want it." I turned back in time to see her face tighten momentarily into a wince.

"It will relieve the pain," I assured her.

"Nothing will relieve the pain. Nothing. Because it ain't that sort of pain. There's my Pa, my Ma, Green, Little Zach and his Sweet Annie. Ben and Joe and all the others I would never let cozy up to me. They're all waiting for me over in Gloryland. I don't know why the Good Man has kept me here so long. H'isn't punishment for killing Ma. I know that now. There must be a reason for it; but I'm a-weary of the waiting. If'n I have this operation like you want, what difference will it make? A few months? Doc, I won't live those months in silence."

> *My Chloe has dimples and smiles, I must own;*
> *But, though she could smile, yet in truth she could frown.*
> *But tell me, ye lovers of liquor divine,*
> *Did you e'er see a frown in a bumper of wine?*

There is something about the ice cold shock of a perfect martini. The pine tree scent of the gin. The smooth liquid sliding down the throat. Then, a half second later, wham! It hits you. And in that half second, there is an hour of insight; though, sometimes, that hour comes very late at night. You can see with the same icy clarity of the drink. You can see the trail of choices behind you. Paths that led up rocky pitches; paths beside still waters. You can see where the paths forked, where, had you turned that way instead of this, you'd not be here today. You can even, sometimes, see where, when the paths forked, people took different trails.

"Paul!"

And you can wonder whether you can ever find that fork again.

I turned to see Brenda drop her briefcase on the sofa. "Paul! I *never* see you drinking."

Subtext: Do you drink a lot in secret when I can't see you? Sub-subtext: Are you an alcoholic? Holding a conversation with Brenda was a challenge. Her words were multi-layered; and you never knew on which layer to answer.

I placed my martini glass, still half-full, carefully down upon the sideboard, beside the others. It spilled a little as I did, defying the laws of gravity. I faced her squarely. "I'm running out of time," I said.

She looked at me for a moment. Then she said, "That's right. I'd wondered if you knew."

"I'm running out of time," I repeated. "She'll die before I know."

"*She. . . .*" Brenda pulled her elbows in tight against her sides. "I don't want to hear this."

"That old woman. To live so long, only to die just now."

"The old woman from the home? *She* has you upset? For God's sake, Paul." And she turned away from me.

"You don't understand. She could save Dee-dee."

Brenda's head jerked a little to the left. Then she retrieved her briefcase and shook herself all over, as if preparing to leave. "How can a dying old woman save a dying old girl?"

"She's yin to Dee-dee's yang. The Universe is neutral. There's a plus sign for every minus. But she wants to go over Jordan and I . . . can't stop her. And I don't understand why I can't."

"You're not making any sense, Paul. How many of those have you had?"

"She's two centuries old, Brenda. Two centuries old. She was a swinger and a sheba and a daisy and a pippin. She hears songs, in her head; but sometimes they're wrong, except they're right. The words are different. Older. 'Old Zip Coon,' instead of 'Turkey in the Straw.' 'Lovely Fan', instead of 'Buffalo Gals.' 'Bright Mohawk Valley,' instead of 'Red River Valley.' She read *Moral Physiology*, when it first came out. Mae did. Do you know the book? *Moral Physiology*, by Robert Dale Owen? No, of course not. It was all about birth control and it sold twenty-five thousand copies even though newspapers and magazines refused to carry the ads *and it was published in 18-god-damned-30.* She voted for Zachary Taylor, and her Pa fought in the Creek War, and her husband died at Resaca, and she saw Abraham-fucking-Lincoln—"

"Paul, can you hear yourself? You're talking crazy."

"Did you know *The Gladiator* debuted in New York in 1831? 'Ho! slaves, arise! Freedom . . . Freedom and revenge!' " I struck a pose, one fist raised.

"I can't stand to watch you like this, Paul. You're sopping drunk."

"And you're out late every night." Which was totally irrelevant to our discussion, but the tongue has a life of its own.

Through teeth clenched tight, she answered: "I have a job to keep."

I took a step away from the sideboard, and there must have been something wrong with the floorboards. Perhaps the support beam had begun to sag, because the floor suddenly tilted. I grabbed for the back of the armchair. The lamp beside it wobbled and I grabbed it with my other hand to keep it still.

Awkwardly twisted, half bent over, I looked at Brenda and spoke distinctly. "Mae Holloway is two centuries old. There is something in her genes. We think. Singer and Peeler and I. We think that with enough time. With enough time. Singer and Peeler can crack the secret. They can tailor a . . . tailor a . . . ." I hunted for the right word, found it scuttling about on the floor and snatched it. "Nanomachine." Triumph. "Tailor a nanomachine that can repair Dee-dee's cells. But Mae is dying. She has a brain tumor, and it's killing her. There's a treatment. An experimental treatment. It looks very good. But Mae won't take it. She doesn't want it. She wants to sleep."

I don't know what I expected. I expected hope, or disbelief. I expected a demand of proof, or for more details. I expected her to say, 'do anything to save my daughter!' I expected anything but indifference.

Brenda brushed imaginary dust from her briefcase and turned away. "Do what you always do, Paul. Just ignore what she wants."

I was in the clinic at the Home the next day when I received the call from the hospital. My head felt as if nails had been driven into it. I was queasy from the hangover. When the phone rang and I picked it up, a tinny voice on the other end spoke crisply and urgently and asked that I come over right away. I don't remember what I said, or even that I said anything; and I don't suppose my caller expected a coherent answer. My numb fingers fumbled the phone several times before it sat right in its cradle. *Heart attack*, I thought. And as quickly as that, the time runs out.

But they hadn't said she was dead. They hadn't said she was dead.

I hope that there was no traffic on the road when I raced to the hospital, for I remember nothing of the journey. Three times along the way I picked up the car phone to call the hospital for more information, and three times I replaced it. It was better not to know. Half an hour, with the lights right and the speed law ignored. That was thirty minutes in which hope was thinkable.

Smythe, the cardio-vascular man, met me in the corridor outside her room. He grabbed me by both my arms and steadied me. I could not understand why he was grinning. What possible reason could there be?

"She'll live, mon," he said. "It was a near thing, but she'll live."

I stared at Smythe without comprehension. He shook me by the arm, hard. My head felt like shattered glass.

"She'll live," he said again. His teeth were impossibly white.

I brushed him off and stepped into the room. *She'll live?* Then there was still time. Everything else was detail. My body felt suddenly weak, as if a stopcock had been pulled and all my sand had drained away. I staggered as far as the bed side, where I sank into a steel and vinyl chair. Smythe waited by the door, in the corridor, giving me the time alone.

Dee-dee lay asleep upon the bed, breathing slowly and softly through a tube set up her nose. An intravenous tube entered her left arm. Remote sensor implants on her skull and chest broadcast her heartbeat and breathing and brain waves to stations throughout the hospital. Smythe was never more than a terminal away from knowing her condition. I reached out and took her right hand in mine and gently stroked the back of it. "Hello, Dee-dee, I came as fast as I could. Why didn't. . . ." I swallowed hard. "Why didn't you wait for me to tuck you in?"

Dee-dee was still unconscious from the anesthetic. She couldn't hear me; but a quiet sob, quickly stifled, drew my attention to the accordion-pleated expandable wall, drawn halfway out on the opposite side of the bed. When I walked around it, I saw Consuela sitting in a chair on the other side. Her features were tightly leashed, but the tracks of tears had darkened both her cheeks. Her hands were pale where they gripped the arms of the chair.

"Connie!"

"Oh, Paul, we almost lost her. We almost lost her."

It slammed against my chest with the force of a hammer, a harder stroke for having missed. *Someday we will.* I took Connie's hand and brushed the backside of it as I had brushed Dee-dee's. "It's all right now," I said.

"She is such a sweet child. She never complains."

Prognosis: The life span is shortened by relentless arterial athermoatosis. Death usually occurs at puberty.

"She's all right now."

"For a little while. But it will become worse, and worse; until. . . ." She leaned her head against me and I cradled her; I rubbed her neck and shoulders, smoothed her hair. With my left hand, I caressed her cheek. *It is not the end; but it is the beginning of the end.*

"We knew it would happen." The emotions are a very odd thing. When all was dark, when I believed myself helpless, I could endure that knowledge. It was my comfort. But now that there was a ray of light, I found it overwhelming me, crushing me so that I could hardly breathe. A sliver of sunshine makes a darkened room seem blacker still. I could live with Fate, but not with Hope. I found that there was a new factor in the equation now. I found that I could fail.

"Where is Brenda?" I asked.

Connie pulled herself from my arms, turned and pulled aside the curtain that separated her from Deirdre.

"She didn't come."

"What?"

"She didn't come."

Something went out of me then, like a light switch turned off. I didn't say anything for the longest time. I drifted away from Connie over toward the window. A thick stand of trees filled the block across the street from the hospital. Leaves fresh and green with spring. Forsythia bursting yellow. A flock of birds banked in unison over the treetops and shied off from the high tension lines behind. I thought of the time when Brenda and I first met on campus, both of us young and full of the future. I remembered how we had talked about making a difference in the world.

I found Brenda at home. I found her in the family room, late at night after I had finally left the hospital. She was still clad in her business suit, as if she had just come from the office. She was standing rigidly by the bookcase, with her eyes dry and red and puffy, with Dee-dee's book, *The Boxcar Children*, in her hands. I had the impression that she had stood that way for hours.

"I tried to come, Paul," she said before I could get any words out. "I tried to come, but I couldn't. I was paralyzed; I couldn't move."

"It doesn't matter," I said. "Connie was there. She'll stay until I get changed and return." I rubbed a hand across my face. "God, I'm tired."

"She's taken my place, hasn't she? She feeds Deirdre, she nurses her, she tutors her. Tell me, Paul, has she taken over *all* my duties?"

"I don't know what you mean."

"I didn't think there was room in your life for anyone beside your daughter. You've shut everyone else out."

"I never pushed you away. You ran."

"It needs more than that. It needs more than not pushing. You could have caught me, if you'd reached. There was an awful row at the office today. Crowe and FitzPatrick argued. They're dissolving the partnership. I was taking too long to say yes to the partnership offer; so Sèan became curious and. . . . He found out Walther had wanted a 'yes' on a lot more, so we filed for harrass. . . . Oh, hell. It doesn't matter any more; none of it."

She was talking about events on another planet. I stepped to her side and took hold of the book. It was frozen to her fingers. I tugged, and pried it from her grasp. Slowly, her hands clenched into balls, but she did not lower her arms. I turned to place the book on the shelf and Brenda said in a small voice, "It doesn't go there, Paul."

"Damn it, Brenda!"

"I'm afraid," she said. "Oh, God, I'm afraid. Someday I will open up the tableware drawer and find her baby spoon; or I'll look under the sofa and find a ball that had rolled there forgotten. Or I'll find one of her dresses bundled up in the wash. And I won't be able to take it. Do you understand? Do you know what it's like? Do you have any feelings at all? How can you look at that shelf and remember that *her* book had once lain there? Look at that kitchen table and remember her high chair and how we played airplane with her food? Look into a room full of toys, with no child any more to play with them? Everywhere I look I see an aching void."

With a sudden rush of tenderness, I pulled her to me, but she remained stiff and unyielding in my arms. Yet, we all mourn in our own ways. "She did not die, Brenda. She'll be OK."

"This time. But, Paul, I can't look forward to a lifetime looking back. At the little girl who grew up and grew old, and went away before I ever got to know her. Paul, it isn't right. It isn't right, Paul. It isn't right for a child to die before the parent."

"So, you'll close her out of your mind? Is that the answer? Create the void now? You'll push all those memories into one room and then close the door? You can't do that. If we forget her, it will be as if she had never lived."

She softened at last and her arms went around me. "What can I do? I've lost her, and I've lost you, and I've lost . . . everything."

We stood there locked together. I could feel her small, tightly-controlled sobs trembling against me. Sometimes the reins have been held so close for so long that you can never drop them, never even know if they have been dropped. The damp of her tears seeped through my shirt. Past her, I could see the shelf with

The Boxcar Children lying flat upon it and I tried to imagine how, in future years, I could ever look on that shelf again without grief.

> *"Tell me the tales that to me were so dear*
> *Long, long ago; long, long ago.*
> *Sing me the songs I delighted to hear*
> *Long, long ago, long ago."*

Dee-dee was wired. There was a tube up her nose and another in her arm. A bag of glucose hung on a pole rack by her bed, steadily dripping into an accumulator and thence through the tube. A catheter took her wastes away. A pad on her finger and a cuff around her arm were plugged into a CRT monitor. I smiled when I saw she was awake.

"Hi, Daddy." Her voice was weak and hoarse, a byproduct of the anaesthesia.

"Hi, Dee-dee. How do you feel?"

"Yucky."

"Me, too. You're a TV star." I pointed to the monitor, where red and yellow and white lines hopped and skipped across the screen. Heart rate, blood pressure. Every time she breathed, the white line crested and dropped. She didn't say anything and I listened for a moment to the sucking sound that the nose tube made. A kid trying for the last bit of soda in the can. The liquid it carried off was brown, which meant that there was still a little blood. "Connie is here." I nodded to the other side of the bed.

Dee-dee turned her eyes, but not her head. "Hello, Connie. I can't see you."

Consuela moved a little into her field of vision. "Good morning, Little One. You have a splendid view from your window."

"Nurse Jeannie told me that. Wish I could see. . . ."

"Then, I will tell you what it looks like. You can see the north end of town—all those lovely, old houses—and far off past them, on the edge of the world, the blue-ridge mountain wall and, in the very center of it, the Gap; and through the Gap, you can see the mountains beyond."

"It sounds beautiful. . . ."

"Oh, it is. I wish I could be here instead of you, just so I could have the view."

I looked up at Connie when she said that and, for a moment, we locked gazes with one another. I could see the truth of her words in her eyes.

And then I saw surprise. Surprise and something else besides. I looked over my shoulder—and Brenda was standing there in the doorway, smartly dressed, on wobbly legs, with her purse clutched tightly in her hands before her.

"The nurses," she said. "The nurses said she could have two visitors at a time." Visiting was allowed every three hours, but only for an hour and only two visitors at a time. I was a doctor and Connie was a nurse and the staff cut us a little slack, but the rules were there for a reason. Consuela stood.

"I will leave."

Brenda looked at her and caught her lower lip between her teeth. She laid her purse with military precision on a small table beside the bed. "I would like to spend some time with Deirdre, Paul. If you don't mind."

I nodded. As I stood up I gave Dee-dee a smile and a little squeeze on her arm. "Mommy's here," I told her.

Connie and I left them alone together (a curious expression, that—"alone together") and waited in the outer nursing area. I didn't eavesdrop, though I did overhear Brenda whisper at one point, "No, darling, it was never anything that *you* did wrong." Maybe it wasn't much, not when weighted against those years of inattention. It wasn't much; but it wasn't nothing. I knew—maybe for the first time—how much it cost Brenda to take on these memories, to take on the risks of remembering; because she was right. If in later years you remembered nothing, you would feel no pain.

And yet, I had seen two centuries of pain come washing back, bringing with it joy.

Children recover remarkably well. Drop them, and they bounce. Maybe not so high as before, but they do rebound. Dee-dee bore a solemn air about her for a day or two, sensing, without being told, that she had almost "gone away." But to a child, a day is a lifetime, and a week is forever; and she was soon in the recovery ward, playing with the other children. Rheumatic children with heart murmurs; shaven-headed children staring leukemia in the face; broken children with scars and cigarette burns. . . . They played with an impossible cheerfulness, living, as most children did, in the moment. But then, the Now was all most of them would ever have.

There came a day when Dee-dee was not in her room when I arrived. Connie sat framed in a bright square of sunlight, reading a book. She looked up when I walked in. "Deirdre has gone to visit a new friend," she said.

"Oh." A strange clash of emotions: Happy she was up and about again, even if confined to a wheelchair; disappointed that she was not there to greet me.

"She will return soon, I think."

"Well," I said, "we had wanted her to become more active."

Consuela closed her book and laid it on the small table beside her. "I suppose you will no longer need my services," she said. She did not look at me when she said it, but out the window at the new-born summer.

"Not need you? Don't be foolish."

"She has her mother back, now."

Every morning before work; every evening after. Pressing lost years into a few hours. "She still needs you."

"The hospital staff cares for her now."

I shook my head. "It's not that she *needs* you, but that she needs *you*. You are not only her nurse."

"If I take on new clients," she went on as if I had not spoken, "I can do things properly. I can visit at the appointed times, perform my duties, and leave; and not allow them such a place in my heart when they are gone."

"If people don't leave a hole in your life when they are gone, Consuela, they were never in your life at all."

She turned away from the window and looked at me. "Or two holes."

I dropped my gaze, looked instead at the rumpled bed.

"In many ways," I heard her say, "you are a cold man, Doctor. Uncaring and thoughtless. But it was the fruit of bitterness and despair. I thought you deserved better than you had. And you love her as deeply as I. If death could be forestalled by clinging tight, Deirdre would never leave us."

I had no answer for her, but I allowed my eyes to seek out hers.

"I thought," she said, "sometimes, at night, when I played my flute, that because we shared that love . . . that we could share another."

"It must be lonely for you here, in a strange country, with a strange language and customs. No family and fewer friends. I must be a wretched man for never having asked."

She shook her head. "You had your own worry. A large one that consumed you."

"Consuela Montejo, if you leave, you would leave as great a hole in my life as in Dee-dee's."

"And in Mrs. Wilkes's." She smiled a little bit. "It is a very odd thing, but I believe that if I stayed I might even grow to like her."

"She was frightened. She thought she could cauterize the wound before she received it. It was only when she nearly lost Dee-dee that she suddenly realized that she had never had her."

Consuela stood and walked to the bed. She touched the sheet and smoothed it out, pulling the wrinkles flat. She shook her head. "It will hurt if I go; it will hurt if I stay. But Mrs. Wilkes deserves this one chance."

I reached out and took her hand, and she reached out and took mine. Had Brenda walked in then, I do not know what she would have made of our embrace. I do not know what I made of it. I think I would have pulled Brenda in with us, the three of us arm in arm in arm.

The really strange thing was how inevitable it all was in hindsight.

When I left Consuela, I went to visit Mae. It had been nearly two weeks since I had last seen her and it occurred to me that the old bat might be lonely, too. And what the hell, she could put up with me and I could put up with her.

I found my Dee-dee in Mae Holloway's room. The two of them had their heads bent close together, giggling over something. Deirdre was strapped to her electric wheelchair and Mae lay flat upon her bed; but I was struck by how alike they looked. Two gnarled and bent figures with pale, spotted skin stretched tight over their bones, lit from within by a pure, childlike joy. Two old women; two young girls. Deirdre looked up and saw me.

"Daddy! Granny Mae has been teaching me the most wonderful songs."

Mae Holloway lifted her head a little. "Yours?" she said in a hoarse whisper. "This woman-child is yours?"

"Yes," I said, bending to kiss Dee-dee's cheek. "All mine." No. Not *all* mine. There were others who shared her.

"Listen to the song Granny Mae taught me! It goes like this."

I looked over Dee-dee's head at the old woman. "She didn't tell you?"

"Noor brought her in, but didn't say aye, yea, or no. Just that she thought we should meet."

Dee-dee began singing in her high, piping voice.

"The days go slowly by, Lorena.
The snow is on the grass again.
The years go slowly by Lorena. . . ."

"Her days are going by too fast, ain't they?" Mae said. I nodded and saw how her eyes lingered on my little girl. "Growing old in the blink of an eye," she said softly. "Oh, I know how that feels."

"Granny Mae tells such interesting stories," Dee-dee insisted. "Did you know she saw Abraham Lincoln one time?" I rubbed her thinning hair. Too young to know how impossible that was. Too young to doubt.

Mae's hand sought out Dee-dee's and clenched hold of it. "Doc, I'll have me that operation."

"What?"

"I'll have me that operation. The one that's supposed to make this tumor of mine go away. I'll have it, even if my music and my memories go with it."

"You will? Why?"

"Because I know why you been poking me and taking my blood. And I know why the Good Lord has kept me here for all this long time."

Noor Khan was waiting in the hallway when I stepped out of the room.

"Ah, Doctor," I said. "How are things at Sunny Dale?"

"Quiet," she said. "Though the residents are all asking when you will be back."

I shrugged. "Old people dislike upsets to their routine. They grew used to having me around."

Khan said, "I never knew about your little girl. I heard it from Smythe. Why did you never tell me?"

I shrugged again. "I never thought it was anyone's business."

Khan accepted the statement. "After you told Wing and me of Mae's remarkable longevity, I knew you were taking blood samples to that genetic engineering firm—"

"Singer and Peeler."

"Yes. I thought you had . . . other reasons."

"What, that I would find the secret of the Tree of Life?" I shook my head. "I never thought to ask for so much. Mae has lived most her life as an old woman. I would not count that a blessing. But to live a normal life? To set right what had come out wrong? Yes, and I won't apologize. Neither would you, if it were your daughter."

"Is Singer close? To a solution?"

"I don't know. Neither do they. We won't know how close we are until we stumble right into it. But we've bought a little time now, thanks to you. Is that why you did it? Because you knew that meeting my daughter would convince Mae to accept the Culver-Blaese gene therapy?"

Khan shook her head. "No. I never even thought of that."

"Then, why?"

"Sometimes," said Khan, looking back into the room where the young girl and the old girl taught each other songs. "Sometimes, there are other medicines, for other kinds of hurts."

> *I seek no more the fine and gay,*
> *For each does but remind me*
> *How swift the hours did pass away*
> *With the girl I left behind me.*

They are all gone now. All gone. Mae, Dee-dee, all of them. Consuela was first. Brenda's partnership arrangement with FitzPatrick—telecommuting, they called it—left no place for her at the house. She came to visit Dee-dee, and she and Brenda often met for coffee—what they talked about I do not know—but she stopped coming after Dee-dee passed on and I have not seen her in years.

Brenda, too. She lives in LA, now. I visit her when I'm on the Coast and we go out together, and catch dinner or a show. But she can't look at me without thinking of *her*; and neither can I, and sometimes, that becomes too much.

There was no bitterness in the divorce. There was no bitterness left in either of us. But Dee-dee's illness had been a fault line splitting the earth. A chasm had run through our lives, and we jumped out of its way, but Brenda to one side and I, to the other. When Dee-dee was gone, there was no bridge across it and we found that we shared nothing between us but a void.

The operation bought Mae six months. Six months of silence in her mind before the stroke took her. She complained a little, now and then, about her quickly evaporating memories, but sometimes I read to her from my notes, or played the tape recorder, and that made her feel a little better. When she heard about seeing Lincoln on the White House lawn, she just shook her head and said, "Isn't that a wonder?" The last time I saw Mae Holloway, she was fumbling after some elusive memory of her Mister that kept slipping like water through the fingers of her mind, when she suddenly brightened, looked at me, and smiled. "They're all a-waiting," she whispered, and then all the lights went out.

And Dee-dee.

Dee-dee.

Still, after all these years, I cannot talk about my little girl.

They call it the Deirdre-Holloway treatment. I insisted on that. It came too late for her, but maybe there are a few thousand fewer children who die now each year because of it. Sometimes I think it was worth it. Sometimes I wonder selfishly why it could not have come earlier. I wonder if there wasn't something I could have done differently that would have brought us home sooner.

Singer found the key; or Peeler did, or they found it together. Three years later, thank God. Had the break-through followed too soon on Deirdre's death, I could not have borne it. The income from the book funded it and it took every penny, but I feel no poorer for it.

It's a mutation, Peeler told me, that codes for an enzyme that retards catabolism. In males, the gene's expression is suppressed by testosterone. In females, there's a sudden acceleration of fetal development in the last months of pregnancy that almost always kills the mother, and often the child as well. After birth, aging slows quickly until it nearly stops at puberty. It only resumes after menopause. Generations of gene-spliced lab mice lived and died to establish that. Sweet

Annie's dear, dead child would have been programmed for the same long future had she lived.

Is the line extinct now? Or does the gene linger out there, carried safely by males waiting unwittingly to kill their mates with daughters?

I don't know. I never found another like Mae, despite my years of practice in geriatrics.

When I retired from the Home, the residents gave me a party, though none of them were of that original group—Jimmy, Rose, Leo, Old Man Morton. . . . By then I had seen them all through their final passage. When the residents began approaching my own age, I knew it was time to take down my shingle.

I find myself thinking more and more about the past these days. About Mae and the Home and Khan—I heard from my neighbor's boy that she is still in practice, in pediatrics now. Sometimes, I think of my own parents and the old river town where I grew up. The old cliffside stairs. Hiking down along the creek. Hasbrouk's grocery down on the corner.

The memories are dim and faded, brittle with time.

And I don't remember the music, at all. My memories are silent, like an old Chaplin film. I've had my house wired, and tapes play continually, but it isn't the same. The melodies do not come from within; they do not come from the heart.

They tell me I have a tumor in my left temporal lobe, and it's growing. It may be operable. It may not be. Wing wants to try Culver-Blaese, but I won't let him. I keep hoping.

I want to remember. I want to remember Mae. Yes, and Consuela and Brenda, too. And Dee-dee most of all. I want to remember them all. I want to hear them singing.

THE HOLE IN THE HOLE

Terry Bisson

Here's a warm, funny, and deliciously bizarre tale, in the tradition of the best of R. A. Lafferty, about some intrepid explorers who dare to venture into the wilds of darkest Brooklyn in search of treasure beyond price . . . and who find far more than they *expect* to find.

Terry Bisson is the author of a number of critically acclaimed novels such as *Fire on the Mountain*, *Wyrldmaker*, the popular *Talking Man*, which was a finalist for the World Fantasy Award in 1986, and, most recently, *Voyage to the Red Planet*. In 1991, his famous story ''Bears Discover Fire'' won the Nebula Award, the Hugo Award, the Theodore Sturgeon Award, *and* the *Asimov's* Reader's Award, the only story ever to sweep them all. His most recent book is a collection, *Bears Discover Fire and Other Stories*. His stories have appeared in our Eighth and Tenth Annual Collections. He lives with his family in Brooklyn, New York.

One

Trying to find Volvo parts can be a pain, particularly if you are a cheapskate, like me. I needed the hardware that keeps the brake pads from squealing, but I kept letting it go, knowing it wouldn't be easy to find. The brakes worked okay; good enough for Brooklyn. And I was pretty busy, anyway, being in the middle of a divorce, the most difficult I have ever handled, my own.

After the squeal developed into a steady scream (we're talking about the brakes here, not the divorce, which was silent), I tried the two auto supply houses I usually dealt with, but had no luck. The counterman at Aberth's just gave me a blank look. At Park Slope Foreign Auto, I heard those dread words, ''dealer item.'' Breaking (no pun intended) with my usual policy, I went to the Volvo dealer in Bay Ridge, and the parts man, one of those Jamaicans who seem to think being rude is the same thing as being funny, fished around in his bins and placed a pile of pins, clips, and springs on the counter.

''That'll be twenty-eight dollars, mon,'' he said, with what they used to call a shit-eating grin. When I complained (or as we lawyers like to say, objected), he pointed at the spring which was spray-painted yellow, and said, ''Well, you see, they're gold, mon!'' Then he spun on one heel to enjoy the laughs of his co-workers, and I left. There is a limit.

So I let the brakes squeal for another week. They got worse and worse.

Ambulances were pulling over to let me by, thinking I had priority. Then I tried spraying the pads with WD-40.

Don't ever try that.

On Friday morning I went back to Park Slope Foreign Auto and pleaded (another legal specialty) for help. Vinnie, the boss's son, told me to try Boulevard Imports in Howard Beach, out where Queens and Brooklyn come together at the edge of Jamaica Bay. Since I didn't have court that day, I decided to give it a try.

The brakes howled all the way. I found Boulevard Imports on Rockaway Boulevard just off the Belt Parkway. It was a dark, grungy, impressive-looking cave of a joint, with guys in coveralls lounging around drinking coffee and waiting on deliveries. I was hopeful.

The counterman, another Vinnie, listened to my tale of woe before dashing my hopes with the dread words: "Dealer item." Then the guy in line behind me, still another Vinnie (everyone wore their names over their pockets) said, "Send him to Frankie in the Hole."

The Vinnie behind the counter shook his head, saying, "He'd never find it."

I turned to the other Vinnie and asked, "Frankie in the Hole?"

"Frankie runs a little junkyard," he said. "Volvos only. You know the Hole?"

"Can't say as I do."

"I'm not surprised. Here's what you do. Listen carefully, because it's not so easy to find these days, and I'm only going to tell you once."

There's no way I could describe or even remember everything this Vinnie told me: suffice it to say that it had to do with crossing over Rockaway Boulevard, then back under the Belt Parkway, forking onto a service road, making a U turn onto Conduit but staying in the center lane, cutting a sharp left into a dead end (that really wasn't), and following a dirt track down a steep bank through a grove of trees and brush.

I did as I was told, and found myself in a sort of sunken neighborhood, on a wide, dirt street running between decrepit houses set at odd angles on weed-grown lots. It looked like one of those left-over neighborhoods in the meadowlands of Jersey, or down South, where I did my basic training. There were no sidewalks but plenty of potholes, abandoned gardens, and vacant lots. The streets were half-covered by huge puddles. The houses were of concrete block, or tarpaper, or board and batten, no two alike or even remotely similar; there was even a house trailer, illegal in New York City (of course, so is crime). There were no street signs, so I couldn't tell if I was in Brooklyn or Queens, or on the dotted line between the two.

The other Vinnie (or third, if you are counting) had told me to follow my nose until I found a small junkyard, which I proceeded to do. Mine was the only car on the street. Weaving around the puddles (or cruising through them like a motorboat) gave driving an almost nautical air of adventure. There was no shortage of junk in the Hole, including a subway car someone was living in, and a crane that had lost its verticality and took up two backyards. Another backyard had a piebald pony. The few people I saw were white. A fat woman in a short dress sat on a high step talking on a portable phone. A gang of kids were gathered around a puddle, killing something with sticks. In the yard behind them was a card table with a crude sign reading "MOON ROCKS R US."

I liked the peaceful scene in the Hole. And driving through the puddles quietened my brakes. I saw plenty of junk cars, but they came in ones or twos, in the yards and on the street, and none of them were Volvos (no surprise).

After I passed the piebald pony twice, I realized I was going in circles. Then I noticed a chain link fence with reeds woven into it. And I had a feeling.

I stopped. The fence was just too high to look over, but I could see between the reeds. I was right. It was a junkyard that had been "lady-birded."

The lot hidden by the fence was filled with cars, squeezed together tightly, side by side and end to end. All from Sweden. All immortal and all dead. All indestructible, and all destroyed. All Volvos.

The first thing you learn in law school is when not to look like a lawyer. I left my tie and jacket in the car, pulled on my coveralls, and followed the fence around to a gate. On the gate was a picture of a snarling dog. The picture was (it turned out) all the dog there was, but it was enough; it slowed you down. Made you think.

The gate was unlocked. I opened it enough to slip through. I was in a narrow driveway, the only open space in the junkyard. The rest was packed so tightly with Volvos that there was barely room to squeeze between them. They were lined up in rows, some facing north and some south (or was it east and west?) so that it looked like a traffic jam in Hell. The gridlock of the dead.

At the end of the driveway, there was a ramshackle garage made of corrugated iron, shingleboard, plywood, and fiberglass. In and around it, too skinny to cast shade, were several ailanthuses—New York's parking lot tree. There were no signs but none were needed. This had to be Frankie's.

Only one living car was in the junkyard. It stood at the end of the driveway, by the garage, with its hood raised, as if it were trying to speak but had forgotten what it wanted to say. It was a 164, Volvo's unusual straight six. The body was battered, with bondo under the taillights and doors where rust had been filled in. It had cheap imitation racing wheels and a chrome racing stripe along the bottom of the doors. Two men were leaning over, peering into the engine compartment.

I walked up and watched, unwelcomed but not (I suspected) unnoticed. An older white man in coveralls bent over the engine while a black man in a business suit looked on and kibitzed in a rough but friendly way. I noticed, because this was the late 1980s, and the relations between black and white weren't all that friendly in New York.

And here we were in Howard Beach. Or at least in a Hole in Howard Beach.

"If you weren't so damn cheap, you'd get a Weber and throw these SUs away," the white man said.

"If I wasn't so damn cheap, you'd never see my ass," the black man said. He had a West Indian accent.

"I find you a good car and you turn it into a piece of island junk."

"You sell me a piece of trash and . . ."

And so forth. But all very friendly. I stood waiting patiently until the old man raised his head and lifted his eyeglasses, wiped along the two sides of his grease-smeared nose, and then pretended to notice me for the first time.

"You Frankie?" I asked.

"Nope."

"This is Frankie's, though?"

"Could be." Junkyard men like the conditional.

So do lawyers. "I was wondering if it might be possible to find some brake parts for a 145, a 1970. Station wagon."

"What you're looking for is an antique dealer," the West Indian said.

The old man laughed; they both laughed. I didn't.

"Brake hardware," I said. "The clips and pins and stuff."

"Hard to find," the old man said. "That kind of stuff is very expensive these days."

The second thing you learn in law school is when to walk away. I was almost at the end of the drive when the old man reached through the window of the 164 and blew the horn: two shorts and a long.

At the far end of the yard, by the fence, a head popped up. I thought I was seeing a cartoon, because the eyes were too large for the head, and the head was too large for the body.

"Yeah, Unc?"

"Frankie, I'm sending a lawyer fellow back there. Show him that 145 we pulled the wheels off of last week."

"I'll take a look," I said. "But what makes you think I'm an attorney?"

"The tassels," the old man said, looking down at my loafers. He stuck his head back under the hood of the 164 to let me know I was dismissed.

Frankie's hair was almost white, and so thin it floated off the top of his head. His eyes were bright blue-green, and slightly bugged out, giving him an astonished look. He wore cowboy boots with the heels rolled over so far that he walked on their sides and left scrollwork for tracks. Like the old man, he was wearing blue gabardine pants and a lighter blue work shirt. On the back it said—

But I didn't notice what it said. I wasn't paying attention. I had never seen so many Volvos in one place before. There was every make and model—station wagons, sedans, fastbacks, 544s and 122s, DLs and GLs, 140s to 740s, even a 940—in every state of dissolution, destruction, decay, desolation, degradation, decrepitude, and disrepair. It was beautiful. The Volvos were jammed so close together that I had to edge sideways between them.

We made our way around the far corner of the garage, where I saw a huge jumbled pile—not a stack—of tires against the fence. It was cooler here. The ailanthus trees were waving though I could feel no breeze.

"This what you're looking for?" Frankie stopped by a 145 sedan—dark green, like my station wagon; it was a popular color. The wheels were gone and it sat on the ground. By each wheel well lay a hubcap, filled with water.

There was a hollow thud behind us. A tire had come over the fence, onto the pile; another followed it. "I need to get back to work," Frankie said. "You can find what you need, right?"

He left me with the 145, called out to someone over the fence, then started pulling tires off the pile and rolling them through a low door into a shed built onto the side of the garage. The shed was only about five feet high. The door was half covered by a plastic shower curtain hung sideways. It was slit like a hula skirt and every time a tire went through it, it went *pop*.

Every time Frankie rolled a tire through the door, another sailed over the fence onto the pile behind him. It seemed like the labors of Sisyphus.

Well, I had my own work. Carefully, I drained the water out of the first hubcap. There lay the precious springs and clips I sought, rusty but usable. I worked my way around the car (a job in itself, as it was jammed so closely with the others). I drained the four hubcaps and collected all the treasure into one of them. It was like panning for gold.

There was a cool breeze and a funny smell. Behind me I heard a steady *pop*, *pop*, *pop*. But when I finished and took the brake parts to Frankie, the pile of tires was still the same size. Frankie was on top of it, leaning on the fence, talking with an Indian man in a Goodyear shirt

The Indian (who must have been standing on a truck on the other side of the fence) saw me and ducked. I had scared him away. I realized I was witnessing some kind of illegal dumping operation. I wondered how all the junk tires fit into the tiny shed, but I wasn't about to ask. Probably Frankie and the old man took them out and dumped them into Jamaica Bay every night.

I showed Frankie the brake parts. "I figure they're worth a couple of bucks," I said.

"Show Unc," he said. "He'll tell you what they're worth."

I'll bet, I thought. Carrying my precious hubcap of brake hardware, like a waiter with a dish, I started back toward the driveway. Behind me I heard a steady *pop*, *pop*, *pop* as Frankie went back to work. I must have been following a different route between the cars—because when I saw it, I knew it was for the first time.

The 1800 is Volvo's legendary (well, sort of) sports car from the early 1960s. The first model, the P1800, was assembled in Scotland and England (unusual, to say the least, for a Swedish car). This one, the only one I had ever seen in a junkyard, still had its fins and appeared to have all its glass. It was dark blue. I edged up to it, afraid that if I alarmed it, it might disappear. But it was real. It was wheelless, engineless, and rusted out in the rocker panels, but it was real. I looked inside. I tapped on the glass. I opened the door.

The interior was the wrong color, but it was real too. It smelled musty, but it was intact. Or close enough. I arrived at the driveway so excited that I didn't even flinch when the old man looked into my hubcap (like a fortune teller reading entrails) and said, "Ten dollars."

I raced home to tell Wu what I had found.

Two

Everybody should have a friend like Wilson Wu, just to keep them guessing. Wu worked his way through high school as a pastry chef, then dropped out to form a rock band, then won a scholarship to Princeton (I think) for math (I think), then dropped out to get a job as an engineer, then made it halfway through medical school at night before becoming a lawyer, which is where I met him. He passed his bar exam on the first try. Somewhere along the line he decided he was gay, then decided he wasn't (I don't know what his wife thought of all this); he has been both Democrat and Republican, Catholic and Protestant, pro and anti gun control. He can't decide if he's Chinese or American, or both. The only constant thing in his life is the Volvo. Wu has never owned another kind of car. He kept a 1984 240DL station wagon for the wife and kids. He kept his P1800, which I had helped him tow from Pennsylvania, where he had bought it at a yard sale for $500 (a whole other story), in my garage. I didn't charge him rent. It was a red 1961 sports coupe with a B18. The engine and transmission were good (well, fair) but the interior had been gutted. Wu had found seats but hadn't yet put them in. He was waiting for the knobs and trim and door panels, the little stuff that is hardest to find, especially for a P1800. He had been looking for two years.

Wu lived on my block in Brooklyn, which was strictly a coincidence since I knew him from Downtown Brooklyn Law School and Legal Aid, where we had both worked before going into private practice. I found him in his kitchen, helping his wife decorate a wedding cake. She's a caterer. "What are you doing in the morning?" I asked, but I didn't wait for him to tell me. I have never been good at surprises (which is why I had no success as a criminal lawyer). "Your long travail is over," I said. "I found an 1800. A P1800. With an interior."

"Handles?"

"Handles."

"Panels?"

"Panels."

"Knobs?" Wu had stopped stirring. I had his attention.

"I see you got your brakes fixed," Wu said the next day as we were on our way to Howard Beach in my car. "Or perhaps I should say, 'I hear.' "

"I found the parts yesterday and put them on this morning," I told him. I told him the story of how I had found the Hole. I told him about the junkyard of Volvos. I told him about stumbling across the dark blue P1800. By then, we were past the end of Atlantic Avenue, near Howard Beach. I turned off onto Conduit and tried to retrace my turns of the day before, but with no luck. Nothing looked familiar.

Wu started to look skeptical; or maybe I should say, he started to look even more skeptical. "Maybe it was all a dream," he said, either taunting me or comforting himself, or both.

"I don't imagine P1800s in junkyards even in dreams," I said. But in spite of my best efforts to find the Hole, I was going in circles. Finally, I gave up and went to Boulevard Imports. The place was almost empty. I didn't recognize the counterman. His shirt said he was a Sal.

"Vinnie's off," he said. "It's Saturday."

"Then maybe you can help me. I'm trying to find a place called Frankie's. In the Hole."

People sometimes use the expression "blank look" loosely. Sal's was the genuine article.

"A Volvo junkyard?" I said. "A pony or so?"

Blank got even blanker. Wu had come in behind me, and I didn't have to turn around to know he was looking skeptical.

"I don't know about any Volvos, but did somebody mention a pony?" a voice said from in the back. An old man came forward. He must have been doing the books, because he was wearing a tie. "My pop used to keep a pony in the Hole. We sold it when horseshoes got scarce during the war."

"Jeez, Vinnie, what war was this?" Sal asked. (So I had found another Vinnie!)

"How many have there been?" the old Vinnie asked. He turned to me. "Now, listen up, kid." (I couldn't help smiling; usually only judges call me "kid," and only in chambers.) "I can only tell you once, and I'm not sure I'll get it right."

The old Vinnie's instructions were completely different from the ones I had gotten from the Vinnie the day before. They involved a turn into an abandoned gas station on the Belt Parkway, a used car lot on Conduit, a McDonald's with a dumpster in the back, plus other flourishes that I have forgotten.

Suffice it to say that, twenty minutes later, after bouncing down a steep bank, Wu and I found ourselves cruising the wide mud streets of the Hole, looking for Frankie's. I could tell by Wu's silence that he was impressed. The Hole is pretty impressive if you are not expecting it, and who's expecting it? There was the non-vertical crane, the subway car (with smoke coming from its makeshift chimney), and the pony grazing in a lot between two shanties. I wondered if it was a descendant of the old Vinnie's father's pony. I couldn't tell if it was shod or not.

The fat lady was still on the phone. The kids must have heard us coming, because they were standing in front of the card table waving hand-lettered signs: "Moon Rocks This Way!" and "Moon Rocks R Us!" When he saw them, Wu put his hand on my arm and said, "Pull over, Irv."—his first words since we had descended into the Hole. I pulled over and he got out. He fingered a couple of ashy-looking lumps, and handed the kids a dollar. They giggled and said they had no change.

Wu told them to keep it.

"I hope you don't behave like that at Frankie's," I said, when he got back into the car.

"Like what?"

"You're supposed to bargain, Wu. People expect it. Even kids. What do you want with phony moon rocks anyway?"

"Supporting free enterprise," he said. "Plus, I worked on Apollo and I handled some real moon rocks once. They looked just like these." He sniffed them. "Smelled just like these." He tossed them out the window into the shallow water as we motored through a puddle.

As impressive as the Hole can be (first time), there is nothing more impressive than a junkyard of all Volvos. I couldn't wait to see Wu's face when he saw it.

I wasn't disappointed. I heard him gasp as we slipped through the gate. He looked around, then looked at me and grinned. "Astonishing," he said. Even the inscrutable, skeptical Wu.

"Thank you," I said. (I could hardly wait till he saw the P1800!)

The old man was at the end of the driveway, working on a diesel this time. Another customer, this one white, looked on and kibitzed. The old man seemed to sell entertainment as much as expertise. They were trying to get water out of the injectors.

"I understand you have an 1800," Wu said, and added: "They're hard to find."

I winced. Wu was no businessman. The old man straightened up, and looked us over. There's nothing like a six-foot Chinaman to get your attention, and Wu is six-two.

"P1800," the old man said. "Hard to find is hardly the word for it. I'd call it your rare luxury item. But I guess it won't cost you nothing to have a look." He reached around the diesel's windshield and honked the horn. Two shorts and a long.

The oversized head with the oversized eyes appeared at the far end of the yard, by the fence.

"Two lawyers coming back," the old man called out. Then he said to me: "It's easier to head straight back along the garage till you get to where Frankie is working. Then head to your right, and you'll find the P1800."

Frankie was still working on the endless pile (not a stack) of tires by the fence. Each one went through the low door of the shed with a *pop*.

I nodded a greeting, and Frankie nodded back. I turned right and edged between the cars toward the P1800, assuming Wu was right behind me. When I saw it, I was relieved—it had not been a dream after all! I expected an appreciative whistle (at the very least), but when I turned, I saw that I had lost Wu.

He was still back by the garage, looking through a stack (not a pile) of wheels against the wall.

"Hey, Wu!" I said, standing on the bumper of the P1800. "You can get wheels anywhere. Check out the interior on this baby!" Then, afraid I had sounded too enthusiastic, I added: "It's rough but it might almost do."

Wu didn't even bother to answer me. He pulled two wheels from the stack. They weren't exactly wheels, at least not the kind you mount tires on. They were more like wire mesh tires, with metal chevrons where the tread should have been.

Wu set them upright, side by side. He slapped one and gray dust flew. He slapped the other. "Where'd you get these?" he asked.

Frankie stopped working and lit a cigarette. "Off a dune buggy," he said.

By this time, I had joined them. "A Volvo dune buggy?"

"Not a Volvo," Frankie said. "An electric job. Can't sell you the wheels separately. They're a set."

"What about the dune buggy?" Wu asked. "Can I have a look at it?"

Frankie's eyes narrowed. "It's on the property. Hey, are you some kind of environment man or something?"

"The very opposite," said Wu. "I'm a lawyer. I just happen to dig dune buggies. Can I have a look at it? Good ones are hard to find."

I winced.

"I'll have to ask Unc," Frankie said.

"Wu," I said, as soon as Frankie had left to find his uncle, "there's something you need to know about junkyard men. If something is hard to find, you don't have to tell them. And what's this dune buggy business, anyway? I thought you wanted interior trim for your P1800."

"Forget the P1800, Irv," Wu said. "It's yours. I'm giving it to you."

"You're what?"

Wu slapped the wire mesh wheel again and sniffed the cloud of dust. "Do you realize what this is, Irv?"

"Some sort of wire wheel. So what?"

"I worked at Boeing in 1970," Wu said. "I helped build this baby, Irv. It's off the LRV."

"The LR what?"

Before Wu could answer, Frankie was back. "Well, you can look at it," he said. "But you got to hold your breath. It's in the cave and there's no air in there."

"The cave?" I said. They both ignored me.

"You can see it from the door, but I'm not going back in there," said Frankie. "Unc won't let me. Have you got a jacket? It's cold."

"I'll be okay," Wu said.

"Suit yourself." Frankie tossed Wu a pair of plastic welding goggles. "Wear these. And remember, hold your breath."

It was clear at this point where the cave was. Frankie was pointing toward the low door into the shed, where he rolled the tires. Wu put on the goggles and ducked his head; as he went through the doorway he made that same weird *pop* the tires made.

I stood there with Frankie in the sunlight, holding the two wire mesh wheels, feeling like a fool.

There was another *pop* and Wu backed out through the shower curtain. When he turned around, he looked like he had seen a ghost. I don't know how else to describe it. Plus he was shivering like crazy.

"Told you it was cold!" said Frankie. "And it's weird. There's no air in there, for one thing. If you want the dune buggy, you'll have to get it out of there yourself."

Wu gradually stopped shivering. As he did, a huge grin spread across his face. "It's weird, all right," he said. "Let me show my partner. Loan me some extra goggles."

"I'll take your word for it," I said.

"Irv, come on! Put these goggles on."

"No way!" I said. But I put them on. I always did what Wu said, sooner or later; he was that kind of guy.

"Don't hold your breath in. Let it all out, and then hold it. Come on. Follow me."

I breathed out and ducked down just in time; Wu grabbed my hand and pulled me through the shed door behind him. If I made a *pop* I didn't hear it. We were standing in the door of a cave—but looking out, not in. The inside was another outside!

It was like the beach, all gray sand (or dust) but with no water. I could see stars but it wasn't dark. The dust was greenish gray, like a courthouse hallway (a color familiar to lawyers).

My ears were killing me. And it was cold!

We were at the top of a long, smooth slope, like a dune, which was littered with tires. At the bottom was a silver dune buggy with no front wheels, sitting nose down in the gray dust.

Wu pointed at it. He was grinning like a maniac. I had seen enough. Pulling my hand free, I stepped back through the shower curtain and gasped for air. This time I heard a "pop" as I went through.

The warm air felt great. My ears gradually quit ringing. Frankie was sitting on his tire pile, smoking a cigarette. "Where's your buddy? He can't stay in there."

Just then, Wu backed out through the curtain with a loud *pop*. "I'll take it," he said, as soon as he had filled his lungs with air. "I'll take it!"

I winced. Twice.

"I'll have to ask Unc," said Frankie.

"Wu," I said, as soon as Frankie had left to find his uncle, "let me tell you something about junkyard men. You can't say 'I'll take it, I'll take it' around them. You have to say, 'Maybe it might do, or . . . ' "

"Irving!" Wu cut me off. His eyes were wild. (He hardly ever called me Irving.) He took both my hands in his, as if we were bride and groom, and began to walk me in a circle. His fingers were freezing. "Irving, do you know, do you realize, where we just were?"

"Some sort of cave? Haven't we played this game before?"

"The Moon! Irving, that was the surface of the Moon you just saw!"

"I admit it was weird," I said. "But the Moon is a million miles away. And it's up in the air . . ."

"Quarter of a million," Wu said. "But I'll explain later." Frankie was back, with his uncle. "That dune buggy's one of a kind," the old man said. "I couldn't take less than five hundred for it."

Wu said, "I'll take it!"

I winced.

"But you've got to get it out of the cave yourself," the old man said. "I don't want Frankie going in there anymore. That's why I told the kids, no more rocks."

"No problem," Wu said. "Are you open tomorrow?"

"Tomorrow's Sunday," said the old man.

"What about Monday?"

I followed Wu through the packed-together Volvos to the front gate. We were on the street before I realized he hadn't even bothered to look at the P1800.

"You're the best thing that ever happened to those two," I said. I was a little pissed off. More than a little.

"There's no doubt about it," Wu said.

"Damn right there's no doubt about it!" I started my 145 and headed up the street, looking for an exit from the Hole. Any exit. "Five hundred dollars for a junk dune buggy?"

"No doubt about it at all. That was either the Hadley Appenines, or Descartes, or Taurus-Littrow," Wu said. "I guess I could tell by looking at the serial numbers on the LRV."

"I never heard of a Hadley or a Descartes," I said, "but I know Ford never made a dune buggy." I found a dirt road that led up through a clump of trees. Through the branches I could see the full Moon, pale in the afternoon sky. "And there's the Moon, right there in the sky, where it's supposed to be."

"There's apparently more than one way to get to the Moon, Irving. Which they are using as a dump for old tires. We saw it with our own eyes!"

The dirt road gave out in a vacant lot on Conduit. I crossed a sidewalk, bounced down a curb, and edged into the traffic. Now that I was headed back toward Brooklyn, I could pay attention. "Wu," I said. "Just because you worked for NAPA—"

"NASA, Irv. And I didn't work for them, I worked for Boeing."

"Whatever. Science is not my thing. But I know for a fact that the Moon is in the sky. We were in a hole in the ground, although it was weird, I admit."

"A hole with stars?" Wu said. "With no air? Smell the coffee, Irv." He found an envelope in my glove compartment and began scrawling on it with a pencil. "No, I suspected it when I saw those tires. They are from the Lunar Roving Vehicle, better known as the LRV or the lunar rover. Only three were built and all three were left on the Moon. Apollo 15, 16, and 17. 1971 and 1972. Surely you remember."

"Sure," I said. The third thing you learn in law school is never to admit you don't remember something. "So how did this loonie rover get to Brooklyn?"

"That's what I'm trying to figure out," Wu said. "I suspect we're dealing with one of the rarest occurrences in the universe. A neotopological metaeuclidean adjacentcy."

"A non-logical metaphysical what?"

Wu handed me the envelope. It was covered with numbers—

$$\int_0^\infty \chi e^{-\Delta 3 \frac{1}{g^2}} F^2 \sqrt{\frac{\Delta \cdot dx}{\frac{1420\,mhz}{CTL}}} \cdot \frac{17\pi}{4\Sigma c_i c_i} = \frac{H}{h}$$

"That explains the whole thing," Wu said. "A neotopological metaeuclidean adjacentcy. It's quite rare. In fact, I think this may be the only one."

"You're sure about this?"

"I used to be a physicist."

"I thought it was an engineer."

"Before that. Look at the figures, Irv! Numbers don't lie. That equation shows how space-time can be folded so that two parts are adjacent that are also, at the same time, separated by millions of miles. Or a quarter of a million, anyway.''

"So we're talking about a sort of back door to the Moon?"

"Exactly."

Three

On Sundays I had visitation rights to the big-screen TV. I watched golf and stock car racing all afternoon with my wife, switching back and forth during commercials. We got along a lot better now that we weren't speaking. Especially when she was holding the remote. On Monday morning, Wu arrived at the door at nine o'clock sharp, wearing coveralls and carrying a shopping bag and a tool box.

"How do you know I don't have court today?" I asked.

"Because I know you have only one case at present, your divorce, in which you are representing both parties in order to save money. Hi, Diane."

"Hi, Wu." (She was speaking to *him*.)

We took my 145. Wu was silent all the way out Eastern Parkway, doing figures on a cocktail napkin from a Bay Ridge nightclub. "Go out last night?" I asked. After a whole day with Diane, I was dying to have somebody to talk to.

"Something was bothering me all night," he said. "Since the surface of the Moon is a vacuum, how come all the air on Earth doesn't rush through the shed door, along with the tires?"

"I give up," I said.

We were at a stoplight. "There it is," he said. He handed me the napkin, on which was scrawled—

$$\frac{H}{h} = \int_{W4P}^{\infty} \frac{|420|)dx \div}{|\Delta 33|} \frac{\sqrt{.32}}{4A(z')} \cdot \sum_{K\cos^2} \frac{dx}{K\cos^2} = \frac{h}{H}$$

"There what is?"

"The answer to my question. As those figures demonstrate, Irv, we're not just dealing with a neotopological metaeuclidean adjacentcy. We're dealing with an *incongruent* neotopological metaeuclidean adjacentcy. The two areas are still separated by a quarter of a million miles, even though that distance has been folded to less than a centimeter. It's all there in black and white. See?"

"I guess," I said. The fourth thing you learn in law school is to never admit you don't understand something.

"The air doesn't rush through because it can't. It can kind of seep through, though, which creates a slight microclimate in the immediate vicinity of the adjacentcy. Which is probably why we don't die immediately of decompression. A tire can roll through, if you give it a shove, but air is too, too . . ."

"Too wispy to shove," I said.

"Exactly."

I looked for the turn off Conduit, but nothing was familiar. I tried a few streets, but none of them led us into the Hole. "Not again!" Wu complained.

"Again!" I answered.

I went back to Boulevard. Vinnie was behind the counter today, and he remembered me (with a little prodding).

"You're not the only one having trouble finding the Hole," he said. "It's been hard to find lately."

"What do you mean, 'lately'?" Wu asked from the doorway.

"Just this last year. Every month or so it gets hard to find. I think it has to do with the Concorde. I read somewhere that the noise affects the tide, and the Hole isn't that far from Jamaica Bay, you know."

"Can you draw us a map?" I asked.

"I never took drawing," Vinnie said, "so listen up close."

Vinnie's instructions had to do with an abandoned railroad track, a wrong way turn onto a one-way street, a dog-leg that cut across a health club parking lot, and several other ins and outs. While I was negotiating all this, Wu was scrawling on the back of a car wash flyer he had taken from Vinnie's counter.

"The tide," he muttered. "I should have known!"

I didn't ask him what he meant; I figured (I knew!) he would tell me. But before he had a chance, we were bouncing down a dirt track through some scruffy trees, and onto the now-familiar dirt streets of the Hole. "Want some more moon rocks?" I asked when we passed the kids and their stand.

"I'll pick up my own today, Irv!"

I pulled up by the gate and we let ourselves in. Wu carried the shopping bag; he gave me the tool box.

The old man was working on an ancient 122, the Volvo that looks like a '48 Ford from the back. (It was always one of my favorites.) "It's electric," he said when Wu and I walked up.

"The 122?" I asked.

"The dune buggy," the old man said. "Electric is the big thing now. All the cars in California are going to be electric next year. It's the law."

"No, it's not," I said. "So what, anyway?"

"That makes that dune buggy worth a lot of money."

"No, it doesn't. Besides, you already agreed on a price."

"That's right. Five hundred," Wu said. He pulled five bills from his pocket and unfolded them.

"I said I couldn't take *less* than five hundred," the old man said. "I never said I couldn't take more."

Before Wu could answer, I pulled him behind the 122. "Remember the second thing we learned in law school?" I said. "When to walk away. We can come back next week—if you still want that thing."

Wu shook his head. "It won't be here next week. I realized something when Vinnie told us that the Hole was getting hard to find. The adjacentcy is warping the neighborhood as well as the cislunar space-time continuum. And since it's lunar, it has a monthly cycle. Look at this."

He handed me the car wash flyer, on the back of which was scrawled—

$$T = \frac{\propto \sqrt{\frac{L}{G}}}{H(h)} = \frac{1}{g^2} F^2$$

"See?" said Wu. "We're not just dealing with an incongruent neotopological metaeuclidean adjacentcy. We're dealing with a *periodic* incongruent neotopological metaeuclidean adjacentcy."

"Which means . . ."

"The adjacentcy comes and goes. With the Moon."

"Sort of like PMS."

"Exactly. I haven't got the figures adjusted for daylight savings time yet, but the Moon is on the wane, and I'm pretty sure that after today, Frankie will be out of the illegal dumping business for a month at least."

"Perfect. So we come back next month."

"Irv, I don't want to take the chance. Not with a million dollars at stake."

"Not with a what?" He had my attention.

"That LRV cost two million new, and only three of them were made. Once we get it out, all we have to do is contact NASA. Or Boeing. Or the Air & Space Museum at the Smithsonian. But we've got to strike while the iron is hot. Give me a couple of hundred bucks and I'll give you a fourth interest."

"A half."

"A third. Plus the P1800."

"You already gave me the P1800."

"Yeah, but I was only kidding. Now I'm serious."

"Deal," I said. But instead of giving Wu two hundred, I plucked the five hundreds out of his hand. "But you stick to the numbers. I do all the talking."

We got it for six hundred. Non refundable. "What does that mean?" Wu asked.

"It means you boys own the dune buggy whether you get it out of the cave or not," said the old man, counting his money.

"Fair enough," said Wu. It didn't seem fair to me at all, but I kept my mouth shut. I couldn't imagine a scenario in which we would get our money back from the old man, anyway.

He went back to work on the engine of the 122, and Wu and I headed for the far end of the yard. We found Frankie rolling tires through the shed door: *Pop, pop, pop*. The pile by the fence was as big as ever. He waved and kept on working.

Wu set down the shopping bag and pulled out two of those spandex bicycling outfits. He handed one to me, and started taking off his shoes.

I'll spare you the ensuing interchange—what I said, what he said, objections, arguments, etc. Suffice it to say that, ten minutes later, I was wearing black and purple tights under my coveralls, and so was Wu. Supposedly, they were to keep our skin from blistering in the vacuum. Wu was hard to resist when he had his mind made up.

I wondered what Frankie thought of it all. He just kept rolling tires through the doorway, one by one.

There were more surprises in the bag. Wu pulled out rubber gloves and wool mittens, a brown bottle with Chinese writing on it, a roll of clear plastic vegetable bags from the supermarket, a box of cotton balls, a roll of duct tape, and a rope.

Frankie didn't say anything until Wu got to the rope. Then he stopped working, sat down on the pile of tires, lit a cigarette and said: "Won't work."

Wu begged his pardon.

"I'll show you," Frankie said. He tied one end of the rope to a tire and tossed it through the low door into the shed. There was the usual *pop* and then a fierce crackling noise.

Smoke blew out the door. Wu and I both jumped back.

Frankie pulled the rope back, charred on one end. There was no tire. "I learned the hard way," he said, "when I tried to pull the dune buggy through myself, before I took the wheels off."

"Of course!" Wu said. "What a fool I've been. I should have known!"

"Should have known what?" Frankie and I both asked at once.

Wu tore a corner off the shopping bag and started scrawling numbers on it with a pencil stub. "Should have known this!" he said, and he handed it to Frankie.

Frankie looked at it, shrugged, and handed it to me—

$$ \frac{t_p \approx \frac{1}{G} \times \frac{e^4}{mpm} = eC^3}{h(H)} $$

"So?" I said.

"So, there it is!" Wu said. "As those figures clearly indicate, you can *pass through* a noncongruent adjacentcy, but you can't *connect* its two aspects. It's only logical. Imagine the differential energy stored when a quarter of a million miles of spacetime is folded to less than a millimeter."

"Burns right through a rope," Frankie said.

"Exactly."

"How about a chain?" I suggested.

"Melts a chain," said Frankie. "Never tried a cable, though."

"No substance known to man could withstand that awesome energy differential," Wu said. "Not even cable. That's why the tires make that *pop*. I'll bet you have to roll them hard or they bounce back, right?"

"Whatever you say," said Frankie, putting out his cigarette. He was losing interest.

"Guess that means we leave it there," I said. I had mixed feelings. I hated to lose a third of a million dollars, but I didn't like the looks of that charred rope. Or the smell. I was even willing to kiss my hundred bucks goodbye.

"Leave it there? No way. We'll *drive* it out!" Wu said. "Frankie, do you have some twelve volt batteries you can loan me? Three, to be exact."

"Unc's got some," said Frankie. "I suspect he'll want to sell them, though. Unc's not much of a loaner."

Why was I not surprised?

Half an hour later we had three twelve volt batteries in a supermarket shopping cart. The old man had wanted another hundred dollars, but since I was now a partner I did the bargaining, and we got them for twenty bucks apiece, charged and ready to go, with the cart thrown in. Plus three sets of jumper cables, on loan.

Wu rolled the two wire mesh wheels through the shed door. Each went *pop* and was gone. He put the tool box into the supermarket cart with the batteries and the jumper cables. He pulled on the rubber gloves, and pulled the wool mittens over them. I did the same.

"Ready, Irv?" Wu said. (I would have said no, but I knew it wouldn't do any good, so I didn't say anything.) "We won't be able to talk on the Moon, so here's the plan. First, we push the cart through. Don't let it get stuck in the doorway where it connects the two aspects of the adjacentcy, or it'll start to heat up. Might even explode. Blow up both worlds. Who knows? Once we're through, you head down the hill with the cart. I'll bring the two wheels. When we get to the LRV, you pick up the front end and—"

"Don't we have a jack?"

"I'm expecting very low gravity. Besides, the LRV is lighter than a golf cart. Only 460 pounds, and that's here on Earth. You hold it up while I mount the wheels—I have the tools laid out in the tray of the tool box. Then you hand me the batteries, they go in front, and I'll connect them with the jumper cables, in series. Then we climb in and—"

"Aren't you forgetting something, Wu?" I said. "We won't be able to hold our breath long enough to do all that."

"Ah so!" Wu grinned and held up the brown bottle with Chinese writing on it. "No problem! I have here the ancient Chinese herbal treatment known as (he said some Chinese words) or 'Pond Explorer.' Han dynasty sages used it to lay underwater and meditate for hours. I ordered this from Hong Kong, where it is called (more Chinese words) or 'Mud Turtle Master' and used by thieves; but no matter, it's the same stuff. Hand me those cotton balls."

The bottle was closed with a cork. Wu uncorked it and poured thick brown fluid on a cotton ball; it hissed and steamed.

"Jesus," I said.

"Pond Explorer not only provides the blood with oxygen, it suppresses the breathing reflex. As a matter of fact, you *can't* breathe while it's under your tongue. Which means you can't talk. It also contracts the capillaries and slows the heartbeat. It also scours the nitrogen out of the blood so you don't get the bends."

"How do you know all this?"

"I was into organic chemistry for several years," Wu said. "Did my masters thesis on ancient oriental herbals. Never finished it, though."

"Before you studied math?"

"After math, before law. Open up."

As he prepared to put the cotton ball under my tongue, he said, "Pond Explorer switches your cortex to an ancient respiratory pattern predating the oxygenation of the Earth's atmosphere. Pretty old stuff, Irv! It will feel perfectly natural, though. Breathe out and empty your lungs. There! When we come out, spit it out immediately so you can breathe and talk. It's that simple."

The Pond Explorer tasted bitter. I felt oxygen (or something) flooding my tongue and my cheeks. My mouth tingled. Once I got used to it, it wasn't so bad; as a matter of fact, it felt great. Except for the taste, which didn't go away.

Wu put his cotton ball under his tongue, smiled, and corked the bottle. Then, while I watched in alarm, he tore two plastic bags off the roll.

I saw what was coming. I backed away, shaking my head—

I'll spare you the ensuing interchange. Suffice it to say that, minutes later, we both had plastic bags over our heads, taped around our necks with duct tape. Once I got over my initial panic, it wasn't so bad. As always, Wu seemed to know what he was doing. And as always, it was no use resisting his plans.

If you're wondering what Frankie was making of all this, so was I. He had stopped working again. While my bag was being taped on, I saw him sitting on the pile of tires, watching us with those blue-green eyes; looking a little bored, as if he saw such goings-on every day.

It was time. Wu grabbed the front of the supermarket cart and I grabbed the handle. Wu spun his finger and pointed toward the shed door with its tattered shower curtain waving slightly in the ripples of the space-time interface. We were off!

I waved goodbye to Frankie. He lifted one finger in farewell as we ran through.

Four

From the Earth to the Moon—in one long step for mankind (and in particular, Wilson Wu). I heard a crackling, even through the plastic bag, and the supermarket cart shuddered and shook like a lawnmower with a bent blade. Then we were on the other side, and there was only a great huge cold empty silence.

Overhead were a million stars. At our feet, gray dust. The door we had come through was a dimly lighted hole under a low cliff behind us. We were looking down a gray slope strewn with tires. The flat area at the bottom of the slope was littered with empty bottles, wrappers, air tanks, a big tripod, and of course, the dune buggy—or LRV—nose down in the dust. There were tracks all around it. Beyond were low hills, gray-green except for an occasional black stone. Everything seemed close; there was no far away. Except for the tires, the junk and the tracks around the dune buggy, the landscape was featureless, smooth. Unmarked. Untouched. Lifeless.

The whole scene was half-lit, like dirty snow under a full moon in winter, only brighter. And more green.

Wu was grinning like a madman. His plastic bag had expanded so that it looked like a space helmet; I realized mine probably looked the same. This made me feel better.

Wu pointed up behind us. I turned and there was the Earth—hanging in the sky like a blue-green, oversized Moon, just like the cover of *The Whole Earth Catalog*. I hadn't actually doubted Wu, but I hadn't actually believed him either, until then. The fifth thing you learn in law school is to be comfortable in that "twilight zone" between belief and doubt.

Now I believed it. We were on the Moon, looking back at the Earth. And it was cold! The gloves did no good at all, even with the wool over the rubber. But there was no time to worry about it. Wu had already picked up the wire mesh wheels and started down the slope, sort of hopping with one under each arm, trying to miss the scattered tires. I followed, dragging the grocery cart behind me. I had expected it to bog down in the dust, but it didn't. The only problem was, the low gravity made it hard for me to keep my footing. I had to wedge my toes under the junk tires and pull it a few feet at a time.

The dune buggy, or LRV, as Wu liked to call it, was about the size of a jeep without a hood (or even an engine). It had two seats side by side, like lawn chairs with plastic webbing, facing a square console the size of a portable TV. Between the seats was a gearshift. There was no steering wheel. An umbrella-shaped antenna attached to the front end made the whole thing look like a contraption out of *E.T.* or *Mary Poppins*.

I picked up the front end, and Wu started putting on the left wheel, fitting it under the round fiberglass fender. Even though the LRV was light, the sudden exertion reminded me that I wasn't breathing, and I felt an instant of panic. I closed my eyes and sucked my tongue until it went away. The bitter taste of the Pond Explorer was reassuring.

When I opened my eyes, it looked like a fog was rolling in: it was my plastic bag, fogging up. I could barely see Wu, already finishing the left wheel. I wondered if he had ever worked on an Indy pit crew. (I found out later that he had.)

Wu crossed to the right wheel. The fog was getting thicker. I tried wiping it off with one hand, but of course, it was on the inside. Wu gave the thumbs up, and I set the front end down. I pointed at my plastic bag, and he nodded. His was fogged up, too. He tossed his wrench into the tool box, and the plastic tray shattered like glass (silently, of course). Must have been the cold. My fingers and toes were killing me.

Wu started hopping up the slope, and I followed. I couldn't see the Earth overhead, or the Moon below; everything was a blur. I wondered how we would find our way out (or in?), back through the shed door. I needn't have worried. Wu took my hand and led me through, and this time I heard the *pop*. Blinking in the light, we tore the bags off our heads.

Wu spit out his cotton, and I did the same. My first breath felt strange. And wonderful. I had never realized breathing was so much fun.

There was a high-pitched cheer. Several of the neighborhood kids had joined Frankie on the pile of tires.

"Descartes," Wu said.

"We left it in there," I said.

"I mean our location. It's in the lunar highlands, near the equator. Apollo 16. Young, Duke, and Mattingly. 1972. I recognize the battery cover on the LRV. The return was a little hairy, though. Ours, I mean, not theirs. I had to follow the tires the last few yards. We'll spray some WD-40 on the inside of the plastic bags before we go back in.''

"Stuff's good for everything," Frankie said.

It was noon, and I was starving, but there was no question of breaking for lunch. Wu was afraid the batteries would freeze; though they were heavy duty, they were made for Earth, not the Moon. With new Pond Explorer and new plastic bags properly treated with WD-40, we went back in. I had also taped plastic bags over my shoes. My toes were still stinging from the cold.

As we went down the slope toward the LRV site, we tossed a few of the tires aside to clear a road. With any luck, we would be coming up soon.

We left the original NASA batteries in place and set the new (well, used, but charged) batteries on top of them, between the front fenders. While Wu hooked them up with the jumper cables, I looked around for what I hoped was the last time. There was no view, just low hills all around, the one in front of us strewn with tires like burnt donuts. The shed door (or adjacentcy, as Wu liked to call it) was a dimly lighted cave under a low cliff at the top of the slope. It wasn't a long hill, but it was steep; about twelve degrees.

I wondered if the umbrella-antenna would make it through the door. As if he had read my mind, Wu was already unbolting it when I turned back around. He tossed it aside with the rest of the junk, sat down, and patted the seat beside him.

I climbed in, or rather "on," since there was no "in" to the LRV. Wu sat, of course, on the left. It occurred to me that if the English had been first on the Moon, he would have been on the right. There was no steering wheel or foot pedals either—but that didn't bother Wu. He seemed to know exactly what he was doing. He hit a few switches on the console, and dials lighted up for "roll," "heading," "power," etc. With a mad grin toward me, and a "thumbs up" toward the top of the slope (or the Earth hanging above it), he pushed the T-handle between us forward.

The LRV lurched. It groaned—I could "hear" it through my seat and my tailbone—and began to roll slowly forward. I could tell the batteries were weak.

If the LRV had lights, we didn't need them. The Earth, hanging over the adjacentcy like a gigantic pole star, gave plenty of light. The handle I had thought was a gearshift was actually a joystick, like on a video game. Pushing it to one side, Wu turned the LRV sharply to the right—all four wheels turned—and started up the slope.

It was slow going. You might think the Earth would have looked friendly, but it didn't. It looked cold and cruel; it seemed to be mocking us. The batteries, which had started out weak, were getting weaker. Wu's smile was gone already. The path we had cleared through the tires was useless; the LRV would never make it straight up the slope.

I climbed down and began clearing an angled switchback. If pulling things on the Moon is hard, throwing them is almost fun. I hopped from tire to tire, slinging them down the hill, while Wu drove behind me.

The problem was, even on a switchback the corners are steep. The LRV was still twenty yards from the top when the batteries gave out entirely. I didn't hear it, of course; but when I looked back after clearing the last stretch, I saw it was stopped. Wu was banging on the joystick with both hands. His plastic bag was swollen, and I was afraid it would burst. I had never seen Wu lose it before. It alarmed me. I ran (or rather, hopped) back to help out.

I started unhooking the jumper cables. Wu stopped banging on the joystick and helped. The supermarket cart had been left at the bottom, but the batteries were light enough in the lunar gravity. I picked up one under each arm and started up the hill. I didn't bother to look back, because I knew Wu would be following with the other one.

We burst through the adjacentcy—the shed door—together; we tore the plastic bags off our heads and spit out the cotton balls. Warm air flooded my lungs. It felt wonderful. But my toes and fingers were on fire.

"Damn and Hell!" Wu said. I had never heard him curse before. "We almost made it!"

"We can still make it," I said. "We only lack a few feet. Let's put these babies on the charger and get some pizza."

"Good idea," Wu said. He was calming down. "I have a tendency to lose it when I'm hungry. But look, Irv. Our problems are worse than we thought."

I groaned. Two of the batteries had split along the sides when we had set them down. All three were empty; the acid had boiled away in the vacuum of the Moon. It was a wonder they had worked at all.

"Meanwhile, are your toes hurting?" Wu asked.

"My toes are killing me," I said.

The sixth thing you learn in law school is that cash solves all (or almost all) problems. I had one last hundred dollar bill hidden in my wallet for emergencies—and if this didn't qualify, what did? We gave the old man ninety for three more batteries, and put them on fast charge. Then we sent our change (ten bucks) with one of the kids on a bike, for four slices of pizza and two cans of diet soda.

Then we sat down under an ailanthus and took off our shoes. I was pleased to see that my toes weren't black. They warmed fairly quickly in the sun. It was my shoes that were cold. The tassel on one of my loafers was broken; the other one snapped when I touched it.

"I'm going to have to bypass some of the electrics on the LRV if we're going to make it up the hill," said Wu. He grabbed a piece of newspaper that was blowing by and began to trace a diagram. "According to my calculations, those batteries will put out 33.9 percent power for sixteen minutes if we drop out the nav system. Or maybe shunt past the rear steering motors. Look at this—"

"I'll take your word for it," I said. "Here's our pizza."

My socks were warm. I taped two plastic bags over my feet this time, while Wu poured the Pond Explorer over the cotton balls. It steamed when it went on, and a cheer went up from the kids on the pile of tires. There were ten or twelve of them now. Frankie was charging them a quarter apiece. Wu paused before putting the cotton ball under his tongue.

"Kids," he said, "Don't try this at home!"

They all hooted. Wu taped the plastic bag over my head, then over his. We waved—we were neighborhood heroes!—and picked up the "new" batteries, which were now charged; and ducked side by side back through the adjacentcy to the junk-strewn lunar slope where our work still waited to be finished. We were the first interplanetary automotive salvage team!

Wu was carrying two batteries this time, and I was carrying one. We didn't stop to admire the scenery. I was already sick of the Moon. Wu hooked up the batteries while I got into the passenger seat. He got in beside me and hit a few switches, fewer this time. The "heading" lights on the console didn't come on. Half the steering and drive enable switches remained unlighted.

Then Wu put my left hand on the joystick, and jumped down and grabbed the back of the LRV, indicating that he was going to push. I was going to drive.

I pushed the joystick forward and the LRV groaned into action, a little livelier than last time. The steering was slow; only the front wheels turned. I was hopeful, though. The LRV groaned through the last curve without slowing down.

I headed up the last straightaway, feeling the batteries weaken with every yard, every foot, every inch. It was as if the weight that had been subtracted from everything else on the Moon had been added to the LRV and was dragging it down. The lights on the console were flickering.

We were only ten yards from the adjacentcy. It was a dim slot under the cliff; I knew it was bright on the other side (a midsummer afternoon!) but apparently the same interface that kept the air from leaking through also dimmed the light.

It looked barely wide enough. But low. I was glad the LRV didn't have a windshield. I would have to duck to make it through.

Fifteen feet from the opening. Ten. Eight. The LRV stopped. I jammed the joystick forward and it moved another foot. I reached back over the seat and jiggled the jumper cables. The LRV groaned forward another six inches—then died. I looked at the slot under the cliff just ahead, and at the Earth overhead, both equally far away.

I wiggled the joystick. Nothing. I started to get down to help push, but Wu stopped me. He had one more trick. He unhooked the batteries and reversed their order. It shouldn't have made any difference, but as I have often noticed, electrical matters are not logical, like law: things that shouldn't work, often do.

I jammed the joystick all the way forward again.

The LRV groaned forward again, and groaned on. I pointed it into the slot and ducked. I saw a shimmering light and I felt the machine shudder. The front of the LRV poked through the shower curtain into the sunlight, and I followed, the sudden heat making my plastic bag swell.

The batteries groaned their last. I jumped down and began to pull on the front bumper. Through the plastic bag I could hear the kids screaming; or were they cheering? There was a loud crackling sound from behind the shower curtain. The LRV was only halfway through, and the front end was jumping up and down.

I tore the bag off my head and spit out the cotton and took a deep breath and yelled: "Wu!"

I heard a hiss and a crackling; I could feel the ground shake under my feet. The pile of tires was slowly collapsing behind me; kids were slipping and sliding, trying to get away. I could hear glass breaking somewhere. I yelled, "Wu!"

The front of the LRV suddenly pulled free, throwing me (not to put too fine a point on it) flat on my ass.

The ground stopped shaking. The kids cheered.

Only the front of the LRV had come through. It was burned in half right behind the seat; cut through as if by a sloppy welder. The sour smell of electrical smoke was in the air. I took a deep breath and ducked toward the curtain, after Wu. But there was no curtain there, and no shed—only a pile of loose boards.

''Wu!'' I yelled. But there he was, lying on the ground among the boards. He sat up and tore the bag off his head. He spit out his cotton and took a deep breath—and looked around and groaned.

The kids were all standing and cheering. (Kids love destruction.) Even Frankie looked pleased. But the old man wasn't; he came around the corner of the garage, looking fierce. ''What the Hell's going on here?'' he asked. ''What happened to my shed?''

''Good question,'' said Wu. He stood up and started tossing aside the boards that had been the shed. The shower curtain was under them, melted into a stiff plastic rag. Under it was a pile of ash and cinders—and that was all. No cave, no hole; no rear end of the LRV. No Moon.

''The cave gets bigger and smaller every month,'' said Frankie. ''But it never did that, not since it first showed up.''

''When was that?'' asked Wu.

''About six months ago.''

''What about my jumper cables?'' said the old man.

We paid him for the jumper cables with the change from the pizza, then called a wrecker to tow our half-LRV back to Park Slope. While we were waiting for the wrecker, I pulled Wu aside. ''I hope we didn't put them out of business,'' I said. I'm no bleeding heart liberal, but I was concerned.

''No, no,'' he said. ''The adjacentcy was about to drop into a lower neotopological orbit. We just helped it along a little. It's hard to figure without an almanac, but according to the tide table for August (which I'm glad now I bothered to memorize) the adjacentcy won't be here next month. Or the month after. It was just here for six months, like Frankie said. It was a temporary thing, cyclical as well as periodic.''

''Sort of like the Ice Ages.''

''Exactly. It always occurs somewhere in this hemisphere, but usually not in such a convenient location. It could be at the bottom of Lake Huron. Or in midair over the Great Plains, as one of those unexplained air bumps.''

''What about the other side of it?'' I asked. ''Is it always a landing site? Or was that just a coincidence?''

''Good question!'' Wu picked up one of the paper plates left over from the pizza and started scrawling on it with a pencil stub. ''If I take the mean lunar latitude of all six Apollo sites, and divide by the coefficient of . . .''

''It was just curiosity,'' I said. ''Here's the wrecker.''

Five

We got the half-LRV towed for half-price (I did the negotiating) but we never did make our million dollars. Boeing was in Chapter Eleven; NASA was under a procurement freeze; the Air & Space Museum wasn't interested in anything that rolled.

"Maybe I should take it on the road," Wu told me after several weeks of trying. "I could be a shopping center attraction: 'Half a Chinaman exhibits half a Lunar Roving Vehicle. Kids and adults half price.' "

Wu's humor masked bitter disappointment. But he kept trying. The JPL (Jet Propulsion Laboratory) wouldn't accept his calls. General Motors wouldn't return them. Finally, the Huntsville Parks Department, which was considering putting together an Apollo Memorial, agreed to send their Assistant Administrator for Adult Recreation to have a look.

She arrived on the day my divorce became final. Wu and I met her in the garage, where I had been living while Diane and I were waiting to sell the house. Her eyes were big and blue-green, like Frankie's. She measured the LRV and shook her head. "It's like a dollar bill," she said.

"How's that?" Wu asked. He looked depressed. Or maybe skeptical. It was getting hard to tell the difference.

"If you have over half, it's worth a whole dollar. If you have less than half it's worth nothing. You have slightly less than half of the LRV here, which means that it is worthless. What'll you take for that old P1800, though? Isn't that the one that was assembled in England?"

Which is how I met Candy. But that's another story.

We closed on the house two days later. Since the garage went with it, I helped Wu move the half-LRV to his back yard, where it sits to this day. It was lighter than any motorcycle. We moved the P1800 (which had plates) onto the street, and on Saturday morning, I went to get the interior for it. Just as Wu had predicted, the Hole was easy to find now that it was no longer linked with the adjacentcy. I didn't even have to stop at Boulevard Imports. I just turned off Conduit onto a likely looking street, and there I was.

The old man would hardly speak to me, but Frankie was understanding. "Your partner came out and explained it all," he said. He showed me a yellow legal pad covered with figures. "He gave me this to explain it more, I guess."

$$H\left(M = \frac{E}{c^2}\right)h$$

Frankie had stacked the boards of the shed against the garage. There was a cindery bare spot where the shed door had been; the cinders had that sour Moon smell. "I was sick and tired of the tire disposalment business, anyway," Frankie confided in a whisper.

The old man came around the corner of the garage. "What happened to your buddy?" he asked.

"He's going to school on Saturday mornings," I said. Wu was studying to be a meteorologist. I was never sure if that was weather or shooting stars. Anyway, he had quit the law.

"Good riddance," said the old man.

The old man charged me sixty-five dollars for the interior panels, knobs, handles, and trim. I had no choice but to pay up. I had the money, since I had sold Diane my half of the furniture. I was ready to start my new life. I didn't want to own anything that wouldn't fit into the tiny, heart-shaped trunk of the P1800. That night Wu helped me put in the seats and then the panels and knobs and handles. We finished at midnight and it didn't look bad, even though I knew the colors would look weird in the daylight—blue and white in a red car. Wu was grinning that mad grin again; it was the first time I had seen it since the Moon. He pointed over the rooftops to the east (toward Howard Beach, as a matter of fact). The Moon was rising. I was glad to see it looking so—far away.

Wu's wife brought us some leftover wedding cake. I gave him the keys to the 145 and he gave me the keys to the P1800. "Guess we're about even," I said. I put out my hand but Wu slapped it aside and gave me a hug instead, lifting me off the ground. Everybody should have a friend like Wilson Wu.

I followed the full Moon all the way to Alabama.

—*Special thanks to Pat Molloy.*

PARIS IN JUNE

Pat Cadigan

Many people spend their lives trying to discover why they've been put on Earth, but perhaps, as the strange and disturbing story that follows suggests, it's really better *not* to know . . .

Pat Cadigan was born in Schenectady, New York, and now lives in Overland Park, Kansas. She made her first professional sale in 1980, and has subsequently come to be regarded as one of the best young writers in SF. She was the co-editor of *Shayol*, perhaps the best of the semiprozines of the late '70s; it was honored with a World Fantasy Award in the "Special Achievement, Non-Professional" category in 1981. She has also served as Chairman of the Nebula Award Jury and as a World Fantasy Award Judge. Her first novel, *Mindplayers*, was released in 1987 to excellent critical response, and her second novel, *Synners*, published in 1991, won the prestigious Arthur C. Clarke Award as the year's best science fiction novel. Her third novel, *Fools*, came out in 1992, and she is currently at work on a fourth, tentatively entitled *Parasites*. Her story "Pretty Boy Crossover" has recently appeared on several critic's lists as among the best science fiction stories of the 1980s, her story "Angel" was a finalist for the Hugo Award, the Nebula Award, *and* the World Fantasy Award (one of the few stories ever to earn that rather unusual distinction) and her collection *Patterns* has been hailed as one of the landmark collections of the decade. Her stories have appeared in our First, Second, Third, Fourth, Fifth, Sixth, Ninth, Tenth, and Eleventh Annual Collections. Her most recent book is a major new collection, *Dirty Work*.

Paris in June . . . If there's a good time to be homeless in Paris, it's June. It's warm enough during the day to stake out a spot by the Seine and wave at the tourists on the Bateaux-Mouches, cool enough at night to be—well, okay, damned cold, especially without blankets. Wind blowing off any water can be cold, and only in Paris can you get weather that is hot and muggy with cold breezes.

But if I had made it easy on myself by choosing June—or Juin—it was still somewhat hard because I spoke almost no French, and understood even less. A few words—*merci, au revoir, est-ce que je peu regarder, bonjour*—but *Is it okay if I look?*, while suitable for the shops on the rue de St. Andredes Artes, isn't what you hear from the person rifling through your clothes while you're still in them.

I wanted to speak French, understand. I found myself falling into French-ish cadences when I spoke, fancied that I heard a lilting quality in my voice that I hadn't had back in London or Scarborough. But I just couldn't manage the tongue.

Nonetheless, I got by. What I do *is* a language, whether you do it on a beach in a quaint British resort town, or on the last tube of the night rocketing under Big Ben, or on the paved banks of the Seine where no stars shine except the ones you bring with you.

I liked it by the Seine best, even without amenities. In Scarborough, I sometimes saw the inside of one of those pretty-as-a-picture hotels, like the Hotel St. Nicholas, and once even the Grand Hotel. Although I did have to leave before dawn could even light the water because the man's wife was driving up from Sussex to join him and he had to air out the room.

In London—fabulous London—I had a good, if brief, thing with two gentlemen who loved each other so much that they had no love left for anything or anyone else. They let me be part of it for awhile but ultimately I had to go and leave them to each other.

Then there was the couple in Queen's Gate Gardens—I didn't get the exact address. Even briefer with them: one little night. But every night spent under a real roof was one more victory. And they were responsible for sending me to Paris, at least indirectly. It was because they took me to the tube in their own car, bought me a little card to ride all day, and wished me good luck. And lo, as they say, I got some.

People fantasize more than they know in situations like that—riding on the tube, I mean—and it was like being in a candy store with a blank check or something, a real embarrassment of riches. I binged. When I stopped to think— or reflect, or maybe just gloat—a lady executive with a beautiful briefcase and a rich overnighter bought me a ticket to Heathrow and took me aboard her Air France flight. She liked me well enough to kiss me good-bye at Customs.

I napped on the Roissybus into town in spite of its being my first time in Paris (everyone needs a little downtime). The driver came back to wake me at L'Opera, where everyone else got off and I discovered that in spite of my binge on the British tube, I seemed to have run out of something important.

Luck shifts all the time, so I didn't worry. I wandered around and the weather held. Pretty town, Paris; Paris in Juin, anyway.

But yes, I did see the beggars. I think their children must have been drugged to sleep so much. There were also the homeless like me, who had no fixed address. Not so bad, really. You may think the tourists on the boats wouldn't care for the view of us there on the banks of their pretty Seine. But all you have to do is smile and wave. Then they smile and wave back, figuring you must be all right after all.

The Batobus Edith Piaf passed by full of people hooting and hollering, and most of them weren't tourists. Then I saw her. She was pulling her clothes back on and giving them all what we used to call the "international symbol of disdain." She was a filthy, skinny blonde with hair cut short the way they do in some hospitals to forestall the lice. She was not, by any stretch of the imagination, a young, pretty little thing and I could tell she was completely bewildered by having to get dressed. The Batobus people were obviously yelling for her to leave it off, and she looked such hate at them that I half-expected their gas tank to suddenly explode and engulf them all in a fireball. But nothing happened. She kept struggling into her dirty shirt and jeans. I was tempted to go down and see about her. Even at this distance I could tell that she was what I was, but she didn't seem to know it.

"Va te faire fautre!"

She was pelting some stupid tourist with pieces of rock or brick and he was completely confused. He had obviously meant to take some shots of the Seine and he'd had the misfortune to pick her spot for it. All he had to do was move maybe ten steps in any direction and that would have cured it. But he was too stupid to remember where he was—that is, not in his own country—and was trying to argue with her. It was quite a show. Yelling, she drove him back a step with a piece of rock, stooped to pick up another and flung it at him with all the strength in her skinny arm. It bounced off his leg and he howled in both pain and fury. She got him in the shoulder with another rock and he howled again, louder. People were stopping to watch, the locals laughing, the tourists looking fishfaced and unhappy the way tourists do when they see people being themselves rather than on display for their entertainment.

The fourth rock got him just above his right eyebrow. Then he didn't want to talk any more. He held his camera off to one side and went for her, so she let him have it smack in the chest with another piece of rock. I was behind him and as he took another step toward her, I pulled him back. At the same time, someone else popped out of the crowd and did the same to her. She scrabbled and fought like something feral, but the group closed up around her as efficiently as an automatic door.

The stupid tourist twisted away from me angrily. "Kesker say?" he demanded in his unbearable hick accent, as if he would actually understand the answer if I gave it to him in French.

"You were on her spot," I told him in English.

He brushed back his stringy brown hair. Too much hair tonic; he must have been one of the last fifty people on the planet using Vitalis. "What spot?"

"Her spot. The one where she lives. How would you like it if she stomped into your living room—no, better, your bedroom—and began taking pictures of whatever struck her fancy?"

He looked like he was going to argue with me and then took a second look. "And what the hell are you supposed to be—the fuckin' beggar police?" I was still wearing the Knights Templar coat I'd come over from the States in because it made me look less like a vagrant and more like an old hippie or just an especially affected eccentric. "Haven't you been to the Louvre yet? You don't recognize me? My picture hangs in there," I said, gesturing at the building visible through the trees from where we were. I still have no idea why I told him that. Perhaps I thought he'd be impressed, or scared. The crowd hiding the little blonde roared with laughter, the sort of noise French royalty must have heard just as the guillotine came down. It was a bad moment, because I wasn't sure who the laughter was meant for.

Fortunately, the stupid tourist wasn't so stupid that he didn't know he was supposed to be scared now. Clutching his camera with one hand, he backed away from me making stay-there motions at me with his other hand. I stayed, but the crowd started to creep toward him on the other side. Panicked, he turned and fled up the steps to the street, while the crowd roared more of that scary laughter at his back. They all watched him go and then as one turned to look at me. Some of them shifted position and I saw her, now firmly in the grip of a copper-haired boy and a piss-yellow-headed woman who could have been his mother or his madame.

The skinny blonde's face was pinched, defiant but also somehow pleading, or maybe just wary. Hers would be an old story: Don't hurt me. All right, don't hurt me much. All right, don't hurt me much without paying twenty francs in advance, okay?

I went toward her and held out my hand, unsure if the rabble would let her come with me or if she would even want to. But I managed to pull her away; it felt exactly like uprooting a weed. It wasn't the explaining that took so long but persuading her to believe it. If you need someone to believe something, make them go for a walk with you. Walking takes up most of the energy they'd use to disbelieve you. You have to be thorough and convincing, of course, but that shouldn't be a problem if you're telling the truth. And if you're a liar, goddamn you to hell, who needs you?

With the blonde, the language barrier was against me. Her English was spotty and my French was worse. Then there were her—to put it mildly—emotional problems.

"But who are they?" she kept asking me in French. "Who?" Apparently even what I told her was not enough to alleviate her revulsion at their pure inhumanity. But why shouldn't they be inhuman, since that is exactly what they were.

All right, I'll confess: I love this. Once I discovered that I was a data-gathering device rather than a true human, I embraced my nature—if nature is a word you can use for a manufactured thing—and fully cooperated with my raison d'être. You are what you are and while it may be pointless to hate it or love it, it's easier to function loving it than not, yes?

(Still feeling fine and français, you see.)

So I walked the skinny blonde homeless thing along the banks of the Seine and told her the facts of our life. And yes, she thought I was a psycho, trying to put one over on her so I could lure her to some place where I could rape and murder her.

I took her to a public facility and I showed her how it was impossible for me to rape anyone. When I discovered my true nature, you see, I decided to dispense with the frills and dodges and I carved off anything I didn't think was absolutely necessary.

It wasn't hard, or even painful. You see, what pain really is, is a failure to understand. My complete understanding was something I can only describe as an *über-satori*—my understanding was not only an embracing of my true nature but a conquering. And let's face it, most humans would regard the complete conquest of pain as unconditional victory within the human condition of being alive.

And then there's most of us, who are compelled to partake of the human experience without ever becoming human. Maybe that was supposed to make me care more about real humans. It didn't.

She tried to beat me up.

She tried to make me believe it was for these outrageous paranoid-schizo lies I was telling her but I knew by the bleak look in her eyes that she not only believed me but my telling her had cleared up the mystery of why she was the way she was as nothing else ever had—her fucking gut was telling her I'd spoken the truth. And her gut also told her to beat me up. I countered her fists with my forearms and when she got too active on me, I just held her by her wrists until she tired. Eventually she was crying into my front and wanting to know *Qu'est-ce que je faire?* over and over between sniffles.

"Well," I told her, "that isn't too hard. You fare the way you'd fare, regardless." Her English wasn't good enough to appreciate the pun, but some things I find irresistible even when I'm the only audience for them. Perhaps that's part of the conquest of existence, too.

"No, seriously now, listen. *Ecoutez*," I said to her mixing a little bad French with sign language and English. "I'll show you all the things you can do voluntarily that you didn't know you were doing all along. There's no way you can't do those things because the mechanism works too well. I'll show you how to yield your information at times more convenient for you so that you can do whatever you want. Almost, anyway; close enough for government work, certainly."

She didn't get that either.

In the middle of my explanation of how to yield, she clapped both hands over her ears and ran away crying. I kind of figured what to expect after that and she didn't disappoint me. The one she sent was named Gaston—I swear—and he was infuriated with me. Who did I think I was to tell the *cherie* she was nothing more than a *poupée*, and what odious cult was I proselytizing for, or had I just drunk too much antifreeze during the last pressing in some cheap vineyard. I admitted to nothing and denied nothing. Gaston was certainly not like us and could never understand. But what he lacked in knowledge—of any kind—he made up in heat. She had obviously decided to bring her formidable talents to bear on him, to make him take her side. Which, ironically, proved I was right. Only we can exert such power over humans, since our chemistry triggers their own obsessions.

Do I sound unbearably smug? I should.

I had to kill Gaston. He pulled a knife on me.

Even if it was a sad, rusty excuse for a jack-knife, I had to kill him to prove my point to her. He still could have killed me, after all, if I'd been weaker, if I'd been some scared tourist, say, or new to this kind of life. And as I'd suspected, when I was tending to the remains, I discovered that Gaston had killed two people in his time. If I reveal that one of them was the man who had raped a person who had once been his woman, would you feel bad for him and terrible anger for me? How about if I tell you that the other was the infant that was the issue of this crime? Will you then see me as Gaston's justice caught up to him at last? How is it that you insist that your lives, all your lives together, do not mean nothing?

It was only after I found that I had been manufactured for the sake of information-gathering that I actually felt free enough to gather some. I thought my little blonde would come around to the same point of view, but when Gaston's body bobbed to the surface of the Seine with the features and other important parts carved off and scared the Bateaux-Mouches tourists, she called the police. But what the hell, they came to us there under the impassive Louvre, and they questioned us, those of us who would allow ourselves to be questioned, and she accused me. Pointed her finger, said I did it, said she could prove it—if they would just undo my culottes, they would find that the parts that should have been there had been carved off in just the very same fashion as Gaston's.

The police knew her as the woman who often entertained the tourists with her nude sunbathing; besides, they had no desire to see me or any other of the vagrants sans culottes. They talked to me, although no more closely than they talked to anyone else, and there was a story in the papers and some pictures. She got herself a knife and threatened to use it on me if I came near her again. She also got herself a couple of protectors and threatened to use them on me as well, though the way it actually went was, they used her and smirked at me over their shoulders while they did.

I shrugged, continued to gather information, and June continued to be beautiful.

When I was full of experiences, it was time to yield to those who had made me. I had the strong sense that they would not come to the Seine, that I would have to find some other place where they could take from me. I didn't understand why, but my understanding was not required.

I took a little walking tour in everwidening circles, rode the Metro, found L'Opera again. Something about the arrangement of the steps and the statues . . . I climbed to the third step from the top and settled in to wait. I hated being in sight of the beggars who worked the streets and the entry-ways to the Metro but those who created me don't argue or bargain—I would yield, or I would cease.

I stayed on the steps for two days without moving. Their sense of time is different from ours, so I didn't know how long it would take—two days, five days, a month, whatever. People went up and down, refusing to see me; the police came and made me move to one side during the day. And the weather held, and held, and held.

On the third morning, clouds moved in just about the time the sky began to lighten and the air became heavily humid. I had been asleep or passed out; I went from oblivion to a state of being completely alert, sitting up on the hard stone steps. It took a few moments for me to understand why: there was no sound. I could see cars moving; some of them glided right past me where I sat, but it was like watching a silent film.

Overhead, the clouds were boiling, also in silence. I laid myself down on the steps spreadeagle. It wasn't comfortable, no, but that wasn't the idea, after all. I watched the clouds continue to boil and then to swirl slowly and unevenly clockwise. Appropriate to the hemisphere, I thought dreamily. A fragment of newspaper caught on my foot and then flew up into the sky, mirroring the motion of the clouds as it did. Far inside, lightning flickered almost too fast for the eye to see and too bright to bear, a harshness that turned the clouds into a negative image of themselves.

The spiral in the sky became tighter, narrower and I felt the familiar pulling from within myself. It felt like what I imagined a tide would, or love.

My two English gentlemen passed before my inner eye, and then the business lady who had brought me to France. She had been hoping for that, I realized now; she had been hoping for love when I had come to her on the Underground, backed her up against that smeared, graffitied rear wall of the carriage rocking and swaying and put my mouth against her eye, I had been bringing love—bringing something, anyway—rather than taking away.

Perhaps knowing she had simply broken even was what had made her kiss me good-bye. It isn't often that human compromise doesn't involve some kind of loss. And all that went up to that flickering, spinning cloud-flower in the sky, too. Feeling what she'd felt, I cried a little or at least tears ran from my eyes, because I was an emotion machine as well, when the information called for that kind of context.

The cloud-flower seemed to grow larger and to lower as well; I thought I could feel the cold vapor swirling on my face, the cold wind doing strange things to my eyes. There was the sensation of hard stone at the back of my head suddenly overridden by a more powerful pulling than before, as if I were about to be turned inside out.

And then nothing. I was lying on the steps with the rain pouring down from the dirt-gray sky, though above me was one new shadow. Just a blur at first, it resolved itself into a familiar figure, soaked completely through and miserable, angry and curious at the same time. She had my forelock in her dirty fist. She pulled me up to a sitting position. Something about the rain she yelled into my face, barely audible over the sound of it beating down on the pavement, making a fist of her free hand, threatening me, then pointing at the sky. I tried to shake my head and then settled for just looking bewildered. "What?" I asked her. "What are you saying? *Qu'est-ce que tu dis?*"

"Rain! Clouds!" she bellowed. "I saw you!" Did she think I'd brought the rain? Most vagrants I've known are superstitious as hell.

"The rain is not my fault," I said carefully, close to her ear. She pulled back, looking supremely irritated.

"I saw you. Sky come down and kiss you!" She stared at me, her eyes hard and demanding and expectant. I burst out laughing. The one person who might have appreciated what she'd said had been dead for almost a quarter of a century and had nothing to do with either one of us anyway.

"Sky comes down to kiss you, too, soon," I said, poking her breastbone with my finger. She slapped my hand away, but not very hard, and blinked at me in the rain, which was becoming an honest-to-god pavement-cleaning and gutter-clogging downpour. I got up and hustled her across the street to a Metro entrance, but she balked at the top of the steps, holding onto the railing with both arms and kicking out at me.

"Okay, okay, I get it: you're a claustrophobe." I pushed her into a doorway just big and deep enough to keep the worst of the rain off us. "Or something bad happened to you down there. More likely, eh?"

She looked up at me, puzzled. I smoothed both hands over her face, letting my fingers slide into her hair. Her body stiffened but she didn't try to get away. In her life, there was always something like this. Living through it was important; how, less so.

I had never tried to yield to a human or to another of my kind before. The idea had never even occurred to me until now. I wasn't even sure I could, although there certainly was enough left in me. They never took everything, maybe because there are so many similar things, or maybe because some of the things just aren't to their taste.

In any case, once the idea was in my head, I wanted to try it. It would be an experience that was mine alone. I'd never thought in terms like that before and it was like the notion was tickling me with an urgency all its own.

The rain was machine-gunning on the sidewalk, splattering us with mist from the impact as I pulled her face close and put my mouth over hers. Her lips were cold and thin like the rest of her, though not entirely unpleasant. Things weren't quite right—I moved her jaw so that her lips encircled my mouth instead. She wasn't sure about this and started to pull away, but I had one fist braced against her upper back and the back of her head cupped in my other hand. She had no organ of taking the way they did, or rather, no specific organ, but what she had should serve.

She struggled a little more, and I could feel the panic start to rise in her. The noise of the rain was almost unbearable now, the kind of white noise people must hear in the depths of madness, I thought, and wondered how long I'd be able to tolerate it myself.

Then I felt it give; the place inside me reserved for them opened gently, sensing the nearness of a recipient, and found her in a matter of seconds. It was not what I or the ability was accustomed to and I had some bad moments when I thought she might reject what I had to yield. But then some instinct took over and she accepted in the same way she had been accepting everything else in her life.

Some time later, we just stood holding onto each other. The rain pounded as if it meant to pulverize the cement. Used transit tickets dissolved into aqua pulp and then disappeared altogether.

"You bastard," she whispered to me in French. "You abortion. If you were human, the best part of you would have run down your father's leg."

I pulled back from her, not understanding. She was radiating a satedness that didn't go with her words. "Some would say I carved off the best parts, or at least the most useful," I said, "but why do you?"

"You pet. Are you really going to give that to these—whatever, these things that live in clouds—"

"They don't live there," I said.

"Shut up. Fuck you, you don't understand. You betray your own kind, surrendering to them when we could be doing this for each other." She stared up at me, her no-color eyes moving so very slightly as she searched my face. "Now do you get it, you stupid robot? You stupid slave!"

She clamped her mouth over mine again, but there wasn't much left and after a few moments she pushed me away. "*C'est bien*, I know what to do now," she told me. "And not as somebody's dog to kick, either. How about it, you want to walk on your hind legs for a change?"

That didn't sound so bad, even though I knew I'd done something very wrong and precipitated something even more wrong. But, I thought, what was it to them anyway? Did they even look at me until they wanted what I had? Did they protect me, did they find me any place to go? For all I knew, they thought as much of me as a maid thinks of a vacuum cleaner when the inside bag needs to be changed.

"Come on, pet," my blonde spat at me. "Let me show you what it's like to be something real, if you think you can face it." She pulled me out of the doorway into the rain, which was still heavy, though not as bad as it had been. I wiped my face with my forearm and she laughed at me. *"Bête! Stupide!"* But she didn't run very far ahead of me before coming back to lead me along.

The word ripped up and down the paved banks of the Seine faster than a tourist-borne chancre. I waited to see what this would bring, who would come forward and either denounce us or beg to join in. Well, nobody did. She and I were the only ones of our kind there, it seemed. If others were in the city, they were far away and/or uninterested.

My little blonde ran a come-on that made all the johns hot and bothered to the extreme and then, just before they would have nailed her by force, she came across. To one of the ones she had originally enlisted to protect her from me, no less; the experience totaled him. He agreed to pimp for both of us for no more reward than to be allowed to partake again.

That she and I would pleasure each other that way was understandable, but what could humans find so enthralling about the human experience? And if they had no natural method or organ of accepting the yield, how did they do it?

She only laughed when I said anything, spoke rapid, incomprehensible French at me, and trotted away to some tourist waiting for what he'd been told would be the ultimate in delectables, unusual even for unseen Paris.

"She says you ask a slave's questions," one of her new bodyguards told me helpfully. "She says you may talk to her directly again when you have evolved a backbone." He thought this was hilarious; I was simply amazed that he knew what it meant. He was a dirty pervert who had evolved a belly to balance off his own backbone. I meant to spit on his pants but for some reason I couldn't get enough wet in my mouth.

I suppose she got rich, by vagrants' standards. I hid out closer to where the tourists took the dinner boats. Many drank themselves into near-stupors, enough to allow themselves to be lured away for interludes they never remembered afterwards. It was more dangerous, though, because the boat owners and the police cared more about who was hanging around there, and less satisfying because it was on the fly and in secret—not like finding people who will take you in, talk to you, and give you a little help when they throw you out again.

I was not working right. So much for my hind legs. I wondered what they would think when I yielded again. And then I wondered if they would even notice.

The big-bellied pervert was the one who came to get me in the middle of the night. I woke up over his shoulder in a familiar though distasteful position, not understanding at first that I was being carried off. He had to let me down to explain that there was something wrong with her and she had been calling for me.

"A good trick," I said, "since she doesn't know my name."

"Nobody knows anyone's name," he told me, "but we all knew who she meant, and we all knew where you were." I let him lead me up the Seine to where she was, on her old spot where she had once confounded the Batobus people with her nude sunbathing. The moon was full, or nearly so, and there were a lot of people with her. Some seemed to be trying to tend to her, while others were grouped around a man who was apparently waiting with great and graceless impatience for something. I knew, of course, what that was.

She lay on the pavement like a used rag and I thought she was unconscious. But she must have smelled me; I saw her push herself up on one elbow. Croaking something in French, she pointed at the man who didn't look all that thrilled to see a creature like me come on the scene.

"She says you're the only one who can take care of him and they'll both die if you don't." This from her pimp/protector.

"Just give him back his money and tell him to go home," I said, squatting down in front of her and lifting her face to the moonlight. Her skin looked bruised. I thought the john had beaten her up but I was wrong; she'd done this to herself, straining to yield what she no longer had.

"I can't," said the john warily. "We have a problem here. What are you, her keeper?"

"Not hardly," I said. He spoke English well but in a slow and deliberate way that suggested he wasn't comfortable with the language.

"Her partner, then?" He didn't sound hopeful about it.

"What if I were?" I asked him, standing up and facing him. "What if I were and you had to do the thing with me if you wanted to do it at all?" His eyes narrowed and I laughed at him. "Go home, monsieur. Give it up. Hit the road, Jacques."

"I told you, I can't." He produced a handkerchief; the blood on it looked black, which was how I knew it was blood. Blood always looks black in the moonlight. "You want to see, I'll show you." He took a few steps back and I saw it happen. He was crying blood.

"It feels worse than it looks," he said, moving toward me quickly. "And pressure in my ears. Any further, I'll bleed from those, too." He dabbed at his face, shaking his head. "I am not a superstitious man or a bad man. But she came to me—"

"Yes, yes, the woman tempted you," I said. "It's going around, eh?"

"She came to me," he said, as if I hadn't spoken, "and sometimes I am a weak man. But what did I do so bad to cry blood?" I looked down at her and she looked back at me, breathing in deep, shuddery gasps. Probably no hope for her, unless there was something I could do—

"I don't want to do a thing with anyone now," the john said. "Especially you. But to end this—" he shrugged. "Is there some other way?"

I had to shake my head.

He spoke through a painful breath. "Then we do this quick. If we can." I could see that he wanted to ask me if that was possible, but he couldn't quite because he was afraid that the answer would be no. I didn't know if we could do it quick or not. I wasn't really ready to yield yet, I didn't know how long it would take me. Especially with an audience. I looked around. Such a big audience, too; every Seine rat seemed to be in on this tonight, and maybe a few regular citizens in vagrant drag as well, for all I knew.

I had a few moments of pity for this weak man and for my blonde, also weak, and for myself, perhaps the weakest of all. I might have wanted to blame her rat's greed and lust, but this was my fault. Careful to stay within a certain distance of her, I pushed the john into the shadows of the willows along the wall.

"Here," I said, backing him up against the stone. He stiffened as I took him by the throat, but he didn't try to push me away. At least he knew that it was going to be something other than an especially adept handjob.

I had thought to make it as quick and painless as possible, but after five minutes fading in and out of a halfassed trance state, I knew I couldn't do it for him. Quirk, mine or hers? Either mine for being unable to do a human, or hers for being able to?

"She—" he croaked, and then began coughing. I loosened my grip on his throat, realizing he was right. She, indeed. She would have to complete the circuit before anything could happen.

I pushed him back against the wall and gestured for him to stay, and then went to get her. Lifted her up onehanded. She'd been siphoning off her own substance so that now her very bones must have been hollow tubes. Hollow tubes with a little soft-chewed leather stretched over them; she dragged along under my arm, her feet bumping the pavement but no complaints about it, none whatsoever.

As soon as he saw me coming back with her, he knew it was right. "What do I do?" he half-whispered to me.

I put her hands on each of his shoulders. "Hold her," I said. "Lean back so she can stay up on you without trying." Her head flopped forward and nestled under his chin, so that they really did look a lot like lovers. I yanked her head back by her hair and managed to maneuver his face into position, so that finally her mouth was on his eye. It was difficult, given our height differences and her limpness, but I was able to position my own mouth on her eye.

I had barely done so when her need seized on me and ran all through me, searching for the best and the most substantial that I had. This would not be a yielding, I realized, no matter how passive I was to it, to her. What there had been in her to gather information had mutated into a drive rapacious, hungry, and without intelligence or compassion.

It found the issue from the dinner boat patrons I had lured: a man who had

had the experience of loving one person but being bound to another for many years, until the one he had been bound to had died; discovering, once he was free to join the other that it had been the barrier and not the hope of consummation that had kept that love alive;

a woman who had filled her emotional needs with material goods so that objects were passions for her now while other people's passions were messy and distasteful;

a man who had done terrible things to his children in the sincere belief that it would prepare them to live in a world that would do far worse;

a woman who stole things without understanding that she was trying to recover something she believed had been stolen from her long ago;

a man who was a man by accident and a woman by intention;

a woman who had carved off in spirit what I had carved off in fact;

a teacher who had never learned a single one of her own lessons;

a priest whose faith had failed when he realized that he loved another priest.

Each was seized, examined, gobbled up, digested, and claimed. I relived each one, felt the explosion of knowledge in the pivotal moment and then felt it ripped away from me and absorbed by my skinny blonde, who then applied it to the man with such force that I thought she might be purposely trying to kill him.

She couldn't help it, I saw; this had become something she had to do, or die. I felt him trembling under the onslaught, unable to produce enough will in himself to want to refuse her. Her need would kill him, and probably me, too, while leaving her alive, though just barely, and still in need.

I didn't want to do it just then but there was no good time; while his body was in spasm, I pulled up both my hands and snapped her neck.

The sudden absence was deafening, blinding, dizzying; we swayed from side to side with her still pressed between us, and I heard him sob, or groan, or just make meaningless noise. He did it again and I realized he had said Gaston—in the act of saving us from her, I had let that come through and he knew now what I had done.

I stepped back and let her fall to the pavement. "You can go safely now, I think," I told him.

He was clutching his head with both hands but he managed to nod.

"Don't even think about telling anyone what you know," I said, "or what you think you know. And don't come down here again looking for anything, or I'll eat you alive myself."

He promised, wiping quite ordinary tears from his eyes, and staggered up the steps to the rue whatever-it-was.

The Seine rats weighted her body with stones and dumped it in the water. One of them bet that it would dissolve down there before it had a chance to float. I cleaned up and gorged myself at the Louvre and at Notre Dame. All tourists, of course, nothing but tourists, who spoke French to me in accents of varying atrociousness and gave me more information about themselves than I had ever thought of asking for. I kept hoping one of them would take me home, wherever that was.

I couldn't stand the smell of that river any more. It was as if the rat had been right and her body really had dissolved, poisoning the entire body of water and everything it touched. The essence of her seemed to be in the air; I didn't understand how the tourists didn't choke, or how the rats themselves could stand it. Till the end of Juin, then, I lived in the Metro with the beggars, emerging when I thought they should come again for my yield.

They didn't. I waited at L'Opera, near the Louvre, below the Eiffel Tower and finally on the banks of the Seine, but they didn't come. They weren't coming—not just taking a long time about it, but really not coming. I went a little crazy, and then a lot crazy. The Seine rats, sensing my trouble with that bizarre and unerring instinct for hurting someone by helping, directed her old johns my way, telling them I was the sole surviving practitioner of her odd art.

Her art. It's a laugh.

I held on as long as I could, but I was made to yield and I did, choosing those as clean as I could find for it. I could do it without her now; the circuit, once completed, stayed completed. Humans did not have much capacity, so it took more of them to yield to, and they weren't as good at it, but they were better than ceasing to be.

Or maybe they weren't. I just didn't have the nerve to test that out.

It's because I turned from them to her, of course; I chose her to yield to and whether they consider this is some unforgivable sin or just a dirty, unnatural act, I'll never know, because they have left me here to go on or to cease on my own, and I can tell by the great empty sky that they will never be there again for me. I'll never even see them come for another of my kind.

(Maybe it was her. Maybe she was defective and they consider me tainted because of my association with her.)

So everything is a little bit looser and messier than it used to be, but the world being what it is won't notice, so I don't imagine it will ever really matter. And since it won't, I tell what I know promiscuously, to anyone, everyone within my range, wherever I am. I've learned to do what she should have, to siphon off here and siphon off there, and I have a Seine rat's instincts as well now, so that I only dispense the exact knowledge nobody wants at the exact moment they don't want it.

This is my indirect message to them, if they still come for the others like me that they made. The information they take is imbued with the mess I've made in it. So they can do something about me, or they can live with their poisoned knowledge.

As for me, with nothing to lose, I will go underground again for the worst of the summer heat and then the onset of cold weather. When spring comes, I'll poke my head up with the other things from under the earth. And when it is Juin once again, I will go back to the Seine, to her old spot, drive away anyone who might be on it before I strip off my clothes and lie down for the entertainment and edification of the commuters on the Edith Piaf Batobus, and I will drink in whatever essence of humanity that I find under the sun.

And when it gets dark and the rats draw close, I will tell them everything. Everything. Everything. And if I'm still alive when the sun comes up, I'll do it all again.

FLOWERING MANDRAKE

George Turner

An Australian writer and critic of great renown, George Turner may be that country's most distinguished science fiction writer, and one of the few Australian SF writers to have established an international reputation that transcends parochial boundaries. Although he has published six mainstream novels, he is best known in the genre for the string of unsentimental, rigorous, and sometimes acerbic science fiction novels that he began to publish in 1978, including *Beloved Son*, *Vaneglory*, *Yesterday's Men*, *Brain Child*, *In the Heart or in the Head*, *The Destiny Makers*, and the widely acclaimed *Drowning Towers*, which won the Arthur C. Clarke Award. His most recent novel is *Genetic Soldier*. His short fiction has been collected in *A Pursuit of Miracles*, and he is the editor of the anthology of Australian science fiction, *The View from the Edge*.

Turner may be the Grandmaster of Australian science fiction, and, true, he is decades older than his next-most-talked-about compatriot, Greg Egan . . . but he has lost none of his imagination or intellectual vigor, as he proves in the powerful and ingenious story that follows, a tale unsurpassed by any Young Turks anywhere for the bravura sweep and daring of its conceptualization.

> Go, and catch a falling star,
> Get with child a mandrake root . . .
>
> From the song, 'Go, and catch', by John Donne.

Four stars make Capella: two G-type suns sharing between them five times the mass of Terra's Sol and two lesser lights seen only with difficulty from a system so far away.

Two of the fifteen orbiting worlds produced thinking life under fairly similar conditions but the dominant forms which evolved on each bore little resemblance to each other save in the possession of upright carriage, a head, and limbs for ambulation and grasping.

When, in time, they discovered each other's existence, they fought with that ferocity of civilized hatred which no feral species can or need to match.

The Red-Bloods fought at first because they were attacked, then because they perceived that the Green Folk were bent not on conquest but on destruction. The Green Folk fought because the discovery of Red-Blood dominance over a planet uncovered traits deep in their genetic structure. Evolution had been for them a million year struggle against domination by emerging red-blooded forms and their eventual supremacy had been achieved only by ruthless self-preservation— the destruction of all competition. They kept small animals for various domestic and manufacturing purposes, even ate them at times for gourmet pleasure rather than need and feared them not at all, but the ancient enmity and dread persisted in racial defensiveness like a memory in the blood.

The discovery of a planet of Red-Bloods with a capacity for cultural competition wreaked psychological havoc. Almost without thought the Green Folk attacked.

Ships exploded, ancient cities drowned in fresh-sprung lava pits, atmospheres were polluted with death.

Beyond the Capellan system no sentient being knew of species in conflict. Galactic darkness swallowed the bright, tiny carnage.

Capella lay some forty-seven light years from the nearest habitable planet, which its people called, by various forms of the name, Terra.

Only one member of crew, a young officer of the Fifth Brachiate, new to his insignia and with little seniority, but infinitely privileged over the Root-kin of his gunnery unit, escaped the destruction of *Deadly Thorn*. His name (if it matters, because it was never heard anywhere again) was Fernix, which meant in the Old Tongue, 'journeying forest father'.

When the Triple Alert flashed he was in the Leisure Mess, sucking at a tubule of the stem, taking in the new, mildly stimulating liquor fermented from the red fluid of animals. It was a popular drink, not too dangerously potent, taken with a flick of excitement for the rumour that it was salted with the life-blood of enemy captives. This was surely untrue but made a good morale boosting story.

Triple Alerts came a dozen a day and these bored old hands of the war no longer leapt to battle stations like sprouts-in-training. Some hostile craft a satellite's orbit distant had detected *Deadly Thorn* and launched a missile; deflector arrays would catch and return it with augmented velocity and the flurry would be over before they reached the doorway.

There was, of course, always the unlucky chance. Deflector arrays had their failings and enemy launchers their moments of cunning.

Fernix was still clearing his mouth when an instant of brilliant explosion filled space around *Deadly Thorn* and her nose section and Command Room blew out into the long night.

He was running, an automaton trained to emergency, when the sirens screamed and through the remaining two-thirds of the ship the ironwood bulkheads thudded closed. He was running for his Brachiate Enclave, where his Root-kin waited for orders, when the second missile struck somewhere forward of him and on the belly plates five decks below.

A brutal rending and splintering rose under him and at his running feet the immensely strong deck-timbers tore apart in a gaping mouth that he attempted uselessly to cross in a clumsy, shaken leap. Off balance and unprepared, he felt himself falling into Cargo Three, the Maintenance Stores hold.

At the same moment ship's gravity vanished and the lighting system failed. *Deadly Thorn* was Dead Thorn. Fernix tumbled at a blind angle into darkness, arms across his head against crashing into a pillar or bulkhead at speed. In fact his foot caught in a length of rope, dragging him to a jarring halt.

Spread arms told him he had been fortunate to land on a stack of tarpaulins when it might as easily have been the sharp edges of tool boxes. Knowledge of the Issue Layout told him precisely where he was in the huge hold. There was a nub of escape pods in the wall not far to his left. He moved cautiously sideways, not daring to lose contact in null-gravity darkness but slithering as fast as he safely might.

Bulkheads had warped in the broken and twisted hull; both temperature and air pressure were dropping perceptibly.

He found the wall of the hold at the outer skin and moved slowly towards the vanished fore section until he felt the swelling of the nub of pods and at last the mechanism of an entry lock. Needing a little light to align the incised lines which would spring the mechanism, he pumped sap until the luminescent buds of his right arm shed a mild greenish radiance on the ironwood.

He thought momentarily, regretfully, of his Root-kin crew able to move only a creeper-length from their assigned beds, awaiting death without him. In this extremity he owed them no loyalty and they would expect none but they would, he hoped, think well of him. They were neuters, expendable and aware of it whereas he, Officer Class free-moving breeder, carried in him the gift of new life. There could be no question of dying with them though sentimental ballads wept such ideas; they, hard-headed pragmatists, would think it the act of an idiot. And they would be right.

He matched the lock lines and stepped quickly in as the fissure opened. As he closed the inner porte the automatic launch set the pod drifting gently into space.

He activated fresh luminescence to find the control panels and light switch. A low-powered light—perhaps forty watts—shone in the small space. To his eyes it was brilliant and a little dangerous; to a culture which made little use of metals, the power-carrying copper wires were a constant threat to wood, however tempered and insulated.

To discover where he was with respect to *Deadly Thorn*, he activated an enzyme flow through the ironwood hull at a point he judged would offer the best vision. As the area cleared he was able to see the lightless hulk occulting stars. The entire forward section was gone, perhaps blown to dust, and a ragged hole gaped amidships under the belly holds. If other pods floated nearby he could not see them.

Poised weightless over the controls, he checked the direction of the three-dimensional compass point in its bowl and saw that the homing beam shone steadily with no flicker from intervening wreckage. His way was clear and his duty certain, to return to the Home World carrying his spores of life.

A final, useless missile must have struck *Deadly Thorn* as he stretched for the controls and never reached them. A silent explosion dazzled his eyes, then assaulted his hearing as the shock wave struck the pod. A huge plate of *Deadly Thorn*'s armour loomed in the faint glow of his light, spinning lazily to strike the pod a glancing blow that set it tumbling end over end.

He had a split second for cursing carelessness because he had not strapped down at once. Then his curled up, frightened body bounced back and forth from the spinning walls until his head struck solidly and unconsciousness took him.

He came to in midair with legs bunched into his stomach and arms clasped round his skull. There was no gravity; he was falling free. But where?

Slow swimming motions brought him to a handhold but he became aware of a brutal stiffness in his right side. He pumped sap to make fingerlight, bent his head to the ribplates and saw with revulsion that he was deformed; the plates had been broken and had healed while he floated, but had healed unevenly in a body curled up instead of stretched. Surgery would rectify that—but first he must find a surgeon.

He was struck unpleasantly by the fact that even his botched joining would have occupied several months of the somatic shutdown which had maintained him in coma while the central system concentrated on healing. (He recalled sourly that the RedBloods healed quickly, almost on the run.)

Deity only knew where in space he might be by now.

But what had broken his body?

There were no sharp edges in the pod. Something broken, protruding spikes?

Shockingly, yes. The compass needle had been wrenched loose and the transparent, glassy tegument, black with his sap, lay shattered around it.

He thought, *I am lost*, but not yet with despair; there were actions to be taken before despair need be faced. He fed the hull, creating windows. Spaces cleared, opening on darkness and the diamond points of far stars. He found no sign of *Deadly Thorn*; he might have drifted a long way from her after the blast. He looked for the Home World, palely green, but could not find it; nor could he see the bluer, duller sister-world of the red-sapped, animal enemy.

Patiently he scanned the sky until a terrifying sight of the double star told him his search was done. It was visible still as a pair but as the twin radiances of a distant star. Of the lesser companions he could see nothing; their dimness was lost in the deep sky.

He had drifted unbelievably far. He could not estimate the distance; he remembered only from some long ago lecture that the double star might appear like this from a point beyond the orbit of the outermost planet, the dark fifteenth world.

The sight spoke not of months of healing but of years.

Only a brain injury . . .

Every officer carried a small grooming mirror in his tunic; with it Fernix examined the front and sides of his skull as well as he was able. Tiny swellings of healed fractures were visible, telling him that the braincase had crushed cruelly in on his frontal lobes and temples. Regrowth of brain tissue had forced them out again but the marks were unmistakeable. In the collision with the wreckage of *Deadly Thorn* he had crashed disastrously into . . . what?

The whole drive panel was buckled and cracked, its levers broken off or jammed down hard in their guides. They were what had assaulted him. Acceleration at top level had held him unconscious until the last drops in the tank were consumed, releasing him then to float and commence healing.

Fearfully he examined the fuel gauges. The Forward Flight gauge was empty, its black needle flush with the bottom.

The Retro fuel gauge still showed full, indicating precisely enough to balance the Forward gauge supply and bring the pod to a halt—enough, he realized drearily, to leave him twice as far from home as he now was, because the buckled panel had locked the steering jet controls with the rest. He could not take the pod into the necessary end for end roll. Only the useless deceleration lever still seemed free in its guides. The linkages behind the panel might still be operable but he had no means of reaching them and no engineering skill to achieve much if he did.

He was more than lost; he was coffined alive.

Something like despair, something like fear shook his mind as he eased himself into the pilot's seat, bruises complaining, but his species was not given to the disintegrative emotions. He sat quietly until the spasm subsided.

His actions now were culturally governed; there could be no question of what he would do. He was an officer, a carrier of breeding, and the next generation must be given every chance, however small, to be born. Very small, he thought. His pod could drift for a million years without being found and without falling into the gravity field of a world, let alone a livable world, but the Compulsion could not be denied. The Compulsion had never been stated in words; it was in the genes, irrevocable.

Calmly now, he withdrew the hull enzymes and blacked out the universe. He started the air pump and the quiet hiss of intake assured him that it was operative still. As the pressure tank filled with the withdrawn atmosphere he made the mental adjustment for Transformation. As with the Compulsion, there were no words for what took place. Psychologists theorized and priests pontificated but when the time and the circumstance came together, the thing happened. The process was as intangible as thought, about whose nature there was also no agreement. The thought and the need and the will formed the cultural imperative and the thing happened.

Before consciousness left him, perhaps for ever, Fernix doused the internal heating, which was not run from the ruined drive panel.

Resuscitation he did not think about. That would take place automatically if the pod ever drifted close enough to a sun for its hull to warm appreciably, but that would not, could not happen. Deity did not play at Chance-in-a-Million with His creation.

Consciousness faded out. The last wisps of air withdrew. The temperature fell slowly; it would require several days to match the cold of space.

The Transformation crept over him as a hardening of his outer skin, slowly, slowly, until his form was sheathed in seamless bark. Enzymes clustered at the underside of his skin, fostering a hardening above and below until tegument and muscle took on the impermeability of ironwood. Officer of the Fifth Brachiate Fernix had become a huge, complex spore drifting in galactic emptiness.

He was, in fact, drifting at a surprising speed. A full tank expended at full acceleration had cut out with the pod moving at something close to six thousandths of the speed of light.

The pod's automatic distress signal shut down. It had never been heard amidst the radio noise of battle fleets. The interior temperature dropped towards zero and the vegetal computers faded out as ion exchange ceased. The pod slept.

Nearly eight thousand Terrestrial years passed before the old saying was disproved: Deity did indeed play at Chance-in-a-Million with His creation.

Vegetal computers were more efficient than a metal-working culture would readily believe, though they could not compete in any way with the multiplex machines of the animal foe—in any, that is, except one.

The pod's computers were living things in the sense that any plant is a living thing. They were as much grown as fashioned, as much trained as programmed, and their essential mechanisms shared one faculty with the entity in Transformation who slept in his armour: They could adopt the spore mode and recover from it in the presence of warmth.

They had no way of detecting the passage of millennia as they slept but their links to the skin of the pod could and did react to the heat of a G-type sun rushing nearer by the moment.

As the outer temperature rose, at first by microscopic increments, then faster and faster, the computer frame sucked warmth from the hull and, still at cryogenic levels, returned to minimal function.

At the end of half a day the chemical warming plant came silently into operation and the internal temperature climbed towards normal. Automatically the Life Maintenance computer opened the air tank to loose a jet of snow that evanesced at once into invisible gases.

The miracle of awakening came to Fernix. His outer tegument metamorphosed, cell by cell, into vegetal flesh as his body heat responded; first pores, then more generalized organs sucked carbon dioxide from the air and return from Transformation began.

Emergence into full consciousness was slow, first as an emptiness in which flashes of dreams, inchoate and meaningless, darted and vanished; then as a closer, more personal space occupied by true dreams becoming ever more lucid as metabolism completed its regeneration; finally as an awareness of self, of small pressures from the restricted pilot's seat, of sap swelling in capillaries and veins, of warmth and the sharp scent of too-pure air. His first coherent thought was that a good life caterer would have included some forest fragrance, mulch or nitrate, in the atmosphere tank.

From that point he was awake, in full muscular and mental control, more swiftly than a Red-Blood could have managed. (But the Red-Bloods had no Transformation refuge that the scientists could discover; in deep cold or without air they died and quickly rotted. They were disgusting.)

He knew that only rising warmth could have recalled him.

A sun?

The Great Twin itself?

That was not possible.

Thanking Deity that the computers were not operated from the drive panel, he directed them to provide enzyme vision and in a moment gazed straight ahead at a smallish yellow sun near the centre of the forward field.

So Deity did . . . He wasted no time on that beyond a transient thought that every chance must come to coincidence at some time in the life of the universe—and that he might as well be winner as any other.

He asked the navigating computer for details: distance, size, luminescence. Slowly, because vegetal processes cannot be hurried, the thing made its observations and calculations and offered them. Obediently it unrolled the stellar chart and almanac—and Fernix knew where he was.

And, he thought, little good *that* brings me.

This was a star not easily naked-eye visible from the Home World, but the astronomers had long ago pinpointed it and its unseen planets. He was forty-seven light years from home (his mind accepted without understanding the abyss of time passed) on a course plunging him into the gravity well of an all-too-welcoming star at some thirty-two miles per second. The computer assured him that on his present course this yellow sun, though a child by comparison with the Great Twin, was powerful enough to grasp him and draw him into its atmosphere of flame.

But he had not come so far across time and space to die sitting still, eaten alive by a pigmy star.

He needed to buy time for thought. Deceleration alone was not enough for useful flight.

There was a blue-green planet, the almanac told him, which might possibly offer livable conditions. The hope was small in a universe where minute changes of temperature, orbit or atmosphere composition could put a world for ever beyond life, but the Deity which had guided him so finely and so far could surely crown His miracle with a greater one.

If he could achieve steering . . .

He was tempted to jemmy the cover off the Drive Panel and expose the linkages but common sense suggested that he would merely cause greater damage. He was coldly aware of ignorance and lack of mechanical talent; the maze of linkages would be to him just that—a maze, impenetrable.

Because he was untrained he failed for several hours to hit on the possibility that the the computer, once programmed to act rather than simply inform the pilot, might operate directly on the machine structures, bypassing linkages and levers. The entertainment media had imprinted him and all but those who actually operated space craft with a mental picture of pilots working by manual control, whereas it might be necessary only to tell the computer what he wanted.

That turned out to be anything but simple. As a gunnery officer he considered himself computer competent but he slept several times before he penetrated the symbols, information needs and connections of the highly specialized machine. Like most junior officers he had been rushed through an inadequate basic training and sent into space innocent of the peacetime auxiliary courses, with no expertise in other than visual navigation.

But, finally, the steering jets turned the pod end for end, the main jet roared triumphantly and the little craft slowed at the limit of deceleration his consciousness could bear. Held firmly in his straps with an arm weighing like stonewood, he questioned the computer about trajectories and escape velocities and how it might take him to the third planet of the yellow star.

It balanced distance against fuel and calculated a slingshot rounding of the central sun which would bring him economically to his goal, his destiny. There would be, Fernix knew, only a single chance and choice.

A Miner's Mate is, more correctly, an Asteroid Mining Navigational and Mass Detection Buoy. One of them sat sedately above a group of fairly large iridium-bearing 'rocks' in the Belt, providing guidance for the occasional incoming or outgoing scow and warning against rogue intruders—meteorites or small asteroids in eccentric orbits. It carried a considerable armament, including two fusion bombs capable of shattering a ten million tonne mass, but large wanderers were rare and collision orbits rarer still. Its warnings commonly did little more than send miners scurrying to the sheltered side of their rock until the danger passed.

Since space debris travels at speeds of miles per second, the sensitivity radius of the Mate's radar and vision systems was necessarily large. It registered the incoming pod at a million kilometres. Being fully automatic, it had no intelligence to find anything peculiar in the fact that it saw the thing before the mass detectors noted its presence. It simply radioed a routine alert to the mines and thereafter conscientiously observed.

The Shift Safety Monitor at the communication shack saw the tiny, brilliant point of light on his screen and wondered briefly what sort of craft was blasting inwards from the outer orbits. Scientific and exploratory probes were continuously listed and there were none due in this area of the System. Somebody racing home in emergency? Automatically he looked for the mass reading and there was none. What could the bloody Mate be doing? The mass of metal that put out such a blast must be easily measurable.

The Monitor's name was John Takamatta; he was a Murri from Western Queensland. This particular group of mines was a Murri venture and he was a trained miner and emergency pilot, now taking his turn on the dreary safety shift. Like most of his people he rarely acted without careful observation first; he waited for the Mate to declare or solve its problem.

The Mate's problem was that it could not recognize timber or any substance that let most of its beam through and diffused it thoroughly in passage. There was metal present but not enough to contain the tubes for such a drive blast and there was ceramic, probably enough for linings, but the amorphous mass surrounding these was matter for conjecture and conjecture was outside its capacity.

However, it tried, feeding back to the Mines computer a flicker of figures which mimicked a state of desperate uncertainty and gave the impression of a large, fuzzy thing of indefinite outline secreting within it some small metal components and ceramic duct lining.

Takamatta tried to enlarge the screen image but the size of the light did not change. It was either very small or far away or both.

The Mate's hesitant figures hovered round something under a tonne but no mass so slight could contain such brilliance. Yet it could only be a ship and there were no ships of that nursery size. He rang the dormitory for the off-duty, sleeping Computer Technician. Albert Tjilkamati would curse him for it but they were related, men of the same Dreaming, and the curse would be routinely friendly.

Albert came, cursed, watched, sent a few test orders to the Mate and decided that it was not malfunctioning, yet the oscillating, tentative figures suggested a human operator floundering with an observation beyond his competence. Once the analogy had occurred to him, he saw the force of it.

"Something it can't recognize, John. Its beam is being diffused and spread from inner surfaces—like light shining into a box of fog. The receptors don't understand. John, man, it's picked up something new in space! We'll be in the newscasts!"

He called Search and Rescue's advance base in the Belt.

The Search and Rescue Watch Officer knew Albert Tjilkamati; if he said 'strange' and 'unusual,' then strange and unusual the thing was.

"OK, Albert; I'll send a probe. Get back to you later."

He eased a torpedo probe out of its hangar, instructed its computers and sent it to intercept the flight path of the stranger. The probe was mainly a block of observational and analytical equipment in a narrow, twelve-metre tube, most of which was fuel tank; it leapt across the sky at an acceleration that would have broken every bone in a human body.

Starting from a point five million kilometres retrograde from the orbit of the Murri Mines, it used the Miner's Mate broadcast to form a base for triangulation and discovered at once that the incoming craft was decelerating at a g-number so high that the probe would have to recalculate its navigating instructions in order to draw alongside. It would, in fact, have to slow down and let the thing catch up with it.

The Watch Officer asked his prime computer for enhancement of the fuzzy mass/size estimates of the Mate, but the machine could not decide what the craft was made of or precisely where its edges were.

At this point, as if aware of observation, the craft's blast vanished from the screen.

The Watch Officer was intrigued but not much concerned; his probe had it on firm trace and would not let go. He notified HQ Mars, which was providentially the nearest HQ to him, of an incoming 'artificial object of unknown origin', accompanied by a full transcript of the Mate's data, stated: 'Intelligence probe despatched' and sat back to contemplate the probable uproar at HQ Mars. The lunatic fringe would be in full babble.

The computer, not Fernix, had cut the pod's blast because its velocity had dropped to the effective rate for rounding the system's sun. There would be corrections later as approach allowed more accurate data on the star's mass and gravity but for two million kilometres the pod would coast.

Fernix drifted into sleep. Transformation sleep conferred no healing, being essentially a reduction of metabolism to preservative zero; nothing was lost or gained during the hiatus. So he had awakened still in reaction to the stress of escape from *Deadly Thorn* and now needed sleep.

He woke again to the stridency of an alarm. The computer flashed characters in urgent orange, proclaiming the presence of a mass in steady attendance above and to the right of the pod and no more than twice its length distant.

He realized sluggishly that the mass must be a ship; only a ship equipped with damping screens could have approached so closely without detection.

The thought brought him fully alert. He opened a narrow vision slit and at first saw nothing; then he observed the slender occulting of stars. The thing was in darkness and probably painted black, else the central sun should have glinted on its nose.

If this was an artefact of the local life, he needed to find out what he could about it, even at the risk of exposing himself—if that was indeed a risk. The crew might well be friendly. He primed a camera for minimum exposure and, to aid it, turned the pod's lighting up full and opened the vision slit to his head's width for a tenth of a second.

It was enough for the camera to take its picture. It was enough, also, for the other to shoot through the gap a beam of intense light to take its own picture and blind Fernix's weak eyes. He flung his arms across his face and grunted with pain until his sight cleared. He stayed in darkness with the slit closed. He reasoned that he had been photographed by a race whose vision stretched further into the shortwave light spectrum than his and not so far into the gentler infra-red.

When the ache in his eyes subsided he examined his own infra-red picture. It showed a slender needle of nondescript colour, dull and non-reflective, without visible portes. The small diameter of the craft inclined him to think it was an unmanned reconnaissance probe. His evolutionary teaching dictated that an intelligent life form must perforce have its brain case and sensory organs raised well above ground level, and no such entity could have stood upright or even sat comfortably in that projectile.

He considered what action he might take.

He had been outplayed at the observation game and could do nothing about that. His weaponless pod was not equipped to fight, which was perhaps as well; nothing would be gained by antagonising these unknown people. Evasive action was out of the question. His fuel supply was low and his computer's decisions had been made on limits too tight for any but last ditch interference from himself; there was none for ad hoc manoeuvre.

He could take no action. The next move must come from outside.

Conclusion reached, he slept.

The Search and Rescue call sign squealed in the shack, the screen cleared and Takamarra looked up from his novel as the Watch Officer hailed him, "John, oh John, have we got something here! This one will puncture holes in your Dreaming!"

John said coldly, "Indeed." He was no traditionalist but did not appreciate light handling of his cultural mores by a white man.

Some fifteen seconds would pass before his reply reached S & R and fifteen more for the Watch Officer's response. In that time he digested the message and concluded that the unlikely was true, that the intruding craft was extra-systemic. Alien. And that the existence of life among the stars *could* have some effect on the credibility of Murri Dreaming.

Then he decided that it would not. Incursion of the white man and knowledge of a huge world beyond the oceans had altered most things in his people's lives but not that one thing, the Dreamings around which the Murri cultures were built. Science and civilization might rock on their foundations as the word went out, *We are not alone*, but the ancient beliefs would not shift by the quiver of a thought.

Willy Grant's voice said, "Get this carefully, John. Make notes. We need the biggest scow you've got because yours is the nearest mining group. We want to pick this little ship out of the sky but we can't get a magnetic grapple on it because what little metal there is appears to be shielded. The best bet is to clamp it in the loading jaws of your Number Three scow if it's available. The thing is only ten metres long and three wide, so it will fit in easily. The scow can dawdle sunwards and let the outsider catch up with it until they are matched for speed. Forty-eight hours at one point five g should do it. This is an Emergency Order, John, so time and fuel compensation will be paid. Relay that to your Manager, but pronto. The scow's computer can talk to mine about course and speed and we'll have your Manager's balls in a double reef knot if he raises objections. Got it?"

"Got it, Willy." He repeated the message for check. "Hang on while I pass it." Minus the threat; the Elder might not appreciate blunt humour.

The Murri Duty Manager preserved the Old Man routine of unimpressed self-possession, which fooled nobody. He turned his eyes from his screen, contemplated infinity in his fingernails for a respectable sixty seconds, raised his white-bearded head with an air of responsible decision-making and said, "Number Three scow is empty and available. It shall be floated off. The S & R computer can then take over." He would not have had the nerve to say otherwise; nobody in space flouted S & R.

Grant, on the other screen, heard the message and beat down the temptation to wink at John; the tribal old dear would be outraged and so would his miners. The Murri were good blokes but in some areas you had to tread carefully. When the Manager had cut out, he said, "Now, John, this'll rock you from here to Uluru. Look!"

He displayed a picture of the intruder illuminated by the probe's beam. It was shaped roughly like an appleseed, symmetrical and smooth, its line broken only by what must be a surprisingly narrow jet throat. Its colour seemed to be a deep brown, almost ebony.

"Now, get this!" He homed the viewpoint to a distance of a few inches from the hull. "What do you make of it?"

What John saw surprised him very much. The hull surface was grained like wood; there was even a spot where some missile (sand-grain meteoroid?) had gouged it to expose a slightly lighter colour and what was surely a broken splinter end.

Willy carried on talking. You do not wait for an answer across a thirty second delay. "Looks like wood, doesn't it? Well, see this!" The view roved back and forth from nose to tail, and the wave pattern of the grain flowed evenly along the whole length. "You'd think they grew the thing and lathed it out of a single block. And why not? A ship doesn't have to be built of steel, does it? I know timber couldn't stand the take-off and landing strains but how about if they are ferried up in bulk in a metal mother ship or built on asteroids and launched at low speed? Or there could be means of hardening and strengthening timber; we don't know because we've never needed to do it. But a race on a metal-poor world would develop alternative technologies. I'd stake a month's pay the thing's made of wood, John.''

In John's opinion he would have won the bet.

Willy did not display the other picture, the shocker taken when the alien tried to photograph the probe. Under instruction he had given Takamatta enough to satisfy immediate curiosity without providing food for the idiot fantasy that flourishes when laymen are presented with too much mystery and too few answers.

Alone he studied the startling hologram, at life size, which his computer had built for him.

It seemed that the alien had also taken a shot of the probe just as the automatic camera took advantage of the widening slit in the intruder's hull. The thing's face—'face' for want of a word—stared at him over what was surely a camera lens.

The alien—being, entity, what you would—seemed generally patterned on an anthropoid model with a skin dappled in grey and green. The head and neck protruded above shoulders from which sprang arms or extensions of some kind—probably arms, Willy thought, because on the thing's camera rested what should be fingers, though they looked more like a bunch of aerial roots dropped by some variety of creeper but thicker and, judging by their outlandish grasping, more flexible than fingers.

In the narrow head he could discern no obvious bone structure under thick—flesh? The face was repulsive in the vague fashion of nightmare when the horror is incompletely seen. There was a mouth, or something in the place of a mouth—an orifice, small and round with slightly raised edges where lips should have been. He thought of a tube which would shoot forward to fix and suck. Nose there was none. The eyes—they had to be eyes—were circular black discs with little holes at their centres.

He guessed hazily that black eyes, totally receptive of all wavelengths of light, could be very powerful organs of vision, given the outlandish nervous system necessary to operate them. Or, perhaps, the central holes were the receptors, like pinhole cameras.

Ears? Well . . . there were flaps on the sides of the head, probably capable of manipulation since the hologram showed one raised and one nearly flush with the grey and green flesh. A third flap, partly open, in what must be called the forehead and revealing under it an intricately shaped opening reminiscent of the outer ear, suggested all-round hearing with a capacity for blocking out sound and/or direction finding. A useful variation.

Hair there seemed to be none but on the crown of the bud-shaped skull sat a plain, yellowish lump like a skittish party hat, a fez six inches or so high and four wide. Yet it seemed to be part of the head, not a decoration. He could make nothing of it.

There remained the faintly purplish cape around the thing's shoulders. Or was it a cape? It hung loosely over both shoulders and its lower edges fell below the rim of the vision slit, but it was parted at the throat and he had an impression that what he saw at the parting was dappled flesh rather than a garment. On closer examination he thought that the 'cape' was actually a huge flap of skin, perhaps growing from the back of the neck. He thought of an elephant's ears, which serve as cooling surfaces.

An idea that had been knocking for expression came suddenly into the light and he said aloud, ''The thing's a plant!''

At once he was, however unwarrantably, certain that he looked on the portrait of a plant shaped in the caricature of a man. The 'cape' was a huge leaf, not for cooling but for transpiration. The seemingly boneless skull and tentacular hands made vegetable sense; the thing would be infinitely flexible in body, acquiring rigidity as and where needed by hydrostatic pressure. He pondered root systems and acquired mobility as an evolutionary problem without a glimmer of an answer, but his impression would not be shifted.

The thing from out there was a motile vegetable.

The setting up of ore refineries on asteroids which were usually worked out in a few years would have been prohibitively expensive, so the main refinery had been located on Phobos, and there the output of all Belt companies was handled without need for the scows to make planetfall. The saving in expensive fuel was most of what made the ventures profitable. Nor was there any waste of manpower on those lonely voyages; the scows were computer-directed from float-off to docking.

An empty scow, not slowed by several hundred tonnes mass of ore, could accelerate at a very respectable g-rate. Number Three scow from the Murri outfit caught its prey dead on time, forty-eight hours after float-off. Forty-eight hours of silent flight, accompanied by a probe which made no move, took toll of nerves. Fernix slept and wondered and theorized from too little knowledge and slept again. At the second waking he fed, sparsely, not knowing how long his supplies must stretch; he injected a bare minimum of trace elements into the mulch tray with just enough water to guarantee ingestion, and rested his feet in it. The splayed pads protruded their tubules like tiny rootlets as his system drew up the moisture. He preferred mouth feeding but in the pod he had no choice.

The brief euphoria of ingestion passed and his mood flickered between fear and hope. Did the probe accompany him for a purpose unknown or did its controllers watch and wait to see what he would do?

He would do nothing. The vacillations of mood rendered him unfit to decide with proper reason. He writhed internally but sat still, did nothing.

His people, slow-thinking and phlegmatic, did not slip easily into neurosis but he was muttering and twitching when new outside action came. He switched into calm observation and appraisal.

The alarm indicated a new presence in space, ahead of him but drawing close.

He chanced a pinhole observation in the direction of the new mass but could see nothing. Whatever the thing was, either he was closing on it or it waited for him. His computer reported that the mass was losing some speed and he decided that it intended to match his course.

His instruments described it as long in body and large in diameter but not of a mass consistent with such size. An empty shell? Such as a cargo vessel with cleared holds?

Shortly he found that the probe had vanished and a quite monstrous ship was slipping back past him; the light of the system's sun shone on its pitted, blue-painted nose. It was old in space and about the size of a raiding destroyer but showed no sign of armament.

It slipped behind him and took up a steady position uncomfortably close to him. He was tempted to discover what it would do if he accelerated or changed course, then thought of his thin-edge supply of fuel. Do nothing, nothing; pray for friendly beings.

He saw with a frisson of tension that it was moving swiftly up to him.

Looming close to collision point, it opened its forward hull in a vast black mouth and gullet, like the sea monsters of his baby tales.

Its forward surge engulfed his pod, swallowed it whole and closed about it as something (grasping bands?) thudded on the pod's shell and held captor and prey to matched speeds. He was imprisoned in a vast, empty space, in darkness.

After a while he cleared the pod's entire shell, turning it into a transparent seed hanging in a white space illuminated by his interior lights. White, he thought, for optimum lighting when they work in here.

The space was utterly vacant. At the far end, roughly amidships he calculated, vertical oblong outlines were visible against her white paint—entry hatches. So the entities stood upright; he had expected no less. Evolutionary observation and theory (formulated so long ago, so far away) suggested that an intelligent, land-based being must stand erect, that it should carry brain and major sensory organs at its greatest height, that it should possess strong limbs for locomotion and grasping in limited number according to the law of minimum replication, that it—

—a dozen other things whose correctness he should soon discover in fact.

He saw that his pod was clamped above and below in a vise powerful enough to hold it steady in a turbulent manoeuvre. It was, his instruments told him, basically iron, as was the hull of the ship.

He was not sure whether or not he should envy a race which could be so prodigal of metal. Their technologies would be very different from those of the Home World.

He waited for them but they did not come.

Could their ship be unmanned, totally remote-controlled? His people had a few such—had had a few such—but their radio-control techniques had been primitive and doubtful. Given unlimited iron and copper for experiment . . .

He waited.

Suddenly the pod was jerked backward as the captor vessel decelerated at a comfortable rate; he could have withstood twice as much.

Homing on a world nearby? He could not tell; his instruments could not penetrate the metal hull.

He thought, I am learning the discipline of patience.

The crew of a ship approaching Phobos would have seen few surface installations though the moonlet housed the HQ Outer Planets Search and Rescue, an Advanced College of Null-Gravity Science, the Belt Mining Co-Operative Ore Refineries, a dozen privately owned and very secretive research organizations and, most extensive of all, the Martian Terra-forming Project Laboratories and Administrative Offices.

All of these were located inside the tunnelled and hollowed rock that was Phobos.

It had been known for a century or more that the moonlet was slowly spiralling inwards for a long fall to Mars, and Martian Terraforming did not want some 6000 cubic kilometres of solid matter crashing on the planet either before or after its hundred-year work was completed. So the interior had been excavated to the extent of nearly twenty per cent of the total mass (the engineers had vetoed more lest stress changes break the rock apart) and the detritus blasted into space at high velocity. The change in mass, even after the installation of men and machinery, had slowed the inward drift but more brutal measures would eventually have to be taken, and one College research unit was permanently engaged in deciding what such measures might be (brute force is easily said) and how they might be applied (less easily said).

Phobos, swinging 6000 kilometres above the Martian surface, was a busy hive where even gossip rarely rose above the intellectual feuds and excitements of dogged dedication—

—until a junior ass in S & R cried breathlessly, careless of eager ears, "Bloody thing looks like a lily pad with head and chest. A plant, bejesus!"

After that, S & R had trouble preventing the information being broadcast throughout the System, but prevent it they did. The last thing a troubled Earth needed as it emerged from the Greenhouse Years and the Population Wars was the political, religious and lunatic fringe upheaval expectable on the cry of *We are not alone*.

Possum Takamatta, John's younger brother, a Communications Operative with S & R, pondered the hologram transmitted from the Belt and asked, "Just what sense do they think an ecologist might make of that?"

"God knows," said ecologist Anne Spriggs of Waterloo, Iowa and Martian Terraforming, who was as pink-and-white as Possum was deep brown-black, "but I know some botany, which is more than anyone else around here does, so I just might make a useful contribution, read guess."

"With no tame expert at hand, they're desperate?"

"Possum, wouldn't you be desperate?"

"Why? I'm just interested. My people knew that 'more things in heaven and earth' line twenty thousand years before Shakespeare. You got any ideas?"

"No, only questions."

"Like?"

"Is it necessarily a plant because it reminds us of a plant? If it is, how does a rooted vegetable evolve into a motile form?"

"Who says it's motile? We've only got this still picture."

"It has to be to go into space. It couldn't take a garden plot with it."

"Why not? A small one, packed with concentrates, eh? And why should it have to become motile? Might have descended from floating algae washed up in swamplands with plenty of mud. Developed feet instead of roots, eh?'

Anne said with frustration, "So much for the ecologist! The local screeneye has more ideas than I do."

He tried soothing because he liked Anne. "You're hampered by knowledge, while I can give free rein to ignorance."

She was not mollified. "Anyway, is it plant or animal? Why not something new? Who knows what conditions formed it or where it's from?"

"From at least Alpha Centauri; that's the nearest. It came in at thirty k per second, and decelerating; if that was anything like its constant speed it's been on its way for centuries. That's a long time for one little lone entity."

"Why not FTL propulsion?"

"Come off it, girl! Do you credit that shit?"

"Not really."

"Nor does anyone else. If it came from anywhere out there, then it's an ancient monument in its own lifetime."

"In the face of that," she said, "I feel monumentally useless. What in hell am I good for?"

"Marry me and find out."

"In a humpy outside Alice Springs?"

"I've a bloody expensive home in Brisbane."

"And I've a fiance in Waterloo, Iowa."

"The hell you say!"

"So watch it, Buster!" She planted a kiss on the tip of his ear. "That's it. Everything else is off limits."

"In Australia we say out of bounds."

"In Australia you also say sheila when you mean pushover."

Not quite right but near enough and she certainly made better viewing than the mess on the screen.

In another part of the cavern system the Base Commander S & R held a meeting in an office not designed to hold thirteen people at once—himself and the twelve managers of the moonlet's private research companies. Commander Ali Musad's mother was Italian, his father Iraki and himself a citizen of Switzerland; S & R took pride in being the least racially oriented of all the service arms.

He had set the office internal g at one-fifth, enough to keep them all on the floor, however crowded; it is difficult to dominate a meeting whose units sit on walls and ceiling and float away at a careless gesture.

He said, "I have a problem and I need your help. As Station senior executive I can give orders to service groups and enforce them; of you ladies and gentlemen representing civilian projects I can only ask."

They resented his overall authority. They remained silent, letting him wriggle on his own hook, whatever it was. Then they might help, cautiously, if advantage offered.

"Some of you will have heard of a . . . presence . . . in space. A foolish boy talked too loudly in a mess room and no doubt the whisper of what he said has gone the rounds."

That should have produced a murmur but did not. Only Harrison of Ultra-Micro asked, "Something about a green man in a sort of lifeboat?"

"Something like that."

"I didn't pay attention. Another comedian at work or has someone picked up a phantom image from a dramacast?"

"Neither. He's real."

Someone jeered softly, someone laughed, most preferred a sceptical lift of eyebrows. Chan of Null-G Germinants suggested that managers had low priority on the rumour chain. "Ask the maintenance staff; they're the slush bearers."

Musad told them, "It isn't silly season slush; it's real; I've seen it. Talk has to be stopped."

Still they did not take him too seriously. "Can't stop gossip, Commander."

"I mean: Stop it getting off Phobos."

"Too late, Commander. If it's a little green men story it's gone out on a dozen private coms by now."

He said stiffly, "It hasn't. I've activated the censor network." The shocked silence was everything he could have desired. "Every com going out is being scanned for key words; anything containing them is being held for my decision."

He waited while anger ran its course of outrage and vituperation. They didn't give a damn about little green men but censorship was an arbitrary interference guaranteed to rouse fury anywhere across the System. The noise simmered down in predictable protests: ". . . abuse of power . . . justifiable only in war emergency . . . legally doubtful on international Phobos . . ."

Melanie Duchamp, the Beautiful Battleaxe of Fillette Bonded Aromatics, produced the growling English that browbeat boardrooms: "You will need a vairy good reason for this."

No honorific, he noted; Melanie was psyching herself for battle. "It was a necessary move. Now I am asking you to ratify it among your company personnel."

"Fat chance," said one, and another, "We'd have mutiny on our hands."

He had expected as much. "In that case I shall order it as a service necessity and take whatever blame comes." And leave them to accept blame if events proved his action the right one. "I can promise worse than mutiny if the news is not controlled."

At that at least they listened. He told them what he knew of the intruding ship, its contents and the speculation about its origin, and then: "Let this news loose on Earth and Luna and we'll have every whining, power-grabbing, politicking ratbag in the System here within days. I don't mean just the service arms and intelligence wood-beetles and scientists and power-brokers; I mean the churches and cults and fringe pseudo-sciences and rich brats with nothing better to do. I also mean your own company executives and research specialists and the same from your merchant rivals—to say nothing of the print and electronic media nosing at your secrets. How do you feel about it?''

It was Melanie who surrendered savagely. ''I will support you—under protest.''

''You don't have to cover your arse, Melanie. I'll take the flack.''

''So? There will be lawsuits, class actions that will cost the companies millions.''

''No! I will declare a Defence Emergency.''

''Then God or Allah help you, Commander.''

Harrison said, ''You can't do it. You say the thing seems to be unarmed; how can you invoke defence?''

''Possible espionage by an alien intruder. If that won't do, the Legal Section will think up something else.''

In the end they agreed if only because he left them no choice. Satisfied that they would keep the lid on civilian protest, he threw them a bone: He would call on them to supply experts in various fields not immediately available among the service personnel on Phobos, because he intended to bring the thing inside and mount as complete an examination as possible before allowing a squeak out of Phobos Communications.

They brightened behind impassive agreement. With their own men at the centre of action they would be first with the news as history was made in their particular corners . . . with profit perhaps . . . and wily Musad was welcome to the lawsuits.

When they had gone he summoned his secretary. ''All on record?''

''Yes, sir.''

''Am I covered?''

''I think so. They will co-operate in case you retaliate by leaving them out of the selection of expert assistance. Which means that you must take at least one from each firm, however useless.''

''Yes. Many messages intercepted?''

''Seven for your attention. Three to media outlets. It seems we have some unofficial stringers aboard.''

''The buggers are everywhere. I don't want media complaints when they find out that their lines were stopped. They stir up too much shit.'' He recalled too late that Miss Merritt was a Clean Thinker. ''Sorry.''

She was unforgiving. ''Nevertheless there will be complaints.'' Her tone added, And serve you right. Clean Thinkers held that censorship was unnecessary in a right-minded community—and so was crude language.

''I think the courts will uphold me.''

''No doubt, sir. Will that be all?''

''Yes, Miss Merritt.'' And to hell with you, Miss Merritt, but you are too efficient to be returned to the pool.

The Number Three scow drifted down through darkness to hover over the moonlet's docking intake, a square hole like a mineshaft, that came suddenly alive with light.

The docking computer took control, edged the huge scow, precisely centred, through the intake and closed the entry behind it.

A backup computer waited, ready to take over in the event of malfunction, and a human operator waited with finger on override, prepared to assume manual control at an unpredictable, unprogrammable happening. This was a first in the history of the human race and almost anything, including the inconceivable, might occur.

Nothing did.

The computer took the scow evenly through the second lock, closed it, moved the vessel sideways through the Repair and Maintenance Cavern to the largest dock and set it smoothly belly-down on the floor. Then, because nobody had thought to tell it otherwise, it followed normal procedure and switched on one-eighth g in the floor area covered by the vessel, sufficient to ensure cargo stability.

Watching in his office screen, Musad cursed somebody's thoughtlessness—his own, where the buck stopped—and opened his mouth for a countermanding order. Then he thought that any damage was already done. Anyway, why should there be damage? No world with an eighth g would have produced a life form requiring an atmosphere, and the probe had certainly reported an atmosphere of sorts. Whatever lived inside the . . . lifeboat? . . . should be comfortable enough.

He shut his mouth and called Analysis. "Full scan, inside and out. There is a living being inside; take care."

Analysis knew more than he about taking care and had prepared accordingly. The first necessity was to establish the precise position of the thing inside—being, entity, e-t, what you would—and ascertain that it was or was not alone. So: a very delicate selection of penetrating radiation in irreducibly small doses, just enough to get a readable shadow and keep it in view.

Analysis had far better instrumentation than the comparatively crude probe and established at once that the thing was alive and moving its . . . limbs? . . . while remaining in seated position facing the nose of the vessel. Able now to work safely round the thing, visitor, whatever, Analysis unleashed its full battery of probe, camera, resolution and dissection.

The results were interesting, exciting, even breathtaking, but no scrap of evidence suggested where the little ship might have come from.

Musad was an administrator, not a scientist; Analysis gave him a very condensed version of its immensely detailed preliminary report—blocked out, scripted, eviscerated, rendered down and printed for him in under three hours—highlighting the facts he had called for most urgently:

The living entity in the captive vessel would be, when it stood, approximately one and a half metres tall. It showed the basic pentagonal structure—head and four limbs—which might well represent an evolutionary optimum design for surface dwellers in a low-g Terrene range. There was a rudimentary skeletal structure, more in the nature of supportive surface plates than armatures of bone, and the limbs appeared tentacular rather than jointed. This raised problems of push-pull capability with no answers immediately available.

Spectroscopic reading was complicated by the chemical structure of the vessel's hull, but chlorophyll was definitely present in the entity as well as in the hull, and the bulky 'cape' on its shoulders showed the visual characteristics of a huge leaf. It was certainly a carbon-based form and seemed to be about ninety per cent water; there was no sign of haemoglobin or any related molecule.

The atmosphere was some forty per cent denser than Terrene air at sea level, a little light in oxygen but heavy with water vapour and carbon dioxide.

Tentative description: Highly intelligent, highly evolved, motile plant species.

We always wondered about aliens and now we've got one. What does he eat? Fertilizer? Or does that snout work like a Venus fly trap?

The small amounts of iron in the vessel—tank linings and a few hand tools— argued a metal-poor environment, ruling out any Sol-system planet as a world of origin.

As if they needed ruling out!

The ceramic lining of the jet would require longer evaluation but appeared to be of an unfamiliar crystalline macro-structure. All the other parts of the vessel, including the hull, were timber. There was nothing unusual about the composition of the various woods but a great deal unusual about about the treatments they had undergone, presumably for hardening and strengthening; no description of these could be hazarded without closer examination. (There followed a dissertation on the possible technology of a timber based culture. Musad skipped over it.)

Dating procedures were at best tentative on materials whose isotopic balance might not match Terrene counterparts, but guesstimates gave a pro tem figure of between seven and ten thousand Terrene years. The signatories declined to draw any conclusions as to the age of the vegetal pilot or where he might have originated.

And all it does is sit there, sit there, sit there, occasionally moving a tentacle in some unguessable activity. So: What next?

He was taken by an idea so absurd that it would not go away, an idea which might, just might stir the creature into some action. It was a sort of 'welcome home' idea—rather, an introduction . . .

He called the Projection Library.

Fernix slept and woke while the deceleration held him comfortably in his seat. He slept again and woke, nerves alert, when deceleration ceased.

He opened a tiny vision hole but saw only his prison still closed around him.

Shortly there was a perceptible forward motion and the slightest of centrifugal effects as the direction changed several times. Then his captor ship settled, gently for so large a transport. His pod shook momentarily and was still.

Suddenly there was gravity, not much of it but enough to aid balance and movement.

Not that he had any intention of moving; he could not afford movement. He needed energy. Food alone was not enough; his thousands of chloroplasts needed sunlight for the miracle of conversion to maintain body temperature, muscle tone, even the capacity to think effectively. There was a spectrum lamp aboard but its batteries would operate for only a limited time; a pod was not intended for pan-galactic voyaging.

Yet full alertness could be demanded of him at any moment; he must pump his body resources to a reasonable ability for sustained effort. He used a third of the lamp's reserve, switched it off and continued at rest in the pilot seat.

There was little assessment he could make of his position. His captors had demonstrated no technological expertise (beyond a squandering of metal) which could not have been duplicated on the Home World, nor had they attempted to harm him. So they were civilized beings, reasonably of a cultural status with which he could relate.

On the panel, radiation detectors flickered at low power. He was, he guessed, being investigated. So, this race was able to operate its instruments *through* the metal hull outside. That proved little; a race evolving on a metal rich world would naturally develop along different lines of scientific interest from one grown from the forests of Home. Different need not mean better.

It was an exciting thought, that on another world a people had emerged from the nurturing trees to conquer the void of space.

The thought was followed by another, more like a dream, in which his people had traversed the unimaginable distance between stars to colonize this faraway system, facing and overcoming the challenges of worlds utterly variant from their own, inventing whole new sciences to maintain their foothold on the universe.

The open-minded intelligence can contemplate the unfamiliar, the never-conceived, and adapt it to new modes of survival.

He had arrived by freakish accident; could not his people have made the crossing during the eons while he crept through space in free fall? The idea of using Transformation for survival while a ship traversed the years and miles had been mooted often.

His reverie was broken by a squealing hiss from outside the pod.

Outside. They were supplying his prison with an atmosphere.

Chemist Megan Ryan was the first to curse Musad for mishandling the approach to the alien ship. Suited up and ready to examine the hull, she heard someone at the closed-circuit screen ask, "What the hell's going on? They've let air into the scow."

She clawed the man out of the way and punched Musad's number to scream at him, "What do you think you're bloody well doing?"

"And who do you think you're talking to, Captain-Specialist?"

She took a deep, furious breath. "To you . . . sir. Who ordered air into the scow?"

"I did." His tone said that if she objected, her reason had better be foolproof.

"But why, why, why?" She was close to stuttering with rage.

His administrative mind groped uneasily at the likelihood of an error of unscientific judgment and decided that this was not a moment for discipline. "To provide air and temperature for the investigating teams to work in. What else?"

She swallowed, conscious of a red face and tears of frustration. "Sir, that ship has been in space for God only knows how long, in the interstellar deep. Its timber hull will have collected impact evidence of space-borne elements and zero-temperature molecules. That evidence will by now have been negated by temperature change and highly reactive gases. Knowledge has been destroyed."

She was right and he would hear about it later from higher echelons; he simply had not thought from a laboratory standpoint. "I'm sorry, Meg, but my first priority for investigation is the traveller rather than the ship. He represents more urgent science than a little basic chemistry."

The wriggling was shameful and he knew it; he had forgotten everything outside the focus of his own excitement, the alien.

She was glaring still as he cut her off.

He spoke to the Library: "Have you got much?"

"A good representative selection, sir. Vegetable environments from different climates. As you requested, no human beings."

"Good. I don't want humans presented to him in stances and occupations he—it—won't understand. Get a computer mockup ready—a naked man, good physique, in a space suit. Set it up so that the suit can be dissolved from around him. I want a laboratory effect, emotionally distancing, to reduce any 'monster' reaction."

"Yes, sir," the screen murmured.

"He's put out a probe of some sort," said another screen. "Sampling the air maybe."

Musad turned to screen 3 and the alien ship. The temperature in the hold had risen to minus thirty Celsius and vapour was clearing rapidly from the warming air. Visibility was already good.

When the air reached normal temperature and pressure for their planet, Fernix reasoned, they would come for him.

They did not come, though temperature and pressure levelled off. He was disappointed but accepted that there would be circumstances which he could not at present comprehend.

He extended a hull probe for atmosphere analysis, to find the outside pressure very low while the water vapour content hovered at the 'dry' end of the scale and the carbon dioxide reading was disturbingly light. He could exist in such an atmosphere only with difficulty and constant re-energizing. Acclimatization would take time.

Through the generations, he reasoned, his people would have made adaptation, for the vegetal germ was capable of swift genetic change. There would be visible differences by now—of skin, of stature, of breathing areas—but essentially they would be his people still . . .

He saw a flash of coloured movement outside his spyhole and leaned forward to observe.

In the prison space, a bare armslength from the pod's nose, a silver-green tree flickered into existence, took colour and solidity to become a dark, slender trunk rising high before spreading into radiating fronds. His narrow field of vision took in others like it on both sides and beyond, ranged at roughly equal distances. Beyond them again, a broad river. The palmate forms were familiar (mutations, perhaps, of ancestral seeds carried across the void?) as was the formal arrangement on a river bank, the traditional files of the rituals of Deity.

As he watched, the scene changed to a vista of rolling highlands thickly covered with conical trees of the deep green of polar growths, and in the foreground a meadow brilliant with some manner of green cover where four-legged, white beasts grazed. Their shape was unfamiliar, but his people had used grazing beasts throughout historical time; children loved them and petted them and wept when they were slaughtered. Only the anthropoid monsters from the sister world could terrify the young and rouse the adults to protective fury.

As the picture faded he wondered had the man-beasts been utterly destroyed. Some would have been preserved for study . . . mated in zoos . . . exhibited . . .

A new view faded in and the hologram placed him at the edge of a great pond on whose surface floated green pads three or four strides across their diameter. He recognized water-dwelling tubers though the evolved details were strange, as were the flitting things that darted on and above them. Forms analogous to insects, he guessed, thinking that some such line was an almost inevitable product of similar environment.

Cautiously he opened the vision slit wider and saw that the huge picture extended away and above as though no walls set limits to it. He looked upwards to an outrageously blue, cloudless sky that hurt his eyes. This world, without cloud cover, would be different indeed.

He realized with a burst of emotion, of enormous pride and fulfilment, that he was being shown the local planet of his people, accentuating the similarities that he would recognize, welcoming him Home as best they could.

The picture changed again and this time he wept.

His pod lay now in the heart of a jungle clearing, brilliant-hued with flowers and fungi that stirred memory though none were truly familiar. Tall, damp trunks lifted to the light, up to the tight leaf cover where the branching giants competed for the light filtered down through cloud cover. For there was cloud cover here, familiarly grey, pressing down and loosing its continuous drizzle to collect on the leaves and slide groundwards in silver-liquid tendrils. Bright insect-things darted, and larger things that flapped extensions like flattened arms to stay aloft in surprisingly effective fashion. These were strange indeed as were the four-legged, furry things that leapt and scurried on the ground, chewing leaves and grubbing for roots.

The whole area could have been a corner of his ancestral estate, transformed yet strangely and truly belonging. He had been welcomed to a various but beautiful world.

With the drunken recklessness of love and recognition he activated the enzyme control and cleared the entire hull of the pod for vision. It was as though he stood in the heart of a Home playground, amid surroundings he already loved.

Soon, soon his people of these new, triumphant years must show themselves . . .

. . . and as though the desire had triggered the revelation, the jungle faded away and a single figure formed beyond the nose of the pod, floating in darkness as only a hologram could, hugely bulky in its pressure suit, face hidden behind the filtering helmet plate but wholly human in its outward structure of head and arms and motor limbs.

He left the seat to lean, yearning, against his transparent hull, face pressed to the invisible surface, arms spread in unrestrained blessing.

The figure spread its arms in a similar gesture, the ancient gesture of welcome and peace, unchanged across the void and down the centuries.

The outlines of the pressure suit commenced to blur, to fade, revealing the creature within.

The naked body was white, stiff-limbed, fang-mouthed, bright-eyed with recognition of its helpless, immemorial foe.

It floated, arms outstretched, in mockery of the ritual of peace.

The Red-Blood.

The enemy.

When the first hologram appeared—the Nile-bank scene of the planting program for binding the loosening soil—Musad watched for reaction from the ship but there was none.

The Swedish panorama, its forest of firs contrasted with the feeding sheep, pleased him better. On any habitable world there must be some environment roughly correlating with this, some scene of bucolic peace.

Then came the Victoria lilies and their pond life—A screen voice said, "It's opened the vision slit a little bit. It's interested."

It? Too clinical. Musad would settle for he. Could be she, of course, or some exotic gender yet unclassified.

The fourth scene, the jungle display, brought a dramatic result. The entire hull of the ship became cloudy, then translucent and—vanished. The interior was revealed from nose to jet.

Musad did not bother scanning the internal fittings; a dozen cameras would be doing that from every angle. He concentrated on the alien.

It—*he* rose swiftly out of his chair, head thrust forward in the fashion of a pointing hound and stepped close to the invisible inner hull. He was not very tall, Musad thought, nor heavily muscled but very limber, as though jointless. (But how could a jointless being stand erect or exert pressure? His basically engineering mind thought vaguely of a compartmentalized hydrostatic system, nerve-operated. Practical but slow in reaction time.) He lifted his tentacular arms, spreading the great 'cape' like a leaf to sunlight, and raised them over his head in a movement redolent of ecstasy.

Could jungle, or something like it be the preferred habitat? *He* was plainly enthralled.

The jungle scene faded and the hold was in darkness save for the low-level radiance of the little ship's interior lighting.

The computer's creation, man-in-space-suit, appeared forward of the ship, floating a metre above the floor. *He* leaned, in unmistakable fascination, close against the inner hull. *He* pressed his face against the invisible timber like a child at a sweetshop window and slowly spread his arms. His 'hands' were bunches of grey-green hoses until the fingers separated and stiffened. Musad could see that the tubular members straightened and swelled slightly; he could detect no muscle but they had plainly hardened as they pressed against the wood. It seemed to Musad that he stood in a posture of unrestrained, longing welcome.

The Library operator must have caught the same impression and in a moment of inspiration had the space-suited figure duplicate the outspread stance of friendship. Then he began to fade the armour, baring the symbolic man within.

He remained perfectly still.

Musad advanced his viewpoint until the alien's face dominated his screen. The face changed slowly. Thin folds of skin advanced across the huge black eyes, closing until only small circles remained. The mouth tube retracted and simultaneously opened wide in another circle, a great 'Oh!' of wonder and surprise. The face resembled nothing more than a child's drawing of a happy clown.

Musad pulled back the view and saw that the 'cape' was now fully raised behind the head, like some vast Elizabethan jewelled collar, save that the leaf-veins shone bright yellow.

"He's happy," Musad said to anyone who might hear him. "He's happy!"

He stepped slowly back from the hull, lowered an arm to one of the panels— and the dark hull was there again, lightless, impenetrable.

Musad could not, never did know that what he had seen was a rictus mask more deeply murderous than simple hatred could rouse and mould.

For Fernix recognition of the Red-Blood was more than a cataclysm; it was a trigger.

On the Home World, when the end came it was recognized.

An end was an end. Intellect lost overriding control and biological forces took over. Genetically dictated reactions awoke and the process of Final Change began.

Pollination, initiated in the peak years of adolescence and suspended until the Time of Flowering, was completed in a burst of inner activity. At the same time stimulant molecules invaded his cerebrum, clarifying and calming thought for the Last Actions. In the domed crown of his skull the bud stirred; the first lines of cleavage appeared faintly on the surface as the pressure of opening mounted. His people flowered once only in life—when, at the moment of leaving it, the pollen was gathered by exultant young partners while the dying one's children were born.

There would be none to gather pollen from Fernix but his salute should be as royal as his lineage.

The initial burst of killing rage against the Red-Blood ebbed slowly. Had the projection been indeed a physical Red-Blood he would have been unable to master the urge to murder; he would have been out of the pod and in attack without conscious thought, obeying an impulse prehistorically ancient. The fading of the thing helped return him to reason.

It had shown him in the opening of its mouth, in what the things called a 'smile', that he was the helpless captive of enemy cruelty. The display of fangs had been the promise of the last insult to honourable extinction, the eating of his body before Final Change could translate him to Deity.

It did not seem to him irrational that he had so simply projected as fact his people's conquest of space and the new worlds; his psychology carried no understanding other than that the vegetal races were naturally dominant in the intellectual universe. The Home World scientists found it difficult to account for the evolution of thinking Red-Bloods on the neighbour planet; such things, they reasoned, could only be sports, the occasional creations of a blind chance, having no destiny.

Fernix, orthodox because he had no training beyond orthodoxy, could only grasp that his people must have been totally destroyed in that long ago war, overwhelmed by unimaginable disaster. Not they had conquered interstellar space but the Red-Bloods. He, Fernix, was alone in a universe empty of his kind.

He knew, as he regained mental balance, that Final Change had begun. There was no fear of death in his people's psychology, only an ineradicable instinct to perpetuate the species; Fernix felt already the changes in his lower limbs heralding the swift growth of embryonic offspring, motile units in one limb, rooted slave-kin in the other.

That they would be born only to die almost at once did not trouble him; he could not abort births governed by autonomic forces and he was not capable of useless railing against the inevitable. He had seen the terror of Red-Bloods as death came to them and been unable to comprehend the working of brains which in extremity rendered their possessors useless and demented. How could such creatures have mastered the great void?

He settled again into the pilot's seat and with quick actions emptied the whole store of trace elements into the feeding bed and thrust his feet deep into the mulch.

With triumphant pleasure he opened the emergency carbon dioxide cock and drained the tank into the pod's atmosphere. His death would be such a flowering of insult as few had ever offered the Red-Bloods. The burst of mocking blossom, in the colour of their own life fluid, would take his people out of history in a blaze of derisive laughter at their barbarian destroyers.

That was not all. One other gesture was possible—the winning of a last battle although the war was long over.

The alien had shut himself in. The shortwave team reported that he had resumed the pilot seat and as far as they could determine had moved little in several hours.

Anne Ryan blamed Musad and was careless who heard her. "It's a vegetable form and he lulls it into euphoria with holograms of arboreal paradise, then confronts it with a bone-and-meat structure as far outside its experience as it is outside ours! It's probably half-paralysed with shock. It needs time to assimilate the unthinkable. We need a brain here, not a bloody bureaucrat."

Melanie's contribution seemed more vicious for being delivered in a strong Breton accent. "The thing showed its teeth! The plant was terrified. It has no teeth, only a sucking tube! So you bare teeth at it and it runs to hide! Who would not?"

Musad thought the women had a point and that he had acted with more authority than prudence. But, what should be done on first contact with the unknowable? The only certainty had been that he must take some action; if he had ordered the scientists to leave the thing alone he would have had rebellion on his hands and eventually questions asked in political arenas; if he had given them their heads they would have mauled each other in battles for priority and he would have ended up cashiered for inefficient management of an undisciplined rabble.

Now, when he had no idea what to do, help came from his own S & R, from the shortwave investigation team. "Something's going on inside, sir, but we don't know what it means. In the first minutes after it closed off the vision we could see it—the shadow of it, that is—gesturing like an angry man. Then it went back to the seat and made motions like pressing little buttons or flicking small levers—maybe. We can't be sure because with so much wood it's hard to get even a shadow picture. At any rate it made some adjustments because the carbon dioxide component in its air went up to eight per cent. The water vapour content seems to have increased, too, and the temperature has risen from thirty-five degrees to forty-six."

"Hothouse conditions!"

"Super-hothouse, sir."

"What's he up to? Forcing his growth?"

"We think more likely some other growth it carries in there. Maybe it has seeds in that thing like a tub at its feet. That's if the things make seeds."

Seeds or sprouts or tubers or buds . . . What do you do when you don't know what you're dealing with? How do you even think?

The diffident, careful tones of the radiographer said, "Sir, it doesn't want any part of us."

"Seems so."

"If it won't come to us, sir, shouldn't we go to it?"

Musad had no false pride. "You have a suggestion, Sergeant?"

"We could put a duroplastic tent round its ship, sir, big enough to allow a bunch of scientists to work in space suits, and fill it with an atmosphere matching the alien's."

"Then?"

"Cut a hole in the hull, sir, and get it out. Cut the ship in half if necessary."

That should at least keep everybody quiet until the next decision—except, perhaps, the alien—and anything he did would be marginally preferable to stalemate. And—oh, God!—he would have to decide who to allow into the tent and who must wait his or her turn.

He noted the Sergeant's name; one man at least was thinking while the rest boiled and complained. Yet he hesitated to give a command which in itself would be controversial.

He was still hesitating when the Analysis team gave an update: "It hasn't moved from the chair in two hours. Now chest movement has ceased; it is no longer breathing. It is probably dead."

That settled it. He ordered positioning of the tent and matching of atmospheres. That done, they must recover the body before serious deterioration set in.

Fernix was not dead. Not quite. The complex overlapping of birth and death made the passing of his kind a drawnout experience.

Fully aerated, he had ceased to breathe. The new ones in his lower limbs drew their nourishment from the mulch and no longer needed him, were in the process of detaching themselves. When they dropped free his life's duty, life's story, life's meaning would be complete . . .

. . . save for the one thing more, planned and prepared.

Now he could only wait with tentacle/finger curled for tightening, remaining perfectly still, having no reason to move, conserving strength for the final action.

His quietly sinking senses told him dully of sounds outside the pod and a fading curiosity wondered what they did out there. He thought of activating hull vision but the thought slipped away.

A sword of white fire cut a section from the hull alongside the control panels a long armslength from him and he was aware, without reacting as alertness ebbed (only the last command holding strength for its moment) of a suited figure entering the pod, followed by another. And another.

Red-Bloods. He no longer hated or cared. They would be dealt with.

One knelt by his lower limbs and unintelligible sounds dribbled from the grille in its helmet. He could not tell what it did.

Came the Last Pain, the splitting of cleavage lines in his bud sheath as the death flower swelled and bloomed from his ruined head.

At the moment of brain death his body obeyed the command stored in its nervous system for this moment. The curled tentacle/finger retracted, giving the computer its last command.

Under the tent the science teams went at it with a will. A small piece of timber was carved, with unexpected difficulty, from the alien craft's hull and rushed to a laboratory. The preliminary report came very quickly: ". . . a technique of molecular fusion—everything packed tight in cross-bonded grids. Not brittle but elastic beyond anything you'd believe. Take a real explosive wallop to do more than make it quiver and settle back."

The ceramic jet lining seemed impervious to common cutting methods and nobody wanted to use force at this stage. Soft radiation told little and they agreed that hard radiation should not be risked until they had found a means of excising small samples.

Chemanalysis had managed to create a computer mockup of the contents of the fuel tank, derived from hazy shortwave and sonar pictures, and was excited by a vision of complex molecular structures which promised incredible power output but must remain illogical until their catalysts were derived.

Carbon Dating, on safer ground with a piece of timber more or less analysed, certified the ship eight thousand years old, give or take a hundred, which made no sense at all of the presence of a living thing within.

Well, it had been living, in some fashion, perhaps still was—in some fashion. But, centuries?

Then the section of hull was cut out and the first group went in. There was surprisingly little to see. The cabin was small because most of the vessel's volume was fuel storage and the living space was parsimoniously uncluttered. There was a timber panel with wooden keys mid-mounted like tiny seesaws, which might be on-off controls, another console-type installation that could reasonably be a keyboard and clusters of incomprehensible recording instruments—some circular, some square and some like bent thermometers. There was also a sort of dashboard set with small levers, badly smashed.

Ecologist Anne Spriggs of Waterloo, Iowa, surveyed the alien with the despair of a preserver arrived too late. The creature was an unpleasant sight, its grey and green skin muted in death to patched and streaky brown, its slender body collapsed upon itself until it resembled nothing so much as a stick-figure doll. It had died with a tentacle resting loosely round one of the on-off seesaw controls.

A tiny movement, low down, brought her kneeling cumbersomely to scrutinize the container of mulch on the floor beneath the creature's lower limbs. The limbs hung oddly above it, their exposed, footless termini lighter coloured than the body, as if only recently exposed. Broken off? Cut off? How and why?

Several brown sticks lay on the surface of the mulch. One of them wriggled. Despite an instant revulsion she reached a gloved hand to pick it up. It was a tuber of some kind, like a brown artichoke formed fortuitously with nubs for vestigial arms and legs and head, and spots for eyes.

Musad spoke in her helmet. "What have you there, Anne?"

"I think it's an embryo alien. It's like—" she shrugged and held it up.

He suggested, "A mandrake."

That was a somehow nasty idea, smelling of small evil.

A rending crack from the dead creature itself startled the suited figures crowding into the hull and those who watched through screens.

They were offered a miracle. The excrescence on the thing's skull opened flaps like huge sepals and a blood-red crimson bolt shot a metre's length of unfolding bloom free of the body. It unfurled not a single flower but a clustered dozen packed in and on each other, each opening the flared trumpet of a monstrous lily.

The flowers expanded in a drunken ecstasy of growth, bending down and over the dead thing that fed them until it was wrapped in a shroud of blood. From the hearts of the trumpets rose green stamens like spears, each crowned with a golden magnet of pollen.

And not another, Anne thought, for such a flourish of procreation to attract and join.

In the surprised stillness someone, somewhere, whistled softly and another hissed an indrawn breath of wonder. Melanie's voice spoke from her office deep in the moonlet, Breton roughness smoothed in awe; "I have never seen so lovely a thing."

An unidentified voice said, "Like a salute from somewhere out there."

And that, Musad thought, would be the line the media would fall on with crocodile tears: A Dying Salute From Infinity . . .

Then Anne Spriggs said with a touch of panic, "It moved!"

"What moved?"

"The body. It moved its hand. On the lever."

"A natural contraction," Musad said. "The whole external form appears to have shrunk."

Fernix had placed a slight delay on the ignition. He wanted the Red-Bloods to see his derisive flowering but he also wanted to be decently dead before the fury struck.

When the fuel spark finally leapt the ignition gap his life was over; he had timed his going with dignity. Home World would have honoured him.

The jet roared, filling the scow's hold with a sea of fire before the craft skidded across the floor to crash through the soft steel of the imprisoning hull.

Those outside the scow had a microsecond's view of death in a blinding, incandescent torpedo that struck the rock wall of the Maintenance Cavern and disintegrated. The cloudburst of fuel from the shattered tank burgeoned in a twenty thousand degree ball of fire, engulfing and destroying the watchers in a hell-breath and licking its tongues of bellowing flame into the adjoining corridors and tunnels, a monstrous blast of heat driving death before it.

Thirty-seven scientists died and more than three hundred general personnel. Nearly a thousand others suffered serious burns.

The material damage ran to the total of a dozen national debts and the lawsuits of the private companies on Phobos made the fortunes of the lawyers on both sides.

Heads fell on the political chopping block, Musad's first among the offerings to the smug virtue of scapegoating.

First contact between intelligent cultures had been made.

NONE SO BLIND

Joe Haldeman

Here's a sly and fascinating little story that examines the personal *cost* of that high-tech competitive Edge we'd all like to have . . .

Born in Oklahoma City, Oklahoma, Joe Haldeman took a BS degree in physics and astronomy from the University of Maryland, and did postgraduate work in mathematics and computer science. But his plans for a career in science were cut short by the U.S. Army, which sent him to Vietnam in 1968 as a combat engineer. Seriously wounded in action, Haldeman returned home in 1969 and began to write. He sold his first story to *Galaxy* in 1969, and by 1976 had garnered both the Nebula Award and the Hugo Award for his famous novel *The Forever War*, one of the landmark books of the '70s. He took another Hugo Award in 1977 for his story "Tricentennial," won the Rhysling Award in 1983 for the best science fiction poem of the year (although usually thought of primarily as a "hard-science" writer, Haldeman is, in fact, also an accomplished poet, and has sold poetry to most of the major professional markets in the genre), and won both the Nebula and the Hugo Award in 1991 for the novella version of "The Hemingway Hoax." His other books include a mainstream novel, *War Year*, the SF novels *Mindbridge*, *All My Sins Remembered*, *There Is No Darkness* (written with his brother, SF writer Jack C. Haldeman II) *Worlds*, *Worlds Apart*, *Buying Time*, and *The Hemingway Hoax*, the "techno-thriller" *Tools of the Trade*, the collections *Infinite Dreams* and *Dealing in Futures*, and, as editor, the anthologies *Study War No More*, *Cosmic Laughter*, and *Nebula Award Stories Seventeen*. His most recent books are the SF novel *Worlds Enough and Time* and a new collection, *Vietnam and Other Alien Worlds*. Upcoming is a major new mainstream novel, *1968*. He has had stories in our First, Third, Eighth, Tenth, and Eleventh Annual Collections. Haldeman lives part of the year in Boston, where he teaches writing at the Massachusetts Institute of Technology, and the rest of the year in Florida, where he and his wife Gay make their home.

It all started when Cletus Jefferson asked himself "Why aren't all blind people geniuses?" Cletus was only thirteen at the time, but it was a good question, and he would work on it for fourteen more years, and then change the world forever.

Young Jefferson was a polymath, an autodidact, a nerd literally without peer. He had a chemistry set, a microscope, a telescope, and several computers, some of them bought with paper route money. Most of his income was from education, though: teaching his classmates not to draw to inside straights.

Not even nerds, not even nerds who are poker players nonpareil, not even nerdish poker players who can do differential equations in their heads, are immune to Cupid's darts and the sudden storm of testosterone that will accompany those missiles at the age of thirteen. Cletus knew that he was ugly and his mother dressed him funny. He was also short and pudgy and could not throw a ball in any direction. None of this bothered him until his ductless glands started cooking up chemicals that weren't in his chemistry set.

So Cletus started combing his hair and wearing clothes that mismatched according to fashion, but he was still short and pudgy and irregular of feature. He was also the youngest person in his school, even though he was a senior—and the only black person there, which was a factor in Virginia in 1994.

Now if love were sensible, if the sexual impulse was ever tempered by logic, you would expect that Cletus, being Cletus, would assess his situation and go off in search of someone homely. But of course he didn't. He just jingled and clanked down through the Pachinko machine of adolescence, being rejected, at first glance, by every Mary and Judy and Jenny and Veronica in Known Space, going from the ravishing to the beautiful to the pretty to the cute to the plain to the "great personality," until the irresistible force of statistics brought him finally into contact with Amy Linderbaum, who could not reject him at first glance because she was blind.

The other kids thought it was more than amusing. Besides being blind, Amy was about twice as tall as Cletus and, to be kind, equally irregular of feature. She was accompanied by a guide dog who looked remarkably like Cletus, short and black and pudgy. Everybody was polite to her because she was blind and rich, but she was a new transfer student and didn't have any actual friends.

So along came Cletus, to whom Cupid had dealt only slings and arrows, and what might otherwise have been merely an opposites-attract sort of romance became an emotional and intellectual union that, in the next century, would power a social tsunami that would irreversibly transform the human condition. But first there was the violin.

Her classmates had sensed that Amy was some kind of nerd herself, as classmates will, but they hadn't figured out what kind yet. She was pretty fast with a computer, but you could chalk that up to being blind and actually needing the damned thing. She wasn't fanatical about it, nor about science or math or history or Star Trek or student government, so what the hell kind of nerd was she? It turns out that she was a music nerd, but at the time was too painfully shy to demonstrate it.

All Cletus cared about, initially, was that she lacked those pesky Y-chromosomes and didn't recoil from him: in the Venn diagram of the human race, she was the only member of that particular set. When he found out that she was actually smart as well, having read more books than most of her classmates put together, romance began to smolder in a deep and permanent place. That was even before the violin.

Amy liked it that Cletus didn't play with her dog and was straightforward in his curiosity about what it was like to be blind. She could assess people pretty well from their voices: after one sentence, she knew that he was young, black, shy, nerdly, and not from Virginia. She could tell from his inflection that either he was unattractive or he thought he was. She was six years older than him and white and twice his size, but otherwise they matched up pretty well, and they started keeping company in a big way.

Among the few things that Cletus did not know anything about was music. That the other kids wasted their time memorizing the words to inane top-40 songs was proof of intellectual dysfunction if not actual lunacy. Furthermore, his parents had always been fanatical devotees of opera. A universe bounded on one end by puerile mumblings about unrequited love and on the other by foreigners screaming in agony was not a universe that Cletus desired to explore. Until Amy picked up her violin.

They talked constantly. They sat together at lunch and met between classes. When the weather was good, they sat outside before and after school and talked. Amy asked her chauffeur to please be ten or fifteen minutes late picking her up.

So after about three weeks' worth of the fullness of time, Amy asked Cletus to come over to her house for dinner. He was a little hesitant, knowing that her parents were rich, but he was also curious about that life style and, face it, was smitten enough that he would have walked off a cliff if she asked him nicely. He even used some computer money to buy a nice suit, a symptom that caused his mother to grope for the Valium.

The dinner at first was awkward. Cletus was bewildered by the arsenal of silverware and all the different kinds of food that didn't look or taste like food. But he had known it was going to be a test, and he always did well on tests, even when he had to figure out the rules as he went along.

Amy had told him that her father was a self-made millionaire; his fortune had come from a set of patents in solid-state electronics. Cletus had therefore spent a Saturday at the University library, first searching patents and then reading selected texts, and he was ready at least for the father. It worked very well. Over soup, the four of them talked about computers. Over the calimari cocktail, Cletus and Mr. Linderbaum had it narrowed down to specific operating systems and partitioning schemata. With the Beef Wellington, Cletus and "Call-me-Lindy" were talking quantum electrodynamics; with the salad they were on an electron cloud somewhere, and by the time the nuts were served, the two nuts at that end of the table were talking in Boolean algebra while Amy and her mother exchanged knowing sighs and hummed snatches of Gilbert and Sullivan.

By the time they retired to the music room for coffee, Lindy liked Cletus very much, and the feeling was mutual, but Cletus didn't know how much he liked Amy, *really* liked her, until she picked up the violin.

It wasn't a Strad—she was promised one if and when she graduated from Juilliard—but it had cost more than the Lamborghini in the garage, and she was not only worth it, but equal to it. She picked it up and tuned it quietly while her mother sat down at an electronic keyboard next to the grand piano, set it to "harp," and began the simple arpeggio that a musically sophisticated person would recognize as the introduction to the violin showpiece *Méditation* from Massenet's *Thaïs*.

Cletus had turned a deaf ear to opera for all his short life, so he didn't know the back-story of transformation and transcending love behind this intermezzo, but he did know that his girlfriend had lost her sight at the age of five, and the next year—the year he was born!—was given her first violin. For thirteen years she had been using it to say what she would not say with her voice, perhaps to see what she could not see with her eyes, and on the deceptively simple romantic matrix that Massenet built to present the beautiful courtesan Thaïs gloriously reborn as the bride of Christ, Amy forgave her Godless universe for taking her sight, and praised it for what she was given in return, and she said this in a language that even Cletus could understand. He didn't cry very much, never had, but by the last high wavering note he was weeping into his hands, and he knew that if she wanted him, she could have him forever, and oddly enough, considering his age and what eventually happened, he was right.

He would learn to play the violin before he had his first doctorate, and during a lifetime of remarkable amity they would play together for ten thousand hours, but all of that would come after the big idea. The big idea—"Why aren't all blind people geniuses?"—was planted that very night, but it didn't start to sprout for another week.

Like most thirteen-year-olds, Cletus was fascinated by the human body, his own and others, but his study was more systematic than others' and, atypically, the organ that interested him most was the brain.

The brain isn't very much like a computer, although it doesn't do a bad job, considering that it's built by unskilled labor and programmed more by pure chance than anything else. One thing computers do a lot better than brains, though, is what Cletus and Lindy had been talking about over their little squids in tomato sauce: partitioning.

Think of the computer as a big meadow of green pastureland, instead of a little dark box full of number-clogged things that are expensive to replace, and that pastureland is presided over by a wise old magic shepherd who is not called a macroprogram. The shepherd stands on a hill and looks out over the pastureland, which is full of sheep and goats and cows. They aren't all in one homogenous mass, of course, since the cows would step on the lambs and kids and the goats would make everybody nervous, leaping and butting, so there are *partitions* of barbed wire that keep all the species separate and happy.

This is a frenetic sort of meadow, though, with cows and goats and sheep coming in and going out all the time, moving at about 3×10^8 meters per second, and if the partitions were all of the same size it would be a disaster, because sometimes there are no sheep at all, but lots of cows, who would be jammed in there hip to hip and miserable. But the shepherd, being wise, knows ahead of time how much space to allot to the various creatures and, being magic, can move barbed wire quickly without hurting himself or the animals. So each partition winds up marking a comfortable-sized space for each use. Your computer does that, too, but instead of barbed wire you see little rectangles or windows or file folders, depending on your computer's religion.

The brain has its own partitions, in a sense. Cletus knew that certain physical areas of the brain were associated with certain mental abilities, but it wasn't a simple matter of "music appreciation goes over there; long division in that corner.'' The brain is mushier than that. For instance, there are pretty well-defined partitions associated with linguistic functions, areas named after French and German brain people. If one of those areas is destroyed, by stroke or bullet or flung frying pan, the stricken person may lose the ability—reading or speaking or writing coherently—associated with the lost area.

That's interesting, but what is more interesting is that the lost ability sometimes comes back over time. Okay, you say, so the brain grew back—but it doesn't! You're born with all the brain cells you'll ever have. (Ask any child.) What evidently happens is that some part of the brain has been sitting around as a kind of back-up, and after a while the wiring gets rewired and hooked into that back-up. The afflicted person can say his name, and then his wife's name, and then ''frying pan,'' and before you know it he's complaining about hospital food and calling a divorce lawyer.

So on that evidence, it would appear that the brain has a shepherd like the computer-meadow has, moving partitions around, but alas, no. Most of the time when some part of the brain ceases to function, that's the end of it. There may be acres and acres of fertile ground lying fallow right next door, but nobody in charge to make use of it—at least not consistently. The fact that it sometimes *did* work is what made Cletus ask ''Why aren't all blind people geniuses?''

Of course there have always been great thinkers and writers and composers who were blind (and in the twentieth century, some painters to whom eyesight was irrelevant), and many of them, like Amy with her violin, felt that their talent was a compensating gift. Cletus wondered whether there might be a literal truth to that, in the micro-anatomy of the brain. It didn't happen every time, or else all blind people *would* be geniuses. Perhaps it happened occasionally, through a mechanism like the one that helped people recover from strokes. Perhaps it could be made to happen.

Cletus had been offered scholarships at both Harvard and MIT, but he opted for Columbia, in order to be near Amy while she was studying at Juilliard. Columbia reluctantly allowed him a triple major in physiology, electrical engineering, and cognitive science, and he surprised everybody who knew him by doing only moderately well. The reason, it turned out, was that he was treating undergraduate work as a diversion at best; a necessary evil at worst. He was racing ahead of his studies in the areas that were important to him.

If he had paid more attention in trivial classes like history, like philosophy, things might have turned out differently. If he had paid attention to literature he might have read the story of Pandora.

Our own story now descends into the dark recesses of the brain. For the next ten years the main part of the story, which we will try to ignore after this paragraph, will involve Cletus doing disturbing intellectual tasks like cutting up dead brains, learning how to pronounce cholecystokinin, and sawing holes in people's skulls and poking around inside with live electrodes.

In the other part of the story, Amy also learned how to pronounce cholecystokinin, for the same reason that Cletus learned how to play the violin. Their love grew and mellowed, and at the age of 19, between his first doctorate and his M.D., Cletus paused long enough for them to be married and have a whirlwind honeymoon in Paris, where Cletus divided his time between the musky charms of his beloved and the sterile cubicles of Institute Marey, learning how squids learn things, which was by serotonin pushing adenylate cyclase to catalyze the synthesis of cyclic adenosine monophosphate in just the right place, but that's actually the main part of the story, which we have been trying to ignore, because it gets pretty gruesome.

They returned to New York, where Cletus spent eight years becoming a pretty good neurosurgeon. In his spare time he tucked away a doctorate in electrical engineering. Things began to converge.

At the age of thirteen, Cletus had noted that the brain used more cells collecting, handling, and storing visual images than it used for all the other senses combined. "Why aren't all blind people geniuses?" was just a specific case of the broader assertion, "The brain doesn't know how to make use of what it's got." His investigations over the next fourteen years were more subtle and complex than that initial question and statement, but he did wind up coming right back around to them.

Because the key to the whole thing was the visual cortex.

When a baritone saxophone player has to transpose sheet music from cello, he (few women are drawn to the instrument) merely pretends that the music is written in treble clef rather than bass, eyeballs it up an octave, and then plays without the octave key pressed down. It's so simple a child could do it, if a child wanted to play such a huge, ungainly instrument. As his eye dances along the little fenceposts of notes, his fingers automatically perform a one-to-one transformation that is the theoretical equivalent of adding and subtracting octaves, fifths, and thirds, but all of the actual mental work is done when he looks up in the top right corner of the first page and says, "Aw hell. Cello again." Cello parts aren't that interesting to saxophonists.

But the eye is the key, and the visual cortex is the lock. When blind Amy "sight-reads" for the violin, she has to stop playing and feel the Braille notes with her left hand. (Years of keeping the instrument in place while she does this has made her neck muscles so strong that she can crack a walnut between her chin and shoulder.) The visual cortex is not involved, of course; she "hears" the mute notes of a phrase with her fingertips, temporarily memorizing them, and then plays them over and over until she can add that phrase to the rest of the piece.

Like most blind musicians, Amy had a very good "ear"; it actually took her less time to memorize music by listening to it repeatedly, rather than reading, even with fairly complex pieces. (She used Braille nevertheless for serious work, so she could isolate the composer's intent from the performer's or conductor's phrasing decisions.)

She didn't really miss being able to sight-read in a conventional way. She wasn't even sure what it would be like, since she had never seen sheet music before she lost her sight, and in fact had only a vague idea of what a printed page of writing looked like.

So when her father came to her in her thirty-third year and offered to buy her the chance of a limited gift of sight, she didn't immediately jump at it. It was expensive and risky and grossly deforming: implanting miniaturized video cameras in her eyesockets and wiring them up to stimulate her dormant optic nerves. What if it made her only half blind, but also blunted her musical ability? She knew how other people read music, at least in theory, but after a quarter-century of doing without the skill, she wasn't sure that it would do much for her. It might make her tighten up.

Besides, most of her concerts were done as charities to benefit organizations for the blind or for special education. Her father argued that she would be even more effective in those venues as a recovered blind person. Still she resisted.

Cletus said he was cautiously for it. He said he had reviewed the literature and talked to the Swiss team who had successfully done the implants on dogs and primates. He said he didn't think she would be harmed by it even if the experiment failed. What he didn't say to Amy or Lindy or anybody was the grisly Frankensteinian truth: that he was himself behind the experiment; that it had nothing to do with restoring sight; that the little video cameras would never even be hooked up. They were just an excuse for surgically removing her eyeballs.

Now a normal person would have extreme feelings about popping out some-body's eyeballs for the sake of science, and even more extreme feelings on learning that it was a husband wanting to do it to his wife. Of course Cletus was far from being normal in any respect. To his way of thinking, those eyeballs were useless vestigial appendages that blocked surgical access to the optic nerves, which would be his conduits through the brain to the visual cortex. *Physical* conduits, through which incredibly tiny surgical instruments would be threaded. But we have promised not to investigate that part of the story in detail.

The end result was not grisly at all. Amy finally agreed to go to Geneva, and Cletus and his surgical team (all as skilled as they were unethical) put her through three 20-hour days of painstaking but painless microsurgery, and when they took the bandages off and adjusted a thousand-dollar wig (for they'd had to go in behind as well as through the eyesockets), she actually looked more attractive than when they had started. That was partly because her actual hair had always been a disaster. And now she had glass baby-blues instead of the rather scary opalescence of her natural eyes. No Buck Rogers TV cameras peering out at the world.

He told her father that that part of the experiment hadn't worked, and the six Swiss scientists who had been hired for the purpose agreed.

"They're lying," Amy said. "They never intended to restore my sight. The sole intent of the operations was to subvert the normal functions of the visual cortex in such a way as to give me access to the unused parts of my brain." She faced the sound of her husband's breathing, her blue eyes looking beyond him. "You have succeeded beyond your wildest expectations."

Amy had known this as soon as the fog of drugs from the last operation had lifted. Her mind started making connections, and those connections made connections, and so on at a geometrical rate of growth. By the time they had finished putting her wig on, she had reconstructed the entire microsurgical proce-dure from her limited readings and conversations with Cletus. She had suggestions as to improving it, and was eager to go under and submit herself to further refinement.

As to her feelings about Cletus, in less time than it takes to read about it, she had gone from horror to hate to understanding to renewed love, and finally to an emotional condition beyond the ability of any merely natural language to express. Fortunately, the lovers did have Boolean algebra and propositional calculus at their disposal.

Cletus was one of the few people in the world she *could* love, or even talk to one-on-one, without condescending. His IQ was so high that its number would be meaningless. Compared to her, though, he was slow, and barely literate. It was not a situation he would tolerate for long.

The rest is history, as they say, and anthropology, as those of us left who read with our eyes must recognize every minute of every day. Cletus was the second person to have the operation done, and he had to accomplish it while on the run from medical ethics people and their policemen. There were four the next year, though, and twenty the year after that, and then 2000 and 20,000. Within a decade, people with purely intellectual occupations had no choice, or one choice: lose your eyes or lose your job. By then the "secondsight" operation was totally automated, totally safe.

It's still illegal in most countries, including the United States, but who is kidding whom? If your department chairman is secondsighted and you are not, do you think you'll get tenure? You can't even hold a conversation with a creature whose synapses fire six times as fast as yours, with whole encyclopedias of information instantly available. You are, like me, an intellectual throwback.

You may have a good reason for it, being a painter, an architect, a naturalist, or a trainer of guide dogs. Maybe you can't come up with the money for the operation, but that's a weak excuse, since it's trivially easy to get a loan against future earnings. Maybe there's a good medical reason for you not to lie down on that table and open your eyes for the last time.

I know Cletus and Amy through music. I was her keyboard professor once, at Juilliard, though now of course I'm not smart enough to teach her anything. They come to hear me play sometimes, in this rundown bar with its band of ageing firstsight musicians. Our music must seem boring, obvious, but they do us the favor of not joining in.

Amy was an innocent bystander in this sudden evolutionary explosion. And Cletus was, arguably, blinded by love.

The rest of us have to choose which kind of blindness to endure.

COCOON

Greg Egan

Only a few years into the decade, it's already a fairly safe bet to predict that Australian writer Greg Egan is going to be recognized (if indeed he hasn't *already* been so recognized) as one of the Big New Names to emerge in SF in the nineties. In the last few years, he has become a frequent contributor to *Interzone* and *Asimov's Science Fiction*, and has made sales as well as to *Pulphouse*, *Analog*, *Aurealis*, *Eidolon*, and other publications. Several of his stories have appeared in various "Best of the Year" series, including this one; in fact, he placed *two* stories in *both* our Eighth and Ninth Annual Collections—the first author ever to do that back-to-back in consecutive volumes; he has also had stories in our Tenth and Eleventh Annual Collections as well. His first novel, *Quarantine*, appeared in 1992 to wide critical acclaim, and was followed in 1994 by a second novel, *Permutation City*. Coming up is a collection of his short fiction, *Axiomatic*, and another novel, tentatively entitled *Distress*.

In the powerful story that follows—one of the year's most controversial—he spins a suspenseful and provocative tale of sexual politics, corporate intrigue, and high-tech eugenics in a troubled future Australia . . .

The explosion shattered windows hundreds of meters away, but started no fire. Later, I discovered that it had shown up on a seismograph at Macquarie University, fixing the time precisely: 3:52 A.M. Residents woken by the blast phoned emergency services within minutes, and our night shift operator called me just after four, but there was no point rushing to the scene when I'd only be in the way. I sat at the terminal in my study for almost an hour, assembling background data and monitoring the radio traffic on headphones, drinking coffee and trying not to type too loudly.

By the time I arrived, the local fire service contractors had departed, having certified that there was no risk of further explosions, but our forensic people were still poring over the wreckage, the electric hum of their equipment all but drowned out by birdsong. Lane Cove was a quiet, leafy suburb, mixed residential and high-tech industrial, the lush vegetation of corporate open spaces blending almost seamlessly into the adjacent national park that straddled the Lane Cove River. The map of the area on my car terminal had identified suppliers of laboratory reagents and pharmaceuticals, manufacturers of precision instruments for scientific and aerospace applications, and no less than twenty-seven biotechnology firms—including Life Enhancement International, the erstwhile sprawling concrete building now reduced to a collection of white powdery blocks clustered around twisted reinforcement rods. The exposed steel glinted in the early light, disconcertingly pristine; the building was only three years old. I could understand why the forensic team had ruled out an accident at their first glance; a few drums of organic solvent could not have done anything remotely like *this*. Nothing legally stored in a residential zone could reduce a modern building to rubble in a matter of seconds.

I spotted Janet Lansing as I left my car. She was surveying the ruins with an expression of stoicism, but she was hugging herself. Mild shock, probably. She had no other reason to be chilly; it had been stinking hot all night, and the temperature was already climbing. Lansing was Director of the Lane Cove complex: forty-three years old, with a Ph.D. in molecular biology from Cambridge, and an M.B.A. from an equally reputable Japanese virtual university. I'd had my knowledge miner extract her details, and photo, from assorted databases before I'd left home.

I approached her and said, "James Glass, Nexus Investigations." She frowned at my business card, but accepted it, then glanced at the technicians trawling their gas chromatographs and holography equipment around the perimeter of the ruins.

"They're yours, I suppose?"

"Yes. They've been here since four."

She smirked slightly. "What happens if I give the job to someone else? And charge the lot of you with trespass?"

"If you hire another company, we'll be happy to hand over all the samples and data we've collected."

She nodded distractedly. "I'll hire you, of course. Since four? I'm impressed. You've even arrived before the insurance people." As it happened, LEI's "insurance people" owned 49 percent of Nexus, and would stay out of the way until we were finished, but I didn't see any reason to mention that. Lansing added sourly, "Our so-called security firm only worked up the courage to phone me half an hour ago. Evidently a fiber-optic junction box was sabotaged, disconnecting the whole area. They're supposed to send in patrols in the event of equipment failure, but apparently they didn't bother."

I grimaced sympathetically. "What exactly were you people making here?"

"Making? Nothing. We did no manufacturing; this was pure R & D."

In fact, I'd already established that LEI's factories were all in Thailand and Indonesia, with the head office in Monaco, and research facilities scattered around the world. There's a fine line, though, between demonstrating that the facts are at your fingertips, and unnerving the client. A total stranger *ought* to make at least one trivial wrong assumption, ask at least one misguided question. I always do.

"So what were you researching and developing?"

"That's commercially sensitive information."

I took my notepad from my shirt pocket and displayed a standard contract, complete with the usual secrecy provisions. She glanced at it, then had her own computer scrutinize the document. Conversing in modulated infrared, the machines rapidly negotiated the fine details. My notepad signed the agreement electronically on my behalf, and Lansing's did the same, then they both chimed happily in unison to let us know that the deal had been concluded.

Lansing said, "Our main project here was engineering improved syncytiotrophoblastic cells." I smiled patiently, and she translated for me. "Strengthening the barrier between the maternal and fetal blood supplies. Mother and fetus don't share blood directly, but they exchange nutrients and hormones across the placental barrier. The trouble is, all kinds of viruses, toxins, pharmaceuticals and illicit drugs can also cross over. The natural barrier cells didn't evolve to cope with AIDS, fetal alcohol syndrome, cocaine-addicted babies, or the next thalidomidelike disaster. We're aiming for a single intravenous injection of a gene-tailoring vector, which would trigger the formation of an extra layer of cells in the appropriate structures within the placenta, specifically designed to shield the fetal blood supply from contaminants in the maternal blood."

"A thicker barrier?"

"Smarter. More selective. More choosy about what it lets through. We know exactly what the developing fetus actually *needs* from the maternal blood. These gene-tailored cells would contain specific channels for transporting each of those substances. Nothing else would be allowed through."

"Very impressive." *A cocoon around the unborn child, shielding it from all of the poisons of modern society.* It sounded exactly like the kind of beneficent technology a company called Life Enhancement would be hatching in leafy Lane Cove. True, even a layman could spot a few flaws in the scheme. I'd heard that AIDS most often infected children during birth itself, not pregnancy—but presumably there were other viruses that crossed the placental barrier more frequently. I had no idea whether or not mothers at risk of giving birth to children stunted by alcohol or addicted to cocaine were likely to rush out *en masse* and have gene-tailored fetal barriers installed—but I could picture a strong demand from people terrified of food additives, pesticides, and pollutants. In the long term—if the system actually worked, and wasn't prohibitively expensive—it could even become a part of routine prenatal care.

Beneficent, and lucrative.

In any case—whether or not there were biological, economic, and social factors which might keep the technology from being a complete success . . . it was hard to imagine anyone objecting to *the principle of the thing.*

I said, "Were you working with animals?"

Lansing scowled. "Only early calf embryos, and disembodied bovine uteruses on tissue-support machines. If it was an animal rights group, they would have been better off bombing an abattoir."

"Mmm." In the past few years, the Sydney chapter of Animal Equality— the only group known to use such extreme methods—had concentrated on primate research facilities. They might have changed their focus, or been misinformed, but LEI still seemed like an odd target; there were plenty of laboratories widely known to use whole, live rats and rabbits as if they were disposable test tubes— many of them quite close by. "What about competitors?"

"No one else is pursuing this kind of product line, so far as I know. There's no race being run; we've already obtained individual patents for all of the essential components—the membrane channels, the transporter molecules—so any competitor would have to pay us license fees, regardless.''

''What if someone simply wanted to damage you, financially?''

''Then they should have bombed one of the factories instead. Cutting off our cash flow would have been the best way to hurt us; this laboratory wasn't earning a cent.''

''Your share price will still take a dive, won't it? Nothing makes investors nervous quite so much as terrorism.''

Lansing agreed, reluctantly. ''But then, whoever took advantage of that and launched a takeover bid would suffer the same taint, themselves. I don't deny that commercial sabotage takes place in this industry, now and then . . . but not on a level as crude as this. Genetic engineering is a subtle business. Bombs are for fanatics.''

Perhaps. But who would be fanatically opposed to the idea of shielding human embryos from viruses and poisons? Several religious sects flatly rejected any kind of modification to human biology . . . but the ones who employed violence were far more likely to have bombed a manufacturer of abortifacient drugs than a laboratory dedicated to the task of *safeguarding* the unborn child.

Elaine Chang, head of the forensic team, approached us. I introduced her to Lansing. Elaine said, ''It was a very professional job. If you'd hired demolition experts, they wouldn't have done a single thing differently. But then, they probably would have used identical software to compute the timing and placement of the charges.'' She held up her notepad, and displayed a stylized reconstruction of the building, with hypothetical explosive charges marked. She hit a button and the simulation crumbled into something very like the actual mess behind us.

She continued, ''Most reputable manufacturers these days imprint every batch of explosives with a trace element signature, which remains in the residue. We've linked the charges used here to a batch stolen from a warehouse in Singapore five years ago.''

I added, ''Which may not be a great help, though, I'm afraid. After five years on the black market, they could have changed hands a dozen times.''

Elaine returned to her equipment. Lansing was beginning to look a little dazed. I said, ''I'd like to talk to you again, later—but I am going to need a list of your employees, past and present, as soon as possible.''

She nodded, and hit a few keys on her notepad, transferring the list to mine. She said, ''Nothing's been lost, really. We had off-site backup for all of our data, administrative and scientific. And we have frozen samples of most of the cell lines we were working on, in a vault in Milson's Point.''

Commercial data backup would be all but untouchable, with the records stored in a dozen or more locations scattered around the world—heavily encrypted, of course. Cell lines sounded more vulnerable. I said, ''You'd better let the vault's operators know what's happened.''

''I've already done that; I phoned them on my way here.'' She gazed at the wreckage. ''The insurance company will pay for the rebuilding. In six months' time, we'll be back on our feet. So whoever did this was wasting their time. The work will go on.''

I said, "Who would want to stop it in the first place?"

Lansing's faint smirk appeared again, and I very nearly asked her what she found so amusing. But people often act incongruously in the face of disasters, large or small; nobody had died, she wasn't remotely hysterical, but it would have been strange if a setback like this hadn't knocked her slightly out of kilter.

She said, "*You* tell *me*. That's your job, isn't it?"

Martin was in the living room when I arrived home that evening. Working on his costume for the Mardi Gras. I couldn't imagine what it would look like when it was completed, but there were definitely feathers involved. Blue feathers. I did my best to appear composed, but I could tell from his expression that he'd caught an involuntary flicker of distaste on my face as he looked up. We kissed anyway, and said nothing about it.

Over dinner, though, he couldn't help himself.

"Fortieth anniversary this year, James. Sure to be the biggest yet. You could at least come and watch." His eyes glinted; he enjoyed needling me. We'd had this argument five years running, and it was close to becoming a ritual as pointless as the parade itself.

I said flatly, "Why would I want to watch ten thousand drag queens ride down Oxford Street, blowing kisses to the tourists?"

"Don't exaggerate. There'll only be a thousand men in drag, at most."

"Yeah, the rest will be in sequined jockstraps."

"If you actually came and watched, you'd discover that most people's imaginations have progressed far beyond that."

I shook my head, bemused. "If people's imaginations had *progressed*, there'd be no Gay and Lesbian Mardi Gras at all. It's a freak show, for people who want to live in a cultural ghetto. Forty years ago, it might have been . . . provocative. Maybe it did some good, back then. But *now*? What's the point? There are no laws left to change, there's no politics left to address. This kind of thing just recycles the same moronic stereotypes, year after year."

Martin said smoothly, "It's a public reassertion of the right to diverse sexuality. Just because it's no longer a *protest march* as well as a celebration doesn't mean it's irrelevant. And complaining about stereotypes is like . . . complaining about the characters in a medieval morality play. The costumes are code, shorthand. Give the great unwashed heterosexual masses credit for some intelligence; they don't watch the parade and conclude that the average gay man spends all his time in a gold lamé tutu. People aren't that literal-minded. They all learnt semiotics in kindergarten, they know how to decode the message."

"I'm sure they do. But it's still the wrong message: it makes exotic what ought to be mundane. Okay, people have the right to dress up any way they like and march down Oxford Street . . . but it means absolutely nothing to me."

"I'm not asking you to join in—"

"Very wise."

"—but if one hundred thousand straights can turn up, to show their support for the gay community, why can't you?"

I said wearily, "Because every time I hear the word *community*, I know I'm being manipulated. If there *is* such a thing as *the gay community*, I'm certainly not a part of it. As it happens, I don't want to spend my life watching *gay and lesbian* television channels, using *gay and lesbian* news systems . . . or going to *gay and lesbian* street parades. It's all so . . . proprietary. You'd think there was a multinational corporation who had the franchise rights on homosexuality. And if you don't *market the product* their way, you're some kind of second-class, inferior, bootleg, unauthorized queer.''

Martin cracked up. When he finally stopped laughing, he said, ''Go on. I'm waiting for you to get to the part where you say you're no more proud of being gay than you are of having brown eyes, or black hair, or a birthmark behind your left knee.''

I protested, ''That's true. Why should I be 'proud' of something I was born with? I'm not proud, *or* ashamed. I just *accept* it. And I don't have to join a parade to prove that.''

''So you'd rather we all stayed invisible?''

''*Invisible!* You're the one who told me that the representation rates in movies and TV last year were close to the true demographics. And if you hardly even *notice it* anymore when an openly gay or lesbian politician gets elected, that's because it's *no longer an issue.* To most people, now, it's about as significant as . . . being left or right handed.''

Martin seemed to find this suggestion surreal. ''Are you trying to tell me that it's now a *non-subject?* That the inhabitants of this planet are now absolutely impartial on the question of sexual preference? Your faith is touching—but . . .'' He mimed incredulity.

I said, ''We're equal before the law with any heterosexual couple, aren't we? And when was the last time you told someone you were gay and they so much as blinked? And yes, I know, there are dozens of countries where it's still illegal—along with joining the wrong political parties, or the wrong religions. Parades in Oxford Street aren't going to change *that.*''

''People are still bashed *in this city*. People are *still* discriminated against.''

''Yeah. And people are also shot dead in peak-hour traffic for playing the wrong music on their car stereos, or denied jobs because they live in the wrong suburbs. I'm not talking about the perfection of human nature. I just want you to acknowledge one tiny victory: leaving out a few psychotics, and a few fundamentalist bigots . . . most people *just don't care.*''

Martin said ruefully, ''If only that were true!''

The argument went on for more than an hour—ending in a stalemate, as usual. But then, neither one of us had seriously expected to change the other's mind.

I did catch myself wondering afterward, though, if I really believed all of my own optimistic rhetoric. *About as significant as being left or right handed?* Certainly, that was the line taken by most Western politicians, academics, essayists, talk show hosts, soap opera writers, and mainstream religious leaders . . . but the same people had been espousing equally high-minded principles of racial equality for decades, and the reality still hadn't entirely caught up on *that* front. I'd suffered very little discrimination, myself—by the time I reached high school, tolerance was hip, and I'd witnessed a constant stream of improvements since then . . . but how could I ever know precisely how much hidden prejudice remained? By interrogating my own straight friends? By reading the sociologists' latest attitude surveys? People will always tell you what they think you want to hear.

Still, it hardly seemed to matter. Personally, I could get by without the deep and sincere approval of every other member of the human race. Martin and I were lucky enough to have been born into a time and place where, in almost every tangible respect, we were treated as equal.

What more could anyone hope for?

In bed that night, we made love very slowly, at first just kissing and stroking each other's bodies for what seemed like hours. Neither of us spoke, and in the stupefying heat I lost all sense of belonging to any other time, any other reality. Nothing existed but the two of us; the rest of the world, the rest of my life, went spinning away into the darkness.

The investigation moved slowly. I interviewed every current member of LEI's workforce, then started on the long list of past employees. I still believed that commercial sabotage was the most likely explanation for such a professional job—but blowing up the opposition is a desperate measure; a little civilized espionage usually comes first. I was hoping that someone who'd worked for LEI might have been approached in the past and offered money for inside information—and if I could find just one employee who'd turned down a bribe, they might have learnt something useful from their contact with the presumed rival.

Although the Lane Cove facility had only been built three years before, LEI had operated a research division in Sydney for twelve years before that, in North Ryde, not far away. Many of the ex-employees from that period had moved interstate or overseas; quite a few had been transferred to LEI divisions in other countries. Still, almost no one had changed their personal phone numbers, so I had very little trouble tracking them down.

The exception was a biochemist named Catherine Mendelsohn; the number listed for her in the LEI staff records had been canceled. There were seventeen people with the same surname and initials in the national phone directory; none admitted to being Catherine Alice Mendelsohn, and none looked at all like the staff photo I had.

Mendelsohn's address in the Electoral Roll, an apartment in Newtown, matched the LEI records—but the same address was in the phone directory (and Electoral Roll) for Stanley Goh, a young man who told me that he'd never met Mendelsohn. He'd been leasing the apartment for the past eighteen months.

Credit rating databases gave the same out-of-date address. I couldn't access tax, banking, or utilities records without a warrant. I had my knowledge miner scan the death notices, but there was no match there.

Mendelsohn had worked for LEI until about a year before the move to Lane Cove. She'd been part of a team working on a gene-tailoring system for ameliorating menstrual side-effects, and although the Sydney division had always specialized in gynecological research, for some reason the project was about to be moved to Texas. I checked the industry publications; apparently, LEI had been rearranging all of its operations at the time, gathering together projects from around the globe into new multi-disciplinary configurations, in accordance with the latest fashionable theories of research dynamics. Mendelsohn had declined the transfer, and had been retrenched.

I dug deeper. The staff records showed that Mendelsohn had been questioned by security guards after being found on the North Ryde premises late at night, two days before her dismissal. Workaholic biotechnologists aren't uncommon, but starting the day at two in the morning shows exceptional dedication, especially when the company has just tried to shuffle you off to Amarillo. Having turned down the transfer, she must have known what was in store.

Nothing came of the incident, though. And even if Mendelsohn *had* been planning some minor act of sabotage, that hardly established any connection with a bombing four years later. She might have been angry enough to leak confidential information to one of LEI's rivals . . . but whoever had bombed the Lane Cove laboratory would have been more interested in someone who'd worked on the fetal barrier project itself—a project which had only come into existence a year after Mendelsohn had been sacked.

I pressed on through the list. Interviewing the ex-employees was frustrating; almost all of them were still working in the biotechnology industry, and they would have been an ideal group to poll on the question of *who would benefit most* from LEI's misfortune—but the confidentiality agreement I'd signed meant that I couldn't disclose anything about the research in question—not even to people working for LEI's other divisions.

The one thing which I *could* discuss drew a blank: if anyone had been offered a bribe, they weren't talking about it—and no magistrate was going to sign a warrant letting me loose on a fishing expedition through a hundred and seventeen people's financial records.

Forensic examination of the ruins, and the sabotaged fiber-optic exchange, had yielded the usual catalogue of minutiae which might eventually turn out to be invaluable—but none of it was going to conjure up a suspect out of thin air.

Four days after the bombing—just as I found myself growing desperate for a fresh angle on the case—I had a call from Janet Lansing.

The backup samples of the project's gene-tailored cell lines had been destroyed.

The vault in Milson's Point turned out to be directly underneath a section of the Harbor Bridge—built right into the foundations on the north shore. Lansing hadn't arrived yet, but the head of security for the storage company, an elderly man called David Asher, showed me around. Inside, the traffic was barely audible, but the vibration coming through the floor felt like a constant mild earthquake. The place was cavernous, dry and cool. At least a hundred cryogenic freezers were laid out in rows; heavily clad pipes ran between them, replenishing their liquid nitrogen.

Asher was understandably morose, but cooperative. Celluloid movie film had been archived here, he explained, before everything went digital; the present owners specialized in biological materials. There were no guards physically assigned to the vault, but the surveillance cameras and alarm systems looked impressive, and the structure itself must have been close to impregnable.

Lansing had phoned the storage company, Biofile, on the morning of the bombing. Asher confirmed that he'd sent someone down from their North Sydney office to check the freezer in question. Nothing was missing—but he'd promised to boost security measures immediately. Because the freezers were supposedly tamper-proof, and individually locked, clients were normally allowed access to the vault at their convenience, monitored by the surveillance cameras, but otherwise unsupervised. Asher had promised Lansing that, henceforth, nobody would enter the building without a member of his staff to accompany them—and he claimed that nobody had been inside since the day of the bombing, anyway.

When two LEI technicians had arrived that morning to carry out an inventory, they'd found the expected number of culture flasks, all with the correct bar code labels, all tightly sealed—but the appearance of their contents was subtly wrong. The translucent frozen colloid was more opalescent than cloudy; an untrained eye might never have noticed the difference, but apparently it spoke volumes to the cognoscenti.

The technicians had taken a number of the flasks away for analysis; LEI were working out of temporary premises, a sub-leased corner of a paint manufacturer's quality control lab. Lansing had promised me preliminary test results by the time we met.

Lansing arrived, and unlocked the freezer. With gloved hands, she lifted a flask out of the swirling mist and held it up for me to inspect.

She said, "We've only thawed three samples, but they all look the same. The cells have been torn apart."

"How?" The flask was covered with such heavy condensation that I couldn't have said if it was empty or full, let alone *cloudy* or *opalescent*.

"It looks like radiation damage."

My skin crawled. I peered into the depths of the freezer; all I could make out were the tops of rows of identical flasks—*but if one of them had been spiked with a radioisotope . . .*

Lansing scowled. "Relax." She tapped a small electronic badge pinned to her lab coat, with a dull gray face like a solar cell: a radiation dosimeter. "*This* would be screaming if we were being exposed to anything significant. Whatever the source of the radiation was, it's no longer in here—and it hasn't left the walls glowing. Your future offspring are safe."

I let that pass. "You think all the samples will turn out to be ruined? You won't be able to salvage anything?"

Lansing was stoical as ever. "It looks that way. There are some elaborate techniques we could use, to try to repair the DNA—but it will probably be easier to synthesize fresh DNA from scratch, and re-introduce it into unmodified bovine placental cell lines. We still have all the sequence data; that's what matters in the end."

I pondered the freezer's locking system, the surveillance cameras. "Are you sure that the source was *inside* the freezer? Or could the damage have been done without actually breaking in—right through the walls?"

She thought it over. "Maybe. There's not much metal in these things; they're mostly plastic foam. But I'm not a radiation physicist; your forensic people will probably be able to give you a better idea of what happened, once they've checked out the freezer itself. If there's damage to the polymers in the foam, it might be possible to use that to reconstruct the geometry of the radiation field."

A forensic team was on its way. I said, "How would they have done it? Walked casually by, and just—?"

"Hardly. A source which could do this in one quick hit would have been unmanageable. It's far more likely to have been a matter of weeks, or months, of low-level exposure."

"So they must have smuggled some kind of device into *their own freezer*, and aimed it at yours? But then . . . we'll be able to trace the effects right back to the source, won't we? So how could they have hoped to get away with it?"

Lansing said, "It's even simpler than that. We're talking about a modest amount of a gamma-emitting isotope, not some billion-dollar particle-beam weapon. The effective range would be a couple of meters, at most. If it *was* done from the outside, you've just narrowed down your suspect list to two." She thumped the freezer's left neighbor in the aisle, then did the same to the one on the right—and said, "Aha."

"What?"

She thumped them both again. The second one sounded hollow. I said, "No liquid nitrogen? It's not in use?"

Lansing nodded. She reached for the handle.

Asher said, "I don't think—"

The freezer was unlocked, the lid swung open easily. Lansing's badge started beeping—and, worse, *there was something in there, with batteries and wires. . . .*

I don't know what kept me from knocking her to the floor—but Lansing, untroubled, lifted the lid all the way. She said mildly, "Don't panic; this dose rate's nothing. Threshold of detectable."

The thing inside looked superficially like a home-made bomb—but the batteries and timer chip I'd glimpsed were wired to a heavy-duty solenoid, which was part of an elaborate shutter mechanism on one side of a large, metallic gray box.

Lansing said, "Cannibalized medical source, probably. You know these things have turned up in *garbage dumps*?" She unpinned her badge and waved it near the box; the pitch of the alarm increased, but only slightly. "Shielding seems to be intact."

I said, as calmly as possible, "These people have access to *high explosives*. You don't have any idea what the fuck might be in there, or what it's wired up to do. This is the point where we walk out, quietly, and leave it to the bomb-disposal robots."

She seemed about to protest, but then she nodded contritely. The three of us went up onto the street, and Asher called the local terrorist services contractor. I suddenly realized that they'd have to divert all traffic from the bridge. The Lane Cove bombing had received some perfunctory media coverage—but *this* would lead the evening news.

I took Lansing aside. "They've destroyed your laboratory. They've wiped out your cell lines. Your data may be almost impossible to locate and corrupt—so the next logical target is you and your employees. Nexus doesn't provide protective services, but I can recommend a good firm."

I gave her the phone number; she accepted it with appropriate solemnity. "So you finally believe me? These people aren't commercial saboteurs. They're dangerous fanatics."

I was growing impatient with her vague references to "fanatics." "Who exactly do you have in mind?"

She said darkly, "We're tampering with certain . . . *natural processes*. You can draw your own conclusions, can't you?"

There was no logic to that at all. God's Image would probably want to *force* all pregnant women with HIV infections, or drug habits, to use the cocoon; they wouldn't try to bomb the technology out of existence. Gaia's Soldiers were more concerned with genetically engineered crops and bacteria than trivial modifications to insignificant species like humans—and they wouldn't have used *radioisotopes* if the fate of the planet depended on it. Lansing was beginning to sound thoroughly paranoid—although in the circumstances, I couldn't really blame her.

I said, "I'm not drawing any conclusions. I'm just advising you to take some sensible precautions, because we have no way of knowing how far this might escalate. But . . . Biofile must lease freezer space to every one of your competitors. A commercial rival would have found it a thousand times easier than any hypothetical sect member to get into the vault to plant that thing."

A gray armor-plated van screeched to a halt in front of us; the back door swung up, ramps slid down, and a squat, multi-limbed robot on treads descended. I raised a hand in greeting and the robot did the same; the operator was a friend of mine.

Lansing said, "You may be right. But then, there's nothing to stop a terrorist from having a day job in biotechnology, is there?"

The device turned out not to be booby-trapped at all—just rigged to spray LEI's precious cells with gamma rays for six hours, starting at midnight, every night. Even in the unlikely event that someone had come into the vault in the early hours and wedged themselves into the narrow gap between the freezers, the dose they received would not have been much; as Lansing had suggested, it was the cumulative effect over months which had done the damage. The radioisotope in the box was cobalt 60, almost certainly a decommissioned medical source—grown too weak for its original use, but still too hot to be discarded—stolen from a "cooling off" site. No such theft had been reported, but Elaine Chang's assistants were phoning around the hospitals, trying to persuade them to re-inventory their concrete bunkers.

Cobalt 60 was dangerous stuff—but fifty milligrams in a carefully shielded container wasn't exactly a tactical nuclear weapon. The news systems went berserk, though: ATOMIC TERRORISTS STRIKE HARBOR BRIDGE, et cetera. If LEI's enemies *were* activists, with some "moral cause" which they hoped to set before the public, they clearly had the worst PR advisers in the business. Their prospects of gaining the slightest sympathy had vanished, the instant the first news reports had mentioned the word *radiation*.

My secretarial software issued polite statements of ''No comment'' on my behalf, but camera crews began hovering outside my front door, so I relented and mouthed a few news-speak sentences for them which meant essentially the same thing. Martin looked on, amused—and then I looked on, astonished, as Janet Lansing's own doorstop media conference appeared on TV.

''These people are clearly ruthless. Human life, the environment, radioactive contamination . . . all mean nothing to them.''

''Do you have any idea who might be responsible for this outrage, Dr. Lansing?''

''I can't disclose that, yet. All I can reveal, right now, is that our research is at the very cutting edge of preventative medicine—and I'm not at all surprised that there are powerful vested interests working against us.''

Powerful vested interests? What was *that* meant to be code for—if not the rival biotechnology firm whose involvement she kept denying? No doubt she had her eye on the publicity advantages of being the victim of ATOMIC TERRORISTS—but I thought she was wasting her breath. In two or more years' time, when the product finally hit the market, the story would be long forgotten.

After some tricky jurisdictional negotiations, Asher finally sent me six months' worth of files from the vault's surveillance cameras—all that they kept. The freezer in question had been unused for almost two years; the last authorized tenant was a small IVF clinic which had gone bankrupt. Only about 60 percent of the freezers were currently leased, so it wasn't particularly surprising that LEI had had a conveniently empty neighbor.

I ran the surveillance files through image-processing software, in the hope that someone might have been caught in the act of opening the unused freezer. The search took almost an hour of supercomputer time—and turned up precisely nothing. A few minutes later, Elaine Chang popped her head into my office to say that she'd finished her analysis of the damage to the freezer walls: the nightly irradiation had been going on for between eight and nine months.

Undeterred, I scanned the files again, this time instructing the software to assemble a gallery of every individual sighted inside the vault.

Sixty-two faces emerged. I put company names to all of them, matching the times of each sighting to Biofile's records of the use of each client's electronic key. No obvious inconsistencies showed up; nobody had been seen inside who hadn't used an authorized key to gain access—and the same people had used the same keys, again and again.

I flicked through the gallery, wondering what to do next. *Search for anyone glancing slyly in the direction of the radioactive freezer?* The software could have done it—but I wasn't quite ready for barrel-scraping efforts like that.

I came to a face which looked familiar: a blonde woman in her midthirties, who'd used the key belonging to Federation Centennial Hospital's Oncology Research Unit, three times. I was certain that I knew her, but I couldn't recall where I'd seen her before. It didn't matter; after a few seconds' searching, I found a clear shot of the name badge pinned to her lab coat. All I had to do was zoom in.

The badge read: C. MENDELSOHN.

There was a knock on my open door. I turned from the screen; Elaine was back, looking pleased with herself.

She said, "We've finally found a place who'll own up to having lost some cobalt 60. What's more . . . the activity of our source fits their missing item's decay curve, exactly."

"So where was it stolen from?"

"Federation Centennial."

I phoned the Oncology Research Unit. Yes, Catherine Mendelsohn worked there—she'd done so for almost four years—but they couldn't put me through to her; she'd been on sick leave all week. They gave me the same canceled phone number as LEI—but a different address, an apartment in Petersham. The address wasn't listed in the phone directory; I'd have to go there in person.

A cancer research team would have no reason to want to harm LEI, but a commercial rival—with or without their own key to the vault—could still have paid Mendelsohn to do their work for them. It seemed like a lousy deal to me, whatever they'd offered her—if she was convicted, every last cent would be traced and confiscated—but bitterness over her sacking might have clouded her judgment.

Maybe. Or maybe that was all too glib.

I replayed the shots of Mendelsohn taken by the surveillance cameras. She did nothing unusual, nothing suspicious. She went straight to the ORU's freezer, put in whatever samples she'd brought, and departed. She didn't glance slyly in any direction at all.

The fact that she had been inside the vault—on legitimate business—proved nothing. The fact that the cobalt 60 had been stolen from the hospital where she worked could have been pure coincidence.

And anyone had the right to cancel their phone service.

I pictured the steel reinforcement rods of the Lane Cove laboratory, glinting in the sunlight.

On the way out, reluctantly, I took a detour to the basement. I sat at a console while the armaments safe checked my fingerprints, took breath samples and a retinal blood spectrogram, ran some perception-and-judgment response time tests, then quizzed me for five minutes about the case. Once it was satisfied with my reflexes, my motives, and my state of mind, it issued me a nine-millimeter pistol and a shoulder holster.

Mendelsohn's apartment block was a concrete box from the 1960s, front doors opening onto long shared balconies, no security at all. I arrived just after seven, to the smell of cooking and the sound of game show applause, wafting from a hundred open windows. The concrete still shimmered with the day's heat; three flights of stairs left me coated in sweat. Mendelsohn's apartment was silent, but the lights were on.

She answered the door. I introduced myself, and showed her my ID. She seemed nervous, but not surprised.

She said, "I still find it galling to have to deal with people like you."

"People like—?"

"I was opposed to privatizing the police force. I helped organize some of the marches."

She would have been fourteen years old at the time—a precocious political activist.

She let me in, begrudgingly. The living room was modestly furnished, with a terminal on a desk in one corner.

I said, "I'm investigating the bombing of Life Enhancement International. You used to work for them, up until about four years ago. Is that correct?"

"Yes."

"Can you tell me why you left?"

She repeated what I knew about the transfer of her project to the Amarillo division. She answered every question directly, looking me straight in the eye; she still appeared nervous, but she seemed to be trying to read some vital piece of information from my demeanor. *Wondering if I'd traced the cobalt?*

"What were you doing on the North Ryde premises at two in the morning, two days before you were sacked?"

She said, "I wanted to find out what LEI was planning for the new building. I wanted to know why they didn't want me to stick around."

"Your job was moved to Texas."

She laughed drily. "The work wasn't *that* specialized. I could have swapped jobs with someone who wanted to travel to the States. It would have been the perfect solution—and there would have been plenty of people more than happy to trade places with me. But no, that wasn't allowed."

"So . . . did you find the answer?"

"Not that night. But later, yes."

I said carefully, "So you knew what LEI was doing in Lane Cove?"

"Yes."

"How did you discover that?"

"I kept an ear to the ground. Nobody who'd stayed on would have told me directly, but word leaked out, eventually. About a year ago."

"*Three years after you'd left?* Why were you still interested? Did you think there was a market for the information?"

She said, "Put your notepad in the bathroom sink and run the tap on it."

I hesitated, then complied. When I returned to the living room, she had her face in her hands. She looked up at me grimly.

"*Why was I still interested?* Because I wanted to know why *every project* with any lesbian or gay team members was being transferred out of the division. I wanted to know if that was pure coincidence. Or not."

I felt a sudden chill in the pit of my stomach. I said, "If you had some problem with discrimination, there are avenues you could have—"

Mendelsohn shook her head impatiently. "LEI was never *discriminatory*. They didn't sack anyone who was willing to move—and they always transferred the entire team; there was nothing so crude as picking out *individuals* by sexual preference. And they had a rationalization for everything: projects were being re-grouped between divisions to facilitate 'synergistic cross-pollination.' And if that sounds like pretentious bullshit, it was—but it was plausible pretentious bullshit. Other corporations have adopted far more ridiculous schemes, in perfect sincerity.''

"But if it wasn't a matter of discrimination . . . why should LEI want to force people out of one particular division—?''

I think I'd finally guessed the answer, even as I said those words—but I needed to hear her spell it out, before I could really believe it.

Mendelsohn must have been practicing her version for non-biochemists; she had it down pat. ''When people are subject to *stress*—physical or emotional—the levels of certain substances in the bloodstream increase. Cortisol and adrenaline, mainly. Adrenaline has a rapid, short-term effect on the nervous system. Cortisol works on a much longer time frame, modulating all kinds of bodily processes, adapting them for hard times: injury, fatigue, whatever. If the stress is prolonged, someone's cortisol can be elevated for days, or weeks, or months.

"High enough levels of cortisol, in the bloodstream of a pregnant woman, can cross the placental barrier and interact with the hormonal system of the developing fetus. There are parts of the brain where embryonic development is switched into one of two possible pathways, by hormones released by the fetal testes or ovaries. The parts of the brain which control body image, and the parts which control sexual preference. Female embryos usually develop a brain wired with a self-image of a female body, and the strongest potential for sexual attraction toward males. Male embryos, vice versa. And it's the sex hormones in the fetal bloodstream which let the growing neurons *know* the gender of the embryo, and which wiring pattern to adopt.

"Cortisol can interfere with this process. The precise interactions are complex, but the ultimate effect depends on the timing; different parts of the brain are switched into gender-specific versions at different stages of development. So stress at different times during pregnancy leads to different patterns of sexual preference and body image in the child: homosexual, bisexual, transsexual.

"Obviously, a lot depends on the mother's biochemistry. Pregnancy *itself* is stressful—but everyone responds to that differently. The first sign that cortisol might have an effect came in studies in the 1980s, on the children of German women who'd been pregnant during the most intense bombing raids of World War II—when the stress was so great that the effect showed through despite individual differences. In the nineties, researchers thought they'd found a gene which determined male homosexuality . . . but it was always maternally inherited—and it turned out to be influencing *the mother's stress response*, rather than acting directly on the child.

"If maternal cortisol, and other stress hormones, were kept from reaching the fetus . . . then the gender of the brain would always match the gender of the body in every respect. All of the present variation would be wiped out.''

I was shaken, but I don't think I let it show. Everything she said rang true; I didn't doubt a word of it. I'd always known that sexual preference was decided before birth. I'd known that I was gay, myself, by the age of seven. I'd never sought out the elaborate biological details, though—because I'd never believed that the tedious mechanics of the process could ever matter to me. What turned my blood to ice was not finally learning *the neuroembryology of desire*. The shock was discovering that LEI planned to reach into the womb and take *control* of it.

I pressed on with the questioning in a kind of trance, putting my own feelings into suspended animation.

I said, "LEI's barrier is for filtering out *viruses and toxins*. You're talking about a natural substance which has been present for millions of years—"

"LEI's barrier will keep out everything they deem *non-essential*. The fetus doesn't *need* maternal cortisol in order to survive. If LEI doesn't explicitly include transporters for it, it won't get through. And I'll give you one guess what their plans are."

I said, "You're being paranoid. You think LEI would invest millions of dollars just to take part in a conspiracy to rid the world of homosexuals?"

Mendelsohn looked at me pityingly. "It's not a *conspiracy*. It's a *marketing opportunity*. LEI doesn't give a shit about the sexual politics. They could put in cortisol transporters, and sell the barrier as an anti-viral, anti-drug, anti-pollution screen. Or, they could leave them out, and sell it as all of that—plus a means of guaranteeing a heterosexual child. *Which do you think would earn the most money?*"

That question hit a nerve; I said angrily, "And you had so little faith in people's choice that you *bombed the laboratory* so that no one would ever have the chance to decide?"

Mendelsohn's expression turned stony. "I did *not* bomb LEI. Or irradiate their freezer."

"No? We've traced the cobalt 60 to Federation Centennial."

She looked stunned for a moment, then she said, "Congratulations. Six thousand other people work there, you know. I'm obviously not the only one of them who'd discovered what LEI is up to."

"You're the only one with access to the Biofile vault. What do you expect me to believe? That having learnt about this project, you were going to do absolutely nothing about it?"

"Of course not! And I still plan to publicize what they're doing. Let people know what it will mean. Try to get the issue debated before the product appears in a blaze of misinformation."

"You said you've known about the work for a year."

"Yes—and I've spent most of that time trying to verify all the facts, before opening my big mouth. Nothing would have been stupider than going public with half-baked rumors. I've only told about a dozen people so far, but we were going to launch a big publicity campaign to coincide with this year's Mardi Gras. Although now, with the bombing, everything's a thousand times more complicated." She spread her hands in a gesture of helplessness. "But we still have to do what we can, to try to keep the worst from happening."

"The worst?"

"Separatism. Paranoia. Homosexuality redefined as *pathological*. Lesbians and sympathetic straight women looking for their *own* technological means to *guarantee* the survival of the culture . . . while the religious far-right try to prosecute them for *poisoning their babies* . . . with a substance *God's* been happily 'poisoning' babies with for the last few thousand years! Sexual tourists traveling from wealthy countries where the technology is in use, to poorer countries where it isn't.''

I was sickened by the vision she was painting—but I pushed on. "These dozen friends of yours—?''

Mendelsohn said dispassionately, "Go fuck yourself. I've got nothing more to say to you. I've told you the truth. I'm not a criminal. And I think you'd better leave.''

I went to the bathroom and collected my notepad. In the doorway, I said, "If you're not a criminal, why are you so hard to track down?''

Wordlessly, contemptuously, she lifted her shirt and showed me the bruises below her rib cage—fading, but still an ugly sight. Whoever it was who'd beaten her—an ex-lover?—I could hardly blame her for doing everything she could to avoid a repeat performance.

On the stairs, I hit the REPLAY button on my notepad. The software computed the frequency spectrum for the noise of the running water, subtracted it out of the recording, and then amplified and cleaned up what remained. Every word of our conversation came through crystal clear.

From my car, I phoned a surveillance firm and arranged to have Mendelsohn kept under twenty-four-hour observation.

Halfway home, I stopped in a side street, and sat behind the wheel for ten minutes, unable to think, unable to move.

In bed that night, I asked Martin, "You're left-handed. How would you feel if no one was ever born left-handed again?''

"It wouldn't bother me in the least. Why?''

"You wouldn't think of it as a kind of . . . genocide?''

"Hardly. What's this all about?''

"Nothing. Forget it.''

"You're shaking.''

"I'm cold.''

"You don't feel cold to me.''

As we made love—tenderly, then savagely—I thought: *This is our language, this is our dialect. Wars have been fought over less. And if this language ever dies out, a people will have vanished from the face of the Earth.*

I knew I had to drop the case. If Mendelsohn was guilty, someone else could prove it. To go on working for LEI would destroy me.

Afterward, though . . . that seemed like sentimental bullshit. I belonged to no tribe. Every human being possessed their own sexuality—and when they died, it died with them. If no one was ever born gay again, it made no difference to *me*.

And if I dropped the case *because I was gay*, I'd be abandoning everything

I'd ever believed about my own equality, my own identity . . . not to mention giving LEI the chance to announce: *Yes, of course we hired an investigator without regard to sexual preference—but apparently, that was a mistake.*

Staring up into the darkness, I said, "Every time I hear the word *community*, I reach for my revolver."

There was no response; Martin was fast asleep. I wanted to wake him, I wanted to argue it all through, there and then—but I'd signed an agreement, I couldn't tell him a thing.

So I watched him sleep, and tried to convince myself that when the truth came out, he'd understand.

I phoned Janet Lansing, brought her up to date on Mendelsohn—and said coldly, "Why were you so coy? *'Fanatics'? 'Powerful vested interests'?* Are there some words you have trouble pronouncing?"

She'd clearly prepared herself for this moment. "I didn't want to plant my own ideas in your head. Later on, that might have been seen as prejudicial."

"Seen as prejudicial *by whom?*" It was a rhetorical question: the media, of course. By keeping silent on the issue, she'd minimized the risk of being seen to have launched a witch-hunt. Telling me to go look for *homosexual terrorists* might have put LEI in a very unsympathetic light . . . whereas my finding Mendelsohn—for other reasons entirely, despite my ignorance—would come across as proof that the investigation had been conducted without any preconceptions.

I said, "You had your suspicions, and you should have disclosed them. At the very least, you should have told me what the barrier was *for*."

"The barrier," she said, "is for protection against viruses and toxins. But anything we do to the body has side effects. It's not my role to judge whether or not those side effects are acceptable; the regulatory authorities will insist that we publicize *all* of the consequences of using the product—and then the decision will be up to consumers."

Very neat: the government would twist their arm, "forcing them" to disclose their major selling point!

"And what does your market research tell you?"

"That's strictly confidential."

I very nearly asked her: *When exactly did you find out that I was gay? After you'd hired me—or before?* On the morning of the bombing, while I'd been assembling a dossier on Janet Lansing . . . had *she* been assembling dossiers on all of the people who might have bid for the investigation? And had she found the ultimate PR advantage, the ultimate seal of impartiality, just too tempting to resist?

I didn't ask. I still wanted to believe that it made no difference: she'd hired me, and I'd solve the crime like any other, and nothing else would matter.

I went to the bunker where the cobalt had been stored, at the edge of Federation Centennial's grounds. The trapdoor was solid, but the lock was a joke, and there was no alarm system at all; any smart twelve-year-old could have broken in.

Crates full of all kinds of (low-level, short-lived) radioactive waste were stacked up to the ceiling, blocking most of the light from the single bulb; it was no wonder that the theft hadn't been detected sooner. There were even cobwebs—but no mutant spiders, so far as I could see.

After five minutes poking around, listening to my borrowed dosimetry badge adding up the exposure, I was glad to get out . . . whether or not the average chest X-ray would have done ten times more damage. *Hadn't Mendelsohn realized that: how irrational people were about radiation, how much harm it would do her cause once the cobalt was discovered?* Or had her own—fully informed—knowledge of the minimal risks distorted her perception?

The surveillance teams sent me reports daily. It was an expensive service, but LEI was paying. Mendelsohn met her friends openly—telling them all about the night I'd questioned her, warning them in outraged tones that they were almost certainly being watched. They discussed the fetal barrier, the options for—legitimate—opposition, the problems the bombing had caused them. I couldn't tell if the whole thing was being staged for my benefit, or if Mendelsohn was deliberately contacting only those friends who genuinely believed that she hadn't been involved.

I spent most of my time checking the histories of the people she met. I could find no evidence of past violence or sabotage by any of them—let alone experience with high explosives. But then, I hadn't seriously expected to be led straight to the bomber.

All I had was circumstantial evidence. All I could do was gather detail after detail, and hope that the mountain of facts I was assembling would eventually reach a critical mass—or that Mendelsohn would slip up, cracking under the pressure.

Weeks passed, and Mendelsohn continued to brazen it out. She even had pamphlets printed, ready to distribute at the Mardi Gras—condemning the bombing as loudly as they condemned LEI for its secrecy.

The nights grew hotter. My temper frayed. I don't know what Martin thought was happening to me, but I had no idea how we were going to survive the impending revelations. I couldn't begin to face up to the magnitude of the backlash there'd be once ATOMIC TERRORISTS met GAY BABY-POISONERS in the daily murdochs—and it would make no difference whether it was Mendelsohn's arrest which broke the news to the public, or her media conference blowing the whistle on LEI and proclaiming her own innocence; either way, the investigation would become a circus. I tried not to think about any of it; it was too late to do anything differently, to drop the case, to tell Martin the truth. So I worked on my tunnel vision.

Elaine scoured the radioactive waste bunker for evidence, but weeks of analysis came up blank. I quizzed the Biofile guards, who (supposedly) would have been watching the whole thing on their monitors when the cobalt was planted, but nobody could recall a client with an unusually large and oddly shaped item, wandering casually into the wrong aisle.

I finally obtained the warrants I needed to scrutinize Mendelsohn's entire electronic history since birth. She'd been arrested exactly once, twenty years before, for kicking an—unprivatized—policeman in the shin, during a protest he'd probably, privately, applauded. The charges had been dropped. She'd had a court order in force for the last eighteen months, restraining a former lover from coming within a kilometer of her home. (The woman was a musician with a band called Tetanus Switchblade; she had two convictions for assault.) There was no evidence of undeclared income, or unusual expenditure. No phone calls to or from known or suspected dealers in arms or explosives, or their known or suspected associates. But everything could have been done with pay phones and cash, if she'd organized it carefully.

Mendelsohn wasn't going to put a foot wrong while I was watching. However careful she'd been, though, she could not have carried out the bombing alone. What I needed was someone venal, nervous, or conscience-stricken enough to turn informant. I put out word on the usual channels: I'd be willing to pay, I'd be willing to bargain.

Six weeks after the bombing, I received an anonymous message by datamail: *Be at the Mardi Gras. No wires, no weapons. I'll find you.*
29:17:5:31:23:11

I played with the numbers for more than an hour, trying to make sense of them, before I finally showed them to Elaine.

She said, "Be careful, James."

"Why?"

"These are the ratios of the six trace elements we found in the residue from the explosion."

Martin spent the day of the Mardi Gras with friends who'd also be in the parade. I sat in my air-conditioned office and tuned in to a TV channel which showed the final preparations, interspersed with talking heads describing the history of the event. In forty years, the Gay and Lesbian Mardi Gras had been transformed from a series of ugly confrontations with police and local authorities, into a money-spinning spectacle advertised in tourist brochures around the world. It was blessed by every level of government, led by politicians and business identities—and the police, like most professions, now had their own float.

Martin was no transvestite (or muscle-bound leather-fetishist, or any other walking cliché); dressing up in a flamboyant costume, one night a year, was as false, as artificial, for him as it would have been for most heterosexual men. But I think I understood why he did it. He felt guilty that he could "pass for straight" in the clothes he usually wore, with the speech and manner and bearing which came naturally to him. He'd never concealed his sexuality from anyone—but it wasn't instantly apparent to total strangers. For him, taking part in the Mardi Gras was a gesture of solidarity with those gay men who *were* visible, obvious, all year round—and who'd borne the brunt of intolerance because of it.

As dusk fell, spectators began to gather along the route. Helicopters from every news service appeared overhead, turning their cameras on each other to prove to their viewers that this was An Event. Mounted crowd-control personnel—in something very much like the old blue uniform that had vanished when I was a child—parked their horses by the fast-food stands, and stood around fortifying themselves for the long night ahead.

I didn't see how the bomber could seriously expect to find me once I was mingling with a hundred thousand other people—so after leaving the Nexus building, I drove my car around the block slowly, three times, just in case.

By the time I'd made my way to a vantage point, I'd missed the start of the parade; the first thing I saw was a long line of people wearing giant plastic heads bearing the features of famous and infamous queers. (Apparently the word was back in fashion again, officially declared nonperjorative once more, after several years out of favor.) It was all so Disney I could have gagged—and yes, there was even Bernadette, the world's first lesbian cartoon mouse. I only recognized three of the humans portrayed—Patrick White, looking haggard and suitably bemused, Joe Orton, leering sardonically, and J. Edgar Hoover, with a Mephisto-phelian sneer. Everyone wore their names on sashes, though, for what that was worth. A young man beside me asked his girlfriend, "Who the hell was Walt Whitman?"

She shook her head. "No idea. Alan Turing?"

"Search me."

They photographed both of them, anyway.

I wanted to yell at the marchers: *So what? Some queers were famous. Some famous people were queer. What a surprise! Do you think that means you own them?*

I kept silent, of course—while everyone around me cheered and clapped. I wondered how close the bomber was, how long he or she would leave me sweating. Panopticon—the surveillance contractors—were still following Men-delsohn and all of her known associates, most of whom were somewhere along the route of the parade, handing out their pamphlets. None of them appeared to have followed me, though. The bomber was almost certainly someone outside the network of friends we'd uncovered.

An anti-viral, anti-drug, anti-pollution barrier, alone—or a means of guaran-teeing a heterosexual child. Which do you think would earn the most money? Surrounded by cheering spectators—half of them mixed-sex couples with chil-dren in tow—it was *almost* possible to laugh off Mendelsohn's fears. Who, here, would admit that they'd buy a version of the cocoon which would help wipe out the source of their entertainment? But applauding the freak show didn't mean wanting your own flesh and blood to join it.

An hour after the parade had started, I decided to move out of the densest part of the crowd. If the bomber couldn't reach me through the crush of people, there wasn't much point being here. A hundred or so leather-clad women on—noise-enhanced—electric motorbikes went riding past in a crucifix formation, behind a banner which read DYKES ON BIKES FOR JESUS. I recalled the small group of fundamentalists I'd passed earlier, their backs to the parade route lest they turn into pillars of salt, holding up candles and praying for rain.

I made my way to one of the food stalls, and bought a cold hot dog and a warm orange juice, trying to ignore the smell of horse turds. The place seemed to attract law enforcement types; J. Edgar Hoover himself came wandering by while I was eating, looking like a malevolent Humpty Dumpty.

As he passed me, he said, "Twenty-nine. Seventeen. Five."

I finished my hot dog and followed him.

He stopped in a deserted side street, behind a supermarket parking lot. As I caught up with him, he took out a magnetic scanner.

I said, "No wires, no weapons." He waved the device over me. I was telling the truth. "Can you talk through that thing?"

"Yes." The giant head bobbed strangely; I couldn't see any eye holes, but he clearly wasn't blind.

"Okay. Where did the explosives come from? We know they started off in Singapore, but who was your supplier here?"

Hoover laughed, deep and muffled. "I'm not going to tell you that. I'd be dead in a week."

"So what *do* you want to tell me?"

"That I only did the grunt work. Mendelsohn organized everything."

"No shit. But what have you got that will prove it? Phone calls? Financial transactions?"

He just laughed again. I was beginning to wonder how many people in the parade would know who'd played J. Edgar Hoover; even if he clammed up now, it was possible that I'd be able to track him down later.

That was when I turned and saw six more, identical, Hoovers coming around the corner. They were all carrying baseball bats.

I started to move. Hoover One drew a pistol and aimed it at my face. He said, "Kneel down slowly, with your hands behind your head."

I did it. He kept the gun on me, and I kept my eyes on the trigger, but I heard the others arrive, and close into a half-circle behind me.

Hoover One said, "Don't you know what happens to traitors? Don't you know what's going to happen to you?"

I shook my head slowly. I didn't know what I could say to appease him, so I spoke the truth. "How can I be a traitor? What is there to betray? Dykes on Bikes for Jesus? The William S. Burroughs Dancers?"

Someone behind me swung their bat into the small of my back. Not as hard as they might have; I lurched forward, but I kept my balance.

Hoover One said, "Don't you know any history, Mr. Pig? Mr. *Polizei?* The Nazis put us in their death camps. The Reaganites tried to have us all die of AIDS. And here you are now, Mr. Pig, working for the fuckers who want to wipe us off the face of the planet. That sounds like betrayal to *me.*"

I knelt there, staring at the gun, unable to speak. I couldn't dredge up the words to justify myself. The truth was too difficult, too gray, too confusing. My teeth started chattering. *Nazis. AIDS. Genocide.* Maybe he was right. Maybe I deserved to die.

I felt tears on my cheeks. Hoover One laughed. "Boo hoo, Mr. Pig." Someone swung their bat onto my shoulders. I fell forward on my face, too afraid to move my hands to break the fall; I tried to get up, but a boot came down on the back of my neck.

Hoover One bent down and put the gun to my skull. He whispered, "Will you close the case? Lose the evidence on Catherine? You know, your boyfriend frequents some dangerous places; he needs all the friends he can get."

I lifted my face high enough above the asphalt to reply. "Yes."

"Well done, Mr. Pig."

That was when I heard the helicopter.

I blinked the gravel out of my eyes and saw the ground, far brighter than it should have been; there was a spotlight trained on us. I waited for the sound of a bullhorn. Nothing happened. I waited for my assailants to flee. Hoover One took his foot off my neck.

And then they all laid into me with their baseball bats.

I should have curled up and protected my head, but curiosity got the better of me; I turned and stole a glimpse of the chopper. It was a news crew, of course, refusing to do anything unethical like spoil a good story just when it was getting telegenic. That much made perfect sense.

But the goon squad made no sense at all. Why were they sticking around, now that the cameras were running? Just for the pleasure of beating me for a few seconds longer?

Nobody was *that* stupid, that oblivious to PR.

I coughed up two teeth and hid my face again. *They wanted it all to be broadcast.* They *wanted* the headlines, the backlash, the outrage. ATOMIC TERRORISTS! BABY-POISONERS! BRUTAL THUGS!

They wanted to demonize the enemy they were pretending to be.

The Hoovers finally dropped their bats and started running. I lay on the ground drooling blood, too weak to lift my head to see what had driven them away.

A while later, I heard hoofbeats. Someone dropped to the ground beside me and checked my pulse.

I said, "I'm not in pain. I'm happy. I'm delirious."

Then I passed out.

On his second visit, Martin brought Catherine Mendelsohn to the hospital with him. They showed me a recording of LEI's media conference, the day after the Mardi Gras—two hours before Mendelsohn's was scheduled to take place.

Janet Lansing said, "In the light of recent events, we have no choice but to go public. We would have preferred to keep this technology under wraps for commercial reasons, but innocent lives are at stake. And when people turn on their own kind—"

I burst the stitches in my lips laughing.

LEI had bombed their own laboratory. They'd irradiated their own cells. And they'd hoped that I'd cover up for Mendelsohn, once the evidence led me to her, out of sympathy with her cause. Later, with a tipoff to an investigative reporter or two, the cover-up would have been revealed.

The perfect climate for their product launch.

Since I'd continued with the investigation, though, they'd had to make the best of it: sending in the Hoovers, claiming to be linked to Mendelsohn, to punish me for my diligence.

Mendelsohn said, "Everything LEI leaked about me—the cobalt, my key to the vault—was already spelt out in the pamphlets I'd printed, but that doesn't seem to cut much ice with the murdochs. I'm the Harbor Bridge Gamma Ray Terrorist now.''

''You'll never be charged.''

''Of course not. So I'll never be found innocent, either.''

I said, ''When I'm out of here, I'm going after them.'' *They wanted impartiality? An investigation untainted by prejudice? They'd get exactly what they paid for, this time. Minus the tunnel vision.*

Martin said softly, ''Who's going to employ you to do that?''

I smiled, painfully. ''LEI's insurance company.''

When they'd left, I dozed off.

I woke suddenly, from a dream of suffocation.

Even if I proved that the whole thing had been a marketing exercise by LEI— even if half their directors were thrown in prison, even if the company itself was liquidated—the technology would still be owned by *someone*.

And one way or another, in the end, it would be *sold*.

That's what I'd missed, in my fanatical neutrality: you can't sell a cure without a disease. So even if I was right to be neutral—even if there was no difference to fight for, no difference to betray, no difference to preserve—the best way to *sell* the cocoon would always be to invent one. And even if it would be no tragedy at all if there was nothing left but heterosexuality in a century's time, the only path which could lead there would be one of lies, and wounding, and vilification.

Would people buy that, or not?

I was suddenly very much afraid that they would.

SEVEN VIEWS OF OLDUVAI GORGE

Mike Resnick

Here's a bittersweet vision of the Future of Humanity, which also gives us a fascinating look at our origins, our present unsettled condition, and our splendid and terrible destiny . . .

Mike Resnick is one of the bestselling authors in science fiction, and one of the most prolific. His many novels include *The Dark Lady*, *Stalking the Unicorn*, *Paradise*, *Santiago*, *Ivory*, *Soothsayer*, *Oracle*, *Lucifer Jones*, *Purgatory*, and *Inferno*. His award-winning short fiction has been gathered in the collection *Will the Last Person to Leave the Planet Please Shut Off the Sun?*. Of late, he has become almost as prolific as an anthologist, producing, as editor, *Inside the Funhouse: 17 SF stories about SF*, *Whatdunits*, *More Whatdunits*, and *Shaggy B.E.M. Stories*, a long string of anthologies coedited with Martin H. Greenberg, *Alternate Presidents*, *Alternate Kennedys*, *Alternate Warriors*, *Aladdin: Master of the Lamp*, and *Dinosaur Fantastic*, among others, as well as two anthologies coedited with Gardner Dozois, *Future Earths: Under African Skies* and *Future Earths: Under South American Skies*. He won the Hugo Award in 1989 for "Kirinyaga," one of the most controversial and talked-about stories in recent years. He won another Hugo Award in 1991 for another story in the Kirinyaga series, "The Manamouki." His most recent books include the novel *A Miracle of Rare Design*, and the anthologies *Alternate Outlaws* and *Alternate Worldcons*, *Deals With the Devil* (coedited with Martin H. Greenberg and Loren D. Estleman), and *By Any Other Fame* and *Sherlock Holmes in Orbit* (both coedited with Martin H. Greenberg). His stories have appeared in our Sixth, Seventh, Ninth, and Eleventh Annual Collections. He lives with his wife Carol in Cincinnati, Ohio.

The creatures came again last night.

The moon had just slipped behind the clouds when we heard the first rustlings in the grass. Then there was a moment of utter silence, as if they knew we were listening for them, and finally there were the familiar hoots and shrieks as they raced to within fifty meters of us and, still screeching, struck postures of aggression.

They fascinate me, for they never show themselves in the daylight, and yet they manifest none of the features of the true nocturnal animal. Their eyes are not oversized, their ears cannot move independently, they tread very heavily on their feet. They frighten most of the other members of my party, and while I am curious about them, I have yet to absorb one of them and study it.

To tell the truth, I think my use of absorption terrifies my companions more than the creatures do, though there is no reason why it should. Although I am relatively young by my race's standards, I am nevertheless many millennia older than any other member of my party. You would think, given their backgrounds, that they would know that any trait someone of my age possesses must by definition be a survival trait.

Still, it bothers them. Indeed, it *mystifies* them, much as my memory does. Of course, theirs seem very inefficient to me. Imagine having to learn everything one knows in a single lifetime, to be totally ignorant at the moment of birth! Far better to split off from your parent with his knowledge intact in your brain, just as *my* parent's knowledge came to him, and ultimately to me.

But then, that is why we are here: not to compare similarities, but to study differences. And never was there a race so different from all his fellows as Man. He was extinct barely seventeen millennia after he strode boldly out into the galaxy from this, the planet of his birth—but during that brief interval he wrote a chapter in galactic history that will last forever. He claimed the stars for his own, colonized a million worlds, ruled his empire with an iron will. He gave no quarter during his primacy, and he asked for none during his decline and fall. Even now, some forty-eight centuries after his extinction, his accomplishments and his failures still excite the imagination.

Which is why we are on Earth, at the very spot that was said to be Man's true birthplace, the rocky gorge where he first crossed over the evolutionary barrier, saw the stars with fresh eyes, and vowed that they would someday be his.

Our leader is Bellidore, an Elder of the Kragan people, orange-skinned, golden fleeced, with wise, patient ways. Bellidore is well-versed in the behavior of sentient beings, and settles our disputes before we even know that we are engaged in them.

Then there are the Stardust Twins, glittering silver beings who answer to each other's names and finish each other's thoughts. They have worked on seventeen archaeological digs, but even *they* were surprised when Bellidore chose them for this most prestigious of all missions. They behave like life mates, though they display no sexual characteristics—but like all the others, they refuse to have physical contact with me, so I cannot assuage my curiosity.

Also in our party is the Moriteu, who eats the dirt as if it were a delicacy, speaks to no one, and sleeps upside-down while hanging from a branch of a nearby tree. For some reason, the creatures always leave it alone. Perhaps they think it is dead, possibly they know it is asleep and that only the rays of the sun can awaken it. Whatever the reason, we would be lost without it, for only the delicate tendrils that extend from its mouth can excavate the ancient artifacts we have discovered with the proper care.

We have four other species with us: one is an Historian, one an Exobiologist, one an Appraiser of human artifacts, and one a Mystic. (At least, *I* assume she is a Mystic, for I can find no pattern to her approach, but this may be due to my own shortsightedness. After all, what I do seems like magic to my companions and yet it is a rigorously-applied science.)

And, finally, there is me. I have no name, for my people do not use names, but for the convenience of the party I have taken the name of He Who Views for the duration of the expedition. This is a double misnomer: I am not a *he*, for my race is not divided by gender; and I am not a viewer, but a Fourth Level Feeler. Still, I could intuit very early in the voyage that "feel" means something very different to my companions than to myself, and out of respect for their sensitivities, I chose a less accurate name.

Every day finds us back at work, examining the various strata. There are many signs that the area once teemed with living things, that early on there was a veritable explosion of life forms in this place, but very little remains today. There are a few species of insects and birds, some small rodents, and of course the creatures who visit our camp nightly.

Our collection has been growing slowly. It is fascinating to watch my companions perform their tasks, for in many ways they are as much of a mystery to me as my methods are to them. For example, our Exobiologist needs only to glide her tentacle across an object to tell us whether it was once living matter; the Historian, surrounded by its complex equipment, can date any object, carbon-based or otherwise, to within a decade of its origin, regardless of its state of preservation; and even the Moriteu is a thing of beauty and fascination as it gently separates the artifacts from the strata where they have rested for so long.

I am very glad I was chosen to come on this mission.

We have been here for two lunar cycles now, and the work goes slowly. The lower strata were thoroughly excavated eons ago (I have such a personal interest in learning about Man that I almost used the word *plundered* rather than *excavated*, so resentful am I at not finding more artifacts), and for reasons as yet unknown there is almost nothing in the more recent strata.

Most of us are pleased with our results, and Bellidore is particularly elated. He says that finding five nearly intact artifacts makes the expedition an unqualified success.

All the others have worked tirelessly since our arrival. Now it is almost time for me to perform my special function, and I am very excited. I know that my findings will be no more important that the others', but perhaps, when we put them all together, we can finally begin to understand what it was that made Man what he was.

"Are you . . ." asked the first Stardust Twin.

". . . ready?" said the second.

I answered that I was ready, that indeed I had been anxious for this moment.

"May we . . ."

". . . observe?" they asked.

"If you do not find it distasteful," I replied.

"We are . . .

". . . scientists," they said. "There is . . ."

". . . very little . . ."

". . . that we cannot view . . ."

". . . objectively."

I ambulated to the table upon which the artifact rested. It was a stone, or at least that is what it appeared to be to my exterior sensory organs. It was triangular, and the edges showed signs of work.

"How old is this?" I asked.

"Three million . . ."

". . . five hundred and sixty-one thousand . . ."

". . . eight hundred and twelve years," answered the Stardust Twins.

"I see," I said.

"It is much . . ."

". . . the oldest . . ."

". . . of our finds."

I stared at it for a long time, preparing myself. Then I slowly, carefully, altered my structure and allowed my body to flow over and around the stone, engulfing it, and assimilating its history. I began to feel a delicious warmth as it became one with me, and while all my exterior senses had shut down, I knew that I was undulating and glowing with the thrill of discovery. I became one with the stone, and in that corner of my mind that is set aside for Feeling, I seemed to sense the Earth's moon looming low and ominous just above the horizon . . .

Enkatai awoke with a start just after dawn and looked up at the moon, which was still high in the sky. After all these weeks it still seemed far too large to hang suspended in the sky, and must surely crash down onto the planet any moment. The nightmare was still strong in her mind, and she tried to imagine the comforting sight of five small, unthreatening moons leapfrogging across the silver sky of her own world. She was able to hold the vision in her mind's eye for only a moment, and then it was lost, replaced by the reality of the huge satellite above her.

Her companion approached her.

"Another dream?" he asked.

"Exactly like the last one," she said uncomfortably. "The moon is visible in the daylight, and then we begin walking down the path . . ."

He stared at her with sympathy and offered her nourishment. She accepted it gratefully, and looked off across the veldt.

"Just two more days," she sighed, "and then we can leave this awful place."

"It is not such a terrible world," replied Bokatu. "It has many good qualities."

"We have wasted our time here," she said. "It is not fit for colonization."

"No, it is not," he agreed. "Our crops cannot thrive in this soil, and we have problems with the water. But we have learned many things, things that will eventually help us choose the proper world."

"We learned most of them the first week we were here," said Enkatai. "The rest of the time was wasted."

"The ship had other worlds to explore. They could not know we would be able to eliminate this one in such a short time."

She shivered in the cool morning air. "I hate this place."

"It will someday be a fine world," said Bokatu. "It awaits only the evolution of the brown monkeys."

Even as he spoke, an enormous baboon, some 350 pounds in weight, heavily muscled, with a shaggy chest and bold, curious eyes, appeared in the distance. Even walking on all fours it was a formidable figure, fully twice as large as the great spotted cats.

"*We* cannot use this world," continued Bokatu, "but someday *his* descendants will spread across it."

"They seem so placid," commented Enkatai.

"They *are* placid," agreed Bokatu, hurling a piece of food at the baboon, which raced forward and picked it up off the ground. It sniffed at it, seemed to consider whether or not to taste it, and finally, after a moment of indecision, put it in its mouth. "But they will dominate this planet. The huge grass-eaters spend too much time feeding, and the predators sleep all the time. No, my choice is the brown monkey. They are fine, strong, intelligent animals. They have already developed thumbs, they possess a strong sense of community, and even the great cats think twice about attacking them. They are virtually without natural predators." He nodded his head, agreeing with himself. "Yes, it is they who will dominate this world in the eons to come."

"No predators?" said Enkatai.

"Oh, I suppose one falls prey to the great cats now and then, but even the cats do not attack when they are with their troop." He looked at the baboon. "That fellow has the strength to tear all but the biggest cat to pieces."

"Then how do you account for what we found at the bottom of the gorge?" she persisted.

"Their size has cost them some degree of agility. It is only natural that one occasionally falls down the slopes to its death."

"Occasionally?" she repeated. "I found seven skulls, each shattered as if from a blow."

"The force of the fall," said Bokatu with a shrug. "Surely you don't think the great cats brained them before killing them?"

"I wasn't thinking of the cats," she replied.

"What, then?"

"The small, tailless monkeys that live in the gorge."

Bokatu allowed himself the luxury of a superior smile. "Have you *looked* at them?" he said. "They are scarcely a quarter the size of the brown monkeys."

"I *have* looked at them," answered Enkatai. "And they, too, have thumbs."

"Thumbs alone are not enough," said Bokatu.

"They live in the shadow of the brown monkeys, and they are still here," she said. "*That* is enough."

"The brown monkeys are eaters of fruits and leaves. Why should they bother the tailless monkeys?"

"They do more than not bother them," said Enkatai. "They avoid them. That hardly seems like a species that will someday spread across the world."

Bokatu shook his head. "The tailless monkeys seem to be at an evolutionary dead end. Too small to hunt game, too large to feed themselves on what they can find in the gorge, too weak to compete with the brown monkeys for better territory. My guess is that they're an earlier, more primitive species, destined for extinction.''

''Perhaps,'' said Enkatai.

''You disagree?''

''There is something about them . . .''

''What?''

Enkatai shrugged. ''I do not know. They make me uneasy. It is something in their eyes, I think—a hint of malevolence.''

''You are imagining things,'' said Bokatu.

''Perhaps,'' replied Enkatai again.

''I have reports to write today,'' said Bokatu. ''But tomorrow I will prove it to you.''

The next morning Bokatu was up with the sun. He prepared their first meal of the day while Enkatai completed her prayers, then performed his own while she ate.

''Now,'' he announced, ''we will go down into the gorge and capture one of the tailless monkeys.''

''Why?''

''To show you how easy it is. I may take it back with me as a pet. Or perhaps we shall sacrifice it in the lab and learn more about its life processes.''

''I do not *want* a pet, and we are not authorized to kill any animals.''

''As you wish,'' said Bokatu. ''We will let it go.''

''Then why capture one to begin with?''

''To show you that they are not intelligent, for if they are as bright as you think, I will not be able to capture one.'' He pulled her to an upright position. ''Let us begin.''

''This is foolish,'' she protested. ''The ship arrives in midafternoon. Why don't we just wait for it?''

''We will be back in time,'' he replied confidently. ''How long can it take?''

She looked at the clear blue sky, as if trying to urge the ship to appear. The moon was hanging, huge and white, just above the horizon. Finally she turned to him.

''All right, I will come with you—but only if you promise merely to observe them, and not to try to capture one.''

''Then you admit I'm right?''

''Saying that you are right or wrong has nothing to do with the truth of the situation. I *hope* you are right, for the tailless monkeys frighten me. But I do not know you are right, and neither do you.''

Bokatu stared at her for a long moment.

''I agree,'' he said at last.

''You agree that you cannot know?''

''I agree not to capture one,'' he said. ''Let us proceed.''

They walked to the edge of the gorge and then began climbing down the steep embankments, steadying themselves by wrapping their limbs around trees and other outgrowths. Suddenly they heard a loud screeching.

"What is that?" asked Bokatu.

"They have seen us," replied Enkatai.

"What makes you think so?"

"I have heard that scream in my dream—and always the moon was just as it appears now."

"Strange," mused Bokatu. "I have heard them many times before, but somehow they seem louder this time."

"Perhaps more of them are here."

"Or perhaps they are more frightened," he said. He glanced above him. "Here is the reason," he said, pointing. "We have company."

She looked up and saw a huge baboon, quite the largest she had yet seen, following them at a distance of perhaps fifty feet. When its eyes met hers it growled and looked away, but made no attempt to move any closer or farther away.

They kept climbing, and whenever they stopped to rest, there was the baboon, its accustomed fifty feet away from them.

"Does *he* look afraid to you?" asked Bokatu. "If these puny little creatures could harm him, would he be following us down into the gorge?"

"There is a thin line between courage and foolishness, and an even thinner line between confidence and over-confidence," replied Enkatai.

"If he is to die here, it will be like all the others," said Bokatu. "He will lose his footing and fall to his death."

"You do not find it unusual that every one of them fell on its head?" she asked mildly.

"They broke every bone in their bodies," he replied. "I don't know why you consider only the heads."

"Because you do not get identical head wounds from different incidents."

"You have an overactive imagination," said Bokatu. He pointed to a small hairy figure that was staring up at them. "Does *that* look like something that could kill our friend here?"

The baboon glared down into the gorge and snarled. The tailless monkey looked up with no show of fear or even interest. Finally it shuffled off into the thick bush.

"You see?" said Bokatu smugly. "One look at the brown monkey and it retreats out of sight."

"It didn't seem frightened to me," noted Enkatai.

"All the more reason to doubt its intelligence."

In another few minutes they reached the spot where the tailless monkey had been. They paused to regain their strength, and then continued to the floor of the gorge.

"Nothing," announced Bokatu, looking around. "My guess is that the one we saw was a sentry, and by now the whole tribe is miles away."

"Observe our companion."

The baboon had reached the floor of the gorge and was tensely testing the wind.

"He hasn't crossed over the evolutionary barrier yet," said Bokatu, amused. "Do you expect him to search for predators with a sensor?"

"No," said Enkatai, watching the baboon. "But if there is no danger, I expect him to relax, and he hasn't done that yet."

"That's probably how he lived long enough to grow this large," said Bokatu, dismissing her remarks. He looked around. "What could they possibly find to eat here?"

"I don't know."

"Perhaps we should capture one and dissect it. The contents of its stomach might tell us a lot about it."

"You promised."

"It would be so simple, though," he persisted. "All we'd have to do would be bait a trap with fruits or nuts."

Suddenly the baboon snarled, and Bokatu and Enkatai turned to locate the source of his anger. There was nothing there, but the baboon became more and more frenzied. Finally it raced back up the gorge.

"What was that all about, I wonder?" mused Bokatu.

"I think we should leave."

"We have half a day before the ship returns."

"I am uneasy here. I walked down a path exactly like this in my dream."

"You are not used to the sunlight," he said. "We will rest inside a cave."

She reluctantly allowed him to lead her to a small cave in the wall of the gorge. Suddenly she stopped and would go no further.

"What is the matter?"

"This cave was in my dream," she said. "Do not go into it."

"You must learn not to let dreams rule your life," said Bokatu. He sniffed the air. "Something smells strange."

"Let us go back. We want nothing to do with this place."

He stuck his head into the cave. "New world, new odors."

"Please, Bokatu!"

"Let me just see what causes that odor," he said, shining his light into the cave. It illuminated a huge pile of bodies, many of them half-eaten, most in various states of decomposition.

"What are they?" he asked, stepping closer.

"Brown monkeys," she replied without looking. "Each with its head staved in."

"This was part of your dream, too?" he asked, suddenly nervous.

She nodded her head. "We must leave this place *now!*"

He walked to the mouth of the cave.

"It seems safe," he announced.

"It is never safe in my dream," she said uneasily. They left the cave and walked about fifty yards when they came to a bend in the floor of the gorge. As they followed it, they found themselves facing a tailless monkey.

"One of them seems to have stayed behind," said Bokatu. "I'll frighten him away." He picked up a rock and threw it at the monkey, which ducked but held its ground.

Enkatai touched him urgently on the shoulder. "More than one," she said.

He looked up. Two more tailless monkeys were in a tree almost directly overhead.

As he stepped aside, he saw four more lumbering toward them out of the bush. Another emerged from a cave, and three more dropped out of nearby trees.

"What have they got in their hands?" he asked nervously.

"You would call them the femur bones of grass-eaters," said Enkatai, with a sick feeling in her thorax. "*They* would call them weapons."

The hairless monkeys spread out in a semi-circle, then began approaching them slowly.

"But they're so *puny!*" said Bokatu, backing up until he came to a wall of rock and could go no farther.

"You are a fool," said Enkatai, helplessly trapped in the reality of her dream. "*This* is the race that will dominate this planet. Look into their eyes!"

Bokatu looked, and he saw things, terrifying things, that he had never seen in any being or any animal before. He barely had time to offer a brief prayer for some disaster to befall this race before it could reach the stars, and then a tailless monkey hurled a smooth, polished, triangular stone at his head. It dazed him, and as he fell to the ground, the clubs began pounding down rhythmically on him and Enkatai.

At the top of the gorge, the baboon watched the carnage until it was over, and then raced off toward the vast savannah, where he would be safe, at least temporarily, from the tailless monkeys.

"A weapon," I mused. "It was a *weapon!*"

I was all alone. Sometime during the Feeling, the Stardust Twins had decided that I was one of the few things they could not be objective about, and had returned to their quarters.

I waited until the excitement of discovery had diminished enough for me to control my physical structure. Then I once again took the shape that I presented to my companions, and reported my findings to Bellidore.

"So even then they were aggressors," he said. "Well, it is not surprising. The will to dominate the stars had to have come from somewhere."

"It is surprising that there is no record of any race having landed here in their prehistory," said the Historian.

"It was a survey team, and Earth was of no use to them," I answered. "They doubtless touched down on any number of planets. If there is a record anywhere, it is probably in their archives, stating that Earth showed no promise as a colony world."

"But didn't they wonder what had happened to their team?" asked Bellidore.

"There were many large carnivores in the vicinity," I said. "They probably assumed the team had fallen prey to them. Especially if they searched the area and found nothing."

"Interesting," said Bellidore. "That the weaker of the species should have risen to dominance."

"I think it is easily explained," said the Historian. "*As* the smaller species, they were neither as fast as their prey nor as strong as their predators, so the creation of weapons was perhaps the only way to avoid extinction . . . or at least the best way."

"Certainly they displayed the cunning of the predator during their millennia abroad in the galaxy," said Bellidore.

"One does not *stop* being aggressive simply because one invents a weapon," said the Historian. "In fact, it may *add* to one's aggression."

"I shall have to consider that," said Bellidore, looking somewhat unconvinced.

"I have perhaps over-simplified my train of thought for the sake of this discussion," replied the Historian. "Rest assured that I will build a lengthy and rigorous argument when I present my findings to the Academy."

"And what of you, He Who Views?" asked Bellidore. "Have you any observations to add to what you have told us?"

"It is difficult to think of a rock as being the precursor of the sonic rifle and the molecular imploder," I said thoughtfully, "but I believe it to be the case."

"A most interesting species," said Bellidore.

It took almost four hours for my strength to return, for Feeling saps the energy like no other function, drawing equally from the body, the emotions, the mind, and the empathic powers.

The Moriteu, its work done for the day, was hanging upside-down from a tree limb, lost in its evening trance, and the Stardust Twins had not made an appearance since I had Felt the stone.

The other party members were busy with their own pursuits, and it seemed an ideal time for me to Feel the next object, which the Historian told me was approximately 23,300 years old.

It was the metal blade of a spear, rusted and pitted, and before I assimilated it, I thought I could see a slight discoloration, perhaps caused by blood . . .

His name was Mtepwa, and it seemed to him that he had been wearing a metal collar around his neck since the day he had been born. He knew that couldn't be true, for he had fleeting memories of playing with his brothers and sisters, and of stalking the kudu and the bongo on the tree-covered mountain where he grew up.

But the more he concentrated on those memories, the more vague and imprecise they became, and he knew they must have occurred a very long time ago. Sometimes he tried to remember the name of his tribe, but it was lost in the mists of time, as were the names of his parents and siblings.

It was at times like this that Mtepwa felt sorry for himself, but then he would consider his companions' situation, and he felt better, for while they were to be taken in ships and sent to the edge of the world to spend the remainder of their lives as slaves of the Arabs and the Europeans, he himself was the favored servant of his master, Sharif Abdullah, and as such his position was assured.

This was his eighth caravan—or was it his ninth?—from the Interior. They would trade salt and cartridges to the tribal chiefs who would in turn sell them their least productive warriors and women as slaves, and then they would march them out, around the huge lake and across the dry flat savannah. They would circle the mountain that was so old that it had turned white on the top, just like a white-haired old man, and finally out to the coast, where dhows filled the harbor. There they would sell their human booty to the highest bidders, and Sharif Abdullah would purchase another wife and turn half the money over to his aged, feeble father, and they would be off to the Interior again on another quest for black gold.

Abdullah was a good master. He rarely drank—and when he did, he always apologized to Allah at the next opportunity—and he did not beat Mtepwa overly much, and they always had enough to eat, even when the cargo went hungry. He even went so far as to teach Mtepwa how to read, although the only reading matter he carried with him was the Koran.

Mtepwa spent long hours honing his reading skills with the Koran, and somewhere along the way he made a most interesting discovery: the Koran forbade a practitioner of the True Faith to keep another member in bondage.

It was at that moment that Mtepwa made up his mind to convert to Islam. He began questioning Sharif Abdullah incessantly on the finer points of his religion, and made sure that the old man saw him sitting by the fire, hour after hour, reading the Koran.

So enthused was Sharif Abdullah at this development that he frequently invited Mtepwa into his tent at suppertime, and lectured him on the subtleties of the Koran far into the night. Mtepwa was a motivated student, and Sharif Abdullah marveled at his enthusiasm.

Night after night, as lions prowled around their camp in the Serengeti, master and pupil studied the Koran together. And finally the day came when Sharif Abdullah could no longer deny that Mtepwa was indeed a true believer of Islam. It happened as they camped at the Olduvai Gorge, and that very day Sharif Abdullah had his smith remove the collar from Mtepwa's neck, and Mtepwa himself destroyed the chains link by link, hurling them deep into the gorge when he was finished.

Mtepwa was now a free man, but knowledgeable in only two areas: the Koran, and slave-trading. So it was only natural that when he looked around for some means to support himself, he settled upon following in Sharif Abdullah's footsteps. He became a junior partner to the old man, and after two more trips to the Interior, he decided that he was ready to go out on his own.

To do that, he required a trained staff—warriors, smiths, cooks, trackers— and the prospect of assembling one from scratch was daunting, so, since his faith was less strong than his mentor's, he simply sneaked into Sharif Abdullah's quarters on the coast one night and slit the old man's throat.

The next day, he marched inland at the head of his own caravan.

He had learned much about the business of slaving, both as a practitioner and a victim, and he put his knowledge to full use. He knew that healthy slaves would bring a better price at market, and so he fed and treated his captives far better than Sharif Abdullah and most other slavers did. On the other hand, he knew which ones were fomenting trouble, and knew it was better to kill them on the spot as an example to the others, than to let any hopes of insurrection spread among the captives.

Because he was thorough, he was equally successful, and soon expanded into ivory trading as well. Within six years he had the biggest slaving and poaching operation in East Africa.

From time to time he ran across European explorers. It was said that he even spent a week with Dr. David Livingstone and left without the missionary ever knowing that he had been playing host to the slaver he most wanted to put out of business.

After America's War Between the States killed his primary market, he took a year off from his operation to go to Asia and the Arabian Peninsula and open up new ones. Upon returning he found that Abdullah's son, Sharif Ibn Jad Mahir, had appropriated all his men and headed inland, intent on carrying on his father's business. Mtepwa, who had become quite wealthy, hired some 500 *askari*, placed them under the command of the notorious ivory poacher Alfred Henry Pym, and sat back to await the results.

Three months later Pym marched some 438 men back to the Tanganyika coast. Two hundred and seventy-six were slaves that Sharif Ibn Jad Mahir had captured; the remainder were the remnants of Mtepwa's organization, who had gone to work for Sharif Ibn Jad Mahir. Mtepwa sold all 438 of them into bondage and built a new organization, composed of the warriors who had fought for him under Pym's leadership.

Most of the colonial powers were inclined to turn a blind eye to his practices, but the British, who were determined to put an end to slavery, issued a warrant for Mtepwa's arrest. Eventually he tired of continually looking over his shoulder, and moved his headquarters to Mozambique, where the Portuguese were happy to let him set up shop as long as he remembered that colonial palms needed constant greasing.

He was never happy there—he didn't speak Portuguese or any of the local languages—and after nine years he returned to Tanganyika, now the wealthiest black man on the continent.

One day he found among his latest batch of captives a young Acholi boy named Haradi, no more than ten years old, and decided to keep him as a personal servant rather than ship him across the ocean.

Mtepwa had never married. Most of his associates assumed that he had simply never had the time, but as the almost-nightly demands for Haradi to visit him in his tent became common knowledge, they soon revised their opinions. Mtepwa seemed besotted with his servant boy, though—doubtless remembering his own experience—he never taught Haradi to read, and promised a slow and painful death to anyone who spoke of Islam to the boy.

Then one night, after some three years had passed, Mtepwa sent for Haradi. The boy was nowhere to be found. Mtepwa awoke all his warriors and demanded that they search for him, for a leopard had been seen in the vicinity of the camp, and the slaver feared the worst.

They found Haradi an hour later, not in the jaws of a leopard, but in the arms of a young female slave they had taken from the Zaneke tribe. Mtepwa was beside himself with rage, and had the poor girl's arms and legs torn from her body.

Haradi never offered a word of protest, and never tried to defend the girl—not that it would have done any good—but the next morning he was gone, and though Mtepwa and his warriors spent almost a month searching for him, they found no trace of him.

By the end of the month Mtepwa was quite insane with rage and grief. Deciding that life was no longer worth living, he walked up to a pride of lions that were gorging themselves on a topi carcass and, striding into their midst, began cursing them and hitting them with his bare hands. Almost unbelievably, the lions backed away from him, snarling and growling, and disappeared into the thick bush.

The next day he picked up a large stick and began beating a baby elephant with it. That should have precipitated a brutal attack by its mother—but the mother, standing only a few feet away, trumpeted in terror and raced off, the baby following her as best it could.

It was then that Mtepwa decided that he could not die, that somehow the act of dismembering the poor Zaneke girl had made him immortal. Since both incidents had occurred within sight of his superstitious followers, they fervently believed him.

Now that he was immortal, he decided that it was time to stop trying to accommodate the Europeans who had invaded his land and kept issuing warrants for his arrest. He sent a runner to the Kenya border and invited the British to meet him in battle. When the appointed day came, and the British did not show up to fight him, he confidently told his warriors that word of his immortality had reached the Europeans and that from that day forth no white men would ever be willing to oppose him. The fact that he was still in German territory, and the British had no legal right to go there, somehow managed to elude him.

He began marching his warriors inland, openly in search of slaves, and he found his share of them in the Congo. He looted villages of their men, their women, and their ivory, and finally, with almost 600 captives and half that many tusks, he turned east and began the months-long trek to the coast.

This time the British were waiting for him at the Uganda border, and they had so many armed men there that Mtepwa turned south, not for fear for his own life, but because he could not afford to lose his slaves and his ivory, and he knew that his warriors lacked his invulnerability.

He marched his army down to Lake Tanganyika, then headed east. It took him two weeks to reach the western corridor of the Serengeti, and another ten days to cross it.

One night he made camp at the lip of the Olduvai Gorge, the very place where he had gained his freedom. The fires were lit, a wildebeest was slaughtered and cooked, and as he relaxed after the meal he became aware of a buzzing among his men. Then, from out of the shadows, stepped a strangely familiar figure. It was Haradi, now fifteen years old, and as tall as Mtepwa himself.

Mtepwa stared at him for a long moment, and suddenly all the anger seemed to drain from his face.

"I am very glad to see you again, Haradi," he said.

"I have heard that you cannot be killed," answered the boy, brandishing a spear. "I have come to see if that is true."

"We have no need to fight, you and I," said Mtepwa. "Join me in my tent, and all will be as it was."

"Once I tear your limbs from your body, *then* we will have no reason to fight,'' responded Haradi. "And even then, you will seem no less repulsive to me than you do now, or than you did all those many years ago."

Mtepwa jumped up, his face a mask of fury. "Do your worst, then!" he cried. "And when you realize that I cannot be harmed, I will do to you as I did to the Zaneke girl!"

Haradi made no reply, but hurled his spear at Mtepwa. It went into the slaver's body, and was thrown with such force that the point emerged a good six inches on the other side. Mtepwa stared at Haradi with disbelief, moaned once, and tumbled down the rocky slopes of the gorge.

Haradi looked around at the warriors. "Is there any among you who dispute my right to take Mtepwa's place?" he asked confidently.

A burly Makonde stood up to challenge him, and within thirty seconds Haradi, too, was dead.

The British were waiting for them when they reached Zanzibar. The slaves were freed, the ivory confiscated, the warriors arrested and forced to serve as laborers on the Mombasa/Uganda Railway. Two of them were later killed and eaten by lions in the Tsavo District.

By the time Lieutenant-Colonel J. H. Patterson shot the notorious Man-Eaters of Tsavo, the railway had almost reached the shanty town of Nairobi, and Mtepwa's name was so thoroughly forgotten that it was misspelled in the only history book in which it appeared.

"Amazing!" said the Appraiser. "I knew they enslaved many races throughout the galaxy—but to enslave *themselves*! It is almost beyond belief!"

I had rested from my efforts, and then related the story of Mtepwa.

"All ideas must begin somewhere," said Bellidore placidly. "This one obviously began on Earth."

"It is barbaric!" muttered the Appraiser.

Bellidore turned to me. "Man never attempted to subjugate *your* race, He Who Views. Why was that?"

"We had nothing that he wanted."

"Can you remember the galaxy when Man dominated it?" asked the Appraiser.

"I can remember the galaxy when Man's progenitors killed Bokatu and Enkatai," I replied truthfully.

"Did you ever have any dealings with Man?"

"None. Man had no use for us."

"But did he not destroy profligately things for which he had no use?"

"No," I said. "He took what he wanted, and he destroyed that which threatened him. The rest he ignored."

"Such arrogance!"

"Such practicality," said Bellidore.

"You call genocide on a galactic scale *practical?*" demanded the Appraiser.

"From Man's point of view, it was," answered Bellidore. "It got him what he wanted with a minimum of risk and effort. Consider that one single race, born not five hundred yards from us, at one time ruled an empire of more than a million worlds. Almost every civilized race in the galaxy spoke Terran.''

"Upon pain of death."

"That is true," agreed Bellidore. "I did not say Man was an angel. Only that, if he was indeed a devil, he was an efficient one."

It was time for me to assimilate the third artifact, which the Historian and the Appraiser seemed to think was the handle of a knife, but even as I moved off to perform my function, I could not help but listen to the speculation that was taking place.

"Given his bloodlust and his efficiency," said the Appraiser, "I'm surprised that he lived long enough to reach the stars."

"It *is* surprising in a way," agreed Bellidore. "The Historian tells me that Man was not always homogeneous, that early in his history there were several variations of the species. He was divided by color, by belief, by territory." He sighed. "Still, he must have learned to live in peace with his fellow man. That much, at least, accrues to his credit."

I reached the artifact with Bellidore's words still in my ears, and began to engulf it . . .

Mary Leakey pressed against the horn of the Landrover. Inside the museum, her husband turned to the young uniformed officer.

"I can't think of any instructions to give you," he said. "The museum's not open to the public yet, and we're a good 300 kilometers from Kikuyuland."

"I'm just following my orders, Dr. Leakey," replied the officer.

"Well, I suppose it doesn't hurt to be safe," acknowledged Leakey. "There are a lot of Kikuyu who want me dead even though I spoke up for Kenyatta at his trial." He walked to the door. "If the discoveries at Lake Turkana prove interesting, we could be gone as long as a month. Otherwise, we should be back within ten to twelve days."

"No problem, sir. The museum will still be here when you get back."

"I never doubted it," said Leakey, walking out and joining his wife in the vehicle.

Lieutenant Ian Chelmswood stood in the doorway and watched the Leakeys, accompanied by two military vehicles, start down the red dirt road. Within seconds the car was obscured by dust, and he stepped back into the building and closed the door to avoid being covered by it. The heat was oppressive, and he removed his jacket and holster and laid them neatly across one of the small display cases.

It was strange. All the images he had seen of African wildlife, from the German Schillings' old still photographs to the American Johnson's motion pictures, had led him to believe that East Africa was a wonderland of green grass and clear water. No one had ever mentioned the dust, but that was the one memory of it that he would take home with him.

Well, not quite the only one. He would never forget the morning the alarm had sounded back when he was stationed in Nanyuki. He arrived at the settlers' farm and found the entire family cut to ribbons and all their cattle mutilated, most with their genitals cut off, many missing ears and eyes. But as horrible as that was, the picture he would carry to his grave was the kitten impaled on a dagger and pinned to the mailbox. It was the Mau Mau's signature, just in case anyone thought some madman had run berserk among the cattle and the humans.

Chelmswood didn't understand the politics of it. He didn't know who had started it, who had precipitated the war. It made no difference to him. He was just a soldier, following orders, and if those orders would take him back to Nanyuki so that he could kill the men who had committed those atrocities, so much the better.

But in the meantime, he had pulled what he considered Idiot Duty. There had been a very mild outburst of violence in Arusha, not really Mau Mau but rather a show of support for Kenya's Kikuyu, and his unit had been transferred there. Then the government found out that Professor Leakey, whose scientific finds had made Olduvai Gorge almost a household word among East Africans, had been getting death threats. Over his objections, they had insisted on providing him with bodyguards. Most of the men from Chelmswood's unit would accompany Leakey on his trip to Lake Turkana, but someone had to stay behind to guard the museum, and it was just his bad luck that his name had been atop the duty roster.

It wasn't even a museum, really, not the kind of museum his parents had taken him to see in London. *Those* were museums; this was just a two-room mud-walled structure with perhaps a hundred of Leakey's finds. Ancient arrowheads, some oddly-shaped stones that had functioned as prehistoric tools, a couple of bones that obviously weren't from monkeys but that Chelmswood was certain were not from any creature *he* was related to.

Leakey had hung some crudely drawn charts on the wall, charts that showed what he believed to be the evolution of some small, grotesque, apelike beasts into *Homo sapiens*. There were photographs, too, showing some of the finds that had been sent on to Nairobi. It seemed that even if this gorge was the birthplace of the race, nobody really wanted to visit it. All the best finds were shipped back to Nairobi and then to the British Museum. In fact, this wasn't a museum at all, decided Chelmswood, but rather a holding area for the better specimens until they could be sent elsewhere.

It was strange to think of life starting here in this gorge. If there was an uglier spot in Africa, he had yet to come across it. And while he didn't accept Genesis or any of that religious nonsense, it bothered him to think that the first human beings to walk the Earth might have been black. He'd hardly had any exposure to blacks when he was growing up in the Cotswolds, but he'd seen enough of what they could do since coming to British East, and he was appalled by their savagery and barbarism.

And what about those crazy Americans, wringing their hands and saying that colonialism had to end? If they had seen what *he'd* seen on that farm in Nanyuki, they'd know that the only thing that was keeping all of East Africa from exploding into an unholy conflagration of blood and butchery was the British presence. Certainly, there were parallels between the Mau Mau and America: both had been colonized by the British and both wanted their independence . . . but there all similarity ended. The Americans wrote a Declaration outlining their grievances, and then they fielded an army and fought the British *soldiers*. What did chopping up innocent children and pinning cats to mailboxes have in common with that? If he had his way, he'd march in half a million British troops, wipe out every last Kikuyu—except for the good ones, the loyal ones—and solve the problem once and for all.

He wandered over to the cabinet where Leakey kept his beer and pulled out a warm bottle. Safari brand. He opened it and took a long swallow, then made a face. If that's what people drank on safari, he'd have to remember never to go on one.

And yet he knew that someday he *would* go on safari, hopefully before he was mustered out and sent home. Parts of the country were so damned beautiful, dust or no dust, and he liked the thought of sitting beneath a shade tree, cold drink in hand, while his body servant cooled him with a fan made of ostrich feathers and he and his white hunter discussed the day's kills and what they would go out after tomorrow. It wasn't the shooting that was important, they'd both reassure themselves, but rather the thrill of the hunt. Then he'd have a couple of his black boys draw his bath, and he'd bathe and prepare for dinner. Funny how he had fallen into the habit of calling them boys; most of them were far older than he.

But while they weren't boys, they *were* children in need of guidance and civilizing. Take those Maasai, for example; proud, arrogant bastards. They looked great on postcards, but try *dealing* with them. They acted as if they had a direct line to God, that He had told them they were His chosen people. The more Chelmswood thought about it, the more surprised he was that it was the Kikuyu that had begun Mau Mau rather than the Maasai. And come to think of it, he'd noticed four or five Maasai *elmorani* hanging around the museum. He'd have to keep an eye on them . . .

"Excuse, please?" said a high-pitched voice, and Chelmswood turned to see a small skinny black boy, no more than ten years old, standing in the doorway.

"What do you want?" he asked.

"Doctor Mister Leakey, he promise me candy," said the boy, stepping inside the building.

"Go away," said Chelmswood irritably. "We don't have any candy here."

"Yes yes," said the boy, stepping forward. "Every day."

"He gives you candy every day?"

The boy nodded his head and smiled.

"Where does he keep it?"

The boy shrugged. "Maybe in there?" he said, pointing to a cabinet.

Chelmswood walked to the cabinet and opened it. There was nothing in it but four jars containing primitive teeth.

"I don't see any," he said. "You'll have to wait until Dr. Leakey comes back."

Two tears trickled down the boy's cheek. "But Doctor Mister Leakey, he *promise!*"

Chelmswood looked around. "I don't know where it is."

The boy began crying in earnest.

"Be quiet!" snapped Chelmswood. "I'll look for it."

"Maybe next room," suggested the boy.

"Come along," said Chelmswood, walking through the doorway to the adjoining room. He looked around, hands on hips, trying to imagine where Leakey had hidden the candy.

"This place maybe," said the boy, pointing to a closet.

Chelmswood opened the closet. It contained two spades, three picks, and an assortment of small brushes, all of which he assumed were used by the Leakeys for their work.

"Nothing here," he said, closing the door.

He turned to face the boy, but found the room empty.

"Little bugger was lying all along," he muttered. "Probably ran away to save himself a beating."

He walked back into the main room—and found himself facing a well-built black man holding a machete-like *panga* in his right hand.

"What's going on here?" snapped Chelmswood.

"Freedom is going on here, Lieutenant," said the black man in near-perfect English. "I was sent to kill Dr. Leakey, but you will have to do."

"Why are you killing anyone?" demanded Chelmswood. "What did we ever do to the Maasai?"

"I will let the Maasai answer that. Any one of them could take one look at me and tell you that I am Kikuyu—but we are all the same to you British, aren't we?"

Chelmswood reached for his gun and suddenly realized he had left it on a display case.

"You all look like cowardly savages to me!"

"Why? Because we do not meet you in battle?" The black man's face filled with fury. "You take our land away, you forbid us to own weapons, you even make it a crime for us to carry spears—and then you call us savages when we don't march in formation against your guns!" He spat contemptuously on the floor. "We fight you in the only way that is left to us."

"It's a big country, big enough for both races," said Chelmswood.

"If we came to England and took away your best farmland and forced you to work for us, would you think England was big enough for both races?"

"I'm not political," said Chelmswood, edging another step closer to his weapon. "I'm just doing my job."

"And your job is to keep two hundred whites on land that once held a million Kikuyu," said the black man, his face reflecting his hatred.

"There'll be a lot less than a million when *we* get through with you!" hissed Chelmswood, diving for his gun.

Quick as he was, the black man was faster, and with a single swipe of his *panga* he almost severed the Englishman's right hand from his wrist. Chelmswood bellowed in pain, and spun around, presenting his back to the Kikuyu as he reached for the pistol with his other hand.

The *panga* came down again, practically splitting him open, but as he fell he managed to get his fingers around the handle of his pistol and pull the trigger. The bullet struck the black man in the chest, and he, too, collapsed to the floor.

"You've killed me!" moaned Chelmswood. "Why would anyone want to kill me?"

"You have so much and we have so little," whispered the black man. "Why must you have what is ours, too?"

"What did I ever do to you?" asked Chelmswood.

"You came here. That was enough," said the black man. "Filthy English!" He closed his eyes and lay still.

"Bloody nigger!" slurred Chelmswood, and died.

Outside, the four Maasai paid no attention to the tumult within. They let the small Kikuyu boy leave without giving him so much as a glance. The business of inferior races was none of their concern.

"These notions of superiority among members of the same race are very difficult to comprehend," said Bellidore. "Are you *sure* you read the artifact properly, He Who Views?"

"I do not *read* artifacts," I replied. "I *assimilate* them. I become one with them. Everything *they* have experienced, *I* experience." I paused. "There can be no mistake."

"Well, it is difficult to fathom, especially in a species that would one day control most of the galaxy. Did they think *every* race they met was inferior to them?"

"They certainly behaved as if they did," said the Historian. "They seemed to respect only those races that stood up to them—and even then they felt that militarily defeating them was proof of their superiority."

"And yet we know from ancient records that primitive man worshipped non-sentient animals," put in the Exobiologist.

"They must not have survived for any great length of time," suggested the Historian. "If Man treated the races of the galaxy with contempt, how much worse must he have treated the poor creatures with whom he shared his home world?"

"Perhaps he viewed them much the same as he viewed my own race," I offered. "If they had nothing he wanted, if they presented no threat . . ."

"They would have had something he wanted," said the Exobiologist. "He was a predator. They would have had meat."

"And land," added the Historian. "If even the galaxy was not enough to quench Man's thirst for territory, think how unwilling he would have been to share his own world."

"It is a question I suspect will never be answered," said Bellidore.

"Unless the answer lies in one of the remaining artifacts," agreed the Exobiologist.

I'm sure the remark was not meant to jar me from my lethargy, but it occurred to me that it had been half a day since I had assimilated the knife handle, and I had regained enough of my strength to examine the next artifact.

It was a metal stylus . . .

*   *   *

February 15, 2103:

Well, we finally got here! The Supermole got us through the tunnel from New York to London in just over four hours. Even so we were twenty minutes late, missed our connection, and had to wait another five hours for the next flight to Khartoum. From there our means of transport got increasingly more primitive—jet planes to Nairobi and Arusha—and then a quick shuttle to our campsite, but we've finally put civilization behind us. I've never seen open spaces like this before; you're barely aware of the skyscrapers of Nyerere, the closest town.

After an orientation speech telling us what to expect and how to behave on safari, we got the afternoon off to meet our traveling companions. I'm the youngest member of the group: a trip like this just costs too much for most people my age to afford. Of course, most people my age don't have an Uncle Reuben who dies and leaves them a ton of money. (Well, it's probably about eight ounces of money, now that the safari is paid for. Ha ha.)

The lodge is quite rustic. They have quaint microwaves for warming our food, although most of us will be eating at the restaurants. I understand the Japanese and Brazilian ones are the most popular, the former for the food—real fish—and the latter for the entertainment. My roommate is Mr. Shiboni, an elderly Japanese gentleman who tells me he has been saving his money for fifteen years to come on this safari. He seems pleasant and good-natured; I hope he can survive the rigors of the trip.

I had really wanted a shower, just to get in the spirit of things, but water is scarce here, and it looks like I'll have to settle for the same old chemical dryshower. I know, I know, it disinfects as well as cleanses, but if I wanted all the comforts of home, I'd have stayed home and saved $150,000.

February 16:

We met our guide today. I don't know why, but he doesn't quite fit my preconception of an African safari guide. I was expecting some grizzled old veteran who had a wealth of stories to tell, who had maybe even seen a civet cat or a duiker before they became extinct. What we got was Kevin Ole Tambake, a young Maasai who can't be twenty-five years old and dresses in a suit while we all wear our khakis. Still, he's lived here all his life, so I suppose he knows his way around.

And I'll give him this: he's a wonderful storyteller. He spent half an hour telling us myths about how his people used to live in huts called manyattas, and how their rite of passage to manhood was to kill a lion with a spear. As if the government would let anyone kill an animal!

We spent the morning driving down into the Ngorongoro Crater. It's a col-lapsed caldera, or volcano, that was once taller than Kilimanjaro itself. Kevin says it used to teem with game, though I can't see how, since any game standing atop it when it collapsed would have been instantly killed.

I think the real reason we went there was just to get the kinks out of our safari vehicle and learn the proper protocol. Probably just as well. The air-conditioning wasn't working right in two of the compartments, the service mechanism couldn't get the temperature right on the iced drinks, and once, when we thought we saw a bird, three of us buzzed Kevin at the same time and jammed his communication line.

In the afternoon we went out to Serengeti. Kevin says it used to extend all the way to the Kenya border, but now it's just a 20-square-mile park adjacent to the Crater. About an hour into the game run we saw a ground squirrel, but he disappeared into a hole before I could adjust my holo camera. Still, he was very impressive. Varying shades of brown, with dark eyes and a fluffy tail. Kevin estimated that he went almost three pounds, and says he hasn't seen one that big since he was a boy.

Just before we returned to camp, Kevin got word on the radio from another driver that they had spotted two starlings nesting in a tree about eight miles north and east of us. The vehicle's computer told us we wouldn't be able to reach it before dark, so Kevin had it lock the spot in its memory and promised us that we'd go there first thing in the morning.

I opted for the Brazilian restaurant, and spent a few pleasant hours listening to the live band. A very nice end to the first full day of safari.

February 17:

We left at dawn in search of the starlings, and though we found the tree where they had been spotted, we never did see them. One of the passengers—I think it was the little man from Burma, though I'm not sure—must have complained, because Kevin soon announced to the entire party that this was a safari, that there was no guarantee of seeing any particular bird or animal, and that while he would do his best for us, one could never be certain where the game might be.

And then, just as he was talking, a banded mongoose almost a foot long appeared out of nowhere. It seemed to pay no attention to us, and Kevin announced that we were killing the motor and going into hover mode so the noise wouldn't scare it away.

After a minute or two everyone on the right side of the vehicle had gotten their holographs, and we slowly spun on our axis so that the left side could see him—but the movement must have scared him off, because though the maneuver took less than thirty seconds, he was nowhere to be seen when we came to rest again.

Kevin announced that the vehicle had captured the mongoose on its automated holos, and copies would be made available to anyone who had missed their holo opportunity.

We were feeling great—the right side of the vehicle, anyway—when we stopped for lunch, and during our afternoon game run we saw three yellow weaver birds building their spherical nests in a tree. Kevin let us out, warning us not to approach closer than thirty yards, and we spent almost an hour watching and holographing them.

All in all, a very satisfying day.

February 18:

Today we left camp about an hour after sunrise, and went to a new location: Olduvai Gorge.

Kevin announced that we would spend our last two days here, that with the encroachment of the cities and farms on all the flat land, the remaining big game was pretty much confined to the gullies and slopes of the gorge.

No vehicle, not even our specially-equipped one, was capable of navigating its way through the gorge, so we all got out and began walking in single file behind Kevin.

Most of us found it very difficult to keep up with Kevin. He clambered up and down the rocks as if he'd been doing it all his life, whereas I can't remember the last time I saw a stair that didn't move when I stood on it. We had trekked for perhaps half an hour when I heard one of the men at the back of our strung-out party give a cry and point to a spot at the bottom of the gorge, and we all looked and saw something racing away at phenomenal speed.

"Another squirrel?" I asked.

Kevin just smiled.

The man behind me said he thought it was a mongoose.

"What you saw," said Kevin, "was a dik-dik, the last surviving African antelope."

"How big was it?" asked a woman.

"About average size," said Kevin. "Perhaps ten inches at the shoulder."

Imagine anything ten inches high being called average!

Kevin explained that dik-diks were very territorial, and that this one wouldn't stray far from his home area. Which meant that if we were patient and quiet— and lucky—we'd be able to spot him again.

I asked Kevin how many dik-diks lived in the gorge, and he scratched his head and considered it for a moment and then guessed that there might be as many as ten. (And Yellowstone has only nineteen rabbits left! Is it any wonder that all the serious animal buffs come to Africa?)

We kept walking for another hour, and then broke for lunch, while Kevin gave us the history of the place, telling us all about Dr. Leakey's finds. There were probably still more skeletons to be dug up, he guessed, but the government didn't want to frighten any animals away from what had become their last refuge, so the bones would have to wait for some future generation to unearth them. Roughly translated, that meant that Tanzania wasn't going to give up the revenues from 300 tourists a week and turn over the crown jewel in their park system to a bunch of anthropologists. I can't say that I blame them.

Other parties had begun pouring into the gorge, and I think the entire safari population must have totaled almost seventy by the time lunch was over. The guides each seemed to have "their" areas marked out, and I noticed that rarely did we get within a quarter mile of any other parties.

Kevin asked us if we wanted to sit in the shade until the heat of the day had passed, but since this was our next-to-last day on safari we voted overwhelmingly to proceed as soon as we were through eating.

It couldn't have been ten minutes later that the disaster occurred. We were clambering down a steep slope in single file, Kevin in the lead as usual, and me right behind him, when I heard a grunt and then a surprised yell, and I looked back to see Mr. Shiboni tumbling down the path. Evidently he'd lost his footing, and we could hear the bones in his leg snap as he hurtled toward us.

Kevin positioned himself to stop him, and almost got knocked down the gorge himself before he finally stopped poor Mr. Shiboni. Then he knelt down next to the old gentleman to tend to his broken leg—but as he did so his keen eyes spotted something we all had missed, and suddenly he was bounding up the slopes like a monkey. He stopped where Mr. Shiboni had initially stumbled, squatted down, and examined something. Then, looking like Death itself, he picked up the object and brought it back down the path.

It was a dead lizard, fully grown, almost eight inches long, and smashed flat by Mr. Shiboni. It was impossible to say whether his fall was caused by stepping on it, or whether it simply couldn't get out of the way once he began tumbling . . . but it made no difference: he was responsible for the death of an animal in a National Park.

I tried to remember the release we had signed, giving the Park System permission to instantly withdraw money from our accounts should we destroy an animal for any reason, even self-protection. I knew that the absolute minimum penalty was $50,000, but I think that was for two of the more common birds, and that ugaama and gecko lizards were in the $70,000 range.

Kevin held the lizard up for all of us to see, and told us that should legal action ensue, we were all witnesses to what had happened.

Mr. Shiboni groaned in pain, and Kevin said that there was no sense wasting the lizard, so he gave it to me to hold while he splinted Mr. Shiboni's leg and summoned the paramedics on the radio.

I began examining the little lizard. Its feet were finely-shaped, its tail long and elegant, but it was the colors that made the most lasting impression on me: a reddish head, a blue body, and gray legs, the color growing lighter as it reached the claws. A beautiful, beautiful thing, even in death.

After the paramedics had taken Mr. Shiboni back to the lodge, Kevin spent the next hour showing us how the ugaama lizard functioned: how its eyes could see in two directions at once, how its claws allowed it to hang upside down from any uneven surface, and how efficiently its jaws could crack the carapaces of the insects it caught. Finally, in view of the tragedy, and also because he wanted to check on Mr. Shiboni's condition, Kevin suggested that we call it a day.

None of us objected—we knew Kevin would have hours of extra work, writing up the incident and convincing the Park Department that his safari company was not responsible for it—but still we felt cheated, since there was only one day left. I think Kevin knew it, because just before we reached the lodge he promised us a special treat tomorrow.

I've been awake half the night wondering what it could be? Can he possibly know where the other dik-diks are? Or could the legends of a last flamingo possibly be true?

February 19:

We were all excited when we climbed aboard the vehicle this morning. Everyone kept asking Kevin what his "special treat" was, but he merely smiled and kept changing the subject. Finally we reached Olduvai Gorge and began walking, only this time we seemed to be going to a specific location, and Kevin hardly stopped to try to spot the dik-dik.

We climbed down twisting, winding paths, tripping over tree roots, cutting our arms and legs on thorn bushes, but nobody objected, for Kevin seemed so confident of his surprise that all these hardships were forgotten.

Finally we reached the bottom of the gorge and began walking along a flat winding path. Still, by the time we were ready to stop for lunch, we hadn't seen a thing. As we sat beneath the shade of an acacia tree, eating, Kevin pulled out his radio and conversed with the other guides. One group had seen three dik-diks, and another had found a lilac-breasted roller's nest with two hatchlings in it. Kevin is very competitive, and ordinarily news like that would have had him urging everyone to finish eating quickly so that we would not return to the lodge having seen less than everyone else, but this time he just smiled and told the other guides that we had seen nothing on the floor of the gorge and that the game seemed to have moved out, perhaps in search of water.

Then, when lunch was over, Kevin walked about fifty yards away, disappeared into a cave, and emerged a moment later with a small wooden cage. There was a little brown bird in it, and while I was thrilled to be able to see it close up, I felt somehow disappointed that this was to be the special treat.

"Have you ever seen a honey guide?" he asked.

We all admitted that we hadn't, and he explained that that was the name of the small brown bird.

I asked why it was called that, since it obviously didn't produce honey, and seemed incapable of replacing Kevin as our guide, and he smiled again.

"Do you see that tree?" he asked, pointing to a tree perhaps seventy-five yards away. There was a huge beehive on a low-hanging branch.

"Yes," I said.

"Then watch," he said, opening the cage and releasing the bird. It stood still for a moment, then fluttered its wings and took off in the direction of the tree.

"He is making sure there is honey there," explained Kevin, pointing to the bird as it circled the hive.

"Where is he going now?" I asked, as the bird suddenly flew down the river bed.

"To find his partner."

"Partner?" I asked, confused.

"Wait and see," said Kevin, sitting down with his back propped against a large rock.

We all followed suit and sat in the shade, our binoculars and holo cameras trained on the tree. After almost an hour nothing had happened, and some of us were getting restless, when Kevin tensed and pointed up the river bed.

"There!" he whispered. I looked in the direction he was pointing, and there, following the bird, which was flying just ahead of him and chirping frantically, was an enormous black-and-white animal, the largest I have ever seen.

"What is it?" I whispered.

"A honey badger," answered Kevin softly. "They were thought to be extinct twenty years ago, but a mated pair took sanctuary in Olduvai. This is the fourth generation to be born here."

"Is he going to eat the bird?" asked one of the party.

"No," whispered Kevin. "The bird will lead him to the honey, and after he has pulled down the nest and eaten his fill, he will leave some for the bird."

And it was just as Kevin said. The honey badger climbed the bole of the tree and knocked off the beehive with a forepaw, then climbed back down and broke it apart, oblivious to the stings of the bees. We caught the whole fantastic scene on our holos, and when he was done he did indeed leave some honey for the honey guide.

Later, while Kevin was recapturing the bird and putting it back in its cage, the rest of us discussed what we had seen. I thought the honey badger must have weighed forty-five pounds, though less excitable members of the party put its weight at closer to thirty-six or thirty-seven. Whichever it was, the creature was enormous. The discussion then shifted to how big a tip to leave for Kevin, for he had certainly earned one.

As I write this final entry in my safari diary, I am still trembling with the excitement that can only come from encountering big game in the wild. Prior to this afternoon, I had some doubts about the safari—I felt it was overpriced, or that perhaps my expectations had been too high—but now I know that it was worth every penny, and I have a feeling that I am leaving some part of me behind here, and that I will never be truly content until I return to this last bastion of the wilderness.

The camp was abuzz with excitement. Just when we were sure that there were no more treasures to unearth, the Stardust Twins had found three small pieces of bone, attached together with a wire—obviously a human artifact. "But the dates are wrong," said the Historian, after examining the bones thoroughly with its equipment. "This is a primitive piece of jewelry—for the adornment of savages, one might say—and yet the bones and wire both date from centuries after Man discovered space travel."

"Do you . . ."

". . . deny that we . . ."

". . . found it in the . . ."

". . . gorge?" demanded the Twins.

"I believe you," said the Historian. "I simply state that it seems to be an anachronism."

"It is our find, and . . ."

". . . it will bear our name."

"No one is denying your right of discovery," said Bellidore. "It is simply that you have presented us with a mystery."

"Give it to . . ."

". . . He Who Views, and he . . ."

". . . will solve the mystery."

"I will do my best," I said. "But it has not been long enough since I assimilated the stylus. I must rest and regain my strength."

"That is . . ."

". . . acceptable."

We let the Moriteu go about brushing and cleaning the artifact, while we speculated on why a primitive fetish should exist in the starfaring age. Finally the Exobiologist got to her feet.

"I am going back into the gorge," she announced. "If the Stardust Twins could find this, perhaps there are other things we have overlooked. After all, it is an enormous area." She paused and looked at the rest of us. "Would anyone care to come with me?"

It was nearing the end of the day, and no one volunteered, and finally the Exobiologist turned and began walking toward the path that led down into the depths of Olduvai Gorge.

It was dark when I finally felt strong enough to assimilate the jewelry. I spread my essence about the bones and the wire and soon became one with them . . .

His name was Joseph Meromo, and he could live with the money but not the guilt.

It had begun with the communication from Brussels, and the veiled suggestion from the head of the multinational conglomerate headquartered there. They had a certain commodity to get rid of. They had no place to get rid of it. Could Tanzania help?

Meromo had told them he would look into it, but he doubted that his government could be of use.

Just *try*, came the reply.

In fact, more than the reply came. The next day a private courier delivered a huge wad of large-denomination bills, with a polite note thanking Meromo for his efforts on their behalf.

Meromo knew a bribe when he saw one—he'd certainly taken enough in his career—but he'd never seen one remotely the size of this one. And not even for helping them, but merely for being willing to explore possibilities.

Well, he had thought, why not? What could they conceivably have? A couple of containers of toxic waste? A few plutonium rods? You bury them deep enough in the earth and no one would ever know or care. Wasn't that what the Western countries did?

Of course, there was the Denver Disaster, and that little accident that made the Thames undrinkable for almost a century, but the only reason they popped so quickly to mind is because they were the *exceptions*, not the rule. There were thousands of dumping sites around the world, and ninety-nine percent of them caused no problems at all.

Meromo had his computer cast a holographic map of Tanzania above his desk. He looked at it, frowned, added topographical features, then began studying it in earnest.

If he decided to help them dump the stuff, whatever it was—and he told himself that he was still uncommitted—where would be the best place to dispose of it?

Off the coast? No, the fishermen would pull it up two minutes later, take it to the press, and raise enough hell to get him fired, and possibly even cause the rest of the government to resign. The party really couldn't handle any more scandals this year.

The Selous Province? Maybe five centuries ago, when it was the last wilderness on the continent, but not now, not with a thriving, semi-autonomous city-state of fifty-two million people where once there had been nothing but elephants and almost-impenetrable thorn bush.

Lake Victoria? No. Same problem with the fishermen. Dar es Salaam? It was a possibility. Close enough to the coast to make transport easy, practically deserted since Dodoma had become the new capital of the country.

But Dar es Salaam had been hit by an earthquake twenty years ago, when Meromo was still a boy, and he couldn't take the chance of another one exposing or breaking open whatever it was that he planned to hide.

He continued going over the map: Gombe, Ruaha, Iringa, Mbeya, Mtwara, Tarengire, Olduvai . . .

He stopped and stared at Olduvai, then called up all available data.

Almost a mile deep. That was in its favor. No animals left. Better still. No settlements on its steep slopes. Only a handful of Maasai still living in the area, no more than two dozen families, and they were too arrogant to pay any attention to what the government was doing. Of that Meromo was sure: he himself was a Maasai.

So he strung it out for as long as he could, collected cash gifts for almost two years, and finally gave them a delivery date.

Meromo stared out the window of his thirty-fourth floor office, past the bustling city of Dodoma, off to the east, to where he imagined Olduvai Gorge was.

It had seemed so simple. Yes, he was paid a lot of money, a disproportionate amount—but these multinationals had money to burn. It was just supposed to be a few dozen plutonium rods, or so he had thought. How was he to know that they were speaking of forty-two *tons* of nuclear waste?

There was no returning the money. Even if he wanted to, he could hardly expect them to come back and pull all that deadly material back out of the ground. Probably it was safe, probably no one would ever know . . .

But it haunted his days, and even worse, it began haunting his nights as well, appearing in various guises in his dreams. Sometimes it was as carefully sealed containers, sometimes it was as ticking bombs, sometimes a disaster had already occurred and all he could see were the charred bodies of Maasai children spread across the lip of the gorge.

For almost eight months he fought his devils alone, but eventually he realized that he must have help. The dreams not only haunted him at night, but invaded the day as well. He would be sitting at a staff meeting, and suddenly he would imagine he was sitting among the emaciated, sore-covered bodies of the Olduvai Maasai. He would be reading a book, and the words seemed to change and he would be reading that Joseph Meromo had been sentenced to death for his greed. He would watch a holo of the Titanic disaster, and suddenly he was viewing some variation of the Olduvai Disaster.

Finally he went to a psychiatrist, and because he was a Maasai, he chose a Maasai psychiatrist. Fearing the doctor's contempt, Meromo would not state explicitly what was causing the nightmares and intrusions, and after almost half a year's worth of futile attempts to cure him, the psychiatrist announced that he could do no more.

"Then am I to be cursed with these dreams forever?" asked Meromo.

"Perhaps not," said the psychiatrist. "*I* cannot help you, but just possibly there is one man who can."

He rummaged through his desk and came up with a small white card. On it was written a single word: MULEWO.

"This is his business card," said the psychiatrist. "Take it."

"There is no address on it, no means of communicating with him," said Meromo. "How will I contact him?"

"He will contact you."

"You will give him my name?"

The psychiatrist shook his head. "I will not have to. Just keep the card on your person. He will know you require his services."

Meromo felt like he was being made the butt of some joke he didn't understand, but he dutifully put the card in his pocket and soon forgot about it.

Two weeks later, as he was drinking at a bar, putting off going home to sleep as long as he could, a small woman approached him.

"Are you Joseph Meromo?" she asked.

"Yes."

"Please follow me."

"Why?" he asked suspiciously.

"You have business with Mulewo, do you not?" she said.

Meromo fell into step behind her, at least as much to avoid going home as from any belief that this mysterious man with no first name could help him. They went out to the street, turned left, walked in silence for three blocks, and turned right, coming to a halt at the front door to a steel-and-glass skyscraper.

"The sixty-third floor," she said. "He is expecting you."

"You're not coming with me?" asked Meromo.

She shook her head. "My job is done." She turned and walked off into the night.

Meromo looked up at the top of the building. It seemed residential. He considered his options, finally shrugged, and walk into the lobby.

"You're here for Mulewo," said the doorman. It was not a question. "Go to the elevator on the left."

Meromo did as he was told. The elevator was paneled with an oiled wood, and smelled fresh and sweet. It operated on voice command and quickly took him to the sixty-third floor. When he emerged he found himself in an elegantly decorated corridor, with ebony wainscotting and discreetly placed mirrors. He walked past three unmarked doors, wondering how he was supposed to know which apartment belonged to Mulewo, and finally came to one that was partially open.

"Come in, Joseph Meromo," said a hoarse voice from within.

Meromo opened the door the rest of the way, stepped into the apartment, and blinked.

Sitting on a torn rug was an old man, wearing nothing but a red cloth gathered at the shoulder. The walls were covered by reed matting, and a noxious-smelling caldron bubbled in the fireplace. A torch provided the only illumination.

"What *is* this?" asked Meromo, ready to step back into the corridor if the old man appeared as irrational as his surroundings.

"Come sit across from me, Joseph Meromo," said the old man. "Surely this is less frightening than your nightmares."

"What do you know about my nightmares?" demanded Meromo.

"I know why you have them. I know what lies buried at the bottom of Olduvai Gorge."

Meromo shut the door quickly. "Who told you?"

"No one told me. I have peered into your dreams, and sifted through them until I found the truth. Come sit."

Meromo walked to where the old man indicated and sat down carefully, trying not to get too much dirt on his freshly pressed outfit.

"Are you Mulewo?" he asked.

The old man nodded. "I am Mulewo."

"How do you know these things about me?"

"I am a *laibon*," said Mulewo.

"A witch doctor?"

"It is a dying art," answered Mulewo. "I am the last practitioner."

"I thought *laibons* cast spells and created curses."

"They also remove curses—and your nights, and even your days, are cursed, are they not?"

"You seem to know all about it."

"I know that you have done a wicked thing, and that you are haunted not only by the ghost of it, but by the ghosts of the future as well."

"And you can end the dreams?"

"That is why I have summoned you here."

"But if I did such a terrible thing, why do you *want* to help me?"

"I do not make moral judgments. I am here only to help the Maasai."

"And what about the Maasai who live by the gorge?" asked Meromo. "The ones who haunt my dreams?"

"When they ask for help, then I will help them."

"Can you cause the material that's buried there to vanish?"

Mulewo shook his head. "I cannot undo what has been done. I cannot even assuage your guilt, for it is a just guilt. All I can do is banish it from your dreams."

"I'll settle for that," said Meromo.

There was an uneasy silence.

"What do I do now?" asked Meromo.

"Bring me a tribute befitting the magnitude of the service I shall perform."

"I can write you a check right now, or have money transferred from my account to your own."

"I have more money than I need. I must have a tribute."

"But—"

"Bring it back tomorrow night," said Mulewo.

Meromo stared at the old *laibon* for a long minute, then got up and left without another word.

He called in sick the next morning, then went to two of Dodoma's better antique shops. Finally he found what he was looking for, charged it to his personal account, and took it home with him. He was afraid to nap before dinner, so he simply read a book all afternoon, then ate a hasty meal and returned to Mulewo's apartment.

"What have you brought me?" asked Mulewo.

Meromo laid the package down in front of the old man. "A headdress made from the skin of a lion," he answered. "They told me it was worn by Sendayo himself, the greatest of all *laibons*."

"It was not," said Mulewo, without unwrapping the package. "But it is a sufficient tribute nonetheless." He reached beneath his red cloth and withdrew a small necklace, holding it out for Meromo.

"What is this for?" asked Meromo, examining the necklace. It was made of small bones that had been strung together.

"You must wear it tonight when you go to sleep," explained the old man. "It will take all your visions unto itself. Then, tomorrow, you must go to Olduvai Gorge and throw it down to the bottom, so that the visions may lie side by side with the reality."

"And that's all?"

"That is all."

Meromo went back to his apartment, donned the necklace, and went to sleep. That night his dreams were worse than they had ever been before.

In the morning he put the necklace into a pocket and had a government plane fly him to Arusha. From there he rented a ground vehicle, and two hours later he was standing on the edge of the gorge. There was no sign of the buried material.

He took the necklace in his hand and hurled it far out over the lip of the gorge.

His nightmares vanished that night.

One hundred thirty-four years later, mighty Kilimanjaro shuddered as the long-dormant volcano within it came briefly to life.

One hundred miles away, the ground shifted on the floor of Olduvai Gorge, and three of the lead-lined containers broke open.

Joseph Meromo was long dead by that time; and, unfortunately, there were no *laibons* remaining to aid those people who were now compelled to live Meromo's nightmares.

I had examined the necklace in my own quarters, and when I came out to report my findings, I discovered that the entire camp was in a tumultuous state.

"What has happened?" I asked Bellidore.

"The Exobiologist has not returned from the gorge," he said.

"How long has she been gone?"

"She left at sunset last night. It is now morning, and she has not returned or attempted to use her communicator."

"We fear . . ."

". . . that she might . . ."

". . . have fallen and . . ."

". . . become immobile. Or perhaps even . . ."

". . . unconscious . . ." said the Stardust Twins.

"I have sent the Historian and the Appraiser to look for her," said Bellidore.

"I can help, too," I offered.

"No, you have the last artifact to examine," he said. "When the Moriteu awakens, I will send it as well."

"What about the Mystic?" I asked.

Bellidore looked at the Mystic and sighed. "She has not said a word since landing on this world. In truth, I do not understand her function. At any rate, I do not know how to communicate with her."

The Stardust Twins kicked at the earth together, sending up a pair of reddish dust clouds.

"It seems ridiculous . . ." said one.

". . . that we can find the tiniest artifact . . ." said the other.

". . . but we cannot find . . ."

". . . an entire exobiologist."

"Why do you not help search for it?" I asked.

"They get vertigo," explained Bellidore.

"We searched . . ."

". . . the entire camp," they added defensively.

"I can put off assimilating the last piece until tomorrow, and help with the search," I volunteered.

"No," replied Bellidore. "I have sent for the ship. We will leave tomorrow, and I want all of our major finds examined by then. It is *my* job to find the Exobiologist; it is *yours* to read the history of the last artifact."

"If that is your desire," I said. "Where is it?"

He led me to a table where the Historian and the Appraiser had been examining it.

"Even *I* know what this is," said Bellidore. "An unspent cartridge." He paused. "Along with the fact that we have found no human artifacts on any higher strata, I would say this in itself is unique: a bullet that a man chose *not* to fire."

"When you state it in those terms, it *does* arouse the curiosity," I acknowledged.

"Are you . . ."

". . . going to examine it . . ."

". . . now?" asked the Stardust Twins apprehensively.

"Yes, I am," I said.

"Wait!" they shouted in unison.

I paused above the cartridge while they began backing away.

"We mean . . ."

". . . no disrespect . . ."

". . . but watching you examine artifacts . . ."

". . . is too unsettling."

And with that, they raced off to hide behind some of the camp structures.

"What about you?" I asked Bellidore. "Would you like me to wait until you leave?"

"Not at all," he replied. "I find diversity fascinating. With your permission, I would like to stay and observe."

"As you wish," I said, allowing my body to melt around the cartridge until it had become a part of myself, and its history became my own history, as clear and precise as if it had all occurred yesterday . . .

"They are coming!"

Thomas Naikosiai looked across the table at his wife.

"Was there ever any doubt that they would?"

"This was foolish, Thomas!" she snapped. "They will force us to leave, and because we made no preparations, we will have to leave all our possessions behind."

"Nobody is leaving," said Naikosiai.

He stood up and walked to the closet. "You stay here," he said, donning his long coat and his mask. "I will meet them outside."

"That is both rude and cruel, to make them stand out there when they have come all this way."

"They were not invited," said Naikosiai. He reached deep into the closet and grabbed the rifle that leaned up against the back wall, then closed the closet, walked through the airlock and emerged on the front porch.

Six men, all wearing protective clothing and masks to filter the air, confronted him.

"It is time, Thomas," said the tallest of them.

"Time for *you*, perhaps," said Naikosiai, holding the rifle casually across his chest.

"Time for all of us," answered the tall man.

"I am not going anywhere. This is my home. I will not leave it."

"It is a pustule of decay and contamination, as is this whole country," came the answer. "We are all leaving."

Naikosiai shook his head. "My father was born on this land, and his father, and his father's father. *You* may run from danger, if you wish; I will stay and fight it."

"How can you make a stand against radiation?" demanded the tall man. "Can you put a bullet through it? How can you fight air that is no longer safe to breathe?"

"Go away," said Naikosiai, who had no answer to that, other than the conviction that he would never leave his home. "I do not demand that you stay. Do not demand that I leave."

"It is for your own good, Naikosiai," urged another. "If you care nothing for your own life, think of your wife's. How much longer can she breathe the air?"

"Long enough."

"Why not let *her* decide?"

"*I* speak for our family."

An older man stepped forward. "She is *my* daughter, Thomas," he said severely. "I will not allow you to condemn her to the life you have chosen for yourself. Nor will I let my grandchildren remain here."

The old man took another step toward the porch, and suddenly the rifle was pointing at him.

"That's far enough," said Naikosiai.

"They are Maasai," said the old man stubbornly. "They must come with the other Maasai to our new world."

"You are not Maasai," said Naikosiai contemptuously. "Maasai did not leave their ancestral lands when the rinderpest destroyed their herds, or when the white man came, or when the governments sold off their lands. Maasai never surrender. *I* am the last Maasai."

"Be reasonable, Thomas. How can you not surrender to a world that is no longer safe for people to live on? Come with us to New Kilimanjaro."

"The Maasai do not run from danger," said Naikosiai.

"I tell you, Thomas Naikosiai," said the old man, "that I cannot allow you to condemn my daughter and my grandchildren to live in this hellhole. The last ship leaves tomorrow morning. They will be on it."

"They will stay with me, to build a new Maasai nation."

The six men whispered among themselves, and then their leader looked up at Naikosiai.

"You are making a terrible mistake, Thomas," he said. "If you change your mind, there is room for you on the ship."

They all turned to go, but the old man stopped and turned to Naikosiai.

"I will be back for my daughter," he said.

Naikosiai gestured with his rifle. "I will be waiting for you."

The old man turned and walked off with the others, and Naikosiai went back into his house through the airlock. The tile floor smelled of disinfectant, and the sight of the television set offended his eyes, as always. His wife was waiting for him in the kitchen, amid the dozens of gadgets she had purchased over the years.

"How can you speak with such disrespect to the Elders!" she demanded. "You have disgraced us."

"No!" he snapped. "*They* have disgraced us, by leaving!"

"Thomas, you cannot grow anything in the fields. The animals have all died. You cannot even breathe the air without a filtering mask. *Why* do you insist on staying?"

"This is our ancestral land. We will not leave it."

"But all the others—"

"They can do as they please," he interrupted. "En-kai will judge them, as He judges us all. I am not afraid to meet my creator."

"But why must you meet him so soon?" she persisted. "You have seen the tapes and disks of New Kilimanjaro. It is a beautiful world, green and gold and filled with rivers and lakes."

"Once Earth was green and gold and filled with rivers and lakes," said Naikosiai. "They ruined this world. They will ruin the next one."

"Even if they do, we will be long dead," she said. "I want to go."

"We've been through all this before."

"And it always ends with an order rather than an agreement," she said. Her expression softened. "Thomas, just once before I die, I want to see water that you can drink without adding chemicals to it. I want to see antelope grazing on long green grasses. I want to walk outside without having to protect myself from the very air I breathe."

"It's settled."

She shook her head. "I love you, Thomas, but I cannot stay here, and I cannot let our children stay here."

"No one is taking my children from me!" he yelled.

"Just because you care nothing for *your* future, I cannot permit you to deny our sons *their* future."

"Their future is here, where the Maasai have always lived."

"Please come with us, Papa," said a small voice behind him, and Naikosiai turned to see his two sons, eight and five, standing in the doorway to their bedroom, staring at him.

"What have you been saying to them?" demanded Naikosiai suspiciously.

"The truth," said his wife.

He turned to the two boys. "Come here," he said, and they trudged across the room to him.

"What are you?" he asked.

"Boys," said the younger child.

"What *else?*"

"Maasai," said the older.

"That is right," said Naikosiai. "You come from a race of giants. There was a time when, if you climbed to the very top of Kilimanjaro, all the land you could see in every direction belonged to us."

"But that was long ago," said the older boy.

"Someday it will be ours again," said Naikosiai. "You must remember who you are, my son. You are the descendant of Leeyo, who killed one hundred lions with just his spear; of Nelion, who waged war against the whites and drove them from the Rift; of Sendayo, the greatest of all the *laibons*. Once the Kikuyu and the Wakamba and the Lumbwa trembled in fear at the very mention of the word Maasai. This is your heritage; do not turn your back on it."

"But the Kikuyu and the other tribes have all left."

"What difference does that make to the Maasai? We did not make a stand only against the Kikuyu and the Wakamba, but against *all* men who would have us change our ways. Even after the Europeans conquered Kenya and Tanganyika, they never conquered the Maasai. When Independence came, and all the other tribes moved to cities and wore suits and aped the Europeans, we remained as we had always been. We wore what we chose and we lived where we chose, for we were proud to be Maasai. Does that not *mean* something to you?"

"Will we not still be Maasai if we go to the new world?" asked the older boy.

"No," said Naikosiai firmly. "There is a bond between the Maasai and the land. We define it, and it defines us. It is what we have always fought for and always defended."

"But it is diseased now," said the boy.

"If I were sick, would you leave me?" asked Naikosiai.

"No, Papa."

"And just as you would not leave me in my illness, so we will not leave the land in *its* illness. When you love something, when it is a part of what you are, you do not leave it simply because it becomes sick. You stay, and you fight even harder to cure it than you fought to win it."

"But—"

"Trust me," said Naikosiai. "Have I ever misled you?"

"No, Papa."

"I am not misleading you now. We are En-kai's chosen people. We live on the ground He has given us. Don't you see that we *must* remain here, that we must keep our covenant with En-kai?"

"But I will never see my friends again!" wailed his younger son.

"You will make new friends."

"Where?" cried the boy. "Everyone is gone!"

"Stop that at once!" said Naikosiai harshly. "Maasai do not cry."

The boy continued sobbing, and Naikosiai looked up at his wife.

"This is *your* doing," he said. "You have spoiled him."

She stared unblinking into his eyes. "Five-year-old boys are allowed to cry."

"Not Maasai boys," he answered.

"Then he is no longer Maasai, and you can have no objection to his coming with me."

"I want to go too!" said the eight-year-old, and suddenly he, too, forced some tears down his face.

Thomas Naikosiai looked at his wife and his children—really *looked* at them—and realized that he did not know them at all. This was not the quiet maiden, raised in the traditions of his people, that he had married nine years ago. These soft sobbing boys were not the successors of Leeyo and Nelion.

He walked to the door and opened it.

"Go to the new world with the rest of the black Europeans," he growled.

"Will you come with us?" asked his oldest son.

Naikosiai turned to his wife. "I divorce you," he said coldly. "All that was between us is no more."

He walked over to his two sons. "I disown you. I am no longer your father, you are no longer my sons. Now go!"

His wife put coats and masks on both of the boys, then donned her own.

"I will send some men for my things before morning," she said.

"If any man comes onto my property, I will kill him," said Naikosiai.

She stared at him, a look of pure hatred. Then she took the children by the hands and led them out of the house and down the long road to where the ship awaited them.

Naikosiai paced the house for a few minutes, filled with nervous rage. Finally he went to the closet, donned his coat and mask, pulled out his rifle, and walked through the airlock to the front of his house. Visibility was poor, as always, and he went out to the road to see if anyone was coming.

There was no sign of any movement. He was almost disappointed. He planned to show them how a Maasai protected what was his.

And suddenly he realized that this was *not* how a Maasai protected his own. He walked to the edge of the gorge, opened the bolt, and threw his cartridges into the void one by one. Then he held the rifle over his head and hurled it after them. The coat came next, then the mask, and finally his clothes and shoes.

He went back into the house and pulled out that special trunk that held the memorabilia of a lifetime. In it he found what he was looking for: a simple piece of red cloth. He attached it at his shoulder.

Then he went into the bathroom, looking among his wife's cosmetics. It took almost half an hour to hit upon the right combinations, but when he emerged his hair was red, as if smeared with clay.

He stopped by the fireplace and pulled down the spear that hung there. Family tradition had it that the spear had once been used by Nelion himself; he wasn't sure he believed it, but it was definitely a Maasai spear, blooded many times in battle and hunts during centuries past.

Naikosiai walked out the door and positioned himself in front of his house—his *manyatta*. He planted his bare feet on the diseased ground, placed the butt of his spear next to his right foot, and stood at attention. Whatever came down the road next—a band of black Europeans hoping to rob him of his possessions, a lion out of history, a band of Nandi or Lumbwa come to slay the enemy of their blood, they would find him ready.

They returned just after sunrise the next morning, hoping to convince him to emigrate to New Kilimanjaro. What they found was the last Maasai, his lungs burst from the pollution, his dead eyes staring proudly out across the vanished savannah at some enemy only he could see.

I released the cartridge, my strength nearly gone, my emotions drained.

So that was how it had ended for Man on earth, probably less than a mile from where it had begun. So bold and so foolish, so moral and so savage. I had hoped the last artifact would prove to be the final piece of the puzzle, but instead it merely added to the mystery of this most contentious and fascinating race.

Nothing was beyond their ability to achieve. One got the feeling that the day the first primitive man looked up and saw the stars, the galaxy's days as a haven of peace and freedom were numbered. And yet they came out to the stars not just with their lusts and their hatred and their fears, but with their technology and their medicine, their heroes as well as their villains. Most of the races of the galaxy had been painted by the Creator in pastels; Men were primaries.

I had much to think about as I went off to my quarters to renew my strength. I do not know how long I lay, somnolent and unmoving, recovering my energy, but it must have been a long time, for night had come and gone before I felt prepared to rejoin the party.

As I emerged from my quarters and walked to the center of camp, I heard a yell from the direction of the gorge, and a moment later the Appraiser appeared, a large sterile bag balanced atop an air trolly.

"What have you found?" asked Bellidore, and suddenly I remembered that the Exobiologist was missing.

"I am almost afraid to guess," replied the Appraiser, laying the bag on the table.

All the members of the party gathered around as he began withdrawing items: a blood-stained communicator, bent out of shape; the floating shade, now broken, that the Exobiologist used to protect her head from the rays of the sun; a torn piece of clothing; and finally, a single gleaming white bone.

The instant the bone was placed on the table, the Mystic began screaming. We were all shocked into momentary immobility, not only because of the suddenness of her reaction, but because it was the first sign of life she had shown since joining our party. She continued to stare at the bone and scream, and finally, before we could question her or remove the bone from her sight, she collapsed.

"I don't suppose there can be much doubt about what happened," said Bellidore. "The creatures caught up with the Exobiologist somewhere on her way down the gorge and killed her."

"Probably ate . . ."

". . . her too," said the Stardust Twins.

"I am glad we are leaving today," continued Bellidore. "Even after all these millennia, the spirit of Man continues to corrupt and degrade this world. Those lumbering creatures can't possibly be predators: there are no meat animals left on Earth. But given the opportunity, they fell upon the Exobiologist and consumed her flesh. I have this uneasy feeling that if we stayed much longer, we, too, would become corrupted by this world's barbaric heritage."

The Mystic regained consciousness and began screaming again, and the Stardust Twins gently escorted her back to her quarters, where she was given a sedative.

"I suppose we might as well make it official," said Bellidore. He turned to the Historian. "Would you please check the bone with your instruments and make sure that this is the remains of the Exobiologist?"

The Historian stared at the bone, horror-stricken. "She was my *friend!*" it said at last. "I cannot touch it as if it were just another artifact."

"We must know for sure," said Bellidore. "If it is not part of the Exobiologist, then there is a chance, however slim, that your friend might still be alive."

The Historian reached out tentatively for the bone, then jerked its hand away. "I can't!"

Finally Bellidore turned to me. "He Who Views," he said. "Have you the strength to examine it?"

"Yes," I answered.

They all moved back to give me room, and I allowed my mass to slowly spread over the bone and engulf it. I assimilated its history and ingested its emotional residue, and finally I withdrew from it.

"It is the Exobiologist," I said.

"What are the funeral customs of her race?" asked Bellidore.

"Cremation," said the Appraiser.

"Then we shall build a fire and incinerate what remains of our friend, and we will each offer a prayer to send her soul along the Eternal Path."

And that is what we did.

The ship came later that day, and took us off the planet, and it is only now, safely removed from its influence, that I can reconstruct what I learned on that last morning.

I lied to Bellidore—to the entire party—for once I made my discovery I knew that my primary duty was to get them away from Earth as quickly as possible. Had I told them the truth, one or more of them would have wanted to remain behind, for they are scientists with curious, probing minds, and I would never be able to convince them that a curious, probing mind is no match for what I found in my seventh and final view of Olduvai Gorge.

The bone was *not* a part of the Exobiologist. The Historian, or even the Moriteu, would have known that had they not been too horrified to examine it. It was the tibia of a *Man*.

Man has been extinct for five thousand years, at least as we citizens of the galaxy have come to understand him. But those lumbering, ungainly creatures of the night, who seemed so attracted to our campfires, are what Man has become. Even the pollution and radiation he spread across his own planet could not kill him off. It merely changed him to the extent that we were no longer able to recognize him.

I could have told them the simple facts, I suppose: that a tribe of these pseudo-Men stalked the Exobiologist down the gorge, then attacked and killed and, yes, ate her. Predators are not unknown throughout the worlds of the galaxy.

But as I became one with the tibia, as I felt it crashing down again and again upon our companion's head and shoulders, I felt a sense of power, of exultation I had never experienced before. I suddenly seemed to see the world through the eyes of the bone's possessor. I saw how he had killed his own companion to create the weapon, I saw how he planned to plunder the bodies of the old and the infirm for more weapons, I saw visions of conquest against other tribes living near the gorge.

And finally, at the moment of triumph, he and I looked up at the sky, and we knew that someday all that we could see would be ours.

And this is the knowledge that I have lived with for two days. I do not know who to share it with, for it is patently immoral to exterminate a race simply because of the vastness of its dreams or the ruthlessness of its ambition.

But this is a race that refuses to die, and somehow I must warn the rest of us, who have lived in harmony for almost five millennia.

It's not over.

DEAD SPACE FOR THE UNEXPECTED

Geoff Ryman

Born in Canada, Geoff Ryman now lives in England. He made his first sale in 1976 to *New Worlds*, but it was not until 1984, when he made his first appearance in *Interzone* (the magazine where almost all of his published short fiction has appeared) with his brilliant novella "The Unconquered Country" that he first attracted any serious attention. "The Unconquered Country," one of the best novellas of the decade, had a stunning impact on the science fiction scene and almost overnight established Ryman as one of the premier writers of his generation, winning him both the British Science Fiction Award and the World Fantasy Award; it was later published in a book version, *The Unconquered Country: A Life History*. His output since then has been sparse, by the high-production standards of the genre, but extremely distinguished, with his novel *The Child Garden: A Low Comedy* winning both the prestigious Arthur C. Clarke Award and the John W. Campbell Memorial Award. His other novels include *The Warrior Who Carried Life* and the critically acclaimed mainstream novel *Was*. His most recent book is a collection of four of his novellas, *Unconquered Countries*.

The idea that science fiction actually *predicts* the future is an overemphasized one, but, in the bleak little story that follows, Ryman gives us a razor-sharp look at working conditions in a near-future society that, as anyone who has ever worked for a major corporation could tell you, is all too likely to come to pass; in fact, it's very nearly here *now* . . .

Jonathan was going to have to fire Simon. It was a big moment in Jonathan's day, a solid achievement from the point of view of the company. Jonathan knew that his handling of the whole procedure had been model—so far. He had warned Simon a month ago that termination was a possibility and that plans should be made. Jonathan knew that he had felt all the appropriate feelings—sympathy, regret, and an echoing in himself of the sick, sad panic of redundancy.

Well, if you have sincere emotion, hang onto it. Use it. Hell, there had even been a sting of tears around the bottom of his eyes as he told Simon. Jonathan's score for that session had been 9.839 out of 10, a personal best for a counselling episode.

Now he had to be even better. The entire Team's average had nose-dived. So had Jonathan's own scores. He, the Team, needed a good score. Next month's printouts were at stake.

So Jonathan waited in the meeting room with a sign up on the door that said IN USE. On his eyes were contact lenses that were marked for accurate measurement, and which flickered and swerved as his eyes moved. There was a bright pattern of stripes and squares and circles on his shirt, to highlight breathing patterns. Galvanic skin resistance was monitored by his watch strap. It was, of course, a voluntary program, designed to give managers and staff alike feedback on their performance.

There was a knock on the door and Simon came in, handsome, neat, running a bit to fat, 52 years old.

It would be the benches for Simon, the park benches in summer with the civic chess board with the missing pieces. Then the leaves and seasonal chill in autumn. Winter would be the packed and steamy public library with the unwashed bodies, and the waiting for a chance to read the job ads, check the terminals, scan the benefits information. It would be bye-bye to clean shirts, ties without food stains, a desk, the odd bottle of wine, pride. For just a moment, Jonathan saw it all clearly in his mind.

Either you were a performer or you weren't.

"Hi, Simon, have a good weekend?"

"Yes, thank you," said Simon, as he sat down, his face impassive, his movements contained and neat.

Jonathan sighed. "I wanted to give you this now, before I sent it to anyone else. I wanted you to be the first to know I'm very sorry."

Jonathan held out a sealed, white, blank envelope. Simon primed for a month, simply nodded.

"I hope you know there's nothing personal in this. I've tried to explain why it's necessary, but just to be clear, there has been a severe drop in our performance and we simply must up our averages, and be seen to be taking some positive action. In terms of more staff training, that sort of thing."

Already this was not going well. The opening line about the weekend could not be less appropriate, and nobody was going to think that being fired was a positive step or care two hoots about the training other people were going to get. Inwardly, Jonathan winced. "Anyway," he shrugged with regret, still holding out the envelope that Simon had not taken. Jonathan tossed it across the table and it spun on a cushion of air across the wood-patterned surface.

Simon made no move to pick it up. "We all get old," he said. "You will, too."

"And when my scores slip," said Jonathan, trying to generate some fellow feeling, "I expect the same thing will happen to me."

"I hope so," said Simon.

Right, counselling mode. Jonathan remembered his training. Unfortunately, so did Simon—they had been on the same courses.

"Are you angry, would you like to talk?" said Jonathan, remembering: keep steady eye contact, or rather contact with the forehead or bridge of the nose, which is less threatening. Lean backwards so less aggression, but echo body language.

Simon smiled slightly and started to pick his nose, very messily, and look at the result. He held the result up towards Jonathan as if to say echo this.

Jonathan nodded as if in agreement. "It's only natural that you should feel some resentment, but it might be more constructive if you expressed it verbally. You know, say what you feel, blow off some steam. If not to me, then to someone, the Welfare Officer perhaps."

"I don't need to blow off steam," said Simon and stood up and walked to the door.

Procedures were not being followed; discipline was important.

"Simon, you haven't taken your letter."

Simon stood at the door for a moment. "It's not my letter. It's not written for me, it's addressed to Personnel so they can stop paying me."

Boy, thought Jonathan, if you were still being marked, you'd be in trouble, buddy.

"You forget," said Simon his blue eyes gray and flinty, "I used to work in Accounts." He picked up the letter, paused, and wiped his finger on it. Then he left the room.

Jonathan sat at the table, trembling with rage. Fuck counselling, he wanted to haul off and slug the guy. He took a deep breath, just like in the handling stress course, then stood up and left the meeting room, remembering to change the sign on the door. VACANT it said.

Back in his own office, he checked his score. It was bad form to check your scores too often; it showed insecurity, but Jonathan couldn't help himself. He verballed to the computer.

"Performance feedback, Dayplan Item One."

His mark was higher than he had thought it would be: 7.2, well over a five and edging towards a 7.5 for a pretty tough situation. But it was not the high score the Team needed.

It was 8:42. Three minutes ahead of schedule.

"Dayplan complete," he verballed, and his day was laid out before him on the screen.

```
 8:30   Simon Hasley (actioned)
 8:45   Dayplan confirmed and in tray
 8:50   Sally meeting prep
 9:00   Sally meeting
 9:30   Sales meeting William
10:00   Dead space for the unexpected...
```

It was important that work was seen to be prioritised, that nothing stayed on the desk, or queued up on the machine. It all had to be handled in the right order. The computer worked that out for you from the priority rating you gave each item, gave you optimum work times and the corporate cost, and if you did not object, those were your targets for the first half of the day.

Right. In-tray. There was a management report on purchasing. Jonathan did not purchase, but he needed to know the new procedures his Finance Officer was supposed to follow. So make that a priority eight, book in a reading for it next week, and ask for the machine to prepare a precis. Next was a memo with spreadsheet from Admin. Admin acted as a kind of prophylactic against Accounts, giving early warning of what would strike Accounts as below par performance. Jonathan's heart sank. Late invoices. Holy shit, not again, an average of 12 days?

Thanks a lot, George, thanks a fucking lot. Shit, piss, fuck, I'll cut off that god-damned asshole's head and stick it up his own greased asshole.

Ho-boy, Jonathan, that's anger. Channel it, use it. Right, we got ourselves a priority one here, schedule it in Dead Space. Jonathan slammed his way into George's network terminal. Which at 8:47 in the morning was not switched on.

```
PRIORITY 1
George, we have a serious issue to discuss. Can you
come to my office at 10:00 am today, Thursday 17th.
Please come with figures on speed of invoicing.
J Rosson, III 723, nc 11723JR.
```

There goes our cash flow down the fucking tube. And interest payments to the Centre. Great.

There was a fretful knocking at his door. Jonathan could guess who it was. Two minutes was all the time he had.

In came Harriet, gray hair flying. What you might call an individual. Jonathan swivelled, knowing his body language showed no surprise or alarm. His greeting was warm, friendly, in control So far, so good.

"Hello, Harriet, good to see you, but I'm afraid I'm up against it this morning. I expect you've heard about Simon."

"Yes, I have actually," said Harriet, eyes bright, smile wide. She was preparing to sit down.

No, my door is not always open. Don't mess with my time management, lady. "I'd love to talk to you about it when I can give you some time. How about 10:10 this morning?"

"This will only take a minute." Harriet was still smiling. A tough old bird.

"I doubt that very much. It's an important issue, and I'd like to talk to you about it properly." With a flourish, he keyed her into his Dayplan. "There we go. 10:10. See you then?"

Harriet accepted defeat with good grace. "Lovely," she said. "I'll look forward to that." She even gave him a sweet little wave as she left.

Poor old cow is scared, thought Jonathan. Well, there are no plans to get rid of her, so that should be a fairly easy session.

Next. Up came a report on a new initiative in timekeeping, a hobby horse of Jonathan's. Was a priority one justified just because he was interested in it? He decided to downgrade it, show he was keeping a sense of proportion, that he was a team player. He gave it a two and booked it in for Friday.

He was behind schedule. Thanks, Harriet. Next was a note of praise for a job well done from that crawler Jason. The guy even writes memos to apologise for not writing memos. Jonathan wastebinned it with a grin. Next was a welfare report on the Team's resident schizophrenic. Jonathan was sure the poor guy had been hired just to give them a bit of an obstacle to show jump. The Welfare Officer was asking him to counsel the man to reduce his smoking in the office. But. He was to remember that the stress of giving up smoking could trigger another schizophrenic episode.

Oh come on, this really must be a monitoring exercise. Jonathan thought a moment. He should therefore show that he knew it was an exercise and not take it too seriously. So, he delegated. He dumped the whole report off his own screen and into the Dayplan of his Supporting Officer.

And so, 8:55. Five minutes to prep for Sally. Jeez, thought Jonathan. I hope I'm not showing. Not showing fear. Which meant, of course, that he was.

Simply, Sally was one of the big boys. She was the same grade as Jonathan, a 1.1 on a level D, but she was younger, whiplash quick, utterly charming, and she always won. Jonathan knew her scores were infinitely better than his own.

Sally had been naughty. Her Division and his Team had to cooperate on projects that were both above and below the line. Without telling him, she had called a meeting on his own grade 2s, flattered them no end, and then got the poor lambs to agree, just as a point of procedure, that all joint projects would be registered with her Division. This would cost his Team about three hundred thousand a year in turnover.

Jonathan had countered with a report on procedures, reminding all concerned that such decisions needed to be made at Divisional level, and suggesting a more thorough procedural review. Sally had countered with enthusiastic agreement, deadly, but said a joint presentation on procedures might eliminate misunderstanding. The difference between discussion and presentation was the difference between procedures up for grabs, and procedures already set and agreed.

When Jonathan pointed this out at a Divisional Liaison, Sally had said "Awwww!" as if he were a hurt, suspicious child. She had even started to counsel him—in front of management! Jonathan had never felt so angry, so outmanoeuvered. Now his Team had noticed pieces of artwork they should have controlled going elsewhere and wanted him to do something about it. Too late, guys. Bloody Harry, his boss, was too dim to see what had happened, or too feeble to fight. Harry had agreed to the presentation.

So, he told himself. The posture has to be teamwork, cooperation between different parts of the same organization, steer like hell to get back what he could. And keep smiling.

He put his phone and mail through to Support and went downstairs.

Sally's office was neater than his own, and had tiny white furniture. It was like sitting on porcelain teacups. He was sure she chose the furniture deliberately to make large men feel clumsy. Sally offered him coffee. Christ, what was his caffeine count already? Too many stimulants, you lost points. Was she trying to jangle him, get him shaky?

"Oh, great, thanks," he said. "White with one sugar."

"Help yourself," she said. Her smile was warm and friendly. What she meant was: help yourself, I'm not your mother.

"Real cream," acknowledged Jonathan as he poured.

"Nothing but the best is good enough for us," said Sally. She was luxuriantly made up, frosted with sheen. She sat down opposite him. Her hair was in different streaks of honey, beige and blonde, and she was slim under her sharp and padded suit. Her entire mien was sociable and open, inviting trust.

"Thanks for the report," she said. "It was very useful, and I really want to thank you for organizing the presentation for us."

Jonathan had fought it every step of the way. "My pleasure," he said. "We really need to get the two teams together to talk. I just want to be clear that what we're aiming to do is work towards a set of procedures for shared work, which keeps everything going to the right people."

Sally nodded. But she didn't speak.

Jonathan double-checked. "Am I right?"

Her smile broadened just a stretch. "Uh-huh. We do have a set of procedures that your own staff agreed."

"Not all my staff, and not the Quality Action Units who should have been involved. The idea is to empower everyone in the organization."

"Well, I'm sure we can iron out any points of difference. Refer them to the Quasi. OK?"

Jonathan played back the same trick, an uncommitted shrug. But it was one up to him.

A peace offering? Sally kept on. "I also thought that we should present to you first. Most of my staff are familiar with what you do, but our CD ROM work is new, and we need to go over it with your team."

Can I let her get away with that? The clock was ticking, his heart was racing. Caffeine and three hundred thousand smackers. Basically, her staff would NOT be there, say just three of them. They would have the floor and the agenda, but his people would outnumber them, and it would be very easy to take pot shots from the audience. On balance, yes, he could go along with that.

So he agreed. They set dates and agreed how to split the cost of wine and food. Sally gave him a warm and enveloping smile as he left.

Climbing back up the stairs, he reckoned he had scored a five. She still had the initiative, she'd gone no distance towards giving up registration of his jobs, but then, it could be argued that Harry had given them away. I got some points across, but anyone could see I was tense. Jeez. Why do I do it to myself?

Right, now it was Billy, then Dead Space, then the brief on the Commission tender, then lunch.

Lunch with Harry, his boss. Harry was shy and hated schmoozing, which was endearing in a boss, if only he didn't wring his hands for hours at a time and utterly fail to make decisions. Jonathan braced himself for an hour of whining. Jonathan used to work out at lunchtime, till he realized that he scored a full .03 higher if he social-grazed instead. He was climbing the stairs now, to keep fit, though he was not too sure if anyone was noticing. For some reason, he was feeling mean when William arrived for the Sales Meeting.

"Template?" Jonathan snapped at him. William's eyes glittered. Look at those lenses dive for cover. William was in his early twenties, uncomely, gay, nervous. He was supposed to have the agreed agenda and a place for agreed action notes. "Ah. It's just here." When William found his sheet, the agenda section was left blank.

Jonathan tapped the white space, and chuckled, and shook his head, like an indulgent father. "Billy, Billy, what am I going to do with you? Couldn't you remember to print it out? Here, use mine and photocopy it to me after the meeting. Did we get the form letters out?"

Billy had. Well, what do you know?

"All sixty? Great. Thanks very much. Now. The new fax number. We sent all our customers the new fax number, right? Fine. Then why did the Commission fax us a copy of a tender brief on the old number?"

Billy's face fell.

"They sent us a tender, Billy, and it went to our old number, which is with Interactive Media now, who are not necessarily our greatest chums, where it sat for a full afternoon. So now we have four days instead of a working week to develop a full tender with designs. Do you see the problem here?"

Billy face went white and distressed.

The real problem, Jonathan cursed to himself, is that management expects me to make sales without any funding, so I have to use poor Billy from Support who is as sweet as a lamb, but Jeez! Jonathan watched as William scrambled through his shaggy files. OK.

Jonathan decided to try a new management technique. He tried to make himself fancy Billy sexually. LLA, Low Level Attraction, could generate good Team bonding. In fact, people with low to middle bisexuality scores had a favoured Starting-Gun Profile.

So Jonathan looked at Billy and tried, but Billy had chalk white skin and lank black hair, and spots, the thick, clotted, dumb kind of spot that never comes to a head.

I hate this guy, this puny, nervy little idiot; I just can't resist trying to break him.

"Um," said Billy, miserable, balancing his spread-eagled file on his lap. "Yeah, well, I, uh, didn't fax the Commission because it was among my problems to be resolved."

"You mean you didn't know the Commission was one of your clients?" Jonathan managed to say it more in sorrow that in anger.

"I think it was that I didn't know who were our contact names there."

Neither, now that he thought about it, did Jonathan. "OK," he sighed. "Look. Talk to Clara, she'll know them, and then just send the notification you've got. Don't apologize or let them know that we didn't tell them in time. If they ask, the number has just changed. I don't want them to know we had this little hiccup. OK?"

"OK," Billy murmured.

"And, Billy, please. Don't try to keep all your correspondence in one file? You'll find it easier if you keep things separate."

Billy thanked him for the advice. Then he suggested that Jonathan might like to come around to his place for drinks.

I don't believe this. This kid was making a pass at him, he was so desperate. OK, we're both playing the same LLA game. How can we both win? Don't be judgmental, turn the attraction, if that was what you could call it, into friendliness, team bonding.

"That's a great idea, Billy. But I've been feeling bad about not inviting you to my place. I think you've met my wife, but you've never even seen my daughter. Are you free next week?"

Billy looked relieved. Jonathan was relieved too, and thanked him for the job he was doing, and in the general thanking and summing up the invitations were forgotten.

Billy left and Jonathan sat back and sighed. He was feeling tired a lot these days. He saw Sally's face, pink glossy lips parted, as she gave a tiny cry. He sat still for a moment, his eyes closed.

It was 9:57. Jonathan couldn't help himself. He checked his scores again. He really must stop doing this. It was like when he got hooked on the I Ching, and had to have Chaos Therapy to kick it. But all he wanted was a breakdown, a fuller breakdown of this morning's score with Simon.

Verbal content 4.79.

OK, I knew I was bad, but that bad?

Body Language 4.5.

What? Oh, come on. What was I supposed to do, pick my nose? Jonathan actioned a more in-depth analysis. Artificiality, his machine told him, a lack of visible sincerity.

Christ! You can't move around this place. If I'd been sincere. I would have said, you fucked up that own-account job 18 months ago, and you've been a liability ever since and you've done nothing any better, so we're ditching you like we should have done even earlier. I was just trying to be fucking kind. What should I have done, told him to fuck off?

So what got me my good score? This breakdown is terrible.

`10:00 Dead Space.`

And the computer flipped itself out into a proactive intervention.

Suddenly, it started to play him the tape of the morning's session with Simon.

There he was, fat, stone-faced, saying, "It's not written for me. It's written for Personnel."

A full analysis scrolled up on the screen. Flesh tones, oxygen use, body language, uncharacteristic verbals, atypical eye use.

Behavior typical of industrial sabotage. Rage mixed with satisfaction.

In other words, Simon had become dangerous. Not a little bit dangerous, very dangerous. Determined, apparently, to get revenge.

`In-house sabotage is one of the greatest problems now facing both manufacturing and service industries.`

Yeah, yeah, yeah, I've been on the course. Jonathan glanced up at the door to make sure it was closed. He could verbal and no-one would hear. George was supposed to be seeing him, but George, thank heaven, was late as usual.

"First." Jonathan asked the computer. "Why didn't you warn me before?"

`Programed to hold all proactive interventions until Dead Space`

"Alright, reprogram. If you get a priority like this again, you are to intervene immediately. Please confirm."

Confirmed

"What are the possible actions taken by Simon Hasley?"

Action taken

"Fine. What is it?"

There was no response at all. It was almost as though the machine had crashed, right in the middle of proactive intervention. It simply went back to what it had been doing before.

The machine had been analyzing Jonathan's performance.

This time he noticed the total score in the upper right hand corner. His total score was 5.2. It had been 7.2. If Jonathan knew anything, he knew his own scores.

Simon was changing them.

"CV, please, full CV on Simon Hasley."

Not available.
File cancelled due to termination of employment

"Simon Hasley is here until 31st August. His files are not cancelled."

Not available.
File cancelled due to termination of employment

"Then open the ex-employee file."

???????????????????

"Action. Restore scores for Dayplan Item One to 7.2."

ACTION NOT AUTHORISED.

Jonathan slammed the top of his desk.

George walked in. To talk about late invoicing. And the bloody machine flipped back to its proactive intervention.

"It's not my letter," Simon was saying. Jeez, how embarrassing, right in front of other staff.

"Stop intervention," Jonathan ordered. "Sit down, George."

Then Jonathan remembered. What had Simon said? Something about Accounts, that he'd worked in Accounts. Accounts with their big system who did all the monitoring. The really big boys. Simon would have swept up after them, wiped their asses, what does he know about the system?

George was talking to him, and Jonathan realized he had not heard a word. He was losing this, he was not handling it.

". . . it's the same story. We have to wait for extra-contractuals before we know what the job costs, and so we can't bill." George was smiling his non-commissioned, sleeves-up, man-on-the-shop-floor smile.

"That's not what the people upstairs think."

"Well, with the best will in the world, they're not down here doing the work are they?"

"They don't have to. George, I'm sorry to pull the rug from under you, but I want to change the agenda for this meeting."

George sucked his teeth, scoring points, tut, bad meeting management.

"You know I would never do this normally, but I've just had an intervention on Simon as you came in. How is he taking it?"

The shop-floor smile was still there. "Like a prince. He's calm, in fact, you could say he looks quite happy about it, like he has a card up his sleeve. You give him a good severance deal or something?"

"We can't afford severance deals. This is in confidence. Simon is changing people's performance scores. He's got access to Accounts somehow. The machine can't change them back."

"You're joking," said George, his pink face going slack. Then he began to chuckle. "No wonder he looks so pleased. He's changing people's scores. Well, well, I didn't know he had it in him."

Managers must never lose their sense of humour. Jonathan managed to find an answering smile. "It's one way of getting your own back." There was sweat on his forehead.

"Changing yours, is he?" George's red moustache seemed to glow redder.

"Screwed both of us. You're in charge of monitoring." Jonathan's own smile was a bit harder. "So. How could he have done it? How can we stop him?"

"Beats me. Unless he got hold of the password when he was in Accounts."

"You mean the access code."

"No. This is different, it really lays open the whole network. I think only the Chairman has it, maybe Head of Accounts. You get hold of that you can change any information you like and then ice it, so it can never be changed. Change it invisibly I mean."

"Great for when the Auditors call."

"I expect so."

"Can you change it on verbal? By mail?"

"By camel, I imagine. It's only a rumour but I've heard a few funny things."

"From Simon?"

George grinned back at him.

And then in waltzed Harriet. It was 10:10 after all, and here he was, still in his previous meeting, so his time management score would be fucked, and Harriet would know that, and wouldn't she just love that?

Harriet loved something. She had gone doo-lally with pleasure. She started to do a dance around Jonathan's desk. "Ring around the rosy, a pocketful of posy, husha, husha, they all fall down." Harriet roared her hearty, Hooray Henry laugh that Jonathan had not heard in so long. "Did you know that that is a song about the plague?"

"Someone's caught a cold," said George and his and Harriet's eyes seemed to harpoon each other, and both of them grinned.

Bad behaviour from staff depressed their own scores, but insubordination knocked the stuffing out of their manager's profile. They knew it. They were enjoying this.

I am fed up with this crap, I am fed up trying to keep people happy. I am not responsible for keeping people happy.

"Harriet. The stress has gotten to you," Jonathan said. "Come back when you're more in control."

"When you are more in control, you mean." Harriet was beaming, and about to chuckle again. "Come on, George, let's leave him to it."

"George. Please. We're not finished. We still have to talk about invoicing."

"Oh Jesus," and both he and Harriet cracked up.

"I want a breakdown of every invoice on this printout and why it's late. Friday will do. And please remember, that you are responsible for ensuring we hold to financial targets. If you don't, you aren't meeting the minimum requirements of your job. I'll give you a box four marking. And if it doesn't improve, I'll write one of those hilarious little warning letters. Oh, and Harriet, your anti-blood pressure medicine. I know about it. It does have strange side effects, doesn't it. I can recommend Medical Leave. I will be recommending a check-up."

In other words, baby, you may just have lost your job. Harriet's smile slipped.

He verballed it. "Action. Store session. Copy. H. Pednorowska's behavior to the Medical Department."

All this counselling shit to one side, the thing he knew he was really good at was being a bit of a bastard.

"Harriet. George. Thanks for coming to see me. Harriet, I'm sorry you're unwell. George, I'm sure you'll be able to cope with your invoicing problem. Please ask Simon to come in and see me."

Their smiles had not quite faded.

"Meeting over, Team."

Gloves off. Simon had slow reaction times. He needed time to think about things. Well, he had had a whole month to work through this, thanks to Jonathan being so nice. It had probably taken him all month, but he had done it. And he's got me by the balls. He can change my scores, and leave no trace, unless the Chairman is prepared to admit the existence of the password. The computer's got me and George on record and knows our suspicions but that's not proof. I have to wrong foot him. I could say that he'd been monitored telling Harriet what he'd done. But what if he hadn't, or asked "how could they read the note, it was in code?" Jonathan would just have to wing it.

Simon came back in. He looked as calm and unperturbed as this morning.

"An impressive display, Simon."

Simon was saying nothing.

"It wasn't age, you idiot," said Jonathan. "It wasn't slowed-down reaction times. Don't you know when you're being let off? They knew, Simon! That's why you were fired. You didn't think you could use the Chairman's password without all the right protocols did you? They were letting you go without any noise. Then you had to go and tamper with my scores this morning, you stupid, dumb, poor, idiot little lamb, and I don't know if I can stop it this time, Simon. I think they're going to send you to jail."

Simon sat unmoving, in silence. But silence was not a denial, or shocked surprise. Would that be enough?

"I mean, as if I didn't signal it, as if I didn't near as dammit tell you, in those private little sessions, you've got a month, keep your nose clean. I don't want to see you go to jail!"

Jonathan raised his hands and let them fall. "I really thought you were smarter than that."

Simon had not moved, not an involuntary flicker of the eyeballs, not a heave of the prison-patterned shirt. Except, he was weeping. He sat very still and a thick, heavy tear that seemed to be made of glucose crept down his cheek.

"They always have one up on you, don't they?" he said.

In the corner of Jonathan's screen, a tiny white square was flashing on and off, in complete silence. A security alert.

"You work your butt off, they keep you dancing for twenty years, and they make a fortune out of you."

This was going to be very sweet indeed, thought Jonathan. Talk about two birds with one stone. Fancy Accounts letting something like the password out. They'd all be for the high jump. Bloody Accounts, who were always breathing down Jonathan's neck about invoices, or performance scores or project costs or unit cost reduction. They would all have their necks wrung like chickens. What a wonderful world this could be.

"It was a dumb thing to do," Simon admitted, laying each word with a kind of finality, like bricks.

"Well. I reckon you'll have revenge. At least on Accounts," said Jonathan.

The door burst open, and Custody came in like it was a drug bust and they were Supercops. In their dumb blue little uniforms.

"What the fuck kept you?" Jonathan demanded.

"By the way, Simon," he added. "We didn't know for sure, until a second ago. Thanks."

Simon didn't move a muscle. When Jonathan checked later, he found he'd scored a ten. Hot damn, it felt good to be so creative.

He got home after fitting in his evening workout. Got up to one hundred on the bench press. Shows what a little adrenalin could do. He got home, to the ethnic wallpaper and the books and the CDs, and he knew he was not a bad man. Life was tough, but that was business. Home was different.

His wife was a painter, and she wore a smock covered in fresh pistachio, magenta, cobalt. He had to lean forward to kiss her lest the smock print paint on his suit. "We should hang that coat of yours in a gallery," he said. It would be nice to live like this too, in a quiet home, but then someone had to bring home the bacon.

"Daddy, Daddy," called Christine from the bedroom. She wouldn't go to sleep until she had seen him, no matter how long she had to wait, and she was not even his child. He went to her room and sat on the bed and kissed her. She smelled of orange juice and children's shampoo. "Play a game with me," she said, and out came the little screen. Mickey had to shoot the basketball through the hoop to escape the aliens. The score was on the screen. "Daddy, I got an eight!" she cried. He chuckled, but a part of his mind said in a slow, dark voice: get them young.

That night he dreamed he had old hands, and they mumbled through job ads. He couldn't feel anything with them. His fingers were dead.

CRI DE COEUR

Michael Bishop

Michael Bishop is one of the most acclaimed and respected members of that highly talented generation of writers who entered SF in the 1970s. His renowned short-fiction has appeared in almost all the major magazines and anthologies, and has been gathered in four collections: *Blooded on Arachne*, *One Winter in Eden*, *Close Encounters with the Deity*, and *Emphatically Not SF, Almost*. In 1981, he won the Nebula Award for his novelette "The Quickening," and in 1983, he won another Nebula Award for his novel *No Enemy But Time*. His other novels include *Transfigurations*, *Stolen Faces*, *Ancient of Days*, *Catacomb Years*, *Eyes of Fire*, *The Secret Ascension*, *Unicorn Mountain*, and *Count Geiger's Blues*. His most recent novel is the baseball fantasy *Brittle Innings*, which has been optioned for a Major Motion Picture. His story "Thus We Remember Carthage" was in our Fifth Annual Collection. Bishop and his family live in Pine Mountain, Georgia.

In the rich, intricate, and compassionate novella that follows, he takes us along with a convoy of immense ark-ships, headed out and away from Earth to the stars, daring the unknown dangers of the interstellar gulfs in search of a new home, a new life. But even out among the stars, as Bishop eloquently demonstrates, love and duty can come into conflict, and the most rewarding territories to explore, and also the most dangerous, are the uncharted reaches of the human heart . . .

Why, once, did moths singe the tapestries of their wings in candle flames? Why, once, did the cinder-laden parachutes of fireworks so excite us? And, again, why did certain crazies—fools or saints—sometimes steep themselves in petrol and torch themselves to carbon?

Why, in short, do we long to blaze?

Ever since I turned twelve, I've known. Only a minuscule fraction of the stuff of our universe glows. The rest, the bulk, drifts in darkness, unmoored or rudely tugged. The cold vast black of interstellar night cloaks it from our eyes, our telescopes, our roachlike searchings. We belong to the part that does not glow, to the swallowing dark.

Why wonder, then, that a yearning to leap into the furnace, to god-fashion ourselves in fire, drives us starward on the engines of a mute cri de coeur?

"Whurh we guhn?" Dean asked me.

"It's a surprise. Have a little patience."

"Huvh uhliddle"—he grinned up at Lily—"payshuhns."

Excitedly, I gripped one of roly-poly Dean's hands. Lily Aloisi-Stark, my son's mother, a systems specialist, held the other. Dean swung between us like a baby orangutan, a creature habituated *in utero* to a starship's sterile bays, bioengineered for life aboard a space ark.

Except that he hadn't been. After more than an E-standard century of travel, U.N.S. *Annie Jump Cannon* and the other two great wheelships of our colonizing armada pulsed a mere three years from a rendezvous with the Epsilon Eridani system. The brakes were on.

Along with U.N.S. *Fritz Zwicky* and U.N.S. *Subrahmanyan Chandrasekhar*, *Annie* was slowing to keep from overshooting our target, a world where Dean might find himself ill-suited to cope. Of course, I had to admit, that might prove true of all of us.

I led Lily and Dean up a rampway and thumb-keyed the panel of the topmost room in G-Tower of *Annie*'s rotating wheel, a structure so large that the sight of any portion of it always summons my awe.

We entered the observatory. A scaffold supporting the enameled barrel of the ArkBoard Visual Telescope (ABVT) reared over our heads.

We rode an electric lift up through this scaffolding to a carpeted platform with chairs, handrails, and a large shielded viewport. At the platform's other end, two men stood talking at the base of a ladder to the ABVT's sighting mechanisms. One man I knew only as a fuel-systems specialist whose up-phases rarely coincided with mine. The other man, however, was my friend Thich Ngoc Bao, our mission's chief astrophysicist.

Bao sprinted up the ladder. The fuel-systems man turned toward us brushing invisible lint from his tunic. Dean, who had fixed all his attention on Bao and the ABVT's shiny ivory tube, paid him no mind.

"Whurh are we?" Dean said.

"The observatory," Lily said.

"I go up . . . *thurh*!" Dean pointed at the ABVT.

"No. Sit." I made him sit down in front of the shielded viewport. Dean burrowed into the chair and rolled his head against its cushion, his eyes hungry for new wonders. Clearly, this place excited him.

"Watch," I said.

The shields on the forward viewport retracted, exposing a window into space two meters tall and at least twice that wide. Dean quivered. Gaping, he pulled himself forward, his pudgy legs banging the chair's undercarriage, his pudgy hands bouncing on his knees.

"Holy crow," he said. "Holy crow."

Lily put a hand on his shoulder. "Happy birthday, DeBoy. Many happy returns."

"Whurh iz," straining hard to see, "New Hohm?"

"There." I nodded at the window. "Straight ahead. Among those fuzzy match flames and haloes."

Actually, between *Annie Jump* and the edge of the Epsilon Eridani orrery there now lies an arc of interstellar debris—tumbling chunks of dirt-ice, frozen gas, a chaos of nomadic mongrel rocks—not unlike the Oort Cloud beyond the orbit of Sol's Pluto. Our armada's astronomers, using radio telescopes as well as ABVTs, detected this belt less than five E-years ago. Today, we call it the Barricado Stream. Given the dimensions of this shadowy region, however, Commander Odenwald and his counterparts on *Zwicky* and *Chandrasekhar* foresee no trouble taking even our prodigious arks through its far-flung hazards into the system's heart.

The tech who'd been talking to Bao strolled over and halted in front of Dean. From this new vantage, he stared at Dean. The relentless blankness of his gaze annoyed me so much that I stared pointedly back at him.

"Hello, Mr.—?" I prompted.

"Mikol. Kazimierz Mikol. Children have no place up here."

"Sez who?" Lily said.

"Regs, I'm afraid. Ask Heraclitus." He hitched his thumb at the nearest toadstool unit. "Check for yourself."

Seeing a quick tautening of the cords under Lily's jaw, I said, "Dean's just come off a short ursidormizine nap. He's six. This is his first observatory visit. Why try to squelch his pleasure?"

Mikol shrugged.

"This is his birthday present," Lily said. "Abel wanted to give him—" She stuck.

Mikol superciliously lifted an eyebrow.

"—the stars," Lily finished in some consternation.

"Oh? Is that right? Who's Abel?"

"I am," I said. "Abel Gwiazda. When I was twelve, my adoptive father gave the stars to me for Christmas on my first Mars trip."

Mikol clasped his hands at his waist and smiled. "Ah. The reenactment of a family tableau. How sweet."

Lily and I exchanged a look.

"Of course, the reg in question has its roots in a wholly legitimate concern for mission efficiency," Mikol said. "In addition—as if it mattered in this case—it means to protect our youngest from the deleterious effects of either cosmic rays or overexcitement, I forget which."

Dean kept gaping at the stars, but I gaped at Mikol. I had never known such rudeness, even under the guise of enforcing shipboard discipline, since coming aboard *Annie Jump Cannon* off Luna in 2062. Reputedly, the U.N.'s planners had selected against egregious social blunderers like Mikol. If so, how had he contrived to get aboard?

Pointing, Dean suddenly cried, "I see . . . New Hohm!"

"No," I said. "New Home's sun, maybe. We're still too far away to make out planets."

"Or even the biggest rocks in the Barricado Stream," Mikol told Dean in a grating adult-to-child voice.

Dean twigged next to nothing of the insult. He grinned at Kazimierz Mikol.

Mikol turned to Lily. "Does the boy like rocks? Take him down to the beach garden in hydroponics."

"Abel's done that already," Lily said. "Dean likes it."

"Likes rocks, does he? Good. Maybe we'll grab one with a Colombo tether while crossing the Barricado."

"Whatever for?" Lily said.

"To abandon him on," Mikol said as a parting shot. He strode to the scaffold lift before Lily or I could blink, much less frame a rejoinder.

Dean, heedless, sat there gnomishly. Starlight, modestly color-shifted from our deceleration, washed over his face like melting diamonds.

I was outraged. I stared after Mikol, thankful only that Lily and I could give our son the stars.

Me? Just as I told Mikol, I am Abel Gwiazda. My adoptive parents came to the United States from Poland in the fourth decade of the twenty-first century. My father, a physicist trained in Krakow, and my mother, the science journalist who broke Poland's so-called "Coca-Cola/Cyclotron" scandal in the late twenties, took positions with the ISCA (International Space & Colonization Authority) in Hutchinson, Kansas. After discovering that they could have no children of their own, they adopted me, a nameless Tanzanian child orphaned in the last of the Drought Riots and smuggled to Puerto Rico by profit-taking babyleggers.

I grew up well-loved, but aimless and deracinated. I spent three years as a teenager in a dome community beneath the great escarpment of Mons Olympica on Mars, learning, more by accident than deliberate application, the agrogeology skills that, upon our joint return to Earth in 2056, I took up formally in Oran, Algeria. With doctorate in hand and recommendations from my well-placed parents, I qualified for, and easily landed a spot in, the Epsilon Eridani Expedition—whose planning, funding, and assembly in lunar orbit occupied the entire world throughout the turbulent fifties. You can't go home again, but you can try to make one Elsewhere, and for me the E's in E^3 stand for that very hope.

A part of any home is family. I can't help it: I feel the call of family intensely. So strongly did I feel it before the making of my son Dean that I (respectfully) sought reproductive contracts with a half dozen women in G-Tower—including Etsuko Endo, Nita Sistrunk, and even the menopausal physicist Indira Sescharchari—before Lily Aliosi-Stark, a kindly woman in her late twenties, agreed. Her only stipulation was that I expect and solicit only minimal help from her in raising the child. To raise a child in the habitat tower of an ark, at least one parent must forgo the balm of ursidormizine slumber, submitting to the pitiless depredations of aging to care for, teach, and discipline that child.

"This is what *you* want," Lily said. "I wish to save myself for New Home. I don't want to set foot there feeling achy and antiquated. Understand?"

I did. So Dean is *my* child. I begot the Down's-syndrome boy on Lily during several bouts of fiery lovemaking. Later, in a burst of self- and partner-mocking irony that startled and then tickled me, Lily called our wild sessions a "screw-bilee." Aboard *Annie*, I have a reputation for straight-laced stoicism stemming from my Reform Catholicism and the twin concerns of my arkbound work, agrogeology and poetry. The former I do for business (ultimately, the business of survival), the latter for love—just as, looking ahead, I persuaded Lily to conceive a child and then finagled authorization from med services for her to carry it to term.

During our lovemaking, Lily said, "Boy or girl, give it your name. I decline to hang another hyphen around the poor kid's neck."

"Gwiazda-Aliosi-Stark?"

"Absolutely not. Throw in a double first name, Claude-Mark or Julia-Cerise, and it'd go down like a swimmer in a titanium wetsuit."

So, months before giving birth, Lily renounced any claim on handing the child her surname. This fact comforted me. What if she had waited until the photoamnioscan at the end of the first trimester revealed the embryo's trisomy 21? (Which, of course, it did.) At that point, the imperfect fetus would have thrown her motives forever in doubt. I would have wondered if she had deferred to me not solely out of her wish to set aside the demands of parenting, but also out of scorn for our botched offspring.

Masoud Nadeq, the chief physician in G-Tower, showed us the results of the photoamnioscan and listed our options, namely, to abort the pregnancy, to bring it to term with no effort at gene rectification, or to intervene at the chromosomal level with the highly limited procedures available on board. During the past seven E-years, nearly two hundred other children have been born on the *Annie Jump Cannon* alone, and Nadeq's records show that only one other couple—cosmic rays, variable gravity, and the other gene-crippling aspects of near-light-speed travel aside—has conceived a Down's-syndrome infant.

Lily: "What did they do?"

Dr. Nadeq: "They chose to terminate."

"Is that what you advised?" I asked.

Dr. Nadeq: "For quite good reasons, expedition guidelines strongly advance that option. In cases like yours, however, there's no unappealable directive to terminate."

I said, "To get a directive, our fetus would have to have two heads or no brain. Is that it?"

Dr. Nadeq: "In a manner of speaking."

Lily: "Then our baby is reprieved."

Dr. Nadeq: "Do you agree, Dr. Gwiazda?"

I said, "Of course. Didn't I lobby this woman to help me call our hatchling's pent-up spirit from the dark?"

Dr. Nadeq: "That's . . . very poetic."

"My avocation. Didn't I run our application through every nook and switch-back in Heraclitus's cybernetic innards?"

Dr. Nadeq: "Then you accept the role of guardian as well as that of sire?"

Lily: "He does."

"I do," I said.

Dr. Nadeq: "Excellent. Sign off on this waiver."

"What waiver?"

Dr. Nadeq: "Of unadulterated community support—once, that is, your child is born and later when we begin to colonize New Home."

I despised the waiver's threat of premeditated abandonment, but I signed off on it. How could I condemn a society under extreme environmental and psychological duress for declining to accept with open arms a handicapped child? Especially when Lily and I chose to bring him to term in full knowledge of his handicap and his potentially disruptive needs?

Even so, the waiver galled. I signed it with a trembling hand.

Most voyagers treat Dean with kindness. To date, this Kazimierz Mikol bastard comprises a boorish minority of one. Despite recycling and other ingenious reclamation schemes (his reasoning must go), we have finite supplies, and once we make planetfall, anyone with a mental and/or physical handicap will represent an outright drag on the colonization process.

Better that Dean had come stillborn from the womb, Mikol must figure. Better, now, that we recommit him to the darkness through an ejector tube.

I think too much on Mikol's hostility. Most people, as I have said, are kind.

Item: Etsuko Endo, a biologist who passes her up-phase time doing adjustment counseling, recently spent four hours casting sticks of different lengths for Dean and helping him lay them out in educational patterns.

"Rhommm-buhz!" he said when Etsuko brought him back to me. "Daddy, I cuhn make a . . . *rhom-buhz*!" So proud. Even as he made, not a rhombus, but a triangle whose unequal sides did not quite touch one another.

Item: Commander Odenwald visited Lily only two hours after Dean was born. Repeatedly since that visit, he has used small portions of his long up-phases (despite enzyme cocktails and downtime cell repairs, his hair has turned cayenne-and-silver) to watch Dean trip-sleep or to guide him around the various facilities in G-Tower. In fact, had I not begged him to leave the observatory to Lily and me, Odenwald would have long ago showed that to Dean, too. I believe, then, that with a simple request I can have Mikol dressed down, if not sent packing to his biorack.

Why bother? If Dean had understood any part of Mikol's insult in the observatory, or read the least shade of disdain in his face, I would do it. But Dean thinks everyone loves him. In a universe of swallowing dark, and despite the eclipse of his reason at conception, he scatters a property so similar to light that it dims my vision.

Until, less than a decade ago, a few of us began to have children, you could seldom find more than twenty people awake at any one time in any single living tower on the ever-clocking wheels of our ships. Ten percent of the expedition's personnel oversaw the armada's running, tracked the stars, maintained ship-to-ship communications, studied their specialties like workaholic monks, and ministered to the quasi-corpses stacked in each ark's bioracks.

Only a few days into these up-phases, loneliness settled. An ineffable strangeness pervaded *Annie*'s labs and corridors, as if a winged fairy tripping along at light-speed had cast a spell over my sleeping arkmates, a dark enchantment over every workroom, crawlspace, and maintenance deck. I could hear this implacable sorcery in the hydrogen hiss of the stars; in the white noise of generators, computer-cooling fans, and hidden air recirculators.

I came aboard U.N.S. *Annie Jump Cannon* as a hotshot Ph.D. of twenty-two. So far, this voyage to Epsilon E has taken a little over 109 standard years—relative, that is, to the arks in our fleet. Had I left an infant child with my parents in Algeria, it would have long since doddered into codgerhood—if it remained alive at all.

As for me, given the periodic metabolic respite of U-sleep, I have aged (Dr. Nadeq tells me) the physiological equivalent of only thirteen years. In short, I am a thirty-five-year-old centenarian. But no one stays upphase much longer than a month each shipboard year (other than Commanders Odenwald, Roosenno, and Joplin, and a few engineering troubleshooters and continuity personnel), so that, among us would-be colonists, youthful centenarians—of many different ages—register as commonplaces, not freaks.

Of course, in this final decade of our approach to Epsilon Eridani, an expedition policy authorizing the conception, *in utero* gestation, and natural birth of children took effect for screened personnel young enough to carry out their parental obligations on New Home. Six years after Lily and I made Dean, this policy lapsed because "children under four will impact negatively on the efficient settlement of the target world that we have hopefully denominated New Home."

Then why permit the arrival of any children at all? Or, at least, the arrival of any offspring under the able-bodied age of, say, sixteen?

Well, the original U.N. planners believed that "in the long term, a generation of colonists reared on the target world's surface from midchildhood, adapting daily to that world, will prove of incalculable benefit to the planting of a permanent human base in an alien solar system." Nobody, of course, had factored Dean into this reckoning.

In any case, with the advent of children, the living towers on our three wheelships seem less like mausoleums and more like chatter-filled atria or aviaries. I have stayed continuously up-phase ever since Dean's birth (Lily, by contrast, opted for ursidormizine slumber soon afterward and comes up-phase only on his birthday). Although Dean takes closely monitored "naps"—to foster cell growth, to husband our various dry-good stores, and to ease the burden on our recirculating systems—I have no desire to down-phase just to match my sleep periods to his. I sleep when I need to, without drugs, and plot ways to sample, test, and seed the unearthly (conjectural) loams, marls, and humuses of New Home.

At other times, of course, I work in G-Tower's polyped, where Dean has become a cherished favorite of his playmates; a mascot, almost. His blockish head, flat nose, spongy tongue, and stubby hands endear him to, rather than estrange him from, the group. The curiosity and altruism of well-loved children has a weird dynamic. It astonishes and uplifts. It soothes. So how can I regret the nearly six extra years that I've aged as a result of going up-phase for Dean?

Simple: I can't.

Meanwhile, the metaphoric seedpods of *Annie*'s towers have begun to rattle and split. Our corridors ring. The children dance, wonder, explore, scuffle, and sing. Kazimierz Mikol, I feel sure, has taken both a powder and a double dose of refined and amplified bear's blood: ursidormizine.

* * *

Our G-Tower mess is draped festively about with acetane banners. Through it drifted a smell like fried ozone and the piped-in strains of an old song called, if repetition of a single phrase means anything, "I'm So Dizzy."

Thich Ngoc Bao, the astrophotographer Nita Sistrunk, and I sat at a table over our trays. Dean huddled in an obsolescent VidPed near the door, spinning the control ball with his palm. (He won't use virch goggles; their simulated environments cut him off too thoroughly from me, and that scares him.) Hiller Nevels, a pilot and maintenance tech, swaggered over from the autodispenser to join us.

". . . detected Eppie's heliopause," Bao was saying. "So we *will* in fact rendezvous with the system."

"You doubted we would?" Nita said.

"Eppie's heliopause?" Hiller said. "What's that?"

"Did *you* never doubt, Nita?" Bao took a bite out of his steaming oystershell pasta and its garlic-spinach filling. He swallowed. "One downphase, I had a six-month-long nightmare, complete with sound and motion effects. *Annie* dropped like a stale doughnut into a Kerr singularity and whirled around its glowing mouth for about twelve eternities. Frame-dragging, you know. I mummified in my biorack. So did everybody else."

"Cheerful talk," Hiller said.

"Eppie's heliopause is the very edge of the Epsilon Eridani system," Nita told Hiller. "Where the star's solar wind hits the charged particles in interstellar vacuum."

"Isn't the Barricado Stream the edge?" Hiller said.

A star's energy influence, Bao explained, extends well beyond its farthest planet or cometary cloud. Low-frequency radio emissions can undulate a dozen billion miles into the obsidian emptiness surrounding a star.

As Bao spoke, I watched Dean swaying in the VidPed, slapping the control ball. I could see his virtual self—a chunky two-dimensional figure with a feathered spear—stalking a herd of electronic ostriches on a veldt whose real-world equivalent long ago turned into tourist hotels, tennis courts, and golf courses.

Dean didn't care about that. The control ball was easy to spin; the figures on the screen made him laugh. His chuckle, along with the way his head lurched gleefully, warmed my heart, almost as if Lily had rubbed my chest with some sort of thermotherapeutic cream.

Without alerting the others, I picked a comppad off my tunic's carrypatch and began to punch out some verses. I struggled, recasting each stanza three or four times before moving on. During this effort, *Annie* and my friends ceased to exist for me.

In the end, I had my entire effort almost, if not quite, the way I wanted it:

> *A starchild in a VidPed cage*
> *Unwraps himself, with deadpan glee.*
> *Such fragile tissues disengage,*
> *Such guileless beauty in debris.*

Bafflingly, he molts and fledges,
Unwrapping in order to dress.
By this divestment, he pledges
To put on a scarecrow success.

Never has he touched a bird:
A maypop, an eggling, a flame.
In the beginning cracked a word,
The broken promise of his name.

I hear lark song where my fellows
Discern but babble, vocal cheats.
Take away your amped-up cellos,
Leave me only DeBoy's bleats.

With no ulterior intent,
He cocks and grins at every sign:
Litmus test or test-tube infant,
Telescope or Colombo twine.

So watch his palm atop the ball,
A misfit's flesh on spinning chrome:
Just now a shade on spectral veldt,
But next my son on our New Home.

I looked up to find my friends eyeing me with amusement. How long had I occupied myself writing my poem? Even Hiller, the last of us to sit down, had polished off his meal and was staring at my comppad.

"Another poem?" Bao said. "Well, you have to let us see it. If it's bad manners to tell secrets in front of one's dinner companions, concealing a poem composed at table is also rude. Surely."

"The rudeness is writing it in front of us," Nita said. "He might as well've sat here picking his nose."

Hiller guffawed. "That depends on the poem. Or the nose."

Bao reached across the table. "Give."

I handed him the comppad. I had no qualms about showing around the product of my creative withdrawal. Keats need not fear even a partial eclipse of his immortality, but no other soul this far from home—with the self-proclaimed exception of the Pakistani sferics specialist Ghulam Sharif on U.N.S. *Fritz Zwicky*—can rival my versifying prowess. Other expedition members may scribble confessional, or hortatory, or occasional poems (if you look, you can find the results of their activity on toadstool units everywhere about), but I (humorously) regard my challengers as amateurs or hacks.

"Prepare to fall at my feet in veneration."

"Cripes," said Nita. "Self-praise is no praise at all."

"I unequivocally agree, Ms. Sistrunk," I said.

"You do?"

"Sure. But *no praise* is also no praise at all. I blow my own horn to add a little dressing to the silence."

Bao began to scroll the comppad. He read each stanza aloud for the others. He did so with a pitch of feeling that humbled me: I could *hear* the hiccups in my poem's flow, the off-speed diction, the bungled metrics—hiccups for which Bao's sensitive reading almost compensated.

"What's an eggling?" Hiller asked.

"A little egg," Nita ventured. "What else?"

I said, "I don't know. Something hard like a stone, dense like a black hole, and life-packed, potentially, like an ovum. See? Eggling."

"What does it mean?" Hiller asked. "Not just eggling, the whole poem?"

"That he loves his son," Bao said. "And looks forward to raising him to manhood on a brave new world."

I could add nothing to that, and when Bao gave me back my comppad, Nita began talking about heliopause again, the savory immenence of planetfall.

Our fleet pulses onward, skimming at a modest moiety of light-speed the interpenetrating membranes of space-time. The Barricado Stream—inside the hard-to-mark heliopause, outside the orbit of a planetary iceball—rushes nearer.

Toward the end of the twentieth century, perturbations in Epsilon Eridani's motion revealed that it most likely dragged planets, if not a gravity sink, around it. Observations made from the Infrared Lunar Astronomical Telescope (IRLAT) on Darkside in the 2030s, along with the fact that Eppie emits an infrared signal hinting at protoplanetary debris, led scientists to posit that the system had five planets, including one in Eppie's zone of habitability, and possibly an outer dust band. We sent out an unmanned probe to confirm these hypotheses, but our armada—dispatched nearly thirty years later, when Ju Tong technology, multinational money, and worsening environmental/social conditions converged to make the launch seem practical if not imperative—has long since outrun the U.N. probe.

Fortunately, shipboard telescopes and Thich Ngoc Bao's relativistic calculus have validated the presence of these worlds. Even more convincingly, so has a probe that we dropped over the side of *Zwicky* before commencing deceleration; as our arks slowed, this probe kept going, making a full-speed transit of the system and thereby detecting the cometary matter in the Barricado Stream by radar echoes.

In any case, New Home does exist, along with a fiery inner planet that a wag among us tagged Red Hot. Three outer planets received equally silly names: Jelly Belly, Jawbreaker, and Cold Cock. Moreover, spectroanalysis carried out on *Chandrasekhar* indicates that New Home has water.

A couple of days ago, because Dean requires extra work and attention if I wish him to reach his full potential, I took him into the geology bay under *Annie*'s observatory deck. I planned not only to do some elementary professional review but also to show him a grabbag of tray specimens: a quartz crystal, a piece of obsidian, a leaf of limestone, a fossil imprint, a geode. Estsuko Endo, after all, has too much to do to spend her every waking moment amusing Dean or devising therapeutic games to educate him.

I don't. My real work begins when our advance scientific teams set down on Epsilon Eridani II (even the hackneyed New Home seems a better name than that) to map, explore, sample, test, and catalogue. Besides, I'm Dean's father: I insisted that this expedition permit him to be.

Dean handled each specimen with clumsy delight. Except for the collection's lone geode, the specimens are small to the point of parody. In fact, many soil and mineral types exist on *Annie* only as wafer-thin cross sections on glass slides for microscope viewing.

I half feared that Dean would slice himself on the crystal. (His fingers have the nimbleness of porcelain.) Or would drop the trilobite fragilely preserved in Ordovician clay. Or would lose the stalagmite tip that rested on his single-creased palm like a Lilliputian dagger.

But, chortling, goggle-eyed, Dean managed to hold on to, examine, and return to me every item. He was as respectful of them as, on his sixth birthday, he'd been of the glittery stars in the observatory's viewport.

"Whuh's thiz?"

"Schist."

"Durdy word?"

"No. *Schist.* A flaky, stress-formed rock. Be careful, you'll peel away a mica layer."

"Sch-schid?"

I started to say, "No, *schist*," when I heard a man behind us laughing, just inside the bay's entrance. I looked over my shoulder to see (for the first time since Dean's visit to the observatory) Kazimierz Mikol.

My gut clenched, a spasm of *déjà vu*. What was Mikol doing in a work-and-study laboratory authorized for, if not expressly limited to, *Annie*'s geology contingent? Would he argue that my six-year-old retardate had no business here? No business, for that matter, anywhere?

"He *does* like rocks, doesn't he?" Mikol said.

That remark instantly soured the look I turned on him. "My sweet Jesus," I murmured.

"You mistake me for someone else," Mikol said. "Look. I came up here at Ms. Endo's request. She wanted me to tell a man in here—identity then unknown to me—that his son—ditto—would have a therapy session with her tomorrow at ten-hundred hours."

"Why didn't she intercom?"

"A whole tribe of ankle biters had her occupied. Besides, your sanctorum was on my way. I need to eyeball the harp strings sweeping down from the arc opposite G-Tower. That all right with you?"

Harp strings meant fuel spokes. I stared hard at Mikol.

"Consider yourself duly messaged, Dr.—?"

"Gwiazda."

"As you like." He pivoted on his heel.

"Wade," Dean said. He meant *wait*, and Mikol turned back to face him.

Dean held up the geode in our collection. He tilted this queer, split rock so that Mikol had to look directly into its crystal-laced cavity. Its hollow glittered like an in-fallen spiderweb in a splash of sunlight, and Mikol stared into it as if hypnotized.

"Spokes," Dean said. "Fyool spokes."

Those words seemed to stun Mikol. He looked from the reflective cavity of the geode to the dull, flat face of the boy that Lily and I, in his view, had selfishly inflicted on the limited resources of our ark.

"He means the crystals," I said. "They must remind him of the spokes to our matter-antimatter rocket."

"I *know* what he meant."

"He saw those spokes only once," I insisted. "The same day Lily and I gave him the stars."

"There's a mobile of the *Annie* in the polyped. He's seen that dozens of times, surely."

"Its spokes don't glow like the real ones. In the glare of the exhaust stream, the real ones are . . . magical."

"That doesn't make his *equating* the two a wonderwork."

Mikol refused to look away from me. And, out of atavistic machismo or scientific curiosity, I refused to look away from him. "But he's just linked you, a fuel-systems specialist, to the 'spokes' in the geode."

"He has ears. He heard me say fuel spokes. So he has a bare-assed modicum of motherwit. Hallelujah."

"What about the associative leap he just made? Not, by the way, from your words to you, but from the geode's crystals to *Annie*'s weblike fuel lines?"

Dean kept pointing the geode. The way he was gripping it, it reminded me of some sort of exotic weapon. I imagined a burst of energy flashing from it and splitting Mikol's chest cavity open, to reveal . . . what? The gemlike perdurability of his heart? The flowing rubies of his blood? The hard-edged latticework of his myocardia?

"Do you think that on that basis I should declare the kid a genius?" he asked me.

"Human would do. Just human."

"Tiglathpileser was human, it's rumored. And Caligula. So were a whole host of twentieth-century tyrants. So presumably were the brain-dead idiots who turned the Earth into a treeless detention camp. Being human, I'm afraid, doesn't automatically confer demigod status on anyone."

"Human beings made these arks."

"Praise Noah for that irrefutable insight! Which onboard system did your genius offspring invent?"

This retort shut my mouth; it also had a spirit-dampening effect on Dean. He lowered the geode and and made a queer, gargling moan in his throat.

No longer in the geode's sights, Mikol backed out of the workroom. I followed him.

In the corridor, Mikol pointed a finger at me to hold me at bay. "Two run-ins with Gwiazda and his hairless baboon," he said. "Well, this second run-in was a lot less amusing than the first. A third meeting may result in the total overthrow of my antihostility training, the blanket neutralization of my daily serenotil boosters."

"What's the matter with you, anyway?"

"Nothing. I dislike mongoloids. In my view, an entirely rational prejudice."

"You've overstepped yourself there," I said.

"Well, so what? I'll go down-phase again after solving my hydrogen-flow problem. And stay zonked until *Annie* enters the Barricado Stream. With any luck, I won't collide with Gwiazda and Son ever again, either aboard this ark or down on New Home, where I plan to homestead a small farm off limits to fat little mongoloids and their selfish Sambo daddies."

"You bastard," I said.

"Check out the little bastard in your lab," Mikol replied. "More than likely, he's accidentally swallowed a rock."

Once again, he strode away before I could seize his arm or mount a reply. Under my breath, though, I murmured, "Honky," not knowing where the word had come from; even so, it seemed a crass betrayal of the Gwiazdas, who, in innocence and love, had bought my life and raised me.

"Whurh's Lily?" Dean asked.

"You know as well as I. Asleep. She's always asleep. It's her calling."

"I wand to see her."

"Uh-uh. You only think you do. We've done this before, Dean. The damned bioracks spook you."

"I *want* to see her," Dean said, struggling to enunciate.

"No you don't."

"Yez. Yez I do. Take me to see her."

Dean and I had long since retired to our mezzanine-level quarters. The hour was nearly midnight (as if you could not legitimately say the same of any hour of our arkboard journey), and I wanted Dean to go as soundly asleep as his mother. But an afternoon birthday party in the polyped, and then an evening of restored and colorized *Our Gang* comedies over our link to Heraclitus's vidfiles, had left him wrought up and obstinate. I could tell that an all-out battle now would snap my brittle self-control faster than would appeasement, even with a visit to the bioracks thrown in as Dean's unwarranted spoils.

(Spoils. Evocative word.)

Actually, Dean seldom tries to stand his ground against me or anyone else. Agreeableness and conciliation define him the way stealth and curiosity define a cat. Better for harmony's sake, I rationalized, to indulge him tonight in this unusual display of resoluteness than to shatter my peace of mind—what peace of mind?—by playing the tyrant.

Ten minutes after midnight, then, we dropped to the lowest level in G-Tower, a fluorescent dungeon of computer monitors and foam-lined ursidormizine pods, and asked the security tech Greta Agostos to pass us through the barred entrance of *Annie*'s hibernaculum.

"On what business?" Greta asked.

"Guess. Dean wants to see his mother."

Greta rubbed her knuckles furiously—but not hard—over Dean's head. "She won't be very talkative, DeBoy. And you and your dad will have to submit to a search. You know, a ticklish patting down."

"The only reason I came," I said.

But that "patting down" remark was a standard security-tech joke. In fact, without even touching us, Greta ran an aural fod—*foreign-object detector*—around our entire bodies with the impersonal deftness the very opposite of sensual. Her fod, by the way, absolved us of trying to smuggle into the hibernaculum any sort of weapon, drug, or softdrink IV-drip.

The security bars retracted upward, and Dean and I passed into the eerie twilight mausoleum of the bioracks. The air in this circular hibernaculum has a wintry blue tinge and a biting regulated chill. You can identify our quasi-corpses, by the way, either by reading their nameplates or by looking through the pods' frost-traced visors.

We walked the hibernaculum's perimeter—tap-tap-tapping on its naked metal floor—until we had reached the biorack of Lily Aliosi-Stark. Her pod rests on the chamber's third strata, not quite two meters up, and I always have to lift Dean so that he can gaze through the rime-crazed faceplate at his mother's pale but lovely profile.

"Sleebin beaudy," Dean whispered, full of awe. "My mama's jes like sleebin beaudy."

"I'd wake her with a kiss, DeBoy, but my lips always freeze to the visor."

"Funny."

"Not if it happens to you. All right if we go home now?"

Dean put his fingertips to Lily's faceplate. He chuckled when they didn't stick to it. Instead, they left milky prints, which faded slowly once he'd drawn his hand away.

"Pood me down."

I put Dean down. He ambled along the bottom two strata of bioracks, back toward the hibernaculum's entrance, until he came to an empty pod featuring this legend on its nameplate: *Abel Walter Gwiazda*. Dean rubbed the letters of our surname with a stubby forefinger. Then, as I had feared—as I'd *known* would happen—Dean gulped raspingly at the chilly air and went as pop-eyed as a strangler's victim. Why had I supposed that this visit would turn out better than all the others?

"Gone," Dean said. "Holy crow, daddy's gone."

"I'm right here, son. Unlike your ever-drowsing mama, you can't expect me to be two places at once."

On the verge of blubbering, Dean repeated, "Gone," at least a dozen times and then began to wail: a fractured banshee keen that filled this weird crypt for the living like a squadron of angry wasps.

I clutched my shoulders, then covered my ears, then grabbed my shoulders again. Dean's wail stung and restung the snarled thread-ends of my untangling nerves.

"Damn you, you little defective! Shut up!"

Dean's eyes dilated to their utmost. He stopped wailing and retreated. Repeatedly, I shoved him in the chest with my knuckles, herding him toward the mausoleum's exit. On my fifth or sixth such shove, Dean stumbled and collapsed sliding on his bottom. I immediately yanked him up.

"The one place you can't endure for three minutes straight is the one place you insist on coming! Why? You don't have a half-wit's glimmering, do you?"

Greta appeared at Dean's back out of the cold indigo fog. She knelt and hugged him from behind. He, in turn, spun about and clung to her as if to the winged savior in a fairy tale unwinding on a private channel in his head. The sight of his fear—the realization of it—staggered me.

"You asked Lily for this, Abel," Greta said. "You asked for just what's got you so hugely browned off tonight."

"I, I didn't know," I managed. "Not really."

"I'm taking Dean out front with me. He'll be okay. Go to Lily. Talk to her. Stay for as long as it takes."

Greta picked up Dean and carried him, totally compliant in her arms, around the hibernaculum's circular walk. As I stood there in the shame of Greta's rebuke, the two of them receded into the thickening blue fog.

I returned to Lily's biorack. Our conversation touched on many things, including the essential loneliness of starfaring. Later, back at the U-dorm's entrance, Dean greeted me as if I had never derided his mother or cravenly abused him—as if, in short, I *deserved* his regard.

Each of our ships carries around sixteen hundred people, two hundred to a habitation tower. Most travel down-phase in banks of computer-monitored bioracks. Over the last few years of our approach, however, with a deliberate effort to bring children into our spacefaring community, we've increased our numbers by almost twenty young persons a tower. I assume that *Zwicky* and *Chandresekhar* boast comparable population surges, but I've made no real effort to stay abreast of their figures. Dean claims most of my time.

After my ugly flare-up in the hibernaculum, I determined to teach Dean everything I could about our ship, our fleet, our aims, our mystical hopes. He now understands that hydrogen flows from the fuel tanks on *Annie*'s thirty-mile-long wheel to the stores of antihydrogen ice in the rocket dragging us along behind it like a colossal, fixed, empty-bottomed parachute. He knows that once we reach New Home, we will have exhausted every scintilla of fuel available to us, and he also understands, I believe, that to return to Earth or to go on to another solar system (Tau Ceti, say, or Sirius) will require the processing and loading of a volume of hydrogen and antihydrogen ice equal to that with which we left the Moon. He knows. . . .

But I delude myself: Dean has profound physical and mental handicaps; and love, the ultimate paternal blessing and folly, has limited power to add to his brain cells or to pack those he has with liberating knowledge.

In the polyped portion of the G-Tower nursery, Dean and I sat behind a partition draped with a banner depicting the galactic cluster including our own Milky Way. I thumb-moused a gyroscopically interphased replica of *Annie Jump Cannon*, hung above us as a mobile, through a dozen different maneuvers. In its nearly invisible filament harness, the tiny ark canted, wheeled, and strained.

Dean was weary of the drills and demonstrations, enduring them out of a puppy-dog loyalty. In fact, I felt that somewhere along the trajectory of this lesson, our roles—of father and son; of mentor and student—had reversed.

"Howfurh?" Dean said.

"What?"

"How furh to New Hohm?"

"I don't know. We're still braking. Commander Odenwald probably has it computed to the nanosecond."

Etsuko came in and sat down opposite Dean in a kiddie chair almost too small even for her. "No matter when we get into orbit around New Home," she told Dean, "you'll probably be at least eight or nine before you visit the planet."

Dean visibly perked—not at Etsuko's words, but at her presence. "Why?" he asked.

"We'll have a lot to do before we let any of you children risk the surface. Surveillance, photography, mapping, testing, a great many things. Understand?"

"Are thurh guhna be monstuhrs?"

"Monsters?"

The wedge of Dean's tongue hung between his lips. Then he said, *"Dyne-o-sours,"* as if the word embodied a vinegary type of lizardly force.

"I doubt that," Etsuko said.

"Then whud? Peepul?"

"I doubt that too."

"And if there were people, intelligent beings, they'd look upon *us* as the monsters," I said. "Invaders from outer space, their worst fork-legged nightmares."

Dean's face clouded. His tongue filled his mouth like a gag.

"Abel, you've scared him."

"No great task." I usually avoid sarcasm—my son has no feel for it—but I hadn't slept for over fifty hours (not even a catnap), and Dean's intractable innocence had worn some holes in my thick-skinned cheerfulness. "But suppose, Etsuko, that we do drop down to New Home and find ourselves confronted by a species of gentle sapients."

"Suppose we do?"

I told her how the aboriginal sapients of New Home would inevitably view us as a scourge. Later, I wrote,

>   *down*
>   *we*
>   *fall*
>
>   *deformed invaders*
>   *droppinginto their midst*
>
>   *so that*
>   *at our coming*
>   *they reel back*
>   *feeling*
>   *blitzed*
>   *appalled*
>   *prey to misshapen raiders*
>
>   *noting*
>   *our beaklike snouts*
>   *our eyes of shiny goo*

the rows of gleaming bones
behind our pouts
the way our fingers
sprout like vermicelli
with half-moon lyre picks
twanging
in their knuckled heads

and they know
  their hot-pink sods
  glass-sheathed trees
  spiraling geyser creeks
  and dog-masked gods
  crunching fire opals
  on the waves of cliffs
  a destiny made manifest
  by a pale of stars

will fall forever
to the uprights—
  who but us—
swarming down from
  who knows where
  who knows why
  and couldn't they
  just die

  we hope so
  oh we hope so
  don't we
  ms. etsuko

Still later, Dean occupied elsewhere, I showed this effort to Etsuko. She read my last little quatrain as an insult.

Without benefit of ursidormizine, I dream of New Home and its dominant species: humanoid creatures unaware that invaders from outer space are eyeing their world. A landing in the capital of their foremost nation-state allows the first U.N. party down (oddly, it includes both me and Kazimierz Mikol) to see that every individual of this species roughly resembles my handicapped son.

"I know what we ought to call this place," Mikol tells me: "Special Olympica."

In a collective journey of a century or more, you cannot expect to reach your destination without losing someone, even if the majority of your expeditionary force spends most of its time in monitored trip-sleep. Seven of *Annie Jump*'s original contingent of sixteen hundred have died in transit, the latest (but one) a woman in A-Tower who failed to survive childbirth, although, blessedly, her infant daughter did not die and still lives in the A-Tower nursery.

Arkboard funerals last only minutes; few among us attend them. Each tower has a chaplain well-versed in the rituals of different faiths, those of mainline world religions as well as those of small local cults. If the deceased ascribed to a particular belief system and left unambiguous instructions, the chaplain observes them during the memorial service and the subsequent ejection of the corpse from the ship. (For reasons that should be self-evident, our regs permit neither cremation nor entombment.)

Granted, most of those who have died, both here and on our sibling arks, have professed a generic sort of agnosticism or a science-centered, mystical atheism (no matter how oxymoronish this last term may sound), but one man aboard *Chandrasekhar* asked for and received a voodoo funeral, complete with chants and sprinklings of (symbolic) rooster's blood. According to associates, he believed that one day, far in this expansion/contraction cycle of our cosmos, another starfaring ship would retrieve his mummified corpse. Technospiritually revived, he would walk its decks as the undead prophet of the universe's next systalic blossoming.

In my view, the shame of this bravura credo resides not in its superstition, but in the fact that only four of this man's arkmates attended his obsequies. Of course, those who sleep cannot send off the sleeper.

The point of this digression? Several weeks after taking Dean to visit his sleeping mother, a woman by the name of Helena Brodkorb, a floral geneticist in D-Tower, died in her biorack. Despite a complex fail-safe system, her monitors had not alerted her tower's med-unit personnel of her measurable physical deterioration under ursidormizine. By the time anyone noticed, she had slipped away.

A small scandal ensued. Odenwald suspended two up-phase med techs and ordered an investigation. He did not intend to have one more sleeper under his command die in a malfunctioning biorack.

This death would have meant little to me, and nothing to Dean, if, a few hours later, I had not learned that Helena Brodkorb was—or had been—Kazimierz Mikol's aunt, an aunt two years younger than he. Further, Ms. Brodkorb had no other kin on *Annie* or our sibling arks. (Effecting a passenger exchange between two huge wheelships moving at point-ten c is a doable but risky venture.) Excepting spouses and the children born during our decade-long approach to Epsilon Eridani, few people in our expedition have relatives aboard our arks. Therefore, Odenwald felt that Mikol, down-phase again in G-Tower, should know that Ms. Brodkorb had died, even if—maybe *especially* if—it reflected badly on arkboard fail-safe systems. Mikol might elect to attend her last rites.

Quickly, then, Mikol was up-phased, and Odenwald personally broke the news of his aunt's demise.

Mikol, groggy from both the ursidormizine and its sudden neutralization, began to weep. (I have this fact from the med techs who revived him.) He had loved Helena Brodkorb. The disorientation common to the newly awakened may have influenced him, but, still, Mikol's tears had a strong emotional, not just a narrow physiological, wellspring.

I had difficulty crediting this report, of course, but it cheered rather than surprised me. I wanted to believe it—not that a smart and productive woman had died, but that Mikol had reacted to her passing less like an automaton programmed for cynical efficiency than like . . . well, someone's warm-blooded nephew.

I have reconstructed Kazimierz Mikol's activities on the day before Helena Brodkorb's memorial service from an account he gave me later. The most surprising things about this turn of events, of course, are that he deliberately sought Dean and me out in a spirit of reconciliation and that he and I did in fact reach a wary accord.

On that morning, then, Mikol dressed in paper coveralls and a pair of plastic slippers. He added a disposable dove-gray tunic. Every item in his make-do wardrobe emitted a soft gray incandescence. Dove gray. Mourning-dove gray. The colors of civilized dolor, gentlemanly grief.

The chaplain in D-Tower had scheduled Helena's funeral for 0900 hours the next day—after a noninvasive autopsy and med-tech analysis. Mikol had received assurances that he would be unable to tell that anyone, or anything, had so much as pinched Helena's eyelid back or calipered her elbow. He would find her lying serenely in state on the retractable lingula, or tongue, of a waste-disposal ejector.

Tomorrow.

In the meantime, Mikol had a small mission to carry out. He tried to recall what amusements—games, toys, icons—young boys found amusing, and which still pleased *him*, as an adult. No rocks, though. No fake beaches in hydroponics. No shiny precious or semiprecious stones. No geode. Nothing, in fact, pertaining to geology, the professional realm of Dean Gwiazda's father.

Mikol thought a long time. Then he took a lift from the transphase lounge to the mezzanine-level cubbyhole of a pilot and maintenance tech. This, not altogether coincidentally, was a pack rat named Hiller Nevels. Hiller gave him the items he wanted as a kind of consolation gift.

Gift in hand, Mikol rode back down and crossed the G-Tower atrium, a lofty cylinder housing vitrofoam benches, a vegetable garden, exotic ferns, parrot-colored orchids and bromeliads, and a regulated population of purple finches. Heedless of its plants and birds, Mikol hiked through this pocket wilderness to the catwalk outside the polyped.

He found Dean and me playing a game of cards (Go Fish, if I remember correctly) at a toadstool unit well removed from the other children. I greeted him with a look betraying my outrage and suspicion:

"Yes?"

"I came"—Mikol told me later that he could feel his words scratching his throat like a rusty sword blade—"I came to make peace."

"Why?" I said.

"You need a reason?"

"If I'm not to regard this as a shabby trick, yes."

"Such generosity of spirit."

The cards on Dean's screen fanned out before him like so many canceled tickets, and he gave Mikol a toothy, distracted smile.

"Dr. Gwiazda, the truth is, I've undergone a—"

"A change of heart?"

"Perhaps."

"Because your aunt has just died?"

"Word certainly travels."

"Yes, it does. At a healthy fraction of light-speed."

Dean pushed away from his toadstool console. *"Hullo!"* he cried. *"Mistuh Mickle!"*

Mikol knelt beside Dean and pulled a small, foam-lined carrypress from his pocket. After thumbnailing its lid open, he held it on his palm so Dean could see the faceted seeds inside it. They looked like four pieces of sparkly gravel. This was a coincidence of appearances, though, not a surrender to the insult theme—*rocks in the head, out on a rock*—that had so far typified his run-ins with Dean and me.

"Whud . . . whud are they?"

"Eye-eyes," Mikol said. "Impact inflatables."

"They're so . . . liddle."

"The better to bring aboard a vessel where closet space is tight. Touch one."

"No!" I said. "Mr. Mikol, those things are illegal aboard *Annie*."

"Not so," Mikol said from his crouch. "Would I endanger our ship? Or hooliganize your son? You see, *these* eye-eyes will fall back to portable grit as quickly as they burst to their full dimensions—the latest in amusement engineering just before our launch."

Dean held a finger over the carrypress: expectant, unsure, ready for direction. His psychic investment in electronic Go Fish had long since bottomed out.

"No," I told him.

"Ease off, Dr. Gwiazda," Mikol said. "I'm trying to make amends, not get the boy bioracked for reckless mischief."

Although still skeptical, I thought this over and nodded at Dean. "Go on, then. Take one. Just one."

Dean's hand trembled over the carrypress. Mikol seized it and guided his forefinger to one of the eye-eyes. Sweat and surface tension lifted the eye-eye clear. Dean stared at the grit on his fingertip in what looked to me like goggle-eyed dumbfoundment.

"Roll it between your thumb and forefinger," Mikol said. "Then throw it against the floor or the wall." He stepped aside to give Dean room.

Dean flicked the eye-eye feebly past my head. It struck the polyped's deck, skittered to a standstill, and began to emit a faint, melodious hiss.

When Mikol picked it up, it quieted. "More *oomph!*" he advised. "Try again." He gave the eye-eye back to Dean, who looked to me for guidance.

"Go ahead. Hurl it. Hard."

Dean obeyed, tossing the eye-eye with such an awkward shoulder snap that I could imagine him whining for weeks about the lingering soreness. A hard expulsion of breath through his nostrils sounded a lot like a squeal.

But the eye-eye hit the wall behind me and impact-inflated on the rebound.

Wham! Revolving in the polyped was a fabriloon replica of an Allosaurus as large as Kazimierz Mikol himself. It hissed as it tumbled, that crimson and turquoise effigy of a giant lizard, and hissed more loudly than the eye-eye from which it had burst. At length, it righted and settled on its hind legs to the deck.

Dean had begun to scream.

Mikol might have guessed that a dinosaur exploding into view would traumatize a child of Dean's makeup, but, of course, he hadn't. He grabbed the effigy and thrust it to one side—as if removing it a few centimeters would calm Dean. It didn't. Dean went on wailing, his hands at chest height in fortuitous parody of the Allosaurus's forepaws.

"It's all right, Dean," Mikol was saying. "Look. It's okay. A make-believe lizard. See. A plaything."

Despite the threat of ear damage, I picked Dean up.

Meanwhile, Etsuko Endo, Thom Koon, and Sidonia Montoya came rushing in to us from the main polyped. A covey of children in bright paper tunics, muu-muus, dhotis, or jumpsuits crowded in behind the adults to satisfy their own curiosity. One little girl patted Dean's rump and said, "Shhh, shhh," as I also tried to shush him, but the others either flocked to the dinosaur or clamped their palms over their ears.

"Holy crow!" Dean screamed. *"Mon-stuhrrr!"*

"He could mean you," I told Kazimierz Mikol.

Mikol moved one hand in a rapid back-and-forth arc to keep the kids from the fabriloon. "I'm sorry, Gwiazda. You can't think I wanted *this*. I figured the instant manifestation of a dinosaur would, well, tickle him." He slapped the knuckles of Danny Chung-Barnett, who had weaseled far enough into the corner to grab the effigy's turquoise scrotum.

"Can't you de-pop it?" Etsuko asked over Dean's spookily modulating wail.

"Of course. See this." Mikol pointed to a navy-blue spot behind the fabriloon's left eye. "Watch."

He jabbed the spot. With a flatulent keen, the Allosaurus collapsed, rekernelized itself, and began to hiss—so that we could find it again. Mikol grabbed up the tiny eye-eye before the Chung-Barnett kid could pounce on and flee with it.

Dean stopped wailing. Chagrined, Mikol told Etsuko, Thom, and Sidonia what had happened. Herding children before them, they went back to the polyped's main activity area, leaving Mikol to struggle with the necessity of apologizing to Dean. To his credit, Mikol apologized.

Insofar as I had perceived him as an enemy, in the next few moments Kazimierz Mikol ceased to exist. The cynic who had viewed my son as a deadly obstacle to our colonizing mission to Epsilon Eridani vanished as suddenly as had the eye-eye dinosaur, leaving behind no speck of grit to flash-reconstitute his hostile persona.

"If carnivorous lizards are out," he said, "what *would* make a good present for Dean?"

"Stars," I said. "Try stars."

* * *

After the debacle in the polyped, Mikol actually resolved to do as I had suggested. He would bestow upon Dean a gift of stars—not by escorting him to an observatory viewport, but instead by allowing Dean to accompany him to Helena Brodkorb's last rites in D-Tower. This trip, over a fifteen-mile arc of the top side of *Annie*'s wheel, would take a good half hour and expose Dean to all the stars salted into the engulfing bowl of space. Seen from the bubbletop on our perimeter car, these stars would prickle, blaze, shimmer, dim, and flare out again: an unceasing festival of light. Dean would watch it all as if bewitched.

"I don't know," I said. "A ride in a perimeter car may terrify him as much as—"

"A fabriloon from the late Cretaceous?"

"Exactly."

"He's had a good look at stars before. You and his mother made sure of that on his birthday."

"But he's never set foot outside G-Tower."

Mikol appealed to Dean. "You don't want to spend the rest of your life in G-Tower. When we go into parking orbit around New Home, you don't plan to nest in the polyped while everybody else is down exploring the planet. Do you?"

"No surh." Puzzlement and hurt clouded Dean's face. "Nod if . . . I doan huvh to."

"Good for you. So. Would you like to go for a little ride in Peeter?"

Peeter was the name I'd given the perimeter car officially allotted to Towers G-H. Take *rim* from *perimeter*, and you have our magnetic conveyance's pet monicker. It's a silly sort of joke. We call *Annie*'s other three perimeter cars Pauli, MARE (Magnetic Arc-Ranging Elevated), and Albertina. In any case, Mikol spoke the name Peeter on purpose—to flatter me?—even though, as he later confessed, he could not decide if it were genuinely clever or only unbearably cute.

"Yez," Dean said. "I wuhd like to ride."

"But he doesn't want to attend the funeral," I said. "Just the sight of sleepers in bioracks—"

"Then he doesn't have to," Mikol cut in. "He can go to the polyped and virch with the other ankle biters."

"Then I'll ride along too."

"Master Gwiazda, do you want your silver-tongued old man to go over to D-Tower with us?"

Solemnly, Dean nodded.

"Then it's settled," Mikol said. "To give ourselves plenty of time, we'll leave at 0750 hours."

Peeter, our magnetic bubbletop, tracked along the front top edge of *Annie Jump*'s breathtaking wheel of underslung hydrogen tanks. From our perches in the car, we could see *Fritz Zwicky* running parallel to us, a ring of diamonds twinkling beyond the silver Möbius strip of our own ark. *Subrahmanyan Chandrasekhar* was an opalescent sheen somewhere off to port. The other two arks were dimly visible to us, of course, only because of their running lights and the mirrored glow from the exhausts of their braking rockets.

Three distinct motions had their common vectors in our rim car: the bubbletop's tortoiselike crawl toward D-Tower, the gravity-producing circumvolution of *Annie*'s fuel ring, and the starward progress of our ark at point-ten *c*. It seemed to me that these countervailing forces should have ripped us from limb to limb, that our brains and entrails should have flown outward like loose meat in a centrifuge. Instead, we journeyed without incident, three casual travelers poking along the edge of a hurricane slingshot at high speed at infinity.

Dean couldn't keep his eyes off the sky. Starlight sluiced over us like quinine water and guava punch. An alien vista of the Milky Way, familiar but wildly intense. Whorls of gas and dust, a trail of spun sugar crystal. Individual stars guttered and prickled, twinkled and blazed. Nearer to hand, across from us, the underside of *Annie*'s fuel wheel gleamed like the tracks of an archangelic railroad.

"All right, cowboy," Mikol said. "Whaddaya think?"

Dean, his eyes aflicker, continued to gape into the sprawl of God's candelabra.

"Mr. Mikol asked you a question, Dean."

"My friends call me Kaz," Mikol said.

"*Kaz*, that is," I said.

(I'd wondered if he had any friends. Bao referred to him only as a professional colleague, and a nettlesomely frosty one at that.)

"Suhr?" Dean said, fuddled.

"Mr. Mikol—Kaz—wants to know what you think of all this."

A second or two lapsed before Dean could find the words he wanted: "Priddy. Holy crow, very priddy."

Kaz patted Dean's knee and laughed.

Peeter inched ahead—in a steep, gleaming silence that held the three of us like prehistoric waterwalkers in a blister of see-through resin. The wheel turned as Peeter inched as *Annie* leapt gully after gully of the interstellar chasm. . . .

Then Kaz—our old nemesis, Kazimierz Mikol—began to talk, his hands in his lap, the methodical wheel of his mind dipping memories from the millstream of his boyhood:

"My grandfather was an immigrant from the liberated Warsaw Pact nations of eastern Europe. He settled in newly democratic Cuba and set up a small factory in the foothills of the Sierra Maestra, manufacturing a vehicle of his own design that ran on a nonpolluting, replenishable fuel distilled from pig shit and sugar-cane fibers. Cuba had lots of pig shit and sugar cane. Grandfather Alexej's oldest son, Milan, who attended university in Poland in the double-twenties, developed the Mikol Process, a type of nanomechanization that brought down the price of the Sabio, our most popular model, so that even streetcleaners in Havana could afford to buy and drive one. In fact, Milan Mikol, my father, stands in relation to my birth century, at least in Cuba, as Henry Ford stood to the twentieth century in North America."

Kaz had apparently aimed this speech at me, for Dean had tuned him out right after the second mention of pig shit. In our bubbletop, Dean hung beneath the stars like an Earth kid on a midsummer swing.

"I grew up with a sister, Marisa, afflicted with a host of weaknesses that forced my mother to devote herself to her like a nurse. You or I would say that Marisa had cerebral palsy, with severe hemiplegia and ataxia. Mama denied this and said her disabilities stemmed not from brain trauma at birth, but from the influence of an individious toxin made in the States and sprayed relentlessly on the cane crops of our province. No matter. Marisa had many handicaps; at first, not even constant attention and coaxing enabled her to learn to speak."

Kaz's story had begun to make me uncomfortable. I looked past Dean, who sat between Kaz and me, and asked, "Why tell me all this?"

"Just listen, okay?" Annoyed, he resumed: "The year I was thirteen, Marisa turned eight, and my mother's youngest sister, Helena, just then ten or eleven, jetted over with the Brodkorbs from Poznan—for a visit and a reunion. Helena spelled Mother with Marisa. She spelled me, too, because, hating the task, I now often found myself acting as a care provider. I may have welcomed little Helena to Ciudad Sabio even more vigorously than my mother had, because Helena's presence freed me to swim, hike, and play *beisbol*.

"That same autumn, a movie company from Florida built an amusement park on Pico Torquino, the tallest mountain in Cuba, only a few kilometers from our Sabio factory. The jewel of this set was a Ferris wheel that the filmmakers erected as close to Torquino's summit as they could safely get it. Then, once production had halted, the company's publicity department let it be known, in and around the Sierra Maestra, that locals could ride the Ferris wheel for the equivalent of fifteen American dollars a person on the last three days of October. After the last ride, the company would dismantle the device and return Torquino to its more or less natural state, prior to production.

"Marisa heard of the Ferris wheel. By this time, she had a computer that gave her a voice—a lilting little girl's voice—and she told Mama that she wanted to ride Vireo Films' greatly ballyhooed amusement. She wanted this boon as a birthday gift, before Vireo's roustabouts broke the wheel down and shipped it back to Florida. But, of course, if my parents granted Marisa this wish, they couldn't allow her to ride the Ferris wheel's gondola alone.

"I would have to go with her. I despised North American films and the nauseating hoopla that went with them, and so I absolutely hated this idea. In fact, I had a perverse nostalgia for the days of Fidel Castro, the sort of socialistic idealism that only the well-off son of a millionaire capitalist could afford to indulge. I didn't want to go. I didn't want to take Marisa.

"Helena intervened. She said *she* would ride with Marisa, if Diego, our household's major-domo, drove the two of them up Pico Torquino to Vireo's make-believe amusement park. (Even at thirteen, I heard this last phrase as an egregious bourgeois tautology.) She said it was fine if I chose to stay home, for the combined altitudes of the peak and the Ferris wheel would probably simply cause my snotty nose to bleed. This insult—reverse psychology?—worked, and I angrily offered myself up as Marisa's guardian on this expedition after all. Two evenings later, Diego drove Marisa, Helena, and me up the mountain so we could ride in one of the bright gondolas of the film company's Ferris wheel."

I began to see—dimly, at least—where Kaz was going with this story.

"We rode the wheel—Marisa, Helena, and I. We rode it an hour after sunset. Marisa sat between me and her pretty young aunt from Poznan. What can I say? My nose didn't bleed, but the combined heights of Torquino and that stately illuminated wheel made me tremble like a palmetto leaf in the salty October wind. Believe me, I shivered uncontrollably. Marisa, however, loved the entire experience.

"When our gondola stopped at the top of the wheel and swung back and forth in its gyros, with the south Cuba coast and the smoky mirror of the sea arrayed below us like glossy infrared photographs, Marisa barked her approval—a clipped, excited gasp; a call from the heart. The wheel itself blazed, and the stars of autumn . . . *Dios mío*, some of them seemed to swim in and out of view, shyly, like bronze or pewter carp."

Kaz fell silent.

I laughed nervously. "Remind me never to challenge you to a duel of similes."

"What I understand now," Kaz finally went on, "is that in that Ferris wheel gondola, poised above the darkened island, I loved Marisa, I loved Helena, and I loved the simple day-to-day astonishments of living. Down from Pico Torquino, however, the world—my world, anyway—seemed to change. The Brodkorbs went back to Poland. My mother returned to fussing over Marisa and ignoring the rest of us.

"By the following February, my parents had divorced. Mama, taking Marisa with her, rejoined her sister's family in Poznan, and my father immersed himself in design revisions, production goals, marketing strategies. He died four years later, on a business trip to New York, when Sashimi, a guild of militant Japanese whalers, exploded a pocket nuclear device in a subway tunnel under Grand Central Station. I was in my first year at Havana Tech, gearing up to study particle physics and vacuum propulsion systems."

Even though it seemed that he had just begun another story, Kaz stopped.

"Is that all?" I asked.

"All my life, I blamed Marisa for the loss of my parents. Two days ago, upon learning of Helena's death, I remembered something I couldn't quite remember. Please don't laugh. You see, this incomplete memory softened me. Only when we boarded Peeter and started crawling toward D-Tower did the memory come totally back to me. I have just told it to you, Dr. Gwiazda."

"Abel."

"Abel, then."

Peeter docked with the observatory complex at the summit of D-Tower. Dean had a crick from staring heavenward during our crossing—so, while ambling through the docking connector, he bemusedly rubbed his neck.

In D-Tower, despite *my* misgivings, I believe it gratified Kaz—oddly gratified him—when Dean insisted on going with us to Helena's memorial service: the voiding. (This last term offends me even more than does *ejection*, but, over our trip's past quarter century, it has gained currency and a certain cachet; the puns it embodies are, if nothing else, vivid and expressive.) Kaz realized that Dean wanted more to keep him, his new-found friend, in sight than to attend the funeral of a stranger, but I set aside my objections, and all three of us turned up on part of the observatory deck given over to, well, voidings.

To Kaz's obvious surprise, thirteen people, including our party from G-Tower, had come to honor Helena, who lay, just as promised, on the lingula of the ejector tube.

Commander Stefan Odenwald himself, looking distinguished but gaunt, headed this group of mourners, which also comprised Chaplain Mother Sevier and eight of Helena's friends and colleagues. The service, which I thought dignified and painfully moving, featured brief prayer readings by Odenwald and Chaplain Mother Sevier, a few words by a fellow geneticist, and a holovid of fifteen-year-old Helena singing *"Dona Nobis Pacem"* in a soprano as clear and chilling as ice water.

The holovid scared Dean, but didn't send him careening away from the ceremony. He grabbed my arm and held to it like Quasimodo clinging to a bell rope, his gaze shifting back and forth between the shimmering image of young Helena crooning like an angel and her aged-looking corpse, recognizable even to Dean as a transfigured but silent version of the beautiful hologhost. Adding to the eeriness of this experience was the fact that young Helena sang her part in rounds with an unseen orpianoogla and an invisible mixed choir. Indeed, their anthem echoed hauntingly throughout the deck.

At its conclusion, Odenwald said, "Mr. Mikol, as Helena Brodkorb's only living relative aboard *Annie Jump Cannon*, you have—if you wish it—the privilege of eulogizing her."

Kaz walked to the lingula, to stand in almost exactly the spot where the hologhost had sung. Bending, he kissed Helena's cold temple.

"From Pico Torquino to Epsilon Eridani," he said, standing erect again, "Helena Brodkorb was not afraid of heights. She dwelt on them. Like Harry Martinson, she knew that 'space can be more cruel than man, / more than its match is human callousness.' And so, unlike me, she was never cruel."

Which was all Kaz could steady himself to say. He put a hand over his mouth and stared at Helena's sunken eyes and lovely complexion. Meanwhile, Dean threaded a path through the other mourners to stand next to Kaz in mute condolence.

Odenwald said, "Shall we commend her now to the stars?"

Kaz nodded.

The lingula on which Helena Brodkorb lay retracted into its tube. A maintenance tech among the mourners used a remote to seal the tube and activate its plunger. Although no one on the deck could see her go, Kaz's dead aunt hurtled outward like a torpedo—far beyond the gravitational attraction of any of the armada's wheelships.

"Because we're decelerating," Commander Odenwald observed, "Helena Brodkorb will reach Epsilon Eridani before us."

"And eventually pass on out of the system into interstellar space again," said a colleague.

The company fell silent again. No one appeared to want to move.

After a time, I said: "May I speak?"

When Chaplain Mother Sevier nodded, I recited:

"So very human,
To grieve and to entomb.
This ardent woman
We cremate in the cold.

No longer may we hold
Her from her spacious home."

"Amen," said Chaplain Mother Sevier, crossing herself.

Finally, we funeral goers broke up and departed.

Back in G-Tower, Kaz opted to remain up-phase for the remainder of our armada's voyage. He has been spelling me with Dean as once, years ago, Helena Brodkorb spelled his mother and him with his handicapped sister, Marisa.

We have entered the Barricado Stream, a region a good deal less clogged with debris than a few of our astronomers had earlier supposed. The probe dropped by *Zwicky* has determined recently that the Stream hosts only one substantial cometary mass per each sphere the approximate size of the Earth's orbit around Sol. Good news. Very good news.

"There's hardly any chance at all we'll hit a comet," Nita Sistrunk said yesterday in the G-Tower mess.

But Bao added, "It isn't the comet-sized bodies we must fear. Remember, though, if *big* masses whirl around out here, there may also be smaller but more perfidious bodies impossible to detect at a distance."

"What do you mean?" I asked.

"You don't really want to know." And Bao deftly changed the direction of our talk.

In any event, more and more personnel aboard our three wheelships have come up-phase. We still have some journeying to do to reach New Home, at least another standard year's worth, but excitement mounts. Also, the staggered awakening of adults from the enchantment of ursidormizine slumber has delighted the children, and each pulse of our matter-antimatter engines seems a quickening heartbeat. The peculiar atmosphere of a seminar-cum-carnival has gripped *Annie*; also *Chandrasekhar* and *Zwicky*.

I wonder if Pharaoh's royal architect had a like sense of culminating accomplishment upon realizing that only a few more blocks would complete his master's pyramid.

Lily has come up-phase. She still can't believe that nasty Kazimierz Mikol has ingratiated himself with Dean—altogether sincerely, however—as a kind of uncle. Nor does she believe that Kaz and I have become friends. And, in fact, I prefer Thich Ngoc Bao's company to his, or Nita Sistrunk's, or Matthew Rashad's, a compatriot among the geologists. Our personalities (mine and Kaz's, that is) scrape against rather than complement each other's.

Nevertheless, we've hammered out a crumpled sort of mutual respect. Lily can't imagine how. I've told her about Helena Brodkorb's death and our rim-car trip to and from D-Tower, but, not having experienced these herself, she remains skeptical of everything about Kaz except his clear, if startling, affection for Dean.

"It's like the tiger and the lamb on the same bed of straw," she says. "A fearful symmetry whose opposing balances I can't quite grasp."

"Don't try," I tell her. "Just enjoy."

Lily simply shakes her head and laughs, a gruff chuckle so like Dean's that I gape. My look prompts more laughter and a sudden peck on my cheek.

"I like you more today than when we first met," she says. "More than on DeBoy's last birthday, even."

"Why is that?"

"You've started going gray," Lily tells me. "I've always liked older men."

Commander Stefan Odenwald stood in *Annie*'s pilot house, supervising its computer-aimed passage through the Barricado. Our other two arks ran parallel to *Annie*'s course at port and starboard distances of about seventy kilometers. Nonetheless, each of the other ships remained dimly visible to everyone in the pilot house, either on TV monitors or through the shielded viewports of the domelike bridge. A simultaneous look at the two vessels depended, of course, on the pilot house's rotating to either the top or the bottom of the fuel wheel's orbit vis-à-vis the headlong motion of the other two ships, but this happened often enough to thrill Dean and me, and seldom enough to increase our anticipation.

For a long time, I guess, Odenwald had realized that Dean enjoyed looking at the stars as much as anyone else aboard; therefore, he had invited us into the pilot house, a structure midway between Towers A-B and G-H on the ever-clocking fuel ring, and had there installed Dean in the thronelike chair that inevitably, and a bit sardonically, we call the Helm, as if it willy-nilly grants its occupant both authority and navigational savvy.

The Helm swallowed Dean. His feet dangled half a meter from the deck, and his chunky little body resembled that of a ventriloquist's dummy. Thankfully, he took no notice of the chair's scale, but turned his neckless head from side to side, ceaselessly ogling the universe.

"You look like—" Odenwald began. He turned to the other officers in the pilot house. "Who? You know, that holovid space explorer, what's-his-name?"

"I'm almost completely ignorant of such entertainments," I admitted—with an undercurrent of pride that Odenwald did not seem to find off-putting. It suggested, as it should, that I had better things to do.

On the other hand, I had often petitioned Odenwald for this audience, here in *Annie*'s control center, for my handicapped son, and surely that petition told him more about me than did any cheap slam at the junk on holovid.

"Cuhn I?" Dean said. "Cuhn I steer?"

"Have you mastered astronavigation, wheelship helming, and the rights and obligations of cybernetic command?"

"No suhr," Dean told Odenwald meekly.

"Well, then, you can't steer. But you're the only person besides myself to occupy that chair since we left lunar orbit in our own solar system."

"So far as you know," I put in.

Odenwald laughed. "Yes. So far as I know."

The TV monitor taking transmission from the *Subrahmanyan Chandrasekhar* showed all of us on the bridge the face of a haggard Caucasian male. I recognized him as one of Commander Joplin's lieutenants, Wolfgang Krieg.

"*Attention!* Commanders Odenwald and Roosenno, *attention!*" the haggard face said. "We appear to be on a collision course with a stream of frozen debris—gravel, call it—that initially composed a single mass about two meters in circumference. This stream of material—"

Odenwald took the mike. "*Initially?*" he said. "What do you mean, initially? What happened to it?"

"When we radar-sighted the object, we could see it would hit us," Krieg said. "Having no time to change course, we used our laser to try to deflect it."

"By vaporizing one side of the body to push it in another direction?" Odenwald theorized.

"Yessir," Krieg said.

"But, instead of moving aside, the object fragmented?"

"Yessir. The resulting stream of debris will strike us in two minutes fifty-three seconds."

Odenwald said, "How may we assist?"

"Get yourselves out of here," Krieg replied. "You might also want to pray."

Odenwald gave an order to activate the siphons to draw fuel from the C-D to E-F hydrogen tanks down the spokes to their matter-antimatter propulsion system. Kaz appeared from nowhere to do exactly that, while Odenwald ran the ignition programs. Bridge officers on *Zwicky* followed suit. Despite their size, both wheelships shoved agilely ahead, out of the energy-saving coast marking the latest stage of our years-long deceleration process.

"Don't look at the exhaust trail!" I told Dean.

But Dean *was* looking at it, a blazing bore of magnesium-white light that had already turned our wheel's opposite inner arc into an eye-stinging mirror. If he kept looking at it, he'd burn out his retinas. Blessedly, just as I started to push his face into his lap, Dean averted his gaze.

At that instant, the monitor receiving from *Chandrasekhar* filled with popping kinetic snow. *Chandrasekhar* itself, one instant past a platinum ring on a bolster of sequined black felt, flashed out like a miniature nova, a wound of radiance even brighter than *Annie*'s exhaust trail. Then, after the flash, in the place where the space ark had been: nothing but blackness. Every light on its rim, every light in its habitat towers, snapped out.

Immediately, though, a series of explosions on the wheel went off in astonishing sequence, like a silent Fourth of July gala with Roman candles, phosphorus bombs, and self-shredding parachutes of light. The sight of these distant fireworks froze me in place, for, as the disaster unraveled, there was nothing that anyone on either of our sibling arks could do—except imagine both the terror and the agony of our companions aboard the splintering ship.

Later, Bao and others postulated, the biggest chunk of the fragmented rock tracking *Chandrasekhar* had hit and severed its rim. Simultaneously, the gravel from Krieg's misguided attempt to deflect this object ripped into the fuel spokes *cum* support cables. Then centrifugal force took over, tearing the vessel apart. Broken tentacles of diamond writhed in the blackness. The electromagnetic levitation tanks holding the antihydrogen ice clear of the ordinary matter making up the ark's set-apart propulsion unit took ricocheting hits of their own, emitting, as a result, such hot bursts of radiation that the sky flared again and many of the ark's buckled compartments actually began to melt.

This catastrophe stunned me. I could think of nothing very like it in the history of spacefaring. The *Challenger* disaster might qualify, or the fate of the Chinese ship *Wuer Kaixi* off Titan late in 2057, but these events seemed so remote, and so happily limited in their life-taking scale, that the emptiness off to starboard, the afterglow of so many doomed lives, left me groping for some competent or humane response.

"Whuh?" Dean murmured. "Whud happen?"

Odenwald looked at him. Dean, in turn, looked to him for some hopeful reordering of the chaos that had inflicted itself on the sky outside our blister.

The incandescence, then the cold.

The kaleidoscopic brightness, then the dark.

"Please tell him, sir," I said. "And don't sugarcoat it."

Voices from *Fritz Zwicky* rattled in the pilot house. Radio operators in the communications well bent to their tasks. Two of Odenwald's lieutenants rushed in from the attached day room and lounge. Their concern—their activity—could not reverse the fate of *Chandrasekhar* or rescue a single person in any of its radiation-drenched habitation towers. All, like data in an irretrievably crashed program, were gone or going, already almost less than ciphers.

But it was Kaz, not Odenwald, who finally knelt in front of Dean's chair. "They hit something, or something hit them. A chunk of ice about like so." Kaz made a circle of his arms. "Maybe even a little smaller. Which split into pieces when the people on *Chandry* tried to move it."

"Bud how . . . ?"

"As fast as we're going, hitting an object that size makes a bang like the burst of a fission device." Kaz looked at me. "Sorry. He's never heard of Hiroshima, right? Or the Sashimi attacks on New York and L.A.?"

"Cuhd id happen to uz?"

Kaz looked to me for permission. I nodded.

"Yes, it could," Kaz said. "At the moment, though, we're outrunning the blast. If this helps at all, Dean, we should go fairly quickly if we hit something."

Dean began to cry. "I'm sorry thad happen," he said. "I'm sorree-sorree."

"Me too," Kaz said.

Odenwald came over and said he wanted Dean and me off the bridge. I picked Dean up, and Odenwald advised us to retreat to the day room while he spoke with Roosenno and some of his lieutenants about the morale and logistical implications of the disaster.

Dean and I left.

Two hours later, when it seemed to Odenwald and his closest advisors, including Bao, that we'd outrun any pursuing debris, our ships cut their engines and drifted back into the coasting mode of our long advance on Epsilon Eridani II.

If we survive the Stream, none of us will ever forget what has happened out here. Ever.

* * *

Mere chance enabled Dean to witness the destruction of another wheelship. Nonetheless, I blame myself for putting him in a place to see the spectacular melting or vaporization of sixteen-hundred human beings.

And Dean? He understands that *Chandrasekhar* and all its passengers have passed into physical oblivion. Kaz and I both tell him it's possible that God has received their souls, but, despite my religion, I remain a militant skeptic on this point, and Dean no longer asks if the victims of the disaster have gone to heaven. It both frets and wearies him to hear me say, "Dean, I don't know."

He also grasps, by the way, the perilousness of traveling at even a mere fraction of light-speed. He knows that *Annie Jump* or *Fritz Zwicky* could blaze out, novalike, as Commander Joplin's wheelship did. This knowledge has penetrated his awareness as deeply as, if not more deeply than, anything else he has ever learned. Sometimes (for me, red-letter occasions for guilt and moroseness), he remembers the catastrophe, bolts upright, and begins to rock and sway.

"Why?" he says. "Why?"

The basic existential inquiry.

And I wonder if Lily and I sinned against Dean, ourselves, or the incessant nag of the life force by bringing him to be in this precarious flying tin can.

Kaz says to ice the gloom-and-doom, the self-debates, the ontological kvetching.

A word to the wise? Not with *this* target audience: I don't qualify.

An arkboard month has passed. We have broken clear of the Barricado Stream— computationally, if not in our hearts. Our learned astronomers inform us that we have wide riding ahead, unobstructed glissading to New Home. Scant solace to the dead, of course, and scant comfort to either Dean or me.

More than once I've tried to eulogize the victims of this prodigious calamity. My words back up on me; my rhymes, even the off ones, don't quite slot; my rhythms, sprung or unsprung, drill like drugged anacephalics in jackboots. At last I wrote a stanza:

> *With a charged, chance suddenness,*
> *The all of spinning* Chandrasekhar,
> *The all of its ark, flashed to dark and spun to less*
> *Than a heat-dead, hooded star:*
> *A nova, an aura, an aroma of light-speed-sizzled thought,*
> *Brains broiled, skin fried, the atomizing mystery and mess,*
> *Actinic sabotage of each blind arrogance we bought*
> *With the hardware-software-psycheware of our ever-shoving-onward*
> *high-tech-tied success.*

Yesterday Bao asked if I've made any headway on the elegy everyone assumes I'll write. Reluctantly, I showed him this stanza. "Read it aloud," he said. There in the G-Tower mess, I lowered both head and voice and recited it.

Only Bao, thank God, could hear me. Kaz would have flung my comppad aside and stalked off, to seek better company in the finch-filled atrium.

"That's pretty," Bao said. A dig.

"So was the little mishap that triggered it."

"True. But I would have never taken you, my friend, for a Hopkins enthusiast."

This remark startled me. Bao had realized from the get-go that the paradigm for my stanza was an elegy by Gerard Manley Hopkins. I sat back and stared at him.

"Nor I you," I said.

Bao laughed. Then, with no physical prompts whatsoever, he recited:

> *"With a mercy that outrides*
> *The all of water, an ark*
> *For the listener; for the lingerer with a love glides*
> *Lower than death and the dark;*
> *A vein for the visiting of the past-prayer, pent in prison,*
> *The-last-breath penitent spirits—the uttermost mark*
> *Our passion-plunged giant risen,*
> *The Christ of the Father compassionate, fetched in the storm of his strides."*

"How can you do that?" I said. "Remember it all?"

Bao laughed again. "Stanza thirty-three. Because I've had Heraclitus call it up repeatedly since the accident. Balm from a long-dead Jesuit."

"I would have never taken you for an incarnationist, Bao, and certainly not one of a papist stamp."

Nothing marred Bao's hollow-cheeked amiability. "The wise take their comfort where they can."

"The wise seldom choke down such bilge."

Bao, grunting, grabbed his chest as if I'd just slipped a blade into his heart. He recovered at once, a fey smile on his lips. "Your stanza clatters where the Jesuit's sings, my dear unable Abel."

"Then I guess I'd better delete it."

"Ah, a wiser man than I'd supposed." He put a hand on my wrist. "Don't, though. Save it, as a ward against hubris." He released me, finished eating his vegetable shell, and, with a smile and a bad parting joke, excused himself. None of Bao's observations on either wisdom or comfort-taking had recast my own opinions; however, sitting and talking with him had cheered me. I kept the lone stanza of my come-a-cropper elegy, but attempted no others.

Later, in a geology carrel, I had Heraclitus call up "The Wreck of the Deutschland" and read it twice from beginning to end. If mere language can redeem a disaster, I believe Hopkins redeemed his.

Fuel rings turning like mountain-high Ferris wheels, *Annie Jump* and *Fritz Zwicky* have completely traversed the Barricado Stream. We have penetrated the orbit of Epsilon Eridani V, the system's outermost planet, an ice ball known to every member of our expedition as Cold Cock. New Home lies nearly 5.7 billion kilometers farther in, in the direction of Eppie herself; and our fleet, calamitously dispossessed of one of its arks, flies at a scant percentage of light-speed, a million kilometers per hour. At this rate, given the need to slow still more, it will take almost a year to reach our destination.

The hydrogen harvesters we deployed shortly after entering the Barricado, great funnels of molecularly strengthened mylar, will not only add calibrated drag to our deceleration, but resupply the exhausted tanks on the rim arcs between habitat towers. From the G-Tower observatory, it sometimes appears that we haul behind us the iridescent bladders of immense Portuguese men-of-war. Floats or wings? No one seems to know how to regard them. Sometimes, we can't see them at all. In any case, gathering hydrogen makes little sense, given that, by the time we reach New Home, our ships will have almost wholly depleted the antihydrogen ice required by our matter-antimatter rockets for further travel.

Ours not to reason why . . .

Days (or arkboard hours comprising their equivalent) ghost past as our last two vessels simultaneously plummet and wheel through this alien system. Up-phase scientists, technicians, engineers, and support personnel work methodically to prepare for planetfall and the colonization of New Home. Much of this preparation—plan comparisons, logistical projections, computer simulations—has to do with adjusting for the loss of the vital skills and labor units destroyed along with Commander Joplin's *Subrahmanyan Chadrasekhar*. On the other hand, our expedition's organizers factored in an atoning redundancy: personnel on any one ark can meet and overcome, by themselves, the environmental challenges of our target world. If a disaster befalls *Zwicky*, then *Annie* has the wherewithal to succeed.

And, of course, vice versa.

Less than halfway to the gas giant Jawbreaker (named for its bands of umber, licorice, and cherry, as well as for the fact that it has more than twice the mass of Jupiter), an astronomy group met with Odenwald in the observatory. This group (as Thich Ngoc Bao told me later that same evening) consisted of Nita Sistrunk, Indira Seschachari, Pete Ohanessian, and Bao himself.

Actually, after putting Dean to bed in our cubicle on the mezzanine level, I hitched a lift to the observatory for some private time to unwind and found Bao slumped in a swivel chair in a consultation bay not far from the ABVT. The door to this bay stood open, and, upon sighting Bao, who had made himself uncharacteristically scarce for the past seventy-two hours, I slipped in and greeted him.

"Hey."

Bao jumped as if I'd popped an eye-eye in front of him. Recognizing me, he composed himself and gave me a wan grin. His skin looked sallow, drum-tight.

"Doctor," I said, "what's up?"

"The jig," said Bao. "Old American expression. The game is over. Our hopes are dashed. Or, at least, a hefty plenty of them."

I sat down in a swiveler across from Bao, in front of an HD screen as big as a door. "We're surfing different wavelengths, friend o' mine."

"Tonight," Bao said, "our group presented to Odenwald the radio, spectrographic, and visual evidence that New Home may not be habitable to human beings."

My gut corkscrewed around itself. "Come again."

"We did so—Indira, Nita, Pete, and I—as if discussing mutation rates in fruit flies. Very professionally. As if our findings had only hypothetical significance to our arkmates and the people on *Zwicky*. In truth, we all felt blown away, Abel—nuked, one could say.''

I leaned forward. ''Bao, are you violating confidentiality telling me this?''

''I hardly think so. Tomorrow morning, the news will have spread all over both ships.''

''Then go ahead. Tell me.''

Bao rocked back, resting his ankle on his knee. ''All right. Nita showed Odenwald a series of photographs—computer amplified and enhanced—revealing New Home as an ugly-looking marble, a hard little sphere rotating under drifting rinds of reddish-brown dust and ejecta. The water we discovered by spectrographic analysis while outside the Barricado lay hidden under enmantling dust. Odenwald stared at us—his magi, so to speak—as if we'd led Herod right to him.''

''Ejecta?'' I said. ''What's going on? Volcanic activity? A worldwide dust storm?''

''Odenwald asked the same question, and Nita said, 'The dust storm's real enough, but Bao worries more about its causes.'

'' 'What do you think's happened?' Odenwald asked me.

''I told him that not long ago—possibly just before we drew within the orbit of the fifth planet—an asteroidal object the size of Mexico City burned through New Home's atmosphere and impacted with the surface. The stratospheric blizzard wrapping the planet derives from material crater-blasted upward by this nomadic body's impact.

''Odenwald turned over one of Nita's lovely gloomy photos, as if its other side would nullify my words. When it didn't, he thoughtfully replaced it in its sequence.

'' 'What does this mean for us?' he asked. 'As refugees in search of a livable world?'

'' 'Nothing good,' Pete Ohanessian said.

'' 'Itemize, please,' Odenwald insisted.

Nita reached over and touched his wrist—trying, you see, to console him. Meanwhile, though, she told him that infrared absorption spectroscopy would give us the best look at current conditions on the planet.

'' 'Dr. Seschachari has the results,' she said. 'Indira?' ''

Here, Indira had showed him a slide. So Bao punched a button, and the very slide in question flashed up on the HD screen behind me. When I swung about in my chair to look at it, an arrow jumped onto the screen over New Home's latest IR absorption spectrum.

Bao resumed his story:

''Indira said, 'This slide compares data taken on the trip out with more recently obtained info. This peak at around ten microns' ''—the arrow landed on it—'' 'is carbon dioxide, and you can see from the corresponding peak here' ''—the arrow bounced again—'' 'that the atmosphere's carbon dioxide content has risen dramatically as a result of the collision. We hypothesize that the vaporization of a lot of carbonate rock—namely, limestone—from the asteroid strike triggered the jump in CO_2. You can also add to that the CO_2 produced by the combustion of biomass—grasses, trees, who knows what else?—in the resulting firestorm. But even more alarming is that the levels of carbon dioxide continue to rise.'

'' 'Why?' Odenwald demanded.''

Indira told him she'd get back to that and noted that the second peak on the spectrum represented the absorption from the NO molecule, nitric oxide. Bao, quoting Dr. Seschachari, said that fumes from nitric oxide present two real problems for would-be colonists. First, the acid has a bite. Only idiots would try to land with it contaminating the ecosphere. Second, and even worse, the nitric acid has apparently begun to release even more carbon dioxide from New Home's limestone. To get an idea of the process, think of sodium carbonate—ordinary baking soda—in a bath of vinegar, fizzing away.

"Cripes, Bao, you've got to be kidding.''

"I wish.'' He got up and began to pace. "Pete Ohanessian took over from Indira and told Odenwald that the most efficient natural mechanism for removing CO_2 from a world's atmosphere is probably photosynthesis. Unfortunately, Abel, we think the asteroid strike and the firestorm have wiped out all but about five percent of New Home's vegetation. God, or Fate, has smashed the thermostat on that planet. When New Home comes out of its Ice Age—below-freezing temperatures everywhere, all a result of the dust cloud shrouding it—Pete thinks the planet could fall victim to the runaway greenhouse effect.''

In this scenario, Bao told me, atmospheric CO_2 provokes warming via standard greenhouse action. Carbon dioxide levels in cold water drop with added temperature, even more CO_2 outgasses as CO_2 once dissolved in polar oceans comes out of solution. Hence, even faster warming. As temperatures keep going up, the seas begin to evaporate, and H_2O is a more powerful greenhouse gas than CO_2. Water and carbon dioxide working together slow the escape of infrared energy into space. The hotter New Home grows, the more water vapor in its atmosphere: a steady ramping up of the greenhouse effect. Many thick blanketlike layers swaddle the planet, letting solar heat in but trapping the heat generated below. Eventually, New Home's equatorial seas start to boil.

"New Home seems to be something of a misnomer," I said.

Bao chuckled mirthlessly. "Well, perhaps not. We've done some very careful modeling to establish how close the planet is to the edge of Epsilon Eridani's habitable zone. It does lie on the inward edge of the zone, but at sufficient distance from Eppie to avoid a complete greenhouse runaway.''

"Won't things ever get back to normal?''

"What's normal?'' Bao said. "But, of course, that's what Odenwald wanted to know. Pete told him that a counterbalancing geological process could reverse the situation.'' Bao grinned a dare at me. "Any idea what it is, *Dr.* Gwiazda?''

The question took me off guard. "Weathering?''

"You're the geology man. I'm asking you.''

"Weathering,'' I said more forcefully.

"Care to explain it?''

"Spectroscopy implies New Home's mantle consists of calcium and magnesium silicates, right?''

"I guess so. Pete, at least, concurs.''

"Then the planet's atmospheric CO_2 will react slowly with these silicates to make calcium and magnesium carbonate. The process speeds up in hot, damp air, binding carbon dioxide into the planet's limestone. Temperatures drop. With this cooling, water vapor precipitates out. The greenhouse effect decreases, along with the temperature. In the end, New Home returns to 'normal.' How long will it take? I don't know. My specialty is soils. And we still don't know the percentage of anorthitic rock in New Home's exposed crust."

Bao smiled. "Maybe you should have briefed Odenwald too."

"What time-scale estimate did Pete offer?"

"He hemmed and hawed. I don't blame him. We lack solid values for anorthitic rock and the rate of vulcanism."

"Come on, Bao."

"A century or so. For sure, less than two hundred years. Maybe as few as fifty."

Hearing this, I thought first of Dean, now asleep in Lily's care. Such news would crush him. Lily, too. It was crushing *me*, like sixteen tons of granite on my chest. Had we traveled more than a century to reach a world that would accept us as colonists only after we had stewed in our bioracks another one hundred years?

"Yes," Bao said. "New Home's something of a misnomer." He punched a button on the arm of his chair and the speakers next to the HD screen activated. A recorded discussion garbled past on fast-forward. Bao stopped it. "After Pete talked, some of my colleagues got silly. Listen."

Nita: "Dead End might be a better name."

Indira: "Or Crater Quake."

Pete: "Or Pot Hole. Or Acid Bath."

Nita: "Gloomandoom!"

Indira: "Bitter Pill! Or maybe—"

Bao: "That's enough!"

Odenwald: "Easy, Bao—I was about to propose an irreverent name of my own."

Bao: "Sir, the purpose of this session is to brief you, not to divert ourselves."

Odenwald: "Maybe we should divert *Annie* to another planet in this system."

Nita: "Which? Jelly Belly? Red Hot?"

Pete: "The gravity on Jawbreaker would crush us. We'd do as well to set down on Eppie herself."

Nita: "Or as ill."

Bao: "We should continue to New Home. First-hand studies of the environmental aftermath of an asteroid strike this large are virtually nonexistent. We should follow up."

Indira: "But for whose sake?"

Odenwald: "You all have your work. I have mine. And my first duty is to break the news."

Nita: "You'll break hearts as well."

Pete: "A better time might be—"

Odenwald: "Traveling at nearly a million klicks per hour, there's no time like the present."

Bao halted the recording.

"Nita was right," I said. "The news has broken my heart. And it's sure to break others."

Bao toasted me with an imaginary shot glass, then slugged back its imaginary contents.

Lily broke the bad tidings to Dean. She insisted on her prerogative in this. In his self-appointed role as goduncle, Kaz tagged along.

We took Dean to a glade in the atrium, a stand of sycamores bonsai'd artfully near a waterfall encased in a sort of panpipe of clear plastic. In this secluded place, the falling water, pump-driven and -recirculated, made its tremulous woodwind and brook music.

Kaz lifted Dean to a notch in one of the sycamores and then tactfully wandered away. Lily took up a post beside Dean, to catch him if he slipped, while I sat on a bench masquerading as a ledge on the face of our miniature cascade.

Finches warbled, and, not far away, another party murmured among themselves, their talk a faint counterpoint to the water noise and the nonstop background hum.

"DeBoy, I have to tell you a very unpleasant thing," Lily began. "New Home won't be our new home, after all." She told him about our discovery of the recent asteroid strike and its meaning for everyone aboard our remaining ships—namely, either a frustrating wait until environmental conditions improved on Eppie's second planet or another long interstellar journey to another solar system with potential for settlement, most likely the Tau Ceti system.

None of this seemed to impress Dean. He sat in the dwarf sycamore gazing upward, and all around, for a glimpse of one of the finches.

"Do you understand me?" Lily asked. "We've come all this way, DeBoy, and New Home may be denied us."

"Yessum." Dean gave her a grudging, shifty-eyed nod.

"It's all right to feel sad. It's even all right to cry."

Our ingrate son kept rubbernecking for birds.

"*Dean!*"

So quickly did Dean's gaze snap back to Lily that he had to grab a limb. "I *like* id here," he said. "Now thad evvybody's ub . . . *up* . . . I like id jes fine."

Almost against my will, I guffawed.

Lily shot me an I'm-going-to-kill-you glare that modulated, almost against *her* will, into a defeated grin.

Whereupon Hiller Nevels, a botanist named Gulnara Golovin, and Milo Pask, a habitat engineer, came strolling toward us, arguing or at least expostulating among themselves. Golovin had her hand consolingly on Pask's arm, and none of the three seemed at all aware of our own family group, not even when Kaz trudged back into the clearing and halted in some puzzlement at the sight of them.

". . . *won't* get over it!" Pask was saying. "To travel over a century and learn on your final approach that a stupid rock from the sky has turned the planet of your dreams into a gas chamber! Why did I come? I'm supposed to build habitat geodesics, water and sewer systems. Now, I can't. I've come all this way for no reason!"

Golovin said, "You can't do your job *now*, that's all this setback means. Wait for the dust and the acid rain to settle out. A kind of normality will return to New Home. What's another year—even two—given all our years in transit? Milo, from the very beginning we knew we were living with a deferred ambition."

"Besides," said Hiller, "we had no guarantee any planet out here would prove a cozy place to camp."

Pask brushed Golovin's hand from his arm and rounded on Hiller. "Maybe not when we set out. But the closer we got to Eppie and the more that thick-headed gook and his star-gazing cronies learned, the more flowery they got about how New Home was Shangri-La and how grandly the place would welcome us. We hadn't come all this way just to rot in our bioracks. So they told us. The incompetent buggers!"

"Except for the asteroid strike, I think they appraised New Home accurately," Golovin said. "I don't see how you can hold them responsible for an act of God."

"We can't even hold *God* responsible for an act of God!" Pask raged. "So I'm scapegoating Thich and his sickening ilk. Do you mind?"

"Irrationality doesn't become you, Milo," Golovin scolded. "Stop it."

"No. But I become it, don't I?" Finally catching sight of Dean, Pask strode over with a weird glimmer in his eyes. "Who could have predicted this turn of events? This kid? Yeah, the kid. *Annie*'s resident . . . gnomic gnome."

Lily said, "Lay off, Milo."

Pask reddened as if she'd disparaged either his engineering skills or his virility, not simply rebuked him for bullying a child.

"What're the odds?" he asked. "What're the odds that New Home would take a lousy asteroid hit during our expedition's final approach?"

"I have no idea," Lily said.

"Well, I'll tell you. Statistically, Dr. Aliosi-Stark, the chances are something like a trillion to one. *A trillion to buggering one!*"

"I don't think so," Lily said.

"You don't, do you?"

"Given the event itself, I'd say that, statistically, the chances are one hundred percent."

Now Pask looked at Lily as if she'd slapped him. His face crumpled. Without attempting to mitigate or hide the fact, he began to cry. Dean followed suit. I took Dean out of the tree and held him. Lily hugged Pask.

"I want to leap into the same swallowing blackness everyone on *Chandrasekhar* leapt into," Pask said.

"You should talk to someone," Lily told him.

"I've talked to Hiller and Gulnara," Pask said. "Now I'm talking to you.

Talk doesn't heal, it just turns into more of itself.'' Regaining a degree of control, he wiped his eyes and reset his twisted features.

Seeing Pask calm himself, Dean quieted.

"That may be," I said. "But you should still sit down for a while with Etsuko Endo. Soon."

Pask wouldn't commit to this, but Golovin agreed to contact Etsuko on his behalf. Then she and Hiller led him out of the glade, and out of the atrium, in search of someone to dismantle his dread.

Kaz took Dean from me, and Dean leaned his head on Kaz's shoulder. "I like it here," Dean said.

Whether he meant this nook of the atrium or life in general aboard the ark, I had no idea.

New Home—or Acid Bath, or Dead End, or Bitter Pill, as the more mordant of our expedition's surviving members insist on calling the world—has no moon. Not long ago, *Annie Jump* and *Fritz Zwicky* took up orbits about ten thousand kilometers out, orbits that bestow on them—in the minds of our astronomy specialists and a few of our anonymous dreamers—exactly that status.

The two great ships, their own wheels rotating, turn about New Home like diamond-lit satellites, *Annie Jump* half a klick farther out—higher—than *Fritz Zwicky* but otherwise in rough parallel with its sibling. If any sentient species lives on the world below, and if roiling dust didn't veil the night sky from the ground, the sight of our two staggered wheels turning overhead would surely prompt stillness and then awe among their unknowable kind.

Aboard *Annie*, I imagine myself swinging in the gondola of a Ferris wheel on a lofty New Home peak, gazing into the night at this manmade binary cluster. In fact, I go on to imagine myself imagining myself as a passenger on one of our glittering rings. Lost in this double fantasy, I prefer the image of myself in New Home's transfigured sky: Orion orating in the heavens, not some mute Sherpa in the Himalayas.

I want to blaze, not to slog and grapple. Given my choice, I want to god-fashion myself in fire—even if the attempt slays me, even if no one but the greedy homunculus in my own breast hears my Promethean cri de coeur.

At 0800 hours tomorrow—measuring time by Greenwich mean time, as we still do aboard *Annie*—we will boost away from New Home and park ourselves nearer her sun, to begin the refueling process that will eventually take us to Tau Ceti.

The majority of us will travel down-phase, in ursidormizine slumber. Commander Stefan Odenwald will yield the bridge and his primary continuity-preserving duties to Hiller Nevels and a fresh team of self-sacrificing trouble-shooters, all volunteers, for Odenwald hopes to wake with legs fresh enough to climb a lovely new peak on the world that we discover and colonize in the Tau Ceti system.

Who can blame him? He has aged beyond any of the rest of us, excepting only Commander Roosenno, who will stay here in the Epsilon Eridani system, and Commander Joanna Diane Joplin, who ceased aging forever in the fatal millrace of the Barricado Stream.

As noted, the personnel aboard *Zwicky* will remain in orbit around New Home for as long as it takes to outlast the surface inferno brought about by the impact of the asteroid that Bao has named Epimenides, after a figure in Greek mythology who, while seeking a lost sheep, fell asleep for fifty-seven years and on awakening resumed his search unaware that so much time had passed. The oracle of Delphi then recruited Epimenides to cleanse Athens of a plague. Bao sees parallels between our slumbers and Epimenides', and between *Zwicky*'s task upon coming awake and that of the ancient Greek shepherd.

Briefly, Roosenno, like Odenwald, plans to send most of his would-be colonists down-phase until planetary conditions permit their revival. Then they will undertake the daunting task of turning New Home into a permanent human colony. Blessedly, the ark-to-ark redundancy of our skills makes the separate agendas of our ships both feasible and attractive. The survival of our kind, we feel, depends not only on diversity, but also on our projection across as much of the inhabitable or terraformable galaxy as we can reach.

How did we make these decisions? Most democratically, in the extraordinary session I will now describe.

Twelve days ago, when Odenwald first broached this plan in the auditorium of *Annie*'s A-Tower, few of us could credit that he wanted us to vote on an "option" as hare-brained as *resuming* our expedition. We had gathered, after dozens and dozens of rim-car trips, to discuss the issue in face-to-face assembly (rather than from separate electronic carrels), and the first question from the floor surprised no one, least of all Stefan Odenwald himself.

"How can we go on to another solar system when by most cogent reckonings, we've nearly exhausted our supplies of antihydrogen ice?" Thom Koon asked this for everyone but about thirty techs and/or scientists already in the know.

At the head of our banner-hung auditorium, Odenwald asked Thich Ngoc Bao to reply. Bao stepped to the podium to address us: "Good evening."

I had Dean in my lap, for Odenwald had told us that no one should miss this gathering; that, in fact, children should also attend.

So when Bao said, "Good evening," we replied in kind, like children answering a teacher.

Dean, waving crazily, called out, *"Bao! Bao! Bao!"* until I brought his arm down and whispered as quietly as the noise level allowed, "Hush, DeBoy. Hush."

Dean hushed.

"Hydrogen is no problem," Bao said confidently, his reedy voice echoing. "We harvested this fuel during the deceleration process, from the Barricado on in."

"What about the antihydrogen?" Thom cried. "Do you guys plan to turn regular hydrogen molecules inside out?"

Bao shifted his weight. "You should know that every ship in our armada, including *Chandrasekhar*"—he briefly shut his eyes—"was built with the capacity to generate antihydrogen for travel *beyond* the Epsilon Eridani system."

This news stunned most of us in the A-Tower auditorium. *I* had certainly never supposed us to have the ability to journey to another system, perhaps even back to Earth. And none of my friends—with the conspicuous exception of Thich Ngoc Bao—had suspected it either.

"How can we do that?" somebody shouted.

"Each ark is also a cyclotron, a particle accelerator," Bao said. "Each accelerator runs right down the underside of the fuel wheel itself, around its circumference. Given enough time and energy, the cyclotron belting *Annie Jump* will produce the hydrogen antiprotons necessary to fuel our journey from here to Tau Ceti."

Across the hall from where Lily, Dean, and I sat, Milo Pask stood up and shouted, "You geniuses kept this a *secret?* Why? Are we nonphysicists mere freeloaders? Idiot peons unworthy of consultation?"

Odenwald rejoined Bao at the podium. "Please recall that when the U.N. originally began planning a mission to Epsilon Eridani, we didn't know for sure if any planet out here would prove suitable for colonization. We thought it highly likely, of course, but didn't really know."

"Sir, what's your *point?*" Milo Pask asked.

"Simply that our mission's first mandate was one of hopeful exploration. Originally, then, U.N. planners allotted us only *two* ships, both of which were to have antimatter factories so that they could return to Earth after exploring the target star system. In that scenario, I'll remind you, *Annie Jump Cannon* didn't even exist."

Pask, peevishly flushed, was still on his feet, and an undercurrent of impatience—lapping the commander, not Pask—ran through the hall.

"During this initial planning," Odenwald went on, "off-Earth telescopes on Luna and the moons of Mars strengthened the case for a habitable planet here in EE. As a result, our mission changed, from one of exploring and establishing a permanent base if conditions allowed, to one of pure colonization. That change led us to add a third ship and extra people, not only because many more nations were clamoring to take part but also because planting a successful colony requires a diverse genepool and a third ship would give us insurance against an act of fate. In this, by the way, you can see how prescient the U.N. planners proved themselves."

"What about the antimatter factories?" Pask yelled.

"When we added *Annie*, mission costs skyrocketed. The most effective way to cut costs was to dump the notion of putting an accelerator on each vessel. Bao here, along with Trachtenberg and Arbib, considered that suicidal; the manufacturers of our wheelships thought it a kind of sacrilege—namely, bad design—and worked fiendishly to come up with a dirtcheap redesign that would save the antimatter factories. They did. Then they shunted their costs into other systems, at least on disk, and actually built the accelerators. Unfortunately, they couldn't test them without betraying their presence, and they had no money for testing anyway. So the planners kept them a secret—to prevent protests, work stoppages, maybe even the collapse of the entire project."

Pask was having none of this. "Why keep the accelerators a secret once we'd fled our Earthbound debts? It all smacks of a sleazy elitism!"

"Damned straight!" people cried.

"*¡Eso es verdad!*"

"Go get 'em, Milo!"

"*¡Claro que si!*"

Like a bidder at a noisy auction, Odenwald raised his arm. "True, once we were on our way, no one on our dirty, anarchic planet was going to stop us. We had what we needed, and we ran so far beyond Earth's jurisdiction as to become a species apart from those left behind. So we stayed mum, both over the radio and aboard our ships, out of respect."

"*Respect?*" several people cried incredulously.

Odenwald increased the gain on his mike. "We didn't want to rub our patrons' noses in either our early defiance or our present freedom. More important, we were afraid the cyclotrons might not work. We had no reason to try them while in transit and no desire to raise false hopes about their capabilities if the trip to Eppie went forward smoothly, as it did until we hit the Barricado. And even the painful loss of *Chandrasekhar* did nothing to persuade Commander Roosenno or me we should tell you the accelerators existed. What for? Epsilon Eridani Two—New Home—still looked to be a viable colony site. So our silence about them was meant to keep everyone up-phase focused on our prime destination, *not* to relegate any of you to the status of mere steerage riders."

"But that's what it did!" Pask shouted. "Knowing we could go from this system to another, and maybe even from Tau Ceti to yet another one, would've eased our minds! It would've saved *me* a lot of anxiety!"

Pask looked around. Odenwald's explanation had quieted the bulk of the hall. Reluctantly, Pask sat down, and Bao moved up to the podium again to speak:

"Recent tests of the accelerators on *Annie Jump* and *Fritz Zwicky* confirm their reliability. Tau Ceti is closer to Eppie than Eppie is to Sol. We can accomplish the trip without undue emotional stress or physical hardship—in about half the time it took to come here. I have nothing else to add unless some of you have technical inquiries that would fall within my areas of expertise."

"Wonderful!" someone not far from me shouted—Thom Koon, I think. "A mere half century!"

"Ursidormizine slumber will turn that half century into a sleep and a forgetting," Bao said smoothly.

Too smoothly, I'm afraid.

The med techs responsible for maintaining the bioracks and their monitoring systems had seats on a catwalk to Bao's left; a dozen of them stood up and booed. Several other maintenance specialists—down on the floor with Lily, Dean, and me—joined the med techs in jeering Bao's proposal.

"*Booooo! Booooo!*" The auditorium echoed with this ugly rumbling. A few people began to stamp their feet.

"It's Bao, not Boo," Bao told us. "You're using the wrong dipthong."

Not many of Bao's auditors—if you could call them that—caught this witticism. In fact, the booing and foot-stamping got louder. Here and there throughout the hall, people stood to voice their dissent, if not their outrage.

When the woman in front of me rose, Dean struggled out of my lap and held himself upright with his feet on my thighs. I could no longer see the podium.

"Quiet!" I heard Odenwald's amplified voice say. *"Resume your seats!"*

In the face of this esteemed authority, the mutiny more or less ended. Silence settled. People sat back down. Tension, however, left an inaudible buzz in the air; and if Pask or some other aggrieved renegade chose to challenge Odenwald, I feared that chaos—out-and-out insurrection—would erupt in full and undefeatable cry.

Meanwhile, Dean continued to balance himself erect on my thighs. When I tried to tug him back down, he seized the chair back in front with one hand and, with the other, fended off my frustrated tugging.

"Bao!" Dean shouted into the silence. *"Bao! Bao! Bao!"* He pistoned his right arm, an emphatic machine, up and down. *"Bao! Bao! Bao!"*

At the mike again, Bao said, "Of all the learned people in this gathering today, only young Gwiazda seems to know how to pronounce my name. Thank you, Dean."

"Bao!" Dean shouted again. "Bao, holy crow, you are really welcome!" Then eased back into my lap.

A ripple of applause and a drizzle of cheers boomed into a tidal swell of acclamation. Singlehandedly, so to speak, Dean had scotched any threat of mayhem.

Lily rolled her eyes at me. She patted Dean on the leg. Under her breath, she murmured, "Way to go, Tiny Tim. And God bless us, every one."

Bao had control of the meeting again. He pointed out that even if we moved *Annie* ten times closer to Eppie than New Home orbited—to make use of the energy generated by the solar cells affixed to the hydrogen tanks covering our fuel wheel—we would still require about eighty-five days to create a single ton of antihydrogen. Given *Annie*'s overall weight and the speeds that we had to achieve to complete our journey to Tau Ceti in fifty years, it would take another half century, up front, to concoct the 370 tons of antimatter necessary for our trip.

If Bao had given us this news a moment ago, an all-out riot would have broken out. As it was, we began to hear hostile—if not downright bloody—murmurings again.

Greta Agostos stood up. "That puts us back to where we were when we left Earth—a century away from our destination! Possibly more!"

"If I could lessen the time and energy requirements," Bao said, "believe me, I would. But some things are givens. You either deal with them or pitch an infantile tantrum. I would strongly urge the former."

"Amen," said Milo Pask. "Amen." And his consent, after the outrage he'd so angrily voiced, seemed to bring a rational truce upon the convocation.

Odenwald took over good-naturedly from Bao, secret-keeper par excellence, and let it be known that Commander Roosenno and he favored a plan whereby *Fritz Zwicky* stayed in orbit around New Home until it became habitable again and *Annie Jump* went on to the Tau Ceti system. However, within certain well-defined parameters, they would permit personnel exchanges between our ships: the trade-offs mustn't drastically unbalance the skills available to either the would-be colonists or the interstellar voyagers. Whatever we did, long stretches of ursidormizine slumber lay ahead of us, as did a host of catch-as-catch-can repairs. Our wheelships, after all, were *old*. On Earth, we'd regard them as antiques.

"But the plan favored by Commander Roosenno and me isn't a *fait accompli*," Odenwald said. "I called you here to vote on, not merely to endorse, it, and I trust you to discuss and pass on the question like intelligent adults."

I squeezed Dean's leg and whispered to Lily, "Do our less than genius kids get a vote too?"

"Ask him," Lily said *sotto voce*.

But before I could, Kaz had risen to his feet. "Sir, why don't we return to Earth—not just *Annie Jump*, but *Fritz Zwicky* too? Tau Ceti may well lack a colonizable planet, and New Home may never recover from its asteroid strike."

"Are you making a motion that we return to Earth?"

"No, sir. I'm putting it forward as an option worthy of debate. The Sol system bred and gave us birth. Neither Tau Ceti nor Epsilon Eridani can say as much, and some of us now have children. Who wishes to doom them to death in an alien star system with no provision for basic human needs—food, air, water, a sense of belonging?"

Kaz sat down, and we debated the matter. Few wanted to return to Earth. In a quick poll, even our children rejected that option. We had fled Earth to explore, to claim new and rejuvenating territories for our species, not to bail out when that very enterprise—as we had known it would do and so had tried to anticipate—threw obstacles in our way. Besides, we all owed the universe a death, and better to pay up seeking a fruitful tomorrow than retreating to a polluted cradle.

When Odenwald actually called the vote, less than a hundred people selected the return-to-Earth option. Not even Kaz voted for it. He had raised the question with an eye on the future of the innocents born in transit to New Home, and I respected his love and scrupulosity in this. He had completely overcome his early bias against Dean.

After that, the final vote was easy. *Annie Jump Cannon*'s personnel overwhelmingly approved Commander Odenwald's plan to resupply ourselves with antihydrogen ice and then to set out for Tau Ceti. A gathering like ours on *Fritz Zwicky* approved Roosenno's plan to remain in orbit, waiting out the dust storm and the greenhouse effect on New Home. If we were all equally lucky, *Annie* would leave for Tau Ceti about the time those on *Zwicky* ventured to the surface for the initial steps of their colony planting.

"*Hooray!*" cried Dean, clapping, when Odenwald announced the results of our vote. "*Bao! Bao! Bao!*"

At the end of this same meeting, Odenwald congratulated us not only on our decisions, but also on having participated in humanity's first successful venture to another solar system. Whatever happens to us in the coming weeks, months, and years, we have made history, and no one can take that achievement away from us.

"So Commander Roosenno and I agree that we should *celebrate* our arrival here," Odenwald told us. "We therefore decree a three-day festival, to begin officially at 0800 hours the day after tomorrow."

And so it has happened—namely, an alternately solemn and gala commemoration of what we've done, featuring personnel exchange between our wheelships and continuous ship-to-ship TV broadcasts. Our revelries have included songfests, skits, mess parties, musical competitions, art shows, vidouts, seminars, and, most important to me, poetry head-to-heads.

Thich Ngoc Bao on *Annie Jump* and Bashemath Arbib on *Fritz Zwicky* organized competitions in the writing of ballads, odes, sonnets, sestinas, and haiku, among other forms, and required contestants to use different astrophysical phenomena as their poems' subjects or controlling metaphors.

Inevitably, Ghulam Sharif and I found ourselves squared off in three categories, the most amusing a haiku-writing contest. We wrote in our cubicles aboard our own ships, but the finished poems flashed onto toadstool units everywhere as well as onto the huge softscreens in our A-Tower auditoriums.

In her broadcast introduction, Arbib explained, "In its classical form, the Japanese haiku evokes a season. So each contestant must write four poems, using astrophysical phenomena for their primary metaphors. . . ."

Ghulam and I had ten minutes for each haiku, after which we screened them simultaneously (despite their staggered display here), on penalty of disqualification. Their progression ran winter, spring, summer, fall:

      Sharif   *Gwiazda*

Interstellar planet
ice glistens in star-lit dark:
does it dream of spring?

                              Each vast aggregate
                              glitters, a many-armed flake:
                              beautiful, unique

Hydrogen ions
chirp and twitter microwaves
making nests: the stars

                              Plasma stirs and jets:
                              a furnace catalyzer
                              in cold birth-throe depths

Swelling blue-white star
outshines the bright galaxy
spraying iron, salt: us

                              Warm fireflies float
                              amid the midnight showers:
                              blaze and drop, then gone

Hoard scant hydrogen
against the final darkness:
stars, like leaves, turn red

> *A jack o'lantern*
> *Hisses on its black sky loam:*
> *baleful, squat, too red*

I leave to you the discovery of the astrophysical concepts used metaphorically in each haiku, but note that both sequences conclude with the word *red* as a combination of coincidence and contest design.

Three hundred persons—150 from *Zwicky*, a like number from *Annie*—selected the winning sequence in a blind electronic vote, Sharif triumphing 167 to 132. (Attribute the lost vote to an abstainer who adjudged both sequences "insufficiently imaginative" to bother choosing.) But I take some consolation from the fact that, in a separate vote, my haiku for summer was the overall favorite.

And then Epsilon Eridani Days, an entertaining success in nearly every way, concluded.

Once again, every member of our great expedition must face the realities of our present circumstances and the obligations of our choices.

Among my friends and acquaintances, Milo Pask, Etsuko Endo, Indira Sescharchari, Masoud Nadeq, and my arkboard lover, Lily Aliosi-Stark, have chosen to transfer to Roosenno's ark to wait for the dust cloud from Epimenides to settle. The defection that stings most painfully, of course, is the last.

"Abel, I've been down-phase in umpity-ump extended comas here on *Annie*," Lily told me a few hours ago. "I could handle another U-nap or two, but after I come up-phase again, I want to *stay* up-phase. I want to get on with my life. Is that so selfish a wish?"

"No more than my own," I said. "What about Dean?"

"We made him together, Abel, but he's yours. You have his life in your hands—insofar as *any* of us has control out here—and I expect you to do right by him."

"He's going with me."

"Of course he is. Nothing else makes sense. But I still expect you to do right by him."

"I won't let him forget you."

"That's one right thing you can try, but sooner or later he'll forget. Don't *force* him to remember. I won't mind if I'm just a nagging piece of grit in his memory. Eventually, if he has you to count on, that's all I should be."

"What crap," I said. "You sound like Joan of Arc praying amidst the flames."

For an instant, Lily's gaze darkened. Then she began to laugh. "I do, don't I? Well, good for me."

Using Colombo tethers and transfer dinghies, those leaving *Annie* carried their bodies across to *Zwicky*, sundering their souls from ours. But before these leavetakings, we took our melancholy last farewells. Dean, Kaz, and I met with Lily at the G-Tower docking station.

"It's like you guys're dying," Lily told us. "I'll never see you—any of you—again."

I kissed Lily. Hard. I kissed her again, caressing her hair. When I let go, Dean—DeBoy, as Lily had always called him—clung to her like a sorrowful young orang. If Kaz had not distracted him, she would have probably had to have emergency surgery to pry him loose.

Later, I watched from the G-Tower observatory as Lily and the others made their slow-motion glides across to or over from *Zwicky*. It seemed to me, though, that the dinghy containing my lover drew across the dark with it, in a harness of fireflies, a vein from my own clamoring heart.

A delusion, of course; a trick of the vacuum.

Nonetheless, it made me remember a haiku that Ghulam Sharif had written in the wake of our contest and sent over to me with a friend as a parting gift:

> *Iron cinders of stars*
> *cool in expanding darkness:*
> *too late for regrets*

"Guh-bye!" cried Dean, one hand on the viewport. "Guh-bye, Mama!"

Odenwald had okayed Dean's presence upstairs, and as his doting goduncle, Kaz had carried him up—for, under the present circumstances, kids had plenty of business in the observatory. Plenty.

"Guh-bye, guh-bye! Holy crow!"

Without Lily bodily before him, DeBoy truly understood only that *Annie Jump Cannon* was going on another long trip and that he was going with.

—with thanks to Geoffrey A. Landis

THE SAWING BOYS

Howard Waldrop

Howard Waldrop is widely considered to be one of the best short-story writers in the business, and his famous story "The Ugly Chickens" won both the Nebula and the World Fantasy Awards in 1981. His work has been gathered in three collections: *Howard Who?*, *All About Strange Monsters of the Recent Past: Neat Stories by Howard Waldrop*, and *Night of the Cooters: More Neat Stories By Howard Waldrop*, with more collections in the works. Waldrop is also the author of the novel *The Texas-Israeli War: 1999*, in collaboration with Jake Saunders, and of two solo novels, *Them Bones* and *A Dozen Tough Jobs*. He is at work on a new novel, tentatively entitled *The Moon World*. His stories have appeared in our First, Third, Fourth, Fifth, and Sixth Annual Collections. Waldrop lives in Austin, Texas.

Certainly nobody other than Waldrop would ever have come up with the wild and funny story that follows, in which a classic European fairy tale is retold in a distinctly *American* way—with a generous dollop of Damon Runyon thrown in for flavor . . .

There was a place in the woods where three paths came together and turned into one big path heading south.

A bearded man in a large straw hat and patched bib overalls came down one. Over his shoulder was a tow sack, and out of it stuck the handle of a saw. The man had a long wide face and large thin ears.

Down the path to his left came a short man in butternut pants and a red checkerboard shirt that said *Ralston-Purina Net Wt. 20 lbs.* on it. He had on a bright red cloth cap that stood up on the top of his head. Slung over his back was a leather strap; hanging from it was a big ripsaw.

On the third path were two people, one of whom wore a yellow-and-black-striped shirt, and had a mustache that stood straight out from the sides of his nose. The other man was dressed in a dark brown barn coat. He had a wrinkled face, and wore a brown Mackenzie cap down from which the earflaps hung, even though it was a warm morning. The man with the mustache carried a narrow folding ladder; the other carried a two-man bucksaw.

The first man stopped.

"Hi yew!" he said in the general direction of the other two paths.

"Howdee!" said the short man in the red cap.

"Well, well, well!" said the man with the floppy-eared hat, putting down his big saw.

"Weow!" said the man with the wiry mustache.

They looked each other over, keeping their distance, eyeing each others' clothing and saws.

"Well, I guess we know where we're all headed," said the man with the brown Mackenzie cap.

"I reckon," said the man in the straw hat. "I'm Luke Apuleus, from over Cornfield County way. I play the crosscut."

"I'm Rooster Joe Banty," said the second. "I'm a ripsaw bender myself."

"I'm Felix Horbliss," said the man in stripes with the ladder. "That thar's Cave Canem. We play this here big bucksaw."

They looked at each other some more.

"I'm to wonderin'," said Luke, bringing his toe sack around in front of him. "I'm wonderin' if'n we know the same tunes. Seems to me it'd be a shame to have to play agin' each other if'n we could help it."

"You-all know 'Trottin' Gertie Home'?" asked Felix.

Luke and Rooster Joe nodded.

"How about 'When the Shine comes Out'n the Dripper'?" asked Rooster Joe.

The others nodded.

"How are you on 'Snake Handler's Two-Step'?" asked Luke Apuleus.

More nods.

"Well, that's a start on it," said Cave Canem. "We can talk about it on the way there. I bet we'd sound right purty together."

So side by side by bucksaw and ladder, they set out down the big path south.

What we are doing is, we are walking down this unpaved road. How we have come to be walking down this unpaved road is a very long and tiresome story that I should not bore you with.

We are being Chris the Shoemaker, who is the brains of this operation, and a very known guy aback where we come from, which is south of Long Island, and Large Jake and Little Willie, who are being the brawn, and Miss Millie Dee Chantpie, who is Chris the Shoemaker's doll, and who is always dressed to the nines, and myself, Charlie Perro, whose job it is to remind everyone what their job is being.

"I am astounded as all get-out," says Little Willie, "that there are so many places with no persons in them nowise," looking around at the trees and bushes and such. "We have seen two toolsheds which looked as if they once housed families of fourteen, but of real-for-true homes, I am not seeing any."

"Use your glims for something besides keeping your nose from sliding into your eyebrows," says Chris the Shoemaker. "You will have seen the sign that said one of the toolcribs is the town of Podunk, and the other shed is the burg of Shtetl. I am believing the next one we will encounter is called Pratt Falls. I am assuming it contains some sort of trickle of fluid, a stunning and precipitous descent in elevation, established by someone with the aforementioned surname."

He is called Chris the Shoemaker because that is now his moniker, and he once hung around shoestores. At that time the cobbler shops was the place where the policy action was hot, and before you can be saying Hey Presto! there is

Chris the Shoemaker in a new loud suit looking like a comet, and he is the middle guy between the shoemakers and the elves that rig the policy.

"Who would have thought it?" asked Little Willie, "both balonies on the rear blowing at the same time, and bending up the frammus, and all the push and pull running out? I mean, what are the chances?"

Little Willie is called that because he is the smaller of the two brothers. Large Jake is called that because, oh my goodness, is he large. He is so large that people have confused him for nightfall—they are standing on the corner shooting the breeze with some guys, and suddenly all the light goes away, and so do the other guys. There are all these cigarettes dropping to the pavement where guys used to be, and the person looks around and Whoa! it is not night at all, it is only Large Jake.

For two brothers they do not look a thing alike. Little Willie looks, you should excuse the expression, like something from the family Rodentia, whereas Large Jake is a very pleasant-looking individual, only the pleasant is spread across about three feet of mook.

Miss Millie Dee Chantpie is hubba-hubba stuff (only Chris the Shoemaker best not see you give her more than one Long Island peek) and the talk is she used to be a roving debutante. Chris has the goo-goo eyes for her, and she is just about a whiz at the new crossword puzzles, which always give Little Willie a headache when he tries to do one.

Where we are is somewhere in the state of Kentucky, which I had not been able to imagine had I not seen it yesterday from the train. Why we were here was for a meet with this known guy who runs a used furniture business on South Wabash Street in Chi City. The meet was to involve lots of known guys, and to be at some hunting lodge in these hills outside Frankfort, where we should not be bothered by prying eyes. Only first the train is late, and the jalopy we bought stalled on us in the dark, and there must have been this wrong turn somewhere, and the next thing you are knowing the balonies blow and we are playing in the ditch and gunk and goo are all over the place.

So here we are walking down this (pardon the expression) road, and we are looking for a phone and a mechanically inclined individual, and we are not having such a hot time of it.

"You will notice the absence of wires," said Chris the Shoemaker, "which leads me to believe we will not find no blower at this watery paradise of Pratt Falls."

"Christ Almighty, I'm gettin' hungry!" says Miss Millie Dee Chantpie of a sudden. She is in this real flapper outfit, with a bandeau top and fringes, and is wearing pearls that must have come out of oysters the size of freight trucks.

"If we do not soon find the object of our quest," says Chris the Shoemaker, "I shall have Large Jake blow you the head off a moose, or whatever they have in place of cows out here."

It being a meet, we are pretty well rodded up, all except for Chris, who had to put on his Fall Togs last year on Bargain Day at the courthouse and do a minute standing on his head, so of course he can no longer have an oscar anywhere within a block of his person, so Miss Millie Dee Chantpie carries his cannon in one of her enchanting little reticules.

Large Jake is under an even more stringent set of behavioral codes, but he just plain does not care, and I do not personally know any cops or even the Sammys who are so gauche as to try to frisk him without first calling out the militia. Large Jake usually carries a powder wagon—it is the kind of thing they use on mad elephants or to stop runaway locomotives only it is sawed off on both ends to be only about a foot long.

Little Willie usually carries a sissy rod, only it is a dumb gat so there is not much commotion when he uses it—just the sound of air coming out of it, and then the sound of air coming out of whomsoever he uses it on. Little Willie has had a date to Ride Old Sparky before, only he was let out on a technical. The technical was that the judge had not noticed the big shoe box full of geetas on the corner of his desk before he brought the gavel down.

I am packing my usual complement of calibers which (I am prouder than anything to say) I have never used. They are only there for the bulges for people to ogle at while Chris the Shoemaker is speaking.

Pratt Falls is another couple of broken boards and a sign saying Feed and Seed. There was this dry ditch with a hole with a couple of rocks in it.

"It was sure no Niagara," says Little Willie, "that's for certain."

At the end of the place was a sign, all weathered out except for the part that said 2 MILES.

We are making this two miles in something less than three-quarters of an hour because it is mostly uphill and our dogs are barking, and Miss Millie Dee Chantpie, who has left her high heels in the flivver, is falling off the sides of her flats very often.

We are looking down into what passes for a real live town in these parts.

"This is the kind of place," says Little Willie, "where when you are in the paper business, and you mess up your double sawbuck plates, and print a twenty-one-dollar bill, you bring it here and ask for change. And the guy at the store will look in the drawer and ask you if two nines and a three will do."

"Ah, but look, gentlemen and lady," says Chris the Shoemaker, "there are at least two wires coming down over the mountain into this metropolis, and my guess is that they are attached to civilization at the other end."

"I do not spy no filling station," I says. "But there does seem to be great activity for so early of a morning." I am counting houses. "More people are already in town than live here."

"Perhaps the large gaudy sign up ahead will explain it," says Little Willie. The sign is being at an angle where another larger dirt path comes into town. From all around on the mountains I can see people coming in in wagons and on horses and on foot.

We get to the sign. This is what it says, I kid you not:

BIG HARMONY CONTEST!
BRIMMYTOWN SQUARE SAT MAY 16
$50 FIRST PRIZE
Brought to you by Watkins Products
and CARDUI, Makers of BLACK DRAUGHT

Extra! Sacred Harp Singing
Rev. Shapenote and the Mt. Sinai Choir.

"Well, well," says Chris. "Looks like there'll be plenty of *étrangers* in this burg. We get in there, make the call on the meet, get someone to fix the jalopy, and be on our way. We should fit right in."

While Chris the Shoemaker is saying this, he is adjusting his orange-and-pink tie and shooting the cuffs on his purple-and-white pinstripe suit. Little Willie is straightening his pumpkin-colored, double-breasted suit and brushing the dust off his yellow spats. Large Jake is dressed in a pure white suit with a black shirt and white tie, and has on a white fedora with a thin black band. Miss Millie Dee Chantpie swirls her fringes and rearranges the ostrich feather in her cloche. I feel pretty much like a sparrow among peacocks.

"Yeah," I says, looking over the town, "they'll probably never notice we been here."

They made their way into town and went into a store. They bought themselves some items, and went out onto the long, columned verandah of the place, and sat down on some nail kegs, resting their saws and ladders against the porch railings.

Cave Canem had a big five-cent RC Cola and a bag of Tom's Nickel Peanuts. He took a long drink of the cola, tore the top off the celluloid bag, and poured the salted peanuts into the neck of the bottle. The liquid instantly turned to foam and overflowed the top, which Canem put into his mouth. When it settled down, he drank from the bottle and chewed on the peanuts that came up the neck.

Rooster Joe took off his red cap. He had a five-cent Moon Pie the size of a dinner plate and took bites off that.

Horbliss had a ten-cent can of King Oscar Sardines. The key attached to the bottom broke off at the wrong place. Rather than tearing his thumb up, he took out his pocketknife and cut the top of the can off and peeled the ragged edge back. He drank off the oil, smacking his lips, then took out the sardines between his thumb and the knife blade and ate them.

Luke had bought a two-foot length of sugarcane and was sucking on it, spitting out the fine slivers which came away in his mouth.

They ate in silence and watched the crowds go by, clumps of people breaking away and eddying into the stores and shops. At one end of town, farmers stopped their wagons and began selling the produce. From the other end, at the big open place where the courthouse would be if Brimmytown were the county seat, music started up.

They had rarely seen so many men in white shirts, even on Sunday, and women and kids in their finest clothes, even if they were only patched and faded coveralls, they were starched and clean.

Then a bunch of city flatlanders came by—the men all had on hats and bright suits and ties, and the woman—a goddess—was the first flapper they had ever seen—the eyes of the flatlanders were moving everywhere. Heads turned to watch them all along their route. They were moving toward the general mercantile, and they looked tired and dusty for all their fancy duds.

"Well, boys," said Luke. "That were a right smart breakfast. I reckon us-all better be gettin' on down towards the musical place and see what the otherns look like."

They gathered up their saws and ladders and walked toward the sweetest sounds this side of Big Bone Lick.

"So," says Little Willie to a citizen, "tell us where we can score a couple of motorman's gloves?"

The man is looking at him like he has just stepped off one of the outermost colder planets. This is fitting, for the citizen looks to us vice versa.

"What my friend of limited vocabulary means," says Chris the Shoemaker to the astounding and astounded individual, "is where might we purchase a mess of fried pork chops?"

The man keeps looking at us with his wide eyes the size of doorknobs.

"Eats?" I volunteer.

Nothing is happening.

Large Jake makes eating motions with his mitt and goozle.

Still nothing.

"Say, fellers," says this other resident, "you won't be gettin' nothing useful out'n him. He's one of the simpler folks hereabouts, what them Victorian painter fellers used to call 'naturals.' What you want's Ma Gooser's place, straight down this yere street."

"Much obliged," says Chris.

"It's about time, too," says Miss Millie Dee Chantpie. "I'm so hungry I could eat the ass off a pigeon through a park bench!"

I am still staring at the individual who has given us directions, who is knocking the ashes out of his corncob pipe against a rain barrel.

"Such a collection of spungs and feebs I personally have never seen," says Chris the Shoemaker, who is all the time looking at the wire that comes down the hill into town.

"I must admit you are right," says Little Willie. And indeed it seems every living thing for three counties is here—there are nags and wagons, preggo dolls with stair-step children born nine months and fifteen minutes apart, guys wearing only a hat and one blue garment, a couple of men with what's left of Great War uniforms with the dago dazzlers still pinned to the chests—yes indeedy, a motley and hilarity-making group.

The streets are being full of wagons with melons and the lesser legumes and things which for a fact I know grow in the ground. The indigenous peoples are selling everything what moves. And from far away you can hear the beginnings of music.

"I spy," says Chris the Shoemaker.

"Whazzat?" asks Little Willie.

"I spy the blacksmith shop, and I spy the general mercantile establishment to which the blower wire runs. Here is what we are doing. William and I will saunter over to the smithy and forge, where we will inquire of aid for the vehicle. Charlie Perro, you will go make the call which will tender our apologies as being late for the meet, and get some further instructions. Jacob, you will take the love of my life, Miss Millie, to this venerable Ma Gooser's eatatorium where we will soon join you in a prodigious repast."

The general mercantile is in the way of selling everything on god's green earth, and the aroma is very mouth-watering—it is a mixture of apple candy and nag tack, coal oil and licorice and flour, roasted coffee and big burlap sacks of nothing in particular. There is ladies' dresses and guy hats and weapons of all kinds.

There is one phone; it is on the back wall; it is the kind Alexander Graham Bell made himself.

"Good person," I says to the man behind the counter, who is wearing specs and a vest and has a tape measure draped over his shoulder, "might I use your telephonic equipment to make a collect long-distance call?"

"Everthin's long-distance from here," he opines. "Collect, you say?"

"That is being correct."

He goes to the wall and twists a crank and makes bell sounds. "Hello, Gertie. This is Spoon. How's things in Grinder Switch? . . . You don't say? Well, there's a city feller here needs to make a co-llect call. Right. You fix him up." He hands me the long earpiece, and puts me in the fishwife care of this Gertie, and parks himself nearby and begins to count some bright glittery objects.

I tells Gertie the number I want. There are these sounds like the towers are falling. "And what's your name," asks this Gertie.

I gives her the name of this known newspaper guy who hangs out at Chases' and who writes about life in the Roaring Forties back in the Big City. The party on the other end will be wise that that is not who it is, but will know I know he knows.

I hear this voice and Gertie gives them my name and they say okay.

"Go ahead," says Gertie.

"We are missing the meet," I says.

"Bleaso!" says the voice. "Eetmay alledoffcay. Ammysays Iseway! Izzyoway and Oemay erehay."

Itshay I am thinking to myself. To him I says:

"Elltay usoway atwhay otay ooday?"

"Ogay Omehay!"

He gets off the blower.

"I used to have a cousin that could talk Mex," says Spoon at the counter. I thank him for the use of the phone. "Proud as a peach of it," he says, wiping at it with a cloth.

"Well, you should be," I tell him. Then I buy two cents worth of candy and put it in a couple of pockets, and then I ease on down this town's Great White Way.

This Ma Gooser's is some hopping joint. I don't think the griddle here's been allowed to cool off since the McKinley Administration. Large Jake and Miss Millie Dee Chantpie are already tucking in. The place is as busy as a chophouse on Chinese New Year.

There are these indistinguishable shapes on the platters.

A woman the size of Large Jake comes by with six full plates along each arm, headed towards a table of what looks like two oxdrivers in flannel shirts. These two oxdrivers are as alike as all get-out. The woman puts three plates in front of each guy and they fall into them mouth first.

The woman comes back. She has wild hair, and it does not look like she has breasts; it looks like she has a solid shelf across her chest under her work shirt. "Yeah?" she says, wiping sweat from her brow.

"I'd like a steak and some eggs," I says, "over easy on the eggs, steak well-done, some juice on the side."

"You'll get the breakfast, if'n you get anything," she says. "Same's everybody else." She follows my eyes back to the two giants at the next table. Large Jake can put away the groceries, but he is a piker next to these two. A couple of the plates in front of them are already shining clean and they are reaching for a pile of biscuits on the next table as they work on their third plates.

"Them's the Famous Singin' Eesup Twins, Bert and Mert," says Ma Gooser. "If'n everybody could pile it in like them, I'd be a rich woman." She turns to the kitchen.

"Hey, Jughead," she yells, "where's them six dozen biscuits?"

"Comin', Ma Gooser!" yells a voice from back in the hell there.

"More blackstrap 'lasses over here, Ma!" yells a corncob from another table.

"Hold your water!" yells Ma. "I only got six hands!" She runs back towards the kitchen.

Chris the Shoemaker and Little Willie comes in and settles down.

"Well, we are set in some departments. The blacksmith is gathering up the tools of his trade and Little William will accompany him in his wagon to the site of the vehicular happenstance. I will swear to you, he picks up his anvil and puts it into his wagon, just like that. The thing must have dropped the wagon bed two foot. What is it they are feeding the locals around here?" He looks down at the plates in front of Large Jake and Miss Millie. "What is *dat?*"

"I got no idea, sweetie," says Miss Millie, putting another forkful in, "but it sure is good!"

"And what's the news from our friends across the ways?"

"Zex," I says.

He looks at me. "*You* are telling *me* zex in this oomray full of oobrays?"

"No, Chris," I says, "the *word* is zex."

"Oh," he says, "and for why?"

"Izzy and Moe," I says.

"*Izzy* and *Moe?!* How did Izzy and Moe get wise to this deal?"

"How do Izzy and Moe get wise to anything," I says, keeping my voice low and not moving my goozle. "Hell, if someone could get *them* to come over, this umray unningray biz would be a snap. If they can dress like women shipwrecks and get picked up by runners' ships, they can get wind of a meet somewhere."

"So what are our options being?" asks Chris the Shoemaker.

"That is why we have all these round-trip tickets," I says.

He is quiet. Ma Gooser slaps down these plates in front of us, and coffee all round, and takes two more piles of biscuits over to the Famous Singing Eesup Twins.

"Well, that puts the damper on my portion of the Era of Coolidge Prosperity," says Chris the Shoemaker. "I am beginning to think this decade is going to be a more problematical thing than first imagined. In fact, I am getting in one rotten mood." He takes a drink of coffee. His beezer lights up. "Say, the flit in the *Knowledge Box* got *nothing* on this." He drains the cup dry. He digs at his plate, then wolfs it all down. "Suddenly my mood is changing. Suddenlike, I am in a working mood."

I drops my fork.

"Nix?" I asks nice, looking at him like I am a tired halibut.

"No, not no nix at all. It is of a sudden very clear why we have come to be in this place through these unlikely circumstances. I had just not realized it till now."

Large Jake has finished his second plate. He pushes it away and looks at Chris the Shoemaker.

"Later," says Chris. "Outside."

Jake nods.

Of a sudden-like, I am not enjoying Ma Gooser's groaning board as much as I should wish.

For when Chris is in a working mood, things happen.

They had drawn spot # 24 down at the judging stand. Each contestant could sing three songs, and the Black Draught people had a big gong they could ring if anyone was too bad.

"I don't know 'bout the ones from 'round here," said Cave Canem, "but they won't need that there gong for the people we know about. We came in third to some of 'em last year in Sweet Tater City."

"Me neither," said Rooster Joe. "The folks I seen can sure play and sing. Why even the Famous Eesup Twins, Bert and Mert, is here. You ever hear them do 'Land Where No Cabins Fall'?"

"Nope," said Luke, "but I have heard of 'em. It seems we'll just have to outplay them all."

They were under a tree pretty far away from the rest of the crowd, who were waiting for the contest to begin.

"Let's rosin up, boys," said Luke, taking his crosscut saw out of his tow sack.

Felix unfolded the ladder and climbed up. Cave pulled out a big willow bow strung with braided muletail hair.

Rooster Joe took out an eight-ounce ball peen hammer and sat back against a tree root.

Luke rosined up his fiddle bow.

"Okay, let's give 'er about two pounds o' press and bend."

He nodded his head. They bowed, Felix pressing down on the big bucksaw handle from above, Rooster Joe striking his ripsaw, Luke pulling at the back of his crosscut.

The same note, three octaves apart, floated on the air.

"Well, that's enough rehearsin'," said Luke. "Now all we got to do is stay in this shady spot and wait till our turn."

They put their instruments and ladder against the tree, and took naps.

When Chris the Shoemaker starts to working, usually someone ends up with cackle fruit on their mug.

When Little Willie and Chris first teamed up when they were oh so very young, they did all the usual grifts. They worked the cherry-colored cat and the old hydrophoby lay, and once or twice even pulled off the glim drop, which is a wonder since neither of them has a glass peeper. They quit the grift when it turns out that Little Willie is always off nugging when Chris needs him, or is piping some doll's stems when he should be laying zex. So they went into various other forms of getting the mazuma.

The ramadoola Chris has come up with is a simple one. We are to get the lizzie going, or barring that are to Hooverize another one; then we cut the lines of communication; immobilize the town clown, glom the loot, and give them the old razoo.

"But Chris," says I, "it is so simple and easy there must be something wrong with your brainstorm. And besides, it is what? Maybe a hundred simoleons in all? I have seen you lose that betting on which raindrop will run down a window-pane first."

"We have been placed here to do this thing," says Chris the Shoemaker. We are all standing on the porch of Ma Gooser's. "We cut the phone," says Chris, "no one can call out. Any other jalopies, Large Jake makes inoperable. That leaves horses, which even we can go faster than. We make the local yokel do a Brodie so there is no Cicero lightning or Illinois thunder. We are gone, and the news takes till next week to get over the ridge yonder."

Miss Millie Dee Chantpie has one of her shoes off and is rubbing her well-turned foot. "My corns is killing me," she says, "and Chris, I think this is the dumbest thing you have ever thought about!"

"I will note and file that," says Chris. "Meantimes, that is the plan. Little William here will start a rumor that will make our presence acceptable before he goes off with the man with the thews of iron. We will only bleaso this caper should the flivver not be fixable or we cannot kipe another one. So it is written. So it shall be done."

Ten minutes later, just before Little Willie leaves in the wagon, I hear two people talking close by, pointing to Miss Millie Dee Chantpie and swearing she is a famous chanteuse, and that Chris the Shoemaker is a talent scout from Okeh Records.

"The town clown," says Chris to me in a while, "will be no problem. He is that gent you see over there sucking on the yamsicle, with the tin star pinned to his long johns with the Civil War cannon tucked in his belt."

I nod.

"Charlie Perro," he says to me, "now let us make like we are mesmerized by this screeching and hollering that is beginning."

The contest is under way. It was like this carnival freak show had of a sudden gone into a production of *No, No Nanette* while you were trying to get a good peek at the India Rubber Woman.

I am not sure whether to be laughing or crying, so I just puts on the look a steer gets just after the hammer comes down, and pretends to watch. What I am really thinking, even I don't know.

There had been sister harmony groups, and guitar and mandolin ensembles, three guys on one big harmonica, a couple of twelve-year-olds playing ocarinas and washboards, a woman on gutbucket broom bass, a handbell choir from a church, three one-man bands, and a guy who could tear newspapers to the tune of "Hold That Tiger!"

Every eight acts or so, Reverend Shapenote and the Mt. Sinai Choir got up and sang sacred harp music, singing the notes only, with no words because their church believed you went straight to Hell if you sang words to a hymn; you could only lift your voice in song.

Luke lay with his hat over his eyes through two more acts. It was well into the afternoon. People were getting hot and cranky all over the town.

As the next act started, Luke sat up. He looked toward the stage. Two giants in coveralls and flannel shirts got up. Even from this far away, their voices carried clear and loud, not strained: deep bass and baritone.

The words of "Eight More Miles To Home" and then "You Are My Sunshine" came back, and for their last song, they went into the old hymn, "Absalom, Absalom":

> *Day-Vid The—He-Wept—and Wept*
> *Saying—Oh My Son—Oh my son . . .*

and a chill went up Luke's back.

"That's them," said Rooster Joe, seeing Luke awake.

"Well," said Luke Apuleus, pulling his hat back down over his eyes as the crowd went crazy, "them is the ones we really have to beat. Call me when they gets to the Cowbell Quintet so we can be moseying up there."

I am being very relieved when Little Willie comes driving into town in the flivver; it is looking much the worse for wear but seems to be running fine. He parks it on Main Street at the far edge of the crowd and comes walking over to me and Chris the Shoemaker.

"How are you standing this?" he asks.

"Why do you not get up there, William," asks Chris. "I know for a fact you warbled for the cheese up at the River Academy, before they let you out on the technical."

"It was just to keep from driving an Irish buggy," says Little Willie. "The Lizzie will go wherever you want it to. Tires patched. Gassed and lubered up. Say the syllable."

Chris nods to Large Jake over at the edge of the crowd. Jake saunters back towards the only two trucks in town, besides the Cardui vehicle, which, being too gaudy even for us, Jake has already fixed while it is parked right in front of the stage, for Jake is a very clever fellow for someone with such big mitts.

"Charlie Perro," says Chris, reaching in Miss Millie Dee Chantpie's purse, "how's about taking these nippers here," handing me a pair of wire cutters, "and go see if that blower wire back of the general mercantile isn't too long by about six feet when I give you the nod. Then you should come back and help us." He also takes his howitzer out of Miss Millie's bag.

"Little William," he says, turning. "Take Miss Millie Dee Chantpie to the car and start it up. I shall go see what the Cardui Black Draught people are doing."

So it was we sets out to pull the biggest caper in the history of Brimmytown.

"That's them," said Rooster Joe. "The cowbells afore us."

"Well, boys," said Luke, "it's do-or-die time."

They gathered up their saws and sacks and ladder, and started for the stage.

Miss Millie Dee Chantpie is in the car, looking cool as a cucumber. Little Willie is at one side of the crowd, standing out like a sore thumb; he has his hand under his jacket on The Old Crowd Pleaser.

Large Jake is back, shading three or four people from the hot afternoon sun. I am at the corner of the general mercantile, one eye on Chris the Shoemaker and one on the wire coming down the back of the store.

The prize moolah is in this big glass cracker jar on the table with the judges so everybody can see it. It is in greenbacks.

I am seeing Large Jake move up behind the John Law figure, who is sucking at a jug of corn liquor—you would not think the Prohib was the rule of the land here.

I am seeing these guys climb onto the stage, and I cannot believe my peepers, because they are pulling saws and ladders out of their backs. Are these carpenters or what? There is a guy in a straw hat, and one with a bristle mustache, and one with a redchecked shirt and red hat, and one with a cap with big floppy earflaps. One is climbing on a ladder. They are having tools everywhere. What the dingdong is going on?

And they begin to play, a corny song, but it is high and sweet, and then I am thinking of birds and rivers and running water and so forth. So I shakes myself, and keeps my glims on Chris the Shoemaker.

The guys with the saws are finishing their song, and people are going ga-ga over them.

And then I see that Chris is in position.

"Thank yew, thank yew," said Luke. "We-all is the Sawing Boys and we are pleased as butter to be here. I got a cousin over to Cornfield County what has one uh them new cat-whisker crystal *raddio* devices, and you should hear the things that comes right over the air from it. Well, I learned a few of them, and me and the boys talked about them, and now we'll do a couple for yew. Here we're gonna do one by the Molokoi Hotel Royal Hawaiian Serenaders called 'Ule Uhi Umekoi Hwa Hwa.' Take it away, Sawing Boys!'' He tapped his foot.

He bent his saw and bowed the first high, swelling notes, then Rooster Joe came down on the harmony rhythm on the ripsaw. Felix bent down on the ladder on the handle of the bucksaw, and Cave pulled the big willow bow and they were off into a fast, swinging song that was about lagoons and fish and food. People were jumping and yelling all over town, and Luke, whose voice was nothing special, started singing:

> "*Ume hoi uli koi hwa hwa*
> *Wa haweaee omi oi lui lui . . .*"

And the applause began before Rooster Joe finished alone with a dying struck high note that held for ten or fifteen seconds. People were yelling and screaming and the Cardui people didn't know what to do with themselves.

"Thank yew, thank yew!" said Luke Apuleus, wiping his brow with his arm while holding his big straw hat in his hand. "Now, here's another one I heerd. We hope you-all like it. It's from the Abe Schwartz Orchestra and it's called 'Beym Rebn in Palestine.' Take it away, Sawing Boys."

They hit halting, fluttering notes, punctuated by Rooster Joe's hammered ripsaw, and then the bucksaw went rolling behind it, Felix pumping up and down on the handle, Cave Canem bowing away. It sounded like flutes and violins and clarinets and mandolins. It sounded a thousand years old, but not like moonshine mountain music; it was from another time and another land.

Something is wrong, for Chris is standing very still, like he is already in the old oak kimono, and I can see he is not going to be giving me the High Sign.

I see that Little Willie, who never does anything on his own, is motioning to me and Large Jake to come over. So over I trot, and the music really washes over me. I know it in my bones, for it is the music of the old neighborhood where all of us but Miss Millie grew up.

I am coming up on Chris the Shoemaker and I see he has turned on the waterworks. He is transfixed, for here, one thousand miles from home, he is being caught up in the mighty coils of memory and transfiguration.

I am hearing with his ears, and what the saws are making is not the Abe Schwartz Orchestra but Itzike Kramtweiss of Philadelphia, or perhaps Naftalie Brandwein, who used to play bar mitzvahs and weddings with his back to the audience so rival clarinet players couldn't see his hands and how he made those notes.

There is maybe ten thousand years behind that noise, and it is calling all the way across the Kentucky hills from the Land of Gaza.

And while they are still playing, we walk with Chris the Shoemaker back to the jalopy, and pile in around Miss Millie Dee Chantpie, who, when she sees Chris crying, begins herself, and I confess I, too, am a little blurry-eyed at the poignance of the moment.

And we pull out of Brimmytown, the saws still whining and screeching their jazzy ancient tune, and as it is fading and we are going up the hill, Chris the Shoemaker speaks for us all, and what he says is:

"God Damn. You cannot be going *anywhere* these days without you run into a bunch of half-assed *klezmorim*."

For Arthur Hunnicutt and the late Sheldon Leonard.

Glossary to "The Sawing Boys" by Howard Waldrop

Balonies—tires

Bargain Day—court time set aside for sentencing plea-bargain cases

Beezer—the face, sometimes especially the nose

Bleaso!—1. an interjection—Careful! You are being overheard! Some chump is wise to the deal! 2. verb—to forgo something, change plans, etc.

The Cherry-colored Cat—an old con game

Cicero Lightning and Illinois Thunder—the muzzle flashes from machine guns and the sound of hand grenades going off

Do a minute—thirty days

Dogs are barking—feet are hurting

Fall Togs—the suit you wear going into, and coming out of, jail

Flit—prison coffee, from its resemblance to the popular fly spray of the time

Flivver—a jalopy

Frammus—a thingamajig or doohickey

Geetas—money, of any kind or amount

Glim Drop—con game involving leaving a glass eye as security for an amount of money; *at least* one of the con men should have a glass eye . . .

Glims—eyes

Goozle—mouth

Hooverize—(pre-Depression)—Hoover had been Allied Food Commissioner during the Great War, and was responsible for people getting the most use out of whatever foods they had; the standard command from parents was "Hooverize that plate!"; possibly a secondary reference to vacuum cleaners of the time.

Irish buggy (also Irish surrey)—a wheelbarrow

Jalopy—a flivver

Lizzie—a flivver

Mazuma—money, of any kind or amount

Mook—face

Motorman's gloves—any especially large cut of meat

Nugging—porking

The Old Hydrophoby Lay—con game involving pretending to be bitten by someone's (possibly mad) dog

Piping Some Doll's Stems—looking at some woman's legs

Push and Pull—gas and oil

Sammys—the Feds

Zex—Quiet (as in bleaso), cut it out, jiggies! Beat it! laying zex—keeping lookout

Rules of pig Latin: initial consonants are moved to the end of the word and -ay is added to the consonant; initial vowels are moved to the end of the word and -way is added to the vowel

THE MATTER OF SEGGRI

Ursula K. Le Guin

Ursula K. Le Guin was a powerful presence in the short-fiction market this year, publishing seven stories in the genre, at least four or five of which were strong enough to have been shoo-ins for inclusion in a best-of-the-year anthology any other year. With difficulty, I managed to limit myself to two of them: "Forgiveness Day," which appears earlier in this anthology, and the story that follows, another brilliant Hanish novella, this one a powerful, somberly eloquent, and disturbing examination of all the terrible things that people can do to each other in the name of love . . .

The first recorded contact with Seggri was in year 242 of Hainish Cycle 93. A Wandership six generations out from Iao (4-Taurus) came down on the planet, and the captain entered this report in his ship's log.

Captain Aolao-olao's Report

We have spent near forty days on this world they call Se-ri or Ye-ha-ri, well entertained, and leave with as good an estimation of the natives as is consonant with their unregenerate state. They live in fine great buildings they call castles, with large parks all about. Outside the walls of the parks lie well-tilled fields and abundant orchards, reclaimed by diligence from the parched and arid desert of stone that makes up the greatest part of the land. Their women live in villages and towns huddled outside the walls. All the common work of farm and mill is performed by the women, of whom there is a vast superabundance. They are ordinary drudges, living in towns which belong to the lords of the castle. They live amongst the cattle and brute animals of all kinds, who are permitted into the houses, some of which are of fair size. These women go about drably clothed, always in groups and bands. They are never allowed within the walls of the park, leaving the food and necessaries with which they provide the men at the outer gate of the castle. The women evinced great fear and distrust of us, and our hosts advised us that it were best for us to keep away from their towns, which we did.

The men go freely about their great parks, playing at one sport or another. At night they go to certain houses which they own in the town, where they may have their pick among the women and satisfy their lust upon them as they will. The women pay them, we were told, in their money, which is copper, for a

417

night of pleasure, and pay them yet more if they get a child on them. Their nights thus are spent in carnal satisfaction as often as they desire, and their days in a diversity of sports and games, notably a kind of wrestling, in which they throw each other through the air so that we marvelled that they seemed never to take hurt, but rose up and returned to the combat with marvelous dexterity of hand and foot. Also they fence with blunt swords, and combat with long light sticks. Also they play a game with balls on a great field, using the arms to catch or throw the ball and the legs to kick the ball and trip or catch or kick the men of the other team, so that many are bruised and lamed in the passion of the sport, which was very fine to see, the teams in their contrasted garments of bright colors much gauded out with gold and finery seething now this way, now that, up and down the field in a mass, from which the balls were flung up and caught by runners breaking free of the struggling crowd and fleeting towards the one or the other goal with all the rest in hot pursuit. There is a "battlefield" as they call it of this game lying without the walls of the castle park, near to the town, so that the women may come watch and cheer, which they do heartily, calling out the names of favorite players and urging them with many uncouth cries to victory.

Boys are taken from the women at the age of eleven and brought to the castle to be educated as befits a man. We saw such a child brought into the castle with much ceremony and rejoicing. It is said that the women find it difficult to bring a pregnancy of a boy child to term, and that of those born many die in infancy despite the care lavished upon them, so that there are far more women than men. In this we see the curse of GOD laid upon this race as upon all those who acknowledge HIM not, unrepentant heathens whose ears are stopped to true discourse and blind to the light.

These men know little of art, only a kind of leaping dance, and their science is little beyond that of savages. One great man of a castle to whom I talked, who was dressed out in cloth of gold and crimson and whom all called Prince and Grandsire with much respect and deference, yet was so ignorant he believed the stars to be worlds full of people and beasts, asking us from which star we descended. They have only vessels driven by steam along the surface of the land and water, and no notion of flight either in the air or in space, nor any curiosity about such things, saying with disdain, "That is all women's work," and indeed I found that if I asked these great men about matters of common knowledge such as the working of machinery, the weaving of cloth, the transmission of holovision, they would soon chide me for taking interest in womanish things as they called them, desiring me to talk as befit a man.

In the breeding of their fierce cattle within the parks they are very knowledgeable, as in the sewing up of their clothing, which they make from cloth the women weave in their factories. The men vie in the ornamentation and magnificence of their costumes to an extent which we might indeed have thought scarcely manly, were they not withal such proper men, strong and ready for any game or sport, and full of pride and a most delicate and fiery honor.

The log including Captain Aolao-olao's entries was (after a 12-generation journey) returned to the Sacred Archives of The Universe on Iao, which were dis-

persed during the period called The Tumult, and eventually preserved in fragmentary form on Hain. There is no record of further contact with Seggri until the First Observers were sent by the Ekumen in 93 / 1333: an Alterran man and a Hainish woman, Kaza Agad and Merriment. After a year in orbit mapping, photographing, recording and studying broadcasts, and analysing and learning a major regional language, the Observers landed. Acting upon a strong persuasion of the vulnerability of the planetary culture, they presented themselves as survivors of the wreck of a fishing boat, blown far off course, from a remote island. They were, as they had anticipated, separated at once, Kaza Agad being taken to the Castle and Merriment into the town. Kaza kept his name, which was plausible in the native context; Merriment called herself Yude. We have only her report, from which three excerpts follow.

From Mobile Gerindu'uttahayudetwe'menrade Merriment's Notes for a Report to the Ekumen, 93 / 1334.

34 / 223. Their network of trade and information, hence their awareness of what goes on elsewhere in their world, is too sophisticated for me to maintain my Stupid Foreign Castaway act any longer. Ekhaw called me in today and said, "If we had a sire here who was worth buying or if our teams were winning their games, I'd think you were a spy. Who are you, anyhow?"

I said, "Would you let me go to the College at Hagka?"

She said, "Why?"

"There are scientists there, I think? I need to talk with them."

This made sense to her; she made their "Mh" noise of assent.

"Could my friend go there with me?"

"Shask, you mean?"

We were both puzzled for a moment. She didn't expect a woman to call a man 'friend,' and I hadn't thought of Shask as a friend. She's very young, and I haven't taken her very seriously.

"I mean Kaza, the man I came with."

"A man—to the college?" she said, incredulous. She looked at me and said, "Where *do* you come from?"

It was a fair question, not asked in enmity or challenge. I wish I could have answered it, but I am increasingly convinced that we can do great damage to these people; we are facing Resehavanar's Choice here, I fear.

Ekhaw paid for my journey to Hagka, and Shask came along with me. As I thought about it I saw that of course Shask was my friend. It was she who brought me into the motherhouse, persuading Ekhaw and Azman of their duty to be hospitable; it was she who had looked out for me all along. Only she was so conventional in everything she did and said that I hadn't realised how radical her compassion was. When I tried to thank her, as our little jitney-bus purred along the road to Hagka, she said things like she always says—"Oh, we're all family," and "People have to help each other" and "Nobody can live alone."

"Don't women ever live alone?" I asked her, for all the ones I've met belong to a motherhouse or a daughterhouse, whether a couple or a big family like Ekhaw's, which is three generations: five older women, three of their daughters living at home, and four children—the boy they all coddle and spoil so, and three girls.

"Oh yes," Shask said. "If they don't want wives, they can be single-women. And old women, when their wives die, sometimes they just live alone till they die. Usually they go live at a daughterhouse. In the colleges, the *vev* always have a place to be alone." Conventional she may be, but Shask always tries to answer a question seriously and completely; she thinks about her answer. She has been an invaluable informant. She has also made life easy for me by not asking questions about where I come from. I took this for the incuriosity of a person securely embedded in an unquestioned way of life, and for the self-centeredness of the young. Now I see it as delicacy.

"A *vev* is a teacher?"

"Mh."

"And the teachers at the college are very respected?"

"That's what *vev* means. That's why we call Eckaw's mother Vev Kakaw. She didn't go to college, but she's a thoughtful person, she's learned from life, she has a lot to teach us."

So respect and teaching are the same thing, and the only term of respect I've heard women use for women means teacher. And so in teaching me, young Shask respects herself? And/or earns my respect? This casts a different light on what I've been seeing as a society in which wealth is the important thing. Zadedr, the current mayor of Reha, is certainly admired for her very ostentatious display of possessions; but they don't call her Vev.

I said to Shask, "You have taught me so much, may I call you Vev Shask?"

She was equally embarrassed and pleased, and squirmed and said, "Oh no no no no no." Then she said, "If you ever come back to Reha I would like very much to have love with you, Yude."

"I thought you were in love with Sire Zadr!" I blurted out.

"Oh, I am," she said, with that eye-roll and melted look they have when they speak of the Sires, "aren't you? Just think of him fucking you, oh! Oh, I get all wet thinking about it!" She smiled and wriggled. I felt embarrassed in my turn and probably showed it. "Don't you like him?" she inquired with a naivety I found hard to bear. She was acting like a silly adolescent, and I know she's not a silly adolescent. "But I'll never be able to afford him," she said, and sighed.

So you want to make do with me, I thought, nastily.

"I'm going to save my money," she announced after a minute. "I think I want to have a baby next year. Of course I can't afford Sire Zadr, he's a Great Champion, but if I don't go to the Games at Kadaki this year I can save up enough for a really good sire at our fuckery, maybe Master Rosra. I wish, I know this is silly, I'm going to say it anyway, I kept wishing you could be its lovemother. I know you can't, you have to go to the college. I just wanted to tell you. I love you." She took my hands, drew them to my face, pressed my palms on my eyes for a moment, and then released me. She was smiling, but her tears were on my hands.

"Oh, Shask," I said, floored.

"It's all right!" she said. "I have to cry a minute." And she did. She wept openly, bending over, wringing her hands, and wailing softly. I patted her arm and felt unutterably ashamed of myself. Other passengers looked round and made little sympathetic grunting noises. One old woman said, "That's it, that's right, lovey!" In a few minutes Shask stopped crying, wiped her nose and face on her sleeve, drew a long, deep breath, and said, "All right." She smiled at me. "Driver," she called, "I have to piss, can we stop?"

The driver, a tense-looking woman, growled something, but stopped the bus on the wide, weedy roadside; and Shask and another woman got off and pissed in the weeds. There is an enviable simplicity to many acts in a society which has, in all its daily life, only one gender. And which, perhaps—I don't know this but it occurred to me then, while I was ashamed of myself—has no shame?

34 / 245. (Dictated) Still nothing from Kaza. I think I was right to give him the ansible. I hope he's in touch with somebody. I wish it was me. I need to know what goes on in the Castles.

Anyhow I understand better now what I was seeing at the Games in Reha. There are 16 adult women for every adult man. One conception in six or so is male, but a lot of nonviable male fetuses and defective male births bring it down to 1 in 16 by puberty. My ancestors must have really had fun playing with these people's chromosomes. I feel guilty, even if it was a million years ago. I have to learn to do without shame but had better not forget the one good use of guilt. Anyhow. A fairly small town like Reha shares its Castle with other towns. That confusing spectacle I was taken to on my tenth day down was Awaga Castle trying to keep its place in the Maingame against a castle from up north, and losing. Which means Awaga's team can't play in the big game this year in Fadrga, the city south of here, from which the winners go on to compete in the *big* big game at Zask, where people come from all over the continent—hundreds of contestants and thousands of spectators. I saw some holos of last year's Maingame at Zask. There were 1280 players, the comment said, and 40 balls in play. It looked to me like a total mess, my idea of a battle between two unarmed armies, but I gather that great skill and strategy is involved. All the members of the winning team get a special title for the year, and another one for life, and bring glory back to their various Castles and the towns that support them.

I can now get some sense of how this works, see the system from outside it, because the college doesn't support a Castle. People here aren't obsessed with sports and athletes and sexy sires the way the young women in Reha were, and some of the older ones. It's a kind of obligatory obsession. Cheer your team, support your brave men, adore your local hero. It makes sense. Given their situation, they need strong, healthy men at their fuckery; it's social selection reinforcing natural selection. But I'm glad to get away from the rah-rah and the swooning and the posters of fellows with swelling muscles and huge penises and bedroom eyes.

I have made Resehavanar's Choice. I chose the option: Less than the truth. Shoggrad and Skodr and the other teachers, professors we'd call them, are intelligent, enlightened people, perfectly capable of understanding the concept of space travel, etc., making decisions about technological innovation, etc. I limit my answers to their questions to technology. I let them assume, as most people naturally assume, particularly people from a monoculture, that our society is pretty much like theirs. When they find how it differs, the effect will be revolutionary, and I have no mandate, reason, or wish to cause such a revolution on Seggri.

Their gender imbalance has produced a society in which, as far as I can tell, the men have all the privilege and the women have all the power. It's obviously a stable arrangement. According to their histories, it's lasted at least two millennia, and probably in some form or another much longer than that. But it could be quickly and disastrously destabilised by contact with us, by their experiencing the human norm. I don't know if the men would cling to their privileged status or demand freedom, but surely the women would resist giving up their power, and their sexual system and affectional relationships would break down. Even if they learned to undo the genetic program that was inflicted on them, it would take several generations to restore normal gender distribution. I can't be the whisper that starts that avalanche.

34 / 266. (Dictated) Skodr got nowhere with the men of Awaga Castle. She had to make her inquiries very cautiously, since it would endanger Kaza if she told them he was an alien or in any way unique. They'd take it as a claim of superiority, which he'd have to defend in trials of strength and skill. I gather that the hierarchies within the Castles are a rigid framework, within which a man moves up or down issuing challenges and winning or losing obligatory and optional trials. The sports and games the women watch are only the showpieces of an endless series of competitions going on inside the Castles. As an untrained, grown man Kaza would be at a total disadvantage in such trials. The only way he might get out of them, she said, would be by feigning illness or idiocy. She thinks he must have done so, since he is at least alive; but that's all she could find out—"The man who was cast away at Taha-Reha is alive."

Although the women feed, house, clothe, and support the Lords of the Castle, they evidently take their noncooperation for granted. She seemed glad to get even that scrap of information. As I am.

But we have to get Kaza out of there. The more I hear about it from Skodr the more dangerous it sounds. I keep thinking "spoiled brats!" but actually these men must be more like soldiers in the training camps that militarists have. Only the training never ends. As they win trials they gain all kinds of titles and ranks you could translate as "generals" and the other names militarists have for all their power-grades. Some of the "generals," the Lords and Masters and so on, are the sports idols, the darlings of the fuckeries, like the one poor Shask adored; but as they get older apparently they often trade glory among the women for power among the men, and become tyrants within their Castle, bossing the "lesser" men around, until they're overthrown, kicked out. Old sires often live alone, it seems, in little houses away from the main Castle, and are considered crazy and dangerous—rogue males.

It sounds like a miserable life. All they're allowed to do after age eleven is compete at games and sports inside the Castle, and compete in the fuckeries, after they're fifteen or so, for money and number of fucks and so on. Nothing else. No options. No trades. No skills of making. No travel unless they play in the big games. They aren't allowed into the colleges to gain any kind of freedom of mind. I asked Skodr why an intelligent man couldn't at least come study in the college, and she told me that learning was very bad for men: it weakens a man's sense of honor, makes his muscles flabby, and leaves him impotent. " 'What goes to the brain takes from the testicles,' " she said. "Men have to be sheltered from education for their own good."

I tried to "be water," as I was taught, but I was disgusted. Probably she felt it, because after a while she told me about "the secret college." Some women in colleges do smuggle information to men in Castles. The poor things meet secretly and teach each other. In the Castles, homosexual relationships are encouraged among boys under fifteen, but not officially tolerated among grown men; she says the "secret colleges" often are run by the homosexual men. They have to be secret because if they're caught reading or talking about ideas they may be punished by their Lords and Masters. There have been some interesting works from the "secret colleges," Skodr said, but she had to think to come with examples. One was a man who had smuggled out an interesting mathematical theorem, and one was a painter whose landscapes, though primitive in technique, were admired by professionals of the art. She couldn't remember his name.

Arts, sciences, all learning, all professional techniques, are *haggyad*, skilled work. They're all taught at the colleges, and there are no divisions and few specialists. Teachers and students cross and mix fields all the time, and being a famous scholar in one field doesn't keep you from being a student in another. Skodr is a vev of physiology, writes plays, and is currently studying history with one of the history vevs. Her thinking is informed and lively and fearless. My School on Hain could learn from this college. It's a wonderful place, full of free minds. But only minds of one gender. A hedged freedom.

I hope Kaza has found a secret college or something, some way to fit in at the Castle. He's very fit, but these men have trained for years for the games they play. And a lot of the games are violent. The women say don't worry, we don't let the men kill each other, we protect them, they're our treasures. But I've seen men carried off with concussions on the holos of their martial-art fights, where they throw each other around spectacularly.

"Only inexperienced fighters get hurt." Very reassuring. And they wrestle bulls. And in that melee they call the Maingame they break each other's legs and ankles deliberately. "What's a hero without a limp?" the women say. Maybe that's the safe thing to do, get your leg broken so you don't have to prove you're a hero any more. But what else might Kaza have to prove?

I asked Shask to let me know if she ever heard of him being at the Reha fuckery. But Awaga Castle services (that's their word, the same word they use for their bulls) four towns, so he might get sent to one of the others. But probably not, because men who don't win at things aren't allowed to go to the fuckeries.

Only the champions. And boys between fifteen and nineteen, the ones the older women call *dippida*, baby animals, like puppies or kitties or lambies. They like to use the dippida for pleasure, and the champions when they go to the fuckery to get pregnant. But Kaza's thirty-six, he isn't a puppy or a kitten or a lamb. He's a man, and this is a terrible place to be a man.

Kaza Agad had been killed; the Lords of Awaga Castle finally disclosed the fact, but not the circumstances. A year later, Merriment radioed her lander and left Seggri for Hain. Her recommendation was to observe and avoid. The Stabiles, however, decided to send another pair of observers; these were both women, Mobiles Alee Iyoo and Zerin Wu. They lived for eight years on Seggri, after the third year as First Mobiles; Iyoo stayed as Ambassador another fifteen years. They made Resehavanar's Choice as "all the truth slowly." A limit of 200 visitors from off-world was set. During the next several generations the people of Seggri, becoming accustomed to the alien presence, considered their own options as members of the Ekumen. Proposals for a planetwide referendum on genetic alteration were abandoned, since the men's vote would be insignificant unless the women's vote were handicapped. As of the date of this report the Seggri have not undertaken major genetic alteration, though they have learned and applied various repair techniques, which have resulted in a higher proportion of full-term male infants; the gender balance now stands at about 12:1.

The following is a memoir given to Ambassador Eritho te Ves in 93 / 1569 by a woman in Ush on Seggri.

You asked me, dear friend, to tell you anything I might like people on other worlds to know about my life and my world. That's not easy! Do I want anybody anywhere else to know anything about my life? I know how strange we seem to all the others, the half-and-half races; I know they think us backward, provincial, even perverse. Maybe in a few more decades we'll decide that we should remake ourselves. I won't be alive then; I don't think I'd want to be. I like my people. I like our fierce, proud, beautiful men, I don't want them to become like women. I like our trustful, powerful, generous women, I don't want them to become like men. And yet I see that among you each man has his own being and nature, each woman has hers, and I can hardly say what it is I think we would lose.

When I was a child I had a brother a year and a half younger than me. His name was Ittu. My mother had gone to the city and paid five years' savings for my sire, a Master Champion in the Dancing. Ittu's sire was an old fellow at our village fuckery; they called him "Master Fallback." He'd never been a champion at anything, hadn't sired a child for years, and was only too glad to fuck for free. My mother always laughed about it—she was still suckling me, she didn't even use a preventive, and she tipped him two coppers! When she found herself pregnant she was furious. When they tested and found it was a male fetus she was even more disgusted at having, as they say, to wait for the miscarriage. But when Ittu was born sound and healthy, she gave the old sire two hundred coppers, all the cash she had.

He wasn't delicate like so many boy babies, but how can you keep from protecting and cherishing a boy? I don't remember when I wasn't looking after Ittu, with it all very clear in my head what Little Brother should do and shouldn't do and all the perils I must keep him from. I was proud of my responsibility, and vain, too, because I had a brother to look after. Not one other motherhouse in my village had a son still living at home.

Ittu was a lovely child, a star. He had the fleecy soft hair that's common in my part of Ush, and big eyes; his nature was sweet and cheerful, and he was very bright. The other children loved him and always wanted to play with him, but he and I were happiest playing by ourselves, long elaborate games of make-believe. We had a herd of twelve cattle an old woman of the village had carved from gourdshell for Ittu—people always gave him presents—and they were the actors in our dearest game. Our cattle lived in a country called Shush, where they had great adventures, climbing mountains, discovering new lands, sailing on rivers, and so on. Like any herd, like our village herd, the old cows were the leaders; the bull lived apart; the other males were gelded; and the heifers were the adventurers. Our bull would make ceremonial visits to service the cows, and then he might have to go fight with men at Shush Castle. We made the castle of clay and the men of sticks, and the bull always won, knocking the stick-men to pieces. Then sometimes he knocked the castle to pieces too. But the best of our stories were told with two of the heifers. Mine was named Op and my brother's was Utti. Once our hero heifers were having a great adventure on the stream that runs past our village, and their boat got away from us. We found it caught against a log far downstream where the stream was deep and quick. My heifer was still in it. We both dived and dived, but we never found Utti. She had drowned. The Cattle of Shush had a great funeral for her, and Ittu cried very bitterly.

He mourned his brave little toy cow so long that I asked Djerdji the cattleherd if we could work for her, because I thought being with the real cattle might cheer Ittu up. She was glad to get two cowhands for free (when Mother found out we were really working, she made Djerdji pay us a quarter-copper a day). We rode two big, goodnatured old cows, on saddles so big Ittu could lie down on his. We took a herd of two-year-old calves out onto the desert every day to forage for the edta that grows best when it's grazed. We were supposed to keep them from wandering off and from trampling streambanks, and when they wanted to settle down and chew the cud we were supposed to gather them in a place where their droppings would nourish useful plants. Our old mounts did most of the work. Mother came out and checked on what we were doing and decided it was all right, and being out in the desert all day was certainly keeping us fit and healthy.

We loved our riding cows, but they were serious-minded and responsible, rather like the grown-ups in our motherhouse. The calves were something else; they were all riding breed, not fine animals of course, just villagebred; but living on edta they were fat and had plenty of spirit. Ittu and I rode them bareback with a rope rein. At first we always ended up on our own backs watching a calf's heels and tail flying off. By the end of a year we were good riders, and took to training our mounts to tricks, trading mounts at a full run, and hornvaulting. Ittu was a marvelous hornvaulter. He trained a big three-year-old roan ox with lyre horns, and the two of them danced like the finest vaulters of the great Castles that we saw on the holos. We couldn't keep our excellence to ourselves out in the desert; we started showing off to the other children, inviting them to come out to Salt Springs to see our Great Trick Riding Show. And so of course the adults got to hear of it.

My mother was a brave woman, but that was too much for even her, and she said to me in cold fury, "I trusted you to look after Ittu. You let me down."

All the others had been going on and on about endangering the precious life of a boy, the Vial of Hope, the Treasurehouse of Life and so on, but it was what my mother said that hurt.

"I do look after Ittu, and he looks after me," I said to her, in that passion of justice that children know, the birthright we seldom honor. "We both know what's dangerous and we don't do stupid things and we know our cattle and we do everything together. When he has to go to the Castle he'll have to do lots more dangerous things, but at least he'll already know how to do one of them. And there he has to do them alone, but we did everything together. And I didn't let you down."

My mother looked at us. I was nearly twelve, Ittu was ten. She burst into tears, she sat down on the dirt and wept aloud. Ittu and I both went to her and hugged her and cried. Ittu said, "I won't go. I won't go to the damned Castle. They can't make me!"

And I believed him. He believed himself. My mother knew better.

Maybe some day it will be possible for a boy to choose his life. Among your peoples a man's body does not shape his fate, does it? Maybe some day that will be so here.

Our Castle, Hidjegga, had of course been keeping their eye on Ittu ever since he was born; once a year Mother would send them the doctor's report on him, and when he was five Mother and her wives took him out there for the ceremony of Confirmation. Ittu had been embarrassed, disgusted, and flattered. He told me in secret, "There were all these old men that smelled funny and they made me take off my clothes and they had these measuring things and they measured my peepee! And they said it was very good. They said it was a good one. What happens when you descend?" It wasn't the first question he had ever asked me that I couldn't answer, and as usual I made up the answer. "Descend means you can have babies," I said, which, in a way, wasn't so far off the mark.

Some Castles, I am told, prepare boys of nine and ten for the Severance, woo them with visits from older boys, tickets to games, tours of the park and the buildings, so that they may be quite eager to go to the Castle when they turn eleven. But we "outyonders," villagers of the edge of the desert, kept to the harsh old-fashioned ways. Aside from Confirmation, a boy had no contact at all with men until his eleventh birthday. On that day everybody he had ever known brought him to the Gate and gave him to the strangers with whom he would live the rest of his life. Men and women alike believed and still believe that this absolute severance makes the man.

Vev Ushiggi, who had borne a son and had a grandson, and had been mayor five or six times, and was held in great esteem even though she'd never had much money, heard Ittu say that he wouldn't go to the damned Castle. She came next day to our motherhouse and asked to talk to him. He told me what she said. She didn't do any wooing or sweetening. She told him that he was born to the service of his people and had one responsibility, to sire children when he got old enough; and one duty, to be a strong, brave man, stronger and braver than other men, so that women would choose him to sire their children. She said he had to live in the Castle because men could not live among women. At this, Ittu asked her, "Why can't they?"

"You did?" I said, awed by his courage, for Vev Ushiggi was a formidable old woman.

"Yes. And she didn't really answer. She took a long time. She looked at me and then she looked off somewhere and then she stared at me for a long time and then finally she said, 'Because we would destroy them.' "

"But that's crazy," I said. "Men are our treasures. What did she say that for?"

Ittu, of course, didn't know. But he thought hard about what she had said, and I think nothing she could have said would have so impressed him.

After discussion, the village elders and my mother and her wives decided that Ittu could go on practicing hornvaulting, because it really would be a useful skill for him in the Castle; but he could not herd cattle any longer, nor go with me when I did, nor join in any of the work children of the village did, nor their games. "You've done everything together with Po," they told him, "but she should be doing things together with the other girls, and you should be doing things by yourself, the way men do."

They were always very kind to Ittu, but they were stern with us girls; if they saw us even talking with Ittu they'd tell us to go on about our work, leave the boy alone. When we disobeyed—when Ittu and I sneaked off and met at Salt Springs to ride together, or just hid out in our old playplace down in the draw by the stream to talk—he got treated with cold silence to shame him, but I got punished. A day locked in the cellar of the old fiber-processing mill, which was what my village used for a jail; next time it was two days; and the third time they caught us alone together, they locked me in that cellar for ten days. A young woman called Fersk brought me food once a day and made sure I had enough water and wasn't sick, but she didn't speak; that's how they always used to punish people in the villages. I could hear the other children going by up on the street in the evening. It would get dark at last and I could sleep. All day I had nothing to do, no work, nothing to think about except the scorn and contempt they held me in for betraying their trust, and the injustice of my getting punished when Ittu didn't.

When I came out, I felt different. I felt like something had closed up inside me while I was closed up in that cellar.

When we ate at the motherhouse they made sure Ittu and I didn't sit near each other. For a while we didn't even talk to each other. I went back to school and work. I didn't know what Ittu was doing all day. I didn't think about it. It was only fifty days to his birthday.

One night I got into bed and found a note under my clay pillow: in the draw to-nt. Ittu never could spell; what writing he knew I had taught him in secret. I was frightened and angry, but I waited an hour till everybody was asleep, and got up and crept outside into the windy, starry night, and ran to the draw. It was late in the dry season and the stream was barely running. Ittu was there, hunched up with his arms round his knees, a little lump of shadow on the pale, cracked clay at the waterside.

The first thing I said was, "You want to get me locked up again? They said next time it would be thirty days!"

"They're going to lock me up for fifty years," Ittu said, not looking at me.

"What am I supposed to do about it? It's the way it has to be! You're a man. You have to do what men do. They won't lock you up, anyway, you get to play games and come to town to do service and all that. You don't even know what being locked up is!"

"I want to go to Seradda," Ittu said, talking very fast, his eyes shining as he looked up at me. "We could take the riding cows to the bus station in Redang, I saved my money, I have twenty-three coppers, we could take the bus to Seradda. The cows would come back home if we turned them loose."

"What do you think you'd do in Seradda?" I asked, disdainful but curious. Nobody from our village had ever been to the capital.

"The Ekkamen people are there," he said.

"The Ekumen," I corrected him. "So what?"

"They could take me away," Ittu said.

I felt very strange when he said that. I was still angry and still disdainful but a sorrow was rising in me like dark water. "Why would they do that? What would they talk to some little boy for? How would you find them? *Twenty-three* coppers isn't enough anyway. Seradda's way far off. That's a really stupid idea. You can't do that."

"I thought you'd come with me," Ittu said. His voice was softer, but didn't shake.

"I wouldn't do a stupid think like that," I said furiously.

"All right," he said. "But you won't tell. Will you?"

"No, I won't tell!" I said. "But you can't run away, Ittu. You can't. It would be—it would be dishonorable."

This time when he answered his voice shook. "I don't care," he said. "I don't care about honor. I want to be free!"

We were both in tears. I sat down by him and we leaned together the way we used to, and cried a while; not long; we weren't used to crying.

"You can't do it," I whispered to him. "It won't work, Ittu."

He nodded, accepting my wisdom.

"It won't be so bad at the Castle," I said.

After a minute he drew away from me very slightly.

"We'll see each other," I said.

He said only, "When?"

"At games. I can watch you. I bet you'll be the best rider and hornvaulter there. I bet you win all the prizes and get to be a Champion."

He nodded, dutiful. He knew and I knew that I had betrayed our love and our birthright of justice. He knew he had no hope.

That was the last time we talked together alone, and almost the last time we talked together.

Ittu ran away about ten days after that, taking the riding cow and heading for Redang; they tracked him easily and had him back in the village before nightfall. I don't know if he thought I had told them where he would be going. I was so ashamed of not having gone with him that I could not look at him. I kept away from him; they didn't have to keep me away any more. He made no effort to speak to me.

I was beginning my puberty, and my first blood was the night before Ittu's birthday. Menstruating women are not allowed to come near the Gates at conservative Castles like ours, so when Ittu was made a man I stood far back among a few other girls and women, and could not see much of the ceremony. I stood silent while they sang, and looked down at the dirt and my new sandals and my feet in the sandals, and felt the ache and tug of my womb and the secret movement of the blood, and grieved. I knew even then that this grief would be with me all my life.

Ittu went in and the Gates closed.

He became a Young Champion Hornvaulter, and for two years, when he was eighteen and nineteen, came a few times to service in our village, but I never saw him. One of my friends fucked with him and started to tell me about it, how nice he was, thinking I'd like to hear, but I shut her up and walked away in a blind rage which neither of us understood.

He was traded away to a castle on the east coast when he was twenty. When my daughter was born I wrote him, and several times after that, but he never answered my letters.

I don't know what I've told you about my life and my world. I don't know if it's what I want you to know. It is what I had to tell.

The following is a short story written in 93 / 1586 by a popular writer of the city of Adr, Sem Gridji. The classic literature of Seggri was the narrative poem and the drama. Classical poems and plays were written collaboratively, in the original version and also by re-writers of subsequent generations, usually anonymous. Small value was placed on preserving a 'true' text, since the work was seen as an ongoing process. Probably under Ekumenical influence, individual writers in the late sixteenth century began writing short prose narratives, historical and fictional. The genre became popular, particularly in the cities, though it never obtained the immense audience of the great classical epics and plays. Literally everyone knew the plots and many quotations from the epics and plays, from books and holo, and almost every adult woman had seen or participated in a staged performance of several of them. They were one of the principal unifying influences of the Seggrian monoculture. The prose narrative, read in silence, served rather as a device by which the culture might question itself, and a tool for individual moral self-examination. Conservative Seggrian women disapproved of the genre as antagonistic to the intensely cooperative, collaborative structure of their society. Fiction was not included in the curriculum of the literature departments of the colleges, and was often dismissed contemptuously— "fiction is for men."

Sem Gridji published three books of stories. Her bare, blunt style is characteristic of the Seggrian short story.

Love Out of Place
by Sem Gridji

Azak grew up in a motherhouse in the Downriver Quarter, near the textile mills. She was a bright girl, and her family and neighborhood were proud to gather the money to send her to college. She came back to the city as a starting manager at one of the mills. Azak worked well with other people; she prospered. She had a clear idea of what she wanted to do in the next few years: to find two or three partners with whom to found a daughter-house and a business.

A beautiful woman in the prime of youth, Azak took great pleasure in sex, especially liking intercourse with men. Though she saved money for her plan of founding a business, she also spent a good deal at the fuckery, going there often, sometimes hiring two men at once. She liked to see how they incited each other to prowess beyond what they would have achieved alone, and shamed each other when they failed. She found a flaccid penis very disgusting, and did not hesitate to send away a man who could not penetrate her three or four times an evening.

The Castle of her district bought a Young Champion at the Southeast Castles Dance Tournament, and soon sent him to the fuckery. Having seen him dance in the finals on the holovision and been captivated by his flowing, graceful style and his beauty, Azak was eager to have him service her. His price was twice that of any other man there, but she did not hesitate to pay it. She found him handsome and amiable, eager and gentle, skilful and compliant. In their first evening they came to orgasm together five times. When she left she gave him a large tip. Within the week she was back, asking for Toddra. The pleasure he gave her was exquisite, and soon she was quite obsessed with him.

"I wish I had you all to myself," she said to him one night as they lay still conjoined, langorous and fulfilled.

"That is my heart's desire," he said. "I wish I were your servant. None of the other women that come here arouse me. I don't want them. I want only you."

She wondered if he was telling the truth. The next time she came, she inquired casually of the manager if Toddra were as popular as they had hoped. "No," the manager said. "Everybody else reports that he takes a lot of arousing, and is sullen and careless towards them."

"How strange," Azak said.

"Not at all," said the manager. "He's in love with you."

"A man in love with a woman?" Azak said, and laughed.

"It happens all too often," the manager said.

"I thought only women fell in love," said Azak.

"Women fall in love with a man, sometimes, and that's bad too," said the manager. "May I warn you, Azak? Love should be between women. It's out of place here. It can never come to any good end. I hate to lose the money, but I wish you'd fuck with some of the other men and not always ask for Toddra. You're encouraging him, you see, in something that does harm to him."

"But he and you are making lots of money from me!" said Azak, still taking it as a joke.

"He'd make more from other women if he wasn't in love with you," said the manager. To Azak that seemed a weak argument against the pleasure she had in Toddra, and she said, "Well, he can fuck them all when I've done with him, but for now, I want him."

After their intercourse that evening, she said to Toddra, "The manager here says you're in love with me."

"I told you I was," Toddra said. "I told you I wanted to belong to you, to serve you, you alone. I would die for you, Azak."

"That's foolish," she said.

"Don't you like me? Don't I please you?"

"More than any man I ever knew," she said, kissing him. "You are beautiful and utterly satisfying, my sweet Toddra."

"You don't want any of the other men here, do you?" he asked.

"No. They're all ugly fumblers, compared to my beautiful dancer."

"Listen, then," he said, sitting up and speaking very seriously. He was a slender man of twenty-two, with long, smooth-muscled limbs, wide-set eyes, and a thin-lipped, sensitive mouth. Azak lay stroking his thigh, thinking how lovely and lovable he was. "I have a plan," he said. "When I dance, you know, in the story-dances, I play a woman, of course; I've done it since I was twelve. People always say they can't believe I really am a man, I play a woman so well. If I escaped—from here, from the Castle—as a woman—I could come to your house as a servant—"

"What?" cried Azak, astounded.

"I could live there," he said urgently, bending over her. "With you. I would always be there. You could have me every night. It would cost you nothing, except my food. I would serve you, service you, sweep your house, do anything, anything, Azak, please, my beloved, my mistress, let me be yours!" He saw that she was still incredulous, and hurried on, "You could send me away when you got tired of me—"

"If you tried to go back to the Castle after an escapade like that they'd whip you to death, you idiot!"

"I'm valuable," he said. "They'd punish me, but they wouldn't damage me."

"You're wrong. You haven't been dancing, and your value here has slipped because you don't perform well with anybody but me. The manager told me so."

Tears stood in Toddra's eyes. Azak disliked giving him pain, but she was genuinely shocked at his wild plan. "And if you were discovered, my dear," she said more gently, "I would be utterly disgraced. It is a very childish plan, Toddra: please never dream of such a thing again. But I am truly, truly fond of you, I adore you and want no other man but you. Do you believe that, Toddra?"

He nodded. Restraining his tears, he said, "For now."

"For now and for a long, long, long time! My dear, sweet, beautiful dancer, we have each other as long as we want, years and years! Only do your duty by the other women that come, so that you don't get sold away by your Castle, please! I couldn't bear to lose you, Toddra.'' And she clasped him passionately in her arms, and arousing him at once, opened to him, and soon both were crying out in the throes of delight.

Though she could not take his love entirely seriously, since what could come of such a misplaced emotion, except such foolish schemes as he had proposed?— still he touched her heart, and she felt a tenderness towards him that greatly enhanced the pleasure of their intercourse. So for more than a year she spent two or three nights a week with him at the fuckery, which was as much as she could afford. The manager, trying still to discourage his love, would not lower Toddra's fee, even though he was unpopular among the other clients of the fuckery; so Azak spent a great deal of money on him, although he would never, after the first night, accept a tip from her.

Then a woman who had not been able to conceive with any of the sires at the fuckery tried Toddra, and at once conceived, and being tested found the fetus to be male. Another woman conceived by him, again a male fetus. At once Toddra was in demand as a sire. Women began coming from all over the city to be serviced by him. This meant, of course, that he must be free during their period of ovulation. There were now many evenings that he could not meet Azak, for the manager was not to be bribed. Toddra disliked his popularity, but Azak soothed and reassured him, telling him how proud she was of him, and how his work would never interfere with their love. In fact, she was not altogether sorry that he was so much in demand, for she had found another person with whom she wanted to spend her evenings.

This was a young woman named Zedr, who worked in the mill as a machine repair specialist. She was tall and handsome; Azak noticed first how freely and strongly she walked and how proudly she stood. She found a pretext to make her acquaintance. It seemed to Azak that Zedr admired her; but for a long time each behaved to the other as a friend only, making no sexual advances. They were much in each other's company, going to games and dances together, and Azak found that she enjoyed this open and sociable life better than always being in the fuckery alone with Toddra. They talked about how they might set up a machine-repair service in partnership. As time went on, Azak found that Zedr's beautiful body was always in her thoughts. At last, one evening in her sin-glewoman's flat, she told her friend that she loved her, but did not wish to burden their friendship with an unwelcome desire.

Zedr replied, "I have wanted you ever since I first saw you, but I didn't want to embarrass you with my desire. I thought you preferred men."

"Until now I did, but I want to make love with you," Azak said.

She found herself quite timid at first, but Zedr was expert and subtle, and could prolong Azak's orgasms till she found such consummation as she had not dreamed of. She said to Zedr, "You have made me a woman."

"Then let's make each other wives," said Zedr joyfully.

They married, moved to a house in the west of the city, and left the mill, setting up in business together.

All this time, Azak had said nothing of her new love to Toddra, whom she had seen less and less often. A little ashamed of her cowardice, she reassured herself that he was so busy performing as a sire that he would not really miss her. After all, despite his romantic talk of love, he was a man, and to a man fucking is the most important thing, instead of being merely one element of love and life as it is to a woman.

When she married Zedr, she sent Toddra a letter, saying that their lives had drifted apart, and she was now moving away and would not see him again, but would always remember him fondly.

She received an immediate answer from Toddra, a letter begging her to come and talk with him, full of avowals of unchanging love, badly spelled and almost illegible. The letter touched, embarrassed, and shamed her, and she did not answer it.

He wrote again and again, and tried to reach her on the holonet at her new business. Zedr encouraged her not to make any response, saying, "It would be cruel to encourage him."

Their new business went well from the start. They were home one evening busy chopping vegetables for dinner when there was a knock at the door. "Come in," Zedr called, thinking it was Chochi, a friend they were considering as a third partner. A stranger entered, a tall, beautiful woman with a scarf over her hair. The stranger went straight to Azak, saying in a strangled voice, "Azak, Azak, please, please let me stay with you." The scarf fell back from his long hair. Azak recognised Toddra.

She was astonished and a little frightened, but she had known Toddra a long time and been very fond of him, and this habit of affection made her put out her hands to him in greeting. She saw fear and despair in his face, and was sorry for him.

But Zedr, guessing who he was, was both alarmed and angry. She kept the chopping-knife in her hand. She slipped from the room and called the city police.

When she returned she saw the man pleading with Azak to let him stay hidden in their household as a servant. "I will do anything," he said. "Please, Azak, my only love, please! I can't live without you. I can't service those women, those strangers who only want to be impregnated. I can't dance any more. I think only of you, you are my only hope. I will be a woman, no one will know. I'll cut my hair, no one will know!" So he went on, almost threatening in his passion, but pitiful also. Zedr listened coldly, thinking he was mad. Azak listened with pain and shame. "No, no, it is not possible," she said over and over, but he would not hear.

When the police came to the door and he realised who they were, he bolted to the back of the house seeking escape. The policewomen caught him in the bedroom; he fought them desperately, and they subdued him brutally. Azak shouted at them not to hurt him, but they paid no heed, twisting his arms and hitting him about the head till he stopped resisting. They dragged him out. The head of the troop stayed to take evidence. Azak tried to plead for Toddra, but Zedr stated the facts and added that she thought he was insane and dangerous.

After some days, Azak inquired at the police office and was told that Toddra had been returned to his Castle with a warning not to send him to the fuckery again for a year or until the Lords of the Castle found him capable of responsible behavior. She was uneasy thinking of how he might be punished. Zedr said, "They won't hurt him, he's too valuable," just as he himself had said. Azak was glad to believe this. She was, in fact, much relieved to know that he was out of the way.

She and Zedr took Chochi first into their business and then into their household. Chochi was a woman from the dockside quarter, tough and humorous, a hard worker and an undemanding, comfortable lovemaker. They were happy with one another, and prospered.

A year went by, and another year. Azak went to her old quarter to arrange a contract for repair work with two women from the mill where she had first worked. She asked them about Toddra. He was back at the fuckery from time to time, they told her. He had been named the year's Champion Sire of his Castle, and was much in demand, bringing an even higher price, because he impregnated so many women and so many of the conceptions were male. He was not in demand for pleasure, they said, as he had a reputation for roughness and even cruelty. Women asked for him only if they wanted to conceive. Thinking of his gentleness with her, Azak found it hard to imagine him behaving brutally. Harsh punishment at the Castle, she thought, must have altered him. But she could not believe that he had truly changed.

Another year passed. The business was doing very well, and Azak and Chochi both began talking seriously about having children. Zedr was not interested in bearing, though happy to be a mother. Chochi had a favorite man at their local fuckery to whom she went now and then for pleasure; she began going to him at ovulation, for he had a good reputation as a sire.

Azak had never been to a fuckery since she and Zedr married. She honored fidelity highly, and made love with no one but Zedr and Chochi.

When she thought of being impregnated, she found that her old interest in fucking with men had quite died out or even turned to distaste. She did not like the idea of self-impregnation from the sperm bank, but the idea of letting a strange man penetrate her was even more repulsive. Thinking what to do, she thought of Toddra, whom she had truly loved and had pleasure with. He was again a Champion Sire, known throughout the city as a reliable impregnator. There was certainly no other man with whom she could take any pleasure. And he had loved her so much he had put his career and even his life in danger, trying to be with her. That irresponsibility was over and done with. He had never written to her again, and the Castle and the managers of the fuckery would never have let him service women if they thought him mad or untrustworthy. After all this time, she thought, she could go back to him and give him the pleasure he had so desired.

She notified the fuckery of the expected period of her next ovulation, requesting Toddra. He was already engaged for that period, and they offered her another sire; but she preferred to wait till the next month.

Chochi had conceived, and was elated. "Hurry up, hurry up!" she said to Azak. "We want twins!"

Azak found herself looking forward to being with Toddra. Regretting the violence of their last encounter and the pain it must have given him, she wrote the following letter to him:

"My dear, I hope our long separation and the distress of our last meeting will be forgotten in the joy of being together again, and that you still love me as I still love you. I shall be very proud to bear your child, and let us hope it may be a son! I am impatient to see you again, my beautiful dancer. Your Azak."

There had not been time for him to answer this letter when her ovulation period began. She dressed in her best clothes. Zedr still distrusted Toddra and had tried to dissuade her from going to him; she bade her "Good luck!" rather sulkily. Chochi hung a mothercharm round her neck, and she went off.

There was a new manager on duty at the fuckery, a coarse-faced young woman who told her, "Call out if he gives you any trouble. He may be a Champion but he's rough, and we don't let him get away with hurting anybody."

"He won't hurt me," Azak said smiling, and went eagerly into the familiar room where she and Toddra had enjoyed each other so often. He was standing waiting at the window just as he had used to stand. When he turned he looked just as she remembered, long-limbed, his silky hair flowing like water down his back, his wide-set eyes gazing at her.

"Toddra!" she said, coming to him with outstretched hands.

He took her hands and said her name.

"Did you get my letter? Are you happy?"

"Yes," he said, smiling.

"And all that unhappiness, all that foolishness about love, is it over? I am so sorry you were hurt, Toddra, I don't want any more of that. Can we just be ourselves and be happy together as we used to be?"

"Yes, all that is over," he said. "And I am happy to see you." He drew her gently to him. Gently he began to undress her and caress her body, just as he had used to, knowing what gave her pleasure, and she remembering what gave him pleasure. They lay down naked together. She was fondling his erect penis, aroused and yet a little reluctant to be penetrated after so long, when he moved his arm as if uncomfortable. Drawing away from him a little, she saw that he had a knife in his hand, which he must have hidden in the bed. He was holding it concealed behind his back.

Her womb went cold, but she continued to fondle his penis and testicles, not daring to say anything and not able to pull away, for he was holding her close with the other hand.

Suddenly he moved onto her and forced his penis into her vagina with a thrust so painful that for an instant she thought it was the knife. He ejaculated instantly. As his body arched she writhed out from under him, scrambled to the door, and ran from the room crying for help.

He pursued her, striking with the knife, stabbing her in the shoulder blade before the manager and other women and men seized him. The men were very angry and treated him with a violence which the manager's protests did not lessen. Naked, bloody, and half-conscious, he was bound and taken away immediately to the Castle.

Everyone now gathered around Azak, and her wound, which was slight, was cleaned and covered. Shaken and confused, she could ask only, "What will they do to him?"

"What do you think they do to a murdering rapist? Give him a prize?" the manager said. "They'll geld him."

"But it was my fault," Azak said.

The manager stared at her and said, "Are you mad? Go home."

She went back into the room and mechanically put on her clothes. She looked at the bed where they had lain. She stood at the window where Toddra had stood. She remembered how she had seen him dance long ago in the contest where he had first been made champion. She thought, "My life is wrong." But she did not know how to make it right.

Alteration in Seggrian social and cultural institutions did not take the disastrous course Merriment feared. It has been slow and its direction is not clear. In 93 / 1602 Terhada College invited men from two neighboring Castles to apply as students, and three men did so. In the next decades, most colleges opened their doors to men. Once they were graduated, male students had to return to their Castle, unless they left the planet, since native men were not allowed to live anywhere but as students in a college or in a Castle, until the Open Gate Law was passed in 93 / 1662.

Even after passage of that law, the Castles remained closed to women; and the exodus of men from the Castles was much slower than opponents of the measure feared. Social adjustment to the Open Gate Law has been slow. In several regions programs to train men in basic skills such as farming and construction have met with moderate success; the men work in competitive teams, separate from and managed by the women's companies. A good many Seggri have come to Hain to study in recent years—more men than women, despite the great numerical imbalance that still exists.

The following autobiographical sketch by one of these men is of particular interest, since he was involved in the event which directly precipitated the Open Gate Law.

Autobiographical Sketch by Mobile Ardar Dez.

I was born in Ekumenical Cycle 93, Year 1641, in Rakedr on Seggri. Rakedr was a placid, prosperous, conservative town, and I was brought up in the old way, the petted boychild of a big motherhouse. Altogether there were seventeen of us, not counting the kitchen staff—a great-grandmother, two grandmothers, four mothers, nine daughters, and me. We were well off; all the women were or had been managers or skilled workers in the Rakedr Pottery, the principal industry of the town. We kept all the holidays with pomp and energy, decorating the house from roof to foundation with banners for Hillalli, making fantastic costumes for the Harvest Festival, and celebrating somebody's birthday every few weeks with gifts all round. I was petted, as I said, but not, I think, spoiled. My birthday was no grander than my sisters', and I was allowed to run and play with them just as if I were a girl. Yet I was always aware, as were they, that our mothers' eyes rested on me with a different look, brooding, reserved, and sometimes, as I grew older, desolate.

After my Confirmation, my birthmother or her mother took me to Rakedr Castle every spring on Visiting Day. The gates of the Park, which had opened to admit me alone (and terrified) for my Confirmation, remained shut, but rolling stairs were placed against the Park walls. Up these I and a few other little boys from the town climbed, to sit on top of the Park wall in great state, on cushions, under awnings, and watch demonstration dancing, bull-dancing, wrestling, and other sports on the great Gamefield inside the wall. Our mothers waited below, outside, in the bleachers of the public field. Men and youths from the Castle sat with us, explaining the rules of the games and pointing out the fine points of a dancer or wrestler, treating us seriously, making us feel important. I enjoyed that very much, but as soon as I came down off the wall and started home it all fell away like a costume shrugged off, a part played in a play; and I went on with my work and play in the motherhouse with my family, my real life.

When I was ten I went to Boys' Class downtown. The class had been set up forty or fifty years before as a bridge between the motherhouse and the Castle, but the Castle, under increasingly reactionary governance, had recently withdrawn from the project. Lord Fassaw forbade his men to go anywhere outside the walls but directly to the fuckery, in a closed car, returning at first light; and so no men were able to teach the class. The townswomen who tried to tell me what to expect when I went to the Castle did not really know much more than I did. However wellmeaning they were, they mostly frightened and confused me. But fear and confusion were an appropriate preparation.

I cannot describe the ceremony of Severance. I really cannot describe it. Men on Seggri, in those days, had this advantage: they knew what death is. They had all died once before their body's death. They had turned and looked back at their whole life, every place and face they had loved, and turned away from it as the gate closed.

At the time of my Severance, our small Castle was internally divided into "collegials" and "traditionals," a liberal faction left from the regime of Lord Ishog and a younger, highly conservative faction. The split was already disastrously wide when I came to the Castle. Lord Fassaw's rule had grown increasingly harsh and irrational. He governed by corruption, brutality, and cruelty. All of us who lived there were of course infected, and would have been destroyed if there had not been a strong, constant, moral resistance, centered around Ragaz and Kohadrat, who had been proteges of Lord Ishog. The two men were open partners; their followers were all the homosexuals in the Castle, and a good number of other men and older boys.

My first days and months in the Scrubs' dormitory were a bewildering alternation: terror, hatred, shame, as the boys who had been there a few months or years longer than I were incited to humiliate and abuse the newcomer, in order to make a man of him—and comfort, gratitude, love, as boys who had come under the influence of the collegials offered me secret friendship and protection. They helped me in the games and competitions and took me into their beds at night, not for sex but to keep me from the sexual bullies. Lord Fassaw detested adult homosexuality and would have reinstituted the death penalty if the Town Council had allowed it. Though he did not dare punish Ragaz and Kohadrat, he punished consenting love between older boys with bizarre and appalling physical mutilations—ears cut into fringes, fingers branded with redhot iron rings. Yet he encouraged the older boys to rape the eleven- and twelve-year-olds, as a manly practice. None of us escaped. We particularly dreaded four youths, seventeen or eighteen years old when I came there, who called themselves the Lordsmen. Every few nights they raided the Scrubs' dormitory for a victim, whom they raped as a group. The collegials protected us as best they could by ordering us to their beds, where we wept and protested loudly, while they pretended to abuse us, laughing and jeering. Later, in the dark and silence, they comforted us with candy, and sometimes, as we grew older, with a desired love, gentle and exquisite in its secrecy.

There was no privacy at all in the Castle. I have said that to women who asked me to describe life there, and they thought they understood me. "Well, everybody shares everything in a motherhouse," they would say, "everybody's in and out of the rooms all the time. You're never really alone unless you have a singlewoman's flat." I could not tell them how different the loose, warm commonalty of the motherhouse was from the rigid, deliberate publicity of the forty-bed, brightly-lighted Castle dormitories. Nothing in Rakedr was private: only secret, only silent. We ate our tears.

I grew up; I take some pride in that, along with my profound gratitude to the boys and men who made it possible. I did not kill myself, as several boys did during those years, nor did I kill my mind and soul, as some did so their body could survive. Thanks to the maternal care of the collegials—the resistance, as we came to call ourselves—I grew up.

Why do I say maternal, not paternal? Because there were no fathers in my world. There were only sires. I knew no such word as father or paternal. I thought of Ragaz and Kohadrat as my mothers. I still do.

Fassaw grew quite mad as the years went on, and his hold over the Castle tightened to a deathgrip. The Lordsmen now ruled us all. They were lucky in that we still had a strong Maingame team, the pride of Fassaw's heart, which kept us in the First League, as well as two Champion Sires in steady demand at the town fuckeries. Any protest the resistance tried to bring to the Town Council could be dismissed as typical male whining, or laid to the demoralising influence of the Aliens. From the outside Rakedr Castle seemed all right. Look at our great team! Look at our champion studs! The women looked no further.

How could they abandon us?—the cry every Seggrian boy must make in his heart. How could she leave me here? Doesn't she know what it's like? Why doesn't she know? Doesn't she want to know?

"Of course not," Ragaz said to me when I came to him in a passion of righteous indignation, the Town Council having denied our petition to be heard. "Of course they don't want to know how we live. Why do they never come into the Castles? Oh, we keep them out, yes; but do you think we could keep them out if they wanted to enter? My dear, we collude with them and they with us in maintaining the great foundation of ignorance and lies on which our civilisation rests."

"Our own mothers abandon us," I said.

"Abandon us? Who feeds us, clothes us, houses us, pays us? We're utterly dependent on them. If ever we made ourselves independent, perhaps we could rebuild society on a foundation of truth."

Independence was as far as his vision could reach. Yet I think his mind groped further, towards what he could not see, the body's obscure, inalterable dream of mutuality.

Our effort to make our case heard at the Council had no effect except within the Castle. Lord Fassaw saw his power threatened. Within a few days Ragaz was seized by the Lordsmen and their bully boys, accused of repeated homosexual acts and treasonable plots, arraigned, and sentenced by the Lord of the Castle. Everyone was summoned to the Gamefield to witness the punishment. A man of fifty with a heart ailment—he had been a Maingame racer in his twenties and had overtrained—Ragaz was tied naked across a a bench and beaten with 'Lord Long,' a heavy leather tube filled with lead weights. The Lordsman Berhed, who wielded it, struck repeatedly at the head, the kidneys, and the genitals. Ragaz died an hour or two later in the infirmary.

The Rakedr Mutiny took shape that night. Kohadrat, older than Ragaz and devastated by his loss, could not restrain or guide us. His vision had been of a true resistance, longlasting and nonviolent, through which the Lordsmen would in time destroy themselves. We had been following that vision. Now we let it go. We dropped the truth and grabbed weapons. "How you play is what you win," Kohadrat said, but we had heard all those old saws. We would not play the patience game any more. We would win, now, once for all.

And we did. We won. We had our victory. Lord Fassaw, the Lordsmen and their bullies had been slaughtered by the time the police got to the Gate.

I remember how those tough women strode in amongst us, staring at the rooms of the Castle which they had never seen, staring at the mutilated bodies, eviscerated, castrated, headless—at Lordsman Berhed, who had been nailed to the floor with 'Lord Long' stuffed down his throat—at us, the rebels, the victors, with our bloody hands and defiant faces—at Kohadrat, whom we thrust forward as our leader, our spokesman.

He stood silent. He ate his tears.

The women drew closer to one another, clutching their guns, staring around. They were appalled, they thought us all insane. Their utter incomprehension drove one of us at last to speak—a young man, Tarsk, who wore the iron ring that had been forced onto his finger when it was redhot. "They killed Ragaz," he said. "They were all mad. Look." He held out his crippled hand.

The chief of the troop, after a pause, said, "No one will leave here till this is looked into," and marched her women out of the Castle, out of the Park, locking the gate behind them, leaving us with our victory.

The hearings and judgments on the Rakedr Mutiny were all broadcast, of course, and the event has been studied and discussed ever since. My own part in it was the murder of the Lordsman Tatiddi. Three of us set on him and beat him to death with exercise-clubs in the gymnasium where we had cornered him.

How we played was what we won.

We were not punished. Men were sent from several Castles to form a government over Rakedr Castle. They learned enough of Fassaw's behavior to see the cause of our rebellion, but the contempt of even the most liberal of them for us was absolute. They treated us not as men, but as irrational, irresponsible creatures, untamable cattle. If we spoke they did not answer.

I do not know how long we could have endured that cold regime of shame. It was only two months after the Mutiny that the World Council enacted the Open Gate Law. We told one another that that was our victory, we had made that happen. None of us believed it. We told one another we were free. For the first time in history, any man who wanted to leave his Castle could walk out the gate. We were free!

What happened to the free man outside the gate? Nobody had given it much thought.

I was one who walked out the gate, on the morning of the day the Law came into force. Eleven of us walked into town together.

Several of us, men not from Rakedr, went to one or another of the fuckeries, hoping to be allowed to stay there; they had nowhere else to go. Hotels and inns of course would not accept men. Those of us who had been children in the town went to our motherhouses.

What is it like to return from the dead? Not easy. Not for the one who returns, nor for his people. The place he occupied in their world has closed up, ceased to be, filled with accumulated change, habit, the doings and needs of others. He has been replaced. To return from the dead is to be a ghost: a person for whom there is no room.

Neither I nor my family understood that, at first. I came back to them at twenty-one as trustingly as if I were the eleven-year-old who had left them, and they opened their arms to their child. But he did not exist. Who was I?

For a long time, months, we refugees from the Castle hid in our motherhouses. The men from other towns all made their way home, usually by begging a ride with teams on tour. There were seven or eight of us in Rakedr, but we scarcely ever saw one another. Men had no place on the street; for hundreds of years a man seen alone on the street had been arrested immediately. If we went out, women ran from us, or reported us, or surrounded and threatened us—"Get back into your Castle where you belong! Get back to the fuckery where you belong! Get out of our city!" They called us drones, and in fact we had no work, no function at all in the community. The fuckeries would not accept us for service, because we had no guarantee of health and good behavior from a Castle.

This was our freedom: we were all ghosts, useless, frightened, frightening intruders, shadows in the corners of life. We watched life going on around us—work, love, childbearing, childrearing, getting and spending, making and shaping, governing and adventuring—the women's world, the bright, full, real world—and there was no room in it for us. All we had ever learned to do was play games and destroy one another.

My mothers and sisters racked their brains, I know, to find some place and use for me in their lively, industrious household. Two old live-in cooks had run our kitchen since long before I was born, so cooking, the one practical art I had been taught in the Castle, was superfluous. They found household tasks for me, but they were all makework, and they and I knew it. I was perfectly willing to look after the babies, but one of the grandmothers was very jealous of that privilege, and also some of my sisters wives were uneasy about a man touching their baby. My sister Pado broached the possibility of an apprenticeship in the clay-works, and I leaped at the chance; but the managers of the Pottery, after long discussion, were unable to agree to accept men as employees. Their hormones would make male workers unreliable, and female workers would be uncomfortable, and so on.

The holonews was full of such proposals and discussions, of course, and orations about the unforeseen consequences of the Open Gate Law, the proper place of men, male capacities and limitations, gender as destiny. Feeling against the Open Gate policy ran very strong, and it seemed that every time I watched the holo there was a woman talking grimly about the inherent violence and irresponsibility of the male, his biological unfitness to participate in social and political decision-making. Often it was a man saying the same things. Opposition to the new law had the fervent support of all the conservatives in the Castles, who pleaded eloquently for the gates to be closed and men to return to their proper station, pursuing the true, masculine glory of the games and the fuckeries.

Glory did not tempt me, after the years at Rakedr Castle; the word itself had come to mean degradation to me. I ranted against the games and competitions, puzzling most of my family, who loved to watch the Main-games and wrestling, and complained only that the level of excellence of most of the teams had declined since the gates were opened. And I ranted against the fuckeries, where, I said, men were used as cattle, stud bulls, not as human beings. I would never go there again.

"But my dear boy," my mother said at last, alone with me one evening, "will you live the rest of your life celibate?"

"I hope not," I said.

"Then . . . ?"

"I want to get married."

Her eyes widened. She brooded a bit, and finally ventured, "To a man."

"No. To a woman. I want a normal, ordinary marriage. I want to have a wife and be a wife."

Shocking as the idea was, she tried to absorb it. She pondered, frowning.

"All it means," I said, for I had had a long time with nothing to do but ponder, "is that we'd live together just like any married pair. We'd set up our own daughterhouse, and be faithful to each other, and if she had a child I'd be its lovemother along with her. There isn't any reason why it wouldn't work!"

"Well, I don't know—I don't know of any," said my mother, gentle and judicious, and never happy at saying no to me. "But you do have to find the woman, you know."

"I know," I said, glumly.

"It's such a problem for you to meet people," she said. "Perhaps if you went to the fuckery . . . ? I don't see why your own motherhouse couldn't guarantee you just as well as a Castle. We could try—?"

But I passionately refused. Not being one of Fassaw's sycophants, I had seldom been allowed to go the fuckery; and my few experiences there had been unfortunate. Young, inexperienced, and without recommendation, I had been selected by older women who wanted a plaything. Their practiced skill at arousing me had left me humiliated and enraged. They patted and tipped me as they left. That elaborate, mechanical excitation and their condescending coldness was vile to me, after the tenderness of my lover-protectors in the Castle. Yet women attracted me physically as men never had; the beautiful bodies of my sisters and their wives, all around me constantly now, clothed and naked, innocent and sensual, the wonderful heaviness and strength and softness of women's bodies, kept me continually aroused. Every night I masturbated, fantasizing my sisters in my arms. It was unendurable. Again I was a ghost, a raging, yearning impotence in the midst of untouchable reality.

I began to think I would have to go back to the Castle. I sank into a deep depression, an inertia, a chill darkness of the mind.

My family, anxious, affectionate, busy, had no idea what to do for me or with me. I think most of them thought in their hearts that it would be best if I went back through the gate.

One afternoon my sister Pado, with whom I had been closest as a child, came to my room—they had cleared out a dormer attic for me, so that I had room at least in the literal sense. She found me in my now constant lethargy, lying on the bed doing nothing at all. She breezed in, and with the indifference women often showed to moods and signals, plumped down on the foot of the bed and said, "Hey, what do you know about the man who's here from the Ekumen?"

I shrugged and shut my eyes. I had been having rape fantasies lately. I was afraid of her.

She talked on about the offworlder, who was apparently in Rakedr to study the Mutiny. "He wants to talk to the resistance," she said. "Men like you. The men who opened the gates. He says they won't come forward, as if they were ashamed of being heroes."

"Heroes!" I said. The word in my language is gendered female. It refers to the semi-divine, semi-historic protagonists of the Epics.

"It's what you are," Pado said, intensity breaking through her assumed breeziness. "You took responsibility in a great act. Maybe you did it wrong. Sassume did it wrong in the *Founding of Emmo*, didn't she, she let Faradr get killed. But she was still a hero. She took the responsibility. So did you. You ought to go talk to this Alien. Tell him what happened. Nobody really knows what happened at the Castle. You owe us the story."

That was a powerful phrase, among my people. "The untold story mothers the lie," was the saying. The doer of any notable act was held literally *accountable* for it to the community.

"So why should I tell it to an Alien?" I said, defensive of my inertia.

"Because he'll listen," my sister said drily. "We're all too damned busy."

It was profoundly true. Pado had seen a gate for me and opened it; and I went through it, having just enough strength and sanity left to do so.

Mobile Noem was a man in his forties, born some centuries earlier on Terra, trained on Hain, widely travelled; a small, yellowbrown, quick-eyed person, very easy to talk to. He did not seem at all masculine to me, at first; I kept thinking he was a woman, because he acted like one. He got right to business, with none of the maneuvering to assert his authority or jockeying for position that men of my society felt obligatory in any relationship with another man. I was used to men being wary, indirect, and competitive. Noem, like a woman, was direct and receptive. He was also as subtle and powerful as any man or woman I had known, even Ragaz. His authority was in fact immense; but he never stood on it. He sat down on it, comfortably, and invited you to sit down with him.

I was the first of the Rakedr mutineers to come forward and tell our story to him. He recorded it, with my permission, to use in making his report to the Stabiles on the condition of our society, "the matter of Seggri," as he called it. My first description of the Mutiny took less than an hour. I thought I was done. I didn't know, then, the inexhaustible desire to learn, to understand, to hear *all* the story, that characterises the Mobiles of the Ekumen. Noem asked questions, I answered; he speculated and extrapolated, I corrected; he wanted details, I furnished them—telling the story of the Mutiny, of the years before it, of the men of the Castle, of the women of the Town, of my people, of my life—little by little, bit by bit, all in fragments, a muddle. I talked to Noem daily for a month. I learned that the story has no beginning, and no story has an end. That the story is all muddle, all middle. That the story is never true, but that the lie is indeed a child of silence.

By the end of the month I had come to love and trust Noem, and of course to depend on him. Talking to him had become my reason for being. I tried to face the fact that he would not stay in Rakedr much longer. I must learn to do without him. Do what? There were things for men to do, ways for men to live, he proved it by his mere existence; but could I find them?

He was keenly aware of my situation, and would not let me withdraw, as I began to do, into the lethargy of fear again; he would not let me be silent. He asked me impossible questions. "What would you be if you could be anything?" he asked me, a question children ask each other.

I answered at once, passionately—"A wife!"

I know now what the flicker that crossed his face was. His quick, kind eyes watched me, looked away, looked back.

"I want my own family," I said. "Not to live in my mothers' house, where I'm always a child. Work. A wife, wives—children—to be a mother. I want life, not games!"

"You can't bear a child," he said gently.

"No, but I can mother one!"

"We gender the word," he said. "I like it better your way. . . . But tell me, Ardar, what are the chances of your marrying—meeting a woman willing to marry a man? It hasn't happened, here, has it?"

I had to say no, not to my knowledge.

"It will happen, certainly, I think," he said (his certainties were always uncertain). "But the personal cost, at first, is likely to be high. Relationships formed against the negative pressure of a society are under terrible strain; they tend to become defensive, over-intense, unpeaceful. They have no room to grow."

"Room!" I said. And I tried to tell him my feeling of having no room in my world, no air to breathe.

He looked at me, scratching his nose; he laughed. "There's plenty of room in the galaxy, you know," he said.

"Do you mean . . . I could . . . That the Ekumen . . ." I didn't even know what the question I wanted to ask was. Noem did. He began to answer it thoughtfully and in detail. My education so far had been so limited, even as regards the culture of my own people, that I would have to attend a college for at least two or three years, in order to be ready to apply to an offworld institution such as the Ekumenical Schools on Hain. Of course, he went on, where I went and what kind of training I chose would depend on my interests, which I would go to a college to discover, since neither my schooling as a child nor my training at the Castle had really given me any idea of what there was to be interested in. The choices offered me had been unbelievably limited, addressing neither the needs of a normally intelligent person nor the needs of my society. And so the Open Gate Law instead of giving me freedom had left me "with no air to breathe but airless Space," said Noem, quoting some poet from some planet somewhere. My head was spinning, full of stars. "Hagka College is quite near Rakedr," Noem said, "did you never think of applying? If only to escape from your terrible Castle?"

I shook my head. "Lord Fassaw always destroyed the application forms when they were sent to his office. If any of us had tried to apply . . ."

"You would have been punished. Tortured, I suppose. Yes. Well, from the little I know of your colleges, I think your life there would be better than it is here, but not altogether pleasant. You will have work to do, a place to be; but you will be made to feel marginal, inferior. Even highly educated, enlightened women have difficulty accepting men as their intellectual equals. Believe me, I have experienced it myself! And because you were trained at the Castle to compete, to want to excel, you may find it hard to be among people who either believe you incapable of excellence, or to whom the concept of competition, of winning and defeating, is valueless. But just there, there is where you will find air to breathe."

Noem recommended me to women he knew on the faculty of Hagka College, and I was enrolled on probation. My family were delighted to pay my tuition. I was the first of us to go to college, and they were genuinely proud of me.

As Noem had predicted, it was not always easy, but there were enough other men there that I found friends and was not caught in the paralysing isolation of the motherhouse. And as I took courage, I made friends among the women students, finding many of them unprejudiced and companionable. In my third year, one of them and I managed, tentatively and warily, to fall in love. It did not work very well or last very long, yet it was a great liberation for both of us, our liberation from the belief that the only communication or commonalty possible between us was sexual, that an adult man and woman had nothing to join them but their genitals. Emadr loathed the professionalism of the fuckery as I did, and our lovemaking was always shy and brief. Its true significance was not as a consummation of desire, but as proof that we could trust each other. Where our real passion broke loose was when we lay together talking, telling each other what our lives had been, how we felt about men and women and each other and ourselves, what our nightmares were, what our dreams were. We talked endlessly, in a communion that I will cherish and honor all my life, two young souls finding their wings, flying together, not for long, but high. The first flight is the highest.

Emadr has been dead two hundred years; she stayed on Seggri, married into a motherhouse, bore two children, taught at Hagka, and died in her seventies. I went to Hain, to the Ekumenical Schools, and later to Werel and Yeowe as part of the Mobile's staff; my record is herewith enclosed. I have written this sketch of my life as part of my application to return to Seggri as a Mobile of the Ekumen. I want very much to live among my people, to learn who they are, now that I know with at least an uncertain certainty who I am.

YLEM

Eliot Fintushel

Here's a funny, pyrotechnic, and fast-paced tale, packed with bizarre new ideas and even stranger characters, that takes us back through time to the Beginning of Everything—which turns out to be a very peculiar place indeed . . .

New writer Eliot Fintushel made his first sale just last year, to *Tomorrow* magazine. Since then, he has appeared in *Tomorrow* again, made a number of sales to *Asimov's Science Fiction*, and is beginning to attract attention from cognoscenti as a writer who is definitely worth keeping an eye on in years to come. Fintushel, a baker's son from Rochester, New York, has won the National Endowment for the Arts' Solo Performer Award twice, and now lives in Glen Ellen, California, with his wife and young daughter.

The Manhattan Muthuhs were a Puerto Rican street gang that fled New York City to become hippies in Santa Fe. They used to sit outside El Centro, the crash pad run by an eccentric Catholic priest, and watch the sun set over the Sangre de Cristo Mountains. As the sky colored and darkened, they would drum wildly on anything a man or woman could hit. Then they would spread their army rolls and crash.

One night, hitching through, I shared a ratty sofa with one of the gang leader's girlfriends, while a dozen Muthuhs snored on the floor. If we rolled off the sofa, we'd fall on two or three of them. I heaved and pressed and jammed and ground, unable to make an end of it with Sunshine's girl, while she sleepily let me poke. Nobody seemed to mind. Over and over and over, the whole time we were at it, a scratched record (I presumed) was playing this phrase:

> *"Is that boy still climbing up the mountain?*
> *Has he faltered, or has he fallen down SCREEE!*
> *Is that boy . . ."*

And we humped and we humped. I still have a urinary tract infection that reappears from time to time, a penicillin-resistant strain of clap, which I got, indirectly, from the head of the Manhattan Muthuhs!

That night, I had my first revelatory headache. I was wedged in a crevice narrower than my skull. Iron was melting and streaming red hot into my eyes, my ears, my mouth and nose. An avalanche thundered around me, and the sky swarmed with snakes, noxious flowers, and searing lights.

My second headache came in 1966, as I walked along the Susquehanna, thinking how nice it would be at the bottom, dead. When the big blackout hit New York, I thought it was me. Then came the news of a mechanical failure at the generating plant in Niagara Falls.

I had a headache like a mine cave-in. Phantasms and fireballs burned the sky all over Broome County. Again I was deafened as if by an avalanche, and I couldn't shake the smell of rock dust—lime and sulfur.

Now, twenty-seven years later, I know—

1. The blackout: it wasn't caused by a power plant breakdown.
2. The song: it wasn't from a skipping record.
3. My "symptoms": they were a perception of reality.

Now I know, because I just had the headache again, like an earthquake demolishing a rock wall, and the wall is down, and I see the truth.

The occasion for my third headache was a visit from an old college friend with whom I once shared an A-frame in the hills above the Susquehanna. Siggy was passing through Sonoma, where I now live, on business. In college, he and I used to talk the way some people dance, cutting incredible figures in the mind, staying up late and planning great works, right up to the day the ambulance came and took him away, babbling and shrieking, to the state hospital; that was a few days before the big blackout. They eventually gave him shock treatment, and his parents, immigrants, concentration camp survivors, took him home to Long Island to recover, while *they* got worse.

It had been a sort of contest between us, which of us would crumble first, he in his mania, or I in my depression. Siggy won.

He seemed okay now, by and large, if somewhat dried out. He had a beer belly and a family and a gold Bulova that he frequently consulted. The wallet photos of his wife and kids could have been cut from an ad for home insurance. He chain-smoked, however, and ate everything in my refrigerator without tasting a morsel. Every pocket in his brown sports jacket had a pack of Luckies in it, except for one with a bag of Bull Durham and papers—for emergencies.

At about two in the morning, he lit a cigarette scavenged from one of his ashtrays and said, "So tell me, Eliot, how long have you been with us?"

I laughed, and he laughed back.

"No, really," he said. "How long?" Pinching the butt between his knuckles, he stretched and yawned, allowing himself to make a grotesque, sleepy face while he waited for me to answer.

"What do you mean?" I said. My head was starting to throb. I looked out the window, alarmed to hear someone start to mow their lawn at two in the morning; then I realized it wasn't a lawn mower.

"You've never given me any reason to doubt your loyalty in all these years," Siggy said. I'd seen reversible jackets before, but this was the first time I'd seen one reverse itself. Now it was red and gold. But the light was changing—maybe that was it. "And your supervisors tell me they can always depend on you, Elly, even when the other guys are frigging the dog."

"Supervisors?" I said. "What *is* this? A scene from some movie? I don't know what I'm supposed to say."

"Just say thank you, my boy. I'm sending you on a very important mission." How had he turned the cigarette into a fresh cigar? I was sure it was one of Siggy's old mind games, and I worried that he was taking it too far, that he would go off the deep end, as he had back in '66. "You're gonna be one big man when you get back, Elly."

I said, "I like my job the way it is." Where did that come from? I just found myself saying it. "I like everything, really. I *am* grateful, Mr. Duba, but couldn't you get someone else?" My head hurt so bad I had to squint to keep the light from stabbing me.

"Duba?" Siggy said. "Who's Duba?" The cigar was back to a cigarette butt. His jacket had again reversed itself. "Have you got anything else to eat in this place?"

Two A.M., and it was already light outside. I looked out the window at the brilliant, blue sky, filled with dirigibles; I could make out the figure of a bull painted on the hull of each one. When I looked back, Duba was peering at me through a thick cloud of cigar smoke. "Come on," he said, "don't put me on. What are you doing, trying to wheedle more dough out of me? I'll give you dough, believe me. You must have a little ambition, a guy like you. You weren't cut out to be a *now lubber*."

"I don't got any ambitions," I said.

"What about Topsy? You could take her along, you know. In fact, I *want* you to take her along. She knows the route, Elly."

There were the flowers in the air, the snakes and the exploding lights, the thunder, and the pain so sharp I could see it, like fissures wedged open in the bones of my face. "Topsy?" I said. "Please don't talk about Topsy."

"Your little secret, huh? Look. Let's level. She's not gonna stay with you, Elly. They never do." Topsy was a chrono-anomaly. She had just shown up in my apt one day when I got home from work. That was about the same time that the helium ratios changed and the dirigibles started showing up—retroactively.

Look, I know it—if not for Topsy, I never would have had a woman at all. I'm a good chess player though. Some people think I'm a *great* chess player, only I don't like to beat everybody all the time, because of how it makes them feel bad.

"On the other hand, Elly," Mr. Duba told me, "if you take her along on this mission, see, she'll love it. She'll love *you*, boy, because you know where you're going? You know where I'm sending you?"

"No, Mr. Duba. Where?" Gee, my head hurt something awful. I was ready to get out of there and go back to the basement offices and sort the rest of the guys' tools. What do I know about missions and stuff? That was hot air, if you ask me, except if I could get to keep Topsy that way.

"*Ylem*, Elly. Right back to the *ylem!* And that's where Topsy comes from, you know. That's her *home*, boy. If you take her there, believe you me, she'll love you to pieces!"

"I know it," I said. "You're right. I'm gonna *do* it." Something happened to me then that I don't like to talk about, but my eyes kind of went out of focus, and I thought for a second that Mr. Duba was somebody else. I thought he was an old pal of mine from college. But I never went to college. Then he was Mr. Duba again, and I felt better.

Topsy was lying in the corner, listening between the stations, like she always done, to radio static. She had a name for it: "relic background radiation." But I could beat her at chess. I could hardly see her, black as the shadow the way she is, even her gums and teeth and the "whites" of her eyes. I told her, wear white at night, but she didn't care about nothing but static. She said, "It's telegrams from home."

How come she remembers stuff that never happened? How come she knows the colors and sizes of stuff that don't exist and the dates of birthdays for people that never was born? It's all on account of how she got here straight out of nowhere from Mr. Bull screwing in the deep past.

When I told her about our mission, she turned off the radio for the first time since a month, day and night, day and night, and she put her arms around me and pulled me close till I went inside of her. Then we did it, like she showed me.

After, she says to me: "That bastard Duba is up to some bad shit, Elly, but maybe it'll get me home." She knows me pretty good. She can see what I'm thinking. She gives me a peck and says, "Elly, you dear, it'll be a home for you too. Nobody'll take advantage of you there, we'll be together forever, and when you win at chess, you won't have to be afraid of making people angry." So I smile big.

My face above it, the breeze from the flushing toilet revived me a little. Siggy laid both hands on my shoulders. "Can I get you anything?" he said. Just the sound of his voice was excruciating, but I had stopped heaving.

"No," I said. "I'm okay. I'm okay." I pushed my head and shoulders, a leaden mantle, up from the toilet seat. "Siggy, what's *ylem?*"

He laughed, "It's Greek to me, partner." I started to close my eyes and let my head slide back down, when he said, "Hey, I was just kidding. It really *is* Greek . . . no, Latin! Don't you remember? We used to toss that word around back in the A-frame days. It's supposed to be before the Big Bang, when everything was in one place the size of a pinhead."

"Does it send out radio signals?"

"Sure, Doubleyew Big Bang FM. Actually, it *does*, in a way. Some guys working for Ma Bell found it in the sixties. Very faint. Very cool. A few degrees above absolute zero. Static. The afterglow of the Big Bang. Very funky. You want some water?"

"Relic background radiation?"

"That's it. So what are you asking *me* for?"

And then we were sitting, Topsy and I, in harsh sunlight, on a barren salt flat a few hundred yards from the base of a rocky cliff, and I really was okay. The only thing was, I was having some trouble making one thought follow the last pretty good, and Topsy was in the middle of jabbering at me like no tomorrow, which I don't like, and she knows it too, so why *do* it is what I want to know, huh? Also, some Zeppelins were grouping up on the other side of us from the cliff, and it made me nervous, and I think they were making Topsy talk fast like that too.

She was showing me some stuff from her pockets, which she had two of, one on either hip, with stuff in them, but *I* didn't get to have but one. She was saying, "This is a Doppler gauge. This dial sets the scale factor. Yours is exactly the same as mine, and we have to make sure they're always set the same, Elly, or things will get very confusing very fast. Are you listening to me?"

"Sure I am, Topsy," I say, "but them dirigibles aren't Mr. Duba's, and I think we should get out of here fast."

"I'm keeping track of them, Elly," she said. "You just concentrate on what I'm saying. Remember the hypodyne?"

"My head feels like it's cracking open," I said to Siggy. "I know this sounds stupid, but I have to ask you: Are my eyes open?"

"No, they're not," he said.

"Well, I can see," I said.

"Tell me what you see, Eliot."

"I'm not here. I mean, I'm not in California. I'm not in this house. I'm not even in this time, I think. I'm in a dark tube. It's like a CAT scan, but the rays are doing something to me. I think they're killing me, Siggy."

"You're fine, Elly. They're not killing you."

Then Topsy's voice: "Listen to Mr. Duba, Elly. It's the hypodyne. I'm next, Elly. I'm right after you. The hypodyne will make you into thoughts, Elly— that's one way to say it. Don't be scared. I'll be with you soon."

"That's right, my boy," Mr. Duba said. "Then you and Topsy here will be hypostatized into the timeship."

"I'm scared." That's what I wanted to say, but nothing come out. I couldn't even find my mouth. I was all hypodyned, I guess. Then when Mr. Duba talked some more, I couldn't even tell if maybe it was me thinking it instead. . . .

"Don't you worry, son. I know exactly how you feel. Like air in a popped balloon, right? It'll only be a minute. Topsy's getting hers right now. She'll be with you before you can say Duba Enterprises, Eenk! Then we'll stat you into the timeship. I know you're going to do us real proud, kiddo. Just look out for Zeppelins, heh, heh!

"No, really, Elly, I know you're going to really give those helium boys something to think about. Do what Topsy tells you, now! I know you will! *This is the Second Bull!*"

("Second Bull?" Siggy asked me. "He said, 'This is the Second Bull?' " Siggy dug his fingers into my shoulders, anchoring me on Sonoma Mountain.

"Yeah," I said, "like the Zen Bulls, I guess:

> *The Bull is sought. The Bull is tracked.*
> *The Bull is glimpsed. The Bull is caught.*
> *The Bull is tamed. The bull is ridden . . .*

. . . and so on. We were tracking Bull. It's a joke.")

Then I felt like I was dishwater going around and around down the drain, like, and when I was all dripped down into the pipes, then I was out cold, and when I woke up, me and Topsy was standing in the shadow of some dirigibles, and she was showing me stuff, and she was saying: "Remember the hypodyne?" and I remembered it.

She said, "We're in the timeship now, Elly. This landscape is a hypostat of the whole history of the universe. See how it looks flat for a ways and then, about two hundred yards from here, it starts sloping up, and then it's a quarter mile or so straight up? Now watch what I do with my Doppler gauge, and you do exactly the same thing, you hear?"

"You bet, Topsy girl," I said. "Easy as pie."

In my pocket I had one of the same things of what Topsy had, which they put there, and I took it out, and I looked at it, and I looked at what she did, and I did it. I punched the OUTPUT button, the blue one. Then I punched a red one and some other ones. Then I set the big thing to REDSHIFT: LOCAL SCALE FACTOR TIMES TWO, and then I fell down. Topsy helped me get up.

"You see, Elly?" she said. "We just changed the lay of the land." The ground we were standing on looked like a mountain-side now. It was slanted real steep. Also, the dirigibles were way back behind us, almost out of sight.

"This is incredible," I said to Siggy. I couldn't see him—I had ice packs over my head and eyes, and even without them, I think I could only have seen the inside of the timeship. "They've got a machine that makes time look like a rock cliff in Utah. And then there's another one that changes the scaling of the slope according to the redshift as you go back in time. It's like different powers on a microscope, only . . . "

"Take it easy," Siggy said. "Don't talk, Eliot."

" . . . Only, 'YOU ARE THERE!' " I said.

"No," he said, "*you* are there, Eliot. We're trying to get you back."

"What?" I said.

"We're trying to get you back," is what Mr. Duba said. I mean, I thought it was Mr. Duba, only Topsy says shush, that it isn't Mr. Duba, because the dirigible people are trying to fool us so they can shoot us or stop us. They are Mr. Duba's competitors, that bum Bull, see, who made all the extra helium so they could corner some markets, when Mr. Duba's stock went sliding, and they did it by going back in *their* timeship to tinker near the *ylem* like what we're gonna do, only ours is better."

"Listen, Elly," Topsy said, "we've got to hurry. Those helium boys are on our tails. Do what I do. Switch back to the old Doppler scaling. And make sure you don't touch anything else unless I tell you. Then hold my hand and run like hell."

We started in to do our buttons, but then Topsy said, "Wait! I have to show you this, Elly." She showed me a round black ball, so black it almost looked like a hole in the palm of her hand. "If anything happens to me, Elly, and I don't make it up the cliff, you take this off me, understand? You take it all the way up to where the redshift is ten billion, almost at the summit. That's where the helium numbers got switched. Wedge it into a crack or lay it on a flake, then come back down. There's no need for you to enter the *ylem* except for me."

I said, "You're not gonna die, Topsy."

Then we did some more buttons, both of us the same. Everything flattened out, and I fell on my keester again, but I got up and reared up to run like hell. Topsy didn't even have to tell me. What am I, *stupid?* Those big helium ships were all over the sky, and they were shooting hard things at us, like rivets or sixteen-penny nails. They made little cracks and explosions of salt all over the place like you wouldn't want to step in or get in the way of, believe me. A guy could die like that.

"Take a memo," Siggy said. The cigar smoke was making me dizzy again, and I thought I might have to run back to the bathroom to vomit.

"Don't," I said. "Please. Shh!" My eyes were covered with ice packed in washcloths, but I had the idea that they were a kind of visor that would give me a real image of the state of the universe to which some land feature corresponded in the hypostat Topsy and I were traversing via the timeship.

"Push that visor up and run, Elly," Topsy was saying.

"I can't," I said. "My head hurts. I'm sick to my stomach."

"Push it up," she said. She was tugging at my hand. I had taken one stride before the visor had slid down and I had gotten mixed up on account of how I saw big lizards everywhere and the ground cracking and making oceans and stuff. "We've gone back a hundred and fifty million years, Elly. Just stay in the hypostat. Never mind the damned visor!"

"I don't give a damn how you *feel*," Siggy told me. "I want you to take a goddamn memo. Do you get it? Okay?"

"Sure, sure," I said. Anything to calm that voice of his. It was pushing me over the edge; I didn't want to throw up. "Sure, Mr. Duba."

"Okay. No copies, understand? This goes to Bull and nobody else. Burn your notes. The usual precautions. . . ."

I thought, do "the usual precautions" include having me killed once the deal with Bull is set? I shifted the washcloths to get more ice directly over my temples.

"Okay. Dearest P *period comma* Nice trick you pulled *exclamation point* I wake up and guess what *question mark* The helium numbers are changed going back to God's early childhood and guess who was there to cash in from time ex minus one *couple of exclamation points* What a burner on me *comma* huh *question mark* I gotta hand it to you *period* Overnight Duba is down a couple of hundred and the sky is clogged with dirigibles *period Underline* Your dirigibles *period* So you got back to the Big Bang *exclamation point*—No, wait, make it a comma; I don't want it to look like I'm too impressed—and you worked over the nucleosynthesis *comma* well I got news for you *comma* hot shot *period* I'm going back there too *comma* I'm gonna change everything back and good *comma* and I don't care if the chrono-anomalies make your head wind up sprouting from your crotch *period* My boys have got it figured out failsafe and you are not even gonna be history *comma* Bull *comma* my man *period* So how about let's make a deal before my people hit the ylem *comma* what do you say *question mark* Otherwise *comma* that's okay by me *comma* only you better get used to having piss up your nose *period* Affectionately et cetera. And get that off to Mr. Bull the day before yesterday—no, make it last Thursday. Use the executive time shuttle if you have to.''

I said, "Yes, Mr. Duba," and I stumbled to the toilet to throw up.

I couldn't help it because the visor kept flipping down by accident, and then I would see some stuff and I would almost fall except I made myself stay up, and I was getting plenty of bloody scratches from them spikes and rivets, even a bad one on the back of my neck where something stuck in there. Once, my foot slid a little on a pebble, and I looked down and so the lousy visor clacked over my eyes again, and when I watched that pebble roll backward under my feet, well, it wasn't a pebble, brother, it was a whole sea full of funny fish boiling and steaming and going back and forth and forth from eggs to skeletons and winding up back there with the big lizards near to where we come from. Then I pushed the visor back up and run. Don't worry, Topsy. Here I come, and I'm fast!

Another time I got scared because the visor fell down and I got the feeling that Topsy was only somebody I read about in a book, because she was a jillion years ago, which she really *was* in a way, because she was so far ahead of me right then, because I stopped for a second to fix that visor.

Then, in maybe fifty yards, I stopped worrying about the stuff the dirigibles was throwing at us—big rocks was falling straight out of the sky and making holes, and Topsy said, "We've gone nearly four and a half billion years." That's what Topsy said. She was maybe fifty million years in front of me, which means behind me really, because of how the farther we went, the earlier it was; it looked like about two feet.

"We've lost time," Topsy said. "Bull can't follow us here except on foot. From here on, every step we take is a quarter of a billion years, Elly. Pretty soon there won't be any planets any more; they won't have formed yet. Not even any solid rock—I mean, in the real world. Here in the hypostat, we can still move all right. . . . ''

" . . . but only on our own power," I said. Siggy was falling asleep under the reading lamp.

"What are you talking about?" he said.

"The hypostat, Siggy," I told him. "Once you get back to this point, where the redshift is about to spring up by powers of powers, you can't use any kind of vessel. You can hardly wear any clothes. The Doppler meter and the visor are a compromise. You see, you have to *mix* yourself with it, Siggy. You have to struggle in the landscape of the hypostat, become one with it. That's the only way to stay inside the timeship. Otherwise you blow out the hull to God knows where, synchronous to nothing in this world and nothing in the next."

"Oh, I get it," Siggy sighed. He smacked his lips and snuggled into the cushions on the sagging easy chair. In two breaths' time, he was asleep.

I'm taking a minute to check my bod, now that I can afford it. I smart all over, but there are bruises and scratches in only a few places. The worst is my left ham, where one of Bull's little projectiles has wedged itself. I can tug at it, but that hurts like hell, and whenever there's bad pain, like it or not, I see where

I am: about four point six billion B.C., with celestial rock heaps piling up around me, free-floating in space, dark snowmen rolling to planet size. I clench my eyes like little black fists, and I pull the spike out. I remember doing this before— I've learned that that's a sure sign that it never happened.

I lift my black arms like wings, to scan along the length of them for other injuries. I survey my legs and my torso. Nothing serious. Elly is dying, but he doesn't know it. The brass-colored dart embedded in the back of his neck is slow poison, Bull's calling card. There's nothing to be done except to hope he can make it to the summit with me before his nerve tissue starts to lose integrity.

Like the terrain of our journey back in time, shaped by the logarithmic rise of the redshift, the rate of recession of galaxies (exploding out of the *ylem*, lo, these billions of years), Elly's illness will be slight at first, then sudden and catastrophic—Witness the sheer cliff some five hundred feet ahead, erupting toward all our origin, Amitabha Buddha, the Densely Packed, *ylem*—my home.

> *Grant, Oh Amitabha, that this pathetic*
> *fool's death will help to bring me back. Grant*
> *that the bastard Duba be foiled in his*
> *machinations, and Bull in his! Let me come home!*

A quake rocked the entire landscape, throwing me into Elly's arms. We struggled to remain erect while up and down went missing, and we found ourselves half-skidding, half-tumbling forward into the collapse of the protosolar nebula. The timeship itself was suffering an attack; our hull was being battered by volleys of HHC.

"HHC?" Siggy asked me. His voice sounded strange, but I couldn't see why; the melting ice packs were pressed around my eyes, and I felt weighed down all over by something irresistibly heavy, like a lead sheet. The place smelled faintly of chlorine. Our voices echoed harshly, as if from foursquare plaster walls.

"HHC," I said. Then, hearing the sound of my own voice, I realized it: *I* was Siggy. "Hypostatized Hubble Constants."

"Mm hmm!"—the new voice.

"The Hubble constant gives you the recession rate of the galaxies, based on their distance," I explained.

"Tell me about it," the dark man said.

"Well, it isn't really a constant . . . ," I said.

" . . . I see. . . . "

" . . . Because it changes as the universe ages. But it's:

$$r = Hd.$$

Do the math . . . "

" . . . Uh huh . . . "

" . . . and you see that H, the Hubble constant, equals r over d. But d is just r times t."

" . . . Distance is rate times time? . . . "

"Yes. So you get H equal to r over r times t."

"The *r*'s would cancel out."

"More or less. So you get:

$$H = l/t$$

You see? That's what they were throwing at us."

"I don't think I follow."

"It's time inverse!" I said. "The Hubble is time inverse! It kills regular time! It neutralizes it, cancels it out! You see what they were trying to do to us?"

"Take it easy. Sit back down, please. Just relax. Breathe. Sit down, please."

"What do you mean, breathe? What do you *think* I'm doing?"

"Nurse . . . !"

I always get up early, even after a very late night; it's just the way I am. When I hear that *Sonoma Index Tribune* whack the front door, my day is beginning, and never mind the clock, the hangover, or the dream sludge sticking my gears.

I was nibbling on a toasted bagel, sipping hot water—"zen tea"—and listening to the rain slashing against the wall. I'd had to settle for margarine, since Siggy had eaten all the cream cheese and the butter. He was just where I had left him, slumped in the easy chair under the reading lamp, which had been left on all night and was still on. Through my ursine yawns and lumberings about the fridge, Siggy snored. But when I unspindled the newspaper, popping off its red rubber band, he woke.

"Eliot!" he said, expanding from the cushions like a crushed sponge in water. "Jeez! I gotta get to work! What time is it? What Bull have you got to?"

"What?"

"I said, my Bulova stopped. What time is it?"

"I don't know," I said.

"You don't know what time it is?"

"Uh uh. I don't want to look yet. I'm not ready to leave infinity."

"You got the paper, though," he said.

"Guilty," I said, scanning the headlines.

I heard Siggy open the window in the bathroom, close it again as rain poured in, flush the toilet, and then urinate. "So what's the news?" he shouted. "Did Bull make that deal with Duba?"

"Yeah," I shouted back. "It looks like they came to some kind of accommodation, the bastards."

"They get you coming and going, don't they? Those dirigibles were just too good a thing. Too cheap. Too accessible."

"Too good for guys like us," I said.

"Now they'll fix prices any way they want to. It's always the little guy who gets the shaft, Eliot."

"Don't I know it!" I said. "Don't I know it! Don't I know it! Don't I know it! Don't I know it!"

The wind was blowing right through the window glass, tearing the paper out of my hand and nailing Siggy to the wall as he emerged from the bathroom, half-zipped. It drove back his hair, throwing his necktie back like a scarf and deforming his face—escape velocity. My head hit the table, and I couldn't lift it against the wind.

The wind said, "I thought you'd see the light, Bull. There's no sense us beating up on each other. This way, everybody wins."

"I almost *had* you, you old coot!" I said. The floor was bucking in waves like a streamer on a fan. I held onto the table for dear life. "One of your guys was all right, I guess. But holy, holy, where'd you pick up the *other* one?"

"In the mail room!" the wind laughed. "You think I wanted to throw away my best people?"

"What about the good one, the black one?" I said. I had to scream just to hear my own voice. The window shattered and glass sprayed across the room. I heard Siggy cry out.

"That woman was *your* gift, big guy," the wind said. "Some joke, huh? When your boys wiggled the equations back near *ylem* to squeeze more helium out of it, we got Topsy."

"A chrono-anomaly! You son of a gun!"

"An orphan of time! Hey, if she lives, I'm gonna help her file a paternity suit against you, Bull! You gotta take *some* responsibility! Heh heh heh! I'll *get* you, big guy, right down to the Zen Bulls tattooed on your fanny! Heh heh!"

That was a good one. I knew I could make some money with this guy. He was on the ball. He even knew about the Bulls. But you had to watch him, of course. I said, "So now that we've shaken hands and smiled upon each other's countenance and squared off our attorneys, now that you've agreed to stay out of the *ylem*, friend Duba, and I've stopped strafing your chrononauts, tell me, what are you going to do with *them?*"

"With Topsy? Elly? The timeship?" the wind said. "Oh, you needn't concern yourself. Measures are being taken."

"They've broken through! It's *leaking*," I said. They were forcing cotton into my mouth and fastening me to the table. I could smell methyl alcohol from the electrodes they attached to tiny, shaved sections of my scalp. I was too groggy to resist. I tried to explain. "It's leaking *time*. Real time is streaming in through leaks in the stern." The causal fissure which formed the spine of our timeship, guaranteeing controlled disjunction between what happened inside and what happened out, had been violated by an HHC.

Elly was lying on his back, kicking gravel.

"Don't!" I shouted. "Every speck of dust you raise is somebody's world out there exploding. Look!" I pushed down his visor; he froze at once.

"It's all mixed up, Topsy," he said. "The lizards and the stars and the lava and the fish and all the moons—Are they moons, Topsy, pocking up with holes?—they're getting me dizzy."

"We've got to make a run for it," I said, "before it gets any worse." Sequences inside the timeship were starting to be blown awry. My mind was squinting to see things in order. In representing them now, I'm just writing them out in the logical, causal order, with question preceding answer, and consequence following act, but the lived reality was quite different. It was only after I had helped Elly to his feet that I made the effort to do so, for example, and the entire sequence was repeated four times at the same o'clock.

Think of a child's puzzle: a drawing divided into vertical bars. The drawing comprises two pictures spliced together in alternating bars. By covering every other bar, you can see one picture or the other. Multiply that a hundredfold and translate it into three dimensions in real time, and you have our fractured timeship world, riddled by eddies of time swirling together with multi-headed HHC's, winking random moments out of existence.

"Come on!" I said. I took Elly's hand. "Let's go!"

I walked along the Susquehanna, thinking how nice it would be at the bottom, dead. When the big blackout hit New York, I thought it was me. Then came the news of a mechanical failure at the generating plant in Niagara Falls.

I had a headache like a mine cave-in. Phantasms and fireballs burned the sky all over Broome County. Again I was deafened as if by an avalanche, and I couldn't shake the smell of rock dust—lime and sulfur.

It was a spray of pulverized limestone and pebbles dislodged from a shelf just above us. Elly and I had gained the base of the cliff, and bits of rock rained down on us. The base curved up slowly for about a hundred fifty feet, from the collapse of our protogalaxy—resulting in the formation of the stars of the Milky Way—back to the final decoupling of matter and energy, less than half a billion years after the Big Bang, at redshift of ten thousand. (The present value was four!)

My brains felt like cold pabulum. I sensed that I was sitting up in a chair, but my mind was telling me that I was horizontal. I could see the dark man talking, but my mind told me that my eyes were closed. I knew that my mom and dad were coming to visit me any time now, and I wanted to get this over with, even if it wasn't happening.

"I'm going to ask you a question, and I don't want you to get excited or angry. I want you to sit still and to think about what I'm going to ask you." So said the dark man. He leaned forward. I knew that if I gave the wrong answer and he told my parents about it, it would break their hearts. "If the New York power outage was caused, as you say, by a rock slide in a timeship billions of years ago, then what do you make of the mechanical failure at the generating plant in Niagara Falls? Was that just some kind of coincidence?"

I said, "Give me a cigarette."

"They're bad for you, Siggy," he said.

I said, "I know it." He handed me a cigarette from the box he kept in the wide drawer of his metal desk, and he lit it for me. I took a deep drag, and as I blew out the smoke in a big, blue billow, I said, "Causal recovery."

"What's that?"

"Causal recovery," I said, watching my smoke swallow his shaggy head. When he left the hospital and went home to wifey and kiddies, he'd still have my smoke in his whiskers. "That's how it always works. It has to do with the way the human mind is made. But it's not *just* the human mind. After all, the human mind is a reflection of the laws and the forms it evolved *from. All* reality conspires together with the human mind to bring about causal recovery. . . . You're getting impatient with me."

"Not at all. I'm waiting to hear you explain to me what 'causal recovery' *is*."

"There is a disruption of the causal order of things. It's not really a disruption; there is never *really* a disruption. But the distance between the world of the cause and the world of the effect is so vast in space or time, or in conception, that it *seems* a perfect disruption. However, in causality as in pneumatics, Nature abhors a vacuum. So there comes into being, *apparently*, a new cause, local to the effect, not one many billions of years ago, or in another world, or in another Mind, but one right *here*, right next to the perceived effect: a Niagara Falls."

"But nobody made up the failure at Niagara Falls. It really happened, Siggy. Do you doubt that?"

"No," I said. I had to stop for a moment. I had to look at my fingertips. They were so yellow! I had not realized how stained they had become from the nicotine. I don't think they were that bad before I entered the state hospital. "Niagara Falls happened, all right. Only, that wasn't what caused the power outage. Both the power outage *and* the plant breakdown had the same cause."

"So that we'd have to interrupt your electrotherapy and complete it the next day?"

"No, goddamnit, I'm not a madman! I don't think the world revolves around *me*. That *was* just an accident. I'm talking about timeships. I'm talking about the evolution of the goddamn universe!"

"Take it easy. You don't see your explanation as a little far-fetched? You don't believe in Occam's Razor?"

"Occam? The simplest explanation is the true one? That what you mean?"

"Yes."

"Doctor, if we really believed in Occam's Razor, we'd all be goddamn solipsists. Please . . . "

"What is it, Siggy?"

"Please don't tell my mother and father that I said any of this."

"We'll see."

The smoke eddied and swelled, sunlit, through the doctor's room, filling it like a cloud of exhaust. It *was* a cloud of exhaust. It was the exhaust of Duba's executive time shuttle retroing forward, mission accomplished, to the time of his completed deal with Bull Interplanetary. It was real pretty—that's what I thought. I like it when there's pretty smoke, if it doesn't make you cough and stuff.

"You bastard!" When I heard Topsy say that, I felt bad, even though rocks was falling on us and before and after was getting mixed around and there was for sure plenty of other stuff I ought to be paying attention to if I knew what's good for me, because I'm not stupid, you know. But I thought she meant me. But she didn't. She meant Mr. Duba. She was looking up at a hole in the sky, and said it again and again: "You bastard! You bastard!" Then she says it backward: "Dratsab uoy! Dratsab uoy! Dratsab uoy!" like the sound was being pumped back into her, what come out before.

She sat down. "Don't sit there, Tops," I tell her, "because there is rocks falling on us."

She says: "You are a dear little man, Elly, but I'm winded. I just feel winded. That wasn't Bull attacking just now. This time it was Duba. See that smoke trail? That's *his* shuttle, for sure, hypodyning the hell out of here now that it's ruined us. Whatever he was using us for, it's finished now. He's just going to dump us."

And she folded in just like an empty sack. She looked like she used to back in my apt when she would lay there inside a shadow, when she would listen to the static between the stations and think about home.

"Cheer up, old Tops," I say. "We gotta get you to home. Don't be so low, because we gotta climb up to the *ylem* now, girl. Then you'll be okay." I sat down next to her then, because my neck hurt and my arms was feeling numb. She laid her big, black hand on my head and smiled while there was lights like fishes and fires all in the sky, swarming into heaps way up behind my Topsy. She looked like an angel to me, boy!

"I just feel so lonely, Elly. I'm sorry. Tell me—Is there really such a thing as Mr. Duba?"

"Sure there is, Tops," I said.

"And we're in a timeship, right? That isn't just some time-anomalous sense-image stuck in my mind?"

"Sure, Topsy," I said.

"And we can get to *ylem*. We can climb up there. That's the idea, right? That isn't just in my time-orphaned brain?"

"That's the idea, Topsy."

"And Siggy is with us?"

I said, "Yeah, sure, Tops," on account of how I didn't want her to feel funny, but I sure didn't follow her on that particular one.

"*Siggy* is with us?" Siggy said. "She said, 'Siggy is with us?' " He laughed and threw some underwear down onto my head from the balcony of the A-frame. "You crazy jerk, Eliot," he laughed. "I'm sure glad I don't have *your* dreams."

"Listen," I said. "It gets better. Then this ash woman, the one that's all black, Topsy, starts to climb up the cliff. She takes one, two steps, and—Whammo!—she's climbing hand over hand past galaxies unclustering, unforming, backward in time, like strings of spittle stretched to mist. Are you listening, Siggy?"

"I'm listening," he shouted from his bedroom, upstairs. "Do you mind if I put on some music?"

"Yes. Then she hits the vertical, at about nineteen and a half billion years back, redshift close to ten thousand by the Doppler gauge."

"Doppler gauge! You're a nutcase, you know that?"

"There's more," I say. Siggy puts on a record . . .

Is that boy . . .

"Come on, can it, Sig! I said, there's more."

. . . SCREEE!

"Thank you," I said. "It's redshift ten thousand by Topsy's Doppler. Every inch of ascent is about twenty million years back in time. Elly . . . "

"Eliot?"

"No, *Elly!* Not *me!* Elly is back a few feet, say, three quarters of a billion years or so closer to now. There are still galaxies forming around him where he is. The air is thick with HHC's from Duba's cannon, viscous with time currents and whirlpools of inverse time. Even with his visor up, Elly sees galaxies and ferns and positrons kaleidoscoping through his field of vision. He's not very smart except at column addition and chess; he doesn't know where to find a foothold. Topsy is talking him through it."

And Siggy said, "Here they come now."

"Huh?"

"Look out the window, champ."

So I looked. From our big picture windows you could look down the mountain and north over Broome County all the way to the airfield. Scrambling up the final cliff, grabbing onto vines and scrub growth for leverage, a jet-black woman in a khaki jumpsuit was leading a man who looked much too much like me.

It was a clean rise, thin as they come, with slight ripples and few visible scoops for a hand or foot to grip. The prominent weakness was a line of cracks zigzagging up out of sight, the hypostatic image of a causal ravine dating back to the Planck Epoch, bare inches from the summit. The sides of the cracks corresponded to causally disjunct parts of the primordial mass; the distance between them was greater than light could travel before they separated even more. Perhaps one could jam one's knuckles or even just the shanks of one's fingers into the line, to pull up, hand over hand, through the earliest millennia. Perhaps not.

There was no shortcut here; that's not how the timeship worked. " . . . you have to *mix* yourself with it, Siggy," I said. "You have to struggle in the landscape of the hypostat, become one with it. That's the only way to stay inside the timeship. Otherwise you blow out the hull to God knows where, synchronous to nothing in this world and nothing in the next."

But there was no "Siggy." That was just another cul de sac in my chrono-anomalous nerve circuits, my mind like crystals of iodine, brown dust from a brown vapor, sublimed by a random puff of time. There was only me with dear Elly, the half-dead half-wit clinging to my black calf, and the defiled timeship, bleeding eons into empty space-time while we muscled our way toward *ylem*.

I tried flattening out the cliff by fiddling with the Doppler, rescaling, reducing the apparent Hubble slope, but that would increase our travel distance. With the timeship crumbling about us—while Duba's hit men trundled home to their bonuses—we could only rush up the vertical and hope to make *ylem* before the leak killed us, well, me; Elly had a different death in store.

I hazarded a peek at my Doppler—close to ten to the fifth; now came trouble. Just above me, the seam was so narrow I could only lock one pinky in it and torque up maybe a hundred fifty million years, which looked like eight inches. I called down to Elly to do the same. His head was starting to loll from the poison in Bull's dart. "Suck your chest into the wall! Stay vertical," I warned him. Down where he was—galaxies dissolving backward in time—there was still a slight rib on which to get a foothold.

I heard pebbles sliding below. Elly's fingers had slipped against a chockstone wedged inside the crack. It was a Bok globule, a cold, dark cloud about to collapse into protostars. He slid down more than a billion years and was flailing and yelling among crowds of infant galaxies. Suddenly he sat quite still.

I called to him: "Are you okay, Elly?"

"It's so pretty!" he said. "It's like big ghosts, Topsy! Look at them. See there how they're lacing their fingers together? One's got a ring on it."

"Push your visor up," I said, but his visor *was* up.

"It's all shining, Topsy. Gee, it's pretty. Big necklaces and diamonds is eating littler ones. You go home. I'm gonna stay and watch, honey."

"What?" I shouted.

"Honey!"

I held Sunshine's girl tight and tried to ignore the Muthuhs snoring and fidgeting on the floor. We beat against each other like a jellyfish pulsing, but I wasn't getting anywhere. She was too sleepy. I was too weak. I began to feel that we were a figment of the imagination of those sleeping gypsies, and in a way, I guess, we were. They were listening behind closed eyes, storing our sounds for their erotic fantasies. In the next room that record was skipping over and over:

> *"Is that boy still climbing up the mountain?*
> *Has he faltered, or has he fallen down SCREEE!*
> *Is that boy . . . "*

And we humped and we humped. Somehow, I couldn't get proper traction. We must have gone on like that for a couple of hours; I just wouldn't give up. Can you believe it? And then my head hurt. It hurt something awful. And everything was so bright, it hurt my eyes. The air, it felt like hot lead all over me. There was barbells exploding in the sky and smoke rings and fiery things like slingshot stones. No, you go on home, Topsy. Follow your static, honey, right back home. I gotta take a snooze.

"What's wrong?"

I opened my eyes and said, "Elly's dead."

The doctor said, "That's what you're seeing? That's what you're experiencing right now?"

"Yes," I said. "Elly's dead. Bull's poison killed him. He didn't make it."

"Who is Bull?" the doctor asked.

"He's in with Duba now. They were fighting at first, but now they're in cahoots. Elly and Topsy were just cannon fodder. The big shots walk away from it with their pockets bulging and their arms around each other's back."

"Do you want to use my handkerchief?"

"No."

"You're mad at them, aren't you?"

"No. It's just the way the world is, I guess."

"Tell me something," the doctor said. "Do you feel like it's your fault that Siggy ended up the way he did?"

"Of course I do," I said. "I was with him the whole time."

"Is that why you tried to kill yourself? Is that why you ended up here as well?"

"Maybe. But there's something else."

"What's that, Eliot?"

"Elly, Doctor—he's dead. And I don't know if Topsy's going to make it."

It was not a skipping record that played that song over and over as I sweated on top of Sunshine's girl. The record player was another instance of *causal recovery*. A bullet from Bull's dirigibles had struck a certain mound of salt inside the timeship. The salt had exploded into the air and was caught up by one of Duba's HHC's.

Of this salt, one crystal was actually the hypostatic image of an event which had not yet unfolded at the time of Bull's attack: Duba sitting in his office at the headquarters of Duba Enterprises, Inc., in a mammoth building that used to be a mountain near the Pennsylvania border, just outside of Binghamton; Duba blowing smoke rings from his fat cigar and humming to himself absentmindedly; he is thinking about Elly's demise, a slight debit to his massive profit from the helium deal. Duba, his mind sugary, fat and lazy with wealth, sings to himself in a breathy voice:

> *"Is that boy still climbing up the mountain?*
> *Has he faltered, or has he fallen down . . . ?"*

That's what the salt crystal was—a voice, a song, a disjointed reverie. It swirled against Hubble time, became pocked, duplicated, altered, melted into other o'clocks and other venues, one of them a crowded room in Santa Fe, New Mexico, twenty billion years past *ylem*, where two weary primates made the beast with two backs.

My arm was pumped to the limit. I jammed the other hand into the fissure, pulled out my right and let it dangle for a minute, shaking blood back into it. This was the part I had been dreading: redshift above ten to the fourth, a week or so from the Big Bang itself, twenty billion years into what I used to think of as the remote past. The hypostats built into the timeship—the life of the cosmos as landscape—were competing with volleys of images and sensations swirling in through the leak in the hull. I wasn't supposed to feel the terrific density and temperature I was passing through; they were supposed to be land features I could deal with in a dispassionate way.

I leaned into the hot rock face, frictioning my foot against a wrinkle in the stone, hoping my toes wouldn't butter down off their hold. I lunged upward. Hovering at the dead point of my maneuver for what must have been millennia on the referent time scale—I threw my right fist back into the crack and gained purchase at redshift ten to the ninth, one minute from the Big Bang.

Then I glimpsed my poppa's tattoo. Straining till I saw blood, I chinned up to my highest hold and saw The Seventh Bull, the size of my face, chiseled into the rock. It was Bull Interplanetary's "Kilroy was here." This was the spot where Bull's operative had managed to alter the primal nucleosynthetic process, to change the percentage of helium produced, creating me, *inter alia*, as a byproduct.

The Seventh Bull was a picture I knew—or thought I knew—from the series of ten Bulls in Buddhist lore:

> *The Bull is sought. The Bull is tracked.*
> *The Bull is glimpsed. The Bull is caught.*
> *The Bull is tamed. The Bull is ridden. . . .*
> *And seventh—The Bull is passed!*

I reached into my pocket, next to the Doppler gauge, and fished out Duba's black ball. I knew what it was now—a dud. I threw it down the cliff and watched it disappear into the blinding clouds of the protosolar nebula. Then, with nothing more than a prayer holding me to the head-wall, I reached up to grab the overhang separating me from the summit. It was like biting a high power line. I mantled over the edge on bent arms, pumping to the limit, till my stomach was scraping against the summit.

I had reached Planck's Epoch, redshift nearly a dectillion, temperature of ten million billion trillion electron volts, density 1,000,000,000,000,000,000, 000,000,000,000,000,000,000,000,000,000,000,000,000,000,000,000, 000,000,000,000,000,000 kilograms per cubic centimeter, but then the whole observable universe was only a billionth of a trillionth of a trillionth of a centimeter across. I was deaf, blind, completely numb to sensations of any kind . . .

I vaulted onto the summit and into the Eighth Bull: Oneself Passed! And I realized—I was numb to the world because I *was* the world. I had passed inside my own Compton wave length, into the absolute freedom of the infinitesimal, Heisenberg's sanctum, the undefilable mystery in the womb of the world, redshift going to infinity, data to zero—or whatever I would make it, I, Topsy the *Primum Mobile*!

That was twenty billion years ago. Topsy has achieved her goal: to have never been born—As my grandfather used to say, "And who is that lucky? Maybe one in a million!" But there are two more Bulls:

> *Ninth: Home (ylem) is passed.*
> *Tenth: And life goes on. . . .*

I'm sitting by the window on Sonoma Mountain, writing these disjointed notes as the sky starts to glow with radiation from our five-billion-year-old progenitor. The sun is hazy, the mountains dark green. My head still hurts like hell. The ice packs are limp rags staining the corners of my notebook with their leakage. No dirigibles remain.

Siggy has the most disagreeable snore on human record, if it's not just my migraine. This is the Ninth Bull: I'm one little person again, star ash, denouement. I'm Eliot, just like it says on the byline of this story. And the Tenth Bull is that in about five minutes I'm going to have to wake Siggy up so he can get to his appointment in San Rafael on time.

I'm all for causal recovery. God bless causal recovery! God bless wives or husbands and children in wallet photos; dull, local explanations for dull local events; even migraine headaches, if you like, to wedge a spanner twixt this God-blessed world and the goddamned inexplicable others.

When I was leaving El Centro in Santa Fe, Sunshine collared me. He wasn't mad that I had been banging his girlfriend. He even liked me. ''Don't go home, man,'' Sunshine told me. ''Don't be like everybody. Stay here with us. Be a hippy.''

But I didn't take Sunshine's advice. After all, what *is* this life, deep as the night sky, mysteriously rich, each moment, each creature immeasurably ancient? A speck of dust touches my brow. It is Duba's black ball tumbling from the peak of time, where Topsy let it go. The radio spits static. It is a quiver of the primeval fireball.

It's quite remarkable enough being like everybody.

ASYLUM

Katharine Kerr

Thomas Wolfe long ago said, "You can't go home again," but, as the subtle and melancholy story that follows demonstrates, sometimes that's even *more* true than usual—as, for instance, when you have no home left to go *back* to . . .

Katharine Kerr is known primarily as a writer of fantasy, having published such well-received novels as *Daggerspell, Darkspell, The Bristling Wood,* and *The Dragon Revenant,* but recently she has branched out into science fiction as well, and very successfully, with novels such as *Polar City Blues, A Time of Exile,* and *A Time of War.* Her most recent books are an anthology, coedited with Martin H. Greenberg, *Weird Tales from Shakespeare,* and a new science fiction novel, *Freeze Frames.*

"I've always loved Britain so much," Janet says. "It's going to be wonderful, this couple of weeks. I haven't had a vacation in so long. Jam tomorrow, jam yesterday."

Rosemary smiles. Ever since they met at Oxford, some 40 years ago now, they've kept in touch across the Atlantic by phone calls and faxes, e-mail and bulletin boards, the occasional paper letter, the even rarer visit. They have shared their careers, their divorces, and their family news during those years, as well as this long-standing joke about Janet's lack of vacations.

"Well, then." Rosemary supplies the punch line. "I'd say that you've finally got your jam today."

"Finally, yeah," Janet says, grinning. "And the view from here is an extra helping. It makes me feel all John of Gauntish. This sceptred isle and like that."

They are standing at a window on the top floor of the Canary Wharf office building, rising among the ruins of the Docklands. Since they are facing west, London stretches out before them into the misty distance on either side the Thames, glittering in the bright sun of a warm autumn day. All along the banks the new retaining walls rise, bleak slabs of concrete, while the river runs fast and high between them. Janet can pick out the complex round the Tower and the new barricades round its ancient walls, protecting them from tides gone mad. Just east of the Tower, near what used to be St Katharine's Docks, huge concrete pylons, hooded like monks in sheet metal, rise out of the river. Boats swarm round, workmen overrun them, all rushing to finish the new barrier before the winter sets in.

"Well," Janet says. "Maybe not John of Gauntish. Rosemary, this is really pretty awful, the floods, I mean."

"If the new barrier holds . . ." Rosemary lets her voice trail away.

Janet considers her friend for a moment. In the glittering light Rosemary looks exhausted. Her pale blonde and grey-streaked hair, carefully coiffed round a face innocent of make-up, somehow emphasizes the dark circles under her eyes. Along with a handful of other MPs, Rosemary fought long and hard to get the barrier built further east, just upriver from the old one, argued and insisted that the East End should be saved, that millions of people and their homes not be abandoned—but in the end, more powerful interests won. Engineers could guarantee the barrier if built at this location, and of course, it cost much less than her counter-proposal. As a sign of social impartiality, the Docklands, an embarrassment to British business for the last 40-odd years, have been left beyond the new barrier as well.

"We'd best go down," Rosemary says.

"Yeah." Janet turns, glancing round the lobby toward elevator doors that hang not quite at a right angle to the floor. "How long do you think this building's going to stand?"

"Well, we don't get earthquakes here, you know, like you do at home." Rosemary smiles briefly. "The Free University will probably be able to use it for some years yet. After all, the predictions are vague—about the warming trend, I mean. No one can pinpoint the rise year by year. It may even have peaked."

"That's true, of course. And if they get the embankment built up along here, well, that'll hold for a while more."

"If they do. If, my dear."

During the ride down neither woman speaks, both listen, rather, to every small creak and rattle that the cage and cables make. Ground water and shifting terrain have begun to damage the ever-so-delicate array of wires and power conduits upon which 20th-century buildings depended. When the doors open smoothly at the ground floor, Janet lets out her breath in relief. She's glad, as well, to get outside to air that needs no artificial circulation.

On the small flagstone plaza students gather, chattering among themselves under the huge canvas banner, lettered in red, announcing the conference at which Janet has just been the featured guest. "Women's Gains: A Century of Progress." A century of crawling forward would be more honest, Janet thinks. Even on this lovely afternoon, the work to be done haunts her. She reminds herself that this is a vacation, that she has left all the files from outstanding cases at home, that her law practice will survive without her for two weeks and her new book will as well. Besides, her assistant back home has her itinerary, and he can always call if he really needs her.

"It was a good speech, you know," Rosemary says abruptly. "It was one of those that makes me think, my god, I know someone famous!"

Much to her own surprise, Janet blushes.

"Oh now really," Rosemary says. "Sorry."

"No problem. And I have to admit, I wallowed in all that applause. But you should talk! Lately you've been in the media lots more than me."

"Only as a crank, my dear. Another Liberal Party crank, flogging her unpopular ideas."

"Well, don't you think that's what I am? Back in the States, I mean. A small 'I' liberal crank at best. A tool of Satan is more like it."

They look at each other, grimace, shrug, and walk across the plaza. In the shade of the low embankment, near the steps up to the RiverBus dock, someone has set up a table and folding chair. A young woman lounges in the chair; a monitor and set of input tablets lie on the table. Nearby stands a man of about 50, short and compact, his dark curly hair streaked with grey, his skin the light brown of Thames mud. At the sight of Rosemary he waves vigorously and grins.

"Jonathan, hullo!" Rosemary drifts over. "Have you met Janet? Janet Corey. Jonathan Richards."

They shake hands and smile. Jonathan wears a stubbornly old-fashioned shirt, white and buttoning up the front, with long sleeves rolled up just below his elbows.

"I'm manning the trenches today." Jonathan waves at the table and the monitor. "Petitions."

"Petitions for what?" Janet asks.

"Raising the banks round the Free University. I'm its bursar, you see, and I'm not looking forward to rowing to work every morning."

"Well, yeah, I guess not." Janet glances at the low dirt bank, topped with a thin layer of asphalt. "That won't hold long, if the predictions come true."

Jonathan nods, glancing at Rosemary, who sighs, reaches up to rub her eyes with the back of one hand.

"We keep introducing the special requisition," Rosemary says. "Perhaps if you do get some show of popular support . . ."

"Just so. Hence the petitions." He grins at Janet. "I'd ask you to sign, but obviously you vote elsewhere."

From the river drifts the sound of an airhorn—the hovercraft on its way to dock. Muttering goodbyes, fumbling in their handbags for pass cards, Rosemary and Janet hurry up the steps. Out on the water the hovercraft is pausing, backing, working its way through the crowd of small boats and barges, which are scurrying out of its way in turn. On the dock, down by the gangplank two men in the blue uniforms of the RiverFleet huddle over a portable media link. Janet can just hear the announcer's midget voice say, "deteriorating situation in Detroit" before music carries it away.

"Er, excuse me," Janet says. "Could you tell me what that was about?"

At the sound of her flat American voice the officer nods agreement. "I hope you're not from Detroit," he says. "There seem to have been more riots. Fuel oil rationing, I believe it was."

"Probably. It usually is. Thanks; thanks very much."

As she follows Rosemary down the gangplank to the boat, Janet wonders at herself, that she would take the news of "just another riot" so calmly.

News, bad news, dogs her holiday. As she leaves London, heading north on the Flying Scotsman, she reads of riots spreading all through the Rust Belt, from Chicago in the west to Baltimore in the east. Pictures of the American National

Guard quelling riots scroll past on the media screens that hang from the girders in the Edinburgh station. By the next morning, British time, the first deaths have occurred; the waiter in the hotel dining room informs her, his voice grave, as she helps herself to whole-grain cereal from a stoneware crock at the buffet. Seven young men, two young women, shot as they tried to loot—food in every case, he thinks it was.

"How dreadful." I'll never get used to this, at least. "How awful. Ohmigawd."

He nods, hesitating, glancing round the nearly empty dining room, where a profusion of white linen lies on sunny tables. In a far corner two elderly men eat behind matching newspapers.

"We had an American gentleman in earlier," he says at last. "He joked about it."

"No! Oh god, that's really awful. What did he say?"

Again the glance round. "He said that in his day, young people had the sense to loot luxury items, like televisions. Said he didn't know what was wrong with them, nowadays."

Janet cannot speak; she merely shakes her head.

"I didn't know what to answer," he says.

"I wouldn't have, either. You know, most Americans who can still afford to travel have, shall we say, rather right-wing leanings these days. The rest of us don't."

He smiles as if relieved, but she feels like a hypocrite, lumping herself in the category of "the rest of us" when she so obviously wears expensive slacks, a silk shirt, when she so undeniably is spending her vacation on expensive foreign soil.

"Shall I bring tea to your table or coffee?" the waiter says.

"Tea, please. Thank you."

For the next few days Janet tries to bury herself in problems of the past in order to ignore those of the present. She climbs up the rock of Din Edin, as she always thinks of it, where the Gododdin built their fortress. She knows too much about Mary Queen of Scots to romanticize her, finds herself avoiding the guided tour through the castle, and merely stands, looking down at the fang-sharp grey city below, while white stormclouds pile and build in the blue sky. That night, while she listens to the news on television, it rains. As an aside, almost an afterthought to the real news, the announcer speculates on how long the Holy Isle of Lindisfarne will remain above sea-level. The restored castle on its smaller version of Din Edin's rock is safe, of course, but on the flat, villagers stubbornly cling to ancestral land which sinks into a rising sea.

On the morrow, guidebook in hand, Janet wanders through the National Museum of Antiquities. She spends much of her time there studying the Pictish standing stones. Across the marble floor of a vast hall, decorated with murals of the Highlands, the newly completed collection stands, tucked away from acid rain as the Highlands themselves cannot be. The present, it seems, cannot be avoided.

In her hotel bedroom that night, while she writes postcards to her only child,

Amanda, to her nephew Richie's family up in the Sierra Nevada, and finally, to friends, she flicks on the news out of habit and lets it rumble half-heard until American voices raised in anger force her to watch. Just a few seconds of footage make it plain that Congress has deadlocked over the question of imposing military law on rioting cities. Janet watches fat senators invoke God's name until at last the screen changes to local news, good news: the child who wandered away from his family last night has been found, chilled to the bone but unharmed.

Janet windows the screen into four, then flips channels, finds at last among the meagre 64 available on British television an international news feed, which turns out to be devoting itself to the droughts in Central Africa.

"Damn!" She flicks the monitor off. "But really, you know, you are supposed to be on vacation?"

Yet, all too soon, America invades her holidays across the bridge of the media. At first the troubles at home appear toward the end of a broadcast and only in the evening programme, but slowly they pull ahead and begin appearing on the morning feed as well. By her fourth night in Scotland, they've taken precedence over the Parliamentary debates about preserving British farmland. On the night that she reaches York, American news—the spreading of riots into Sunbelt cities, where fuel oil shortages provide no excuse—has inched in front of the ongoing discussion of whether King William should abdicate. By the time she reaches the Lake Country, the lead story and the headline in the newspapers as well have become REGULAR ARMY UNITS SUPPLEMENT NATIONAL GUARD IN AMERICAN CITIES.

Military law declared, generals replace mayors all across the nation—and in many pulpits though not all, preachers and priests announce that God is punishing America for pride and sin. The Times runs a special feature on the situation, which Janet reads, twice, sitting in the lounge of a small hotel, at a diamond-paned window, under a wood ceiling certified Tudor. Janet stares at the pictures of torn streets, impassive soldiers, smug preachers, for a very long time. All at once, she finds herself afraid.

The outcome reaches her in Cardiff. She has just emerged from the National Museum and crossed to the park where Iolo Morgannwg's gorsedd circle stands, a miniature henge of reddish stone. The morning's rain has stopped, leaving the pale grey civic buildings clean and gleaming, the sky a parade of sun and cloud, the grass between the slabs of Iolo's fancy bejewelled with drops. By the kerb a small electric truck dispenses whipped ice cream, and Janet debates buying a cone, setting her ever-present fear of cholesterol levels against the girlishness of this day. Not far away a group of teenagers huddle round a media kiosk—a newsstand, she suddenly realizes, not a video viewer, and without really thinking she drifts closer, hears the announcer mentioning Washington D.C. and drifts closer still. One of the boys looks up; she sees a familiar face, dark bangs, blue eyes, the busboy from her small hotel.

"You're the American, aren't you?"

"Yes, as a matter of fact."

Silently he steps to one side to let her have his place in the huddle. The announcer, mercifully, is speaking English.

". . . riots feared in San Francisco. Units of the National Guard are moving into the city's centre in spite of scattered resistance."

Earthquake. Her first thought is natural disaster, the quake hit at last, the waiting over, and looters in the street. The announcer drones on.

"Although news lines are down all across the nation, it would seem that the only resistance to the coup does lie in California. Leaders of the junta report that the control of other major cities passed peacefully into their hands early this morning."

Nightmare, not earthquake.

"How well those reports may be trusted remains to be seen. An emergency session of the European parliament has been called for later today. Earlier, the prime minister made this announcement outside Number Ten Downing street . . ."

"Ohmigawd." Janet hears her voice tremble and skip. "Ohmigawd."

The young men are watching her, she realizes. One steps forward and touches her elbow. "I'll flag you down a cab."

She can only nod, not speak, merely stands and trembles until at last the compu-cab pulls up to the kerb.

Back at her hotel room the telephone blinks, signalling messages. Janet hits the button, stands in the middle of the room and listens, merely stands and looks at striped wallpaper while Rosemary's voice, harsh with unfamiliar urgency, asks if she'd heard the news. A second call, from her daughter, Mandi, left behind in San Francisco—for this Janet watches the phonevid. Mandi's face is dead pale, her hands shake, even as she assures her mother that she's all right. When Mandi begs her to call as soon as she can, Janet finds herself speaking aloud, "of course, dear," in answer. A third message—this from her assistant, a terrible connection, Eddie's voice chattering fast over the sound of traffic. The phonevid shows only static.

"I'm calling from a payphone. I hope to god you get this. Don't come home. They ransacked the office this morning. It's Seven Days in May. They took the files. Don't come home. Stay where you are."

Other voices break into the background of the call. Eddie curses. A click, the message over. Janet sits down in a blue-flowered chair next to the telephone, rewinds the tape, and listens to all three messages again. Clever of Eddie, to use the name of an old video to tell her everything she needs to know. The army's been in her office. Half her discrimination cases pended against various military bureaucracies. There is no doubt now who will win them.

Her mouth is dry, her hands shake, and she feels abruptly cold, gets up to find a sweater, stares numbly round the room while she tries to remember what made her stand up, sits down again. She should call Mandi, reaches for the phone, stops herself. Doubtless they, this vast, suddenly ominous "they," will have tapped Mandi's phone by now. Will they go to Mandi's flat and take her away like the files?

"Her engagement will save her." Janet hears her own voice tremble, continues speaking aloud just to hear a voice in the room. "She's Army now herself, really. She's going to marry an officer. He'll take care of her. Jack's a good guy.''

Unless he has chosen to honour his sworn oath to the Constitution and refused to go along with the coup? Jack's stationed in California, after all, named by the announcer as the one place offering any resistance. But who's resisting? Military units? Street gangs? Libertarian and survivalist fighter packs? All of these in some patched-together coalition?

"I've got to call my daughter."

Janet reaches for the phone, pulls her hand back. If she calls, she might implicate Mandi in . . . in what? Something, anything, being the daughter of a liberal, who knows now what the word, crime, may mean. They've taken my files. They know all about me. They know about my daughter. When the phone rings, Janet screams. She gulps a deep breath and picks it up on the third pair of rings.

"Janet? Thank god." Rosemary's voice, slightly breathless, precedes her image, irising onto the phonevid. "You've heard?"

"Sure have."

"Well, look, the maglev train runs from Cardiff to London every hour up until seven o'clock tonight. Call me once you've bought your ticket and I'll arrange to have you met at Euston. It's going to take a while, so we have to start the process as soon as possible, and of course you'll have to declare, so you'll need to be at my office tomorrow morning."

"Declare? Rosemary, wait, slow down. What process?"

"Applying for political asylum, of course. Janet, my dear friend! I've just been briefed by the Foreign Office. You can't go back. You'll be arrested the moment you step off the plane. They're rounding up anyone who might oppose them. It's horrid."

Janet stares at the stripes, blue and white and grey.

"Janet? Janet, look at the camera. Are you all right?"

"Yeah, sure, sorry."

"Well, this has all been a bit of a shock, I'm sure."

Janet restrains the urge to laugh like a madwoman.

"At any rate," Rosemary goes on. "Do get packed up and get yourself down to the station. Wait, someone's talking . . ." A long pause while Rosemary chews on her lower lip. "Good god! Janet, listen. I'll have a ticket waiting for you there. They might have taken over your accounts. Your cards might not work. I'll contact your hotel, too."

"Already? They might have cut people's cards off already? Oh God, they must have been planning this thing for years!"

"Yes, it would certainly seem so. The Foreign Office are shocked, really shocked. They've been keeping an eye on something called the Eagle Brotherhood, but they had no idea of just how high it reached. Well, I'll brief you later. Just get to London, so you can declare."

"Of course. Should I keep an eye out for assassins?"

"Good God, don't joke!"

"Okay. Sorry. I'm on my way. Oh, Rosemary, wait!"

"Yes, still here."

"Don't worry about the train ticket. I've got a BritTravel pass. They couldn't have touched that."

"Right. I'll just ring up your hotel, then."

Janet crams clothes and her bedtime book into her suitcases, checks the bathroom and finds her various toiletries, crams them into plastic bags and stuffs them into a side pocket of the biggest case. She carries the luggage down herself, reaches the hotel desk to find the clerk talking to Rosemary, writing down her charge numbers to settle the bill. The clerk pauses, her dark eyes narrow with worry, with sympathy.

"It's all been taken care of, ma'am."

"Thank you. Could you call a cab for me? Or wait, will they take a BritTravel card?"

"They will, yes. Best of luck to you, ma'am."

"Thanks."

Janet restrains the urge to add "I'll need it" like a character in an old video.

On the maglev, the trip to London takes a bare hour. Through polarized glass Janet sees the countryside shoot by, clear in the far distance, blurred close to the train. Although she's used to thinking on her feet, having practised for years in front of hostile judges, today she cannot think, can only worry about her daughter, her assistant, her sometime lover and closest friend, Robert, and all the other friends in their politically active circle, all left behind in San Francisco. I alone have escaped to tell you. She leans her face against the cool glass and trembles, too tormented to weep.

At Euston she hauls her bags off the train, finds a luggage cart and ladles them in, then trudges down the long platform, leaning on the cart handle for support like some bag lady, drifting through the streets with all she owns before her. As she emerges into the cavernous station hall, she sees two things: the enormous media screen on the far wall, and Jonathan Richards, wearing an old-fashioned tweed jacket flung over an old-fashioned blue shirt, hurrying to meet her. On the screen a man in uniform stands in the Oval Office next to a pale and shaking president. Across the boom and bustle of the hall the general's words die before they reach her.

"Hullo," Jonathan says. "I'd hoped to see you again on a better day than this."

"Yeah, really."

"Rosemary rang me up and pressed me into service. She's afraid that sending an official car would attract too much attention."

Janet starts to answer, but her mouth seems to have frozen into place. Attract too much attention? From whom? Does the coup have the power to pluck its enemies from the streets of foreign cities?

"Rather a nasty situation all round," Jonathan says. "Here, I'll push that cart. The wheels always stick on these beasts." Nodding, Janet relinquishes the handle. As she follows him through the crowd she is trying to convince herself that she's simply too unimportant to be a target, but her new book rises in her memory, and its brisk sales—*Christian Fascism: The Politics of Righteousness*. She thinks: *You saw this coming, you've seen it for years, why are you so surprised?*

Jonathan has spoken to her.

"I'm sorry," Janet says. "I missed that."

He smiles, his eyes weary. "Quite understandable. I'm just abandoning the cart. We go down the steps here."

Books and papers heap the back seat of Jonathan's small electric Morris. He slings the luggage in on top of them, hands Janet into the front seat, then hurries round behind the wheel. As they pull out, Janet realizes that night's fallen. Street lamps halo out bright in a rising mist.

"Where are we going?"

"Rosemary's flat."

"Ah. Thank you. I mean, really, thanks for coming down like this."

"Quite all right."

During the drive out to Kew, where Rosemary lives in a huge walled complex of townhouses and gardens, Janet says very little. Her mind searches for its old humour, tries to find some quip or irony, fails, trails away into wonderings about Mandi and Robert. Suddenly she remembers that Robert talked about leaving the city during her vacation, about going up to her mother's old house in the mountains. If he has, he will be safe; up in Goldust her family knows him, and they will take him in if he needs it. If he left. Will she ever know?

"Jonathan? Have you heard if the phone lines to the States are down?"

"It seems to depend on where you want to call. The various media have their own links, of course. The new programme that I was listening to on the radio implied that private calls are difficult, and the farther west you want to go, the worse it is."

"I was thinking that might be the case, yeah."

"We'll get some sort of underground news network set up down at the university as soon as we can. Hackers." He glances her way briefly. "For a respectable sort of person I happen to know a remarkable number of hackers."

"They'll see it as the best game in the world."

When they reach the flat, Rosemary's housekeeper lets them in, takes the luggage from Jonathan and takes it away. They wander into Rosemary's yellow and white parlour, all slender Eurostil furniture and wall paintings. Rosemary loves florals, and on the display screens glow Renoirs and Monets, each garden blooming for some minutes, then fading to allow the next to appear. Jonathan heads straight for a white wooden cabinet.

"Drink?" he says.

"Gin and tonic, please. I bet Rosemary's on the phone."

"She'll be hoarse before the night's out, yes."

Janet sinks into the corner of the pale leather sofa only to find herself confronted with a picture of her daughter, a snapshot she herself took on the day that Mandi graduated from college. Rosemary has had it enlarged and printed out, then framed in a yellow acrylic oval. In her dark red robes and mortar board Mandi looks overwhelmed, no matter how brightly she smiles for her mother's camera.

She is pale and blue-eyed, like her grandmother, and her long blonde hair streams over her shoulders. All at once Janet's eyes fill with tears. She shakes them away and looks up to find Jonathan holding out a glass.

"I'm so sorry," he says.

She nods and takes the drink.

"You must be worried sick about your daughter."

"I am, yeah." She takes a sip before she goes on. "But actually. I was thinking of my mother. I'm really glad she didn't live to see this."

Jonathan sighs and flops into an armchair opposite. He is drinking something golden-brown, scotch, most likely, sips it and seems to be searching for something to say. Wearing a crumpled blue suit, Rosemary steps in to the room. Her red scarf slides from her shoulder and falls without her noticing.

"Hullo!" She smiles at Janet. "It is so good to see you safe."

"Thanks. Really, thank you for all the help. I don't know what I'd have done without it."

"I'm sure you'd have thought of something, but I'm glad I'm placed as I am. Sorry I was on the phone when you arrived. I've been being courted. Rather nice, really."

"By the party whip, I assume?" Jonathan hands her a drink.

"Exactly." Rosemary sinks down into the other corner of the sofa. "Thank you, darling." She pauses for a long sip. "This is the situation. Emergency session tonight in a few hours. Labour want to threaten an immediate boycott of all American goods and services and to call for immediate restoration of democracy. The Tories, of course, do not. Enough Labour members may bolt to make our votes important. The Labour leaders are willing to be accommodating. I pretended to have doubts about the boycott for the sake of the British middle class." Rosemary smiles briefly. "And so you'll get the embankment, Jonathan, to protect the Free University."

"Brilliant!"

"Tremendous!"

Jonathan and Janet raise their glasses and salute her.

"Corrupt, actually," Rosemary says. "But there we are." She turns Janet's way. "I'm having some information transmitted to my terminal for you. About applying for asylum. We'd best get that underway tomorrow. They're setting up a board to handle the applications, you see."

"Do you think there'll be a crush?" Jonathan said. "Most of the Yanks I've met lately will be overjoyed at the developments."

Rosemary shrugs.

"The coup wouldn't have struck without being sure of having a broad base of support," Janet says. "They've been building it for years. Mostly by playing on the crime issue—you know, the need for order in our embattled streets. And of course, moral values. The so-called family values."

"It's always order, isn't it?" Jonathan says. "The excuse, I mean, for military governments. We must have order. Keep the people in line."

Janet nods agreement.

"Anyway, we'll have dinner before I go," Rosemary says. "Have you remembered to eat today?"

"No." Janet allows herself a smile. "Not since breakfast. Kind of a long time ago now."

"Thompson will be serving soon, I should think. You know, I have no idea what sort of questions the Board will want answered during the asylum proceedings. Your books and career should be enough to satisfy them you're in danger. I hope they don't want an actual threat or your presence on some sort of list. How long do you have left on your tourist visa?"

"Close to two months."

"Splendid! Surely that should be enough, even for a bureaucracy."

"Even for a British bureaucracy?" Jonathan puts in, grinning.

Rosemary groans and holds out her glass for a refill.

"It's a good question, though," Janet says. "I'll have to have some visible means of support, won't I?"

"Oh here." Jonathan pauses on his way to the liquor cabinet. "Surely that won't be a factor in the Board's decision."

"It might," Rosemary breaks in. "The junta are bound to put pressure on our government in turn. They do have all the bombs, you know. I imagine they'll be able to force a very strict adherence to the rules and regulations for this sort of thing."

Jonathan thinks, chewing on his lower lip.

"Well, here," he says at last. "The Free University sponsor lecture series. There's no doubt that you'd be a major attraction, Janet. First, a series of public lectures featuring your book. Christian fascism—its roots and rise. Then a proper course for the student body: American Fascism, the historical background. I foresee no difficulty in getting the Committee to approve it."

"No doubt they'll thank you." Rosemary turns a good bit brighter. "And of course, the book! It's only just come out here, and my god, what a publicity event!"

Janet tries to laugh and fails.

"But what about the money from that?" Rosemary goes on. "Does it go to your agent in America?"

"No, fortunately. She has a co-agent here in London, and David gets all monies received and converts them to pounds before he sends them on. I'll call him tomorrow. He can just send my agent her cut and let me have the rest. Oh my god. My agent!"

"Oh now here," Rosemary says. "You don't think she'll be arrested?"

Janet shrugs helplessly. She has absolutely no idea which of her acquaintances might be endangered by the simple act of knowing her.

"It sounds to me," Jonathan says, "that one way or another you'll do very well for yourself."

"Yeah, it does, doesn't it? If I don't mind being a professional exile."

Although Janet meant the phrase as irony, it cracks out of her mouth like a pistol shot. Rosemary sighs and watches her, worried. Jonathan busies himself with refilling glasses.

"Well, sorry," Janet says. "It's not like I have a lot of choice."

"Just so, darling. Do you want to try to ring Mandi? It can't put her into any worse danger than she's already in."

"Just from having a mother like me? Oh god. But yeah, I do. I'll just go into the other room."

"The green guest room. The one you had before."

Janet sits on the edge of a narrow bed in a pool of yellow light and punches code into the handset. Halfway through, at the code for the San Francisco Bay Area, a string of whistles and shrieks interrupt.

"I'm sorry, but we cannot complete your call as dialled. Please attempt to ring through at a later time."

"Damn!"

Later that night, when Rosemary has gone off to the Houses of Parliament and Jonathan to his home, Janet lies on the bed in her green and white guest room and watches the late news. Footage of tanks rolling down American streets, soldiers standing on guard in front of banks, here and there the ruins of a shelled building—and yet it seems clear that the coup has faced little resistance, except out in the American west. The east, the south, and the capital belong, heart and soul, to the coup and the Christian right. Utah as well has declared for the new government, as have the southern counties of California but up in the mountains, the Rockies, the Sierra Nevada, the rain forests of the Cascades—in the high places even the spokesmen for the junta admit that a campaign of "pacification" lies ahead of them. There are no reports at all from Alaska. All network links seem to be down. Since the Native Americans there have been sabotaging government installations for the past 15 years, Janet can guess that they've found sudden allies among the whites.

It doesn't matter, Janet knows. In the end the coup will win, because the areas that resist matter little to the economic life of the country. They can be cut off and starved out until their cities fall to the neo-fascists. Perhaps Alaska will stay free, an instant republic. Down in the continental United States, up in the mountains, a guerilla war may continue for years, an annoyance but no threat to the new government, fought by a patchwork army of libertarians, survivalists, and honourable men.

The newscast changes to a parade through Washington, rank after rank of soldiers, Army and Marines marching through the rain. Past the Lincoln Memorial—Janet lays down the remote to wipe tears from her eyes. Yet she cannot stop watching, finds herself staring at the screen, puzzling over some small detail. She finds the close-up function, slides it on, zeroes her little white square over one soldier, clicks—and sees upon his shoulder the new patch added to his dress uniform, a white cross on a blue ground. She punches the screen back to normal so hard that the remote squalls in protest.

The end of the newscast shows the Senate voting extraordinary powers to the new chief of government security, that is, to the head of the coup, an Air Force general named James Rogers, and, almost as an afterthought, establishing a new office of public security, to be headed by a certain Colonel Nicholas Harrison. One picture catches Janet by surprise—she hadn't expected Rogers to be black, just somehow hadn't expected it.

Janet flicks off the terminal. For a long time she lies on the bed, staring at the blank screen, until at last she falls asleep with the lights on.

*   *   *

Morning brings coffee (real coffee served in a big mug by the ever-efficient Thompson), the sound of rain pounding on the windows, and memories. On the nightstand lies a telephone, its little screen a green gleam of temptation. Call my daughter. Don't dare. Thompson opens one pair of curtains to grey light, smiles, and leaves again.

Janet gets up, flicks on the news, and dresses, gulping down the coffee in the intervals between zipping up her jeans and pulling a sweater over her head. The American coup has taken over the television as well as the United States. Janet windows the screen into four, finds a silent feed station for one, mutes the sound on two other programmes, and lets the BBC announcer drone at low volume while she unpacks her suitcases.

Except for Seattle the coup now controls every city in the continental United States. The BBC expect Seattle to surrender at any moment, guarded as it is by only two regiments of National Guard and some armed citizens. Since Russia and Japan have both offered their protection to the new Republic of Alaska, it will probably stand. In all three programme windows video rolls endlessly, tanks, Congress, dead bodies, fighter planes, refugees streaming north into Canada from Seattle and Detroit. On the silent feed maps flash; Janet takes a moment to click on the western states and freeze their image upon the screen. She zeroes in on San Francisco, clicks to magnify, sees a street map covered in a thin wash of red, too cheerfully raspberry for even metaphorical blood. The junta holds the city, the bridges are secured.

The search function throws a box on to the screen.

"Do you wish to see a news feed from the city you have selected?"

"Yes."

The BBC disappears, and an ITV reporter pops into focus, standing in Civic Centre. Behind her rises City Hall, grey and domed in a foggy morning, but the high steps are strewn with corpses. Janet begins to tremble. She sits down on the edge of the bed and clasps her mug in both hands while the reporter, pale and dishevelled, speaks in a low voice of a night of horror, of teenagers firing handguns at tanks, of teenagers shot down by those who were once their countrymen. The camera starts to pan through the pollarded trees of the skimpy plaza. A siren breaks into the feed; the reporter shouts something into her microphone; the feed goes dead.

Janet raises the remote and clicks the monitor off. She cannot watch any more of those pictures. Yet she must see more, she must know more. She raises the remote again, then hurls it onto the carpet. *You'll feel better if you cry. Why can't you cry?*

She cannot answer.

"More coffee?"

Thompson at the door, holding a tray—a silver pot, a pitcher of milk, a plate of something covered by a napkin.

"Yes, thanks. Is Mrs White at home?"

"No, ma'am. She's gone to her office."

"Ah. I thought so."

Thompson sets the tray on the dresser, then stoops and picks up the remote.

Janet takes it from him and without thinking, flips the monitor on again. An ITV executive stands before a studio camera, speaking very fast and very high while sweat beads on his high forehead. As far as he can determine, his crew in San Francisco have been arrested, hauled away like common criminals despite every provision of the UNESCO media pact signed just last year in Nairobi. Janet changes the station out from under his indignation. This time a search on the strings "San Francisco" and "northern California" turn up nothing, not on one of the 64 channels.

Janet makes the BBC and the silent feed into insets at the top of the screen, punches up the terminal program, then glances round for a more convenient input device than the TV wand. On the dresser, next to the silver tray, lies a remote keyboard. She picks it up, looks under the napkin—croissants, which normally she loves. Today they look disgusting. She sits on the floor with her back against the foot of the bed and rests the keyboard in her lap while she runs a quick search on documents filed under her name. She finds two directories created and set aside, coded for use, ASYLUM and JANETSWORK. Once again, Rosemary proves herself the hostess who thinks of everything.

When Janet brings up the first directory, she finds more than a meg of docs listed, including the full text of the Special Circumstances Immigration Act of 2028 and a sub-directory of material pertaining to the famous Singh case that triggered the writing of said legislation.

"It's a good thing I'm a lawyer. Hey, I better get used to saying solicitor."

Janet cannot laugh, wishes she could cry. In her mind sound the words, "call your daughter." All morning, as she studies the government-supplied infofiles and readies her application on the official forms, she pauses every ten minutes to try Mandi's number, but the phone lines stay stubbornly down. While she works, she glances often at the two inset windows, where footage of the States in chaos silently rolls by. Finally, toward noon, she transmits the completed application to the office LOC number listed on the form. As an afterthought, she prints out a copy, wondering if perhaps she should go down and apply in person as well. When she calls Rosemary's office, she gets Rosemary herself. Even on the tiny phonevid Janet can see dark smudges under her friend's eyes.

"I'm surprised you're there."

"I just popped in to the office for a minute," Rosemary says, yawning. "Have you transmitted the application?"

"I did, yeah. Yesterday you said something about going down to New White-hall. Do you think I—"

"No, don't! I've heard that pictures are being taken of Americans entering the building."

"Taken? By whom? Wait, no, of course you can't tell me."

Rosemary's image smiles, very faintly.

"I'll just check to make sure the transmission's been received, then," Janet says. "And stay here."

"Yes. That would be best. I'll be back for dinner. If you'd just tell Thompson?"

"Of course."

Rosemary smiles again and rings off.

Janet returns the monitor screen to four windows of news. When she runs the search program, she finds one station with taped video from San Francisco, looping while serious voices discuss the news blackout. Colonel Harrison has issued a statement assuring the world media that the blackout is both regretted and temporary, that the telephone service has been disrupted by rebel sabotage and that it will be restored as soon as possible. No one believes him. As the video reels by, about an hour's worth all told, Janet watches like a huntress, her eyes moving back and forth, studying details, searching desperately for the images of people she knows, seeing none, even though she stays in front of the monitor all day, watching the same loop, over and over.

"Rosemary was quite right," Jonathan says. "The committee are beside themselves with joy. How soon can you give the first lecture? That was their only question."

"Wonderful," Janet says. "In a couple of days, I guess. I'll have to call Eleanor—that's my editor—and see if she can send me a copy of the book. I didn't have one with me, and I don't have any cash, and I can't stand asking Rosemary for pocket money. She's done too much for me already, feeding me and like that. Maybe I can squeeze an advance out of HCM. God knows the book's been selling like crazy over here."

"HCM?"

"HarperCollinsMitsubishi. My British publisher."

Jonathan nods his understanding. On a day streaked with sun and shadow they are walking through the gardens in the centre of the condominium complex. Although the trees have dropped their leaves, the grass thrives, stubbornly green. All round the open space rise white buildings, staggered like drunken ziggurats.

"No word from the immigration people yet?" Jonathan says.

"None. But it's only been a couple of days since I filed the application."

"They probably haven't even looked at it, then. The morning news said that over two thousand Americans have applied for political asylum in various countries. Quite a few business people were caught in Europe, I gather. A lot of them have come here."

"Yeah. I heard that three times that number are just going home." Janet hears her voice growl with bitterness. "Happy as clams with their new theocracy."

"Um, well, yes." Jonathan sighs, hesitates before continuing. "At any rate, I've got the University's contracts for the public series and then for the course of study. I'll transmit them to you tonight, so you can look them over. We'll need to get handbills out for the lectures, by the way, and some notice to the media. We'd best start thinking of a general title."

"That's true. I wonder if I'll get hecklers? Oh well, they'll be easier to handle than the ones back home."

"Rosemary told me once that you'd—well, had some trouble with thugs."

"Oh yeah. They beat the hell out of me. It was after an abortion rights rally, maybe what? Thirty years ago now. I had bruises for weeks. And a broken arm."

"Horrible, absolutely horrible! It's lucky you weren't killed."

"A lot of people were, back in those days. Doctors, nurses. Doctor's wives, even." Janet shudders reflexively. She can still remember images of fists swinging toward her face and hear voices shrieking with rage, chanting Jesus Jesus Jesus. "All in the name of God. No, that's not fair. In the name of the warped little conception of God that these people have."

"The history of an illusion. Living history, unfortunately."

"Yeah, very much alive and well in the US of A. I suppose abortion's the first thing the new government's going to outlaw."

"They have already. The Times had a list, this morning, of the various acts they've pushed through your Congress. Quite a lot for just a few days' work. The junta released the list, you see. They're holding press conferences for official news as well."

"I should look that over." Janet tries to muster an ironic laugh, can't. "Well, there goes my life's work, right down the drain. What do you bet that I've been on the wrong side of every law they've just passed?"

"Doesn't sound like my idea of a fair wager at all." He hesitates, frowning down at the gravelled walk. "Rosemary said there's been no word of your daughter."

"That's right, yeah. Well, no news is good news. The Red Cross doesn't have her name on any of the casualty lists. It hasn't appeared on any of the lists of political prisoners, either."

"That's something, then. Some of my young friends are working on getting a network pieced together. Perhaps they'll run across something."

"How can they even reach the States with the phone lines down?"

"Satellite feeds of some sort. Military, probably. I've asked them not to tell me more. And then they can maybe get in through Canada. Somehow. As I say, I don't really want to know."

That evening Janet goes over the contracts from the Free University, finds them fair and the proposed payment, generous. Since the money will come from a special fund, the cheque will no doubt be slow in coming. She decides to call her agent tomorrow and ask him to see about an advance from the publishers.

"But who knows when we'll get it?' Janet says. "Rosemary, I hate sponging on you like this."

"Oh please!" Rosemary rolls her eyes heavenward. "Who was it who fed and housed my wretched son when he was going through his loathsome phase? He leeched for absolutely months."

"Oh, he was no trouble, really, since I wasn't his mother."

They share a laugh at the now-respectable Adrian's expense.

"Well, you're not any trouble, either," Rosemary goes on. "In fact, that reminds me. I had a phonecard made up for you—on my account, that is. It'll be weeks before you can open your own, and you'll need access."

"Well, I will, yeah. Thanks. I wonder when I'll be able to phone home."

They both find themselves turning in their chairs, glancing toward Mandi's picture on the end table.

"Sometimes I'm sorry that I waited so long to have a child," Janet says. "Here I am in my 60s, and she's just getting married. God, I hope she's still getting married. Jack means the world to her."

"She's not like us, no."

In the photo Mandi smiles, tremulous under her mortarboard, the English literature major with no desire to go to graduate school.

"I just hope she's happy." Janet's voice shakes in her throat. "I just hope she's all right. You know what the worst thing is? Wondering if she hates me, wondering if she hates what I am."

"Oh, surely not!"

"If they won't let her marry Jack? If they call her a security risk?"

"Oh God, they wouldn't!"

"Who knows? Look at the things that happened back in the 1950s, with that McCarthy creature. Witch hunts. It could happen again. I won't know how she feels until I get through."

Rosemary is watching her carefully, patiently. Janet concentrates upon the changing gardens on the display screen, view after view of Giverny fading one into the other.

"They'll have to restore the telephones soon," Rosemary remarks at last. "Business people are howling world-wide. The more centrist Tories are coming round, even. Imagine! Tories actually entertaining thoughts of a commercial boycott! I hear the European parliament is considering a strong resolution to embargo. It's supposed to come to a head tonight. Then we'll take it up tomorrow here, if it passes. Of course, it's just a call for embargo, not a binding act."

"The junta won't care."

"What? Half of America's wealth is in trade!"

"I know these people. They'll be willing to plunge the country into poverty, if that's what it takes to keep it isolated and under control. Of course, if they do that, they'll lose a lot of their support among the middle class and the corporate types. So what? It's a little late for those people to be changing their damn minds now."

"Yes. Rather."

"Well, I mean, that's just my opinion."

"It's one of the best we have, isn't it?"

"What?"

"Well, you have lived there." Rosemary shakes her head. "It's so odd—I read your book, and yet I thought you were being something of an alarmist. I suppose I didn't want, I suppose no one wanted to believe it possible, like that ancient novel, what was it called, the Wells?"

"*Nineteen Eighty-Four?*"

"No, that's Orwell. The other Wells fellow. It Can't Happen Here. That was it. I think."

"Well, it hasn't happened here, just there."

"Yes." Rosemary hesitates for a long moment, then sighs. "Yes, but that's quite bad enough."

Janet was always good at waiting. In discrimination cases waiting served as a weapon, asking the court for a postponement here, a recess there, playing a hard game with powerful opponents who knew that every day they waited without settling was another day for her team to gather evidence, to sway public opinion, to demand another investigation, to serve another writ. But none of those waits ever involved her daughter.

Over that first fortnight of exile, Janet evolves a ritual. Every morning she scans the news, both media and hard copy, for information about the American telephone shut-down, as the papers have taken to calling it. Then, on the off-chance that she missed something, she calls Mandi's number four times a day, mid-morning, mid-afternoon, dinner hour, late night. She never gets through. Since the junta has stopped all out-going calls, Mandi cannot call her. Janet assumes her daughter knows where she is, that she must realize, by now, that her mother will be sheltering with the woman Mandi's always considered her aunt. Every now and then some military spokesman announces that service will be restored soon, very soon. Oddly enough, the infamous Colonel Harrison has disappeared, and a new chief of public security appears now and again on the news. Janet assumes that Harrison has fallen victim to some sort of internal purge; fascists always do fall out among themselves, sooner or later.

Some news does get released: the names of casualties, the names of those imprisoned. Unlike South American dictatorships, which at least realize their crimes to be unspeakable, this junta sees no reason to conceal their victims in silences and mass graves, not when they believe themselves the agents of God on earth. Amanda Elizabeth Hansen-Corey never appears among the names, not on either list. Janet reads each three times through, very slowly, to be absolutely certain of it. By doing so she finally spots Eddie's name, spelled out formally as Jose Eduardo Rodriguez, who has been sentenced to six months imprisonment for assisting an enemy of the state.

"Oh, Eddie! How horrible, how unfair!"

Only much later does Janet realize the full significance of the charge. She herself, of course, is the enemy of the state to whom they referred. She has now been publicly branded as a criminal.

The students at the Free University call their building Major's Last Erection, a name that's been handed down for the last 40 years or so, even though few people remember who the major in question was. A prime minister, Janet tells them, not an army officer at all. Few seem to care. Several times a week she goes down to Canary Wharf, ostensibly to meet with Jonathan and the Curriculum Committee, but in reality to sit around and drink tea with a group of women students. Like most of the students at the university, Rachel, Mary, Vi, and Sherry come from working-class backgrounds; indeed, they all work, waitressing part-time, mostly, to keep themselves in school.

Vi—small, skinny, and very pale, with ash-blonde hair and watery blue eyes—always wears black, black jeans, black shirts, black cloth jackets, since she can't afford leather. Unlike the rest, she knows computers from the inside rather than merely being able to use what BritLink offers the average citizen. Her father was a repairman for the computer end of the Underground; he helped his daughter put together her own system from obsolete parts when she was seven years old.

"It was for my birthday, like," Vi tells Janet. "I was ever so pleased with it, too, all those lovely games it could play. 'Course, I'd never seen a real system then, mind.'' She grins with a flash of gold tooth. ''But it was a good time, anyway, and it got me off to a good start.''

Good start, indeed. When the other girls leave for their jobs, Vi takes Janet up to the thirteenth floor of the office building and a room officially labelled, ''Computer Laboratory.'' They march through the ranks of official students learning programming and pass through a door into a smaller room, where Vi's boyfriend, Harry, has put together another system from spare parts—but these, state of art and pilfered, probably. Janet never asks. Vi is installing a remote feed to a satellite hook-up in the pub where Rachel works over in Southwark, just a few blocks from the cathedral. This particular pub features sports on television and thus owns its weak link-up quite legitimately, but it's also close to various corporate offices with strong links and remote feeds to other satellite systems.

''Piece of cake,'' Vi says. ''Once we link up to the Goal Posts' feed, we can bleed into anything within a couple of kills.''

''Kills?''

''Sorry. Kilometres. And then.'' Vi smiles with a flash of gold. ''And then we'll see. You don't want to know any more.''

''That's very true.'' Janet grins at her. ''I don't.''

At Janet's first public lecture so many people turn up to buy tickets that the University Audio/Visual crew set up a video link to a second auditorium to accommodate the overflow. At the second lecture, scheduled for the largest hall available, two unobtrusive men in dark blue suits appear upon the platform as Janet arranges her notes. Jonathan introduces them as Sergeant Ford, Officer Patel.

''The Foreign Office thought you'd best have some protection,'' Ford remarks. ''You never know these days, do you now?''

''Ah, well, no, I suppose not.'' Janet is annoyed to find her hands shaking. She shoves them into the pockets of her blue blazer. ''You're from the Foreign Office?''

''No, ma'am. Scotland Yard. They just had a word with us, like.''

''I see. Well, thank you.''

During the lecture Ford sits on the platform while Patel stands at the back of the hall. After the lecture they follow, staying close but not too close, as she goes to lunch with Jonathan and several students. When she returns to the condominium, Patel escorts her while Ford follows in an unmarked car. At the gate to the complex, Patel has a few murmured words with a new security guard. Janet has never seen security guards at the gate before. From then on, she sees guards every day.

On the 17th day of her exile Janet receives a telephone call from the Immigration Office. Her application for political asylum is being processed. If her application is accepted, she will be issued a ''red card,'' a visa allowing employment, good for a two years' stay in Britain, at which point her case will need to be reviewed. Janet, who knows all this, senses trouble.

''Is something missing on the application?''

''Well, not exactly.'' The blonde and pink-cheeked girl on the phonevid looks sorrowful. ''It would be a good thing, you see, if you had a bank account or some sort of financial arrangement. We can't legally require this, but . . .''

Janet has heard many such ''buts,'' fading with a dying fall, in her career. ''I understand. Thank you very much. I'll attend to it.''

''Fine. Just transmit a one oh oh four seven, will you?''

''A what?''

''A change or correction to an application form. The parameters should have been transmitted with your packet.''

''Yes, of course. I do remember seeing the file now.''

On the high street in Kew stands an imposing Eurostil building, all glass front and slender columns, a branch of Barclay-Shanghai-Consolidated. Armed with several large checks, one from her publisher, another from the Free University's public affairs fund, Janet walks in one sunny afternoon to open a checking account. Does she have references?

Well, she can give them. But does she have the references with her, signed and ready? By British citizens, please. With the situation in America so dodgy, they are worried about money transfers and suchlike. Surely she understands? No, she does not understand. She has cheques drawn upon British banks in her possession, paper cheques, stamped and validated for instant deposit. Ah. Another manager must be called.

This manager, tall and grey, sports incredibly refined vowels. Janet tells her story once again, waves the cheques about, mentions Rosemary's name several times. He understands, he tells her, but with the situation in America so dodgy, they would prefer to have a British co-signer. Janet tells him, with some vehemence, that she is not a minor child or a halfwit. The manager bows several times in an oddly Japanese manner and apologizes as well. He drops his voice, leans forward in a waft of lemon-drop scent.

''The real problem is that you've not got your red card.''

''If I don't have a bank reference, I won't get one.''

He blinks rapidly several times and looks round the cream-coloured lobby. Janet does, as well, and spots a large brightly coloured poster.

''It says there that any one can open a Christmas Savings Club account. 'From nine to 90 years of age, all are welcome.' It must be a special deal, huh?''

The manager blinks again and stares.

''I want to open a Christmas Club account,'' Janet says, as calmly as she can manage. ''According to your own advertising, I may do so any time before 15th November. It is November 11th today.''

''Ah, why, so it is.'' He sighs in a long drawn-out gush of defeat. ''If you'll just step up to this counter?''

Janet deposits over a thousand pounds in her Christmas Savings Club account and receives in return a bank number, an electronic access number, and a passbook with a picture of Father Christmas on the front. Later that day, she brings up the bank's public information files on her terminal and spends several hours studying them. As she suspected, holders of one account may open another electronically. She opens herself a checking account, transfers most of her Christmas Club monies into it at a mere one per cent penalty, and has two numbers to transmit to Immigration on Form 10047.

On the 27th day after the junta killed the United States of America, their underlings restore full international telephone service to the corpse. Thompson brings Janet the news with her breakfast.

"They say the service isn't at top quality yet, Ma'am."

"As long as I can get through, I don't care."

Janet checks the time: seven o'clock here, minus eight makes damn! eleven at night there. Mandi will most likely be asleep, but Janet cannot wait. Even reaching her daughter's answering machine will be better than nothing.

Picking up the handset gives her a moment of doubt. Will this call bring Rosemary trouble? For a moment she considers the shiny plastic oblong, studded with buttons. Somewhere inside it lies the white strip of encoded optics that sum up Rosemary's identity as a communicating being. Somewhere in a vast computer is the Platonic ideal of this actual number, the electronic archetype which gives this physical object its true meaning, its being. Frail things, these archetypes, and so easy to destroy with one electric pulse, one change of code. What if the junta is automatically wiping codes that dial certain numbers? Could they do that?

Not to a British citizen's account, surely. Janet punches in Mandi's familiar number. Although the call seems to go through smoothly, after two rings a long beep interrupts. A switch of some sort—Janet can hear a different ring, oddly faint. Her hands turn sweaty—FBI? Military police? At last a voice, a taped voice:

"I'm sorry. The number you have reached is no longer in service. Please access the directory files for the area which you have attempted to call."

A click. A pause. The message begins again. Janet hangs up with a fierce curse.

Gulping coffee, she throws on a pair of jeans and a striped rugby shirt, then sits on the floor cross-legged with the keyboard and the remote wand in her lap. Switching the terminal over to remote phone mode takes a few irritating minutes, but at last she can dial on-screen and start the long process of accessing the international directory number. The British memory banks still show Mandi's numbers as functioning. She should have expected that, she supposes. When would they have had time to update? If indeed the junta will ever allow them to update.

On her next pass Janet tries the normal directory number for San Francisco. Much to her shock she reaches it. For all their talk of rebel sabotage, obviously the junta had disabled the phone system at some central source, some master switch or whatever it might be, so that it could be restored cleanly and all at once when they had need of it again. In this directory she finds Mandi's old number clearly marked as out of service.

When Janet tries a search on Mandi's name, she turns up nothing. A moment of panic—then it occurs to her to try Amanda Elizabeth Hansen-Owens, Mrs. Sure enough, such a name appears, cross-referenced to John Kennedy Owens,

Captain. *My daughter is married. I wasn't there.* In the next column, however, where a telephone number should appear, Janet finds only code: UNL-M. She windows the screen in half, leaving Mandi's entry visible, and in the Help utility finds at last the decipherment of codes. UNL-M. Unlisted, military. For a long time Janet stares at the screen. She wipes it clear and turns it off, lays the keyboard and the wand down on the carpet beside her.

At least Mandi has been allowed to marry her officer. At least. Even if the little bastard has hidden her away from her mother. Don't be ridiculous! She'll call you. She's not dumb. *She knows you're at Rosemary's. Or that Rosemary will know where you are.*

Or, Janet supposes, she herself could call friends in California and see if they know Mandi's new number. Mandi had a job in a bookshop—perhaps she could call there? But she was going to quit when she married, because she would be living on base, too far away. Perhaps her old employer will have her new number? The thought of Eddie's prison sentence stops Janet from calling him. She should wait until the situation settles down, until the normal traffic on the telephone lines picks up. Surely the junta won't be able to tap every call, surely they wouldn't bother, not just on the off-chance that she and all those other enemies of the state might say something subversive in a casual conversation.

At lunch, in a little Italian restaurant near the Houses of Parliament, Janet tells Rosemary of her morning's frustrations.

"I'm honestly afraid to put people at risk by calling them," Janet finishes up. "Or am I just being paranoid?"

"I don't know. You're quite possibly being realistic. A dreadful thought, that, but there we are." Rosemary contemplates her wine glass with a vague look of distaste. "Poor Eddie. I only met him briefly, of course, during that last flying visit, but he was such a nice fellow. It's so awful, thinking of him in prison."

"I'd hate to have the same thing happen to Mandi's boss or any of my friends."

"Well, of course. Or your nephew. What was his name? The one who's so good with horses."

"Richie. Although, you know, he's probably the safest person I could call. He lives way the hell up in the Sierras, and I can't imagine anyone suspecting him of subversion, up in that tiny little town."

"True. What about Robert?"

"Yeah. What about Robert?" Janet lays down her fork. "I went back later and looked for his number on the directory. It's been taken out of service, too. But I've never found his name on the lists. Of the prisoners, I mean." Janet's voice breaks. "Or the casualties."

Her mouth full, Rosemary nods in the best sympathy she can muster. Janet leans back in her chair, turns a little, too, to look over the crowded restaurant, and sees Patel standing at the door.

"It must be time for me to head out to the Free You," Janet says. "There's my bodyguard."

"Well, he can wait while you finish."

"I'm not hungry any more. I don't know who I'm more worried about, Mandi or Robert. Robert, I guess. At least I know now she's married."

"And she'll call. She must know that I'd provide for you, one way or another."

"Yeah. You're right. She'll call."

But Mandi never does call, not that day, not the next, not for the entire week after service is restored. Janet wakes every morning to a winter come at last, stands by her window and looks out on slate grey skies, afraid to leave the flat and miss her daughter's call, which never comes.

"I suppose she's just afraid," Rosemary says.

"I hope she doesn't hate me."

"Why should she? She's been allowed to marry Jack."

"Well, maybe so. Do you know what I really think? She's disowned me. They may even have made her do it, for all I know. But I do know she's got too much to lose by associating with me."

"Oh my god! No!" Janet shrugs, finding no words.

"I'm so sorry," Rosemary says at last. "But I think you're right."

"Yeah? So do I."

With Officer Patel trailing behind, they are walking across the plaza in front of the Free University. Around them students in long hair and American blue jeans drift by. Some wear crumbling leather jackets; others, bulging canvas coats decorated mostly with pockets. A few carry books as well as the standard terminal units.

"It's very odd, this place," Rosemary says. "Do you suppose they actually learn anything?"

"I'm about to find out. It's not exactly a new idea, though, a free university. The ones back home have been around for a long while, anyway. Well, I suppose the junta's closed them now."

"I suppose so, yes." Rosemary pauses, watching a particularly grubby couple saunter by. "Better to give them this than to have them rioting again, anyway. Not that they were real riots, compared to yours."

"Um. Maybe so." Janet stops walking and points to a small crowd, standing by the steps up to the RiverBus dock. "There's your photo op."

"Right. I see Jonathan. I suppose I'll have to wear that silly hard-hat he's carrying, even though nothing's been built yet."

Today the work starts on the new flood barrier round the university. Wearing plastic hardhats, men in suits stand uneasily next to men in work clothes wearing solid metal ones. Sandbags, the first, temporary line of defence against the river, lie scattered about and rather randomly. The media, minicams and mikes at the ready, cluster near a van serving tea in foam cups. When Rosemary trots over, Jonathan does indeed hand her the yellow hat. She puts it on as the cameras close in.

In the middle of the night Janet wakes from a dream of San Francisco in late afternoon, when light as gold and thick as honey pours down the hills and dances on the trees. There is no light in the world like the muted sun of Northern

California. Sitting up in bed she weeps, knowing that she will never see it again. She will never see her daughter again, either. She knows it at that moment with a cold hard twist of sickness in the pit of her stomach.

And she weeps the more.

The phone call from Immigration comes some ten days before Christmas. Janet's application has gone through. Would she please pick up her red card in person? They require a witnessed signature and a look at her old passport. For the occasion Janet puts on a grey suit that she's just bought at Harrods—severe trousers, a softened jacket with pleats—and wears it with a peach-coloured silk shirt suitable for a woman her age. As she combs her hair, she looks in the mirror and sees her face as a map: all the roads she's taken are engraved on her cheeks and round her eyes. For the first time in her life she feels old. *There's nothing for me to do in Britain but die here.* The image in the mirror saddens and droops. What can she do against the men who taken over her homeland? She can write and lecture, yes, but it's so little, so weak, so futile. Perhaps she should just give up, live out her last years as an exile, write poetry, maybe, teach for a pittance at the Free University and keep her mouth shut. *My big mouth. Look at all the trouble it's gotten me into.*

She turns and hurls the comb across the room. It bounces on the bed, then slides to the floor with a rattle.

"I will not give up. I'm only a mosquito, maybe, on their ugly hide, but goddamn it, I'll draw what blood I can."

During the cab ride down to the Immigration offices, Janet begins planning her next book. Since her research material has no doubt been confiscated by the junta, she will have to write a personal memoir, hazy on hard facts, but if she works on the prose, she can make it sting. She will dedicate it to Mandi, she thinks, then changes her mind. She refuses to make danger be her last gift to her daughter.

Picking up her red card turns out to be easy and anti-climatic. Two clerks look at her passport, one asks her to sign various documents. In front of the pair Janet promises, quite sincerely, that she will refrain from attempting to overthrow the British government. The first clerk hands her a packet of paper documents and the small red card, laminated in plastic.

"Keep this with you at all times," he says. "And your passport, I suppose. We've not had any guide lines on that, but you might as well."

"Thanks, then, I will."

When she leaves the building, Janet finds herself thinking of her mother, of her mother's house up in Goldust, her nephew's house, now. It was a wonderful place to be a child, that house, with the mountains hanging so close and the big trees all round. She remembers hunting for lizards in rock walls and rescuing birds from her mother's cats, remembers thunderstorms bursting and booming over the high mountains as well as drowsy days of sun and the scent of pine. What if she had never left the mountains? What if she'd married Jimmy, the boy in high school who loved her, married him and settled down to get pregnant the way most girls did up in the mountains, or maybe taken a job in the drugstore till the babies came. She wouldn't be an exile now, drifting down the streets of a city that will never be hers, no matter how much she loves it. She would have gone crazy, probably. She reminds herself sharply of that. She always knew that she would have to leave Goldust from the day she learned to read and found a wider world beyond the hills.

But Mandi would have been happy in that house. She loved visiting her grandmother. Mandi might have been happy living in Goldust, too, safe and tucked away from the world.

Driven by her memories, Janet finds herself drifting to the nearest card phone, built into a red plastic slab inside a red plastic kiosk, sheltered from the sound of traffic plunging past. While she fumbles through her wallet, out the door she sees long lawns behind wrought iron fences. It should be safe to call Richie, it really should. Why would the authorities bother her nephew, a rural teamster? But he might know where Mandi is, he really just might know.

When Janet slides the card through the slot, she can feel her shoulders tense and hunch. With shaking fingers she punches in the code, hears other beeps, and then rings. The phone is ringing. By the most slender of all links she's connected again, for this brief moment, to the Sierra, to Goldust, to what was once her mother's house. She can picture the yellow telephone, sitting on Richie's old-fashioned wood slab desk, right next to the pictures of his family in their red acrylic frames. Three rings, four—a click, and the room changes. She can think of it no other way, that the piece of space at the other end of the line has changed, grown larger, as if she could see the shabby wicker furniture, scattered with cats.

"Hello." The sound of Richie's voice brings tears to her eyes. "You have reached 555–5252. Richie, Allie, and Robert aren't home right now. Please leave us a message, and we'll call you back."

Another click, a long tone. Janet hesitates, then hangs up fast. She cannot risk leaving a message, tangible evidence to some kangaroo court, perhaps, that Richie knows a traitor. As she takes her card out of the slot, the names she heard finally register. And Robert. Not just Richie's name, not just his wife's name, but Robert's name as well.

"He made it to the mountains. Oh thank god."

Janet reaches for her wallet to put the card away, but her fingers slip on the vinyl, and she nearly drops her purse. She glances round: two people have queued up to use the phone. Her paranoia stands at the head of the line. What are they really, this Pakistani woman in the pale grey suit, this Englishman in pinstripes? Agents, maybe? She pretends to drop her purse to gain a little time, squats, cooing unheard apologies, collects her things, shoves the card away along with the wallet and the handkerchief, her stylus and her notebook, her US passport that used to mean so much. With a gulp of breath she stands, settles the purse on her shoulder, and lays a hand on the door. The Englishman is looking at his watch. The Pakistani woman is studying a tiny address book.

Janet gulps again, then swings the door wide and steps out. The Pakistani woman slips into the booth; the Englishman drifts closer to the door; neither so much as look her way as she strides off, heading blindly toward the gate into the park, searching for the safety of green and growing things. In the rising wind leafless trees rustle. Out on the ponds ducks glide. Janet smiles at them all like an idiot child. Robert is free, will most likely stay that way, because indeed, the junta have no reason to hunt him down, the apolitical artist, the popular teacher of the least political subject in the world.

But no news of Mandi. She watches the ducks glide back and forth, the midges hovering at the water's edge, while she tries to make up her mind once and for all. Will she dare call Richie again? It was stupid of her to endanger him at all, stupid and selfish. At least if the military police do try to trace that call, all they'll get is the number of a public phone near Green Park. *My daughter. I don't dare call my daughter.* She doesn't want me to. She feels her joy at Robert's safety crumple like a piece of paper in a fist. She sobs, staring at an alien lawn, at the roots of alien trees. Overhead white clouds pile and glide as the wind picks up strong.

Rain falls in curtains, twisting across the Thames. In yellow slickers men bend and haul, throw and pile sandbags in a levee six bags across and as high as they can make it. The thin yellow line, Janet thinks to herself. In a slicker of her own she stands on the RiverBus dock and watches a red lorry, heaped with sandbags, drive down the grey street toward the workers. Struggling with a bent umbrella Vi scurries to join her. Drops gleam in her pale blonde hair.

"Dr Richards tells me you got your red card."

"Yesterday morning, yeah. There apparently wasn't any problem. Just the usual bureaucracy stuff. The guy who needed to sign the red card was on vacation. That's all."

"That's super."

"Well, yeah. I'm glad, of course." Janet turns away to watch the men unloading the lorry. "I wasn't looking forward to being deported and thrown in prison."

"We wouldn't a let that happen. Me and the girls, we'd a thought of something. Hidden you out, y'know? here and there. There's a lot of us, y'know, all over this bleeding island. Girls like me and Rach and Mary and the lot. We think you're super, y'know, we really do, and we're networked."

"Do you?" For a moment Janet cannot speak. She recovers herself with a long swallow. "Thanks. I'm kind of glad I don't have to take you up on that."

" 'Course not. It wouldn't a been any fun." Vi grins, a twisted little smile. "But you've got the asylum, so it doesn't matter, right?"

"Right. But tell everyone I really appreciate it."

"I will, don't worry. Look." Vi pauses for a glance round. "We've got the feed working. Is there anything you want us to search for?"

I could ask them to get Mandi's number. I bet they could. Piece of cake, breaking into a military phone book. Yet she cannot ask, her mouth seems paralysed. What if they find the number, what if she calls only to have Mandi cut her off, what if Mandi makes it clear, undeniably once and for finally all that she never ever wants her mother to call again? Vi is waiting, smiling a little. Janet could ask her. They'd find the number, she and Harry.

"Well, actually," Janet says. "What I really need is my notes and stuff, all my research banks. But the military confiscated my computer, I'm sure of that. If it's not even plugged in, you won't be able to reach it."

"Oh, I dunno. What if they downloaded everything to some central bank, like? I'll bet they're like the Inquisition was, filing everything away, keeping all the heresies nice and tidy."

"I never thought of that."

"But now, that'll take us a while to figure out. I know, you start writing down everything you can remember, file names, codes, anything at all. That'll give us something to match, like, if we find their central banks." Vi grins again. "And that's what we'll want, anyway, their central banks."

"Yeah, I just bet it is."

"And if you think of anything else, you just tell me, and we'll see what we can do."

"I will, Vi. Thanks. Thanks a whole lot."

But she knows now that she'll never ask for Mandi's number, knows that having it would be too great a temptation to call, to late one night break down and punch code only to hear her daughter hang up the handset as fast as she can.

"Bleeding cold out here," Vi says. "Coming inside?"

"In a minute."

She hears the umbrella rustle, hears Vi walk a few steps off. The girl will wait, she supposes, until she decides to go in. Yellow slickers flapping, the workmen turn and swing, heaving the sandbags onto the levee. The Thames slides by, brown under a grey sky.

"Riverrun," Janet says. "These fragments I have shored against my ruins."

She turns and follows Vi inside.

RED ELVIS

Walter Jon Williams

As the twig is bent, the adage assures us, so the tree inclines. And, as the ingenious story that follows makes quite clear, *some* of the directions in which the tree can bend are very surprising indeed . . .

Walter Jon Williams was born in Minnesota and now lives in Albuquerque, New Mexico. His stories have appeared in our Third, Fourth, Fifth, Sixth, Ninth, and Eleventh Annual Collections. His novels include *Ambassador of Progress*, *Knight Moves*, *Hardwired*, *The Crown Jewels*, *Voice of the Whirlwind*, *House of Shards*, *Days of Atonement*, and the critically acclaimed *Aristoi*. His short fiction has been gathered in the collection *Facets*. A new novel, *Metropolitian*, has just been published.

Here it is, the white house south of the city on US 51. The Memphis Palace of Labor. The district is called Whitehaven and is tony, but the Palace itself sits on the highway opposite some ugly strip malls, a John Deere dealer, and a burger joint.

It's a big house made of Tennessee fieldstone, with a portico and a green lawn and some little mean shacks out back for the servants. It's not the sort of place you'd expect at all, not for the person who lived there. It's the sort of house a boss would live in.

There's a long, long line of mourners out front, stretching from the front door across the drive and for half a mile down Highway 51. The harmonies of a black gospel choir sound faintly from the interior.

Join the long, slow line of mourners who file past the coffin. Hear the music that rings somehow inside you.

Remember who the dead man was, and why you're here.

The boy knows that he had a brother who is just like him, except that he is an angel. They were twins—identical twins, because there was the same webbing between two of their toes—and the eldest lived and the youngest was born dead. And the boy's Mamma tells him that this fact makes him special, that even before he was born, he made his brother an angel.

But that doesn't mean that the boy can't talk to his brother when he wants to. His Mamma takes him to the cemetery often, and the two of them sit by the brother's grave and pray to him and sing songs and tell him everything that happened since they last visited.

The boy likes the cemetery. It's so much more pleasant than the family's little two-room shanty in East Tupelo, where the wind cries like a wailing haunt through the gray clapboard walls and the furniture needs mending and the slop bucket under the sink always smells poorly.

In the cemetery, the boy can always talk to his brother and tell him everything. In the cemetery, someone is always bringing flowers.

Something bad has happened and the boy has lost his Daddy. Men with badges came and took him away. He hears new words—there is "forgery" and "arrest," along with a word whose very utterance is an occasion for terror—"Parchman." Parchman is where Daddy is going, and a man named Orville Bean is sending him there. Orville Bean is Daddy's boss.

The boy screams and weeps and clings to his Mamma's leg. The men with badges told Mamma that the family has to leave the house. The boy always thought the house belonged to Mamma, but now it belongs to Orville Bean. Suddenly the gray two-room shack is the most precious thing the boy has ever known.

Mamma pets him and calls him by his special name, but the boy won't be stilled. Grandpa and Grandma, who have come to help Mamma move the furniture, watch the boy's agony with a certain surprise.

"That Mr. Bean sure is cruel," Grandpa says. "Boss don't have no mercy on a working man."

That night the boy prays to his brother to rescue Daddy, to fly him out of Parchman on angels' wings, but his brother doesn't answer.

Mamma's real name is Satnin, though everyone else calls her Gladys. She and the boy are never apart. She won't let the boy do anything that might hurt him, like swim or dive, or play with other children outside of Mamma's sight. He sleeps with Satnin every night so that nothing can harm him.

Satnin teaches him things to keep him safe. He learns to touch iron after he sees a black cat, and that if you have a spell cast on you, you can take the spell off with a Jack, which is a red cloth filled with coal dust and dirt and a silver dime. The boy learns that most dreams aren't true but that some are, and that Satnin's dreams are almost always true. When she dreams about something bad that's going to happen, she'll do something to prevent it, like make a cake, with special ingredients, that she'll feed to a dog to carry the bad luck away.

After Daddy comes back from Parchman, he gets a job in a war plant in Memphis, so he's home only on weekends. The boy spends all his time with his mother.

When the boy grows old enough for school, his Mamma walks with him to school every morning, then home in the afternoon. They still visit the cemetery regularly so that the boy can talk to his brother, who is an angel.

Sometimes the boy thinks he can hear his brother's voice. "I will always be with you," his brother says. "I am in Heaven and you are special and I will watch out for you always."

* * *

The boy is a Christian, which is good because when he dies, he will go to
Heaven and see his brother. The boy and Satnin and Daddy go to the Assembly
of God Church in East Tupelo, and they sing along with Daddy's cousin Sayles,
who is in the choir. The Reverend Smith is a nice, quiet man who teaches the
boy a few chords on the guitar.

In the Church, the boy receives his baptism of the spirit and gives away
everything he owns to other children. His comic books and his bike and all his
money. His Daddy keeps bringing the bike back, but the boy only gives it away
again. Finally his Daddy gives up and lets the boy give the bike away for good.

"You are a good boy to give everything away," his brother whispers. "We
will live together in Heaven and be happy forever."

The family moves to Memphis so that Daddy can find work. The boy is sad
about leaving his brother behind in the cemetery, but his brother tells him that
he is really in Heaven, not the cemetery, and the boy can still talk to him anytime
he likes.

The family lives in the Lauderdale Courts, part of the projects run by the
Housing Authority. Everyone in the projects works except for Satnin, who spends
all her time with her boy. Daddy has a job at United Paint, but he can't earn
too much or the Housing Authority will make the family move.

"They never let a workingman get ahead," he says.

The boy goes to Humes High School, where he's in the ninth grade. Mamma
still walks him to and from school every day, but the boy has his own bed now,
and he sleeps alone. He has nightmares almost every night and doesn't know
why.

Sometimes he takes his guitar outside to the steps of the Lauderdale Courts
and sings. People from the projects always stop what they're doing and form a
half circle around him and listen. It's as if they're bewitched. Their staring
makes the boy so self-conscious that he sings only after dark, so that he doesn't
have to see the way they look at him.

He looks in the mirror and sees this little cracker kid in overalls, nothing he
wants to be. He tries to make what he sees better. One time he has Satnin give
his fine, blond hair a permanent. Another time he cuts his hair off except for a
Mohawk strip down the middle.

One day, during summer vacation, the boy goes to the picture show and sees
The City Across the River, with a new actor named Tony Curtis. He watches
entranced at the story of the poor working kids who belong to a gang called the
"Amboy Dukes," and who wear flashy clothes and have their hair different
from anyone the boy has ever seen. Tony Curtis's hair is perfect, long and shiny,
winged on the sides, with a curl in the front and upturned in back. He talks in
a funny jivey way, singsong, almost like he has his own language. It's like the
language the boy's brother speaks in dreams.

The boy watches the movie three times.

Next day he goes to a hairdresser. He knows he'll never get the haircut he
wants in a barbershop. "Give me that Tony Curtis cut," he says to the astonished
beautician. The boy describes what he wants and the beautician tells him the

cut is called a D.A. The beautician cuts his hair, but she warns him that his blond hair is too fine to stay in the shape he wants it, and sells him a tin of Royal Crown Pomade. The pomade darkens his hair by several shades but keeps it in place and makes it gleam.

The only place the boy can think to find the right clothes is on Beale Street. It's in the colored part of town where people are killed every week, then carried away so their bodies will be found somewhere else. The boy is a little nervous going there alone, but it's daylight and it looks safe enough, and as he walks down the street, he can see colored men dressed just as he wants to be, in raw-silk jackets dyed lime green or baby blue, with Billy Eckstine collars worn turned up.

The boy finds what he wants in Lansky Brothers' store. Pleated, shiny-black pants worn high on the floating ribs, with red or yellow seams. Double-breasted jackets in glowing colors, with huge vents and sparkles in them, big enough to move around in.

He spends all his money at Lansky Brothers.

Next time he looks in the mirror, he likes what he sees.

Maybe everyone in Heaven looks like this.

In his nightmares, the boy is surrounded by enemies, all of them jeering and laughing at him. He fights them, lashing out with his fists, and often wakes with smarting knuckles from having jumped out of bed and punched the wall.

When the nightmares come true, he doesn't fight. He can't—there are too many of them, the biggest, toughest kids in school, surrounding him and calling him names. They say he dresses like a nigra pimp. They call him a sissy, a queer. He doesn't quite know what a queer is, but he knows it's bad. They threaten to cut his hair off. They knock him around every day, a jeering circle of crackers in overalls with muscles bulging out of their plaid shirts—they're everything the boy wants to get away from, everything he doesn't want to be.

In his dreams, he fights back, screaming wildly, sometimes running out of the apartment and into the hall-way before he wakes. His mother makes him a charm to wear around his neck, a charm that smells of asafoetida and has a black-cat bone in it, but it doesn't keep the dreams away. His mother says he gets it from his father, who also has bad nightmares from time to time.

One day the other boys are pushing him around in the toilets. The air is blue with tobacco smoke. The boy has been bounced into the walls a few times and is being held in a headlock by one football lineman while another waves a pair of shears and threatens to cut his hair.

"I'd stop that if I were you." The voice comes from a newcomer, a big kid with a Yankee accent and the thick neck of an athlete. He's got a big jaw and a look that seems a little puzzling and unbalanced, as if his eyes are pointing in slightly different directions. His name is Schmidt and he's just transferred here from Detroit.

"You cut his hair," Schmidt says, "you better cut mine, too."

The big kids drop the boy and stand aside and mumble. The boy straightens his clothes and tries to thank Schmidt for intervening.

"Call me Leon," the big boy says.

The boy and Leon become friends. Leon plays guitar a little and sings, and the two of them go together to a party. Leon sings a Woody Guthrie song, and the boy plays accompaniment. Then the boy turns all the lights off, so he won't get self-conscious, and sings an Eddie Arnold tune, "Won't You Tell Me, Molly Darling." All the party noise stops as the other kids listen. The boy finishes the tune.

"Your turn," he says to Leon.

"Brother," Leon says, "no way I'm gonna follow that."

The boy sings all night, with Leon strumming accompaniment and singing harmony. The darkness is very friendly. The other kids listen in silence except for their applause.

Maybe, he thinks, this is what Heaven is like.

Leon is an orphan. His father died in a strike against Henry Ford just after he was born, and he'd moved South after his mother married again, this time to a truck driver whose outfit was based in Memphis.

Hearing the story of Leon's father dying after a beating by Ford strikebreakers, the boy hears an echo of his grandfather's voice: *Boss don't have no mercy on a workingman.*

Leon is always reading. The boy never had a friend who read before. The authors seem very intimidating, with names like Strachey and Hilferding and Sternberg.

"You heard Nat Dee yet?" Leon asks. He turns his radio to WDIA. He has to turn up the volume because WDIA broadcasts at only two hundred and fifty watts.

The voice the boy hears is colored and talks so fast the boy can barely make out the words. He's announcing a song by Bukka White, recorded in Parchman Prison in Mississippi.

Parchman Prison, the boy thinks.

Nat Dee's voice is a little difficult, but the boy understands the music very well.

The singer launches himself at the microphone stand like it's his worst enemy. He knocks it down and straddles it, grabbing it near the top as if he's wringing its neck. He wears a pink see-through blouse and a blazing pink suit with black velvet trim. His eyes are made ghostly with mascara and heavy green eye shadow. He's playing the Gator Bowl in front of fourteen thousand people.

The second he appeared, a strange sound went up, a weird keening that sent hairs crawling on the necks of half the men in the audience. The sound of thousands of young girls working themselves into a frenzy.

The sound sometimes makes it difficult for the singer to hear his band, but he can always turn and see them solid behind him, Leon mimicking the Scotty Moore guitar arrangements from the records, Bill Black slapping bass, and drummer D.J. laying down the solid beat that the singer's music thrives on.

The singer has finally wrung the mike stand into submission. He rears back perilously far, right on the edge of balance, and he hops forward with little thrusts of his polished heels, holding the mike stand up above his head like a jazzman wailing sax. He thrusts his pelvis right at the audience, and the long rubber tube he's stuck down his pants in front is perfectly outlined by the taut fabric.

The eerie sound that rises from the audience goes up in intensity, in volume. State police in front of the stage are flinging little girls back as they try to rush forward. All over the South, people are denouncing his act as obscene.

Incredibly, the singer is only one of the half-dozen opening acts for Hank Snow. But some of the other performers, the Davis Sisters and the Wilburn Brothers, complain that they can't follow him onstage, so he was given the coveted slot just before the intermission.

After the recess, the headliners Slim Whitman and Hank Snow will step onstage and try to restore the program to some kind of order. Some nights they have their work cut out for them.

The singer still has nightmares every night. Satnin persuaded him to hire his cousins, Gene and Junior Smith, to sleep in the same room with him and keep him from injuring himself.

When the singer finishes his act, he's soaked in sweat. He grins into the mike, tosses his head to clear his long hair from his eyes, speaks to the audience. "Thank you, ladies and gentlemen," he says. Then he gives a wink. "Girls," he promises, "I'll see you backstage."

The screaming doubles in volume. The singer waves good-bye and starts to head off, and then out of the slant of his eye, he sees the line of state cops go down before an avalanche of little girls as if they were made of cardboard.

The singer runs for it, his terrified band at his heels. He dives down into the tunnels under the Gator Bowl, where the concrete echoes his pursuers' shrill screams. The flimsy door to his dressing room doesn't keep them out for a second. His cousins Gene and Junior Smith go down fighting. The terrified singer leaps onto the shower stall, and even there, one frantic girl in white gloves and crinolines manages to tear off one of his shoes. The singer stares at her in fascination, at the desperate, inhuman glitter in her eyes as she snatches her trophy, and he wonders what kind of beast he's liberated in her, what it is that's just exploded out of all the restraining apparel, the girdle and nylons and starched underskirts.

He doesn't know quite what it is, but he knows he likes it.

Eventually reinforcements arrive and the girls are driven out. The dressing room looks as if it has been through a hurricane. Junior Smith, a veteran of Korea, appears as if he's just relived Porkchop Hill. The singer limps on one shoe and one pink sock as he surveys the damage.

Leon wanders in, clutching his guitar. The band's first impulse had been to protect their instruments rather than their singer.

"I wouldn't make no more promises to them girls," Leon says. He talks more Southern every day.

Hank Snow arrives with a bottle of Dr Pepper in his hand. One of his business associates is with him, a bald fat man who carries an elephant-headed cane.

"I never seen nothing like it," Snow says. "Boy, you're gonna go far in this business if your fans don't kill you first."

"Junior," the singer says, "see if you can find me a pair of shoes, okay?"

"Sure, boss," Junior says.

Hank Snow points to the fat man. "I'd like to introduce a friend of mine—he manages Hank Snow Productions for me. Colonel Tom Parker."

The Colonel has a powerful blue gaze and a grip of iron. He looks at the singer in a way that makes him feel uncomfortable—it's the same look the little girl gave him, like he wants more than anyone can say, more than the singer can ever give. "I've been hearing a lot about you," the Colonel says. "Maybe you and me can do some business."

Colonel Parker does the singer a lot of good. He straightens out the tangled mess of the singer's management, puts him under exclusive contract, gets his records played north of the Mason-Dixon line, and gets a big advance from RCA that lets the singer buy his Satnin a Cadillac. Then he buys several more for himself and his band.

"I want to look good for this car," Satnin says. "I'm going to lose some weight."

Suddenly the singer is supporting his whole family. His Daddy quits his job and never takes another. Gene and Junior work for him. His Grandmother is living with his parents. Sometimes he thinks about it and gets a little scared.

But mostly he doesn't have much time to think. He and his band are on tour constantly, mostly across the South, their nights spent speeding from one engagement to another in a long line of Cadillacs, each one a different color and fronted by a half ton of solid chrome. Sometimes the cops stop him, but it's only for autographs.

"That Colonel, he's a snake-oil salesman for sure," Leon says. He's sitting in the shotgun seat while the singer drives across Georgia at three in the morning. "You better keep an eye on him."

"Ain't gonna let him cheat me," the singer says. The speedometer reads a hundred twenty-five. He laughs. "He sure is good with that hypnotism thing he does. Did you see Gene on his hands and knees, barking like a dog?"

Leon gazes at him significantly. "Do me a big favor. Don't ever let him hypnotize you."

The singer gives him a startled look, then jerks his attention back to the road. "Can't hypnotize me any way," he says, thinking of the power of the Colonel's ice-blue eyes.

"Don't let him try. He's done you a lot of good, okay. But that's just business. He doesn't own you."

"He's gonna get me a screen test with Hal Wallis."

"That's good. But don't let the Colonel or Wallis or any of those tell you what to do. You know best."

"Okay."

"*You* pick your music. *You* work out the arrangements. You need to insist on that, because these other people—" Leon waves a hand as if pulling difficult ideas out of the air. "You've got the magic, okay? They don't even know what the magic *is*. They're just bosses, and they'll use you for every dollar you can give them."

"Boss don't have no mercy on a workingman," the singer says.

Leon favors him with a smile. "That's right, big man. And don't you forget it."

The singer buys the big white house out on Highway 51, the place called Graceland. Because he's on the road so much, he doesn't spend a lot of time there. His parents live out back and install a chicken coop and a hog pen so they have something to do.

On the road, he's learned that he likes the night. He visits the South's little sin towns, Phenix City or Norfolk or Bossier City, cruising for girls he can take back to his cheap motel rooms.

When he's home in Memphis, there's no place he can go at night—Beale Street is still for colored people. So he has the state cops close off a piece of highway for motorcycle racing. He dresses up in his leathers, with his little peaked cap, and cranks his panhead Harley to well over a hundred. He does incredibly dangerous stunts at high speed—standing up on the foot pegs with his hands outstretched, away from the handlebars; reaching out to hold hands with the guy he's racing with. He's a hairbreadth from death or injury the whole time.

He thinks about the kids in school who called him a sissy, and snarls. When he's wound up the Harley and is howling down the road with the huge engine vibrating between his legs, he knows that the cry of wind in his ears is really his brother's voice, calling him home.

"What is this business?" the singer demands. "Some old burlesque comic? An Irish tenor? *Performing midgets?*"

"The Heidelberg Troupe of Performing Midgets." The Colonel grins around his cigar. "Great act. Know 'em from my carny days."

"*Carny* days?" Leon asks. "What're you trying to do, turn us into a freak show?"

The Colonel scowls at Leon. He knows who's put the singer up to this. "Why should we hire a rock act to open?" he says. "It costs money to hire Johnny Cash or Carl Perkins, and all they do is imitations of our boy anyway. We can get the vaudeville acts a lot cheaper—hell, they're happy to have the work."

"They'll make me look ridiculous," the singer says. His blond hair is dyed black for the movies he's making for Hal Wallis. He wants badly to be the next James Dean, but the critics compare him to Sonny Tufts.

The Colonel chomps down on his cigar again. "Gotta have opening acts," he says. "Since nobody's gonna pay attention to 'em anyway, we might as well have the cheap ones. More money for the rest of us that way."

"That was something—" the singer begins. He casts an uneasy look toward Leon, then turns back to the Colonel. "We had an idea. Why do we need opening acts at all?"

Puzzlement enters the Colonel's blue eyes. "Gotta have 'em," he says. "The marks'll feel cheated 'less they get their money's worth. And you gotta have an intermission between the opening acts and the main show so you can sell drinks and programs and souvenirs."

"So we'll give them their money's worth *without* an opening act," Leon says.

"We'll just play two sets' worth of music with an intermission in between."
He looks at the singer. "The big man's willing."

"Hell, yes," the singer says.

"Save all the money you'd waste on those opening acts," Leon says. "And
you don't have to pay good money to ship a dozen midgets around the country,
either."

The Colonel considers this. He looks at the singer. "You're really willin' to
do this?"

The singer shrugs. "Sure. I *like* being onstage."

"You'll have to do more than the five or six songs you do now."

"Plenty of songs out there."

The Colonel's eyes glitter. Everyone knows he gets kickbacks from writers
who offer their songs to the singer. He nods slowly.

"Okay," he says. "This sure seems worth a thought."

And then his eyes move to Leon and turn cold.

Someday there's going to be an accounting.

The story in *Billboard* says that the singer has cut a special deal with the Army,
that when he's drafted, he's going into Special Services and entertain the troops.
It says he won't even have to cut his hair.

It's an absolute lie. The singer has an understanding with his draft board,
that's true, but it's only that he should get some advance notice if he's going to
be called up.

He hasn't even had his physical yet.

"Where is this coming from?" the singer demands.

Leon thinks for a moment. "This is *Billboard*, not some fan magazine. They
must have got the story from somewhere."

"Who could have told them such a thing?"

Leon looks like he wants to say something but decides not to. The singer has
enough on his mind.

Satnin is grieved and ailing. She's turning yellow with jaundice and nobody
knows why. Her weight keeps going up in spite of the dozens of diet pills she
takes every day. When her boy isn't with her, she stays drunk all the time. The
thought of her mortality makes the singer frantic with anxiety.

The story about the draft keeps getting bigger. When the singer goes on tour,
reporters ask him about the Army all the time. He can't figure out what's getting
them so stirred up.

He keeps in touch with Memphis by phone. And when Satnin goes into a
hospital, he cancels the tour and is on the next train.

She rallies a bit when she sees her boy. But within twenty-four hours, she
fails and dies.

The next sound that comes from her hospital room is even more eerie than
the sound of the singer's massed fans. Hospital personnel and bystanders stop,
listen in rising horror, then flee.

The family is keening over Satnin. It's an Appalachian custom, and the good
burghers of Memphis have never heard such a thing. The singer's powerful voice

rises, dominates the rest of his family, his wails of grief echoing down the corridor. Waiting outside, Leon can feel the hairs rise on his neck. It's the most terrifying thing he's ever heard.

The funeral takes place in the big house on Highway 51. It's a circus. The gates are open, and strangers wander around the house and grounds and take things. The Colonel tries to keep order, but nobody listens to him. Reporters take the best seats at the service and snap pictures of everything.

The singer is frantic and crazed with grief. He keeps dragging people over to admire Satnin in her coffin. He spends hours talking to the corpse in some language of his own. Leon calls for a doctor to give him a sedative, but the doctor can't make it through the mass of people waiting outside the gates. The crowds are so huge that the state police have to close the highway.

At the funeral, the singer throws himself into the grave and demands to be buried with his Mamma. His friends have to drag him away.

Unbelievably, a reporter chooses this moment to ask the singer about the Army. The singer stares in disbelief.

"Ain't gonna go in no Army!" he shouts, and then his friends pull him away to his limousine. The doctor finally arrives and puts him to sleep.

The next day, there are headlines.

"We ain't at war," the singer says. "Why does anyone care about the damn Army anyway? Why cain't they leave a man alone?"

It's two days since the funeral, and the singer has spent the intervening time in a drugged stupor. He sits in a huge velour-covered chair in a room swathed in red velvet. Newspapers open to their screaming headlines surround his chair.

"Somebody's planting these stories," Leon tells him. "We all know that. And if you think about it, you know who it's got to be."

The singer just stares at him with drug-dulled eyes.

"The Colonel," Leon says. "It's got to be the Colonel."

The singer thinks about it. "Don't make no sense," he says. "Colonel don't make no money when I'm in the service."

"But he gets control," Leon says. "You can't look after your affairs if you're away. You'll have to put him in charge of everything and trust him. He'll have to renegotiate your RCA contract, your movie contract. When you get back, he'll be the one in charge."

The singer stares at him and says nothing.

"He's just some goddam carnival barker, brother," Leon says. "All he does now is arrange your bookings—anyone can do that. He isn't even a real colonel. He just wants to be the boss in the big house and keep you working in his cotton fields for the rest of your life."

"Orville Bean," the singer says. Leon doesn't understand, but this doesn't stop him.

"And you don't need the damn Army," Leon says. "All it does is protect bosses like the Colonel and their money. What's the Army ever done for you?"

"Ain't gonna go in no Army," the singer says.

"The draft board *has* to call you up after all this. The newspapers won't let them do anything else. What're you gonna tell 'em?"

"Have the Colonel work out something."

"The Colonel *wants* you in the Army."

The singer closes his eyes and lolls his head back in the big velour chair. He wishes everyone would go away and leave him alone. He strains his mind, trying to find an answer.

Make the Colonel do what you want.

The singer starts awake. He's heard the voice plainly, but he knows Leon hasn't spoken.

He realizes it was his brother's voice, calling to him from the Beyond.

The singer calls the Colonel on the phone and tells him that if he receives his draft notice, the first thing he'll do is fire Thomas Andrew Parker. The Colonel is staggered.

He says it's too late. The singer only repeats his demand and hangs up.

He manages to avoid seeing the Colonel for another week, and then the Colonel comes anyway. The singer agrees to meet him and wishes that Leon wasn't in town visiting his mom.

The Colonel walks into the den, leaning hard on his elephant-head cane, and drops heavily into a chair. He looks pale and sweaty and he keeps massaging his left arm. He explains that he's talked to every man on the draft board, that public opinion is forcing them to call the singer up. The Colonel has offered them colossal bribes, but it appears they're all honest citizens.

"Ain't changed my mind," the singer says. "You keep me out of the Army, or you and me are through."

"I can't," the Colonel protests. His powerful blue eyes are hollow.

"Then you and me are finished the second that notice gets here."

"Listen. There's a chance. The medical—" the Colonel starts, and then he gasps, his mouth open, and clutches at his left arm. His mouth works and he doesn't say anything.

Heart attack. His brother's voice. *Don't do anything.*

The singer knows the Colonel already had a heart attack a few years ago. He's old and fat and deserves exactly what he's going to get.

The Colonel's eyes plead with the singer. The singer just watches him. The Colonel begins moving slowly, his hand reaching for the elephant-head cane he's propped against a table.

Take the cane, the angel voice says. The singer takes the cane and holds it while the Colonel topples off his chair and starts to crawl toward the door. And then the Colonel falls over and doesn't move anymore.

"Ain't gonna have no more bosses," the singer says.

"Not gonna fight for no rich people," the singer says to reporters.

He doesn't give a damn about the firestorm that follows. He takes his motorcycle out onto the highways and blasts along at full speed and tries to listen to what his brother is telling him.

Leon tells him a lot, too. He reads him passages from a book called *Capital*.

He explains about workers and bosses and how bosses make money by exploiting workers. It's everything the singer ever learned from his family, from his days as a truck driver after high school. Leon explains how he's a Marxist-Leninist.

"Isn't that the same as a Communist?" the singer asks. Leon's answer is long and involved and has a lot of historical digressions. But the angel voice that whispers inside the singer speaks simple sense:

Doesn't matter what people call it, it only matters that it's true.

There are bonfires out on Highway 51 now, the singer's records going up in flames. To the American public it looks as if their worst fears are confirmed, that the singer, driving girls into a sexual frenzy with his degenerate Negro music, is an agent of Moscow as well as of Satan. Outside the gate of the house are weeping girls begging him to repent. His brother's grave in East Tupelo is vandalized, so the singer has both his brother's body and Satnin's exhumed and reburied at Graceland.

Every booking has been canceled. The movie contract is gone. The singer doesn't care, because for the first time in his life, the nightmares are gone and he can sleep at night. The singer is going to Party meetings and making the members nervous, because crowds of reporters are still following him around and snapping pictures of everyone.

Johnny Cash and Jerry Lee Lewis tell anyone who'll listen that they're country singers. Ricky Nelson starts covering Dean Martin tunes. Little Richard goes into the church. Rock and roll is finished.

"Plenty of bookings in Europe, comrade," Leon says.

So the singer plays Europe, but he's playing clubs, not auditoriums or stadiums. His Daddy and Grandma stay home and take care of his house. The singer's European audiences are a strange mixture of teenage girls and thin intellectuals who wear glasses and smoke cigarettes. Gene and Junior Smith are still with him, protecting him from fanatics who might want to hurt him, or the strange, intense people who want to discourse on the class origins of his appeal. It seems to the singer that the Left doesn't understand rock and roll. Leon calmly says that sooner or later, they'll figure it out.

All the professional songwriters who kept him supplied with material are long gone. So are Scotty and the others who helped with the arrangements. He picks his own tunes. He has a new band, working-class British kids who worship the ground he walks on. The Party wants him to sing folk songs and songs about the Struggle. He obliges, but he rocks them up, and that doesn't seem to please them, so he just goes back to singing the blues.

He records in little studios in Italy and Germany that are even more primitive than the Sun studio in Memphis. He teaches them a trick or two—he knows how to create the Sun sound by putting a second mike behind his head and arranging for a slight delay between the two to produce Sam Phillips' trademark echo effect.

The records are carried into America in the holds of freighters. There's a surprising demand for them. There's even a story in the papers about a Navy sailor courtmartialed for having some of his 45s in his locker.

His voice fills out. He's got three and a half octaves and he uses them brilliantly—his chest voice is powerful and evocative, his high notes clear and resonant. He wishes he had a bigger audience now that he knows so much more about the music.

Don't matter who listens so long as you sing it right, his brother says. The singer knows his brother always speaks the truth.

The singer is appalled by his tour of the East. It's taken him forever to get permission, and he's succeeded only because some kind of propaganda coup is necessary. Comrade Khrushchev has just built a wall in Berlin to keep out American spies, and he's demanded solidarity from Socialists everywhere.

Still, the singer can't believe the people he's got opening for him. Jugglers. Trained seals. A couple of clowns. A drill team from the Czech Army, and a couple of folk-singers so old and so drunk they can barely stagger onto the stage every night.

At least there are no midgets.

With the tour is a platoon of big men in baggy pants and bulky jackets, supposedly there to protect the singer from counterrevolutionaries, but all they really do is insulate the singer from anyone in the countries he's touring.

Just like Colonel Parker, his brother whispers.

The audiences are polite, but clearly they like the jugglers best. The singer works like hell to win them over, but his real fans, the young people, seem to be excluded. At one point his rage explodes, and in the middle of a song he turns to Leon and screams, *"Look what you've got me into!"*

Leon doesn't respond. He knows there's nothing he can say.

When the singer returns to the West, he announces he's leaving the Party. His remaining audiences get smaller.

But he's singing better than ever. He gets together with French and British blues fanatics, men with huge collections of vinyl bought from American sailors, and he listens carefully. He knows how to take a minor tune, a B-side or a neglected work, and reinvent it, jack it up and rock it till it cries with power and glows like neon. And people with names like Dylan and Fariña cross the Atlantic to meet with him, to tell him how much he means to them.

He doesn't abandon the Left. He studies Marx and Gandhi and Strachey and Hilferding. He leads his band and followers in discussion groups and self-criticism sessions, American hill people and Yorkshire kids educating themselves in revolution. Leon suggests inviting others to run the meetings, intellectuals, but the singer doesn't like the idea.

Years pass. The singer's audiences grow older. He's disappointed that the young girls are gone, that he can't tease them and drive them mad with the way he moves.

And then rock and roll is back, exploding out of the sweaty-walled European clubs where it's been living all these years, blasting into the minds and hearts of a newer, younger generation.

For the first time in years, the singer hears his brother's voice: *Now's your time.*

* * *

The singer runs onto the stage, drops onto his knees as he passes the mike, slides across half the stage. He looks at the girls in the audience from under his taunting eyelids.

"Well . . ." he intones.

The eerie sound comes up from the audience again, adolescent girls in the thrall of a need they can't explain. The singer had forgotten how much he missed them.

"Well . . ." he sings again, as if he's forgotten where he was. The wail goes up again.

When he finally gets around to singing, he thinks he can hear his brother on harmony.

Most of his new audience isn't familiar with the old material, with the old songs and moves—it's all spanking new to them. And the new material is good, written by Lennon and McCartney and Dylan and Richards and Jagger, all of them offering their best in homage to their idol. They swarm into his recording sessions to sing backup or strum out chords. He isn't as popular as he once was—there's still a lot of resistance, and he doesn't get much airplay and is never invited to appear on television—but his new fans think the American Legion pickets outside his concerts are quaint, and his old fans have never forgotten him.

He hasn't forgotten much either. He remembers who shunned him, who helped when the chips were down. The few who dared to support him in public. He works to advance the Struggle. He not only marches with Dr. King, he gives him a bright yellow Cadillac so he doesn't have to march at all. He directs public scorn at the Vietnam War. FBI men in dark suits and hats follow him around and tap his phones. They can't do anything to him because he's never done anything illegal—in the confusion of the headlines and statements and his jump to Europe, his local draft board never actually issued his induction notice.

Outnumbering the FBI are the fans who camp outside his house, living there just as they did a decade before, people who seem to have a tenuous existence only in the singer's shadow. It's as if he's their god, the only thing that gives them meaning.

Only one way to become a god, his brother whispers.

He knows what his brother means.

When Dr. King comes to Memphis, it's only natural for the singer to climb on his bike and pay a courtesy call.

Maybe the magic will work one last time.

What was he doing on the balcony, exactly? Demonstrating his moves, jumping around, playing the clown for his bewildered host? Or was there a whisper in his ear, a soft murmur that told him exactly where the bullet would be found as it hissed through the air?

Bleeding, both lungs punctured, he shoves the confused Dr. King into the motel room and to safety. He falls, coughing blood, his moist breath whistling through the hole in his side.

King remembers, forever afterward, the peculiar inward look on the singer's face as he dies.

The singer remembers his baptism of the spirit, the way he gave everything away. Now he's giving everything away again. He hears his brother's voice.

Welcome, his brother says, *to where we can live forever*.

You stand with the long line of mourners as it files up to the big white house. The singer's will was a surprise: there's an education foundation, and the house is to be renamed the Memphis Palace of Labor. It will become a library and center for research on labor issues.

File through a series of rooms on your way to view the coffin. Rooms so strangely decorated that they're like a window into the singer's mind. The Joe Hill room, the Gandhi room, the Karl Marx room. A pink bust of Marx sits in a shrine in the corner of his chamber, flanked by smoked-mirror glass and red-velvet curtains. Joe Hill—a life-sized statue of a noble-looking man in a cap and bib overalls—gazes defiantly at the scarlet velour walls of his chamber and at a piano gilded with what appears to be solid gold.

You have the feeling that the staid trustees of the foundation will redecorate at the first chance they get.

The singer lies in state under a portrait of the wizened figure of Gandhi, in a room whose walls seem to be upholstered in white plastic. Dr. King is chief mourner and speaks the eulogy. A choir from a local black church mourns softly, then spits fire. The crowd claps and stamps in answer.

And at last the moment comes when the huge bronze coffin is closed and the singer, Jessie Garon Presley, is carried out to be laid to rest in the garden. On his one side is his Mamma, and on the other his twin, Elvis, with whom he will live forever.

CALIFORNIA DREAMER

Mary Rosenblum

One of the most popular and prolific of the new writers of the '90s, Mary Rosenblum made her first sale in 1990 to *Asimov's Science Fiction*, and has since become a mainstay of that magazine, and one of its most frequent contributors, with almost twenty sales there to her credit; her linked series of "Drylands" stories have proved to be one of the magazine's most popular series. She has also sold to *The Magazine of Fantasy & Science Fiction*, *Pulphouse*, *New Legends*, and elsewhere. Her first novel, *The Drylands*, appeared in 1993 to wide critical acclaim, winning the prestigious Compton Crook Award for Best First Novel of the year; it was followed in short order by her second novel, *Chimera*. A third novel, *The Stone Garden*, was published late in 1994, and she has finished a fourth novel. Coming up soon is her first short-story collection, *Synthesis and Other Stories*. A graduate of Clarion West, Mary Rosenblum lives with her family in Portland, Oregon.

In the tough-minded, compassionate, and deceptively quiet story that follows, she examines the seemingly simple idea that what something is worth depends on what you're willing to *pay* for it—and the fact that *some* of those prices can go very high indeed . . .

The relief boat came once a week. This morning it had been a sturdy salmon fisher, hired down from Oregon. The crew had unloaded the usual relief supplies; canned milk and shrink-wrapped cheese, cans of peanut butter and stuff like that. It had unloaded mail.

Mail. Letters. Junk mail, for God's sake. No power yet, no telephones, but the US Postal Service had come through. Neither rain nor snow nor earthquake . . . Ellen struggled to swallow the hurting lump in her throat as she walked slowly homeward. Back on the beach—the new, Wave-scoured beach—people were sorting through envelopes and catalogues and cards. Crying and laughing. Britty Harris had gone into hysterics over a postcard from her vacationing brother. *Wish you were here*, he had scrawled on the back of a glossy picture of Fisherman's Wharf.

Wish you were here. Neither Fisherman's Wharf nor her brother were there anymore.

There had been no ghost mail from Rebecca. The lump swelled, threatening to turn into more tears. Ellen ducked her head and walked faster. Her shadow stretched seaward; a tall, thin caricature of herself. Perhaps she was *becoming* a caricature; turned hollow and surreal by the force of the Quake. Changed.

Beanpole, Rebecca had called her, and said, *Why can't I be thin like you?* at least once a week. Then Ellen would tell her to quit eating so much junk food and Rebecca would call her a Jewish mother and they would both laugh, because Scandinavian-blonde Ellen had grown up Catholic, and Rebecca *was* Jewish. It had been a ritual between them—a lightly spoken touchstone of love. As she turned up the walkway to the house, the unshed tears settled into Ellen's stomach, hard as beach pebbles.

It was a cottage, more than a house. Weathered gray shingles, weathered gray roof. Rebecca's house, because she'd always wanted to live near the sea, even though she had called it *ours*. Scraggly geraniums bloomed in a pot on the tiny front porch. The pot—generic red earthenware—was cracked. Ellen had watched it crack, clinging to this very railing as the earth shuddered and the house groaned in a choir of terrifying voices.

Earthquake, Ellen had thought in surprise. *That's not supposed to happen* here.

They'd heard it was the Big One on Jack's generator-run radio. But it was only after the relief boats started coming that they got to see the news photos of San Francisco and L.A. Ellen stomped sand from her shoes on the three wooden steps, went inside. A long worktable filled half of the single main room. Boxes of beads, feathers, and assorted junk cluttered the floor, and unfinished collages leaned against the wall. Rebecca's workspace. Rebecca's *life*. The room looked . . . unfamiliar. The Quake had changed everything, had charged the air with something like electricity. Angles and familiar lines looked sharp and strange and new, as if the unleashed force had transformed flowerpots and people and houses on some subtle, molecular scale.

Ellen set the bundled mail down on the stained formica of the kitchen counter and worked one of the rubber bands loose. Bank statements. Mail order catalogues, bright with spring dresses and shoes. A sale flyer from an art supply dealer. The second rubber band snapped as Ellen slid her fingers beneath it. The unexpected sting filled her eyes with tears. They spilled over and ran down her cheeks. She sobbed once, clutching the stupid, useless envelopes, fighting the tide that would rise up if she let it, and sweep her away.

Mail. It meant that Rebecca was dead. Ellen's tears made round, wrinkled spots on a glossy sportswear catalogue. All these endless weeks, she had told herself that Rebecca had survived, had cowered in the safety of some doorway or park while San Francisco dissolved in rubble and flame. She had told herself that Rebecca was in some schoolhouse shelter, frantic with worry because she couldn't call. As long as Ellen believed this—as long as she really—*believed*— then, Rebecca was alive.

How could you believe in a miracle, with a sportswear catalogue in your hands?

I have never lived without Rebecca, Ellen thought in terror.

That wasn't quite true. She had passed through childhood without Rebecca, had only met her in college. Rebecca had been struggling through art-majors' bio, as it was called. Ellen had helped her, because she was a bio major and Rebecca's outraged frustration made her laugh. *You need someone to take care of you,* Ellen had said lightly. They had moved in together a month later. Fifteen years ago. Ellen looked up at the cupboard above the sink.

The bottle of pills was up there, on the top shelf behind the glasses, with the aspirin and antacids. Sleeping pills, prescribed for Rebecca years ago, after she hurt her knee skiing. Would Ellen die if she took them all? She had a hard time swallowing capsules. They would stick to the back of her throat; hard, gelatinous lumps of oblivion. She would have to drink glasses of water to get them down.

Someone knocked on the door.

Rebecca? The traitorous rush of hope made her dizzy. ''Coming!'' Ellen flung the door open.

''Mom's sick.'' A girl stared up at her, dirty-faced, tousle-headed; a stranger. ''Please come.''

Not Rebecca. ''Who are *you*?'' Ellen said numbly. ''Where did you come from?''

''I'm Beth. Our car ran out of gas and we got lost. Please hurry.''

Ellen blinked at the girl. Eleven? Twelve? Gawky and blonde, but you noticed her eyes first. They were a strange color; depthless blue, like the sky after sunset.

''All right.'' Ellen sighed and stepped out onto the porch. ''Take me to your mom.''

The girl turned unhesitatingly inland, trotting up through the scraggly spring grass toward the forested ridge above the cottage. ''Wait a minute,'' Ellen called, but the girl didn't slow down, didn't even look back. Ellen hesitated, then ducked her head and broke into a run, was panting after only a dozen uphill yards, because Rebecca had run every morning and Ellen hadn't.

The girl crouched in the tree shadows, cradling a woman in her arms. The woman's face was flushed and she breathed in short, raspy breaths. Her hair stuck to her face, dark and stringy, as if she had been sweating, but when Ellen touched her cheek, her skin felt hot and dry.

''How long has your mother been sick?'' Ellen asked the girl.

''A couple of days. It rained on us and it was cold. Mom let me wear her jacket, but then she started shivering.''

''We've got to get her down to the house somehow.'' This was a crisis and Ellen could handle crises. She'd had fifteen years of practice, because Rebecca *didn't* handle them. She squatted beside the sick woman, shook her gently. ''Can you wake up?''

Miraculously, the woman's eyelids fluttered.

''Come on, honey. Got to get you on your feet.'' Ellen slid her arm beneath the woman's shoulders.

Another miracle. The woman mumbled something incoherent and struggled to her feet. Ellen kept her arm around her, frightened by her fierce heat, supporting her. Step by step, she coaxed the woman down the slope, staggering like a drunk beneath her slack weight.

It took forever to reach the house, but they finally made it. Ellen put the woman into Rebecca's empty (forever, Oh God) bed. The rasp of her breathing scared Ellen. Pneumonia? In the old days, before antibiotics, people had died from flu and pneumonia. The Quake had smashed the comfortable present as it smashed through the California hills. It had warped time back on itself, had brought back the old days of candles and no roads and death from measles or cholera. Seal Cove had no doctor. Big chunks of the California coast had fallen into the sea and you couldn't *get* there from here.

"I'll walk down to the store." Ellen poured water into a bowl from the kitchen jug, got a clean washcloth down from the shelf. "Jack can call Eureka on the radio. They'll send a helicopter to take your mom to the hospital. I'm going to give her some aspirin and I want you to wipe her all over while I'm gone." She handed the washcloth to Beth. "We need to get her fever down."

"Okay." The girl looked up at Ellen, her eyes dark and fierce. "She'll be all right. I love her."

She'll be all right. I love her. That incantation hadn't saved Rebecca. Ellen swallowed. "What's your mom's name, honey?"

"Laura Sorenson." The girl dipped the folded washcloth into the water. "She'll get well. She *has* to."

Her hands were trembling as she wiped her mother's face. Ellen groped for reassuring words and found only emptiness. "I'll be back in a little while," she said.

Clouds were boiling up over the horizon again by the time Ellen returned to the house. The wind gusted onshore, whipping the waves, snatching wisps of spume from the gray curl of the breakers. There had been a lot of storms lately, as if the Quake's terrible power had been absorbed into the atmosphere, was being discharged in raging wind and waves.

"Jack called the relief people up in Eureka." Ellen flinched as the wind slammed the screen door behind her. "They'll send the helicopter for your mom, just as soon as it gets back in." If the weather didn't stop it. She closed the wooden door against the building storm. "How is she?"

"Asleep." Beth hovered protectively in the bedroom doorway. "Better, I think."

Ellen edged past her and bent over the bed. She was worse, struggling to breathe, burning with fever. The woman's eyelids fluttered and Ellen shivered. There was a disinterested glaze to her eyes; as if the woman was on a boat, watching a shoreline recede into the distance. She is dying, Ellen thought and shivered again. "Beth?" Distract her. "Come have something to eat, okay? I don't want you getting sick, too."

"If you want." Beth sat reluctantly at the kitchen table. "What a pretty woman." She nodded at the watercolor on the wall. "Did you paint it?" she asked with a child's transparent effort to be polite.

"No." Some art student had painted it, years ago. Rebecca was smiling, head tilted, one hand in her dark, thick, semitic hair that had just been starting to go gray. The student had caught the impatience, the *intensity* that kept her up all night working, sent her weeping into Ellen's bed in the dawn, full of exhaustion and triumph and doubts. *Tell me it's not awful*, she would whisper. *God, El, I need you.* "It's a picture of my friend." Ellen busied herself peeling back shrink-wrap and slicing the yellow block of salmon-boat cheese. "Is a cheese sandwich all right?"

"Fine."

Silence. The rasp of the dying woman's breathing filled the kitchen. "She was an artist," Ellen said too loudly. "She did collages. When they started selling, I quit my job and we moved out here." *You supported me,* Rebecca had said, grinning. *While I was a starving artist. Now you get to be my kept woman.* "I took care of her. She needed a full-time keeper when she was working."

Beth nodded politely, eyes on the bedroom door. "Where is she now?"

"She's dead." The words caught Ellen by surprise. "She was in . . . San Francisco. When the Quake happened." She set the plate of sandwiches down in front of Beth with a small thump, aware of the pill bottle up on the top shelf. "I'll get you some water."

"I'm really sorry." Beth touched her hand. "That your friend died."

"Me, too," Ellen whispered.

Storm wind whined around the corners of the house, banging a loose piece of gutter against the eaves. Shadows were creeping into the corners. She switched on the fluorescent lantern, hung it on its hook above the table. The shadows cast by its gentle swinging made the watercolor Rebecca smile, but her eyes looked sad. "In a hundred years, we'll have forgotten how California looked before the Quake," Ellen murmured. "Everything will seem so *normal.*"

"We lived in Berkeley." Beth lifted a corner of bread, stared at the yellow slab of cheese beneath. "We had an apartment near the doctor's office where Mom was a nurse. I was across the street telling Cara about Mr. Walther's giving me a referral at school and all of a sudden we fell down. I saw our building *sway*, like it was made out of rubber. Pieces cracked out of it and started falling. Cars were crashing into things and Cara was screaming. Her voice sounded so *small.* All you could hear was this giant roar. I thought . . . Mom was dead."

"She wasn't dead." Beth had won that terrible lottery and Ellen had lost. Outside, the wind rattled the screen door against its hook. Beth was trembling and Ellen's twinge of anger metamorphosed suddenly into sympathy. "C'mon, eat." She put her arm around Beth's shoulders. *Eat*, she had said a hundred times a week to Rebecca. *You can't live on corn chips and pop, you idiot.* "Take your time. I'll check on your mom," she said.

The lantern streaked Rebecca's bedroom with dim light and shadow. Beth's mother—Laura—lay still beneath the light sheet. She didn't react as Ellen wiped her hot face with a washcloth. Her breathing was shallow and uneven. Outside, wind fluttered the shingles with the sound of cards riffling in a giant hand. No helicopter would land to save her.

"Ellen?" Beth's butterfly touch made Ellen jump, raised gooseflesh on her arms. "What's wrong?"

"Nothing."

"Don't lie to me." Beth's face was pale. "You think she's dying."

Ellen opened her mouth, but the lie wouldn't come.

"She can't die," Beth whispered. "She *can't*. I need her."

Need couldn't save the one you loved. "Your mom's sleeping and you need some sleep, too." Ellen steered Beth firmly out of the room. "You can sleep in my bed tonight. I'll sit up with your mom."

"She'll be better when she wakes up." Beth's shoulders stiffened. "She *has* to be."

"I'm sure she will be," Ellen said, but Beth's eyes told her she knew the lie for what it was.

Ellen found an extra nightshirt and tucked Beth into her own bed. Such bitter, bitter irony, to survive the Quake just to die from the busy breeding of invisible bacteria. "Go to sleep," Ellen whispered. "Your mom will be fine."

"She was making fudge." Beth looked up at Ellen, golden hair spread across the pillow. "She always makes fudge on Wednesday, because Wednesday's her day off and fudge is our favorite thing in the whole world. The corner where our apartment is cracked and just fell down. This big chunk of concrete landed on a man and you couldn't even see what happened to him. Just dust, lots of dust. It hid everything and then there was smoke and fire and Cara was screaming that everyone was dead, that Mom was dead. She ran away, but I waited for the firetrucks. They didn't come and then the whole building fell in and Cara's building was on fire and I had to run away after all."

Terror filled those depthless eyes. "It's all right, honey." Ellen stroked her face. "Your mom got out, remember?"

"Cara was lying," Beth said shrilly. "She always lied. I knew Mom wasn't dead, but I couldn't find her. I saw a body lying in a pile of bricks. It was a man with black hair. He didn't have any pants on and one of his legs was gone. Some firemen in yellow coats told me they'd help me, but they didn't. They took me to this park and it wasn't even in Berkeley. There were tents and lots of people. I told them I couldn't stay, that I had to look for my mother, but they wouldn't listen to me. There was a fence around the park. And soldiers. They wouldn't let me out. They said that Mom would come look for me there, but how could she *know?*"

"She found you. She's right here, Beth." And dying. Ellen put her arms around the shaking girl, held her close, rocking her gently.

"I found *her*," Beth whispered. "We're going to Grandpa's house, up in Oregon. We'll be safe there. *You* think she's dying." Beth pushed Ellen away. "She's *not* dying. I won't let her die."

"There, there," Ellen soothed, but tears stung her eyes. "You sleep now." She kissed Beth gently on the forehead. "I'll take good care of your mom."

"She won't die." Beth turned onto her side and closed her eyes.

But she *was* dying. Ellen sat beside her bed, wiping her fever-hot body with the wet cloth. Had Rebecca's last moments been full of terror and pain? Had she bled to death, trapped under fallen ceilings and walls, or had she burned, screaming? Outside, the wind hurled itself inland, slamming against the house with the Quake's absorbed power, shaking it to its foundations. Ellen rinsed the cloth.

It was warm with the woman's heat. She didn't look like Beth. She had dark hair and an olive tint to her skin. The lantern cast long shadows across the floor and something creaked in the main room. Rebecca's ghost?

Need shapes our lives, Ellen thought dully. Need for food, for attention, for power. The need for love. That's the foundation, the rock on which we build everything. "How can I live without Rebecca?" she whispered.

The woman's eyelids twitched. "Joseph?" she whispered. "Have to get back . . . Love . . . don't worry . . ." The feeble words fluttered to silence.

Joseph? Ellen wiped the woman's forehead. Beth's father? Beth hadn't mentioned a Joseph or a father.

Ellen woke to gray dawn light and the morning sounds of surf. Her head was pillowed on the sick woman's thigh and the wash cloth made a damp spot on the quilt. Afraid, Ellen jerked upright.

"Hello," Laura Sorenson whispered.

Still alive! "Good morning." Guilty and relieved, Ellen stifled a yawn. "I didn't mean to fall asleep. How are you feeling?"

"Tired. What . . . happened?"

"You're in my house. You've been sick." Ellen touched the woman's forehead. No fever. "Beth's here, too, and she's fine. Your daughter's a brave girl."

"Beth? I . . . don't have a daughter." She clutched weakly at the sheet. "Why did you call me Laura? That's not . . . my name."

"Just take it easy." Ellen patted Laura's shoulder, hiding dismay. "You had a high fever."

"Oh." Fear flickered in the woman's dark eyes. "Did I hit my head? What day is this? I feel as if . . . I've been dreaming for a long time."

"You were just sick," Ellen murmured. "It's March 25. Don't worry about it now. I'll get you some water, or would you rather have some orange juice?"

"March?" the woman whispered brokenly. "It *can't* be. Why can't I *remember?*"

In the kitchen, Ellen spooned orange crystals into a glass from a white can, trying to recall the effects of a prolonged high fever. Seizures, she remembered, but Laura hadn't gone into convulsions. Amnesia? Ellen shook her head, stirred the fake juice to orange froth. She carried the glass back to the bedroom and found Beth already there, her arms around her mother.

"Mom, it's *me*," Beth was saying in a broken voice.

"It's . . . coming back." Laura stroked her daughter's back. "Beth. Honey, it'll be all right."

There was a tentative quality to the gesture and a frightened expression in her eyes. "Here's your juice," Ellen said, holding out the glass. "How are you doing?"

Beth almost snatched the glass from Ellen's hand. "I told you she'd get well," she said.

Voyeur, outsider, Ellen watched Beth help her mother drink. Side by side, they looked even less alike. There was a protective possessiveness to Beth's posture; a confidence that was lacking in Laura. Beth might be the mother; Laura the fragile child.

"Thank you." The woman sank back on the pillows, trying for a smile. "Thank you for taking us in. We must be a horrible burden."

"Not at all." Ellen collected the empty glass. "I'm just glad you're better."

Laura stroked her daughter's hair. "Beth said I was in our apartment when it happened. I'm . . . starting to remember." She spoke hesitantly, like an actor groping for half-learned lines. "What about . . . Joseph? Oh . . . God, Joseph!"

"What's wrong? Who's Joseph," Mom?" Beth stroked a strand of hair back from her mother's face. "Someone at the office?"

"No. I . . . don't know. I don't know a Joseph, do I? It was a . . . dream, I guess. From the fever." She squeezed Beth's hand, her fingers trembling.

"You'll sort it out." Ellen touched Laura's shoulder, moved by the anguish in her face. "I've got to run into town." She had almost forgotten the helicopter. "I'll be back in an hour. There's more water in the jugs beside the kitchen counter."

Laura nodded weakly, but her eyes never left her daughter's face. She is afraid, Ellen thought.

Of what?

At the store, Jack eyed her over the fake tortoiseshell rim of his glasses as he called Eureka and canceled the helicopter. "They were busy anyway," he drawled. "Guess the storm hit real bad up there. Your visitor wasn't too sick, huh?"

Dumb woman, his expression said. *Don't know just sick from dying.*

"She *was* dying," Ellen snapped, but she hadn't died, had she? "I guess I was wrong," she said lamely. "Thanks for calling Eureka." She turned away from Jack's cool, judgmental face. She had no real friends in this Godforsaken town. Ellen-and-Rebecca had been a complete and seamless universe. She could feel the shattered bits of that universe crunching beneath her feet. "I'd better get back," she said.

"Oh yeah." Jack crossed his arms on the top of the old-fashioned wood-and-glass counter. "Aaron McDevitt was in yesterday, to pick up his share of the food. He said he found a car up on the old logging road acrost Bear Ridge." He cleared his throat. "Aaron brought this in." He fished around behind the counter, laid a brown handbag on the scarred wood, put a woman's wallet down beside it. "Wasn't no money in it," he said.

Aaron would have made sure of that. Ellen picked up the leather wallet. The bag was leather, too. It looked expensive. She opened the wallet. Credit cards from stores and oil companies. A check guarantee card. All in the name of Julia DeMarco. Ellen started to say that it didn't belong to Laura, but she closed her mouth without speaking. Laura's dark, oval face smiled at her from a California driver's license.

Julia DeMarco?

"This is . . . her bag." Ellen folded up the wallet, stuffed it back into the bag. "I'll take it to her. Thanks," she said too quickly. "Thank Aaron, too, when you see him."

She left the store, feeling guilty, as if she was partner to some crime. There were hundreds of reasons to lie about your name—some good, lots of them bad. Ellen stopped at the bottom of her driveway and opened the bag again. It held the usual stuff; checkbook, wallet, makeup items and a leatherbound datebook. Ellen found a leather card case full of business cards, printed on creamy stock.

Julia DeMarco
Attorney at Law

The address was San Francisco. Beth had told Ellen that her mother was a nurse in Berkeley. The datebook listed court dates, appointments, and reminders to pick up dry cleaning or visit the dentist. Ellen paged through it. *Joseph's Birthday* was written neatly at the top of the page for next Wednesday. Joseph. A dream, Laura had said with her face full of anguish. Ellen stuffed everything back into the bag and hurried up the lane to the house.

Inside, the watercolor Rebecca glowed on the wall. Ellen tossed the bag onto the cluttered worktable and went into the bedroom.

"Hi." Laura smiled wanly at Ellen. "Beth went to get more water. She said she saw a pool up above the house."

"The spring." Ellen nodded. "That was nice of her."

"Beth's a good kid. She had to grow up a little too early. There was a divorce—a custody battle. I think . . . it was ugly. I think it . . . hurt Beth."

Again, the sense of lines being recited. "You're remembering?" Ellen asked.

"I don't know." Laura's eyes flickered. "I remember scenes or faces—and I don't know them, but I *do*. I'm not making any sense, am I?" Her laugh was fragile, edged with hysteria. "Did our building burn down? I remember it burning and . . . I remember picking up pieces of a broken vase and thinking how *lucky* I was. I keep wanting to remember that it was a house, but it was an apartment, wasn't it?"

Ellen took a quick breath. "Who's Julia DeMarco?"

"I . . . don't know. Do I?" Laura whispered. "Joseph . . .? Oh, God." She buried her face in her hands. "Why do I want to cry? What's *wrong* with me? I don't even know where we are or why we're *here*."

"Take it easy." Ellen stroked Laura's back. "You'll straighten everything out eventually." Would she? Who *are* you? she wondered, but she didn't say it out loud.

"Hi, Mom." Beth stuck her head through the doorway, a wet jug in each hand. "What's wrong?" She dropped the jugs, ran to the bedside. "Mom, what's *wrong*?"

"Nothing . . . nothing." Laura straightened, struggling to smile for her daughter. "I'm still feeling . . . shaky."

"Oh, Mom." Beth clutched her mother. "You'll remember again. You have to."

"Of course I will, sweetheart." Laura buried her face in her daughter's hair. "It's all right, Beth. Really."

Was it? Ellen tiptoed out of the room. Perhaps it would be all right. Perhaps Laura Sorenson would wake up tomorrow and remember the burning apartment.

And what about Julia DeMarco? What about Joseph? Not my business, Ellen told herself fiercely. Not at all. She got a pot down from the kitchen cupboard, filled it with water from the dripping jug.

"What are you doing?" Beth asked from the doorway.

"Fixing brunch."

"I'll help you." Beth perched herself on the table. "What can I do?"

"Nothing just yet." Ellen measured dusty flakes of oatmeal into the water. "Why were you going to your grandfather's house? Half the roads in the state are closed. Why didn't you and your mom stay in San Francisco?"

"We . . . couldn't."

Aha. "Why not?"

No answer.

Ellen lit the little white-gas camping stove, set the pot of oatmeal on to boil.

"They wouldn't let me go," Beth spoke up suddenly. She sat rigidly straight, hands tucked beneath her thighs, eyes fixed on her knees. "I saw her one afternoon, but she was outside the fence and she didn't see me. When I told them, they said she was dead, that she'd died in our building. They said I'd have to wait for my father to come. He'd never let me go back to Mom. Never. The firemen told me they'd help me find Mom, but they lied. They just took me to that place." She looked at Ellen at last. "The man at the gate hit me, when I tried to run after her."

Such terrible eyes, dark as the Quake-storm yesterday. They were full of desperate need. Full of power. Power to tear apart the landscape of reality, to reshape it like the Quake had reshaped the hills? A hissing startled Ellen and she snatched her gaze away from those depthless eyes, grabbing a potholder. Sticky oatmeal foamed over the lip of the pot and bubbled down the side.

Oh, yes, she understood the power of need. Ellen stirred the boiling cereal, Rebecca's absence a gaping wound in her heart.

"Grandpa won't let Dad take me," Beth went on in a flat monotone. "He won't let them take Mom. We'll be safe there. We'll be happy. They want to take her away." Beth's voice cracked suddenly, became the cry of a frightened child. "They *can't!*"

"Honey, it's all right." Ellen's arms went around her. She knew that terror, had felt it every dark, post-Quake night, as she waited to hear from Rebecca. It had seeped into the marrow of her bones and would never go away. "It's all right," she murmured. Beth was sobbing her thin body shaking as Ellen held her close.

Nothing was all right. The Quake had shattered the earth. It had shattered buildings and freeways, it had buckled lives, smashed them into ruin. So much *power*, but it was an innocent power; destruction without choice or anger. The sky had absorbed some of that power, had transformed it into the wild, unseasonable storms that were battering the coast. Children were such *sponges*. They absorbed experiences so easily . . .

Beth's sobs were diminishing. Ellen stroked her hair back from her damp and swollen face. "Why don't you ask your mom if she wants honey or canned milk on her cereal," she said.

"She puts milk on it." Beth hiccoughed. "And brown sugar."

"I think I have a little brown sugar left." How did Julia DeMarco like her oatmeal? Ellen fished in the cupboard, found a plastic bag with a few brown lumps left in it. It didn't matter, she thought as she crumbled rock hard lumps onto the steaming cereal. Beth's mother had liked brown sugar on her oatmeal and Beth needed her mother. Desperately. With all the power of the Quake.

She had found her, on the other side of a barbed-wire fence. She had reshaped Julia DeMarco into Laura Sorenson, as innocent and destructive as the Quake that had reshaped California.

"I'll fix yours," Beth said gravely. "Do you want honey and milk on it?"

"Thank you," Ellen said. She picked up the tray, carried it into the bedroom.

"I could eat at the table with you." Laura sat up straighter as Ellen put the tray down on her lap. "I'm feeling much better."

She wore a gold wedding ring on her left hand. "You can get up any time." Was Joseph searching frantically for Julia DeMarco, praying that she was still alive?

"I'll come eat with you." Beth came in with her bowl, her eyes bright with love.

How many days had Beth huddled behind the barbed wire of a refugee camp, filling the black hole of her loss with the Quake's power, waiting for a mother who would never come? Ellen tiptoed into the kitchen. In the bedroom, Beth laughed and Laura joined in tentatively. Maybe Julia had been a volunteer at the refugee center, or had been hired to untangle the miles of legal red tape. Ellen wondered why Beth had chosen her. Perhaps the choice had been as random as the Quake's violence.

She's not dying, Beth had said and those words had been an incantation. This woman couldn't die any more than she could remain Julia DeMarco. Beth needed her mother. Julia DeMarco had had no choice at all.

A bowl of oatmeal cooled on the table, flanked neatly by spoon and napkin. With honey and milk. Sunlight streamed through the window into the cluttered room, and the watercolor Rebecca smiled gently from the wall. "I will always love you," Ellen whispered to her. Standing on her toes, she took the bottle of pills down from the cabinet shelf.

The helicopter from Eureka landed at dusk. The blades flattened the grass in the front yard and whipped a small sandstorm into the air. "In here," Ellen told the tired-looking paramedics who climbed out of the hatch. "She's unconscious." She had put three of the sleeping capsules into Laura's hot chocolate, had been terrified that it might be too much.

The paramedics took Laura's blood pressure, shone a light into her eyes, frowned, and asked Ellen questions. "She seemed to be getting better," Ellen told them. "And then, all of a sudden, she just collapsed. I had Jack call you right away."

"Does she have any ID?" the taller of the two men asked her. He had black hair and dark circles beneath his eyes.

"She had this." Ellen handed them Julia DeMarco's handbag. "Off and on, she'd forget who she was. She was confused. I don't know how she ended up out here.''

"Lady, we've seen stranger things." The dark-haired paramedic shrugged. "She's pretty unresponsive. We'll take her in."

They lifted her onto a stretcher with remarkable gentleness and loaded her into the belly of the waiting helicopter; Laura Sorenson, Julia DeMarco. Tomorrow, she would wake up in the Eureka hospital and for a while, she would wonder where she was and who she was. But she would remember. Someone would contact Joseph. He would hurry out to Eureka in an ecstasy of fear and relief, and he would help her to remember. Happy birthday, Joseph.

Outside, the helicopter thundered into the sky. Ellen left the lantern on—a flagrant waste of precious batteries, but she couldn't face the darkness. The room looked strange in the feeble glow of yellow light—streaked with shadows and memories. Each item, each tool in Rebecca's cluttered workspace, carried echoes of laughter and tears and *life*. Memories. Ellen picked up a leather-gouge, envisioning Rebecca bent over her work table. How can you be sure that what you remember really happened? She tucked the gouge into a box and reached for a basket of feathers.

She spent the night sorting through shells, beads, and tools; sorting through the moments of their life together. On the wall, Rebecca's watercolor eyes were full of life and love, full of death. Ellen packed everything into the cartons left over from hauling home the relief supplies. In the gray predawn light, she stacked the last of the filled cartons in a corner of the shed out behind the house.

The first beams of sunlight streaked the sparse grass in the front yard and stretched shadows westward toward the beach. In a few weeks, they would have power again, and running water. Slowly, the scars would be covered by new buildings, new grass, new roads, new lives. Scars on the soul were harder to heal. Ellen closed the shed door, snapped the padlock shut.

Beth waited in the neat, uncluttered house, a little unsteady on her feet. "What are you doing? Where's Mom?" She rubbed at her eyes, words slurring a little.

A whole capsule had been just right. "I couldn't sleep." Ellen's heart began to pound, but she kept her tone casual. "I thought I'd clean up Grandpa's house."

Beth's eyes widened.

"I was going to take a walk on the beach," Ellen said quickly. "Do you want to come along?"

Beth nodded slowly, silent and wary.

The rising sun burned on the rim of the hills as they walked across the smooth white sand. The Wave had washed out the road in some places, left it hanging like an asphalt cliff in others. Beth remained silent, her twilight eyes full of shadows and unconscious power. I should be afraid, Ellen thought, but she wasn't afraid. She had lost her capacity for fear when she had contemplated the pills, with her hands full of mail.

The watercolor cracked as she pulled it from her pocket and unfolded it. Rebecca smiled at her, eyes sparkling in the morning light. "Rebecca, I love you,'' Ellen whispered. ''I will always love you, but you were the strong one. Not me. I am not strong enough to use the pills and I am not strong enough to live without you. Forgive me.'' She wrapped the stiff paper around a beach stone and fastened it with one of the thick rubber-bands that had come on the mail. The rising sun stretched her shadow seaward as she drew her arm back and hurled the painting-wrapped stone far out into the offshore swell.

The Quake had released so much power. It charged the air like electricity, it shimmered in Beth's twilight eyes. Innocent power. The power to reshape reality, like the Quake had reshaped the land. Rebecca had needed her, but Rebecca was dead. Beth needed her mother. Ellen could feel that need seeping into the hole Rebecca had left in her life, filling her up like the tide. Behind her, waves curled and broke, dissolving the painting. She didn't want to look at Rebecca's face one day, and see a stranger.

What will I remember tomorrow? Ellen reached for Beth's hand, shivering a little at the cool touch of the girl's fingers. She could feel the change shuddering through her, an invisible Quake across the landscape of the soul. ''There's chocolate in the cupboard. We've got margarine from the last relief boat and canned milk,'' Ellen smiled. ''We could try to make fudge. It's Wednesday, after all.''

Beth's slow smile was like the sun rising, bringing color to the gray world. ''It *is* Wednesday.'' She put her arm around Ellen's waist, face turned up to hers, eyes full of twilight and love. ''I'm so *glad* we're here,'' she said.

''Me, too,'' Ellen whispered. She could almost remember it—the apartment and the doctor's office where she had worked. Tomorrow, or the next day, she *would* remember it. Beth needed her. She would take care of her daughter and they would be happy together.

Beth had said so.

SPLIT LIGHT

Lisa Goldstein

There are turning points in everyone's lives, but, as the evocative and insightful story that follows demonstrates, sometimes those personal turning points change everything forever for the *world* at large as well . . .

Lisa Goldstein is a Bay Area writer who won the American Book Award for her first novel, *The Red Magician*, and who has subsequently gone on to become one of the most critically acclaimed fantasists of her day with novels such as *Tourists*, *The Dream Years*, *A Mask for the General*, and *Strange Devices of the Sun and Moon*. Her stories have appeared in *Asimov's Science Fiction, Interzone, Pulphouse, Full Spectrum, Snow White, Blood Red, The Magazine of Fantasy & Science Fiction*, and elsewhere. Her most recent books are a new novel, *Summer King, Winter Fool*, and a collection of her short fiction, *Travellers in Magic*.

SHABBETAI ZEVI (1626–1676), the central figure of the largest and most momentous messianic movement in Jewish history subsequent to the destruction of the Temple . . .

Encyclopedia Judaica

He sits in a prison in Constantinople. The room is dark, his mind a perfect blank, the slate on which his visions are written. He waits.

He sees the moon. The moon spins like a coin through the blue night sky. The moon splinters and falls to earth. Its light is the shattered soul of Adam, dispersed since the fall. All over the earth the shards are falling; he sees each one, and knows where it comes to rest.

He alone can bind the shards together. He will leave this prison, become king. He will wear the circled walls of Jerusalem as a crown. All the world will be his.

His name is Shabbetai Zevi. "Shabbetai" for the Sabbath, the seventh day, the day of rest. The seventh letter in the Hebrew alphabet is zayin. In England they call the Holy Land "Zion." He is the Holy Land, the center of the world. If he is in Constantinople, then Constantinople is the center of the world.

He has never been to England, but he has seen it in his visions. He has ranged through the world in his visions, has seen the past and fragments of the future. But he does not know what will happen to him in this prison.

When he thinks of his prison the shards of light grow faint and disappear. The darkness returns. He feels the weight of the stone building above him; it is as heavy as the crown he felt a moment ago. He gives in to despair.

A year ago, he thinks, he was the most important man in the world. Although he is a Jew in a Moslem prison he gives the past year its Christian date: it was 1665. It was a date of portent; some Christians believe that 1666 will be the year of the second coming of Christ. Even among the Christians he has his supporters.

But it was to the Jews, to his own people, that he preached. As a child he had seen the evidence of God in the world, the fiery jewels hidden in gutters and trash heaps; he could not understand why no one else had noticed them, why his brother had beaten him and called him a liar. As a young man he had felt his soul kindle into light as he prayed. He had understood that he was born to heal the world, to collect the broken shards of light, to turn mourning into joy.

When he was in his twenties he began the mystical study of Kabbalah. He read, with growing excitement, about the light of God, how it had been scattered and hidden throughout the world at Adam's fall, held captive by the evil that resulted from that fall. The Jews, according to the Kabbalist Isaac Luria, had been cast across the world like sand, like sparks, and in their dispersal they symbolized the broken fate of God.

One morning while he was at prayer he saw the black letters in his prayer book dance like flame and translate themselves into the unpronounceable Name of God. He understood everything at that moment, saw the correct pronunciation of the Name, knew that he could restore all the broken parts of the world by simply saying the Name aloud.

He spoke. His followers say he rose into midair. He does not remember; he rarely remembers what he says or does in his religious trances. He knows that he was shunned in his town of Smyrna, that the people there began to think him a lunatic or a fool.

Despite their intolerance he grew to understand more and more. He saw that he was meant to bring about an end to history, and that with the coming of the end all things were to be allowed. He ate pork. He worked on the Sabbath, the day of rest, the day that he was named for or that was named for him.

Finally the townspeople could stand it no longer and banished him. He blessed them all before he went, ''in the name of God who allows the forbidden.''

As he left the town of his birth, though, the melancholy that had plagued him all his life came upon him again. He wandered through Greece and Thrace, and ended finally in Constantinople. In Constantinople he saw a vision of the black prison, the dungeon in which he would be immured, and in his fear the knowledge that had sustained him for so long vanished. God was lost in the world, broken into so many shards no one could discover him.

In his frantic search for God he celebrated the festivals of Passover, Shavuot and Sukkot all in one week. He was exiled again and resumed his wandering, travelling from Constantinople to Rhodes to Cairo.

In Cairo he dreamed he was a bridegroom, about to take as his bride the holy city of Jerusalem. The next day the woman Sarah came, unattended, to Cairo.

The door to his prison opens and a guard comes in, the one named Kasim. "Stand up!" Kasim says.

Shabbetai stands. "Come with me," Kasim says.

Shabbetai follows. The guard takes him through the dungeon and out into Constantinople. It is day; the sun striking the domes and minarets of the city nearly blinds him.

Kasim leads him through the crowded streets, saying nothing. They pass covered bazaars and slave markets, coffee houses and sherbet shops. A caravan of camels forces them to stop.

When they continue on Shabbetai turns to study his guard. Suddenly he sees to the heart of the other man, understands everything. He knows that Kasim is under orders to transfer him to the fortress at Gallipoli, that the sultan himself has given him this order before leaving to fight the Venetians on Crete. "How goes the war, brother?" Shabbetai asks.

Kasim jerks as if he has been shot. He hurries on toward the wharf, saying nothing.

At the harbor Kasim hands Shabbetai to another man and goes quickly back to the city. Shabbetai is stowed in the dark hold of a ship, amid sour-smelling hides and strong spices and ripe oranges. Above him he hears someone shout, and he feels the ship creak and separate from the wharf and head out into the Sea of Marmara.

Darkness again, he thinks. He is a piece of God, hidden from sight. It is only by going down into the darkness of the fallen world that he can find the other fragments, missing since the Creation. Everything has been ordained, even this trip from Constantinople to Gallipoli.

Visions of the world around him encroach upon the darkness. He sees Pierre de Fermat, a mathematician, lying dead in France; a book is open on the table in which he has written, "I have discovered a truly remarkable proof which this margin is too small to contain." He sees Rembrandt adding a stroke of bright gold to a painting he calls "The Jewish Bride." He sees a great fire destroy London; a killing wind blows the red and orange flames down to the Thames.

He is blinded again, this time by the vast inrushing light of the world. He closes his eyes, a spark of light among many millions of others, and rocks to the motion of the ship.

Sarah's arrival in Cairo two years ago caused a great deal of consternation. No one could remember ever seeing a woman travelling by herself. She stood alone on the dock, a slight figure with long red hair tumbling from her kerchief, gazing around her as if at Adam's Eden.

Finally someone ran for the chief rabbi. He gave the order to have her brought to his house, and summoned all the elders as well.

"Who are you?" he asked. "Why are you travelling alone in such a dangerous part of the world?"

"I'm an orphan," Sarah said. "But I was raised in a great castle by a Polish nobleman. I had one servant just to pare my nails, and another to brush my hair a hundred times before I went to bed.''

None of the elders answered her, but each one wore an identical expression of doubt. Why would a Polish nobleman raise a Jewish orphan? And what on earth was she doing in Cairo?

Only Shabbetai saw her true nature; only he knew that what the elders suspected was true. She had been the nobleman's mistress, passed among his circle of friends when he grew tired of her. The prophet Hosea married a prostitute, he thought. "I will be your husband," he said. "If you will have me."

He knew as he spoke that she would marry him, and his heart rejoiced.

They held the wedding at night and out of doors. The sky was dark blue silk, buttoned by a moon of old ivory. Stars without number shone.

After the ceremony the elders came to congratulate him. For Sarah's sake he pretended not to see the doubt in their eyes. "I cannot tell you how happy I am tonight," he said.

After the ceremony he brought her to his house and led her to the bedroom, not bothering to light the candles. He lay on the bed and drew her to him. Her hair was tangled; perhaps she never brushed it.

They lay together for a long time. "Shall I undress?" she asked finally. Her breath was warm on his face.

"The angels sang at my birth," he said. "I have never told anyone this. Only you."

She ran her fingers through her hair, then moved to lift her dress. He held her tightly. "We must be like the angels," he said. "Like the moon. We must be pure.''

"I don't understand."

"We cannot fall into sin. If I am stained like Adam I will not be able to do the work for which I was sent here."

"The—work?''

"I was born to heal the world," he said.

The moon appeared before him in the darkened room. Its silver-white light cast everything in shadow.

The moon began to spin. No, he thought. He watched as it shattered and plummeted to earth, saw the scattered fragments hide themselves in darkness.

He cried aloud. He felt the great sadness of the world, and the doubt he had struggled with all his life returned.

"It's broken," he said. "It can never be repaired. I'll never be able to join all the pieces together."

Sarah kissed him lightly on the cheek. "Let us join together, then," she said. "Let two people stand for the entire world."

"No—''

"I heard you tell your followers that everything is permitted. Why are we not permitted to come together as husband and wife?"

"I can't," he said simply. "I have never been able to."

He expected scorn, or pity. But her expression did not change. She held him in her arms, and eventually he drifted off to sleep.

* * *

With Sarah at his side he was able to begin the mission for which he was born. Together they travelled toward Jerusalem, stopping so that he could preach along the way.

He spoke in rough huts consecrated only by the presence of ten men joined by prayer. He spoke in ancient synagogues, with lamps of twisted silver casting a wavering light on the golden letters etched into the walls. Sometimes he stood at a plain wooden table, watched by unlettered rustics who know nothing of the mysteries of Kabbalah; sometimes he preached from an altar of faded white and gold.

His message was the same wherever they went. He was the Messiah, appointed by God. He proclaimed an end to fast days; he promised women that he would set them free from the curse of Eve. He would take the crown from the Turkish sultan without war, he said, and he would make the sultan his servant.

The lost ten tribes of Israel had been found, he told the people who gathered to hear him. They were marching slowly as sleepwalkers toward the Sahara desert, uncertain of the way or of their purpose, waiting for him to unite them.

When he reached Jerusalem he circled the walls seven times on horseback, like a king. Once inside the city he won over many of the rabbis and elders. Letters were sent out to the scattered Jewish communities all over the world, to England, Holland and Italy, proclaiming that the long time of waiting was over; the Messiah had come.

A great storm shook the world. Families sold their belongings and travelled toward Jerusalem. Others set out with nothing, trusting in God to provide for them. Letters begging for more news were sent back to Jerusalem, dated from "the first year of the renewal of the prophecy and the kingdom." Shabbetai signed the answering letters "the firstborn son of God," and even "I am the Lord your God Shabbetai Zevi," and such was the fervor of the people that very few of them were shocked.

The boat docks at Gallipoli, and Shabbetai is taken to the fortress there. Once inside he sees that he has been given a large and well-lit suite of rooms, and he understands that his followers have succeeded in bribing the officials.

The guards leave him and lock the door. However comfortable his rooms are, he is still in a prison cell. He paces for several minutes, studying the silver lamps and deep carpets and polished tables and chairs. Mosaics on the wall, fragments of red, green and black, repeat over and over in a complex pattern.

He sits on the plump mattress and puts his head in his hands. His head throbs. With each pulse, it seems, the lamps in the room dim, grow darker, until, finally, they go out.

He is a letter of light. He is the seventh letter, the zayin. Every person alive is a letter, and together they make up the book of the world, all things past, present and to come.

He thinks he can read the book, can know the future of the world. But as he looks on, the book's pages turn; the letters form and reshape. Futures branch off before him.

He watches as children are born, as some die, as others grow to adulthood.

Some stay in their villages, farm their land, sit by their hearths with their families surrounding them. Others disperse across the world and begin new lives.

The sight disturbs him; he does not know why. A page turns and he sees ranks of soldiers riding to wars, and men and women lying dead in the streets from plague. Kingdoms fall to sword and gun and cannon.

Great wars consume the world. The letters twist and sharpen, become pointed wire. He sees millions of people herded beyond the wire, watches as they go toward their deaths.

The light grows brighter. He wants to close his eyes, to look away, but he cannot. He watches as men learn the secrets of the light, as they break it open and release the life concealed within it. A shining cloud flares above a city, and thousands more die.

No, he thinks. But the light shines out again, and this time it seems to comfort him. Here is the end of history that he has promised his followers. Here is the end of everything, the world cleansed, made anew.

The great book closes, and the light goes out.

In Jerusalem he preached to hundreds of people. They filled the synagogue, dressed in their best clothes, the men on his right hand and the women on his left. Children played and shouted in the aisles.

He spoke of rebuilding the temple, of finding the builder's stone lost since the time of Solomon. As he looked out over his audience he saw Sarah stand and leave the congregation. One of his followers left as well, a man named Aaron.

He stopped, the words he had been about to speak dying before they left his mouth. For a moment he could not go on. The people stirred in their seats.

He hurried to an end. After the service he ran quickly to the house the rabbis had given him. Sarah was already there.

"What were you doing here?" he asked.

"What do you mean?" she said. Her expression was innocent, unalarmed.

"I saw you leave with Aaron."

"With Aaron? I left to come home. I didn't feel well."

"You were a whore in Poland, weren't you?" he asked harshly. "Was there a single man in the country you didn't sleep with?"

"I was a nobleman's daughter," she said. Her voice was calm. He could not see her heart; she held as many mysteries as the Kabbalah.

"A nobleman's—" he said. "You were his mistress. And what did you do with Aaron? What did you do with all of them, all of my followers?"

"I told you—"

"Don't lie to me!"

"Listen. Listen to me. I did nothing. I have not known a man since I came to Cairo."

"Then you admit that in Poland—"

"Quiet. Yes. Yes. I was his mistress."

"And Aaron? You want him, don't you? You whore—You want them all, every man you have ever known."

"Listen," she said angrily. "You know nothing of women, nothing at all. I was his mistress in Poland, yes. But I did not enjoy it—I did it because I was an orphan, and hungry, and I needed to eat. I hated it when he came to me, but I managed to hide my feelings. I had to, or I would have starved."

"But you wanted me. On our wedding night, you said—"

"Yes. You are the only man who has ever made me feel safe."

A great pity moved him. He felt awed at the depths to which her life had driven her, the sins she had been forced to take upon herself. Could she be telling the truth? But why would she stay with him, a man of no use to her or any other woman?

"You lied to your nobleman," he said carefully. "Are you lying to me now?"

"No," she said.

He believed her. He felt free, released from the jealousy that had bound him. "You may have Aaron, you know," he said.

"What?"

"You may have Aaron, or any man you want."

"I don't—Haven't you heard me at all? I don't want Aaron."

"I understand everything now. You were a test, but through the help of God I have passed it. With the coming of the kingdom of God all things are allowed. Nothing is forbidden. You may have any man, any woman, any one of God's creatures."

"I am not a test! I am a woman, your wife! You are the only man I want!"

He did not understand why she had become angry. His own anger had gone. He left the house calmly.

From Jerusalem he travelled with his followers to Smyrna, the place where he was born. There are those who say that he was banished from Jerusalem too, that the rabbis there declared him guilty of blasphemy. He does not remember. He remembers only the sweetness of returning to his birthplace in triumph.

Thousands of men and women turned out to greet him as he rode through the city gates. Men on the walls lifted ram's horns to their lips and sounded notes of welcome. People crowded the streets, cheering and singing loudly; they raised their children to their shoulders and pointed him out as he went past.

He nodded to the right and left as he rode. A man left the assembly and stepped out in front of the procession.

Shabbetai's horse reared. "Careful, my lord!" Nathan said, hurrying to his side. Nathan was one of the many who had joined him in Jerusalem, who had heard Shabbetai's message and given up all his worldly goods.

But Shabbetai had recognized the fat, worried-looking man, and he reined in his horse. "This is my brother Joseph," he said. "A merchant."

To his surprise Joseph bowed to him. "Welcome, my lord," he said. "We hear great things of you."

Shabbetai laughed. When they were children he had told Joseph about his visions, and Joseph had beaten him for lying. Seeing his brother bent before him was more pleasing than Shabbetai could have imagined. "Rise, my friend," he said.

In the days that followed the city became one great festival. Business came to a standstill as people danced in the streets, recited psalms to one another when they met, fell into prophetic trances proclaiming the kingdom of God.

Only Sarah did not join in the city's riot. He urged her to take a lover, as so many people in the city were doing, but she refused. When he called for an end to fast days she became the only one in the city to keep the old customs.

Despite her actions he felt more strongly than ever that he was travelling down the right road, that he was close to the fulfillment of his mission. He excommunicated those who refused to believe in him. He sang love songs during prayer, and explained to the congregation the mystical meaning behind the words of the songs. He distributed the kingdoms of the earth among his followers.

His newly-made kings urged him to take the crown intended for him, to announce the date of his entrance into Constantinople. He delayed, remembering the evil vision of the dark prison.

But in his euphoria he began to see another vision, one in which he took the crown from the sultan. He understood that history would be split at Constantinople, would travel down one of two diverging paths. He began to make arrangements to sail.

Two days before they were to leave Sarah came to him. "I'm not going with you," she said.

"What do you mean?" he asked. "I will be king, ruler of the world, and you will be at my side, my queen. This is what I have worked for all these years. How can you give that up?"

"I don't want to be queen."

"You don't—Why not?"

"I don't feel safe with you any longer. I don't like the things you ask me to do."

"What things?"

"What things? How can you ask me that when you tell me to lie with every one of your followers? You're like the nobleman, passing me around when you get tired of me."

"I did nothing. It was you who lusted after Aaron."

"I didn't—"

"And others too," he said, remembering the glances she had given men in the congregation. She *had* pitied him, and hated him too, just as he had always thought. "Do you think I didn't notice?"

"I've done nothing," she said. "I—"

"I won't grant you a divorce, you know."

"Of course not. If we're married you still own me, even if I'm not there. That dream you told me about, where you took Jerusalem as your bride—you want to master Jerusalem, make her bow to your will. You want to control the entire world. But have you ever thought about how you will govern once you have the sultan's crown? You want to be ruler of the earth, but what kind of ruler will you be?"

"What do you know about statecraft, about policy? I have been ordained by God to be king. And you—you have been chosen to be queen."

"No," she said. "I have not."

She turned to leave. "I excommunicate you!" he said, shouting after her. "I call upon God to witness my words—you are excommunicated!"

She continued walking as if she did not hear him.

He watched her go. Perhaps it was just as well that she was leaving. He had known for a long time that she could not grasp the vastness of the task he had been given; she had never studied Kabbalah, or had visions of the light of God. His work in the world was far more important than her private feelings, or his.

He and his followers set sail on December 30, 1665. Word of his departure had gone before him. His boat was intercepted in the Sea of Marmara, and he was brought ashore in chains.

He sits in his prison in Gallipoli and waits for the light. He has not had a vision in many days; perhaps, he thinks, they have left him. He wonders if they have been consumed by the great fires he has seen in the future.

What had gone wrong? He and his followers had been so certain; he had seen the signs, read all the portents. He was destined to be the ruler of the world.

He puts his head in his hands and laughs harshly. Ruler of the world! And instead he sits in prison, waiting to be killed or released at the whim of the Turkish sultan.

The light of God is broken, dispersed throughout the world. And like the light his own mind is broken, splitting.

There is a knock on the door, and Nathan enters. "How did you find me?" Shabbetai asks.

Nathan appears surprised. "Don't you know?" he asks.

Shabbetai says nothing.

"I bribed a great many people to get you here," Nathan says. "Are you comfortable?"

"I—Yes. Quite comfortable."

"The sultan has returned from Crete," Nathan says. "There are rumors that he will want to see you."

"When?"

"I don't know. Soon, I think. He is alarmed by the support you have among the people of Turkey." Nathan pauses and then goes on. "Some of your followers are worried. They don't believe that we can hold out against the combined armies of the sultan."

"Tell them not to fear," Shabbetai says. He is surprised at how confident he sounds. But there is no reason to worry Nathan and the others, and perhaps the visions will return. "Tell them that God watches over me."

Nathan nods, satisfied.

A few days later Shabbetai is taken by guards from Gallipoli to Adrianople. They pass through the city and come to a strong high wall. Men look down at them from the watchtowers.

Soldiers with plumed helmets stand at the wall's gate. The soldiers nod to them and motion them through. Beyond the gate is a courtyard filled with fountains and cypress trees and green plots of grass where gazelles feed.

They turn left, and come to a door guarded by soldiers. They enter through this door and are shown before the sultan and his council.

"Do you claim to be the Messiah?" a councilor asks Shabbetai.

"No," he says.

"What?" the councilor says, astonished.

"No. Perhaps I was the Messiah once. But the light has left me—I see no more and no less than other people."

The sultan moves his hand. The councilor nods to him and turns toward Shabbetai. "I see," he says. "You understand that we cannot just take your word for this. We cannot say, Very well, you may go now. Your followers outside are waiting for you—you have become a very dangerous man."

"We are prepared to offer you a choice," the sultan says. "Either convert to Islam or be put to death immediately."

The light returns, filling the room. Shabbetai gasps; he had begun to think it lost forever. The light breaks. Two paths branch off before him.

On one path he accepts death. His followers, stunned, sit in mourning for him for the required seven days. Then Nathan pronounces him a martyr, and others proclaim that he has ascended to heaven.

His following grows. Miracles are seen, and attested to by others. An army forms; they attack the Turks. A long and bloody war follows. The sultan, the man sitting so smugly before him, is killed by one of his own people, a convert to what is starting to be called Sabbatarianism.

After a decade the Turks surrender, worn out by the fighting against the Sabbatarians on one side and the Venetians on the other. Shabbetai's followers take Constantinople; Hagia Sophia, once a church and then a mosque, is converted a third time by the victorious army.

The Sabbatarians consolidate their power, and spread across Europe and Asia. First hundreds and then thousands of heretics are put to death. Holy wars flare. Men hungry for power come to Constantinople and are given positions in the hierarchy of the new religion.

Finally, using the terrifying tools of the far future, the Sabbatarians set out to kill everyone who is not a believer. The broken light that Shabbetai saw in his vision shines across the sky as city after city is laid waste. Poisons cover the earth. At the end only a few thousand people are left alive.

Shabbetai turns his gaze away from the destruction and looks down the other path. Here he becomes a convert to Islam; he changes his name to Aziz Mehmed Effendi. The sultan, pleased at his decision, grants him a royal pension of 150 piasters a day.

His followers are shocked, but they soon invent reasons for his apostasy. Nathan explains that the conversion was necessary, that the Messiah must lose himself in darkness in order to find all the shards of God hidden in the world.

Over the years his followers begin to lose hope. Sarah dies in 1674. Two years later he himself dies. Several groups of Sabbatarians continue to meet in secret; one group even survives to the mid-twentieth century.

He turns back to the first path. Once again he is drawn to the vision of annihilation. An end to breeding and living and dying, an end to the mad ceaseless activity that covers the earth. Perhaps this is what God requires of him.

He remembers Sarah, her desire to lie with him. She thought him powerless; very well, he will show her something of power. Flame will consume her descendants, all the children he had been unable to give her.

The moon spins before him, fragments into a thousand pieces. He understands that his vision is not an allegory but real, that people will become so strong they can destroy the moon.

His head pounds. He is not powerless at all. He is the most powerful man in the world. All the people he has seen in his travels, the bakers and learned men and farmers and housewives and bandits, all of them depend for their lives on his next word.

He thinks of Sarah again, her tangled hair, her breath warm on his cheek. If he lets the world live all her children will be his, although she will not know it. Every person in the world will be his child. He can choose life, for himself and for everyone; he can do what he was chosen to do and heal the world.

The light blazes and dies. He looks up at the sultan and his men and says, calmly, "I will choose Islam."

LES FLEURS DU MAL

Brian Stableford

One of the most respected as well as one of the most prolific British SF writers, Brian Stableford is the author of more than thirty books, including *Cradle of the Sun*, *The Blind Worm*, *Days of Glory*, *In The Kingdom of the Beasts*, *Day of Wrath*, *The Halcyon Drift*, *The Paradox of the Sets*, *The Realms of Tartarus*, and the critically acclaimed trilogy consisting of *The Empire of Fear*, *The Angel of Pain*, and *The Carnival of Destruction*. His short fiction has been collected in *Sexual Chemistry: Sardonic Tales of the Genetic Revolution*. His nonfiction books include *The Sociology of Science Fiction* and, with David Langford, *The Third Millennium: A History of the World A.D. 2000–3000*. Upcoming is a new novel, *Serpent's Blood*, which is the start of another projected trilogy. His stories have appeared in our Sixth (two separate stories) and Seventh Annual Collections. A biologist and sociologist by training, Stableford lives in Reading, England.

In the ornate and engrossing novella that follows, Stableford takes us deep into a high-tech future whose decadent, ultrarich inhabitants have almost the power of gods . . . but even gods occasionally dabble in obsession and revenge, and *murder*. And when murder most foul (and most peculiar) begins to stalk through this calm and prosperous future Utopia, it's up to two very unusual detectives to cry "The game's afoot!" and track the killer down—if they *can*.

Prologue: 14 April, 2550

Oscar stood before the full-length mirror, carefully inspecting every detail of his face. He caressed the flawless flesh with sensitive fingertips, rejoicing in its gloss. "Ivory and rose-leaves," he murmured.

Oscar always addressed his own reflection in the most admiring terms while it remained full of youth. When it grew old, as it had three times before, it lost its capacity to inspire admiration, and became a mocking reminder of the hazards that he and all men of his era still faced: decay, senescence, decomposition.

His revitalized hair was a glossy chestnut brown. To describe his complexion in terms of ivory and rose-leaves was a trifle hyperbolic, but the skin was pale and even. Authentically young men never had skin as perfect as that, because they could not help accumulating petty flaws while growing to maturity; only the rejuvenated could attain perfection, thanks to the artistry of their cosmetic engineers.

It was a nice paradox, Oscar thought, that only those who had been old could look *truly* young. He had flown in the face of professional advice by attempting a third rejuvenation so soon, at the age of 133. Many older men than he had not yet undergone their second rejuvenation, refusing to risk deep somatic engineering while their bodies had not quite descended to the depths of decrepitude. Oscar was far less brave than they; his fear of personal dilapidation was pathological.

"It is only shallow people," he informed his reflection, confident in the knowledge that he had an appreciative audience, "who do not judge by appearances." He bathed in the luxury of his own narcissism, admiring his grey eyes, his soft lips, his pearly white teeth.

He reached out to pluck a green carnation from the wall beside the mirror. He twirled it between his delicate fingers, admiring it with as much satisfaction as he admired his own image. The flower was his own creation. It was a joke, of course, but a serious joke. The games which Oscar played in consequence of his name—which had been given to him in all innocence by parents whose knowledge of the earlier Oscar Wilde was limited to a vague awareness that he had been a writer of note—were no mere matter of public relations. His identification with the ideas and ideals of his *alter ego* had long ago become a kind of fetish. He was not afraid to acknowledge that fact, nor to take pride in it. Life, if it were to be lived to the full in modern conditions, required a definite style and aesthetic shape: a constant flow of delicate ironies, tensions, and innovations.

He placed the flower in the buttonhole of his neatly tailored suit.

Furnishing hotel interiors was vulgar hackwork unbefitting a real artist, but a real artist had to make a living, and the commonplaceness of such commissions was offset by such flourishes of unorthodoxy as having it written into every contract that one suite of rooms should be fitted with green carnations instead of the more fashionable roses and amaranths. His clients did not mind his making such demands; they were, after all, paying for his fashionability as well as his technical dexterity, and he could not have been nearly so fashionable were it not for his extravagantly extrovert eccentricity.

He turned one way and then the other, shrugging his shoulders to make sure that his jacket hung perfectly upon his remodeled body.

Oscar did not doubt for a moment, as his greedy eyes devoured the glory of his reflection, that he would be equal to the challenge of his third youth. He was no crass businessman, apt to fall back into the same old routines at the first opportunity, wearing a new face as if it were merely a mask laid over the old. Nor was he the kind of man who would go to the opposite extreme, reverting to the habits and follies of first youthfulness, playing the sportsman or the rake. He was an *artist*. Artists had always been the pioneers who led mankind into the psychological unknown, and the current technology of rejuvenation was, after all, little more than a century old. No one knew for sure how many times a man might be successfully restored to youth, although it was tragically obvious that many failed at the second or third attempt. Oscar was firmly resolved that if the only thing required to secure eternal life was the correct attitude of mind, then he would be the first man to live forever.

He closed his eyes for a moment while he savored the pleasures of anticipation, but his delicious reverie was shattered by the comcon bell. He sighed, and crossed the room to the nearest telescreen, pausing only to make sure that his cravat was in order before exposing himself to the unit's camera-eye. His precautions were unnecessary; no face appeared on the screen. There was only a teletext message, cold and impersonal. It was a request that he should call on a man he knew only slightly, and did not like at all. It seemed an unromantic and unpromising beginning to the new phase of his life. He reached out to send a message refusing the invitation, but paused before his fingers could descend upon the keys. The fax light was blinking. He pressed the RECEIVE button. He expected a copy of the message displayed on the screen, but what emerged from the humming printer was a seat reservation for the midnight maglev to San Francisco. Oscar had no intention of going to San Francisco; no such thought had crossed his mind. He could not imagine why anyone, least of all Gabriel King, should send him such a gift, with or without an explanation.

"Curiouser and curiouser," he murmured.

He decided to obey the summons after all. He had never been able to resist temptation, and there was nothing in the world quite as tempting as a mystery.

1

While she waited for the forensic experts to conclude their examination of Gabriel King's apartment, Charlotte Holmes tried to collect her thoughts. This was by far the biggest case of her fledgling career. Routine police work was incredibly dull, at least for site-investigation officers, and there had been nothing in her training or experience to prepare her for anything half as bizarre as *this*. Murder was nowadays the rarest of crimes, and such murders as *did* happen usually occurred when rage or spite smashed through the barriers erected by years of biofeedback training. Premeditated murders had fallen out of fashion as soon as it became impossible for the perpetrators to avoid apprehension.

She went to the window at the end of the corridor and looked out over the city. She was on the thirty-ninth floor, and there was quite a view. Central Park looked much as it must have looked in the days before the Devastation, but the rotting skyline was a product of the moment, whose like would probably never be seen again. Charlotte assumed that Gabriel King must have taken up residence in New York so that he might bid for a lion's share of the work involved in the deconstruction of the city. He had always been bigger in demolition than in construction, because he controlled a number of key patents in decay biotechnology. The Decivilization Movement had been a great boon to his business, although its prophets detested Gabriel King as much as they detested all old-style entrepreneurs, especially wealthy multiple rejuvenates. King could easily have made enemies among the people whose crusade he was furthering, and among the business rivals who had competed with him for the contracts—but who among them could have thought up the murder weapon she had just been studying through a camera-eye?

Her waistphone buzzed, and she took the handscreen from its holster. No image appeared. Hal Watson rarely allowed his face to be seen; he was a dealer in data, and preferred to remain invisible within the webs of information that he spun. "Two names," he said. As he spoke, the names appeared on the screen in capital letters: WALTER CZASTKA; OSCAR WILDE. "They're the top people involved in the engineering of flowering plants," the voice continued. "We'll need one of them as a consultant, to double-check the forensic investigation. Czastka's in Micronesia, on an island he's leased in order to build an artificial ecosystem. Wilde's here in New York, but he's just gone through his third rejuvenation and may be incommunicado. Try Czastka first."

"I'll call him," said Charlotte. "What about the girl?"

"Nothing yet. Camscan's under way. Might be able to pick her up somewhere, figure out where she came from or where she went. Has the team come out of the apartment yet?"

"No," said Charlotte, glumly. "I'll stay until they do."

"Don't worry," Hal said. "It'll open up once we have the forensics. With luck, we might crack the case before the story leaks out."

Charlotte sighed, and began punching the buttons on the handset. She tried Czastka first, as instructed. The fact that he was on the other side of the world wasn't of any real consequence, because he'd have to use a camera to inspect the murder-weapon anyhow, and probably wouldn't be able to do much more until the lab had turned up a geneprint. The image which came onto the screen was a grade A sim.

"Charlotte Holmes," she said. "UN Police. Sending authority." The privacy-breaking codes cut no ice. The sim told her that Czastka was temporarily unreachable. That probably meant that he was messing about somewhere on his island, without a beeper. It wasn't worth the hassle of getting Czastka's house-system to send out a summoner while there was an obvious alternative.

This time, she got a low-grade AI receptionist, which informed her that Oscar Wilde was not in his hotel room at present. She sent her authorization code. The pretty face flickered as the new subroutine was engaged. "Mr. Wilde is in a cab," said the higher-grade receptionist, her simulated voice still honey-sweet. "Sending contact code; destination Trebizond Tower."

Charlotte was just about to retransmit the contact code when she realized that Trebizond Tower was the building on whose thirty-ninth floor she was standing.

"What a coincidence," she murmured, reflectively. Before she had finished wondering what the coincidence might possibly signify, another voice-call came through. This one was from the uniformed officer she had posted at the bottom of the elevator shaft to keep the public at bay.

"There's an Oscar Wilde here," said the officer, laconically. "He says he got a message half an hour ago to come up to King's apartment."

Charlotte frowned. Gabriel King had been dead for quite some time, and no call could possibly have been made from his apartment. "Send him up," she said, tersely. She had an uncomfortable feeling of being out of her depth. She was only a legman, after all; Hal was the real investigator. She hesitated over calling Hal to tell him what had happened, but decided against it. Instead, she went to the elevator to meet the new arrival.

When the man emerged, she felt a curious jolt of astonishment. Hal had mentioned that Wilde was a recent rejuvenate, but she hadn't adapted her expectations to take account of it. Expert witnesses and other consultants usually looked fairly old, but Oscar Wilde looked ten years younger than *she* did; in fact, he was quite the most beautiful man she had ever seen. He bowed gracefully, and then looked up, briefly, at the discreet plastic eye set in the wall, whose security camera recorded every face which passed by.

Public eyes and private bubblebugs were everywhere in a city like New York, and native New Yorkers were entirely used to living under observation; those who had grown up with the situation took it completely for granted. In some unintegrated nations, it still wasn't common for all walls to have eyes and ears, but within the borders of the six superpowers, citizens had long since been required to learn to tolerate the ever-presence of the benevolent mechanical observers which guaranteed their safety. Wilde was neither a native New Yorker nor a genuinely young man, but he didn't give the impression that he resented the presence of the eye at all. If anything, his self-consciousness suggested that he *liked* to be watched.

"Mr. Wilde?" she said, tentatively. "I'm Charlotte Holmes, UN Police Department."

"Please call me Oscar," said the beautiful man. "What exactly has happened to poor Gabriel?"

"He's dead," Charlotte replied, shortly. "I understand that you received a call from him, or his simulacrum?"

"The message came as text only, with a supplementary fax. It was an invitation—or perhaps a *command*. It was sufficiently impolite to warrant disobedience, but sufficiently intriguing to be tempting."

"That message wasn't sent from this apartment," she told him, bluntly.

"Then you must trace it," he replied, affably, "and discover where it did come from. It would be interesting to know, would it not, who sent it and why?"

They were interrupted by the emergence of the forensic team from the apartment. Charlotte waited patiently while they removed their sterile suits. Oscar looked curiously at all the protective gear, undoubtedly wondering why it had been necessary to use it.

"It's sealed," said the team-leader. "We set up a camera on remote control, and we stripped all the bubbled data there was. We connected his personal machines to the Net so that Hal can trawl the data."

Oscar wore a quizzical expression. Charlotte didn't want to enlighten him yet as to what had happened; she was anxious to see what his reaction would be when she showed him what was in the apartment. She led the way to the screen mounted in the wall outside the apartment door, and punched in the instruction codes.

The camera was still at the scene, but it had been left pointing tastefully away from the *corpus delicti*. The room was furnished in an unusually utilitarian manner; there was no decorative plant life integrated into the walls, nor any kind of inert decoration. There were mural screens on the blank walls, but they displayed plain shades of pastel blue. Apart from the food delivery point, the room's main feature was a particularly elaborate array of special-function telescreens. Charlotte juggled the camera while Oscar peered over her shoulder, raptly. On one of three sofas lay all that remained of the late Gabriel King. The "corpse" was no more than a skeleton, whose white bones were intricately entwined with gorgeous flowers. Charlotte zoomed in, and moved aside to let her companion look closely at the strange garlands and the reclining skeleton.

The stems and leaves of the marvelous plant were green, but the petals of each bloom were black. The waxy stigma at the center of each bell was dark red, and had the form of a *crux ansata*. Oscar Wilde took over the controls, moving them delicately so that he could inspect the structure and texture of the flowers at the minutest level. He followed the rim of a corolla, then passed along a stem which bore huge thorns, paler in color than the flesh from which they sprouted. Each thorn was tipped with red, as though it had drawn blood. The stems wound around and around the long bones of the corpse, holding the skeleton together even though every vestige of flesh had been consumed. The plant had supportive structures like holdfasts which maintained the shape of the whole organism and the coherence of the skeleton. The skull was very strikingly embellished, with a single stem emerging from each of the empty eye-sockets.

"Can you be certain that it's Gabriel?" asked Oscar, finally.

"Pretty certain," Charlotte said. "In the absence of retinas the analysts checked the skull-shape and the dental profile. A DNA scan on the bone-marrow will confirm it. It seems that the flowers are composed of what used to be his flesh. You might say that their seeds devoured him as they grew."

"Fascinating," he said, in a tone which had more admiration in it than horror.

"Fascinating!" she echoed, in exasperation. "Can you imagine what an organism like that might *do* if it ever got loose? We're looking at something that could wipe out the entire human race!"

"I think not," said Oscar, calmly. "These are single-sexed flowers from a dioecious species, incapable of producing fertile seed. How long ago did Gabriel die?"

"Between two and three days," she told him, grimly. "He seems to have felt the first symptoms about seventy hours ago; he was incapacitated soon afterward, and died a few hours later."

Oscar licked his lips, as though savoring his own astonishment. "Those delightful flowers must have a voracious appetite," he said.

Charlotte eyed him carefully, wondering exactly what his reaction might signify. "You're something of a flower-designer yourself, I believe." Her gaze flickered momentarily to the green carnation in his lapel. "Could you make plants like those?"

Oscar met her eyes frankly. She was as tall as he, and their stares were perfectly level. He frowned as he considered the matter, then said: "Until I saw this marvel, I would have opined that *no* man could. Clearly, I have underrated one of my peers." He seemed genuinely perplexed, although the level of his concern for the victim and for the fact that a crime had been committed left something to be desired.

Charlotte stared hard at the beautiful man, wondering whether anyone in the world were capable of committing an act like this and then turning up in person to confront and mock the officers investigating the crime. She decided that if he could be guilty of the *first* madness, the second might not be too hard to believe. "I can't help feeling that your appearance here is a very strange coincidence, Mr. Wilde," she said.

"It is indeed," said Oscar, blithely. "Given that it seems to be impossible that I was summoned by the victim, I can only conclude that I was summoned by the murderer."

"I find that hard to believe."

"It *is* hard to believe. But when we have eliminated the impossible, are we not committed to believing the improbable? Unless, of course, you think that *I* did this to poor Gabriel, and have come to gloat over his fate? I disliked the man, but I did not dislike him as much as *that*—and if I had decided to murder him, I certainly would not have revisited the scene of my crime in this reckless fashion. A showman I might be, a madman never." He turned back to the screen, and looked again at the deadly flowers, which were still displayed there in intimate close-up.

Charlotte did not want to be put off. "As it happens," she said, "we would have shown all this material to you anyway. We need an expert report on the nature and potential of the organism, and I was given two possible names. I couldn't get through to Walter Czastka. I was trying to call you at your hotel while you were on the way over here."

"I'm offended by the fact that you tried Walter first," Oscar murmured, "but I forgive you."

"Mr. Wilde. . . ."she began, feeling that her patience was being tested too far.

"Yes, of course," he said, "This is a serious matter—a murder investigation. I think I can hazard a guess as to why the summons was sent. I suspect that I was brought here to identify the murderer."

"How?" she demanded.

"By his style," he replied.

"That's ridiculous!" she said, petulantly. "If the murderer had wanted to identify himself, all he had to do was call us. How would he know that you could recognize his work—and why, if he knew it, would he want you to *do* it?"

"Those are interesting questions," admitted Oscar. "Nevertheless, I can only suppose that I was sent an invitation to this mysterious event in order that I might play a part in its unraveling." He paused, and looked at her reproachfully, radiating injured innocence. "You really do suspect that I'm responsible for this, don't you?" he said.

"If not *you*," she countered, "then who?"

He opened his arms wide in a gesture of exaggerated helplessness. "I cannot claim to be absolutely certain," he said, "but if appearances and may expert judgment *are* to be trusted, these flowers are the work of the man who has always been known to me as Rappaccini!"

2

Charlotte called Hal Watson. "Oscar Wilde's here," she said, making an effort to be businesslike. "Can you trace the call that was made to his hotel room asking him to come? He says the flowers might have been made by a man named Rappaccini."

"Of course," Oscar added, with annoying casualness, "Rappaccini is not his real name. Some long-standing members of the Institute of Genetic Art still prefer to exhibit their work pseudonymously—a hangover from the days of prejudice."

"Are you one of them?" she asked.

Oscar shook his head. "I am fortunate enough to have a real name that *sounds* like a pseudonym—my identity thus becomes a kind of double bluff."

"Perhaps," she said, "your identification of Rappaccini as the man who made the flowers is also a double bluff."

Oscar shook his head. "I fear that I have an ironclad alibi. Three days ago I was in the hospital, and the flesh of my outer tissues was unbecomingly fluid. I had been there for some time."

"That doesn't prove anything," Charlotte pointed out. "You might have made the seeds months ago, and made sure that they were delivered—or began to take effect—while you were in the hospital."

"I suppose I might have," said Oscar, wearily, "but I assure you that your investigation will proceed more smoothly if you forget about me and concentrate on Rappaccini."

"Why should a man take the trouble to summon someone capable of identifying him to the scene of the crime?" she asked, with a trace of asperity. "Why didn't he simply leave his calling card?"

"Why didn't he simply shoot Gabriel King with a revolver?" countered the geneticist. "Why go to the effort of designing and making this fabulous plant? There is something very strange going on here, dear Charlotte."

There certainly is, she thought, staring at him, as if by effort she could penetrate the lovely mask to see the secret self within. Oscar, seemingly unalarmed by her scrutiny, began to play with the keys that controlled the camera in the apartment. He zoomed in on something which lay on the glass-topped table. It was a small cardboard rectangle. It had been lacquered over as a safety-measure, but it was still possible to read what was written on it. The words were in French, but Oscar effortlessly read out what Charlotte took to be a translation.

" 'Stupidity, error, sin and poverty of spirit,' " he said, " 'possess our hearts and work within our bodies, and we nourish our fond remorse as beggars suckle their own parasites.' Perhaps the murderer *did* leave his calling card, Inspector Holmes. A man like Gabriel King would hardly have a note of such lines as those."

"Do you recognize them?" asked Charlotte.

"A poem by Baudelaire. *Au lecteur*—that is, 'To the Reader.' From *Les Fleurs du Mal*. A play on words, I think."

Charlotte's audio-link to Hal Watson was still open. "Did you catch that, Hal?" she asked.

"I checked the words already," Hal replied. "He's right."

Charlotte wondered how many men there were in the world who could recognize seven-hundred-year-old poems written in French. Surely, she thought, Oscar Wilde *must* be the person behind all this. But if so, what monstrous game was he playing?

"What significance do you attach to the card?" she asked him, sharply.

"If my earlier reasoning was correct, it must be a message directed to me," replied Oscar. "*All* this is communication—not merely the card, and the message which summoned me, but the flowers, and the crime itself. The whole affair is to be *read*, and hence understood. I am here because Rappaccini expects me to be able to interpret and comprehend what he is doing."

Charlotte tried to remain impassive, but she knew that her amazement was showing. She was grateful when the phone in her hand crackled.

"I'm blocked on Rappaccini for the moment," said Hal. "His real name is recorded as Jafri Biasiolo, but there's hardly any official data on Biasiolo at all beyond his birth-date, way back in 2420. It's old data, of course, and may be just a sketchy construction of disinformation."

Old data tended to be incomplete, often corrupted by all kinds of errors—although she noticed that Hal had said "disinformation," which meant lies, rather than "misinformation." In Hal's view, old data was senile data, too decrepit to be of much use in a slick modern police inquiry. But Gabriel King had been nearly a hundred and fifty years old, and Oscar Wilde—in spite of appearances—must be well over a hundred. If Rappaccini really had been born in 2420, the motive for this affair might go all the way back to the final years of the Aftermath. The Net had been of holes in those days.

"What about the call which summoned Wilde here?" she asked.

"Placed three days ago from a blind unit, time-triggered to arrive when it did. I've got nowhere with the woman yet. No picture-match, no route to or from the apartment-house. This is going to take longer than I had hoped."

Charlotte digested this information. She was not unduly surprised by the news that the real person behind "Rappaccini" might be difficult to identify. It was easy enough nowadays to establish electronic identities whose telescreen appearances could be maintained and controlled by AI simulacra. Virtual individuals could play so full a role in modern society that their real puppet-masters could easily remain hidden—until they came under the scrutiny of a highly skilled investigator. Hal could get through any conventional information-wall, and work his way through any data-maze, but it would take time. She had a gut feeling that told her that the creator of "Rappaccini" was right in front of her, taunting her with his presence, but she didn't dare say so to Hal. He was no respecter of gut feelings.

"Can you patch the security tape through to the wallscreen here?" she said. "I'd like Mr. Wilde to see it. He seems to know everything else—perhaps he can tell us who the woman is."

"Ah," said Oscar, softly. "*Cherchez la femme!* Without a woman the crime could not be deemed complete!"

"Hal Watson's a top cracksman," Charlotte told him, trying to shake his casual composure. "He can get into all the little electronic backwaters all the locked-up mines of information. It's impossible to hide anything from him. It's only a matter of time before we get to the bottom of this.''

Wilde did not seem in the least intimidated. ''I'm delighted to find the two of you working in partnership,'' he said. ''It demonstrates that even the higher echelons of the International Bureau of Investigation are home to a sense of humor and a sense of tradition.''

He was trying to be clever again, but this time she knew what he meant. Everyone made jokes about it.

On the biggest of the display screens on the far wall there appeared an image of the corridor outside the apartment. The tape had already been edited; no sooner had it started than a young woman came into view, reaching out to activate the doorchime. Her lustrous brown hair was worn unfashionably long. She had clear blue eyes and finely-chiseled features. Even in this day and age, when cosmetic engineers could so easily remold superficial flesh, her beauty was striking. It was not merely the shape of her face, but the undefinable presence which she brought to it. Charlotte could not quite make up her mind weather she was authentically young, or whether she was a successful product of rejuvenative engineering, whose perfection of manner arose from long and careful practice. The woman stepped forward as the door opened, and passed beneath the eye.

The viewpoint abruptly shifted to the second security camera in the hall. King was visible now, with his back to the camera, and Charlotte watched carefully as the girl moved forward, her eyes gazing into his, and raised her head slightly so that he could kiss her on the lips. King did not seem surprised, and he responded to the unspoken invitation. The kiss did not seem particularly passionate; it might, Charlotte thought have been a polite greeting between people who had some history of intimacy, but were meeting as friends, or it might have been a friendly kiss exchanged in hopeful anticipation of future intimacy. There was no sound-track on the tape, but few words were spoken before King stood aside to let his visitor precede him into the sitting room. The tape cut again, and they saw the woman re-emerge from the doorway. She was alone, and seemed quite composed as she walked to the main door of the apartment, opened it, and went out.

''She was inside for about half an hour,'' said Charlotte, drily. ''King was still perfectly healthy when she left, and it wasn't until some twelve or thirteen hours later that he called up a diagnostic program. He never had a chance to hit his panic button—the progress of the plant was too swift. We'll know more when we've decanted his bubblebugs, but we won't know what went on in the bedroom. The girl might have nothing at all to do with it, but she *was* the last person to see him alive. We don't know how she fed him the seeds, if indeed she did feed them to him. Do you recognize her?''

''I'm afraid not,'' said Oscar. ''I can only offer the obvious suggestion.''

''Which is?''

''Rappaccini's daughter.''

Charlotte said nothing, but simply waited for clarification.

''It's another echo of the nineteenth century,'' said Oscar, with a slight sigh.

"Rappaccini borrowed his pseudonym from a story by Nathaniel Hawthorne entitled 'Rappaccini's Daughter.' You don't know the period, I take it?"

"Not very well," she said awkwardly. "Hardly at all" would have been nearer the truth.

"Then it's as well that I'm here. Otherwise, this exotic performance would be entirely wasted."

"You think that the man you know as Rappaccini is acting the part of his namesake—just as you make a show of acting the part of yours?"

Oscar shrugged. "In the story, Rappaccini committed no murder—but he did cultivate fatal flowers: *fleurs du mal*. Our Rappaccini has signed his work, for those who have the wit to read the signature. I have a strong suspicion that we have probably seen the murder committed, by means of that gentle kiss which our mysterious visitor delivered. She, of course, would have to be immune to them."

"This is too much," Charlotte explained.

"I quite agree. As lushly extravagant as a poem in prose by Baudelaire himself. But we have been instructed to expect a Baudelairean dimension. I can hardly wait for the next installment of the story."

"You think this is going to happen again?"

"I'm almost sure of it," said Oscar, with infuriating calm. "If Rappaccini intends to present us with a real psychodrama, he will hardly stop when he has only just begun.

"The next murder, by the way, might well be committed in San Francisco."

"Why San Francisco?"

"Because the item which was faxed through to me when I was summoned here was a reservation for the midnight maglev to San Francisco." So saying, he took a sheet of paper from his pocket, and held it out for her inspection.

She took it from him, and stared at it dumbly.

"Why didn't you show me this immediately?" she said.

"My mind was occupied with other things. Anyhow, your colleague Dr. Watson must have obtained a copy of the message when he tried to trace it. Perhaps he has already begun to investigate. I do hope that you will not try to prevent my using the ticket—and that you will allow me to assist you throughout the investigation."

"Why should I?" she replied. She was uncomfortably aware of the fact that she could not prevent his going anywhere in the world he pleased.

"Because the person who committed this murder has gone to extraordinary lengths to make me party to the investigation. If I am supposed to go to San Francisco, there must be a reason. This is only the beginning, dear Charlotte, and if you wish to get to the end with all possible speed, you must stay with me. You can, of course, count on my complete cooperation and my absolute discretion."

And you, Charlotte said, silently, while she stared into his lovely eyes, *can count on being instantly arrested, the moment Hal digs up anything that proves your involvement in this unholy mess.*

3

IBI headquarters in New York were in the "new" UN complex built in 2431. There had once been talk of the UN taking over the whole of Manhattan Island, but that had gone the way of most dream-schemes during the troubled years of the Aftermath. Now, an even more grandiose plan to move the core of the UN bureaucracy to Antarctica was well-advanced. The same sentence of death had been passed on the IBI complex that had been passed on the whole of New York City, but Gabriel King's brand of controlled rot had not yet been allowed to set in.

"How well did you know Gabriel King?" Charlotte asked Oscar, while they were *en route* in the police car. He had suggested that he come with her until the time appointed for his departure, and she had been quick to agree although she knew that Hal would not approve.

"I supply his company with decorative materials for various building projects. I haven't *met* him for more than twenty years. He and I are by no means kindred spirits."

"And how well do you know Rappaccini?"

"I know the work far better than the man, but there was a period before and after the Great Exhibition when we met regularly. We were often bracketed together by critics who observed a kinship in our ideas, methods, and personalities but I was never convinced of the similarity. Our conversations were never intimate; we discussed art and genetics, never ourselves. It was a long time ago."

She would have pursued the line of questioning further, but the distance between the Trebizond Tower and the UN complex was short, and they arrived before she had a chance to do any serious probing. She asked Oscar to wait in her office while she consulted her colleague in private. "I brought Wilde with me," she told Hal, brusquely.

Even in the dim light, she was easily able to see the expression of distaste which flitted across Hal's face, but all he said was: "Why?"

"Because he knows too much about this business," she said, wishing that it didn't sound so feeble, so *intuitive*. "I know it sounds crazy, but I think he set this whole thing *up*, then turned up in person to watch us wrestle with it!"

"So you think his introduction of the 'Rappaccini' name is a red herring?"

"Yes, I do. It's all far too convenient. Is it possible that Rappaccini is entirely his invention?"

"I'll check it out," Hal said. "But we don't need him *here*."

"He wants to go to San Francisco on the midnight maglev."

"Let him. What difference does it make? We can find him, if need be, in San Francisco or on the moon."

"Suppose he were to murder someone *else*," said Charlotte, desperately. It was pointless. Modern detective work was sifting data, carefully sorting the relevant from the irrelevant, and the real information from misinformation and disinformation. Talking to people, being a real-time activity, was generally considered to be an inordinately wasteful use of IBI time, to be kept to an absolute minimum even by lowly scene-of-crime officers. "Can I bring him down here?" Charlotte asked, defensively. "I'd like you to see for yourself what he's like—then perhaps you'll understand what I mean."

Hal shrugged in world-weary fashion.

Charlotte collected Oscar from her office, and brought him down into Hal's Underworld. The room was crowded with screens and comcons, but there were enough workstations for them to sit reasonably comfortably.

"Oscar Wilde—Hal Watson," she said, with awkward formality. "Mr. Wilde thinks that his unique insight may be of some help in the investigation."

"I hope so," said Oscar, smoothly. "There are times when instant recognition and artistic sensitivity facilitate more rapid deduction than the most powerful analytical engines. I am an invader in your realm, of course—and I confess that I feel like one of those mortals of old who fell asleep on a burial mound and woke to find himself in the gloomy land of the fairy folk—but I really do feel that I can help you. I have some hours in hand before the midnight maglev leaves."

"I'm always grateful for any help I can get," said Hal, not bothering to feign sincerity. Charlotte saw that her colleague was unimpressed by Oscar Wilde's recently renewed handsomeness. Hal, whose machine-assisted perceptions ground up all the richness and complexity of the social world into mere atoms of data, had not the same idea of beauty as common men. The cataract of encoded data which poured through his screens was *his* reality, and, for him, beauty was to be found in patterns woven out of information or enigmas smoothed into comprehension, not in the hard and soft sculptures of stone and flesh. Unfortunately, the unshadowy world of hard and superabundant data had yet to be persuaded to explain how it had produced the eccentric masterpiece of mere appearances which was the murder of Gabriel King.

"Rappaccini is proving evasive," Hal told Charlotte, while his eyes continued to scan his screens. "His business dealings are fairly elaborate, but he holds a flag-of-convenience citizenship in the Kalahari Republic, and has no recorded residence. His telephonic addresses are black boxes, and he conducts all his affairs through the medium of AIs. The Rappaccini name first became manifest in 2480, when he registered with the Institute of the Genetic Arts in Sydney. He participated in a number of public exhibitions, including the Great Exhibition of 2505, sometimes putting in personal appearances. Unlike other genetic engineers specializing in flowering plants, he never got involved in designing gardens or in the kind of interior decoration that provides you with a living, Mr. Wilde. He seems to have specialized in the design of funeral wreaths."

"Funeral wreaths?" echoed Charlotte, incredulously. The manufacture of funeral wreaths seemed an absurd profession for anyone to follow, even in the guise of a part-time *persona*. Now that serial rejuvenation supposedly guaranteed everyone an extended lifespan, funerals were not the everyday occurrences they once had been. On the other hand, their very rarity meant that the ceremony devoted to the commemoration of revered public figures was usually very lavish.

"Rappaccini's flowers have always been grown under contract by middlemen in various parts of Australia." Hal went on, while his fingers roamed in desultory fashion over his keyboards. "I'm checking the routes by which seeds used to be delivered, trying to backtrack them to the laboratories of origin, but he hasn't put out anything new in thirty years. His agents are still making up wreaths and crediting him with royalties, but they've had no personal contact since 2520. He still has a considerable credit balance, and he probably has more in accounts I haven't identified yet. His last manifestation as an active electronic *persona* was in 2527. Incoming telephone calls have been handled since then by a simulacrum which doesn't seem to have referred enquiries elsewhere. Our best hope of discovering the real person behind the network of sims is a thorough interrogation of the financial records. The real person has to have *some* means of recovering or redirecting credit accumulated by the dummy. I also have AIs trawling out the data relating to every recorded public appearance Rappaccini has ever made. We'll pin him down, even if it takes a week. I have all the data in the world to work with—I just need time to find, extract, and combine the relevant items. If your artistic intuition throws up any other helpful suggestions, just let me know, and I'll let loose another pack of data-hounds."

"Mr. Wilde hasn't been able to guess why Rappaccini should want to murder Gabriel King," said Charlotte. "Do we have anything on a possible motive?"

"I'm investigating King's background," said Hal. "If there's a motive there, I'll find it. For the time being, I'm more interested in the method. We know that the murderer has to be a first-class genetic engineer, so I've got AIs looking at the people who have the necessary expertise, trying to eliminate them one by one. It's not easy, of course—there are too many commercial engineers whose work involves the relevant technical skills. Even a structural engineer like Gabriel King might be able to adapt what he knew."

"I don't think so," Oscar said, dubiously.

"Maybe not," said Hal. "Naturally, we'll start with the people whose expertise is most relevant. Walter Czastka—and yourself, of course, Dr. Wilde."

"My life," said Oscar, airily, "is an open book. I fear that the sheer profusion of data will test the stamina of your programs—but that may make it all the easier for them to eliminate me from consideration. The idea that Walter Czastka might be Rappaccini is too absurd to contemplate."

"Why?" asked Charlotte.

"A matter of style," said Oscar. "Walter never had any."

"According to the database, he's the top man in the field—or was."

"I presume you mean that he has made more money than anyone else out of engineered flowers. Walter is a mass-producer, not an artist. I fear that if Rappaccini is leading a double life, you will not find his secret identity among the ranks of flower-designers. You'll have to cast your net further afield. He might be an animal engineer, perhaps a human engineer . . . but there are thousands of experts in each category."

"My AIs are indefatigable," Hal assured him. He was interrupted by a quiet beep from one of his comcons. His fingers raced back and forth across the relevant keyboard for a few seconds while he stared thoughtfully at a screen half-hidden from Charlotte's view. After half a minute or so, he said: "You might be interested to see this, Dr. Wilde." He pointed to the biggest of his display screens, mounted high on the wall directly in front of them.

A picture appeared on the left of the screen. It showed a tall man with silver hair, a dark beard trimmed into a goatee, and a prominent nose. "Rappaccini in 2481," Hal said "Taken at the offices of his growers during an early meeting." He pressed more keys and another image appeared in the center of the screen, showing two men side by side. One of them was clearly the same man whose image was already on the screen.

"Isn't that . . . ?" Charlotte began.

"I fear that it is," said Oscar, regretfully. "I looked a lot older then, of course. Taken in 2505, I believe, at the Sydney Exhibition."

It proves nothing that they've been photographed together, Charlotte thought. *That may only be an actor, hired to lend flesh to the illusion.* Somehow, though, she couldn't quite believe it.

"It was 2505," agreed Hal. A third picture appeared, again showing Rappaccini alone. "2520," Hal said. "His last public appearance."

Charlotte compared the three pictures. There was hardly any difference between them. The man had not undergone a full rejuvenation between 2481 and 2520, although he had probably employed light cosmetic reconstruction to maintain the appearance of dignified middle-age.

"If he really was born in 2420, he seems to have delayed rejuvenation far longer than usual," said Hal, pensively. "He must have had a full rejuve very soon after the last picture was taken—I'll get a program to trawl the records. A picture-search program might be able to connect up the face, but that kind of data's very messy. It's proving difficult to track the woman who visited Gabriel King's apartment—there are plenty of cameras in the streets, but a bit of everyday make-up and a wig can cause a good deal of confusion. Faces aren't as widely different as they used to be, now that so many people use light cosmetic engineering to follow fashion-trends. We'll trace her eventually, but . . . again, it's a matter of time."

As he spoke, three signals began beeping and blinking within the space of a second's hesitation, and his attention was instantly diverted. Charlotte and Oscar left the computer-man to the company of his assiduous AIs.

"It's good to know," observed Oscar, as the elevator carried them up, "that there are so many patient recording angels sorting religiously through the multitudinous sins of mankind. Alas, I fear that the capacity of our fellow men for *committing* sins may still outstrip their best endeavors."

"On the contrary," Charlotte retorted. "The crime rate keeps going down and down as the number of spy-eyes and bubblebugs scattered around the world goes up and up."

"I spoke of *sins*, not crimes," said Oscar. "What your electronic eyes do *not* see the law may not grieve about, but the capacity for sin will lurk in the hearts of men long after its expression has been banished from their actions."

"People can do what they like in the privacy of their virtual realities," she said. "There's no sin in that."

"If there were no sin in our adventures in imagination," Oscar replied, evidently determined to have the last word, "there would be no enjoyment in them. It is mainly our sense of sin which sustains our appetite for virtual experience. No matter how perfect an image we present to the world, in our appearances and our actions, we are as vicious at heart as we have ever been. If you cannot understand that, my dear, I fear that you will never be a real detective.''

4

While he still had time to spare, Charlotte took Oscar to dinner in the IBI's restaurant, where he decided that what his appetite demanded was Tournedos Béarnaise and a bottle of St. Emilion. IBI food technology was easily adequate to the task of meeting these requirements. Its beef was grown from a celebrated local tissue-culture which had long rejoiced in the pet name of Baltimore Bess: a veritable mountain of muscle, ''rejuvenated'' a hundred times or more by means of the techniques whose gradual perfection in the last two centuries had paved the way for the rejuvenation of human beings. The St. Emilion was authentic, although the whole Bordeaux region had been replanted as recently as 2430, when connoisseurs had decided that the native root-stocks had suffered too much deterioration due to the environmental degradations of the Third Biotech War.

''This crime,'' said Charlotte, as soon as she felt the time was ripe for talk of business, ''is the work of a very remarkable mind.''

''Very,'' Oscar agreed. ''I have, of course, a very remarkable mind myself, but genius is always unique. I wear my genius openly, and can barely understand the temperament that would hide away an entire life behind a series of electronic masks, but the man who has invented Rappaccini is clearly a dissimulator. I suspect that this crime has been planned for a very long time. The fictitious Rappaccini might have been *invented* with this murder in mind, and every detail of him has been tailored to its requirements. Absurd as it may seem, I cannot help but wonder whether my involvement as a witness was planned along with the crime.''

Charlotte studied his face soberly. She wondered whether he had designed his own features. It was rare to see such flamboyant femininity in the lines of a male's face, but she had to admit that it suited him.

''What was your impression of the man who posed as Rappaccini?'' she asked.

''I liked him. He had an admirable hauteur—as if he considered himself a more profound person by far than the other exhibitors at the Great Exhibition. He was a man of civilized taste and conversation. He appeared to like me, and we shared a taste for all things antiquarian—particularly relics of the nineteenth century, to which we were both linked by our names.''

''Do you remember anything *useful?*'' asked Charlotte, with some slight impatience. ''Anything which might help us to identify the man behind the name.''

''I fear not. We never became *friends.* We were both solitary workers, deeply interested in the purely aesthetic aspects of our work. One could not say that of all the exhibitors at Sydney, or even of the majority. Walter Czastka is more typical—he has always worked with an army of apprentices, far more interested in industry than art.''

"You don't seem to like Walter Czastka," she observed.

Oscar hesitated briefly before replying. "I don't *dislike* Walter," he said, "although I find him rather dull. He's an able man, in his way, but a hack. Whereas I aspire to perfection in my work, he aims to be prolific. He certainly has Creationist ambitions—he has taken out a lease on a small island in the Pacific, just as I have—but I can't imagine what he is doing with it."

"Walter Czastka knew Gabriel King very well," Charlotte observed, having scanned several pages of data copied to her by Hal Watson while they ate. "They were both born in 2401, and they attended the same university. Czastka has done a great deal of work for King's companies—far more than you. Most murders, you know, involve people who know one another well."

"Walter has not sufficient imagination to have committed this crime," said Oscar, firmly, "even if he had a motive. I doubt that he did; he and Gabriel are—or were—cats of a similar stripe."

"What do you mean by that?"

"I mean that they were both hacks. A modern architect, working with thousands of subspecies of gantzing bacteria, can raise buildings out of almost any materials, shaped to almost any design. The integration of pseudo-living systems to provide water and other amenities adds a further dimension of creative opportunity. A true artist could make buildings that would stand forever as monuments to contemporary creativity, but Gabriel King's main interest was always in *productivity*—razing whole towns to the ground and re-erecting them with the least possible effort. His business was the mass-production of third-rate homes for second-rate people."

"I thought the whole point of bacterial cementation processes is that they facilitate the provision of decent homes for the very poor," said Charlotte.

"That is the utilitarian view," agreed Oscar. "But it is two hundred years out of date. Future generations will look back at ours with pity for the recklessness with which we have wasted our aesthetic opportunities. One day, the building of a home will be part of a person's cultivation of his own personality. Making a home will be one of the things every man is expected to do for himself, and there will be no more Gabriel King houses with Walter Czastka sub-systems."

"We can't *all* be Creationists," objected Charlotte.

"Oh, but we *can*," retorted Oscar. "We can all be everything we *want* to be, or we should at least make every effort to do so. Even men like me, who were born when rejuvenation technology was still in its infancy, should do their utmost to believe that the specter of death is impotent to set a limit upon our achievements. The children of tomorrow will surely live for centuries if only they have the will to do so. You and I, Charlotte, must be prepared to set them a good example. The men of the past had an excuse for all their failures—that man born of woman had but a short time to live, and full of misery—but only cowardice inhibits us now. There is no excuse for any man who fails to be a true artist, and declines to take full responsibility for both his mind and his environment. Too many of us still aim for mediocrity, and are content with its achievement. You don't intend to be a policewoman *all* your life, I hope?"

Charlotte was slightly discomfited by this question. "I'm continuing my education,'' she said. ''My options are still open.'' Her waistphone began to buzz. She plucked it from its holster and accepted the call. She held it close to her ear so that Oscar would not be able to eavesdrop, assuming that Hal had ferreted out some further morsel of information about Rappaccini. What he actually had to say was rather more disturbing. When she had replaced the phone, she looked at her companion, trying to control the bleakness of her expression.

''Do you know a man named Michi Urashima?'' she asked, as blandly as she could.

''Of course I do,'' said Oscar. ''I hope you aren't going to tell me that he's dead. He was a better man by far than Gabriel King.''

''Not everyone would agree with you,'' she said, shortly. Urashima was an expert in computer graphics and image-simulation, famed for the contributions to synthetic cinema he had made before becoming involved in outlawed brainfeed research—which had led to a much-publicized fall from grace.

''How was he killed?'' Oscar asked, sadly. ''The same method?''

''Yes,'' she said, tersely. ''In San Francisco. There's no need for you to take the maglev now.''

''On the contrary,'' he said. ''There is every reason. This affair is still in its early stages, and if we want to witness the further stages of its unfolding, we must follow the script laid down for us. You will come with me, I hope?''

''Scene-of-crime officers don't operate nationwide,'' she said. ''Police work isn't done that way in this day and age.'' She knew even as she said it, though, that she still wanted—and still intended—to cling to her suspect.

''Police work may not be,'' he replied, with an infuriating wave of his hand, ''but psychodrama is. The mystery in this, my dear Charlotte, is not *who* has done it, but *why*. I am the man appointed by the murderer himself to the task of following the thread of explanation to the heart of the maze. If you want to *understand* the crime as well as solving it, you must come with me.''

''All right,'' she said, hypocritically. ''You've convinced me. I'll stick with you till the bitter end.''

5

Charlotte rose earlier than was her habit; the maglev *couchette* was not the kind of bed which encouraged one to sleep in. She called Hal to get an update on the investigation, then wandered along to the dining car to dial up some croissants, coffee, and pills. It was a pity, she thought, that there was no quicker way than the maglev to travel between New York and San Francisco. She had an uncomfortable feeling that she might end up chasing a daisy-chain of murders all around the globe, always twenty-four hours behind the breaking news. But the maglev was the fastest form of transportation within the bounds of United America since the last supersonic jet had flown four centuries before. The power-crises of the Aftermath were ancient history now, but the inland airways were so cluttered with private flitterbugs and helicopters, and the green zealots so avid in their crusades against large areas of concrete, that commercial aviation had never really gotten going again. Even intercontinental travelers tended to prefer the plush comfort of airships to the hectic pace of supersonics. Electronic communication had so completely taken over the lifestyles and folkways of modern man that most business was conducted via comcon.

By the time Charlotte had finished her breakfast, the train was only four hours out of San Francisco. Oscar joined her then, looking neat and trim although the green carnation in his buttonhole was now rather bedraggled. "Such has been the mercy of our timetable," he observed, "that we have slept through Missouri and Kansas."

She knew what he meant. Missouri and Kansas were distinctly lacking in interesting scenery since the re-stabilization of the climate had made their great plains prime sites for the establishment of vast tracts of artificial photosynthetics. Nowadays, the greater part of the Midwest looked rather like sections of an infinite undulating sheet of a dull near-black violet which offended unpracticed eyes. The SAP-fields of Kansas always gave Charlotte the impression of looking at a gigantic piece of frilly corrugated cardboard. Houses and factories alike had retreated beneath the dark canopy, and parts of the landscape were almost featureless. By now, though, the maglev passengers had the more elevating scenery of Colorado to look out upon. Most of the state had been returned to wilderness, and its centers of population had taken advantage of the versatility of modern building techniques to blend in with their surroundings. Chlorophyll green was infinitely easier on the human eye than SAP-violet, presumably because millions of years of adaptive natural selection had helped to make it so.

While Oscar ordered eggs duchesse for breakfast, Charlotte activated the wallscreen beside their table and called up the latest news. The fact of Gabriel King's death was recorded, but there was nothing as yet about the exotic circumstances. The IBI never liked to advertise crimes until they were solved, but the exotic circumstances of King's death would make it a hot topic of gossip, and she knew that it was only a matter of time before bootleg copies of the security tapes leaked out.

"My dear Charlotte," said Oscar, "you have the unmistakable look of one who woke too early and has been working too hard."

"I couldn't sleep," she told him. "I took a couple of boosters with breakfast. They'll clear my head soon enough."

Oscar shook his head. "No one who looks twenty when he is really a hundred and thirty-three can possibly be less than worshipful of the wonders of medical science," he said, "but, in my experience, the use of it to maintain one's sense of equilibrium is a false economy. We must have sleep in order to dream, and we must dream in order to discharge the chaos from our thoughts, so that we may reason effectively while we are awake. Now, what about the second murder? Any progress?"

She frowned. She was supposed to be the one asking the questions. "Did you know Urashima personally, or just by reputation?" she countered, determined not to let him get the upper hand.

"We met on several occasions," said Oscar, equably. "He was an artist, like myself. I respected his work. Although I didn't know him well, I would have been glad to count him a friend."

"He'd been inactive of late," she said, watching her suspect closely. "He hadn't worked commercially since his conviction for illegal experimentation thirteen years ago. He served four years house arrest and control of communication. He was probably still experimenting, though, and he may well have been engaged in illegal activities.''

"His imprisonment was an absurd sentence for an absurd crime," Oscar opined. "He placed no one in danger but himself."

"He was playing about with brainfeed equipment," she said. "Not just memory boxes or neural stimulators, but mental cyborgization. And he didn't just endanger, himself; he was pooling information with others."

"Of course he was," said Oscar. "What on earth is the point of hazardous exploration unless one makes every effort to pass on the legacy of one's discoveries?"

"Have *you* ever experimented with that sort of stuff?" Charlotte asked, vaguely. Like everyone else, she bandied about phrases like "psychedelic synthesizer" and "memory box," but she had little or no idea of the way such legendary devices were supposed to work. Ever since the first development of artificial synapses capable of linking up human nervous systems to silicon-based electronic systems, numerous schemes for hooking up the brain to computers had been devised, but almost all the experiments had gone disastrously wrong, often ending up with badly brain-damaged subjects. The brain was the most complex and sensitive of all organs, and disruption of brain-function was the one kind of disorder that twenty-sixth century medical science was impotent to correct. The UN had forced a world-wide ban on devices for connecting brains directly to electronic apparatus, for whatever purpose, but the main effect of the ban had been to drive research underground. Even an expert fisherman like Hal Watson would not have found it easy to figure out what sort of work might be going on, where, and why.

"You've just heard me express my dislike of everyday chemical boosters," Oscar pointed out. "There is nothing I value more than my genius, and I would never knowingly risk my clarity and agility of mind. That does not mean that I disapprove of what Michi Urashima did. He was not an infant, in need of protection from himself. His perennial fascination was the simulation of experience, and for him, the building of better visual images was only a beginning. He wanted to allow his audience to *live* in his illusions, not merely to stand outside and watch. If we are ever to make a proper interface between natural and artificial intelligence, we will need the genius of men like Michi. Now, have you anything to tell me about his death which may help to unravel the puzzle which confronts us?"

"Perhaps," she said, grudgingly. "Did you know that Michi Urashima was at college with Gabriel King—and, for that matter, with Walter Czastka?" She permitted herself a slight smile of satisfaction when Oscar raised an interested eyebrow.

"I did not," he said. "Was Rappaccini, perhaps, also at this particular institution of learning? Has he been harboring some secret grudge for a hundred and thirty years? Where was this remarkable college, where so many of our great men first met?"

"Wollongong, in Australia."

"Wollongong!" he exclaimed, in mock horror. "If only it were Oxford, or the Sorbonne, or even Sapporo . . . but it *is* an interesting coincidence."

Charlotte regarded him speculatively. "Hal transmitted a copy of the scene-of-crime tape," she said. "Urashima's last visitor was a woman. She'd changed her appearance quite considerably, but we're pretty sure that she's the same one who visited Gabriel King."

Oscar nodded. "Rappaccini's daughter," he said. "I expected it."

"The main thrust of Hal's investigation is to identify and track the woman," Charlotte went on. "He's set up programs to monitor every security camera in San Francisco. If she's already gone, we might still be able to pick up her trail. The problem is that she left Urashima's house more than three days ago; if she moved fast, she may have delivered more packages in the interim."

"We must certainly assume that she did," Oscar agreed. "Did she leave another calling card, by any chance?"

"Not this time. But she kissed Michi Urashima, exactly as she kissed Gabriel King." She had decanted the tape on to a disc, so she only had to slot it in. Like the tape she had displayed for Oscar outside Gabriel King's apartment, it had been carefully edited from the various spy-eyes and bubblebugs that had been witness to Michi Urashima's murder.

The similarity between the two records was almost eerie. The woman's hair was silvery blonde now, but still abundant. It was arranged in a precipitate cataract of curls. The eyes were the same electric blue but the cast of the features had been altered subtly, making her face thinner and apparently deeper. The changes were sufficient to deceive a standard picture-search program, but because Charlotte *knew* that it was the same woman, she could *see* that it as the same woman. There was something in the way her eyes looked steadily forward, something in her calm poise that made her seem remote, not quite in contact with the world through which she moved. She was wearing a dark blue costume now, which hung loose about her seemingly fragile frame. It was the kind of outfit which would not attract much attention in the street. As before, the woman said nothing, but moved naturally into a friendly kiss of greeting before preceding her victim into an inner room beyond the reach of conventional security cameras. Her departure was similarly recorded by the spy-eye. She seemed perfectly composed and serene.

There were more pictures to follow, showing the state of Urashima's corpse as it had eventually been discovered. There were long, lingering close-ups of the fatal flowers. The camera's eye moved into a black corolla as if it was venturing into the interior of a great greedy mouth, hovering around the *crux ansata* tip of the blood-red style like a moth fascinated by a flame. There was, of course, a sterile film covering the organism, but it was quite transparent; its presence merely served to give the black petals a weird sheen, adding to their supernatural quality.

Charlotte let the tape run through without comment, then flipped the switch. "The flowers aren't genetically identical to the ones used to kill King. Our lab people think that the germination of the seeds may have been keyed to some trigger unique to the victim's genotype—that each species was designed to kill a specific victim, while being harmless to everyone else. That would explain how the girl can carry the seeds around. She traveled to San Francisco on a scheduled maglev. The card she used to buy the ticket connects to a credit account held in the name of Jeanne Duval. It's a dummy account, of course. She didn't use the Duval account to reach New York, and she'll presumably use another to leave San Francisco.''

"You might set the search programs you're using to find her to pick up the names Daubrun and Sabatier," Oscar advised. "Jeanne Duval was one of Baudelaire's mistresses, and it's possible she has the others on her list of *noms de guerre*.''

Charlotte transmitted this information to Hal. The maglev was taking them down the western side of the Sierra Nevada now, and she had to swallow air to counter the pressure on her eardrums.

"By the time we get to San Francisco," she said, "there won't be anything to do there except to wait for the next phone call.''

"Perhaps not," said Oscar. "But even if she's long gone, we'll be in the right place to follow in her footsteps.''

The buzzer on Charlotte's waistphone sounded, and she snatched it up.

"One of Rappaccini's bank accounts became active," Hal told her. "A debit went through ten minutes ago. The credit was drawn from another account, which had a guarantee arrangement with the Rappaccini account.''

"Never mind the technical details," she said. "What did the credit buy? Have the police at the contact point managed to get the user?''

"I'm afraid not. The debit was put through by a courier service. They don't collect until they've actually made delivery. We've got a picture of the woman from their spy-eye, looking just the same as she did when she went to Urashima's apartment, but it's three days old. It must have been taken before the murder, immediately after she arrived in San Francisco.''

Charlotte groaned softly. "What did she send, and where to?''

"A package she brought in. We don't know what's in it. It was addressed to Oscar Wilde, Green Carnation Suite, Majestic Hotel, San Francisco. It's there now, waiting.''

"We don't have the authority to open that package without your permission," Charlotte told Oscar. "Can I send an instruction to the San Francisco police, telling them to inspect it immediately?''

"Certainly not," Oscar said, without hesitation. "It would spoil the surprise. We'll be there in less than an hour.''

Charlotte frowned. "You're inhibiting the investigation," she said. "I want to know what's in that package. It *could* be a packet of seeds.''

"I think not," said Oscar, airily. "If Rappaccini wished to murder me, he surely wouldn't treat me less generously than his other victims. If they're entitled to a fatal kiss, it would be unjust and unaesthetic to send my *fleurs du mal* by mail.''

"In that case," she said, "it's probably another ticket. If we open it now, we might be able to find out where her next destination is in time to stop her making her delivery.''

"I fear not," said Oscar. "The delayed debit was timed to show up *after* the event. The third victim is probably dead already. The package is addressed to me and I shall open it. That's what Rappaccini intended. I'm sure he has his reasons."

"Mr. Wilde," she said, in utter exasperation, "you seem to be incapable of taking this matter seriously."

"On the contrary," he replied, with a sigh. "I believe that I am the only one who is taking it seriously *enough*. You seem to be unable to look beyond the mere fact that people are being killed. If we are to come to terms with this strange performance, we must take *all* its features as seriously as they are intended to be taken. I am as deeply involved in this as the victims, though I cannot as yet understand why Rappaccini has chosen to involve me."

"You'd better make sure that nothing you do fouls up our investigation," said Charlotte, ominously, "because we won't hesitate to throw the book at you if we find a reason."

"I fear," said Oscar, sadly, "that Rappaccini has already thrown more than enough books into this affair himself."

6

The promised package lay on a table in the reception room of the Green Carnation Suite. It was round, about a hundred centimeters in diameter and twenty deep. Charlotte had taken the precaution of arming herself with a spraygun loaded with a polymer which, on discharge, formed itself into a bimolecular membrane and clung to anything it touched.

Oscar reached out to take hold of the knot in the black ribbon which secured the emerald green box. It yielded easily to his nimble fingers, and he drew the ribbon away. He lifted the lid and laid it to one side. As Charlotte had half-expected since seeing the shape of the container, it contained a Rappaccini wreath: an intricate tangle of dark green stalks and leaves. The stalks were thorny, the leaves slender and curly. There was an envelope in the middle of the display, and around the perimeter were thirteen black flowers like none that she had ever seen before. They looked like black daisies.

Oscar Wilde extended an inquisitive forefinger, and was just about to touch one of the flowers, when it moved.

"Look out!" said Charlotte.

As though the first movement was a kind of signal, *all* the "flowers" began to move. It was a most alarming effect, and Oscar reflexively snatched back his hand as Charlotte pressed the trigger of the spraygun and let fly. When the polymer hit them, the flowers' movements became suddenly jerky. They thrashed and squirmed in obvious distress. The limbs which had mimicked sepals struggled vainly for purchase upon the thorny green ring on which they had been mounted. Now that Charlotte could count them she was able to see that each of the creatures had eight hairy legs. What had seemed to be a cluster of florets was a much-embellished thorax.

"Poor things," said Oscar, as he watched them writhe. "They'll asphyxiate, you know, with that awful stuff all over them."

"I may have just saved your life," observed Charlotte, drily. "Those things are probably poisonous."

Oscar shook his head. "This was no attempted murder. It's a work of art—probably an exercise in symbolism."

"According to you," she said, "the two are not incompatible."

"Not even the most reckless of dramatists," said Oscar, affectedly, "would destroy his audience at the end of act one. We are perfectly safe, my dear, until the final curtain falls. Even then Rappaccini will want us alive and well. He surely will not risk interrupting a standing ovation and cutting short the cries of *encore!*"

Charlotte reached out to pick up the sticky envelope at the center of the ruined display, and contrived to open it. She took out a piece of paper. It was a rental car receipt, overstamped in garish red ink: ANY ATTEMPT TO INTERROGATE THE PROGRAMMING OF THIS VEHICLE WILL ACTIVATE A VIRUS THAT WILL DESTROY ALL THE DATA IN ITS MEMORY. It was probably a bluff, but she didn't suppose that Oscar Wilde would let her call it—and she still didn't have any legal reason to overturn his decisions.

As soon as she had updated Hal, she got through to the rental car company and demanded all the information they had. They told her that they had delivered the car to the hotel three days earlier, and that they had no knowledge of any route or destination which might have been programmed into its systems after dispatch. Hal quickly ascertained that the account which had been used to pay for the car had enough credit to cover three days' storage and a journey of two thousand kilometers.

"That could take you as far north as Juneau or as far south as Guadalajara," Hal pointed out, unhelpfully. "I can't tell how many more accounts there might be on which Rappaccini and the woman might draw, but I've traced several that are held under other names; it's possible that one of them is his real name."

"What are they?" Oscar asked.

"Samuel Cramer, Gustave Moreau, and Thomas Griffiths Wainewright."

Oscar sighed heavily. "Samuel Cramer is the protagonist of a novella by Baudelaire," he said. "Moreau was a French painter. Wainewright was the subject of a famous essay by my namesake called 'Pen, Pencil and Poison.' It's just a series of jokes, presumably intended to amuse me."

The car which awaited them was roomy and powerful. Once it was free of the city's traffic control computers it would be able to zip along the transcontinental at two hundred kph. If they *were* headed for Alaska, Charlotte thought, they'd be there some time around midnight.

As soon as they were both settled into the back seat, Oscar activated the car's program. It slid smoothly up the ramp and into the street. Then he called up a lunch menu from the car's synthesizer, and looked it over critically.

"I fear," he said, "that we are in for a somewhat Spartan trip."

Charlotte took out her handscreen and began scrolling through some pages of data that one of Hal's AIs had compiled from various dossiers. It had found many links between Gabriel King and Michi Urashima—more links than anyone could reasonably have expected. It seemed that the construction engineer and the graphic artist had remained in close touch throughout their long lives. Many of Urashima's experiments had been funded by King, and the two of them had embarked upon several ventures in partnership. Charlotte could see that the AI searches had only just begun to get down into the real dirt. No one whose career was as long as King's was likely to be completely clean, but a man in his position could keep secrets even in today's world, just as long as no one with state-of-the-art equipment actually had a reason to probe. It was only to be expected that this murder would expose a certain amount of dirty linen, but this particular collection seemed overabundant. It seemed entirely probable that Gabriel King had been a major stockholder in the clandestine brainfeed business, and that he had not only funded Urashima but had established all kinds of shields to hide his work and its spinoff. Was there a motive for multiple murder in there? But if there was, where did Rappaccini and Oscar Wilde fit in? Why all the bizarre frills? And who was the mystery woman?

When Charlotte had digested the dossier's contents, she plugged her waistphone into the car's transmitter and phoned Hal.

"Anything new on the woman?" Charlotte inquired.

"No identification yet," said Hal. "We haven't picked up a visual trace since she left Urashima's apartment. I've loosened up the match criteria, but she must have done a first-rate job of disguising herself. Where are you?"

Charlotte realized, guiltily, that she had not even bothered to take note of the direction in which they were headed. She squinted out of the window, but there was nothing to be seen now except the eight lanes of the superhighway.

"We're headed south," said Oscar, helpfully.

"She may have gone south," Charlotte said to Hal. "Better check all plausible destinations between here and Mexico City." She signed off.

"It might be as well," Oscar said, ruminatively, "if I were to have a word with Walter Czastka."

"No, you don't!" Charlotte said, suddenly remembering that she should have called Czastka herself, several hours ago. "That's *my* job. Walter Czastka may be a suspect."

"I know Walter," said Oscar. "He was a difficult man even in his prime, and he's not in his prime now. It really would be better if I did it. You can listen in."

She weighed up the pros and cons. It might, she thought, be interesting to see what Oscar Wilde and Walter Czastka had to say to one another. "You're a free man," she said, in the end. "Go ahead." She moved to the edge of her seat, out of range of the tiny eye mounted above the car's wallscreen. She watched Oscar punch out the codes on the keyboard. He didn't need to call a directory to get the number.

She could see the image on the screen even though she was out of camera-range. She knew immediately that the face that appeared was that of Walter Czastka himself. No one would ever have programmed so much ostentatious world-weariness into a simulacrum.

"Hello, Walter," said Oscar.

Czastka peered at the caller without the least flicker of recognition. He looked unwell. Charlotte could not imagine that he had ever been handsome, and he obviously thought it unnecessary to compromise with the expectations of others by having his face touched up by tissue-control specialists. In a world where almost everyone was beautiful, or at least distinguished, Walter Czastka was an anomaly—but there was nothing monstrous about him. His sad eyes were faded blue, and his stare had a rather disconcerting quality. Charlotte knew that Czastka was exactly the same age as Gabriel King and Michi Urashima, but he looked far worse than either of them. Perhaps rejuvenation hadn't taken properly.

"Yes?" he said.

"Don't you know me?" asked Oscar, in genuine surprise.

For a moment, Czastka simply looked exasperated, but then his stare changed as enlightenment dawned. "Oscar Wilde!" he said, his tone redolent with awe. "My God, you look . . . I didn't look like that after *my* last rejuvenation! But that must be your third—how could you need . . .?"

Oddly enough, Oscar did not swell with pride in reaction to this display of naked envy. "Need," he murmured, "is a relative thing. I'm sorry, Walter; I didn't mean to startle you."

"You'll have to be brief, Oscar," said Czastka, curtly. "I'm expecting the UN police to call—they tried to get past my AI yesterday, but didn't bother to leave a message to say what they wanted. They're taking their time about getting back to me. Damn nuisance."

"The police can break in on us if they really want to," said Oscar, gently. "Have you heard the news about Gabriel King?"

"No. Is it something I should be interested in?"

"He's dead, Walter. Murdered by illegal biotechnics—a very strange kind of flowering plant."

Charlotte couldn't read Czastka's expression. "Murdered by a plant?" he repeated, disbelievingly.

"I've seen the pictures," said Oscar. "The police might want you to take a look at the forensic reports. They have a suspicion that you or I might have designed the murder-weapon, but I'm morally certain that it's Rappaccini's work. Do you remember Rappaccini?"

Charlotte began to regret having given Oscar Wilde permission to make this call. Perhaps it would have been better to ask Czastka to make a separate judgment. If both of them, without collusion, identified Rappaccini as the designer . . . but how could she be sure that they weren't in collusion already?

"Of course I remember Rappaccini," snapped Czastka. "I'm not senile, you know. Specializes in funeral wreaths—a silly affectation, I always thought. I dare say you know him better than I do, you and he being birds of a feather. Are you saying that he murdered Gabriel King?"

"Michi Urashima is dead too," Oscar said. "He and Gabriel were killed by seeds which grew inside them and consumed their flesh. This is important, Walter. Genetic art may have come a long way since the protests at the Great Exhibition, but the green zealots wouldn't need much encouragement to put us back on their hate list. Neither of us wants to go back to the days when we had petty officials looking over our shoulders while we worked. When the police release the full details of this case, there's going to be a lot of adverse publicity. I'm trying to help the police find Rappaccini. I wondered whether you might remember anything that might provide a clue to his real identity.''

Czastka's face had a curious ochreous pallor as he stared at his interlocutor. ''King and Urashima—both dead?'' He didn't seem to be keeping up with Oscar's train of thought.

''Both dead,'' Oscar confirmed. ''I think there might be others. You knew Gabriel and Michi from way back, didn't you?''

''So what?'' said Czastka, grimly. ''I didn't know Urashima as well as you did, and all my dealings with King were strictly business. We were never friends—or enemies.'' Charlotte noted that Czastka's eyes had narrowed, but she couldn't tell whether he was alarmed, suspicious, or merely impatient.

''No one's accusing you of anything,'' said Oscar, carefully. ''I've told the police that you couldn't possibly be the man behind Rappaccini—and I think they're more inclined at present to suspect that *I* might be. We all need to find out who he really is. Can you help?''

''No,'' said Czastka, without hesitation. ''I never knew him. I've had some dealings with his company, but I haven't set eyes on him since the Great Exhibition.''

''What about his daughter?'' said Oscar, abruptly.

If he intended to surprise the other man, it didn't work. Czastka's stare was as stony as it was melancholy. ''What daughter?'' he said. ''I never met a daughter—not that I remember. It was all a long time ago. I can't remember anything at all. It's nothing to do with me. Leave me alone, Oscar—and tell the police to leave me alone!''

Charlotte could see that Oscar Wilde was both puzzled and disappointed by the other man's reaction. As Czastka closed the connection, Oscar's face wrinkled into a frown.

''That wasn't much help, was it?'' she said, unable to resist the temptation to take him down a peg. ''He doesn't even *like* you.''

''As soon as I told him about the murders, he froze,'' Oscar said, thoughtfully. ''He's hiding something, but I can't imagine *what*—or why. I would never have thought it of him. There's something very strange about this. Perhaps your clever associate and his indefatigable assistants should start attacking the problem from the other end.''

''What's *that* supposed to mean?'' she demanded.

''The Wollongong connection. We ought to find out how many other people there are in the world who were at Wollongong at the relevant time. Walter and the two victims are uncommonly old men, even in a world where serial rejuvenation is commonplace. It's possible that such a list might contain the names of other potential victims—and the university records might offer a clue as to a possible motive.''

Charlotte called Hal to relay the suggestion, but he scornfully informed her that he had already put two AIs to work on it. ''One more thing,'' he added. ''Rappaccini's pseudonymous bank accounts have been used over the years to purchase materials that were delivered for collection to the island of Kauai, in Hawaii. They were collected by boat. There are fifty or sixty islets west and south of Kauai, natural and artificial. Some are leased to Creationists for experiments in the construction of artificial ecosystems.'' Charlotte had already turned to look at Oscar, and was on the point of forming a predatory grin when Hal continued: "Oscar Wilde's island is half an ocean away in Micronesia—but Walter Czastka's is nearby. All the supplies that Czastka purchases in his own name are picked up from Kauai, by boat.''

7

Charlotte winced as the car lurched slightly, throwing her sideways. They had left the superhighway and were climbing into the hills along roads which did not seem to have been properly maintained. This had been a densely populated region in the distant past, but California had suffered several plague attacks in the Second Biotech War, and rural areas like this one had been so badly hit as to cause a mass exodus of refugees. Most of those who had survived had never returned, preferring to relocate to more promising land. Three quarters of the original ghost towns of the Sierra Nevada were ghost towns still, even after three hundred years. The car had not been designed for climbing mountains and it had slowed considerably when it first began to follow the winding road up into the foothills of the mountain range. It was picking up speed again now. Charlotte called up a map of the region on to the car's wallscreen, but it was stubbornly unhelpful in the matter of providing clues as to where they might be going or why.

"The region up ahead is real wasteland,'' she told Oscar. "Nobody lives there. Nothing grows except lichens and the odd stalk of grass. The names on the map are just distant memories.''

"*Something* must be up there,'' Oscar said, shifting uncomfortably as the car took another corner. "Rappaccini wouldn't bring us up here if there were nothing to see.''

Charlotte wiped the map from the screen, and replaced it with a list which Hal had beamed through to her. There were twenty-seven names on it: the names of all the surviving men and women who had attended the University of Wollongong while Gabriel King, Michi Urashima, and Walter Czastka had been students there. The names, that is, of all the *supposed* survivors; Hal's patient AIs had so far only managed to obtain positive confirmation of the continued existence of twenty-three. The business of trying to contact them all was proving uncommonly difficult; they all had high-grade sims to answer their phones, and most of the sims had been programmed for maximum unhelpfulness. IBI priority codes were empowered to demand maximum co-operation from every AI in the world, but no AI could do more than its programming permitted.

"These people are crazy!'' she complained.

"They're all *old*,'' Oscar pointed out. "Every single one of them is a double rejuvenate. They were born during the Aftermath, when the climate was still disturbed, the detritus of the plague wars hadn't yet finished claiming casualties, the Net was still highly vulnerable to software sabotage, and cool fusion and artificial photosynthesis were brand new. All of them were conceived by living mothers, and I doubt if one in five was carried to term in an artificial womb. They're strangers in today's world, and many of them don't have any sense of belonging any more. Half of them have nothing left to desire except to die in peace, and more than half—as your associates must have found out in trying to cross-examine them—have no memory at all of the long-gone years they spent at the University of Wollongong.''

She looked at him curiously. ''But you're not much younger than they are,'' she said, ''and you're a *triple* rejuvenate. *You* obviously don't feel like that.''

''The fact that *I* do not,'' he said, drily, ''is the greatest proof of my genius. I am a very unusual individual—as unusual, in my way, as Rappaccini.''

Charlotte's waistphone buzzed, and she lifted it from its holster reflexively.

''You can take Paul Kwiatek off your list,'' Hal's voice said, dully. ''They just found him dead. Same method, same visitor.''

Oscar leaned over to speak into the mouthpiece. ''Who's dead?'' he asked Hal.

''Paul Kwiatek. Another Wollongong graduate, born 2401.''

Charlotte snatched up the phone again. Determined to be businesslike, she said: ''Where?''

''Bologna, Italy.''

''Bologna! But . . . when?''

''Some time last week. It looks as though he was killed before King. The woman probably flew to New York on an intercontinental flight from Rome. I'll try to figure out where she was before that—there might be other bodies we haven't found yet. We're stepping up our attempts to contact and question the others on the list, but I don't know how to work out which of them are potential victims, let alone potential murderers.''

''Czastka knows *something*.'' said Charlotte. ''He might be the key.''

''We've just talked to him,'' Hal said, in his infuriating fashion. ''He denies knowing anything at all that would connect him with King, Urashima and Kwiatek, and he denies having received the equipment and supplies paid for by the Rappaccini accounts. So far, there's no proof that he's lying. We're worried about another name on the Wollongong list—Magnus Teidemann. He's supposed to be out in the wilderness somewhere in mid-Africa, but he's been ominously silent for some time. If he's dead, it could take us a week to find the body. I've ordered a search. That's all for now.'' He broke the connection, without waiting for Charlotte to respond.

Charlotte had already recalled the list, and had begun tracing a path through the back-up information. ''Paul Kwiatek,'' she said to Oscar. ''Software engineer. Should I call up a more detailed biog, or do you know him?''

''No,'' said Oscar, ''but I know Teidemann by repute. He was a major force in the UN a hundred years ago, one of the inner circle of world-planners. Gabriel King probably knew him personally. The unfolding network of cross-connections is going to deluge your friend's AIs with data. There's too much of it to sort out and unravel, unless we can somehow cut the Gordian knot at a stroke.''

''It doesn't work like that,'' she told him, although she wasn't entirely convinced. "The machines are so fast that a profusion of data doesn't trouble them. The real problem is the *age* of the data. If the motive for the murders really does go back a hundred and fifty years . . . but if it does, why wait until *now* to carry them out? Why murder men who are already on the threshold of extinction?"

"Why indeed?" echoed Oscar Wilde.

"It's insane," Charlotte opined, being unable to see any other explanation. "It's some weird obsession." Such things were not unheard of, even in these days of chemical retuning and biofeedback training. The brain was no longer the great mystery it once had been, but it kept stubborn and jealous guard over many of its secrets.

"Obsession might sustain memories which would otherwise fade away," Oscar admitted. "If there were no obsession involved, no murderer could nurse a plan as elaborate as this for as long as Rappaccini must have nursed it."

Charlotte returned to her contemplation of the list displayed on the screen. Apart from Teidemann's, none of the names meant anything at all to her. Only a handful were listed as genetic engineers of any kind, and none seemed to have the right kind of background to be Rappaccini—except, of course, for Walter Czastka. As she scanned the subsidiary list of addresses, her eye was caught by the word "Kauai." She stopped scrolling. One Stuart McCandless, ex-Chancellor of the University of Oceania, had retired to Kauai. She was tempted to call Hal and trumpet her discovery, but she knew what his response would be. His AIs would have turned up the coincidence; investigation of the data-trail would be in hand. She wished, briefly, that she were back in New York. There, at least, she would be involved in the routine pursuit of inquiries, making calls. What was she accomplishing out here, in the middle of nowhere?

She glanced out of the side-window as the car swung slowly and carefully around a bend into one of the ghost-towns whose names were still recorded on the map in spite of the fact that no one had lived in them for centuries. The ancient stone buildings had been weathered by dust-storms, but they still retained the sharp angles which proudly proclaimed their status as human artifacts. The land around them was quite dead, incapable of growing so much as a blade of grass, and every bit as desolate as an unspoiled lunar landscape, but the shadowy scars of human habitation still lay upon it.

In the long-gone days when the earth had lain temporarily unprotected by an ozone layer, this would have been a naked place. Even then, it would probably have been almost empty; this part of the state, within a couple of hundred kilometers of Los Angeles, had been very hard hit even by the first and least of the three plague wars—whose victims, not knowing that there was far worse to come, had innocently called it the Great Plague War.

8

The wallscreen blanked out. While Charlotte was still wondering what the interruption signified, the car's AI relayed a message in large, flamboyant letters:

WELCOME, OSCAR: THE PLAY WILL COMMENCE IN TEN MINUTES.
THE PLAYHOUSE IS BENEATH THE BUILDING TO YOUR RIGHT.

"Play?" said Charlotte, bitterly. "Have we come all this way just to watch
a *play?*"

"It appears so," said Oscar, as he opened the door and climbed out into
the sultry heat of the deepening evening. "Do you carry transmitter-eyes and
bubblebugs in that belt you're wearing?"

"Of course," she said.

"I suggest that you place a few about your person," said Oscar. "I have only
the one bubblebug of my own, which I shall mount on my forehead."

Charlotte turned to stare at the building to their right. It did not look in the
least like a theater. It might once have been a general store. It was roofless now,
nothing more than a gutted shell.

"Why bring us out here to the middle of nowhere?" she demanded, angrily.
"Why didn't he just record it on tape for transmission in a theater in San
Francisco or New York?" As she spoke, she planted two electronic eyes above
her own eyebrows.

Oscar quickly located a downward-leading flight of stone steps inside the
derelict building. Charlotte planted head-high nanolights every six or seven
steps to illuminate their passage, which had been hollowed out using bacterial
deconstructors far more modern than the building itself. By the time they reached
the bottom of the stair, there were several meters of solid rock separating her
from the car; she knew that her transmitter-eye would only function as a re-
cording-device. At the bottom, there was a door made from some kind of synthetic organic material; it had no handle, but when Oscar touched it with his
fingertips, it swung inward. "All doors in the world of theater are open to Oscar
Wilde," he muttered sarcastically.

Beyond the doorway was a well of impenetrable shadow. Charlotte automatically reached up to the wall inside the doorway, placing another nanolight there,
but the darkness seemed to soak up its luminance effortlessly, and it showed
her nothing but a few square centimeters of matte-black wall. The moment Oscar
took a tentative step forward, however, a small spotlight winked on, picking
out a two-seater sofa upholstered in black.

"Very considerate," said Oscar, drily. He invited her to move ahead of him,
and she did. Five seconds after they were seated, the spotlight winked out.
Charlotte could not suppress a small gasp of alarm. The nanolight she had set
beside the door shone like a single distant star in an infinite void.

When light returned, it was cleverly directed away from them; Charlotte could
not see Oscar, nor her own body. It was as if she had become a disembodied
viewpoint, like a bubblebug, looking out upon a world from which her physical
presence had been erased. She seemed to be ten or twelve meters away from the
event which unfolded before her eyes, but the distance was illusory. Cinematic
holograms of the kind to which Michi Urashima had devoted his skills before
turning to more dangerous toys were adept in the seductive art of sensory deception.

The "event" was a solo dance. The performer was a young woman, whose face was made up to duplicate the appearance that the image's living model had presented to Michi Urashima's spy-eyes. Only her hair and costume were different; the hair was now long, straight and jet-black, and she was dressed in sleek, translucent chiffons which were gathered in multicolored profusion about her lissome form, secured at strategic points by gem-faced catches. The music to which she danced, lithely and lasciviously, was raw and primitive. Charlotte knew by now that the original Oscar Wilde had written a play called *Salomé*. Forearmed by that knowledge, she quickly guessed what she was to watch.

As the virtual Salomé began the dance of the seven veils, the first impression Charlotte formed was that the dance was utterly artless. Modern dance, with all the artifice of contemporary biotechnology as a resource, was infinitely smoother and more complicated than *this*—but she judged that its primitive quality was deliberate. In the nineteenth century, Charlotte knew, there had been something called "pornography." Nowadays, in a world where most sexual intercourse took place in virtual reality, with the aid of clever machinery, the idea of pornography was redundant; everyone now accepted that in the realm of mechanized fantasy, nothing was perverse and nothing was taboo. Charlotte thought she understood, dimly, the historical implications of Salomé's silly prancing, but she found it neither stimulating nor instructive. The gradual removal of the veils was simply a laborious way of counting down to a climax she was already expecting. She waited for Salomé to acquire a mute partner for her mesmerized capering.

The dancer *did* look as if she were mesmerized. She looked as if she were lost in some kind of dream, not really aware of who she was or what she was doing. Charlotte remembered that the young woman had given a similar impression during the brief glimpse of her that Gabriel King's cameras had caught. The dance slowed, and finally stopped. Salomé stood with bowed head for a few moments, and then reached out into the shadows that crowded around her, and brought out of the darkness a silver platter, on which sat the decapitated head of a man. Charlotte was not surprised, but she still flinched. The virtual head looked more startlingly real than a real head would probably have done, by virtue of the artistry which had gone into the design of its horror-stricken expression and the bloodiness of the crudely severed neck. She recognized the face which the virtual head wore: it was Gabriel King's.

The dancer plucked the head from its resting-place, entwining her delicate fingers in its hair. The salver disappeared, dissolved into the shadow. The dance began again.

How differently, Charlotte wondered, was Oscar Wilde seeing this ridiculous scene? Could he see it as something daring, monstrous and clever? Would he be able to sigh with satisfaction, in that irritating way of his, when the performance was over, and claim that Rappaccini was indeed a genius?

The macabre dance now seemed mechanical. The woman appeared to be unaware of the fact that she was supposedly brandishing a severed head. She moved its face close to her own, and then extended her arms again, maintaining the same distant and dreamy expression. Then the features of the severed head changed. It acquired an Oriental cast. Charlotte recognized Michi Urashima, and suddenly became interested again, eager for any hint of further change. She fixed her gaze steadfastly upon the horrid head. She had seen no picture of Paul Kwiatek, so she could only infer that the third appearance presented by the severed head was his, and she became even more intent when the third set of features blurred and shifted. The number and nature of the metamorphoses might well be crucial to the development of the investigation. She felt a surge of triumph as she realized that this revelation might vindicate her determination to stay with Oscar Wilde. She did not recognize the fourth face, but she was confident that the bubblebug set above her right eye would record it well enough for computer-aided recognition. How many more would there be?

The fifth face was darker than the fourth—naturally dark, she thought, not cosmetically melanized. She did not recognize this face, either, but she knew the sixth. She had seen it within the last few hours, looking considerably older and more ragged than its manifestation here, but unmistakably the same. It was Walter Czastka.

There was no seventh face. Salomé slowed in her paces, faced the sofa where Oscar and Charlotte sat watching, and took her bow. Then the lights came on. Charlotte had assumed that the performance was over, and its object attained, but she was wrong. What she had so far witnessed was merely a prelude. The lights that came on brought a new illusion, infinitely more spectacular than the last.

Charlotte had attended numerous theatrical displays employing clever holographic techniques, and knew well enough how a black-walled space which comprised no more than a few hundred cubic meters could be made to seem far greater, but she had never seen a virtual space as vast and as ornate as this. Here was the palace in which Salomé had danced, painted by a phantasmagoric imagination: a crazily vaulted ceiling higher than that in any reconstructed medieval cathedral, with elaborate stained-glass windows in mad profusion, offering all manner of fantastic scenes. Here was a polished floor three times the size of a sports-field, with a crowd of onlookers that must have numbered tens of thousands. But there was no sense of this being an actual *place:* it was an edifice born of nightmarish dreams, whose awesome and impossible dimensions weighed down upon a mere observer, reducing Charlotte in her own mind's eye to horrific insignificance.

Salomé, having bowed to the two watchers who had watched her dance at closer range than any of the fictitious multitude, turned to bow to another watcher: Herod, seated upon his throne. There had never been a throne like it in the entire history of empires and kingdoms; none but the most vainglorious of emperors could even have *imagined* it. It was huge and golden, hideously overburdened with silks and jewels, an appalling monstrosity of avaricious self-indulgence. It was, Charlotte knew, *intended* to appall. *All* of this was a calculated insult to the delicacy of effective illusion: a parody of grandiosity; an exercise in profusion for profusion's sake.

The king on the throne had drawn himself three times life-size, as a bloated, overdressed grotesque. The body was like nothing any longer to be seen in a world which had banished obesity four hundred years before, but the face, had it only been leaner, would have been the face which Rappaccini wore in the photographs that Hal Watson had shown her the day before. Oscar took her wrist in his hand and squeezed it. "Tread carefully," he whispered, his invisible lips no more than a centimeter from her ear. "This simulation may be programmed to tell us everything, if only we can question it cunningly enough."

Herod/Rappaccini burst into mocking laughter, his tumultuous flesh heaving. "Do you think that I have merely human ears, Oscar? You can hardly see yourselves, I know, but you are not hidden from *me*. Your friend is charming, Oscar, but she is not one of us. She is of an age that has forgotten and erased its past."

Mad, thought Charlotte. *Absolutely and irredeemably mad.* She wondered whether she might be in mortal danger, if the man beside her really was the secret designer of all of this.

"Moreau might have approved," Oscar said, off-handedly, "but his vision always outpaced his capacity for detail. Michi Urashima would not have been satisfied so easily, although I detect his handiwork in some of the effects. Did Gabriel King supply the organisms which hollowed out this Aladdin's cave, perchance?"

"He did," answered Rappaccini, squirming in his huge uncomfortable seat like a huge slug. "I have made art with his sadly utilitarian instruments. I have taken some trouble to weave the work of all my victims into the tapestry of their destruction."

"It's overdone," said Oscar, bluntly. "As a show of apparent madness, it is too excessive to be anything but pretense. Can we not talk as civilized men, since that is what we are?"

Rappaccini smiled. "That is why I wanted you here, dear Oscar," he said. "Only you could suspect me of cold rationality in the midst of all this. But you understand civilization far too well to wear its gifts unthinkingly. You may well be the only man alive who understands the world's decadence. Have the patient bureaucrats of the United Nations Police Force discovered my true name yet?"

"No," said Oscar.

"We soon will," Charlotte interposed, defiantly. The sim turned its bloodshot eye upon her, and she flinched from the baleful stare.

"The final act has yet to be played," Rappaccini told her. "You may already know my true names, but you will have difficulty in identifying the one which I presently use as my own." The sardonic gaze moved again, to meet Oscar's invisible stare. "You will thank me for this, Oscar. You would never forgive me if I were not just a little *too* clever for you."

"If you wanted to kill six men," said Oscar, "why did you wait until they were almost dead? At any time in the last seventy years, fate might have cheated you. Had you waited another month, you might not have found Walter Czastka alive."

"You underestimate the tenacity of men like these," Rappaccini replied. "You think they are ready for death because they have ceased to live, but longevity has ingrained its habits deeply in the flesh. Without me to help them, they might have protracted their misery for many years yet. But I am nothing if not loyal to those deserving of my tenderness. I bring them not merely death, but glorious transfiguration! The *fact* of death is not the point at issue here. Did you think me capable of pursuing mere revenge? It is the *manner* of a man's death that is all-important in our day and age, is it not? We have rediscovered the ancient joys of mourning, and the awesome propriety of solemn ceremony and dark symbol. Wreaths are not enough—not even wreaths which are spiders in disguise. The end of death *itself* is upon us, and how shall we celebrate it, save by making a new compact with the Grim Reaper? Murder is almost extinct, and it should *not* be. Murder must be rehabilitated, made romantic, flamboyant, gorgeous, and glamorous! What have my six victims left to do but set an example to their younger brethren? And who but *I* should appoint himself their deliverer, their ennobler, the proclaimer of their fame?''

"I fear," said Oscar, coldly, "that this performance might not make the impact that you intend. It reeks of falsity.''

Rappaccini smiled again. "You know better than that, Oscar," he said. "You know in your heart that this marvelous appearance is real, and the hidden actuality a mere nothing. This is no cocoon of hollowed rock; it is my palace. You will see a finer rock before the end.''

"Your representations are deceptive, Dr. Rappaccini," Charlotte put in. "Your daughter showed us Gabriel King's head first and foremost, but Kwiatek died before him, and Teidemann was probably dead even before Kwiatek. It was optimistic, too—we've already warned Walter Czastka, and if the other one can still be saved, we'll save him too.''

Rappaccini's sim turned back to her. She had not been able to deduce, so far, how high a grade of artificial intelligence it had. She did not expect any explicit confirmation of her guess that Magnus Teidemann was a victim, or that the woman really was Rappaccini's daughter, but she felt obliged to try.

"All six will go to their appointed doom," the sim told her.

She wanted to get out now, to transmit a tape of this encounter to Hal Watson, so that he could identify the fifth face, but she hesitated.

"What can these men possibly have done to you?" she asked, trying to sound contemptuous although there was no point. "What unites them in your hatred?''

"I do not hate them at all," replied the sim, "and the link between them is not recorded in that silly Net which was built to trap the essence of human experience. I have done what I have done because it was absurd and unthinkable and comical. Great lies have been banished from the world for far too long, and the time has come for us not merely to tell them, but to *live* them also. It is by no means easy to work against the grain of synthetic wood, but we must try.''

And with that, darkness fell, lit only by the tiny star which marked the door through which they had entered the Underworld.

9

Night had fallen by the time Charlotte and Oscar emerged into the open, but there was a three-quarter moon and the stars shone very brightly through the clear, clean air. The car had gone. Charlotte's hand tightened around the bubblebugs which she had carefully removed from their stations above her eyebrows. She had been holding them at the ready, anxious to plug them into the car's systems so that their data could be decanted and relayed back to Hal Watson. She murmured a curse.

"Don't worry," said Oscar, who had come out behind her. "Rappaccini will not abandon us. A vehicle of some kind will be along very shortly to carry us on our way."

"Where to?" she asked, unable to keep the asperity out of her voice.

"Westward. We may have one more port of call *en route*, but our final destination will surely be the island where Walter Czastka is. His death is intended to form the climatic scene of this little drama."

"Let's hope it's not too late to prevent that," said Charlotte bitterly. "And let's hope the fifth man is still alive when we get a chance to find out who he is. He may be dead already, of course—your ghoulish friend displayed his victims in the order in which their bodies were discovered, not the order in which they were killed."

"He was never my friend," Oscar objected, "and I am not sure that I like his determination to involve me in this. There is an element of mockery in it."

"Mockery," she said, tersely, "isn't a crime. Murder *is*." She took out her waistphone and tried to send a signal. There was a chance that the power-cell had enough muscle to reach a relay-station. Nothing happened. She turned back to her enigmatic companion.

"Did you understand all that stuff?" she asked him, point-blank.

"I think so," Oscar admitted. "My ancient namesake's *Salomé* provided the format, but the set owed more to Gustave Moreau's paintings then Oscar Wilde's humble play. . . ." He broke off. His words had gradually been overlaid by another sound, whose monotonous drone now threatened to drown him out entirely.

"There!" said Charlotte, pointing at a shadow eclipsing the stars. It was descending rapidly toward them, growing hugely as it did so. It was a VTOL airplane, whose engines were even now switching to the vertical mode so that it could land helicopter-fashion. Charlotte and Oscar hurried into the shelter of the building from which they had come, to give it space to land.

The plane had only an AI pilot. While Oscar climbed in behind her Charlotte plugged her waistphone into the comcon and deposited her bubblebugs in the decoder. "Hal," she said, as soon as the connection was made. "Data coming in: crazy message from Rappaccini, delivered by sim. Conclusive proof of Rappaccini's involvement. Pick out the face of the fifth victim and identify it. Send an urgent warning to Walter Czastka. And tell us what course this damn plane is following, when you can track it." The plane had already taken off again.

Hal acknowledged, but paused only briefly before saying: "I'm sure all this is very interesting, but I've closed the file on Rappaccini. We're concentrating all our efforts on the woman."

"What?" said Charlotte, dumbfounded. "What do you mean, *closed the file?* The tape is proof of Rappaccini's involvement. Have you found out his real name?'' Hal was too busy decanting the data and setting up programs to deal with it; there was a frustrating pause. Charlotte looked around. The airplane was a small one, built to carry a maximum of four passengers; there was a frustrating pause. Charlotte looked around. The airplane was a small one, built to carry a maximum, of four passengers; there was a second comcon and a second pair of seats behind the one into which she and Oscar had climbed. Behind the second row of seats there was a curtained section containing four bunks. Oscar was busy inspecting the menu on the food-dispenser, frowning.

"It all depends what you mean by a *real name*," said Hal, finally. "He really was born Jafri Biasiolo. The dearth of information about Biasiolo is the result of poor data-gathering toward the end of the Aftermath. After his first rejuvenation—which changed his appearance to the one that we saw earlier—he began to use the name Rappaccini for all purposes. Later, as he approached his second rejuve, he established half a dozen fake identities under various pseudonyms, including Gustave Moreau. After the rejuve, when he had his appearance considerably modified again, he began using the Moreau name as a primary, and Rappaccini became exclusively virtual. Moreau leased an islet west of Kauai, where he's spent most of the last twenty-five years, never leaving for more than four or five weeks at a time. There's no evident connection between Moreau and the victims, except that Walter Czastka's his nearest neighbor. So far as we know, Biasiolo never had any connection with the university at Wollongong."

"I don't understand," said Charlotte. "Surely we have enough to arrest Moreau, with all the stuff I've just sent through. Why close the file?"

"Because he's *dead*," Hal replied, smugly. "Ten weeks ago in Honolulu. Details of his birth might be lost in the mists of obscurity, but every detail of his death was scrupulously recorded. There's no doubt that it was him. The common links to his island were closed down before that—he's been shipping equipment and material back to Kauai for over a year. There's nothing there now except the ecosystem which he built. The island's off-limits until the UN can get an inspection team in."

"But he's still *responsible* for all this," Charlotte protested. "He must have set it all up before he died. He and the girl—his daughter."

"Moreau never had a daughter in any of his incarnations. He was sterilized before his first rejuve—even though it wasn't actually a legal requirement back then, it was a point of political principle. He made the customary deposits in a reputable sperm bank, but they've never been touched."

"Oh, come *on*, Hal! He's a top-class genetic engineer—his sterilization doesn't mean a thing. Look at the tape. She's playing Salomé to his Herod!"

"That's not *evidence*," said Hal, sharply. "Anyhow, the exact relationship of the girl to Moreau is neither here nor there. The point is that *she's* the active mover in all this. She's the only one we can put on trial, and she's the one we need to find before the newscasters start billing this mess as the Crime of the Century. If there's any *real* help you can give me, I'd be grateful, but all this theatrical stuff is just more news-fodder, which we can do without. Okay?"

Charlotte could understand why Hal was edgy. News of how Gabriel King and the others had died must have leaked out, and he was very sensitive about cases being publicized before arrests had been made. It wasn't his image or his reputation within the department that he was worried about; it was a point of principle, a private obsession.

"We *are* helping, aren't we?" she whispered, after the inset had disappeared. The question, by necessity, was addressed to Oscar Wilde.

"He won't find her before we do," Oscar said softly. "We've been given the fast track to the climax of the psychodrama. And she *is* his daughter—if not a literal daughter, then a figurative one. I see now why the simulacrum said that we'd have difficulty identifying his true name. Moreau was his *true* name, by then, but he knew that the coincidence would make me assume that it was a mere pseudonym. I must talk to Walter again."

Before he could touch the keyboard, however, another call came in.

"The fifth face is Stuart McCandless," said Hal's voice. "We've spoken to him once but we're trying to get through to him again; his house AI's sent out a summoner. Your plane's heading west, on course for Kauai. You might be able to speak to him in person soon."

Charlotte placed her fingers on the rim of the keyboard, but Oscar put his hand on top of hers, gently insistent. "I have to call Walter," he said. "Dr. Watson will have priority on the call to McCandless."

She let him go ahead, although she knew that she shouldn't let her authority slip away so easily. She, after all, was the investigator. She no longer thought that Oscar was a murderer, but that didn't affect the fact that *he* was the one who was only along for the ride.

Oscar's call was fielded by a sim, which looked considerably healthier than the real Walter had. "Oscar Wilde," he said, curtly. "I need to talk to Walter urgently."

"I'm not taking any calls at present," said the simulacrum, flatly.

"Don't be ridiculous, Walter," said Oscar, impatiently. "This is no time to go into a sulk."

The sim flickered, and its image was replaced by Czastka's actual face. "What do you want?" he said, his voice taut with aggravation.

"You're a player in this game whether you like it or not, Walter," Oscar said, soothingly. "We really do have to try to figure it out."

"I'm not in any danger," said Walter, tiredly. "There's no one else on the island, and no one can land without the house systems knowing about it. I'm perfectly safe. I never heard of anyone called Biasiolo, I've never met Moreau, and I know of no connection between myself and the other names the police gave me that could possibly constitute a motive for murder."

"I don't think the motive is conventional," said Oscar. "This whole business is a publicity stunt, a weird artistic statement, but there must be *some* kind of connection—something that happened at Wollongong."

Czastka looked ominously pale. "I told your friends, Oscar—*I don't remember.* Nobody remembers what they were doing a hundred and thirty years ago. *Nobody.*"

"I don't believe that, Walter," said Oscar, softly. "We forget almost everything, but we can always remember the things which matter most, if we try hard enough. This is something which *matters*, Walter. It matters now, and it mattered then. If you try, you can remember.''

''I *can't*.'' The word was delivered with such bitterness and anguish that Charlotte flinched.

''What about you and Gustave Moreau, Walter?'' Oscar asked. ''Didn't you know he was your neighbor?''

''I've never even *seen* the man,'' said Czastka. ''All I know about him is the joke the wise guys on Kauai keep repeating. The island of Dr. Moreau, get it? You must—you've probably even *read* the damn thing. You must know, too, that we keep ourselves to ourselves out here. All I want is to keep to myself. *I just want to be left alone.*''

Oscar paused for thought. ''Do you *want* to die, Walter?'' he asked, finally. His inflection suggested that it was not a rhetorical question.

''No,'' said Czastka, sourly. ''I want to live forever, just like you. I want to be young again, just like you. But when I do die, I don't want flowers by Rappaccini at my funeral, and I don't want anything of yours. When I die, I want all the flowers to be mine. Is that clear?''

''I think we're on our way to see you,'' said Oscar, placidly. ''We can talk then.''

''Damn you, Wilde,'' said the old man, vehemently. ''I don't want you on my island. You stay away, you hear? *Stay away!*'' He broke the connection without waiting for any response.

Oscar turned sideways to look at Charlotte. His face looked slightly sinister in the dim light of the helicopter's cabin. ''Your turn,'' he said. His smile was very faint.

It didn't take as long to get through as Charlotte had expected. Evidently, whoever had called on Hal's behalf had been brisk and business-like. Stuart McCandless wasn't answering his phone in person, but when Charlotte fed his sim her authority codes it summoned him without delay.

''Yes?'' he said, his dark and well-worn face peering at her with slightly peevish surprise. ''I've hardly begun on the data you people dumped into my system. It's going to take some time to look at it all.''

''I'm Charlotte Holmes, Dr. McCandless,'' she said. ''I'm in an airplane that has apparently been programmed by Gustave Moreau, *alias* Rappaccini. He seems intent on providing my companion—Oscar Wilde—with a good seat from which to observe this unfolding melodrama. We're heading out into the ocean from the American coast. We're heading your way and I thought we ought to talk. Have you ever met Moreau?''

McCandless shook his head vigorously. ''I've already answered these questions,'' he said, irritably.

''Have you looked at the tapes of the girl who visited Gabriel King and Michi Urashima? Do you recognize her?''

''I'd be able to study your tapes more closely if you'd allow me time to do it, Ms. Holmes. I'm looking at them now, but in these days of changing appearances it's almost impossible to recognize *anyone*. I don't know whether the person in those pictures is twenty years old or a hundred. I've had dozens of students who were similar enough to be able to duplicate her appearance with a little effort. There's a visitor here now who could only need a little elementary remodeling.''

Charlotte felt Oscar Wilde's hand fall upon hers, but she didn't need the hint. She was already trying to work out how to phrase the next question. "Who is your visitor, Dr. McCandless?" she asked, in the end.

"Oh, there's not the slightest need to worry," McCandless replied. "I've known her for some time. Her name is Julia Herold. I told your colleague in New York all about her."

"Could you ask her to come to the phone?" asked Charlotte. She glanced sideways, very briefly, at Oscar.

"Oh, very well," McCandless said. He turned away, saying, "Julia?"

Moments later he moved aside, surrendering his place in front of the camera to a young woman, apparently in her early twenties. The woman stared into the camera. Her abundant hair was golden red, and very carefully sculptured, and her eyes were a vivid green. *A wig and a bimolecular overlay*, Charlotte thought. "I'm sorry to disturb you, Miss Herold," she said, slowly. "We're investigating a series of murders, and it's difficult to determine what information may be relevant."

"I understand," said the woman, calmly.

Charlotte felt a strange pricking sensation at the back of her neck. *It's her*, she thought. *It has to be her*. Hal Watson was undoubtedly checking the woman out at this very moment, with all possible speed, and if he found anything to justify action, he would act swiftly—but until he did, there was nothing she could do. *She's playing with us*, Charlotte thought. *She has McCandless in the palm of her hand and there's no way we can save him. But she'll never get away. She can't make another move without our knowing about it.*

"May I talk to Dr. McCandless again?" she asked, dully.

They switched places again. Charlotte wanted to say *Whatever you do, don't kiss her!* but she knew how stupid it would sound. "Dr. McCandless," she said, uncomfortably, "we think that something might have happened when you were a student yourself. Something that links you, however tenuously, with Gabriel King, Michi Urashima, Paul Kwiatek, Magnus Teidemann, and Walter Czastka. We desperately need to know what it was. We understand how difficult it is to remember, but . . ."

McCandless controlled his irritation. "I'm checking back through my records, trying to turn something up," he said. "I hardly know Czastka, although he lives close by. The others I know only by repute. I didn't even know that I was contemporary with Urashima or Teidemann. There were thousands of students at the university. We didn't all graduate in the same year. We were never in the same place at one time, unless. . . ."

"Unless what, Dr. McCandless?" said Charlotte, quickly.

The dark brow was furrowed and the eyes were glazed, as the man reached for some fleeting, fugitive memory. "The beach party . . . ?" he muttered. Then, the face became hard and stern again. "No," he said, firmly. "I really can't remember."

Charlotte saw a slender hand descend reassuringly upon Stuart McCandless's shoulder, and she saw him take it in his own, thankfully. She knew that there was no point in asking what he had half-remembered. He was shutting her out.

It's happening now, she thought, before our very eyes. She's going to kill him within the next few minutes, and we can't do a thing to stop it. But we can surely stop her before she gets to Walter Czastka.

"Dr. McCandless," she said, desperately. "I have reason to believe that you're in mortal danger. I advise you to isolate yourself completely—and I mean *completely*, Dr. McCandless."

"I know what you mean," he retorted testily. "I know how the mind of a policeman works. But I can give you my absolute assurance that I'm in no danger whatsoever. Now, may I get on with the work that your colleague asked me to do?"

"Yes," she said. "I'm sorry." She let him break the connection; she didn't feel that she could do it herself.

When the screen blanked, she turned and said: "He's as good as dead, isn't he?"

"The seeds may already be taking root in his flesh," said Oscar, gently. "It might have been too late, no matter what anyone could have said or done."

"What was it that he started to say?" she asked. "And why did he stop?"

"Something that came to mind in spite of his resistance. Something, perhaps, that Walter might half-remember too, if only he wanted to. . . ."

Charlotte shook her head, tiredly. She called Hal. "Julia Herold," she said, shortly. "Have you tied her in with Moreau yet?"

"No," said Hal, simply. "She's a student. Her career seems quite ordinary, all in order. According to the Net, she wasn't in New York when Gabriel King received his visitor, nor in San Francisco when Urashima was infected. I'm double-checking—if it's disinformation, I'll get through it in a matter of hours."

"She was there," said Charlotte. "Whatever the superficial data-flow says, she was there. It's all in place, Hal—everything except the reason. You've got to stop her leaving the island. Whatever else happens, you mustn't let her get to Czastka."

"Who's her father?" Oscar put in. "Whose child is she?"

"Egg and sperm were taken from the banks," said Hal. "Both donors long-dead. Six co-parents filed the application—no traceable link to anyone involved in this. The sperm was logged in the name of Lothar Kjeldsen, born 2355, died 2417. The ovum was Maria Inacio's, born 2402, died 2423. No duplicate pairing registered, no other posthumous offspring registered to either parent. I'm checking for disinformation input, in case the entire Herold identity is virtual."

"The mother was born at the same time as the men on the victim list. Could she have known them?"

"It's possible. She was an Australian resident at the appropriate time. There's no trace of her in the University records, but she might have been living next door. What would it prove if she was? She's been dead for a hundred and thirty years. She drowned in Honolulu—presumed accidental, possibly a suicide. This isn't getting us anywhere, Dr. Wilde, and I have a whole panel lighting up on me—I'm cutting off."

The screen went blank yet again.

"She's Rappaccini's daughter," said Oscar, softly. "I don't know which bit of the record's been faked, or how, but she's Rappaccini's daughter. And she'll get to Walter, even if she has to swim."

10

Charlotte stared out of the viewport beside her. Behind them, in the east, the dawn was breaking. Ahead of them, in the west, the sky was still dark and ominous. Beneath them, the sea was only just becoming visible as fugitive rays of silvery light caught the tops of lazy waves. In these latitudes, the sea was almost unpolluted by the vast amount of synthetic photosynthetic substances which were daily pumped out from the artificial islands of the Timor Sea; even by day it did not display the defiant greenness of Liquid Artificial Photosynthesis. Even so, this region of the ocean could not be reckoned a marine wilderness. The so-called seven seas were a single vast system, now half-gentled by the hand of man. The Continental Engineers, despite the implications of their name, had better control of evolution's womb than extinction's rack. Even the wrathful volcanoes which had created the Hawaiian islands were now sufficiently manipulable that they could be forced to yield upon demand the little virgin territories which the likes of Walter Czastka and Oscar Wilde had rented for their experiments in Creation.

"In my namesake's novel, *The Picture of Dorian Gray*," Oscar said, ruminatively, "the eponymous anti-hero made a diabolical bargain, exchanging fates with a portrait of himself, with the consequence that his picture was marred by all the afflictions of age and dissolution while the real Dorian remained perpetually young. He cast aside all conventional ideas of morality, determined to savor the entire gamut of pleasurable sensation."

"I'm sure it's great fun," said Charlotte, ironically.

Oscar ignored the remark. "At that time, of course," he said, "the story of Dorian Gray was the purest of fantasies, but we live in a different era now. It is perhaps too early to declare that yours is the last generation which will be subject to the curse of aging, but I am living proof of the fact that even *my* generation has set aside much of the burden with which ugliness, disease, and the aging process afflicted us in days of old. We are corruptible, but we also have the means to set aside corruption, to reassert, in spite of all the ravages of time and malady, the image which we would like to have of ourselves. Nowadays, everyone who has the means may have beauty, and even those of limited means have a right of access to the elementary technologies of rejuvenation. I am young now for the fourth time, and no matter how often doctors and doubters tell me that my flesh is too weak to weather a fourth rejuvenation, I will not be prevented from attempting it. Nothing will induce me to become like Walter Czastka when I might instead gamble my mortality against the chance of yet another draught from the fountain of youth."

"So what?" said Charlotte. "Why tell me?"

"Because," he said, tolerantly, "that's why Rappaccini expects me to under-

stand what sort of artwork he is designing. That's why he expects me to become
its interpreter and champion, explaining to the world what it is that he has done.
Because I'm Oscar Wilde—and because I'm Dorian Gray. Men like the first
Oscar Wilde and the first Gustave Moreau were fond of likening their own era
to the days of the declining Roman Empire, when its aristocracy had grown
effete and self-indulgent, so utterly enervated by luxury that its members could
find stimulation only in orgiastic excess. They argued that the ruling class of
the nineteenth century had been similarly corrupted by comfort, to the extent
that anyone among them who had any sensitivity at all lived under the yoke of
a terrible *ennui*, which could only be opposed by sensual and imaginative excess.
All that remained for men of genius to do was mock the meaningless of confor-
mity and enjoy the self-destructive exultation of moral and artistic defiance.

"They were right, of course. Theirs *was* a decadent culture, absurdly distracted
by its luxuries and vanities, unwittingly lurching toward its historical terminus.
The 'comforts' of the nineteenth century—hygiene, medicine, electricity—were
the direct progenitors of what we now call the Devastation. Few men had the
vision to understand what was happening, and even fewer had the capacity to
care. Addicted to their luxuries as they were, even terror could not give them
foresight. Blindly and stupidly, they laid the world to waste, and used all the
good intentions of their marvelous technology to pave themselves a road to Hell.
In the Aftermath, of course, the work of renewal began. Collective control of
fertility was achieved, and the old world of hateful tribes was replaced by the
world of the Net, which bound the entire human race into a single community.
And we were able once again to cultivate our comforts . . . to the extent that
Rappaccini seemingly believes that the revolution is complete, and that the wheel
has come full circle."

"But that's nonsense!" said Charlotte. "There's no way that there could be
another Devastation. There couldn't possibly be another population explosion,
or another plague war."

"That's not what Rappaccini fears," said Oscar. "What he's trying to make
us see, I think, is the horror of a world inhabited entirely by the *old:* a world
made stagnant by the dominion of minds that have lost their grip on memory
and imagination alike, becoming slaves to habit, imprisoned by their own narrow
horizons. He's telling us that, in one way or another, we must kill our old men.
The argument of his artwork is that if we can't liberate our renewable bodies
from the frailty of our mortal minds, then the technological conquest of death
will be a tragedy and not a triumph. He has undertaken to murder six men who
are nearing a hundred and fifty years of age, not one of whom has dared to risk
a third rejuvenation, even though it would seem that they have little or nothing
to lose—and he has chosen for his audience a man who *has* taken that gamble,
hopefully soon enough to avoid the kind of mental sclerosis which has claimed
his victims. Can you begin to see what he's about?"

"I can see that he's stark, staring mad," said Charlotte.

Oscar smiled wryly. "Perhaps he is," he said. "His fear is real enough—
but perhaps the threat isn't as overwhelming as he seems to think. Perhaps the
old men will never take over the world, no matter how many they are or how

old they grow. Old age is, after all, self-defeating. Those who lose the ability to live also lose the will to live. But the creative spark can be maintained, if it's properly nurtured. The victory of *ennui* isn't inevitable. If and when we really can transform every human egg-cell to equip it for eternal physical youth, those children will discover ways to adapt themselves to that condition by cultivating eternal *mental* youth. My way of trying to do that is, I admit, primitive— but I am here to help prepare the way for those who come after me. They will be the true children of our race: the first truly *human* beings.''

Charlotte felt her eyes growing heavy; she felt drained. If only she had been more alert, she thought, she might have obtained a firmer grasp on Oscar Wilde's arguments. After all, she too retained an echo of the 1890s in her name. Could the small phonetic step which separated ''Charlotte'' from ''Sherlock'' really signify such a vast abyss of incomprehension? She knew that she needed sleep, and she felt in need of a soporific. Unfortunately, she was four thousand kilometers away from the ingenious resources of her intimate technology. She looked uncertainly at Oscar Wilde. He was watching her, with a serious expression in his liquid, luminous eyes.

''We ought to get some sleep,'' Charlotte said. ''It'll be late tomorrow before we get to Hawaii.'' She hesitated, wondering how to proceed, her gaze drifting to the curtain which screened the cabin's bunkspace.

''How my namesake's heart would have warmed to our Virtual Realities and the wonders of our intimate technology!'' Oscar said, as though continuing his reverie. ''I fear, though, that we have not yet learned to use our intimate technologies as fully or as consciencelessly as we might. Even in a world of artificial wombs and long-dead parents, we cling to the notion that sexual intercourse is essentially a form of communication, or even communion, rather than an entirely personal matter, whose true milieu is the arena of fantasy, where all idiosyncrasies may be safely unfettered.''

Charlotte couldn't help blushing, although she presumed that he had preempted her proposition mainly in order to spare her blushes.

''Thanks for telling me,'' she said, sharply. ''I suppose that if Rappaccini had you on his list of victims, you'd be in no danger.''

''Not so,'' he said. ''A kiss is, after all, just a kiss—and I can appreciate a lovely face as well as any man. It is only in matters of *true* passion that I am an exclusive and unrepentant Narcissus.''

11

When Charlotte awoke, the sun was high, but Oscar had darkened the viewports in order to conserve a soft crepuscular light within the cabin of the speeding plane. She sat up and drew the curtain aside to look over the backs of the seats. Her waistphone was still plugged in to the comcon; data was parading across the main screen at the command of Oscar's deft fingertips.

''Good morning,'' he said, instantly aware of her movement although he had not turned. ''It *is* still morning, thanks to the time-harvesting effects of westward travel. We're less than half an hour from Kauai, but I fear that we'll be unable to do much there except bear witness to the completion of the fifth phase of Rappaccini's grand plan.''

Because she was slightly befuddled by sleep, it took her a second or two to work out what he meant. ''McCandless is dead!'' she said, finally.

''Quite dead,'' he confirmed. ''The local police had him removed to an intensive-care unit as soon as he showed signs of illness, but there was absolutely nothing to be done for him. The progress of his devourers will be tracked with infinite patience by a multitude of observers—the doctors have sent a fleet of nanocameras into his tissues—but to no avail. What remains of Teidemann's body has been found too.''

Charlotte donned the tunic of her police uniform. ''What about Julia Herold? Have they got her in custody?''

''Alas, no.''

Charlotte knew that she ought to have been astonished and outraged, but all that she really felt was a sense of bitter resignation.

''How could they possibly fail to intercept her?''

''She had already left when McCandless began to show signs of distress,'' said Oscar, who did not seem overly disappointed. ''She went for a moonlight swim, and never surfaced again. The eyes set to follow her were mounted on flitterbugs, and by the time suitable submarine eyes entered the water she was beyond reach. Flying eyes are, of course, watching avidly for her to surface, but she must have had breathing apparatus secreted off-shore, and some kind of mechanized transport.''

''A submarine?'' said Charlotte, incredulously.

''More likely a towing device of some kind. The officer in charge of the failed operation pointed out that there was little more he could have done without a warrant for her arrest. One has now been issued. The Kauai police have sent helicopters to lie in wait for her, but Walter has forbidden them permission to land, and they're not empowered to override his wishes unless and until they actually see her. There's one more police helicopter awaiting our arrival on Kauai.''

''Have you talked to Czastka?''

''No. He's refusing all calls. He presumably still thinks that all he needs to do is keep his house sealed. 'Julia Herold,' by the way, is a fiction of disinformation. Your Dr. Watson has proved that the person in McCandless' house was indeed the same one who visited Gabriel King in New York and Michi Urashima in San Francisco. He is confident that he will be able to prove that she delivered the fatal flowers to Teidemann and Kwiatek too. He assures me that it is only a matter of time before he discloses an authentic personal history.''

''Is that everything?''

''By no means. It required all my skills as an organizer to present these edited highlights so economically.''

Charlotte looked resentfully at the bright and beautiful young man, who seemed unafflicted by the least sign of weariness. She switched the nearest viewport to reflector mode so that she could straighten her hair, and studied the faint wrinkles that were becoming apparent in the corners of her eyes. They could be removed easily enough by the most elementary tissue-manipulation, but they still served as a reminder of the biological clock that was ticking away inside her. *Thirty years to rejuve number one*, she thought, *and counting*. It was not a kind of paranoia to which she was usually prone, but she could not help comparing her flawed features with Oscar's fully-restored perfection.

As soon as they had set down at the Kauai heliport, Charlotte opened the door, and leapt down to the blue plastic apron. The promised helicopter was waiting less than a hundred meters away. Its police markings were a delight to her eyes, holding the promise of *control*. From now on she would no longer be a passenger but an active participant; a pursuer, an active instrument of justice. Oscar kept pace with her in spite of the fact that his gait seemed much lazier.

"I should leave you here," she said, while climbing aboard. "I can, you know—this isn't public transport."

"You wouldn't be so cruel," he said. He was right.

The helicopter lifted as soon as they were strapped in. Charlotte reached into the equipment-locker under the seat, and brought forth a handgun. She checked the mechanism before clipping it to her belt.

"You're not thinking of using that, I hope?" said Oscar.

"Now the proof's in place," Charlotte answered, tautly, "I can employ any practical measure which may be necessary to apprehend her. The bullets are non-lethal. We're the *police*, remember."

They were traveling at a slower speed than they had previously, but flew so low that their progress seemed more rapid. The downdraft of their blades carved the roiling waves into all manner of curious shapes. High in the sky above them, a silver airship was making its stately progress from Honolulu to Yokohama. Oscar tuned in a broadcast news report. There were pictures of Gabriel King's skeleton, neatly entwined with winding stems bearing black flowers in horrid profusion. This was only the beginning; the AI voice-over promised that details of several more murders would soon be revealed. Charlotte knew that an operation of the size that was now being mounted would attract the attention of half the newshawks in United America and a good few in not-very-united Eastasia. Flocks of flying eyes would be migrating this way from every direction. The privacy which Walter Czastka so passionately desired to conserve was about to be rudely shattered.

Oscar blanked the newscast as soon as it moved on to more mundane matters, and his fingers punched out Walter Czastka's telephone code. The AI sim which answered had clearly been reprogrammed since Charlotte had last seen it.

"Damn you, Oscar Wilde," it said, without bothering with any conventional identification or polite preliminary. "Damn you and Rappaccini to the darkest oblivion imaginable."

Charlotte turned the camera-eye so that her own image filled the viewfield. "Dr. Czastka," she said, "this is Charlotte Holmes of the UN Police. I need to speak to you, urgently."

"Damn you, Oscar Wilde," replied the sim, stubbornly. "Damn you and Rappaccini to the darkest oblivion imaginable."

Charlotte looked at Oscar, whose face had creased into an anxious frown. "I have a horrible suspicion," he said, "that we might be too late." Charlotte looked at her wristwatch. They were still twenty minutes away from the island. She punched in another code, connecting herself to the commander of the task-force that had surrounded it.

"What's happening?" she demanded.

"No sign of her yet," the answer came back. "If anything happens, Inspector, you'll be the first to know." There was nothing to do but wait, so she sat back in her seat and stared down at the agitated waves. They were still a few minutes away when the voice came back on line. "We have camera-contact," it said. "Relaying pictures."

The screen showed a female figure in a humpbacked wetsuit walking out of the sea, looking for all the world as if she were enjoying a leisurely stroll. She paused at the high tide line to remove the suit and its built-in paralung, then knelt beside the discarded wetsuit and removed something from a inner pocket. Over the voice-link they could hear the officer who had spoken to them instructing her to desist.

Suddenly, the air around the girl was filled by a dense smoke, which swirled in the breeze as it dispersed.

"Alate spores," Oscar guessed. "Millions of them."

Julia Herold stood, with her arms upraised in a gesture of seeming surrender. She had apparently done what she'd come to do.

"Stay in the copters," Charlotte instructed. "The stuff she's released is probably harmless to anyone but Czastka, but there's no need for everyone to take the risk. I'll pick her up myself."

"As you wish," said the other officer, sourly. He evidently thought that Charlotte was intent on appropriating what little glory there might be in making the arrest.

"I think we may have mistaken the exact form that the final murder was intended to take," said Oscar, quietly. "It's not Walter those spores are after—it's his ecosystem. She came here to destroy his private Creation."

As the helicopter swept in to land Charlotte scanned the trees which fringed the beach. Lush undergrowth nestled about the boles of palmlike trees. She half-expected to see the green leaves already flecked with darker colors, but nothing was happening yet.

"Nothing can stop it," said Oscar, softly, his voice reduced now almost to a whisper. "Each murder is one hundred percent specific to its victim. Walter's own body is safe inside the house, but that's not what he cares about . . . it's not what he *is*. Rappaccini's instruments are going to devour his entire ecosphere—every last molecule."

For the first time, Charlotte realized, Oscar Wilde was genuinely horrified. The equanimity that had hardly been rippled by the sight of Gabriel King's hideously embellished skeleton was ruffled now. For the first time, Oscar was identifying with one of Rappaccini's victims, seeing Rappaccini as a criminal as well as an artist. But even as Charlotte observed his outrage, Oscar's expression was changing.

"Look!" he said. "Look what kind of demi-Eden Walter Czastka has been endeavoring to build here." The helicopter had set down some thirty meters from the woman, who still stood there, with her arms upraised. She was taking no notice of them or the other hovering machines; her green eyes were quite blank. Charlotte climbed down, keeping one eye on the woman while she obeyed Oscar's instruction to look inland. She could not see anything surprising or alarming.

"Poor Walter!" said Oscar, sadly. "What a petty Arcadia this is! Immature and incomplete though it undoubtedly is, its limitations already show. Here is the work of a hack trying desperately to exceed his own potential—but here is the work of a man who has not even the imagination of blind and stupid nature. I can see now why Walter tried to keep me away. The mysterious Julia does not have to kiss poor Walter, because Walter is already dead, and he knows it. Even if his heart still beats within his withered frame, he is dead. Rappaccini's worms are feeding on his carcass."

"It looks perfectly ordinary to me," said Charlotte, staring up at the uneven line made by the crowns of Walter Czastka's palmlike trees, as they extended their ample canopies to bask in the life-giving light of the sun.

"Precisely," said Oscar Wilde, with a heavy sigh.

Charlotte moved to confront the woman, who stood statue-still, looking up into the brilliant blue sky.

"Julia Herold," she began, "I arrest you for . . ."

She heard a strange squawking sound behind her, and guessed that someone was trying to attract her attention by shouting over the voice-link to the helicopter's comcon. She picked up her waistphone impatiently. "It's okay," she said. "I've got her. It's all over."

"Look behind you!" said the voice from the other end, trying to shout at her although the volume control on her waistphone compensated automatically. *"Corrosion and corruption, woman, look behind you!"*

Uncomprehendingly, Charlotte looked behind her.

Falling toward her from the vivid brightness of the early afternoon sun was a black shadow. At first she could judge neither its size nor its shape, but as it swooped down, the truth became abundantly and monstrously clear. She could not believe the evidence of her eyes. She knew full well that what she was seeing was flatly impossible, and her mind stubbornly refused to accept the truth of what she saw.

It was a bird, but it was a bird like none that had ever taken to the skies of earth in the entire evolutionary history of flight, bigger by far than the helicopters whose automatic pilots were taking evasive action to avoid it. The pinion-feathers of its black wings were the size of samurai swords, and its horrible head was naked, like a vulture's. Its beak was agape, and it cried out as it swooped down upon her. Its cry was a terrible inhuman shriek, which made her think of the wailing of the damned in some Dantean Hell.

Wise panic took hold of her and threw her aside like a rag doll, lest she be struck by the diving impossibility. She had no time to fire her gun, nor even to think about firing it. Her reflexes rudely cast her down, tumbling her ignominiously onto the silvery sand.

Julia Herold didn't move a muscle. Charlotte understood, belatedly, that the raising of her arms was not a gesture of surrender at all. With confident ease, the girl interlaced her fingers with the reaching talons of the huge bird, and was lifted instantly from her feet.

According to all the best authorities, Charlotte knew, no bird could lift an adult human being from the ground—but *this* bird could. It was climbing again now, beating its fabulous night-black wings with extravagant majesty, circling back into the dazzling halo of brilliance that surrounded the tropical sun.

Charlotte reached up her own hand to take the one that Oscar Wilde was extending to her. "Do you remember when Rappaccini's simulacrum said to us, 'This is no cocoon of hollowed rock; it is my palace. You will see a finer rock before the end'?" he asked, resignedly. "The second 'rock' was actually 'roc.' A cheap shot, in *my* judgment."

"Get back in the helicopter," she said, grimly. "I don't know how far or how fast that thing can fly, but she is *not* going to get away."

"I don't think she's even trying," said Oscar, with a sigh. "She's merely escorting us to the much-joked-about island of Dr. Moreau, so that we may cast a critical eye over her father's Creation."

12

Moreau's island was more or less identical in size and shape to Walter Czastka's. By the time it was in view, Charlotte had Hal Watson on the line, watching the drunken flight of the giant bird through the helicopter's camera-eyes. Huge though it was, the woman's weight was burden enough to make flight very difficult, and Charlotte wondered whether the creature had sufficient strength left to make landfall.

"It is clear," said Oscar, "that the murders were committed partly in order to lay a trail. We shall be the first to reach its end, but by no means the last. Every news service in the world must have dispatched spy-eyes by now. We are about to attend an exhibition, dear Charlotte—one which will put the so-called Great Exhibition of 2505 to shame."

"We picked up enough body-cells at McCandless's house to produce a DNA-spectrum," Hal put in. "The lab people didn't expect any kind of correlation with the people who were registered as Julia Herold's parents, but they found one. According to her genes, Herold is Maria Inacio, saving some slight somatic modifications compatible with cosmetic transformation. Inacio's alleged death in 2423 must be disinformation."

"No," said Oscar, softly. "Maria Inacio was born in 2402; there's no way that she could be Rappaccini's daughter. You won't find Julia Herold's birth recorded anywhere, Dr. Watson. She was born from an artificial womb on the island, not more than twenty years ago."

"A clone!" said Charlotte. "An unregistered clone! But she's *not* his daughter. You were wrong about that."

"In the literal sense, yes," admitted Oscar, as the bird summoned the last vestiges of its strength for one last surge toward the silver strand where the waves were breaking over Dr. Moreau's island, "but he's raised her from infancy within the confines of his own Garden of Eden, and I'll wager that he has exactly the same degree of genetic relatedness to her as he would have to a daughter: fifty percent."

"You mean," said Charlotte, "that she's his *sister!*"

"No," said Oscar, clenching his fist in a tiny gesture of sympathetic triumph as the bird dropped the girl into the sand and lurched exhaustedly to a sprawling landing twenty meters further on. "I mean that Maria Inacio was Rappaccini's *mother.*"

"I suppose you've worked out who his father was, as well?" said Charlotte, as the helicopter zoomed in to land. The helicopter's safety-minded AIs gave the beached roc a wide berth, putting them down sixty meters away from the point where the woman had been dropped; she had already picked herself up and disappeared into the trees fringing the beach. Charlotte unplugged her waistphone from the comcon. She didn't bother unshipping any transmitter-eyes. Hal would soon have plenty of eyes with which to see. The whole world was coming to *this* party.

"We can narrow it down to one of six," said Oscar, as he opened the door and climbed out of the slightly tilted helicopter. "Perhaps that's as far as Rappaccini cared to narrow it down. It's possible, if McCandless's half-recollection of a beach-party at which all six of the victims might or might not have been present means anything at all, that Maria Inacio was uncertain which of them was the father of her child. I strongly suspect, though, that a genetic engineer of Rappaccini's skill and dedication could not have been content with any such uncertainty."

Charlotte looked uneasily along the strand at the chimerical creature that was peering at them dolefully from an unnaturally large and bloodily crimson eye. "It was Walter Czastka," she said, knowing that she could claim no credit simply for filling in the blank.

"It was Walter Czastka," he echoed. "Poor Walter! To harbor such genius in his genes, and such mediocrity in his poor mortal body."

Charlotte wasn't about to waste time feeling sorry for Walter Czastka—not, at any rate, for *that* reason—but she couldn't help feeling a pang of sympathy for poor Maria Inacio, dead before her life had really begun, leaving nothing behind but a child of uncertain parentage. Such things couldn't happen nowadays, when all children were sterilized as a matter of course—and only a tiny minority ever applied for desterilization in order to exercise their right of reproduction while they were still alive—but Maria Inacio had been a child of the Aftermath. Hers had been the last generation of women victimized by their own fertility.

Charlotte and Oscar walked side by side to the place where Rappaccini's mother/daughter had disappeared. They kept a wary eye on the roc, but the bird made no move toward them. It seemed to be in considerable distress. As they paused before moving into the trees, Charlotte saw the bloodshot eyes close. They walked into the forest, following a grassy pathway that had all the appearance of an accident of nature, but which had in fact been designed with the utmost care, as had every blade of grass.

The trunk of every tree had grown into the shape of something else, as finely wrought in bronze-barked wood as any sculpture. No two were exactly alike: here was the image of a dragon rampant, here a mermaid, here a trilobite, and here a shaggy faun. Many were the images of beasts that natural selection had designed to walk on four legs, but all of those stood upright here, rearing back to extend their forelimbs, separately or entwined, high into the air. These upraised forelimbs provided bases for spreading crowns of many different colors. Some few of the crowns extended from an entire host of limbs rather than a single pair, originating from the maws of krakens or the stalks of hydras.

The animals whose shapes were reproduced by the trunks of the trees all had open eyes, which seemed always to be looking at Charlotte no matter where she was in relation to them, and although she knew that they were all quite blind, she could not help feeling discomfited by their seeming curiosity. Her own curiosity, however, was more than equal to theirs. Every tree of the forest was in flower, and every flower was as bizarre as the plant which bore it. There was a noticeable preponderance of reds and blacks. Butterflies and birds moved ceaselessly through the branches, each one wearing its own coat of many colors, and the tips of the branches moved as though stirred by a breeze, reaching out towards these visitors as though to touch their faces. There was no wind: the branches moved by their own volition, according to their own mute purpose.

Charlotte knew that almost all of what she saw was illicit. Creationists were banned from engineering insects and birds, lest their inventions stray to pollute the artwork of other engineers, or to disrupt the domestic ecosystems of the recently renewed world-at-large. When the final accounting was complete, and all of Rappaccini's felonies and misdemeanors had been tabulated by careful AIs, he would probably turn out to have been the most prolific criminal who had ever lived upon the surface of the earth. Rappaccini had given birth to an extraordinary fantasy, fully aware that it would be destroyed almost as soon as others found out what he had done—but he had found a way to show it off first, and to command that attention be paid to it by every man, woman, and child in the world. Had he, perhaps, hoped that his contemporaries might be so overawed as to reckon him a *god*, far above the petty laws of humankind? Had he dared to believe that they might *condone* what he had done, once they saw it in all its glory?

Rappaccini's creative fecundity had not been content with birds and insects. There were monkeys in the trees, which did not hide or flee from the visitors of their demi-paradise, but came instead to stare with patient curiosity. The monkeys had the slender bodies of gibbons and lorises, but they had the wizened faces of old men. Nor was this simply the generic resemblance that had once been manifest in the faces of long-extinct New World monkeys; *these* faces were actual human faces, writ small. Charlotte recognized a family of Czastkas and an assortment of Kings and Urashimas, but there were dozens she did not know. She felt that her senses were quite overloaded. The moist atmosphere was a riot of perfumes, and the murmurous humming of insect wings composed a subtle symphony.

Is it beautiful? Charlotte asked herself, as she studied the sculpted trees staring at her with their illusory eyes, marveling at their hectic crowns and their luminous flowers. *Or is it mad?*

It *was* beautiful: more beautiful than anything she had ever seen or ever hoped to see. It was much more beautiful than the ghostly echoes of Ancient Nature that modern men called wilderness, doubtless more beautiful than Ancient Nature itself—even in all its pre-Devastation glory—could ever have been. Charlotte could see, even with her unschooled eyes, that it was the work of a *young* man. However many years Rappaccini had lived, however many he had spent in glorious isolation in the midst of all this strange fecundity, he had never grown old. This was not the work of a man grown mournful in forgetfulness; this was the work of a man whose only thought was of the future that he would not live to see: its novelty, its ambition, its progress. This was Moreau's island, by which its creator meant *morrow's* island.

It was mad, too, but its madness was essentially divine.

In the heart of the island, she expected to find a house, but there was none. There was only a mausoleum. She knew that Moreau's body could not be inside it, because he had died in Honolulu, but it was nevertheless his tomb. It was hewn from a white marble whose austerity stood in imperious contrast to the fabulous forest around it. It bore neither cross, nor carven angel, nor any inscription.

"Like you and I, dear Charlotte," Oscar said, "Jafri Biasiolo was delivered by history to the very threshold of true immortality, and yet was fated not to live in the Promised Land. How he must have resented the fading of the faculties which had produced *all this!* How wrathful he must have become, to see his fate mirrored in the faces and careers of all those who might—had the whim of chance dictated it—have been his father. When the true immortals emerge from the womb of biotechnical artifice, they will no longer care about who their fathers were or might have been, for they will indeed be *designed*, by men like gods, from common chromosomal clay. He, alas, was not."

Charlotte looked around curiously as she spoke, wondering where the woman might be. "*He* may be dead," she reminded Oscar, grimly, "but his accomplice and executioner will have to stand trial."

"Yes, of course," he murmured. "She must settle her own account with the recording angels of the Celestial Net." So saying, he walked around the massive mausoleum. Charlotte followed him.

The woman was sitting on the pediment on the further side of the tomb, facing a crowd of leaping lions and prancing unicorns, vaulting hippogriffs and rearing cobras, all hewn in living wood beneath a roof of rainbows. Hundreds of man-faced monkeys were solemnly observing the scene. Her vivid green eyes were staring vacuously into space. It was as though she could not see the fantastic host which paraded itself before her. She was quite bald, and the dome of her skull was starred with a thousand tiny contact-points, glistening in the sunlight. The golden red wig that she had worn lay like stranded sea-weed between her feet. In her left hand, she held a flower: a gorgeously gilded rose. In her right hand was a curious skull-cap, made of exceedingly fine metal mesh.

Oscar Wilde picked up the gilded rose, and placed it carefully in his buttonhole, where he was accustomed to wearing a green carnation. Charlotte picked up the skull-cap, and turned it over in her hands, marveling at its thinness, its lightness, and its awesome complexity.

"What is it?" she asked, as her eyes dutifully compared its shape to the contours of the girl's strangely decorated skull.

"I imagine," said Oscar, "that it is your murderer's accomplice and executioner: Rappaccini's daughter. The Virtual Individual which has moved this Innocent Eve through the world, fascinating her appointed victims and luring them to the acceptance of her fatal kisses, is the vengeful ghost of Rappaccini himself, left behind to settle *all* his accounts on earth. When your Court of Judgment sits, *that* will be the only guilty party that can be summoned to appear before it. No part of this project originated within the mind and purpose of the girl herself. You may add trafficking in illegal brainfeed equipment to the seemingly endless list of Dr. Moreau's crimes."

Charlotte let out her breath in a long, deep sigh that sounded exactly like one of Oscar Wilde's. She looked up into the little tent of blue sky above the mausoleum, which marked the clearing in which they were standing. Already, the sky was full of flying eyes.

This is Rappaccini's funeral, she thought, *and all of this was his last gift to himself: his last and finest wreath. It's a great symbolic circle woven out of life and death, laying claim to the only kind of immortality he could design for himself. Everybody in the world has been invited, to mock or mourn or marvel as they please.*

The eyes, she knew, had ears as well. The words that she and Oscar spoke could be heard by thousands of people all over the world, and would in time be relayed to billions. Oscar was looking upward too, with a curious smile on his face.

"It was, after all," he said, wryly, "a perfect murder."

HONORABLE MENTIONS
1994

Brian W. Aldiss, "The Dream of Antigone," *Blue Motel*.
———, "Else the Isle with Calibans," *Weird Tales from Shakespeare*.
———, "The God Who Slept with Women," *Asimov's*, May.
———, "The Madonna of Futurity," *Universe 3*.
———, "The Monster of Everyday Life," *Interzone*, Feb.
Ray Aldridge, "Filter Feeders," *F&SF*, Jan.
Michael Armstrong, "Mother to Elves," *F&SF*, June.
Eleanor Arnason, "The Lovers," *Asimov's*, July.
Isaac Asimov, "March Against the Foe," *Asimov's*, April.
A. A. Attanasio, "The Dark One: A Mythograph," *Crank! 4*.
———, "Remains of Adam," *Asimov's*, Jan.
Virginia Baker, "Dierdra, Alive and Dead," *Tomorrow*, June.
Neal Barrett Jr., "Donna Rae," *The King Is Dead*.
———, "Manhattan 99," *Asimov's*, Mid-Dec.
Barrington J. Bayley, "Gnostic Endings," *Interzone*, July.
Stephen Baxter, "The Blood of Angels," *Asimov's*, Dec.
———, "Mittelwelt," *Interzone*, April.
———, "The Logic Pool," *Asimov's*, June.
Chris Beckett, "Jazamine in the Green Wood," *Interzone*, Aug.
M. Shayne Bell, "Naked Asylum," *Tomorrow*, June.
———, "Mrs. Lincoln's China," *Asimov's*, July.
Gregory Benford, "Doing Alien," *F&SF*, March.
———, "Not of an Age," *Weird Tales from Shakespeare*.
———, "Soon Comes Night," *Asimov's*, Aug.
Maria Billion, "How My Son Became a Dragon Slayer," *Prairie Fire*.
Terry Bisson, "Dead Man's Curve," *Asimov's*, June.
———, "Tell Them They Are All Full of Shit," *Crank! 4*.
———, "Necronauts," *Playboy*, Aug.
E. Michael Blake, "Moths to the Blue Flame," *Universe 3*.
Terry Boren, "Transcript of 'Yandal,' " *Universe 3*.
Bruce Boston, "Curse of the Cyberhead's Wife," *SF Age*, Sept.
Mark Bourne, "Great Works of Western Literature," *F&SF*, Sept.
Ben Bova, "Inspiration," *F&SF*, April.
———, "Sam's War," *Analog*, July.
Richard Bowes, "The Shadow and the Gunman," *F&SF*, Feb.
Steven R. Boyett, "Epiphany Beach," *F&SF*, April.
———, "The Madonna of Port Lligat," *Asimov's*, June.
Ray Bradbury, "From the Dust Returned," *F&SF*, Sept.
R. V. Branham, "Apocalypse's Children," *Asimov's*, Sept.
David Brin, "The Other Side of the Hill," *SF Age*, Nov.
J. Brooke, "Three Things to Watch for When You're in the Market for a Used Tumor," *Aboriginal SF*, Spring.
Keith Brooke, "Professionals," *Interzone*, Aug.
Eric Brown, "Downtime in the MKCR," *Interzone*, May.
Molly Brown, "Women on the Brink of a Cataclysm," *Interzone*, Jan.
John Brunner, "Good With Rice," *Asimov's*, March.
Edward Bryant, "The Fire That Scours," *Omni*, Oct.

Stephen L. Burns, "Song from a Broken Instrument," *Analog*, Feb.
Pat Cadigan, "Not Just Another Deal," *Deals with the Devil*.
————, "Serial Monogamist," *Little Deaths*.
Steve Carper, "Reflections in an Empty Pool," *Tomorrow*, Dec.
Jonathan Carroll, "A Wheel in the Desert, the Moon on Some Springs," *Omni*, March.
Susan Casper, "Up the Rainbow," *Asimov's*, Dec.
Graham Charnock, "Harringay," *New Worlds 4*.
Rob Chilson, "Dead Men Rise Up Never," *Asimov's*, Aug.
————, "Midnight Yearnings," *F&SF*, Aug.
Eric Choi, "Dedication," *Asimov's*, Nov.
Sarah Clemens, "Holes," *Little Deaths*.
Rick Cook & Peter L. Manly, "Symphony for Skyfall," *Analog*, July.
Greg Costikyan, "The West Is Red," *Asimov's*, May.
Gary Couzens, "Second Contact," *F&SF*, March.
Don D'Ammassa, "Jack the Martian," *Harsh Mistress SF*, Spring.
Tony Daniel, "Angel of Mercy," *Asimov's*, Sept.
Jack Dann, "Counting Coup," *Tales from the Great Turtle*.
Chan Davis, "The Names of Yanils," *Crank! 3*.
Stephen Dedman, "Desired Dragons," *Alien Shores*.
Bradley Denton, "We Love Lydia Love," *F&SF*, Oct./Nov.
Cory Doctorow, "Resume," *On Spec*, Spring.
Paul Di Filippo, "Bad Beliefs," *Pirate Writings*, Fall.
————, "The Double Felix," *Interzone*, Sept.
————, "McGregor," *Universe 3*.
Thomas M. Disch, "The Man Who Read a Book," *Interzone*, Sept.
Gardner Dozois, "A Cat Horror Story," *F&SF*, Oct./Nov.
L. Timmel Duchamp, "Things of the Flesh," *Asimov's*, Jan.
————, "When Joy Came to the World," *F&SF*, Jan.
George Alec Effinger, "Good Night, Duane Allman," *Deals with the Devil*.
Greg Egan, "Our Lady of Chernobyl," *Interzone*, May.
Phyllis Eisenstein, "No Refunds," *Asimov's*, Feb.
Kandis Elliot, "Basket Case," *Asimov's*, Nov.
————, "Cretaceous Park," *Asimov's*, April.
————, "Laddie of the Lake," *Asimov's*, Feb.
Kate Elliott, "My Voice Is in My Sword," *Weird Tales from Shakespeare*.
Harlan Ellison, "The Pale Silver Dollar of the Moon Pays Its Way and Makes Change," *The King Is Dead*.
Stuart Falconer, "Fugue and Variations," *Interzone*, July.
Gregory Feeley, "Aweary of the Sun," *Weird Tales from Shakespeare*.
————, "Passion for the Souls Below," *Deals with the Devil*.
Eliot Fintushel, "A Ram in the Thicket," *Tomorrow*, Dec.
Marina Fitch, "Sarah at the Tidepool," *F&SF*, April.
Alan Dean Foster, "Our Lady of the Machine," *Amazing*, Spring.
Maggie Flinn, "On Dreams: A Love Story," *Asimov's*, June.
Leanne Frahm, "Land's End," *Alien Shores*.
Robert Frazier & James Patrick Kelly, "Grandfather Christmas," *Asimov's*, Dec.
Valerie J. Freireich, "Soft Rain," *Asimov's*, Aug.
Esther M. Friesner, "Death and the Librarian," *Asimov's*, Dec.
————, "Patterns," *Tales from the Great Turtle*.
————, "Royal Tiff Yields Face of Jesus!," *Alien Pregnant by Elvis*.
————, "Titus!," *Weird Tales from Shakespeare*.
R. Garcia y Robertson, "Into A Sunless Sea," *Tomorrow*," Oct.
————, "Wendy Darling, RFC," *F&SF*, April.
————, "Werewolves of Luna," *Asimov's*, Mid-Dec.
David Garnett, "A Friend Indeed," *Interzone*, Nov.

Peter T. Garratt, "The Collectivization of Transylvania," *Interzone*, March.

David Gerrold, "The Martian Child," *F&SF*, Sept.

Gary M. Gibson, "Touched By an Angel," *Interzone*, March.

Owl Goingback, "Animal Sounds," *Tales from the Great Turtle*.

Stephen Goldin, "The Height of Intrigue," *Analog*, Nov.

Lisa Goldstein, "The Narcissus Plague," *Asimov's*, July.

———, "Rites of Spring," *Asimov's*, March.

Kathleen Ann Goonan, "Revelation Station," *Strange Plasma 7*.

———, "Susannah and the Snowbears," *Blue Motel*.

Lee Goodloe and Jerry Oltion, "Waterworld," *Analog*, March.

Alan Gordon, "Digital Music," *Asimov's*, Sept.

Ed Gorman, "The Old Ways," *Tales from the Great Turtle*.

Colin Greenland, "The Travelling Companion," *Strange Plasma 8*.

Nicola Griffith, "Yaguara," *Little Deaths*.

George Guthridge, "The Tower," *Amazing*, Fall.

Joe Haldeman, "The Cure," *Universe 3*.

Jack C. Haldeman II, "South of Eden, Somewhere Near Salinas," *By Any Other Fame*.

Elizabeth Hand, "Last Summer at Mars Hill," *F&SF*, Aug.

Charles L. Harness, "The Tetrahedron," *Analog*, Jan.

M. John Harrison, "Isabel Avens Returns to Stepney in the Spring," *Little Deaths*.

Daniel Hatch, "All Justice Fled," *Pirate Writings*, Fall.

Gerald Hausman, "Turtle Woman," *Tales from the Great Turtle*.

Nina Kiriki Hoffman, "Haunted Humans," *F&SF*, July.

Alexander Jablokov, "Focal Plane," *Future Boston*.

———, "Seating Arrangement," *Future Boston*.

———, "Summer and Ice," *Asimov's*, May.

———, "Syrtis," *Asimov's*, April.

Ben Jeapes, "The Data Class," *Interzone*, Feb.

Alex Jeffers, "Composition with Barbarian and Animal," *Universe 3*.

Phillip C. Jennings, "Going West," *Universe 3*.

———, "Original Sin," *Asimov's*, April.

———, "The Valley of the Humans," *Asimov's*, Nov.

Janet Kagan, "Space Cadet," *By Any Other Fame*.

Michael Kandel, "Ogre," *Black Thorn, White Rose*.

James Patrick Kelly, "Big Guy," *Asimov's*, June.

Leigh Kennedy, "Golden Swan," *Interzone*, Jan.

Katharine Kerr, "Cui Bono?," *Alternate Outlaws*.

Garry Kilworth, "Black Drongo," *Omni*, May.

———, "Nerves of Steel," *New Worlds 4*.

———, "Wayang Kulit," *Interzone*, Dec.

Stephen King, "The Man in the Black Suit," *The New Yorker*, Oct. 31.

Damon Knight, "Fortyday," *Asimov's*, May.

Kathe Koja, "Queen of Angels," *Omni*, April.

Nancy Kress, "Ars Longa," *By Any Other Fame*.

———, "Words Like Pale Stones," *Black Thorn, White Rose*.

R. A. Lafferty, "Holy Woman," *Strange Plasma 7*.

———, "I Don't Care Who Keeps the Cows," *Crank! 4*.

Geoffrey A. Landis, "The Singular Habits of Wasps," *Analog*, April.

———, "What We Really Do at NASA," *SF Age*, July.

Joe Lansdale, "Bubba Ho-Tep," *The King Is Dead*.

Tanith Lee, "Mirror, Mirror," *Weird Tales*, Spring.

———, "One for Sorrow," *Weird Tales*, Spring.

Ursula K. Le Guin, "Another Story," *Tomorrow*, Aug.

———, "Betrayals," *Blue Motel*.

———, "Solitude," *F&SF*, Dec.

———, "Unchosen Love," *Amazing*, Fall.
Jonathan Lethem, "Mood Bender," *Crank! 3*.
Megan Lindholm, "The Fifth Squashed Cat," *Xanadu 2*.
Alison Lurie, "In the Shadow," *Asimov's*, Mid-Dec.
Ian R. MacLeod, "Sealight," *F&SF*, May.
Bruce McAllister, "Assassin," *Omni*, Feb.
Sally McBride, "The Fragrance of Orchids," *Asimov's*, May.
Wil McCarthy, "The Blackery Dark," *Asimov's*, Oct.
———, "Dirtyside Down," *Universe 3*.
Jack McDevitt, "Standard Candles," *F&SF*, Jan.
———, "Windrider," *Asimov's*, July.
Ian McDonald, "Blue Motel," *Blue Motel*.
———, "Legitimate Targets," *New Worlds 4*.
Terry McGarry, "The Only Gift a Portion of Thyself," *Amazing*, Fall.
Maureen F. McHugh, "The Ballad of Ritchie Valenzuela," *Alternate Outlaws*.
———, "Virtual Love," *F&SF*, Jan.
Patricia A. McKillip, "Transmutations," *Xanadu 2*.
Sean McMullen, "The Miocene Arrow," *Alien Shores*.
Barry N. Malzberg, "Allegro Marcato," *By Any Other Fame*.
———, "The Only Thing You Learn," *Universe 3*.
———, "Understanding Entropy," *SF Age*, July.
Daniel Marcus, "Angel from Budapest," *Asimov's*, March.
———, "Conversations with Michael," *Asimov's*, Dec.
———, "Heart of Molten Stone," *SF Age*, Sept.
———, "Winter Rules," *F&SF*, Sept.
Jim Marino, "Secret Identities," *Strange Plasma 8*.
Beth Meacham, "A Dream Can Make a Difference," *By Any Other Fame*.
Michael Moorcock, "Freestates," *New World 4*.
Derryl Murphy, "The History of Photography," *Prairie Fire*.
Pat Murphy, "Games of Deception," *Asimov's*, April.
Pati Nagle, "Coyote Ugly," *F&SF*, April.
Jamil Nasir, "The Lord of Sleep," *Asimov's*, Mid-Dec.
Resa Nelson & Sarah Smith, "Fennario," *Future Boston*.
Kim Newman, "The Pale Spirit People," *Interzone*, Jan.
G. David Nordley, "The Day of Their Coming," *Asimov's*, March.
———, "His Father's Voice," *Analog*, Sept.
———, "Karl's Marine and Spacecraft Repair," *Analog*, Dec.
———, "Of Fire and Ice," *Mindsparks*, Fall.
———, "Out of the Quiet Years," *Asimov's*, July.
———, "Network," *Analog*, Feb.
Jerry Oltion, "Fermat's Last Theorem," *Analog*, Mid-Dec.
Robert Onopa, "Blue Flyers," *Tomorrow*, Dec.
Richard Parks, "Laying the Stones," *Asimov's*, Nov.
Paul Park, "The Tourist," *Interzone*, Feb.
Michael H. Payne, "A Bag of Custard," *Asimov's*, Feb.
———, "One Thin Dime," *Tomorrow*, Oct.
Frederik Pohl, "Redemption in the Quantum Realm," *Asimov's*, April.
———, "What Dreams Remain," *Future Quartet*.
Steven Popkes, "Doctor Couney's Island," *Asimov's*, Dec.
———, "The Test," *Future Boston*.
———, "Whistle in the Dark," *Asimov's*, June.
Tom Purdom, "Dragon Drill," *Asimov's*, Oct.
———, "Legacies," *Asimov's*, Jan.
Robert Reed, "The Dimensions of the Deed," *Tomorrow*, Dec.
———, "The Shape of Everything," *F&SF*, Oct./Nov.

————, "Stride," *Asimov's*, Nov.

————, "Treasure Buried," *F&SF*, Feb.

Laura Resnick, "Confessional," *Deals with the Devil*.

Mike Resnick, "A Little Knowledge," *Asimov's*, April.

————, "Barnaby in Exile," *Asimov's*, Feb.

————, "The Summer of My Discontent," *Weird Tales from Shakespeare*.

Caroline Rhodes, "Snake Medicine," *Tales from the Great Turtle*.

Mark Rich, "The Asking Place," *SF Age*, July.

Carrie Richerson, "Artistic License," *F&SF*, Dec.

————, "The Emerald City," *Pulphouse 17*.

Uncle River, "The Nature of Prosperity," *Interzone*, Oct.

Keith Roberts, "Unlikely Meeting," *Interzone*, Oct.

Frank M. Robinson, "Dealer's Choice," *Deals with the Devil*.

————, "One Month in 1907," *Alternate Outlaws*.

Kim Stanley Robinson, "A Martian Childhood," *Asimov's*, Feb.

Madeleine E. Robins, "Somewhere in Dreamland Tonight," *F&SF*, July.

Michaela Roessner, "Welcome to the Dog Show," *Strange Plasma 8*.

Mary Rosenblum, "The Mermaid's Comb," *Asimov's*, June.

————, "Rat," *Asimov's*, Oct.

————, "Selkies," *Asimov's*, March.

———— and Greg Abraham, "Mr. Sartorius," *Asimov's*, Mid-Dec.

Rudy Rucker and Bruce Sterling, "Big Jelly," *Asimov's*, Nov.

Kristine Kathryn Rusch, "Elvis at the White House," *Alien Pregnant by Elvis*.

————, "Monuments to the Dead," *Tales from the Great Turtle*.

Geoff Ryman, "A Fall of Angels," *Unconquered Countries*.

————, "Fan," *Interzone*, March/*Unconquered Countries*.

Pamela Sargent, "All Rights," *Amazing*, Fall.

————, "Climb the Wind," *Asimov's*, March.

Jessica Amanda Salmonson, "The Hell Gamblers, *Xanadu 2*.

Felicity Savage, "Brixtow White Lady," *F&SF*, March.

Charles Sheffield, "The Bee's Kiss," *Asimov's*, Nov.

Rick Shelley, "We Three," *Analog*, March.

Lucius Shepard, "The Last Time," *Little Deaths*.

Delia Sherman, "Young Woman in a Garden," *Xanadu 2*.

Josepha Sherman, "Ancient Magics, Ancient Hope," *Weird Tales from Shakespeare*.

W. M. Shockley, "Water," *Louis L'Amour Western Magazine*, July.

D. William Shunn, "Rise Up, Ye Women That Are At Ease," *Washed by a Wave of Wind*.

Robert Silverberg, "Via Roma," *Asimov's*, April.

Chris Simmons, "Moonwatcher Breaks the Bones," *Alien Shores*.

Dave Smeds, "A Marathon Runner in the Human Race," *F&SF*, March.

David Alexander Smith, "Sail Away," *Future Boston*.

Dean Wesley Smith, "Jukebox Gifts," *F&SF*, Jan.

Martha Soukup, "Good Girl, Bad Dog," *Alternate Outlaws*.

Bud Sparhawk, "Hurricane!," *Analog*, Sept.

————, "Iridium Dreams," *Analog*, April.

William Browning Spencer, "The Lights of Armagedden," *Argonaut 19*.

Norman Spinrad, "Where the Heart Is," *Tomorrow*, Oct.

Brian Stableford, "The Bad Seed," *Interzone*, April.

————, "Busy Dying," *F&SF*, Feb.

————, "Changlings," *Interzone*, July.

————, "The Scream," *Asimov's*, July.

————, "The Tree of Life," *Asimov's*, Sept.

————, "The Unkindness of Ravens," *Interzone*, Dec.

————, "What Can Chloë Want?," *Asimov's*, March.

Allen Steele, "Riders in the Sky," *Alternate Outlaws.*
———, "See Rock City," *Omni,* Aug.
———, "2,437 UFOs Over New Hampshire," *Alien Pregnant by Elvis.*
———, "Whinin' Boy Blues," *Asimov's,* Feb.
Neal Stephenson, "Spew," *Wired,* Oct.
Sue Storm, "Home," *Xizquil 12.*
Michael Swanwick, "The Changeling's Tale," *Asimov's,* Jan.
———, "The Mask," *Asimov's,* April.
Lucy Sussex, "Kay & Phil," *Alien Shores.*
Judith Tarr, "Cowards Die: A Tragicomedy in Several Fits," *Alternate Outlaws.*
———, "Mending Souls," *Deals with the Devil.*
Braulio Tavares, "Stuntmind," *On Spec,* Fall.
John Alfred Taylor, "Full Circle," *Asimov's,* March.
———, "The Man in the Dinosaur Coat," *Asimov's,* July.
Michael Teasdale, "Half the World Away," *On Spec,* Fall.
Steve Rasnic Tem, "Lost Cherokee," *Tales from the Great Turtle.*
Mark W. Tiedemann, "Drink," *Asimov's,* July.
Lisa Tuttle, "And the Poor Get Children," *New Worlds 4.*
Steven Utley, "Edge of the Wind," *Asimov's,* Jan.
———, "Living It," *Asimov's,* Aug.
———, "Michael Bates," *Pulphouse 17.*
———, "One Kansas Night," *Asimov's,* June.
———, "Two Women of the Prairie," *Louis L'Amour's Western Magazine,* May.
Jeff VanderMeer, "London Burning," *Worlds of Fantasy & Horror, 1.*
Ray Vukcevich, "No Comet," *F&SF,* July.
Holly Wade, "La Pucelle," *Asimov's,* Sept.
Susan Wade, "The Black Swan," *Black Thorn, White Rose.*
———, "The Convertible Coven," *F&SF,* March.
Howard Waldrop, "Why Did?," *Omni,* April.
Lawrence Watt-Evans, "The Bride of Bigfoot," *Alien Pregnant by Elvis.*
Don Webb, "Sabbath of the Zeppelins," *Asimov's,* April.
Andrew Weiner, "Messenger," *Asimov's,* April.
———, "On Becoming an Alien," *Prairie Fire.*
K. D. Wentworth, "Shore Leave," *Aboriginal SF,* Spring.
Leslie What, "Clinging to a Thread," *F&SF,* April.
Rick Wilber, "American Jokes," *SF Age,* July.
Cherry Wilder, "Willow Cottage," *Interzone,* March.
Kate Wilhelm, "Bloodletting," *Omni,* June.
———, "I Know What You're Thinking," *Asimov's,* Nov.
Connie Willis, "Adaptation," *Asimov's,* Dec.
———, "Why the World Didn't End Last Tuesday," *Asimov's,* Jan.
Chris Willrich, "Little Death," *Asimov's,* Mid-Dec.
Robin Wilson, "Something of Consequence," *SF Age,* Sept.
———, "To the Vector Belong . . . ," *F&SF,* Sept.
Amy Wolfe, "The Lazarus Chronicle," *Realms of Fantasy,* Dec.
Dave Wolverton, "Wheatfields Beyond," *Washed by a Wave of Wind.*
Patricia C. Wrede, "Stronger Than Time," *Black Thorn, White Rose.*
Jane Yolen, "Granny Rumple," *Black Thorn, White Rose.*
———, "The Lady's Garden," *F&SF,* May.
———, "The Woman Who Loved a Bear," *Tales from the Great Turtle.*
Roger Zelazny, "Godson," *Black Thorn, White Rose.*

ALSO AVAILABLE FROM ST. MARTIN'S PRESS

	Quantity	Price

The Year's Best Science Fiction:
Thirteenth Annual Collection ($17.95)
ISBN: 0-312-14452-0 (trade paperback)

Modern Classics of Science Fiction
edited by Gardner Dozois ($16.95)
ISBN: 0-312-08847-7 (trade paperback)

Modern Classic Short Novels of Science Fiction
edited by Gardner Dozois ($15.95)
ISBN: 0-312-11317-X (trade paperback)

Those Who Can: A Science Fiction Reader
edited by Robin Wilson ($13.95)
ISBN: 0-312-14139-4 (trade paperback)

Paragons: Twelve SF Writers Ply Their Craft
edited by Robin Wilson ($14.95)
ISBN: 0-312-15623-5 (trade paperback)

Writing Science Fiction and Fantasy
edited by the editors of *Asimov's* and *Analog* ($9.95)
ISBN: 0-312-08926-0 (trade paperback)

The Encyclopedia of Science Fiction
by John Clute and Peter Nicholls ($29.95)
ISBN: 0-312-13486-X (trade paperback)

POSTAGE & HANDLING

(Books up to $12.00 – add $3.00; books up to $15.00 – add $3.50;
books above $15.00 – add $4.00 – plus $1.00 for each additional book)

8% Sales Tax (New York State residents only)

Amount enclosed:

Name _____

Address _____

City _____ State _____ Zip _____

Send this form or a copy with payment to:
Publishers Book & Audio, P.O. Box 070059, 5448 Arthur Kill Road, Staten Island, NY 10307.
Telephone (800) 288-2131. Please allow three weeks for delivery.
For bulk orders (10 copies or more) please contact the St. Martin's Press Special Sales Department
toll free at 800-221-7945 ext. 645 for information. In New York State call 212-674-5151.